HESIOD

THE HOMERIC HYMNS AND HOMERICA

WITH AN ENGLISH TRANSLATION BY

HUGH G. EVELYN-WHITE, M.A.

SOMETIME SCHOLAR OF WADHAM COLLEGE, OXFORD

LONDON : WILLIAM HEINEMANN

NEW YORK : THE MACMILLAN CO.

MCMXIV

PREFACE

This volume contains practically all that remains of the post-Homeric and pre-academic epic poetry.

I have for the most part formed my own text. In the case of Hesiod I have been able to use independent collations of several MSS. by Dr. W. H. D. Rouse; otherwise I have depended on the *apparatus criticus* of the several editions, especially that of Rzach (1902). The arrangement adopted in this edition, by which the complete and fragmentary poems are restored to the order in which they would probably have appeared had the Hesiodic corpus survived intact, is unusual, but should not need apology; the true place for the *Catalogues* (for example), fragmentary as they are, is certainly after the *Theogony*.

In preparing the text of the *Homeric Hymns* my chief debt—and it is a heavy one—is to the edition of Allen and Sikes (1904) and to the series of articles in the *Journal of Hellenic Studies* (vols. xv. *sqq.*) by T. W. Allen. To the same scholar and to the

PREFACE

Delegates of the Clarendon Press I am greatly indebted for permission to use the restorations of the *Hymn to Demeter,* lines 387–401 and 462–470, printed in the Oxford Text of 1912.

Of the fragments of the Epic Cycle I have given only such as seemed to possess distinct importance or interest, and in doing so have relied mostly upon Kinkel's collection and on the fifth volume of the Oxford Homer (1912).

The texts of the *Batrachomyomachia* and of the *Contest of Homer and Hesiod* are those of Baumeister and Flach respectively: where I have diverged from these, the fact has been noted.

Owing to the circumstances of the present time I have been prevented from giving to the *Introduction* that full revision which I should have desired.

RAMPTON, NR. CAMBRIDGE.
Sept. 9th, 1914

CONTENTS

CONTENTS

INTRODUCTION

General

THE early Greek epic—that is, epic poetry as a natural and popular, and not (as it became later) an artificial and academic literary form—passed through the usual three phases, of development, of maturity, and of decline.

No fragments which can be identified as belonging to the first period survive to give us even a general idea of the history of the earliest epic, and we are therefore thrown back upon the evidence of analogy from other forms of literature and of inference from the two great epics which have come down to us. So reconstructed, the earliest period appears to us as a time of slow development in which the characteristic epic metre, diction, and structure grew up slowly from crude elements and were improved until the verge of maturity was reached.

The second period, which produced the *Iliad* and the *Odyssey*, needs no description here: but it is very important to observe the effect of these poems on the course of post-Homeric epic. As the supreme perfection and universality of the *Iliad* and the *Odyssey* cast into oblivion whatever pre-Homeric poets had essayed, so these same qualities exercised a paralysing influence over the successors of Homer. If they continued to sing like their great predecessor of romantic themes, they were drawn as by a kind of magnetic attraction into the Homeric style and manner of treatment, and became mere echoes of the Homeric voice: in a word, Homer had so completely exhausted the epic *genre,* that after him further efforts were doomed to be merely conventional. Only the rare and exceptional genius of Vergil and Milton could use the Homeric medium without loss of individuality: and this quality none of the later epic poets seem to have possessed. Freedom from the domination of the great tradition could only be found by seeking new subjects, and such freedom was really only illusionary, since romantic subjects alone are suitable for epic treatment.

In its third period, therefore, epic poetry shows two divergent tendencies. In Ionia and the islands the epic poets followed the Homeric tradition, singing of romantic subjects in the now stereotyped heroic style, and showing originality only in their choice of legends hitherto neglected or summarily and imperfectly treated. In continental Greece,[1] on the other hand, but especially in Boeotia, a new form of epic sprang up, which for the romance and πάθος of the Ionian School substituted the practical and matter-of-fact. It dealt in moral and practical maxims, in information on technical subjects which are of service in daily life—agriculture, astronomy, augury, and the calendar—in matters of religion and in tracing the genealogies of men. Its attitude is summed up in the words of the Muses to the writer of the *Theogony*: "We can tell many a feigned tale to look like truth, but we can, when we will, utter the truth" (*Theog.* 26–27). Such a poetry

[1] *sc.* in Boeotia, Locris and Thessaly: elsewhere the movement was forced and unfruitful.

could not be permanently successful, because the subjects of which it treats—if susceptible of poetic treatment at all—were certainly not suited for epic treatment, where unity of action which will sustain interest, and to which each part should contribute, is absolutely necessary. While, therefore, an epic like the *Odyssey* is an organism and dramatic in structure, a work such as the *Theogony* is a merely artificial collocation of facts, and, at best, a pageant. It is not surprising, therefore, to find that from the first the Boeotian school is forced to season its matter with romantic episodes, and that later it tends more and more to revert (as in the *Shield of Heracles*) to the Homeric tradition.

The Boeotian School

How did the continental school of epic poetry arise? There is little definite material for an answer to this question, but the probability is that there were at least three contributory causes. First, it is likely that before the rise of the Ionian epos there existed in Boeotia a purely popular and indigenous poetry of a crude form: it comprised, we may suppose, versified proverbs and precepts relating to life in general, agricultural maxims, weather-lore, and the like. In this sense the Boeotian poetry may be taken to have its germ in maxims similar to our English

> "Till May be out, ne'er cast a clout,"

or

> "A rainbow in the morning
> Is the Shepherd's warning."

Secondly and thirdly we may ascribe the rise of the new epic to the nature of the Boeotian people and, as already remarked, to a spirit of revolt against the old epic. The Boeotians, people of the class of which Hesiod represents himself to be the type, were essentially unromantic ; their daily needs marked the general limit of their ideals, and, as a class, they cared little for works of fancy, for pathos, or for fine thought as such. To a people of this nature the Homeric epos would be inacceptable, and the post-Homeric epic, with its conventional atmosphere, its trite and hackneyed diction, and its insincere sentiment, would be anathema. We can imagine, therefore, that among such folk a settler, of Aeolic origin like Hesiod, who clearly was well acquainted with the Ionian epos, would naturally see that the only outlet for his gifts lay in applying epic poetry to new themes acceptable to his hearers.

Though the poems of the Boeotian school [1] were unanimously assigned to Hesiod down to the age of Alexandrian criticism, they were clearly neither the work of one man nor even of one period : some, doubtless, were fraudulently fathered on him in order to gain currency ; but it is probable that most came to be regarded as his partly because of their general character, and partly because the names of their real authors were lost. One fact in this attribution is remarkable—the veneration paid to Hesiod.

[1] The extant collection of three poems, *Works and Days*, *Theogony*, and *Shield of Heracles*, which alone have come down to us complete, dates at least from the 4th century A.D. : the title of the Paris Papyrus (Bibl. Nat. Suppl. Gr. 1099) names only these three works.

INTRODUCTION

Life of Hesiod.—Our information respecting Hesiod is derived in the main from notices and allusions in the works attributed to him, and to these must be added certain traditions concerning his death and burial gathered from later writers.

Hesiod's father (whose name, by a perversion of *Works and Days*, 299 Πέρση δῖον γένος to Πέρση, Δίου γένος, was thought to have been Dius) was a native of Cyme in Aeolis, where he was a seafaring trader and, perhaps, also a farmer. He was forced by poverty to leave his native place, and returned to continental Greece, where he settled at Ascra near Thespiae in Boeotia (*Works and Days*, 636 ff.). Either in Cyme or Ascra, two sons, Hesiod and Perses, were born to the settler, and these, after his death, divided the farm between them. Perses, however, who is represented as an idler and spendthrift, obtained and kept the larger share by bribing the corrupt "lords" who ruled from Thespiae (*Works and Days*, 37–39). While his brother wasted his patrimony and ultimately came to want (*Works and Days*, 34 ff.), Hesiod lived a farmer's life until, according to the very early tradition preserved by the author of the *Theogony* (22–23), the Muses met him as he was tending sheep on Mt. Helicon and "taught him a glorious song"—doubtless the *Works and Days*. The only other personal reference is to his victory in a poetical contest at the funeral games of Amphidamas at Chalcis in Euboea, where he won the prize, a tripod, which he dedicated to the Muses of Helicon (*Works and Days*, 651–9).

Before we go on to the story of Hesiod's death, it will be well to inquire how far the "autobiographical" notices can be treated as historical, especially as many critics treat some, or all of them, as spurious. In the first place attempts have been made to show that "Hesiod" is a significant name and therefore fictitious: it is only necessary to mention Goettling's derivation from ἵημι and ὁδός (which would make "Hesiod" mean the "guide" in virtues and technical arts), and to refer to the pitiful attempts in the *Etymologicum Magnum* (*s.v.* Ἡσίοδος), to show how prejudiced and lacking even in plausibility such efforts are. It seems certain that "Hesiod" stands as a proper name in the fullest sense. Secondly, Hesiod claims that his father—if not he himself—came from Aeolis and settled in Boeotia. There is fairly definite evidence to warrant our acceptance of this: the dialect of the *Works and Days* is shown by Rzach[1] to contain distinct Aeolisms apart from those which formed part of the general stock of epic poetry. And that this Aeolic speaking poet was a Boeotian of Ascra seems even more certain, since the tradition is never once disputed, insignificant though the place was, even before its destruction by the Thespians.

Again, Hesiod's story of his relations with his brother Perses have been treated with scepticism (*see* Murray, *Anc. Gk. Literature,* pp. 53–54): Perses, it is urged, is clearly a mere dummy, set up to be the target for the poet's exhortations. On such a matter precise evidence is naturally not forthcoming; but all probability is against the sceptical view. For (1) if the quarrel between the brothers were a fiction, we should expect it to be detailed at length and not noticed allusively and rather obscurely—as we find

[1] *Der Dialekt des Hesiodos*, p. 464: examples are αἴνημι (*W.* and *D.* 683) and ἀρώμεναι (*ib.* 22).

it; (2) as MM. Croiset remark, if the poet needed a lay-figure the ordinary practice was to introduce some mythological person—as, in fact, is done in the *Precepts of Chiron.* In a word, there is no more solid ground for treating Perses and his quarrel with Hesiod as fictitious than there would be for treating Cyrnus, the friend of Theognis, as mythical.

Thirdly, there is the passage in the *Theogony* relating to Hesiod and the Muses. It is surely an error to suppose that lines 22-35 all refer to Hesiod: rather, the author of the *Theogony* tells the story of his own inspiration by the same Muses who *once* taught Hesiod glorious song. The lines 22–3 are therefore a very early piece of tradition about Hesiod, and though the appearance of Muses must be treated as a graceful fiction, we find that a writer, later than the *Works and Days* by perhaps no more than three-quarters of a century, believed in the actuality of Hesiod and in his life as a farmer or shepherd.

Lastly, there is the famous story of the contest in song at Chalcis. In later times the modest version in the *Works and Days* was elaborated, first by making Homer the opponent whom Hesiod conquered, while a later period exercised its ingenuity in working up the story of the contest into the elaborate form in which it still survives. Finally the contest, in which the two poets contended with hymns to Apollo,[1] was transferred to Delos. These developments certainly need no consideration: are we to say the same

[1] T. W. Allen suggests that the conjoined Delian and Pythian hymns to Apollo (*Homeric Hymns* III) may have suggested this version of the story, the Pythian hymn showing strong continental influence.

of the passage in the *Works and Days*? Critics from Plutarch downwards have almost unanimously rejected the lines 654–662, on the ground that Hesiod's Amphidamas is the hero of the Lelantine war between Chalcis and Eretria, whose death may be placed *circa* 705 B.C.—a date which is obviously too low for the genuine Hesiod. Nevertheless, there is much to be said in defence of the passage. Hesiod's claim in the *Works and Days* is modest, since he neither pretends to have met Homer, nor to have sung in any but an impromptu, local festival, so that the supposed interpolation lacks a sufficient motive. And there is nothing in the context to show that Hesiod's Amphidamas is to be identified with that Amphidamas whom Plutarch alone connects with the Lelantine War: the name may have been borne by an earlier Chalcidian, an ancestor, perhaps, of the person to whom Plutarch refers.

The story of the end of Hesiod may be told in outline. After the contest at Chalcis, Hesiod went to Delphi and there was warned that the "issue of death should overtake him in the fair grove of Nemean Zeus." Avoiding therefore Nemea on the Isthmus of Corinth, to which he supposed the oracle to refer, Hesiod retired to Oenoë in Locris where he was entertained by Amphiphanes and Ganyctor, sons of a certain Phegeus. This place, however, was also sacred to Nemean Zeus, and the poet, suspected by his hosts of having seduced their sister,[1] was murdered there. His body, cast into the sea, was brought to shore by dolphins and buried at Oenoë (or, according to Plutarch, at Ascra): at a later time his bones were removed to Orchomenus. The whole

[1] She is said to have given birth to the lyrist Stesichorus.

story is full of miraculous elements, and the various authorities disagree on numerous points of detail. The tradition seems, however, to be constant in declaring that Hesiod was murdered and buried at Oenoë, and in this respect it is at least as old as the time of Thucydides. In conclusion it may be worth while to add the graceful epigram of Alcaeus of Messene (*Palatine Anthology*, vii 55).

Λοκρίδος ἐν νέμεϊ σκιερῷ νέκυν Ἡσιόδοιο
  Νύμφαι κρηνιάδων λοῦσαν ἀπὸ σφετέρων,
καὶ τάφον ὑψώσαντο· γάλακτι δὲ ποίμενες αἰγῶν
  ἔρραναν, ξανθῷ μιξάμενοι μέλιτι·
τοίην γὰρ καὶ γῆρυν ἀπέπνεεν ἐννέα Μουσῶν
  ὁ πρέσβεις καθαρῶν γευσάμενος λιβάδων.

"When in the shady Locrian grove Hesiod lay dead, the Nymphs washed his body with water from their own springs, and heaped high his grave; and thereon the goat-herds sprinkled offerings of milk mingled with yellow-honey: such was the utterance of the nine Muses that he breathed forth, that old man who had tasted of their pure springs."

The Hesiodic Poems.—The Hesiodic poems fall into two groups according as they are didactic (technical or gnomic) or genealogical: the first group centres round the *Works and Days*, the second round the *Theogony*.

I. *The Works and Days.*—The poem consists of four main sections (*a*) After the prelude, which Pausanias failed to find in the ancient copy engraved on lead seen by him on Mt. Helicon, comes a general exhortation to industry. It begins with the allegory of the two Strifes, who stand for wholesome Emulation and Quarrelsomeness respectively. Then by means of the Myth of Pandora the poet shows how evil and the need for work first arose, and goes on to describe the Five Ages of the World, tracing the gradual increase of evil, and emphasizing the present miserable condition of the world, a condition in which struggle is inevitable. Next, after the Fable of the Hawk and Nightingale, which serves as a condemnation of violence and injustice, the poet passes on to contrast the blessings which Righteousness brings to a nation, and the punishment which Heaven sends down upon the violent, and the section concludes with a series of precepts on industry and prudent conduct generally. (*b*) The second section shows how a man may escape want and misery by industry and care both in agriculture and in trading by sea. Neither subject, it should be carefully noted, is treated in any way comprehensively. (*c*) The third part is occupied with miscellaneous precepts relating mostly to actions of domestic and everyday life and conduct which have little or no connection with one another. (*d*) The final section is taken up with a series of notices on the days of the month which are favourable or unfavourable for agricultural and other operations.

It is from the second and fourth sections that the poem takes its name. At first sight such a work seems to be a miscellany of myths, technical advice, moral precepts, and folklore maxims without any unifying principle; and critics have readily taken the view that the whole is a cento of fragments or short poems worked up by a redactor. Very probably Hesiod used much material of a far older date, just as Shakespeare used the *Gesta Roman-*

orum, old chronicles, and old plays; but close inspection will show that the *Works and Days* has a real unity and that the picturesque title is somewhat misleading. The poem has properly no technical object at all, but is moral: its real aim is to show men how best to live in a difficult world. So viewed the four seemingly independent sections will be found to be linked together in a real bond of unity. Such a connection between the first and second sections is easily seen, but the links between these and the third and fourth are no less real: to make life go tolerably smoothly it is most important to be just and to know how to win a livelihood; but happiness also largely depends on prudence and care both in social and home life as well, and not least on avoidance of actions which offend supernatural powers and bring ill-luck. And finally, if your industry is to be fruitful, you must know what days are suitable for various kinds of work. This moral aim—as opposed to the currently accepted technical aim of the poem—explains the otherwise puzzling incompleteness of the instructions on farming and seafaring.

Of the Hesiodic poems similar in character to the *Works and Days,* only the scantiest fragments survive. One at least of these, the *Divination by Birds,* was, as we know from Proclus, attached to the end of the *Works* until it was rejected by Apollonius Rhodius: doubtless it continued the same theme of how to live, showing how man can avoid disasters by attending to the omens to be drawn from birds. It is possible that the *Astronomy* or *Astrology* (as Plutarch calls it) was in turn appended to the *Divination.* It certainly gave some account of the principal constellations, their dates of rising and setting, and the legends connected with them, and probably showed how these influenced human affairs or might be used as guides. The *Precepts of Chiron* was a didactic poem made up of moral and practical precepts, resembling the gnomic sections of the *Works and Days,* addressed by the Centaur Chiron to his pupil Achilles. Even less is known of the poem called the *Great Works*: the title implies that it was similar in subject to the second section of the *Works and Days,* but longer. Possible references in Roman writers[1] indicate that among the subjects dealt with were the cultivation of the vine and olive and various herbs. The inclusion of the judgment of Rhadamanthys (frag. 1): "If a man sow evil, he shall reap evil," indicates a gnomic element, and the note by Proclus[2] on *Works and Days* 126 makes it likely that metals also were dealt with. It is therefore possible that another lost poem, the *Idaean Dactyls,* which dealt with the discovery of metals and their working, was appended to, or even was a part of the *Great Works,* just as the *Divination by Birds* was appended to the *Works and Days.*

II. *The Genealogical Poems.*—The only complete poem of the genealogical group is the *Theogony,* which traces from the beginning of things the descent and vicissitudes of the families of the gods. Like the *Works and Days* this poem has no dramatic plot; but its unifying principle is clear and simple. The gods are classified chronologically: as soon as one generation is catalogued, the poet goes on to detail

[1] See Kinkel *Epic. Graec. Frag.* i. 158 ff.
[2] See *Great Works*, frag. 2

the offspring of each member of that generation. Exceptions are only made in special cases, as the Sons of Iapetus (ll. 507–616) whose place is accounted for by their treatment by Zeus. The chief landmarks in the poem are as follows: after the first 103 lines, which contain at least three distinct preludes, three primeval beings are introduced, Chaos, Earth and Eros —here an indefinite reproductive influence. Of these three, Earth produces Heaven to whom she bears the Titans, the Cyclopes and the hundred-handed giants. The Titans, oppressed by their father, revolt at the instigation of Earth, under the leadership of Cronos, and as a result Heaven and Earth are separated,[1] and Cronos reigns over the universe. Cronos knowing that he is destined to be overcome by one of his children, swallows each one of them as they are born, until Zeus, saved by Rhea, grows up and overcomes Cronos in some struggle which is not described. Cronos is forced to vomit up the children he had swallowed, and these with Zeus divide the universe between them, like a human estate. Two events mark the early reign of Zeus, the war with the Titans and the overthrow of Typhoeus, and as Zeus is still reigning the poet can only go on to give a list of gods born to Zeus by various goddesses. After this he formally bids farewell to the cosmic and Olympian deities and enumerates the sons born of goddess to mortals. The poem closes with an invocation of the Muses to sing of the "tribe of women."

This conclusion served to link the *Theogony* to what must have been a distinct poem, the *Catalogues of Women*. This work was divided into four (Suidas

[1] See note on p. 93.

says five) books, the last one (or two) of which was known as the *Eoiae* and may have been again a distinct poem: the curious title will be explained presently. The *Catalogues* proper were a series of genealogies which traced the Hellenic race (or its more important peoples and families) from a common ancestor. The reason why women are so prominent is obvious: since most families and tribes claimed to be descended from a god, the only safe clue to their origin was through the mortal woman beloved by that god; and it has also been pointed out that *mutterrecht* still left its traces in northern Greece in historical times.

The following analysis (after Marckscheffel[1]) will show the principle of its composition. From Prometheus and Pronoia sprang Deucalion and Pyrrha, the only survivors of the deluge, who had a son Hellen (frag. 1), the reputed ancestor of the whole Hellenic race. From the daughters of Deucalion sprang Magnes and Macedon, ancestors of the Magnesians and Macedonians, who are thus represented as cousins to the true Hellenic stock. Hellen had three sons, Dorus, Xuthus and Aeolus, parents of the Dorian, Ionic and Aeolian races, and the offspring of these was then detailed. In one instance a considerable and characteristic section can be traced from extant fragments and notices: Salmoneus, son of Aeolus, had a daughter Tyro who bore to Poseidon two sons, Pelias and Neleus; the latter of these, king of Pylos, refused Heracles purification for the murder of Iphitus, whereupon Heracles attacked and sacked Pylos, killing amongst the other sons of Neleus Periclymenus, who had the power of changing himself into all manner of shapes.

[1] *Hesiodi Fragmenta*, pp. 119 f.

From this slaughter Neleus alone escaped (frags. 13, and 10–12). This summary shows the general principle of arrangement of the *Catalogues*: each line seems to have been dealt with in turn, and the monotony was relieved as far as possible by a brief relation of famous adventures connected with any of the personages—as in the case of Atalanta and Hippomenes (frag. 14). Similarly the story of the Argonauts appears from the fragments (37–42) to have been told in some detail.

This tendency to introduce romantic episodes led to an important development. Several poems are ascribed to Hesiod, such as the *Epithalamium of Peleus and Thetis*, the *Descent of Theseus into Hades*, or the *Circuit of the Earth* (which must have been connected with the story of Phineus and the Harpies, and so with the Argonaut-legend), which yet seem to have belonged to the *Catalogues*. It is highly probable that these poems were interpolations into the *Catalogues* expanded by later poets from more summary notices in the genuine Hesiodic work and subsequently detached from their contexts and treated as independent. This is definitely known to be true of the *Shield of Heracles*, the first 53 lines of which belong to the fourth book of the *Catalogues*, and almost certainly applies to other episodes, such as the *Suitors of Helen*,[1] the *Daughters of Leucippus*, and the *Marriage of Ceyx*, which last Plutarch mentions as "interpolated in the works of Hesiod."

To the *Catalogues*, as we have said, was appended another work, the *Eoiae*. The title seems to have

[1] Possibly the division of this poem into two books (see p. 199) is a division belonging solely to this "developed poem," which may have included in its second part a summary of the Tale of Troy.

arisen in the following way[1]: the *Catalogues* probably ended (cp. *Theogony* 963 ff.) with some such passage as this: "But now, ye Muses, sing of the tribes of women with whom the Sons of Heaven were joined in love, women pre-eminent above their fellows in beauty, such (οἵη) as was Niobe (?)." Each succeeding heroine was then introduced by the formula ἢ οἵη "Or such as was . . ." (cp. frags. 88, 92, etc.). A large fragment of the *Eoiae* is extant at the beginning of the *Shield of Heracles*, which may be mentioned here. The "supplement" (ll. 57–480) is nominally devoted to a description of the combat between Heracles and Cycnus, but the greater part is taken up with an inferior description of the shield of Heracles, in imitation of the Homeric shield of Achilles (*Iliad* xviii. 478 ff.). Nothing shows more clearly the collapse of the principles of the Hesiodic school than this ultimate servile dependence upon Homeric models.

At the close of the *Shield* Heracles goes on to Trachis to the house of Ceyx, and this warning suggests that the *Marriage of Ceyx* may have come immediately after the ἢ οἵη of Alcmena in the *Eoiae*: possibly Halcyone, the wife of Ceyx, was one of the heroines sung in the poem, and the original section was "developed" into the *Marriage*, although what form the poem took is unknown.

Next to the *Eoiae* and the poems which seemed to have been developed from it, it is natural to place the *Great Eoiae*. This, again, as we know from fragments, was a list of heroines who bare children to the gods: from the title we must suppose it to have been much longer than the simple *Eoiae*, but its

[1] Goettling's explanation.

extent is unknown. Lehmann, remarking that the heroines are all Boeotian and Thessalian (while the heroines of the *Catalogues* belong to all parts of the Greek world), believes the author to have been either a Boeotian or Thessalian.

Two other poems are ascribed to Hesiod. Of these the *Aegimius* (also ascribed by Athenaeus to Cercops of Miletus), is thought by Valckenaer to deal with the war of Aegimius against the Lapithae and the aid furnished to him by Heracles, and with the history of Aegimius and his sons. Otto Müller suggests that the introduction of Thetis and of Phrixus (frags. 1–2) is to be connected with notices of the allies of the Lapithae from Phthiotis and Iolchus, and that the story of Io was incidental to a narrative of Heracles' expedition against Euboea. The remaining poem, the *Melampodia*, was a work in three books, whose plan it is impossible to recover. Its subject, however, seems to have been the histories of famous seers like Mopsus, Calchas, and Teiresias, and it probably took its name from Melampus, the most famous of them all.

Date of the Hesiodic Poems.—There is no doubt that the *Works and Days* is the oldest, as it is the most original, of the Hesiodic poems. It seems to be distinctly earlier than the *Theogony*, which refers to it, apparently, as a poem already renowned. Two considerations help us to fix a relative date for the *Works.* (1) In diction, dialect and style it is obviously dependent upon Homer, and is therefore considerably later than the *Iliad* and *Odyssey*: moreover, as we have seen, it is in revolt against the romantic school, already grown decadent, and while the digamma is still living, it is obviously growing weak, and is by no means uniformly effective.

(2) On the other hand while tradition steadily puts the Cyclic poets at various dates from 776 B.C. downwards, it is equally consistent in regarding Homer and Hesiod as "prehistoric." Herodotus indeed puts both poets 400 years before his own time; that is, at about 830–820 B.C., and the evidence stated above points to the middle of the ninth century as the probable date for the *Works and Days.* The *Theogony* might be tentatively placed a century later; and the *Catalogues* and *Eoiae* are again later, but not greatly later, than the *Theogony*: the *Shield of Heracles* may be ascribed to the later half of the seventh century, but there is not evidence enough to show whether the other "developed" poems are to be regarded as of a date so low as this.

Literary Value of Hesiod.—Quintilian's[1] judgment on Hesiod that "he rarely rises to great heights . . . and to him is given the palm in the middle-class of speech" is just, but is liable to give a wrong impression. Hesiod has nothing that remotely approaches such scenes as that between Priam and Achilles, or the pathos of Andromache's preparations for Hector's return, even as he was falling before the walls of Troy; but in matters that come within the range of ordinary experience, he rarely fails to rise to the appropriate level. Take, for instance, the description of the Iron Age (*Works and Days,* 182 ff.) with its catalogue of wrongdoing and violence ever increasing until Aidôs and Nemesis are forced to

[1] x. 1. 52.

leave mankind who thenceforward shall have "no remedy against evil." Such occasions, however, rarely occur and are perhaps not characteristic of Hesiod's genius: if we would see Hesiod at his best, in his most natural vein, we must turn to such a passage as that which he himself—according to the compiler of the *Contest of Hesiod and Homer*—selected as best in all his work, "When the Pleiades, Atlas' daughters, begin to rise . . ." (*Works and Days*, 383 ff.). The value of such a passage cannot be analysed: it can only be said that given such a subject, this alone is the right method of treatment.

Hesiod's diction is in the main Homeric, but one of his charms is the use of quaint allusive phrases derived, perhaps, from a pre-Hesiodic peasant poetry: thus the season when Boreas blows is the time when "the Boneless One gnaws his foot by his fireless hearth in his cheerless house"; to cut one's nails is "to sever the withered from the quick upon that which has five branches"; similarly the burglar is the "day-sleeper," and the serpent is the "hairless one." Very similar is his reference to seasons through what happens or is done in that season: "when the House-carrier, fleeing the Pleiades, climbs up the plants from the earth," is the season for harvesting; or "when the artichoke flowers and the clicking grass-hopper, seated in a tree, pours down his shrill song," is the time for rest.

Hesiod's charm lies in his child-like and sincere naïveté, in his unaffected interest in and picturesque view of nature and all that happens in nature. These qualities, it is true, are those pre-eminently of the *Works and Days*: the literary virtues of the *Theogony* are of a more technical character, skill in ordering and disposing long lists of names, sure judgment in seasoning a monotonous subject with marvellous incidents or episodes, and no mean imagination in depicting the awful, as is shown in the description of Tartarus (ll. 736–745). Yet it remains true that Hesiod's distinctive title to a high place in Greek literature lies in the very fact of his freedom from classic form, and his grave, and yet child-like, outlook upon his world.

The Ionic School

The Ionic School of Epic poetry was, as we have seen, dominated by the Homeric tradition, and while the style and method of treatment are Homeric, it is natural that the Ionic poets refrained from cultivating the ground tilled by Homer, and chose for treatment legends which lay beyond the range of the *Iliad* and *Odyssey*. Equally natural it is that they should have particularly selected various phases of the tale of Troy which preceded or followed the action of the *Iliad* and *Odyssey*. In this way, without any preconceived intention, a body of epic poetry was built up by various writers which covered the whole Trojan story. But the entire range of heroic legend was open to these poets, and other clusters of epics grew up dealing particularly with the famous story of Thebes, while others dealt with the beginnings of the world and the wars of heaven. In the end there existed a kind of epic history of the world, as known to the Greeks, down to the death of Odysseus, when the heroic age ended. In the Alexandrian Age these poems were arranged in chronological order, apparently by Zenodotus of Ephesus, at the beginning of the 3rd century B.C. At a later time the term *Cycle*, "round" or "course" was given to this collection.

Of all this mass of epic poetry only the scantiest fragments survive; but happily Photius has preserved to us an abridgment of the synopsis made of each poem of the "Trojan Cycle" by Proclus, *i.e.* Eutychius Proclus of Sicca.

The pre-Trojan poems of the Cycle may be noticed first. The *Titanomachy*, ascribed both to Eumelus of Corinth and to Arctinus of Miletus, began with a kind of Theogony which told of the union of Heaven and Earth and of their offspring the Cyclopes and the Hundred-handed Giants. How the poem proceeded we have no means of knowing, but we may suppose that in character it was not unlike the short account of the Titan War found in the Hesiodic *Theogony* (617 ff.).

What links bound the *Titanomachy* to the Theban Cycle is not clear. This latter group was formed of three poems, the *Story of Oedipus*, the *Thebaïs*, and the *Epigoni*. Of the *Oedipodea* practically nothing is known, though on the assurance of Athenaeus (vii. 277 E) that Sophocles followed the Epic Cycle closely in the plots of his plays, we may suppose that in outline the story corresponded closely to the history of Oedipus as it is found in the *Oedipus Tyrannus*. The *Thebaïs* seems to have begun with the origin of the fatal quarrel between Eteocles and Polyneices in the curse called down upon them by their father in his misery. The story was thence carried down to the end of the expedition under Polyneices, Adrastus and Amphiaraus against Thebes. The *Epigoni* (ascribed to Antimachus of Teos) recounted the expedition of the "After-Born" against Thebes, and the sack of the city.

The Trojan Cycle.—Six epics with the *Iliad* and the *Odyssey* made up the Trojan Cycle—The *Cyprian Lays,* the *Iliad,* the *Aethiopis,* the *Little Iliad,* the *Sack of Troy,* the *Returns,* the *Odyssey,* and the *Telegony.*

It has been assumed in the foregoing pages that the poems of the Trojan Cycle are later than the Homeric poems; but, as the opposite view has been held, the reason for this assumption must now be given. (1) Tradition puts Homer and the Homeric poems proper back in the ages before chronological history began, and at the same time assigns the purely Cyclic poems to definite authors who are dated from the first Olympiad (776 B.C.) downwards. This tradition cannot be purely arbitrary. (2) The Cyclic poets (as we can see from the abstracts of Proclus) were careful not to trespass upon ground already occupied by Homer. Thus, when we find that in the *Returns* all the prominent Greek heroes except Odysseus are accounted for, we are forced to believe that the author of this poem knew the *Odyssey* and judged it unnecessary to deal in full with that hero's adventures.[1] In a word, the Cyclic poems are "written round" the *Iliad* and the *Odyssey.* (3) The general structure of these epics is clearly imitative. As MM. Croiset remark, the abusive Thersites in the *Aethiopis* is clearly copied from the Thersites of the *Iliad*: in the same poem Antilochus, slain by Memnon and avenged by Achilles, is obviously modelled on Patroclus. (4) The geographical knowledge of a poem like

[1] Odysseus appears to have been mentioned once only—and that casually—in the *Returns.*

the *Returns* is far wider and more precise than that of the *Odyssey.* (5) Moreover, in the Cyclic poems epic is clearly degenerating morally—if the expression may be used. The chief greatness of the *Iliad* is in the character of the heroes Achilles and Hector rather than in the actual events which take place : in the Cyclic writers facts rather than character are the objects of interest, and events are so packed together as to leave no space for any exhibition of the play of moral forces. All these reasons justify the view that the poems with which we now have to deal were later than the *Iliad* and *Odyssey,* and if we must recognize the possibility of some conventionality in the received dating, we may feel confident that it is at least approximately just.

The earliest of the post-Homeric epics of Troy are apparently the *Aethiopis* and the *Sack of Ilium,* both ascribed to Arctinus of Miletus who is said to have flourished in the first Olympiad (776 B.C.). He set himself to finish the tale of Troy, which, so far as events were concerned, had been left half-told by Homer, by tracing the course of events after the close of the Iliad. The Aethiopis thus included the coming of the Amazon Penthesilea to help the Trojans after the fall of Hector and her death, the similar arrival and fall of the Aethiopian Memnon, the death of Achilles under the arrow of Paris, and the dispute between Odysseus and Aias for the arms of Achilles. The *Sack of Ilium*[1] as analysed by Proclus was very similar to Vergil's version in

[1] MM. Croiset note that the *Aethiopis* and the *Sack* were originally merely parts of one work containing lays (the Amazoneia, Aethiopis, Persis, etc.), just as the *Iliad* contained various lays such as the Diomedeia.

Aeneid ii, comprising the episodes of the wooden horse, of Laocoon, of Sinon, the return of the Achaeans from Tenedos, the actual Sack of Troy, the division of spoils and the burning of the city.

Lesches or Lescheos (as Pausanias calls him) of Pyrrha or Mitylene is dated at about 660 B.C. In his *Little Iliad* he undertook to elaborate the *Sack* as related by Arctinus. His work included the adjudgment of the arms of Achilles to Odysseus, the madness of Aias, the bringing of Philoctetes from Lemnos and his cure, the coming to the war of Neoptolemus who slays Eurypylus, son of Telephus, the making of the wooden horse, the spying of Odysseus and his theft, along with Diomedes, of the Palladium : the analysis concludes with the admission of the wooden horse into Troy by the Trojans. It is known, however (Aristotle, *Poetics,* xxiii ; Pausanias, x, 25–27), that the *Little Iliad* also contained a description of the *Sack of Troy.* It is probable that this and other superfluous incidents disappeared after the Alexandrian arrangement of the poems in the Cycle, either as the result of some later recension, or merely through disuse. Or Proclus may have thought it unnecessary to give the accounts by Lesches and Arctinus of the same incident.

The *Cyprian Lays,* ascribed to Stasinus of Cyprus [1] (but also to Hegesinus of Salamis) was designed to do for the events preceding the action of the *Iliad* what Arctinus had done for the later phases of the Trojan War. The *Cypria* begins with the first causes of the war, the purpose of Zeus to relieve the overburdened earth, the apple of discord, the rape of Helen. Then

[1] No date is assigned to him, but it seems likely that he was either contemporary or slightly earlier than Lesches.

follow the incidents connected with the gathering of the Achaeans and their ultimate landing in Troy; and the story of the war is detailed up to the quarrel between Achilles and Agamemnon with which the *Iliad* begins.

These four poems rounded off the story of the *Iliad,* and it only remained to connect this enlarged version with the *Odyssey.* This was done by means of the *Returns,* a poem in five books ascribed to Agias or Hegias of Troezen, which begins where the *Sack of Troy* ends. It told of the dispute between Agamemnon and Menelaus, the departure from Troy of Menelaus, the fortunes of the lesser heroes, the return and tragic death of Agamemnon, and the vengeance of Orestes on Aegisthus. The story ends with the return home of Menelaus, which brings the general narrative up to the beginning of the *Odyssey.*

But the *Odyssey* itself left much untold: what, for example, happened in Ithaca after the slaying of the suitors, and what was the ultimate fate of Odysseus? The answer to these questions was supplied by the *Telegony,* a poem in two books by Eugammon of Cyrene (*fl.* 568 B.C.). It told of the adventures of Odysseus in Thesprotis after the killing of the Suitors, of his return to Ithaca, and his death at the hands of Telegonus, his son by Circe. The epic ended by disposing of the surviving personages in a double marriage, Telemachus wedding Circe, and Telegonus Penelope.

The end of the Cycle marks also the end of the Heroic Age.

The Homeric Hymns.

The collection of thirty-three Hymns, ascribed to Homer, is the last considerable work of the Epic School, and seems, on the whole, to be later than the Cyclic poems. It cannot be definitely assigned either to the Ionian or Continental schools, for while the romantic element is very strong, there is a distinct genealogical interest; and in matters of diction and style the influences of both Hesiod and Homer are well-marked. The date of the formation of the collection as such is unknown. Diodorus Siculus (*temp.* Augustus) is the first to mention such a body of poetry, and it is likely enough that this is, at least substantially, the one which has come down to us. Thucydides quotes the Delian *Hymn to Apollo,* and it is possible that the Homeric corpus of his day also contained other of the more important hymns. Conceivably the collection was arranged in the Alexandrine period.

Thucydides, in quoting the Hymn to Apollo, calls it *προοίμιον,* which ordinarily means a "prelude" chanted by a rhapsode before recitation of a lay from Homer, and such hymns as Nos. vi, x, xxxi, xxxii, are clearly preludes in the strict sense; in No. xxxi, for example, after celebrating Helios, the poet declares he will next sing of the "race of mortal men, the demi-gods." But it may fairly be doubted whether such Hymns as those to *Demeter* (ii), *Apollo* (iii), *Hermes* (iv), *Aphrodite* (v), can have been real preludes, in spite of the closing formula "and now I will pass on to another hymn." The view taken by Allen and Sikes, amongst other scholars, is doubtless right, that these longer hymns are only technically preludes and show to what disproportionate lengths a simple literary form can be developed. The Hymns to *Pan* (xix), to *Dionysus* (xxvi), to *Hestia and Hermes* (xxix), seem to have been designed for use at definite religious festivals, apart from recitations. With the exception perhaps of the *Hymn to Ares* (viii), no item in the collection can be regarded as either devotional or liturgical.

The Hymn is doubtless a very ancient form; but if no examples of extreme antiquity survive this must be put down to the fact that until the age of literary consciousness, such things are not preserved.

First, apparently, in the collection stood the *Hymn to Dionysus,* of which only two fragments now survive. While it appears to have been a hymn of the longer type,[1] we have no evidence to show either its scope or date.

The *Hymn to Demeter,* extant only in the MS. discovered by Matthiae at Moscow, describes the seizure of Persephone by Hades, the grief of Demeter, her stay at Eleusis, and her vengeance on gods and men by causing famine. In the end Zeus is forced to bring Persephone back from the lower world; but the goddess, by the contriving of Hades, still remains partly a deity of the lower world. In memory of her sorrows Demeter establishes the Eleusinian mysteries (which, however, were purely agrarian in origin).

This hymn, as a literary work, is one of the finest

[1] Cp. Allen and Sikes, *Homeric Hymns* p. xv. In the text I have followed the arrangement of these scholars, numbering the Hymns to Dionysus and to Demeter, I and II respectively: to place *Demeter* after *Hermes*, and the Hymn to Dionysus at the end of the collection seems to be merely perverse.

in the collection. It is surely Attic or Eleusinian in origin. Can we in any way fix its date? Firstly, it is certainly not later than the beginning of the sixth century, for it makes no mention of Iacchus, and the Dionysiac element was introduced at Eleusis at about that period. Further, the insignificance of Triptolemus and Eumolpus point to considerable antiquity, and the digamma is still active. All these considerations point to the seventh century as the probable date of the hymn.

The *Hymn to Apollo* consists of two parts, which beyond any doubt were originally distinct, a Delian hymn and a Pythian hymn. The Delian hymn describes how Leto, in travail with Apollo, sought out a place in which to bear her son, and how Apollo, born in Delos, at once claimed for himself the lyre, the bow, and prophecy. This part of the existing hymn ends with an encomium of the Delian festival of Apollo and of the Delian choirs. The second part celebrates the founding of Pytho (Delphi) as the oracular seat of Apollo. After various wanderings the god comes to Telphusa, near Haliartus, but is dissuaded by the nymph of the place from settling there and urged to go on to Pytho where, after slaying the she-dragon who nursed Typhaon, he builds his temple. After the punishment of Telphusa for her deceit in giving him no warning of the dragoness at Pytho, Apollo, in the form of a dolphin, brings certain Cretan shipmen to Delphi to be his priests; and the hymn ends with a charge to these men to behave orderly and righteously.

The Delian part is exclusively Ionian and insular both in style and sympathy; Delos and no other is Apollo's chosen seat: but the second part is as definitely continental; Delos is ignored and Delphi alone is the important centre of Apollo's worship. From this it is clear that the two parts need not be of one date—The first, indeed, is ascribed (Scholiast on Pindar *Nem.* ii, 2) to Cynaethus of Chios (*fl.* 504 B.C.), a date which is obviously far too low; general considerations point rather to the eighth century. The second part is not later than 600 B.C.; for (1) the chariot-races at Pytho, which commenced in 586 B.C., are unknown to the writer of the hymn, (2) the temple built by Trophonius and Agamedes for Apollo (ll. 294–299) seems to have been still standing when the hymn was written, and this temple was burned in 548. We may at least be sure that the first part is a Chian work, and that the second was composed by a continental poet familiar with Delphi.

The *Hymn to Hermes* differs from others in its burlesque, quasi-comic character, and it is also the best-known of the Hymns to English readers in consequence of Shelley's translation.

After a brief narrative of the birth of Hermes, the author goes on to show how he won a place among the gods. First the new-born child found a tortoise and from its shell contrived the lyre; next, with much cunning circumstance, he stole Apollo's cattle and, when charged with the theft by Apollo, forced that god to appear in undignified guise before the tribunal of Zeus. Zeus seeks to reconcile the pair, and Hermes by the gift of the lyre wins Apollo's friendship and purchases various prerogatives, a share in divination, the lordship of herds and animals, and the office of messenger from the gods to Hades.

The hymn is hard to date. Hermes' lyre has seven strings and the invention of the seven-stringed lyre is ascribed to Terpander (*flor.* 676 B.C.). The hymn must therefore be later than that date, though Terpander, according to Weir Smyth,[1] may have only modified the scale of the lyre; yet while the burlesque character precludes an early date, this feature is far removed, as Allen and Sikes remark, from the silliness of the *Battle of the Frogs and Mice,* so that a date in the earlier part of the sixth century is most probable.

The *Hymn to Aphrodite* is not the least remarkable, from a literary point of view, of the whole collection, exhibiting as it does in a masterly manner a divine being as the unwilling victim of an irresistible force. It tells how all creatures, and even the gods themselves, are subject to the will of Aphrodite, saving only Artemis, Athena, and Hestia; how Zeus to humble her pride of power caused her to love a mortal, Anchises; and how the goddess visited the hero upon Mt. Ida. A comparison of this work with the Lay of Demodocus (*Odyssey* viii, 266 ff.), which is superficially similar, will show how far superior is the former in which the goddess is but a victim to forces stronger than herself. The lines (247–255) in which Aphrodite tells of her humiliation and grief are specially noteworthy.

There are only general indications of date. The influence of Hesiod is clear, and the hymn has almost certainly been used by the author of the *Hymn to Demeter,* so that the date must lie between these two periods, and the seventh century seems to be the latest date possible.

The *Hymn to Dionysus* relates how the god was seized by pirates and how with many manifestations of power he avenged himself on them by turning them into dolphins. The date is widely disputed, for while

[1] *Greek Melic Poets,* p. 165.

Ludwich believes it to be a work of the fourth or third century, Allen and Sikes consider a sixth or seventh century date to be possible. The story is figured in a different form on the reliefs from the choragic monument of Lysicrates, now in the British Museum.

Very different in character is the *Hymn to Ares*, which is Orphic in character. The writer, after lauding the god by detailing his attributes, prays to be delivered from feebleness and weakness of soul, as also from impulses to wanton and brutal violence.

The only other considerable hymn is that to *Pan*, which describes how he roams hunting among the mountains and thickets and streams, how he makes music at dusk while returning from the chase, and how he joins in dancing with the nymphs who sing the story of his birth. This, beyond most works of Greek literature, is remarkable for its fresh and spontaneous love of wild natural scenes.

The remaining hymns are mostly of the briefest compass, merely hailing the god to be celebrated and mentioning his chief attributes. The Hymns to *Hermes* (xvii) to the *Dioscuri* (xvii) and to *Demeter* (xiii) are mere abstracts of the longer hymns iv, xxxiii, and ii.

The Epigrams of Homer

The Epigrams of Homer are derived from the pseudo-Herodotean *Life of Homer*, but many of them occur in other documents such as the *Contest of Homer and Hesiod*, or are quoted by various ancient authors. These poetic fragments clearly antedate the "Life" itself, which seems to have been so written round them as to supply appropriate occasions for their composition. Epigram iii. on Midas of Larissa was otherwise attributed to Cleobulus of Lindus, one of the Seven Sages; the address to Glaucus (xi) is purely Hesiodic; xiii, according to MM. Croiset, is a fragment from a gnomic poem. Epigram xiv is a curious poem attributed on no very obvious grounds to Hesiod by Julius Pollux. In it the poet invokes Athena to protect certain potters and their craft, if they will, according to promise, give him a reward for his song; if they prove false, malignant gnomes are invoked to wreck the kiln and hurt the potters.

The Burlesque Poems

To Homer were popularly ascribed certain burlesque poems in which Aristotle (*Poetics* iv) saw the germ of comedy. Most interesting of these, were it extant, would be the *Margites*. The hero of the epic is at once sciolist and simpleton, "knowing many things, but knowing them all badly." It is unfortunately impossible to trace the plan of the poem, which presumably detailed the adventures of this unheroic character: the metre used was a curious mixture of hexametric and iambic lines. The date of such a work cannot be high: Croiset thinks it may belong to the period of Archilochus (*c.* 650 B.C.), but it may well be somewhat later.

Another poem, of which we know even less, is the *Cercopes*. These Cercopes ("Monkey-Men") were a pair of malignant dwarfs who went about the world mischief-making. Their punishment by Heracles is represented on one of the earlier metopes from Selinus. It would be idle to speculate as to the date of this work.

Finally there is the *Battle of the Frogs and Mice.* Here is told the story of the quarrel which arose between the two tribes, and how they fought, until Zeus sent crabs to break up the battle. It is a parody of the warlike epic, but has little in it that is really comic or of literary merit, except perhaps the list of quaint arms assumed by the warriors. The text of the poem is in a chaotic condition, and there are many interpolations, some of Byzantine date.

Though popularly ascribed to Homer, its real author is said by Suidas to have been Pigres, a Carian, brother of Artemisia, "wife of Mausolus," who distinguished herself at the battle of Salamis. Suidas is confusing the two Artemisias, but he may be right in attributing the poem to about 480 B.C.

The Contest of Homer and Hesiod

This curious work dates in its present form from the lifetime or shortly after the death of Hadrian, but seems to be based in part on an earlier version by the sophist Alcidamas (*c.* 400 B.C.). Plutarch (*Conviv. Sept. Sap.*, 40) uses an earlier (or at least a shorter) version than that which we possess.[1] The extant *Contest,* however, has clearly combined with the original document much other ill-digested matter on the life and descent of Homer, probably drawing on the same general sources as does the Herodotean *Life of Homer.* Its scope is as follows: (1) the descent (as variously reported) and relative dates of Homer

[1] Cp. Marckscheffel, *Hesiodi fragmenta*, p. 35. The papyrus fragment recovered by Petrie (*Petrie Papyri*, ed. Mahaffy, p. 70, No. xxv.) agrees essentially with the extant document, but differs in numerous minor textual points.

and Hesiod; (2) their poetical contest at Chalcis; (3) the death of Hesiod; (4) the wanderings and fortunes of Homer, with brief notices of the circumstances under which his reputed works were composed, down to the time of his death.

The whole tract is, of course, mere romance; its only values are (1) the insight it gives into ancient speculations about Homer; (2) a certain amount of definite information about the Cyclic poems; and (3) the epic fragments included in the stichomythia of the *Contest* proper, many of which—did we possess the clue—would have to be referred to poems of the Epic Cycle.

BIBLIOGRAPHY

Hesiod.—The classification and numeration of MSS. here followed is that of Rzach (1908). It is only necessary to add that on the whole the recovery of Hesiodic papyri goes to confirm the authority of the mediaeval MSS. At the same time these fragments have produced much that is interesting and valuable, such as the new lines, *Works and Days* 169 a–d, and the improved readings *ib.* 278, *Theogony* 91, 93. Our chief gains from the papyri are the numerous and excellent fragments of the Catalogues which have been recovered.

Works and Days :—

A Vienna, Rainer Papyri L.P. 21—9 (4th cent.).
B Geneva, Naville Papyri Pap. 94 (6th cent.).
Oxyrhynchus Papyri 1090.[1]
C Paris, Bibl. Nat. 2771 (11th cent.).
D Florence, Laur. xxxi 39 (12th cent.).
E Messina, Univ. Lib. Preexistens 11 (12th–13th cent.).
F Rome, Vatican 38 (14th cent.).
G Venice, Marc. ix 6 (14th cent.).
H Florence, Laur. xxxi 37 (14th cent.).
I ,, ,, xxxii 16 (13th cent.).
K ,, ,, xxxii 2 (14th cent.).
L Milan, Ambros. G 32 sup. (14th cent.).
M Florence, Bibl. Riccardiana 71 (15th cent.).
N Milan, Ambros. J 15 sup. (15th cent.).
O Paris, Bibl. Nat. 2773 (14th cent.).
P Cambridge, Trinity College (Gale MS.), O. 9. 27 (13th–14th cent.).
Q Rome, Vatican 1332 (14th cent.).

These MSS. are divided by Rzach into the following families, issuing from a common original :—

Ωa = C	Ψa = D	Φa = E
Ωb = FGH	Ψb = IKLM	Φb = NOPQ

[1] Not included in Rzach's list.

BIBLIOGRAPHY

Theogony :—

A Paris, Bibl. Nat. Suppl. Graec. (papyrus) 1099 (4th–5th cent.).
B London, British Museum clix (4th cent.).
R Vienna, Rainer Papyri L.P. 21–9 (4th cent.).
C Paris, Bibl. Nat. Suppl. Graec. 663 (12th cent.).
D Florence, Laur. xxxii 16 (13th cent.).
E ,, ,, , Conv. suppr. 158 (14th cent.).
F Paris, Bibl. Nat. 2833 (15th cent.).
G Rome, Vatican 915 (14th cent.).
H Paris, Bibl. Nat. 2772 (14th cent.).
I Florence, Laur. xxxi 32 (15th cent.).
K Venice, Marc. ix 6 (15th cent.).
L Paris, Bibl. Nat. 2708 (15th cent.).

These MSS. are divided into two families:

Ωa = CD Ψ = KL
Ωb = EF
Ωc = GHI

Shield of Heracles :—

P Oxyrhynchus Papyri 689 (2nd cent.).
A Vienna, Rainer Papyri L.P. 21–29 (4th cent.).
Q Berlin Papyri, 9774 (1st cent.).
B Paris, Bibl. Nat., Suppl. Graec. 663 (12th cent.).
C ,, ,, ,, ,, ,, ,, (12th cent.).
D Milan, Ambros. C 222 (13th cent.).
E Florence, Laur. xxxii 16 (13th cent.).
F Paris, Bibl. Nat. 2773 (14th cent.).
G ,, ,, ,, 2772 (14th cent.).
H Florence, Laur. xxxi 32 (15th cent.).
I London, British Museum Harleianus (14th cent.).
K Rome, Bibl. Casanat. 356 (14th cent.).
L Florence, Laur. Conv. suppr. 158 (14th cent.).
M Paris, Bibl. Nat. 2833 (15th cent.).

These MSS belong to two families:

Ωa = BCDF Ψa = E
Ωb = GHI Ψb = KLM

To these must be added two MSS. of mixed family:

N Venice, Marc. ix 6 (14th cent.).
O Paris, Bibl. Nat. 2708 (15th cent.).

BIBLIOGRAPHY

Editions of Hesiod :—

Demetrius Chalcondyles, Milan (?) 1493 (?) (*editio princeps*, containing, however, only the *Works and Days*).
Aldus Manutius (Aldine edition), Venice, 1495 (complete works).
Juntine Editions, 1515 and 1540.
Trincavelli, Venice, 1537 (with scholia).

Of modern editions the following may be noticed :—

Gaisford, Oxford, 1814–1820; Leipzig, 1823 (with scholia: in Poett. Graec. Minn II).
Goettling, Gotha, 1831 (3rd edition, Leipzig 1878).
Didot Edition, Paris, 1840.
Schömann, 1869.
Koechly and Kinkel, Leipzig, 1870.
Flach, Leipzig, 1874–8.
Rzach, Leipzig, 1902 (larger edition), 1908 (smaller edition).

On the Hesiodic poems generally the ordinary Histories of Greek Literature may be consulted, but especially the *Hist. de la Littérature Grecque* I pp. 459 ff. of MM. Croiset. The summary account in Prof. Murray's *Anc. Gk. Lit.* is written with a strong sceptical bias. Very valuable is the appendix to Mair's translation (Oxford, 1908) on *The Farmer's Year in Hesiod*. Recent work on the Hesiodic poems is reviewed in full by Rzach in Bursian's *Jahresberichte* vols. 100 (1899) and 152 (1911).

For the *Fragments* of Hesiodic poems the work of Markscheffel, *Hesiodi Fragmenta* (Leipzig, 1840), is most valuable: important also is Kinkel's *Epicorum Graecorum Fragmenta* I (Leipzig, 1877) and the editions of Rzach noticed above. For recently discovered papyrus fragments see Wilamowitz, *Neue Bruchstücke d. Hesiod Katalog* (Sitzungsb. der k. preuss. Akad. für Wissenschaft, 1900, pp. 839–851.) A list of the papyri belonging to lost Hesiodic works may here be added: all are from the *Catalogues*.

(1) Berlin Papyri 7497 [1] (2nd cent.). } Frag. 7.
(2) *Oxyrhynchus Papyri* 421 (2nd cent.). }

[1] See Schubart, *Berl. Klassikertexte* v. 1. 22 ff.; the other papyri may be found in the publications whose name they bear.

(3) *Petrie Papyri* iii 3. } Frag.
(4) *Papiri greci e latine.* No. 130 (2nd to 3rd cent.) } 14.
(5) Strassburg Papyri, 55 (2nd cent.) Frag. 58.
(6) Berlin Papyri 9739[1] (2nd cent.) } Frag. 58.
(7) ,, ,, 10560[1] (3rd cent.) }
(8) ,, ,, 9777[1] (4th cent.) Frag. 98.
(9) *Papiri greci e latine,* No. 131 (2nd–3rd cent.) Frag. 99.

The Homeric Hymns :—The text of the Homeric hymns is distinctly bad in condition, a fact which may be attributed to the general neglect under which they seem to have laboured at all periods previously to the Revival of Learning. Very many defects have been corrected by the various editions of the Hymns, but a considerable number still defy all efforts ; and especially an abnormal number of undoubted lacunae disfigure the text. Unfortunately no papyrus fragment of the Hymns has yet emerged, though one such fragment (*Berl. Klassikertexte* v. 1. pp. 7 ff.) contains a paraphrase of a poem very closely parallel to the *Hymn to Demeter.*

The mediaeval MSS.[2] are thus enumerated by Dr. T. W. Allen :—

A Paris, Bibl. Nat. 2763.
At Athos, Vatopedi 587.
B Paris, Bibl. Nat. 2765.
C Paris, Bibl. Nat. 2833.
Γ Brussels, Bibl. Royale 11377–11380 (16th cent.).
D Milan, Ambros. B 98 sup.
E Modena, Estense iii E 11.
G Rome, Vatican, Regina 91 (16th cent.).
H London, British Mus. Harley 1752.
J Modena, Estense, ii B 14.
K Florence, Laur. 31, 32.
L ,, ,, 32, 45.
L_2 ,, ,, 70, 35.
L_3 ,, ,, 32, 4.
M Leyden (the Moscow MS.) 33 H (14th cent.).
Mon. Munich, Royal Lib. 333 c.
N Leyden, 74 c.
O Milan, Ambros. C 10 inf.

[1] See note on page xlv.

[2] Unless otherwise noted, all these MSS. are of the 15th century.

P Rome, Vatican Pal. graec. 179.
Π Paris, Bibl. Nat. Suppl. graec. 1095.
Q Milan, Ambros. S 31 sup.
R_1 Florence, Bibl. Riccard. 53 K ii 13.
R_2 ,, ,, ,, 52 K ii 14.
S Rome, Vatican, Vaticani graec. 1880.
T Madrid, Public Library 24.
V Venice, Marc. 456.

The same scholar has traced all the MSS. back to a common parent from which three main families are derived (M had a separate descent and is not included in any family) :—

x^1 = ET.
x^2 = LΠ (and more remotely) AtDSHJK.
y = ELΠT (marginal readings).
p = ABCΓGL^{2}L^{3}NOPQR_1R_2V Mon.

Editions of the Homeric Hymns, &c.

Demetrius Chalcondyles, Florence, 1488 (with the Epigrams and the battle of the Frogs and Mice in the *ed. pr.* of Homer).
Aldine Edition, Venice, 1504.
Juntine Edition, 1537.
Stephanus, Paris, 1566 and 1588.

More modern editions or critical works of value are :—

Martin (Variarum Lectionum libb. iv), Paris, 1605.
Barnes, Cambridge, 1711.
Ruhnken, Leyden, 1782 (Epist. Crit. and Hymn to Demeter).
Ilgen, Halle, 1796 (with Epigrams and the Battle of Frogs and Mice).
Matthiae, Leipzig, 1806 (with the Battle of Frogs and Mice).
Hermann, Berlin, 1806 (with Epigrams).
Franke, Leipzig, 1828 (with Epigrams and the Battle of the Frogs and Mice).
Dindorff (Didot edition), Paris, 1837.
Baumeister (Battle of the Frogs and Mice), Göttingen, 1852.
,, (Hymns), Leipzig, 1860.
Gemoll, Leipzig, 1886.
Goodwin, Oxford, 1893.
Ludwich (Battle of the Frogs and Mice), 1896.
Allen and Sikes, London, 1904.
Allen (Homeri Opera v), Oxford, 1912.

Of these editions that of Messrs Allen and Sikes is by far the best: not only is the text purged of the load of conjectures for which the frequent obscurities of the Hymns offer a special opening, but the Introduction and the Notes throughout are of the highest value. For a full discussion of the MSS. and textual problems, reference must be made to this edition, as also to Dr. T. W. Allen's series of articles in the *Journal of Hellenic Studies* vols. xv ff. Among translations those of J. Edgar (Edinburgh, 1891) and of Andrew Lang (London, 1899) may be mentioned.

The Epic Cycle. The fragments of the Epic Cycle being drawn from a variety of authors, no list of MSS. can be given. The following collections and editions may be mentioned :—

Muller, Leipzig, 1829.
Dindorff (Didot edition of Homer), Paris, 1837-56.
Kinkel (Epicorum Graecorum Fragmenta i, Leipzig, 1877.
Allen (Homeri Opera v), Oxford, 1912.

The fullest discussion of the problems and fragments of the epic cycle is F. G. Welcker's *der epische Cyclus* (Bonn, vol. i, 1835 : vol. ii, 1849 : vol i, 2nd edition, 1865). The Appendix to Monro's *Homer's Odyssey* xii–xxiv (pp. 340 ff.) deals with the Cylic poets in relation to Homer, and a clear and reasonable discussion of the subject is to be found in Croiset's *Hist. de la Littérature Grecque* vol. i.

HESIOD

ΗΣΙΟΔΟΥ ΕΡΓΑ ΚΑΙ ΗΜΕΡΑΙ

Μοῦσαι Πιερίηθεν ἀοιδῇσιν κλείουσαι
δεῦτε, Δί᾽ ἐννέπετε, σφέτερον πατέρ᾽ ὑμνείουσαι·
ὅντε διὰ βροτοὶ ἄνδρες ὁμῶς ἄφατοί τε φατοί τε,
ῥητοί τ᾽ ἄρρητοί τε Διὸς μεγάλοιο ἕκητι.
ῥέα μὲν γὰρ βριάει, ῥέα δὲ βριάοντα χαλέπτει,
ῥεῖα δ᾽ ἀρίζηλον μινύθει καὶ ἄδηλον ἀέξει,
ῥεῖα δέ τ᾽ ἰθύνει σκολιὸν καὶ ἀγήνορα κάρφει
Ζεὺς ὑψιβρεμέτης, ὃς ὑπέρτατα δώματα ναίει.
κλῦθι ἰδὼν ἀίων τε, δίκῃ δ᾽ ἴθυνε θέμιστας
τύνη· ἐγὼ δέ κε, Πέρση, ἐτήτυμα μυθησαίμην.

Οὐκ ἄρα μοῦνον ἔην Ἐρίδων γένος, ἀλλ᾽ ἐπὶ γαῖαν
εἰσὶ δύω· τὴν μέν κεν ἐπαινέσσειε νοήσας,
ἣ δ᾽ ἐπιμωμητή· διὰ δ᾽ ἄνδιχα θυμὸν ἔχουσιν.
ἣ μὲν γὰρ πόλεμόν τε κακὸν καὶ δῆριν ὀφέλλει,
σχετλίη· οὔτις τήν γε φιλεῖ βροτός, ἀλλ᾽ ὑπ᾽ ἀνάγκης
ἀθανάτων βουλῇσιν Ἔριν τιμῶσι βαρεῖαν.
τὴν δ᾽ ἑτέρην προτέρην μὲν ἐγείνατο Νὺξ ἐρεβεννή,
θῆκε δέ μιν Κρονίδης ὑψίζυγος, αἰθέρι ναίων,
γαίης ἐν ῥίζῃσι, καὶ ἀνδράσι πολλὸν ἀμείνω·
ἥτε καὶ ἀπάλαμόν περ ὁμῶς ἐπὶ ἔργον ἔγειρεν.

HESIOD'S WORKS AND DAYS

Muses of Pieria who give glory through song, come hither, tell of Zeus your father and chant his praise. Through him mortal men are famed or unfamed, sung or unsung alike, as great Zeus wills. For easily he makes strong, and easily he brings the strong man low; easily he humbles the proud and raises the obscure, and easily he straightens the crooked and blasts the proud, — Zeus who thunders aloft and has his dwelling most high. Attend thou with eye and ear, and make judgements straight with righteousness. And I, Perses, would tell of true things.

So, after all, there was not one kind of Strife alone, but all over the earth there are two. As for the one, a man would praise her when he came to understand her; but the other is blameworthy: and they are wholly different in nature. For one fosters evil war and battle, being cruel: her no man loves; but perforce, through the will of the deathless gods, men pay harsh Strife her honour due. But the other is the elder daughter of dark Night, and the son of Cronos who sits above and dwells in the aether, set her in the roots of the earth: and she is far kinder to men. She stirs up even the shiftless to toil; for a

εἰς ἕτερον γάρ τίς τε ἰδὼν ἔργοιο χατίζει [1]
πλούσιον, ὃς σπεύδει μὲν ἀρώμεναι ἠδὲ φυτεύειν
οἶκόν τ' εὖ θέσθαι· ζηλοῖ δέ τε γείτονα γείτων
εἰς ἄφενος σπεύδοντ'· ἀγαθὴ δ' Ἔρις ἥδε βροτοῖσιν.
καὶ κεραμεὺς κεραμεῖ κοτέει καὶ τέκτονι τέκτων,
καὶ πτωχὸς πτωχῷ φθονέει καὶ ἀοιδὸς ἀοιδῷ.
Ὦ Πέρση, σὺ δὲ ταῦτα τεῷ ἐνικάτθεο θυμῷ,
μηδέ σ' Ἔρις κακόχαρτος ἀπ' ἔργου θυμὸν ἐρύκοι
νείκε' ὀπιπεύοντ' ἀγορῆς ἐπακουὸν ἐόντα.
ὤρη γάρ τ' ὀλίγη πέλεται νεικέων τ' ἀγορέων τε,
ᾧτινι μὴ βίος ἔνδον ἐπηετανὸς κατάκειται
ὡραῖος, τὸν γαῖα φέρει, Δημήτερος ἀκτήν.
τοῦ κε κορεσσάμενος νείκεα καὶ δῆριν ὀφέλλοις
κτήμασ' ἐπ' ἀλλοτρίοις· σοὶ δ' οὐκέτι δεύτερον ἔσται
ὧδ' ἔρδειν· ἀλλ' αὖθι διακρινώμεθα νεῖκος
ἰθείῃσι δίκῃς, αἵ τ' ἐκ Διός εἰσιν ἄρισται.
ἤδη μὲν γὰρ κλῆρον ἐδασσάμεθ', ἀλλὰ τὰ [2] πολλὰ
ἁρπάζων ἐφόρεις μέγα κυδαίνων βασιλῆας
δωροφάγους, οἳ τήνδε δίκην ἐθέλουσι δίκασσαι.
νήπιοι, οὐδὲ ἴσασιν ὅσῳ πλέον ἥμισυ παντὸς
οὐδ' ὅσον ἐν μαλάχῃ τε καὶ ἀσφοδέλῳ μέγ' ὄνειαρ.
Κρύψαντες γὰρ ἔχουσι θεοὶ βίον ἀνθρώποισιν·
ῥηιδίως γάρ κεν καὶ ἐπ' ἤματι ἐργάσσαιο,
ὥστε σε κεὶς ἐνιαυτὸν ἔχειν καὶ ἀεργὸν ἐόντα·
αἶψά κε πηδάλιον μὲν ὑπὲρ καπνοῦ καταθεῖο,
ἔργα βοῶν δ' ἀπόλοιτο καὶ ἡμιόνων ταλαεργῶν.
ἀλλὰ Ζεὺς ἔκρυψε χολωσάμενος φρεσὶν ᾗσιν,
ὅττι μιν ἐξαπάτησε Προμηθεὺς ἀγκυλομήτης·
τοὔνεκ' ἄρ' ἀνθρώποισιν ἐμήσατο κήδεα λυγρά.

[1] CF: χατίζων, other MSS. [2] Guyet: ἄλλα τε, MSS.

man grows eager to work when he considers his neighbour, a rich man who hastens to plough and plant and put his house in good order; and neighbour vies with his neighbour as he hurries after wealth. This Strife is wholesome for men. And potter is angry with potter, and craftsman with craftsman, and beggar is jealous of beggar, and minstrel of minstrel.

Perses, lay up these things in your heart, and do not let that Strife who delights in mischief hold your heart back from work, while you peep and peer and listen to the wrangles of the court-house. Little concern has he with quarrels and courts who has not a year's victuals laid up betimes, even that which the earth bears, Demeter's grain. When you have got plenty of that, you can raise disputes and strive to get another's goods. But you shall have no second chance to deal so again: nay, let us settle our dispute here with true judgement which is of Zeus and is perfect. For we had already divided our inheritance, but you seized the greater share and carried it off, greatly swelling the glory of our bribe-swallowing lords who love to judge such a cause as this. Fools! They know not how much more the half is than the whole, nor what great advantage there is in mallow and asphodel.[1]

For the gods keep hidden from men the means of life. Else you would easily do work enough in a day to supply you for a full year even without working; soon would you put away your rudder over the smoke, and the fields worked by ox and sturdy mule would run to waste. But Zeus in the anger of his heart hid it, because Prometheus the crafty deceived him; therefore he planned sorrow and mischief against

[1] That is, the poor man's fare, like "bread and cheese."

κρύψε δὲ πῦρ· τὸ μὲν αὖτις ἐὺς πάις Ἰαπετοῖο
ἔκλεψ᾽ ἀνθρώποισι Διὸς πάρα μητιόεντος
ἐν κοΐλῳ νάρθηκι λαθὼν Δία τερπικέραυνον.
τὸν δὲ χολωσάμενος προσέφη νεφεληγερέτα Ζεύς·
Ἰαπετιονίδη, πάντων πέρι μήδεα εἰδώς,
χαίρεις πῦρ κλέψας καὶ ἐμὰς φρένας ἠπεροπεύσας,
σοί τ᾽ αὐτῷ μέγα πῆμα καὶ ἀνδράσιν ἐσσομένοισιν.
τοῖς δ᾽ ἐγὼ ἀντὶ πυρὸς δώσω κακόν, ᾧ κεν ἅπαντες
τέρπωνται κατὰ θυμὸν ἑὸν κακὸν ἀμφαγαπῶντες.
Ὣς ἔφατ᾽· ἐκ δ᾽ ἐγέλασσε πατὴρ ἀνδρῶν τε θεῶν τε.
Ἥφαιστον δ᾽ ἐκέλευσε περικλυτὸν ὅττι τάχιστα
γαῖαν ὕδει φύρειν, ἐν δ᾽ ἀνθρώπου θέμεν αὐδὴν
καὶ σθένος, ἀθανάτῃς δὲ θεῇς εἰς ὦπα ἐίσκειν
παρθενικῆς καλὸν εἶδος ἐπήρατον· αὐτὰρ Ἀθήνην
ἔργα διδασκῆσαι, πολυδαίδαλον ἱστὸν ὑφαίνειν·
καὶ χάριν ἀμφιχέαι κεφαλῇ χρυσέην Ἀφροδίτην
καὶ πόθον ἀργαλέον καὶ γυιοκόρους μελεδώνας·
ἐν δὲ θέμεν κύνεόν τε νόον καὶ ἐπίκλοπον ἦθος
Ἑρμείην ἤνωγε, διάκτορον Ἀργεϊφόντην.
Ὣς ἔφαθ᾽· οἱ δ᾽ ἐπίθοντο Διὶ Κρονίωνι ἄνακτι.
αὐτίκα δ᾽ ἐκ γαίης πλάσσεν κλυτὸς Ἀμφιγυήεις
παρθένῳ αἰδοίῃ ἴκελον Κρονίδεω διὰ βουλάς·
ζῶσε δὲ καὶ κόσμησε θεὰ γλαυκῶπις Ἀθήνη·
ἀμφὶ δέ οἱ Χάριτές τε θεαὶ καὶ πότνια Πειθὼ
ὅρμους χρυσείους ἔθεσαν χροΐ· ἀμφὶ δὲ τήν γε
Ὧραι καλλίκομοι στέφον ἄνθεσιν εἰαρινοῖσιν·
[πάντα δέ οἱ χροῒ κόσμον ἐφήρμοσε Παλλὰς Ἀθήνη.]
ἐν δ᾽ ἄρα οἱ στήθεσσι διάκτορος Ἀργεϊφόντης
ψεύδεά θ᾽ αἱμυλίους τε λόγους καὶ ἐπίκλοπον ἦθος

men. He hid fire; but that the noble son of Iapetus stole again for men from Zeus the counsellor in a hollow fennel-stalk, so that Zeus who delights in thunder did not see it. But afterwards Zeus who gathers the clouds said to him in anger:

"Son of Iapetus, surpassing all in cunning, you are glad that you have outwitted me and stolen fire —a great plague to you yourself and to men that shall be. But I will give men as the price for fire an evil thing in which they may all be glad of heart while they embrace their own destruction."

So said the father of men and gods, and laughed aloud. And he bade famous Hephaestus make haste and mix earth with water and to put in it the voice and strength of human kind, and fashion a sweet, lovely maiden-shape, like to the immortal goddesses in face; and Athene to teach her needlework and the weaving of the varied web; and golden Aphrodite to shed grace upon her head and cruel longing and cares that weary the limbs. And he charged Hermes the guide, the Slayer of Argus, to put in her a shameless mind and a deceitful nature.

So he ordered. And they obeyed the lord Zeus the son of Cronos. Forthwith the famous Lame God moulded clay in the likeness of a modest maid, as the son of Cronos purposed. And the goddess bright-eyed Athene girded and clothed her, and the divine Graces and queenly Persuasion put necklaces of gold upon her, and the rich-haired Hours crowned her head with spring flowers. And Pallas Athene bedecked her form with all manner of finery. Also the Guide, the Slayer of Argus, contrived within her lies and crafty words and a deceitful nature at the

[τεῦξε Διὸς βουλῇσι βαρυκτύπου· ἐν δ' ἄρα φωνὴν]
θῆκε θεῶν κῆρυξ, ὀνόμηνε δὲ τήνδε γυναῖκα
Πανδώρην, ὅτι πάντες Ὀλύμπια δώματ' ἔχοντες
δῶρον ἐδώρησαν, πῆμ' ἀνδράσιν ἀλφηστῇσιν.
Αὐτὰρ ἐπεὶ δόλον αἰπὺν ἀμήχανον ἐξετέλεσσεν,
εἰς Ἐπιμηθέα πέμπε πατὴρ κλυτὸν Ἀργεϊφόντην
δῶρον ἄγοντα, θεῶν ταχὺν ἄγγελον· οὐδ' Ἐπιμηθεὺς
ἐφράσαθ', ὥς οἱ ἔειπε Προμηθεὺς μή ποτε δῶρον
δέξασθαι πὰρ Ζηνὸς Ὀλυμπίου, ἀλλ' ἀποπέμπειν
ἐξοπίσω, μή πού τι κακὸν θνητοῖσι γένηται.
αὐτὰρ ὁ δεξάμενος, ὅτε δὴ κακὸν εἶχ', ἐνόησεν.
Πρὶν μὲν γὰρ ζώεσκον ἐπὶ χθονὶ φῦλ' ἀνθρώπων
νόσφιν ἄτερ τε κακῶν καὶ ἄτερ χαλεποῖο πόνοιο
νούσων τ' ἀργαλέων, αἵ τ' ἀνδράσι Κῆρας ἔδωκαν.
[αἶψα γὰρ ἐν κακότητι βροτοὶ καταγηράσκουσιν.]
ἀλλὰ γυνὴ χείρεσσι πίθου μέγα πῶμ' ἀφελοῦσα
ἐσκέδασ'· ἀνθρώποισι δ' ἐμήσατο κήδεα λυγρά.
μούνη δ' αὐτόθι Ἐλπὶς ἐν ἀρρήκτοισι δόμοισιν
ἔνδον ἔμιμνε πίθου ὑπὸ χείλεσιν, οὐδὲ θύραζε
ἐξέπτη· πρόσθεν γὰρ ἐπέλλαβε[1] πῶμα πίθοιο
[αἰγιόχου βουλῇσι Διὸς νεφεληγερέταο.]
ἄλλα δὲ μυρία λυγρὰ κατ' ἀνθρώπους ἀλάληται·
πλείη μὲν γὰρ γαῖα κακῶν, πλείη δὲ θάλασσα·
νοῦσοι δ' ἀνθρώποισιν ἐφ' ἡμέρῃ, αἳ δ' ἐπὶ νυκτὶ
αὐτόματοι φοιτῶσι κακὰ θνητοῖσι φέρουσαι
σιγῇ, ἐπεὶ φωνὴν ἐξείλετο μητίετα Ζεύς.
οὕτως οὔτι πη ἔστι Διὸς νόον ἐξαλέασθαι.

[1] CHK and Plutarch: ἐπέλαβε, DFIL: ἐπέμβαλε, EHNOPQ.

will of loud thundering Zeus, and the Herald of the gods put speech in her. And he called this woman Pandora,[1] because all they who dwelt on Olympus gave each a gift, a plague to men who eat bread.

But when he had finished the sheer, hopeless snare, the Father sent glorious Argus-Slayer, the swift messenger of the gods, to take it to Epimetheus as a gift. And Epimetheus did not think on what Prometheus had said to him, bidding him never take a gift of Olympian Zeus, but to send it back for fear it might prove to be something harmful to men. But he took the gift, and afterwards, when the evil thing was already his, he understood.

For ere this the tribes of men lived on earth remote and free from ills and hard toil and heavy sicknesses which bring the Fates upon men; for in misery men grow old quickly. But the woman took off the great lid of the jar[2] with her hands and scattered all these and her thought caused sorrow and mischief to men. Only Hope remained there in an unbreakable home within under the rim of the great jar, and did not fly out at the door; for ere that, the lid of the jar stopped her, by the will of Aegis-holding Zeus who gathers the clouds. But the other countless plagues wander amongst men; for earth is full of evils and the sea is full. Of themselves diseases come upon men continually by day and by night, bringing mischief to mortals silently; for wise Zeus took away speech from them. So is there no way to escape the will of Zeus.

[1] The All-endowed.

[2] The jar or casket contained the gifts of the gods mentioned in l. 82.

Εἰ δ' ἐθέλεις, ἕτερόν τοι ἐγὼ λόγον ἐκκορυφώσω
εὖ καὶ ἐπισταμένως· σὺ δ' ἐνὶ φρεσὶ βάλλεο σῇσιν.
ὡς ὁμόθεν γεγάασι θεοὶ θνητοί τ' ἄνθρωποι.
Χρύσεον μὲν πρώτιστα γένος μερόπων ἀνθρώπων
ἀθάνατοι ποίησαν Ὀλύμπια δώματ' ἔχοντες.
οἳ μὲν ἐπὶ Κρόνου ἦσαν, ὅτ' οὐρανῷ ἐμβασίλευεν·
ὥστε θεοὶ δ' ἔζωον ἀκηδέα θυμὸν ἔχοντες
νόσφιν ἄτερ τε πόνων καὶ ὀιζύος· οὐδέ τι δειλὸν
γῆρας ἐπῆν, αἰεὶ δὲ πόδας καὶ χεῖρας ὁμοῖοι
τέρποντ' ἐν θαλίῃσι κακῶν ἔκτοσθεν ἁπάντων·
θνῆσκον δ' ὥσθ' ὕπνῳ δεδμημένοι· ἐσθλὰ δὲ πάντα
τοῖσιν ἔην· καρπὸν δ' ἔφερε ζείδωρος ἄρουρα
αὐτομάτη πολλόν τε καὶ ἄφθονον· οἳ δ' ἐθελημοὶ
ἥσυχοι ἔργ' ἐνέμοντο σὺν ἐσθλοῖσιν πολέεσσιν.
ἀφνειοὶ μήλοισι, φίλοι μακάρεσσι θεοῖσιν.
Αὐτὰρ ἐπεὶ δὴ τοῦτο γένος κατὰ γαῖ' ἐκάλυψε,—
τοὶ μὲν δαίμονες ἁγνοὶ ἐπιχθόνιοι καλέονται [1]
ἐσθλοί, ἀλεξίκακοι,[2] φύλακες θνητῶν ἀνθρώπων,
[οἵ ῥα φυλάσσουσίν τε δίκας καὶ σχέτλια ἔργα
ἠέρα ἑσσάμενοι πάντῃ φοιτῶντες ἐπ' αἶαν,]
πλουτοδόται· καὶ τοῦτο γέρας βασιλήιον ἔσχον—,
δεύτερον αὖτε γένος πολὺ χειρότερον μετόπισθεν
ἀργύρεον ποίησαν Ὀλύμπια δώματ' ἔχοντες,
χρυσέῳ οὔτε φυὴν ἐναλίγκιον οὔτε νόημα.
ἀλλ' ἑκατὸν μὲν παῖς ἔτεα παρὰ μητέρι κεδνῇ
ἐτρέφετ' ἀτάλλων, μέγα νήπιος, ᾧ ἐνὶ οἴκῳ.
ἀλλ' ὅτ' ἄρ' ἡβήσαι τε καὶ ἥβης μέτρον ἵκοιτο,

[1] ἁγνοί, καλέονται, Plato (*Cratylus*), Aristeides, Olympiodorus, Theodoret. ἐπιχθόνιοι Plato (*Repub.*), Olymp., Theod.: the MSS. read εἰσὶ Διὸς μεγάλου διὰ βουλάς.

[2] Plato, Aristeides, Themistius and others: ἐπιχθόνιοι, MSS.

Or if you will, I will sum you up another tale well and skilfully—and do you lay it up in your heart,—how the gods and mortal men sprang from one source.

First of all the deathless gods who dwell on Olympus made a golden race of mortal men who lived in the time of Cronos when he was reigning in heaven. And they lived like gods without sorrow of heart, remote and free from toil and grief: miserable age rested not on them; but with legs and arms never failing they made merry with feasting beyond the reach of all evils. When they died, it was as though they were overcome with sleep, and they had all good things; for the fruitful earth unforced bare them fruit abundantly and without stint. They dwelt in ease and peace upon their lands with many good things, rich in flocks and loved by the blessed gods.

But after the earth had covered this generation—they are called pure spirits dwelling on the earth, and are kindly, delivering from harm, and guardians of mortal men; for they roam everywhere over the earth, clothed in mist and keep watch on judgements and cruel deeds, givers of wealth; for this royal right also they received;—then they who dwell on Olympus made a second generation which was of silver and less noble by far. It was like the golden race neither in body nor in spirit. A child was brought up at his good mother's side an hundred years, an utter simpleton, playing childishly in his own home. But when they were full grown and were come to the full measure of their prime, they

παυρίδιον ζώεσκον ἐπὶ χρόνον, ἄλγε' ἔχοντες
ἀφραδίῃς· ὕβριν γὰρ ἀτάσθαλον οὐκ ἐδύναντο
ἀλλήλων ἀπέχειν, οὐδ' ἀθανάτους θεραπεύειν
ἤθελον οὐδ' ἔρδειν μακάρων ἱεροῖς ἐπὶ βωμοῖς,
ἣ θέμις ἀνθρώποις κατὰ ἤθεα. τοὺς μὲν ἔπειτα
Ζεὺς Κρονίδης ἔκρυψε χολούμενος, οὕνεκα τιμὰς
οὐκ ἔδιδον μακάρεσσι θεοῖς, οἳ Ὄλυμπον ἔχουσιν.
  Αὐτὰρ ἐπεὶ καὶ τοῦτο γένος κατὰ γαῖ' ἐκάλυψε,—
τοὶ μὲν ὑποχθόνιοι μάκαρες θνητοῖς καλέονται,
δεύτεροι, ἀλλ' ἔμπης τιμὴ καὶ τοῖσιν ὀπηδεῖ—,
Ζεὺς δὲ πατὴρ τρίτον ἄλλο γένος μερόπων ἀνθρώπων
χάλκειον ποίησ', οὐκ ἀργυρέῳ οὐδὲν ὁμοῖον,
ἐκ μελιᾶν, δεινόν τε καὶ ὄβριμον· οἷσιν Ἄρηος
ἔργ' ἔμελεν στονόεντα καὶ ὕβριες· οὐδέ τι σῖτον
ἤσθιον, ἀλλ' ἀδάμαντος ἔχον κρατερόφρονα θυμόν,
ἄπλαστοι· μεγάλη δὲ βίη καὶ χεῖρες ἄαπτοι
ἐξ ὤμων ἐπέφυκον ἐπὶ στιβαροῖσι μέλεσσιν.
τῶν δ' ἦν χάλκεα μὲν τεύχεα, χάλκεοι δέ τε οἶκοι
χαλκῷ δ' εἰργάζοντο· μέλας δ' οὐκ ἔσκε σίδηρος.
καὶ τοὶ μὲν χείρεσσιν ὕπο σφετέρῃσι δαμέντες
βῆσαν ἐς εὐρώεντα δόμον κρυεροῦ Ἀίδαο
νώνυμνοι· θάνατος δὲ καὶ ἐκπάγλους περ ἐόντας
εἷλε μέλας, λαμπρὸν δ' ἔλιπον φάος ἠελίοιο.
  Αὐτὰρ ἐπεὶ καὶ τοῦτο γένος κατὰ γαῖ' ἐκάλυψεν,
αὖτις ἔτ' ἄλλο τέταρτον ἐπὶ χθονὶ πουλυβοτείρῃ
Ζεὺς Κρονίδης ποίησε, δικαιότερον καὶ ἄρειον,

lived only a little time and that in sorrow because of their foolishness, for they could not keep from sinning and from wronging one another, nor would they serve the immortals, nor sacrifice on the holy altars of the blessed ones as it is right for men to do wherever they dwell. Then Zeus the son of Cronos was angry and put them away, because they would not give honour to the blessed gods who live on Olympus.

But when earth had covered this generation also—they are called blessed spirits of the underworld by men, and, though they are of second order, yet honour attends them also—Zeus the Father made a third generation of mortal men, a brazen race, sprung from ash-trees[1]; and it was in no way equal to the silver age, but was terrible and strong. They loved the lamentable works of Ares and deeds of violence; they ate no bread, but were hard of heart like adamant, fearful men. Great was their strength and unconquerable the arms which grew from their shoulders on their strong limbs. Their armour was of bronze, and their houses of bronze, and of bronze were their implements: there was no black iron. These were destroyed by their own hands and passed to the dank house of chill Hades, and left no name: terrible though they were, black Death seized them, and they left the bright light of the sun.

But when earth had covered this generation also, Zeus the son of Cronos made yet another, the fourth, upon the fruitful earth, which was nobler and more

[1] Eustathius refers to Hesiod as stating that men sprung "from oaks and stones and ashtrees." Proclus believed that the Nymphs called Meliae (*Theogony*, 187) are intended. Goettling would render: "A race terrible because of their (ashen) spears."

ἀνδρῶν ἡρώων θεῖον γένος, οἳ καλέονται
ἡμίθεοι, προτέρη γενεὴ κατ' ἀπείρονα γαῖαν.
καὶ τοὺς μὲν πόλεμός τε κακὸς καὶ φύλοπις αἰνή,
τοὺς μὲν ὑφ' ἑπταπύλῳ Θήβῃ, Καδμηίδι γαίῃ,
ὤλεσε μαρναμένους μήλων ἕνεκ' Οἰδιπόδαο,
τοὺς δὲ καὶ ἐν νήεσσιν ὑπὲρ μέγα λαῖτμα θαλάσσης·
ἐς Τροίην ἀγαγὼν Ἑλένης ἕνεκ' ἠυκόμοιο.
ἔνθ' ἤτοι τοὺς μὲν θανάτου τέλος ἀμφεκάλυψε,
τοῖς δὲ δίχ' ἀνθρώπων βίοτον καὶ ἤθε' ὀπάσσας
Ζεὺς Κρονίδης κατένασσε πατὴρ ἐς πείρατα γαίης.
καὶ τοὶ μὲν ναίουσιν ἀκηδέα θυμὸν ἔχοντες
ἐν μακάρων νήσοισι παρ' Ὠκεανὸν βαθυδίνην,
ὄλβιοι ἥρωες, τοῖσιν μελιηδέα καρπὸν
τρὶς ἔτεος θάλλοντα φέρει ζείδωρος ἄρουρα. 173
τηλοῦ ἀπ' ἀθανάτων· τοῖσιν Κρόνος ἐμβασιλεύει.[1] 169
τοῦ γὰρ δεσμὸ]ν ἔλυσε πα[τὴρ ἀνδρῶν τε θεῶν τε. 169a
τοῖσι δ' ὁμῶς ν]εάτοις τιμὴ [καὶ κῦδος ὀπηδεῖ. 169b
Πέμπτον δ' αὖτις ἔτ' ἄ]λλο γένος θῆκ' [εὐρύοπα Ζεὺς 169c
ἀνδρῶν, οἳ] γεγάασιν ἐπὶ [χθονὶ πουλυβοτείρῃ.] 169d
Μηκέτ' ἔπειτ' ὤφελλον ἐγὼ πέμπτοισι μετεῖναι 174
ἀνδράσιν, ἀλλ' ἢ πρόσθε θανεῖν ἢ ἔπειτα γενέσθαι.
νῦν γὰρ δὴ γένος ἐστὶ σιδήρεον· οὐδέ ποτ' ἦμαρ
παύονται[2] *καμάτου καὶ ὀιζύος, οὐδέ τι νύκτωρ*

[1] Preserved only by Proclus, from whom some inferior MSS. have copied the verse. The four following lines occur only in Geneva Papyri No. 94. For the restoration of ll. 169 b-c see *Class. Quart.* vii. 219–220.

[2] B: *παύονται*, MSS.

righteous, a god-like race of hero-men who are called demi-gods, the race before our own, throughout the boundless earth. Grim war and dread battle destroyed a part of them, some in the land of Cadmus at seven-gated Thebe when they fought for the flocks of Oedipus, and some, when it had brought them in ships over the great sea gulf to Troy for rich-haired Helen's sake: there death's end enshrouded a part of them. But to the others father Zeus the son of Cronos gave a living and an abode apart from men, and made them dwell at the ends of earth. And they live untouched by sorrow in the islands of the blessed along the shore of deep swirling Ocean, happy heroes for whom the grain-giving earth bears honey-sweet fruit flourishing thrice a year, far from the deathless gods, and Cronos rules over them; for the father of men and gods released him from his bonds. And these last equally have honour and glory.

And again far-seeing Zeus made yet another generation, the fifth, of men who are upon the bounteous earth.

Thereafter, would that I were not among the men of the fifth generation, but either had died before or been born afterwards. For now truly is a race of iron, and men never rest from labour and sorrow by day, and from perishing by night; and the gods shall lay

φθειρόμενοι. χαλεπὰς δὲ θεοὶ δώσουσι μερίμνας·
ἀλλ' ἔμπης καὶ τοῖσι μεμείξεται ἐσθλὰ κακοῖσιν.
Ζεὺς δ' ὀλέσει καὶ τοῦτο γένος μερόπων ἀνθρώπων,
εὖτ' ἂν γεινόμενοι πολιοκρόταφοι τελέθωσιν.
οὐδὲ πατὴρ παίδεσσιν ὁμοίιος οὐδέ τι παῖδες,
οὐδὲ ξεῖνος ξεινοδόκῳ καὶ ἑταῖρος ἑταίρῳ,
οὐδὲ κασίγνητος φίλος ἔσσεται, ὡς τὸ πάρος περ.
αἶψα δὲ γηράσκοντας ἀτιμήσουσι τοκῆας·
μέμψονται δ' ἄρα τοὺς χαλεποῖς βάζοντες ἔπεσσι
σχέτλιοι οὐδὲ θεῶν ὄπιν εἰδότες· οὐδέ κεν οἵ γε
γηράντεσσι τοκεῦσιν ἀπὸ θρεπτήρια δοῖεν
χειροδίκαι· ἕτερος δ' ἑτέρου πόλιν ἐξαλαπάξει.
οὐδέ τις εὐόρκου χάρις ἔσσεται οὔτε δικαίου
οὔτ' ἀγαθοῦ, μᾶλλον δὲ κακῶν ῥεκτῆρα καὶ ὕβριν
ἀνέρες αἰνήσουσι·[1] δίκη δ' ἐν χερσί, καὶ αἰδὼς
οὐκ ἔσται· βλάψει δ' ὁ κακὸς τὸν ἀρείονα φῶτα
μύθοισιν σκολιοῖς ἐνέπων, ἐπὶ δ' ὅρκον ὀμεῖται.
ζῆλος δ' ἀνθρώποισιν ὀιζυροῖσιν ἅπασι
δυσκέλαδος κακόχαρτος ὁμαρτήσει, στυγερώπης.
καὶ τότε δὴ πρὸς Ὄλυμπον ἀπὸ χθονὸς εὐρυοδείης
λευκοῖσιν φάρεσσι καλυψαμένα χρόα καλὸν
ἀθανάτων μετὰ φῦλον ἴτον προλιπόντ' ἀνθρώπους
Αἰδὼς καὶ Νέμεσις· τὰ δὲ λείψεται ἄλγεα λυγρὰ
θνητοῖς ἀνθρώποισι· κακοῦ δ' οὐκ ἔσσεται ἀλκή.

[1] Tr. : ἀνέρα τιμήσουσι, MSS.

sore trouble upon them. But, notwithstanding, even these shall have some good mingled with their evils. And Zeus will destroy this race of mortal men also when they come to have grey hair on the temples at their birth.[1] The father will not agree with his children, nor the children with their father, nor guest with his host, nor comrade with comrade; nor will brother be dear to brother as aforetime. Men will dishonour their parents as they grow quickly old, and will carp at them, chiding them with bitter words, hard-hearted they, not knowing the fear of the gods. They will not repay their aged parents the cost of their nurture, for might shall be their right: and one man will sack another's city. There will be no favour for the man who keeps his oath or for the just or for the good; but rather men will praise the evil-doer and his violent dealing. Strength will be right and reverence will cease to be; and the wicked will hurt the worthy man, speaking false words against him, and will swear an oath upon them. Envy, foul-mouthed, delighting in evil, with scowling face, will go along with wretched men one and all. And then Aidôs and Nemesis,[2] with their sweet forms wrapped in white robes, will go from the wide-pathed earth and forsake mankind to join the company of the deathless gods: and bitter sorrows will be left for mortal men, and there will be no help against evil.

[1] *i.e.* the race will so degenerate that at the last even a new-born child will show the marks of old age.

[2] Aidôs, as a quality, is that feeling of reverence or shame which restrains men from wrong: Nemesis is the feeling of righteous indignation aroused especially by the sight of the wicked in undeserved prosperity (*cf. Psalms*, lxxii. 1–19).

Νῦν δ' αἶνον βασιλεῦσιν ἐρέω φρονέουσι καὶ αὐτοῖς·
ὧδ' ἴρηξ προσέειπεν ἀηδόνα ποικιλόδειρον
ὕψι μάλ' ἐν νεφέεσσι φέρων ὀνύχεσσι μεμαρπώς·
ἣ δ' ἐλεόν, γναμπτοῖσι πεπαρμένη ἀμφ' ὀνύχεσσι,
μύρετο· τὴν ὅγ' ἐπικρατέως πρὸς μῦθον ἔειπεν·
Δαιμονίη, τί λέληκας; ἔχει νύ σε πολλὸν ἀρείων·
τῇ δ' εἶς, ᾗ σ' ἂν ἐγώ περ ἄγω καὶ ἀοιδὸν ἐοῦσαν·
δεῖπνον δ', αἴ κ' ἐθέλω, ποιήσομαι ἠὲ μεθήσω.
ἄφρων δ', ὅς κ' ἐθέλῃ πρὸς κρείσσονας ἀντιφερίζειν·
νίκης τε στέρεται πρός τ' αἴσχεσιν ἄλγεα πάσχει.
Ὣς ἔφατ' ὠκυπέτης ἴρηξ, τανυσίπτερος ὄρνις.

Ὦ Πέρση, σὺ δ' ἄκουε δίκης, μηδ' ὕβριν ὄφελλε·
ὕβρις γάρ τε κακὴ δειλῷ βροτῷ· οὐδὲ μὲν ἐσθλὸς
ῥηιδίως φερέμεν δύναται, βαρύθει δέ θ' ὑπ' αὐτῆς
ἐγκύρσας ἄτῃσιν· ὁδὸς δ' ἑτέρηφι παρελθεῖν
κρείσσων ἐς τὰ δίκαια· Δίκη δ' ὑπὲρ Ὕβριος ἴσχει
ἐς τέλος ἐξελθοῦσα· παθὼν δέ τε νήπιος ἔγνω.
αὐτίκα γὰρ τρέχει Ὅρκος ἅμα σκολιῇσι δίκῃσιν.
τῆς δὲ Δίκης ῥόθος ἑλκομένης, ᾗ κ' ἄνδρες ἄγωσι
δωροφάγοι, σκολιῇς δὲ δίκῃς κρίνωσι θέμιστας.
ἡ δ' ἕπεται κλαίουσα πόλιν καὶ ἤθεα λαῶν,
ἠέρα ἑσσαμένη, κακὸν ἀνθρώποισι φέρουσα,
οἵ τε μιν ἐξελάσωσι καὶ οὐκ ἰθεῖαν ἔνειμαν.
Οἳ δὲ δίκας ξείνοισι καὶ ἐνδήμοισι διδοῦσιν
ἰθείας καὶ μή τι παρεκβαίνουσι δικαίου,
τοῖσι τέθηλε πόλις, λαοὶ δ' ἀνθεῦσιν ἐν αὐτῇ·

And now I will tell a fable for princes who themselves understand. Thus said the hawk to the nightingale with speckled neck, while he carried her high up among the clouds, gripped fast in his talons, and she, pierced by his crooked talons, cried pitifully. To her he spoke disdainfully: "Miserable thing, why do you cry out? One far stronger than you now holds you fast, and you must go wherever I take you, songstress as you are. And if I please I will make my meal of you, or let you go. He is a fool who tries to withstand the stronger, for he does not get the mastery and suffers pain besides his shame." So said the swiftly flying hawk, the long-winged bird.

But you, Perses, listen to right and do not foster violence; for violence is bad for a poor man. Even the prosperous cannot easily bear its burden, but is weighed down under it when he has fallen into delusion. The better path is to go by on the other side towards justice; for Justice beats Outrage when she comes at length to the end of the race. But only when he has suffered does the fool learn this. For Oath keeps pace with wrong judgements. There is a noise when Justice is being dragged in the way where those who devour bribes and give sentence with crooked judgements, take her. And she, wrapped in mist, follows to the city and haunts of the people, weeping, and bringing mischief to men, even to such as have driven her forth in that they did not deal straightly with her.

But they who give straight judgements to strangers and to the men of the land, and go not aside from what is just, their city flourishes, and the people

εἰρήνη δ᾽ ἀνὰ γῆν κουροτρόφος, οὐδέ ποτ᾽ αὐτοῖς
ἀργαλέον πόλεμον τεκμαίρεται εὐρύοπα Ζεύς·
οὐδέ ποτ᾽ ἰθυδίκῃσι μετ᾽ ἀνδράσι λιμὸς ὀπηδεῖ
οὐδ᾽ ἄτη, θαλίῃς δὲ μεμηλότα ἔργα νέμονται.
τοῖσι φέρει μὲν γαῖα πολὺν βίον, οὔρεσι δὲ δρῦς
ἄκρη μέν τε φέρει βαλάνους, μέσση δὲ μελίσσας·
εἰροπόκοι δ᾽ ὄιες μαλλοῖς καταβεβρίθασιν·
τίκτουσιν δὲ γυναῖκες ἐοικότα τέκνα γονεῦσιν·
θάλλουσιν δ᾽ ἀγαθοῖσι διαμπερές· οὐδ᾽ ἐπὶ νηῶν
νίσσονται, καρπὸν δὲ φέρει ζείδωρος ἄρουρα.
Οἷς δ᾽ ὕβρις τε μέμηλε κακὴ καὶ σχέτλια ἔργα,
τοῖς δὲ δίκην Κρονίδης τεκμαίρεται εὐρύοπα Ζεύς.
πολλάκι καὶ ξύμπασα πόλις κακοῦ ἀνδρὸς ἀπηύρα,
ὅς κεν ἀλιτραίνῃ[1] καὶ ἀτάσθαλα μηχανάαται.
τοῖσιν δ᾽ οὐρανόθεν μέγ᾽ ἐπήγαγε πῆμα Κρονίων
λιμὸν ὁμοῦ καὶ λοιμόν· ἀποφθινύθουσι δὲ λαοί.
οὐδὲ γυναῖκες τίκτουσιν, μινύθουσι δὲ οἶκοι
Ζηνὸς φραδμοσύνῃσιν Ὀλυμπίου· ἄλλοτε δ᾽ αὖτε
ἢ τῶν γε στρατὸν εὐρὺν ἀπώλεσεν ἢ ὅ γε τεῖχος
ἢ νέας ἐν πόντῳ Κρονίδης ἀποαίνυται αὐτῶν.

Ὦ βασιλῆς, ὑμεῖς δὲ καταφράζεσθε καὶ αὐτοὶ
τήνδε δίκην· ἐγγὺς γὰρ ἐν ἀνθρώποισιν ἐόντες
ἀθάνατοι φράζονται, ὅσοι σκολιῇσι δίκῃσιν
ἀλλήλους τρίβουσι θεῶν ὄπιν οὐκ ἀλέγοντες.
τρὶς γὰρ μύριοί εἰσιν ἐπὶ χθονὶ πουλυβοτείρῃ
ἀθάνατοι Ζηνὸς φύλακες θνητῶν ἀνθρώπων·
οἵ ῥα φυλάσσουσίν τε δίκας καὶ σχέτλια ἔργα
ἠέρα ἑσσάμενοι, πάντη φοιτῶντες ἐπ᾽ αἶαν.

[1] Aeschines: ὅς τις ἀλιτραίνει, MSS.

prosper in it: Peace, the nurse of children, is abroad in their land, and all-seeing Zeus never decrees cruel war against them. Neither famine nor disaster ever haunt men who do true justice; but light-heartedly they tend the fields which are all their care. The earth bears them victual in plenty, and on the mountains the oak bears acorns upon the top and bees in the midst. Their woolly sheep are laden with fleeces; their women bear children like their parents. They flourish continually with good things, and do not travel on ships, for the grain-giving earth bears them fruit.

But for those who practise violence and cruel deeds far-seeing Zeus, the son of Cronos, ordains a punishment. Often even a whole city suffers for a bad man who sins and devises presumptuous deeds, and the son of Cronos lays great trouble upon the people, famine and plague together, so that the men perish away, and their women do not bear children, and their houses become few, through the contriving of Olympian Zeus. And again, at another time, the son of Cronos either destroys their wide army, or their walls, or else makes an end of their ships on the sea.

You princes, mark well this punishment you also; for the deathless gods are near among men and mark all those who oppress their fellows with crooked judgements, and reck not the anger of the gods. For upon the bounteous earth Zeus has thrice ten thousand spirits, watchers of mortal men, and these keep watch on judgements and deeds of wrong as they roam, clothed in mist, all over the earth. And

ἡ δέ τε παρθένος ἐστὶ Δίκη, Διὸς ἐκγεγαυῖα,
κυδρή τ' αἰδοίη τε θεῶν,[1] οἳ Ὄλυμπον ἔχουσιν.
καί ῥ' ὁπότ' ἄν τίς μιν βλάπτῃ σκολιῶς ὀνοτάζων,
αὐτίκα πὰρ Διὶ πατρὶ καθεζομένη Κρονίωνι
γηρύετ' ἀνθρώπων ἄδικον νόον, ὄφρ' ἀποτίσῃ
δῆμος ἀτασθαλίας βασιλέων, οἳ λυγρὰ νοεῦντες
ἄλλῃ παρκλίνωσι δίκας σκολιῶς ἐνέποντες.
ταῦτα φυλασσόμενοι, βασιλῆς, ἰθύνετε †δίκας[2]
δωροφάγοι, σκολιέων δὲ δικέων[3] ἐπὶ πάγχυ λάθεσθε.
Οἷ γ' αὐτῷ κακὰ τεύχει ἀνὴρ ἄλλῳ κακὰ τεύχων,
ἡ δὲ κακὴ βουλὴ τῷ βουλεύσαντι κακίστη.
Πάντα ἰδὼν Διὸς ὀφθαλμὸς καὶ πάντα νοήσας
καί νυ τάδ', αἴ κ' ἐθέλῃσ', ἐπιδέρκεται, οὐδέ ἑ λήθει,
οἵην δὴ καὶ τήνδε δίκην πόλις ἐντὸς ἐέργει.
νῦν δὴ ἐγὼ μήτ' αὐτὸς ἐν ἀνθρώποισι δίκαιος
εἴην μήτ' ἐμὸς υἱός· ἐπεὶ κακὸν ἄνδρα δίκαιον
ἔμμεναι, εἰ μείζω γε δίκην ἀδικώτερος ἕξει·
ἀλλὰ τά γ' οὔ πω ἔολπα τελεῖν Δία μητιόεντα.
Ὦ Πέρση, σὺ δὲ ταῦτα μετὰ φρεσὶ βάλλεο σῇσι,
καί νυ δίκης ἐπάκουε, βίης δ' ἐπιλήθεο πάμπαν.
τόνδε γὰρ ἀνθρώποισι νόμον διέταξε Κρονίων
ἰχθύσι μὲν καὶ θηρσὶ καὶ οἰωνοῖς πετεηνοῖς
ἐσθέμεν[4] ἀλλήλους, ἐπεὶ οὐ δίκη ἐστὶ μετ'[5] αὐτοῖς·

[1] *Ox. Pap.* 1090 : θεοῖς, MSS.
[2] CHD etc. (*Ox. Pap.* βασιλῆς) : other MSS. read μύθους.
[3] *Ox Pap.* : δικῶν MSS.
[4] Clement of Alexandria, Rzach : ἔσθειν, MSS.
[5] A, Plutarch, Aelian : μετ' αὐτῶν, Clement, Porphyry : μετ' αὐ . . . , *Ox. Pap.* : ἐν αὐτοῖς, MSS.

there is virgin Justice, the daughter of Zeus, who is honoured and reverenced among the gods who dwell on Olympus, and whenever anyone hurts her with lying slander, she sits beside her father, Zeus the son of Cronos, and tells him of men's wicked heart, until the people pay for the mad folly of their princes who, evilly minded, pervert judgement and give sentence crookedly. Keep watch against this, you princes, and make straight your judgements, you who devour bribes; put crooked judgements altogether from your thoughts.

He does mischief to himself who does mischief to another, and evil planned harms the plotter most.

The eye of Zeus, seeing all and understanding all, beholds these things too, if so he will, and fails not to mark what sort of justice is this that the city keeps within it. Now, therefore, may neither I myself be righteous among men, nor my son—for then it is a bad thing to be righteous—if indeed the unrighteous shall have the greater right. But I think that all-wise Zeus will not yet bring that to pass.

But you, Perses, lay up these things within your heart and listen now to right, ceasing altogether to think of violence. For the son of Cronos has ordained this law for men, that fishes and beasts and winged fowls should devour one another, for right is not in them; but to mankind he gave right which

ἀνθρώποισι δ' ἔδωκε δίκην, ἣ πολλὸν ἀρίστη
γίγνεται· εἰ γάρ τίς κ' ἐθέλῃ τὰ δίκαι' ἀγορεῦσαι
γιγνώσκων, τῷ μέν τ' ὄλβον διδοῖ εὐρύοπα Ζεύς·
ὃς δέ κε μαρτυρίῃσι ἑκὼν ἐπίορκον ὀμόσσας
ψεύσεται, ἐν δὲ δίκην βλάψας νήκεστον ἀασθῇ,
τοῦ δέ τ' ἀμαυροτέρη γενεὴ μετόπισθε λέλειπται·
ἀνδρὸς δ' εὐόρκου γενεὴ μετόπισθεν ἀμείνων.
  Σοὶ δ' ἐγὼ ἐσθλὰ νοέων ἐρέω, μέγα νήπιε Πέρση.
τὴν μέν τοι κακότητα καὶ ἰλαδὸν ἔστιν ἑλέσθαι
ῥηιδίως· λείη μὲν ὁδός, μάλα δ' ἐγγύθι ναίει·
τῆς δ' ἀρετῆς ἱδρῶτα θεοὶ προπάροιθεν ἔθηκαν
ἀθάνατοι· μακρὸς δὲ καὶ ὄρθιος οἶμος ἐς αὐτὴν
καὶ τρηχὺς τὸ πρῶτον· ἐπὴν δ' εἰς ἄκρον ἵκηται,
ῥηιδίη δὴ ἔπειτα πέλει, χαλεπή περ ἐοῦσα.
  Οὗτος μὲν πανάριστος, ὃς αὐτὸς πάντα νοήσῃ
φρασσάμενος, τά κ' ἔπειτα καὶ ἐς τέλος ᾖσιν ἀμείνω·
ἐσθλὸς δ' αὖ κἀκεῖνος, ὃς εὖ εἰπόντι πίθηται·
ὃς δέ κε μήτ' αὐτὸς νοέῃ μήτ' ἄλλου ἀκούων
ἐν θυμῷ βάλληται, ὃ δ' αὖτ' ἀχρήιος ἀνήρ.
ἀλλὰ σύ γ' ἡμετέρης μεμνημένος αἰὲν ἐφετμῆς
ἐργάζευ, Πέρση, δῖον γένος, ὄφρα σε λιμὸς
ἐχθαίρῃ, φιλέῃ δέ σ' ἐυστέφανος Δημήτηρ
αἰδοίη, βιότου δὲ τεὴν πιμπλῆσι καλιήν·
λιμὸς γάρ τοι πάμπαν ἀεργῷ σύμφορος ἀνδρί.
τῷ δὲ θεοὶ νεμεσῶσι καὶ ἀνέρες, ὅς κεν ἀεργὸς
ζώῃ, κηφήνεσσι κοθούροις εἴκελος ὀργήν,
οἵ τε μελισσάων κάματον τρύχουσιν ἀεργοὶ
ἔσθοντες· σοὶ δ' ἔργα φίλ' ἔστω μέτρια κοσμεῖν,
ὥς κέ τοι ὡραίου βιότου πλήθωσι καλιαί.
ἐξ ἔργων δ' ἄνδρες πολύμηλοί τ' ἀφνειοί τε·

proves far the best. For whoever knows the right and is ready to speak it, far-seeing Zeus gives him prosperity; but whoever deliberately lies in his witness and forswears himself, and so hurts Justice and sins beyond repair, that man's generation is left obscure thereafter. But the generation of the man who swears truly is better thenceforward.

To you, foolish Perses, I will speak good sense. Badness can be got easily and in shoals: the road to her is smooth, and she lives very near us. But between us and Goodness the gods have placed the sweat of our brows: long and steep is the path that leads to her, and it is rough at the first; but when a man has reached the top, then indeed she is easy, though otherwise hard to reach.

That man is altogether best who considers all things himself and marks what will be better afterwards and at the end; and he, again, is good who listens to a good adviser; but whoever neither thinks for himself nor keeps in mind what another tells him, he is an unprofitable man. But do you at any rate, always remembering my charge, work, high-born Perses, that Hunger may hate you, and venerable Demeter richly crowned may love you and fill your barn with food; for Hunger is altogether a meet comrade for the sluggard. Both gods and men are angry with a man who lives idle, for in nature he is like the stingless drones who waste the labour of the bees, eating without working; but let it be your care to order your work properly, that in the right season your barns may be full of victual. Through work men grow rich in flocks and substance, and working they

καὶ ἐργαζόμενοι πολὺ φίλτεροι[1] ἀθανάτοισιν.
ἔργον δ' οὐδὲν ὄνειδος, ἀεργίη δέ τ' ὄνειδος.
εἰ δέ κε ἐργάζῃ, τάχα σε ζηλώσει ἀεργὸς
πλουτεῦντα· πλούτῳ δ' ἀρετὴ καὶ κῦδος ὀπηδεῖ.
δαίμονι δ' οἷος ἔησθα, τὸ ἐργάζεσθαι ἄμεινον,
εἴ κεν ἀπ' ἀλλοτρίων κτεάνων ἀεσίφρονα θυμὸν
εἰς ἔργον τρέψας μελετᾷς βίου, ὥς σε κελεύω.
αἰδὼς δ' οὐκ ἀγαθὴ κεχρημένον ἄνδρα κομίζει,
αἰδώς, ἥ τ' ἄνδρας μέγα σίνεται ἠδ' ὀνίνησιν.
αἰδώς τοι πρὸς ἀνολβίῃ, θάρσος δὲ πρὸς ὄλβῳ,
Χρήματα δ' οὐχ ἁρπακτά, θεόσδοτα πολλὸν ἀμείνω.
εἰ γάρ τις καὶ χερσὶ βίῃ μέγαν ὄλβον ἕληται,
ἢ ὅ γ' ἀπὸ γλώσσης ληίσσεται, οἷά τε πολλὰ
γίγνεται, εὖτ' ἂν δὴ κέρδος νόον ἐξαπατήσῃ
ἀνθρώπων, αἰδῶ δέ τ' ἀναιδείη κατοπάζῃ·
ῥεῖα δέ μιν μαυροῦσι θεοί, μινύθουσι δὲ οἶκον
ἀνέρι τῷ, παῦρον δέ τ' ἐπὶ χρόνον ὄλβος ὀπηδεῖ.
Ἶσον δ' ὅς θ' ἱκέτην ὅς τε ξεῖνον κακὸν ἔρξῃ,
ὅς τε κασιγνήτοιο ἑοῦ ἀνὰ δέμνια βαίνῃ
κρυπταδίης εὐνῆς ἀλόχου, παρακαίρια ῥέζων,
ὅς τέ τευ ἀφραδίῃς ἀλιταίνεται ὀρφανὰ τέκνα,
ὅς τε γονῆα γέροντα κακῷ ἐπὶ γήραος οὐδῷ
νεικείῃ χαλεποῖσι καθαπτόμενος ἐπέεσσιν·
τῷ δ' ἦ τοι Ζεὺς αὐτὸς ἀγαίεται, ἐς δὲ τελευτὴν
ἔργων ἀντ' ἀδίκων χαλεπὴν ἐπέθηκεν ἀμοιβήν.
ἀλλὰ σὺ τῶν μὲν πάμπαν ἔεργ' ἀεσίφρονα θυμόν.
κὰδ δύναμιν δ' ἔρδειν ἱέρ' ἀθανάτοισι θεοῖσιν

[1] CFH: ἐργαζόμενος . . . φίλτερος, other MSS. Line 310, ἔσσεαι ἠδὲ βροτοῖς· μάλα γὰρ στυγέουσιν ἀεργούς, is omitted by ACD and Stobaeus.

are much better loved by the immortals.[1] Work is no disgrace: it is idleness which is a disgrace. But if you work, the idle will soon envy you as you grow rich, for fame and renown attend on wealth. And whatever be your lot, work is best for you, if you turn your misguided mind away from other men's property to your work and attend to your livelihood as I bid you. An evil shame is the needy man's companion, shame which both greatly harms and prospers men: shame is with poverty, but confidence with wealth.

Wealth should not be seized: god-given wealth is much better; for if a man take great wealth violently and perforce, or if he steal it through his tongue, as often happens when gain deceives men's sense and dishonour tramples down honour, the gods soon blot him out and make that man's house low, and wealth attends him only for a little time. Alike with him who does wrong to a suppliant or a guest, or who goes up to his brother's bed and commits unnatural sin in lying with his wife, or who infatuately offends against fatherless children, or who abuses his old father at the cheerless threshold of old age and attacks him with harsh words, truly Zeus himself is angry, and at the last lays on him a heavy requittal for his evil doing. But do you turn your foolish heart altogether away from these things, and, as far as you are able, sacrifice to the death-

[1] The alternative version is: "and, working, you will be much better loved both by gods and men; for they greatly dislike the idle."

ἁγνῶς καὶ καθαρῶς, ἐπὶ δ᾽ ἀγλαὰ μηρία καίειν·
ἄλλοτε δὲ σπονδῇσι θύεσσί τε ἱλάσκεσθαι,
ἠμὲν ὅτ᾽ εὐνάζῃ καὶ ὅτ᾽ ἂν φάος ἱερὸν ἔλθῃ,
ὥς κέ τοι ἵλαον κραδίην καὶ θυμὸν ἔχωσιν,
ὄφρ᾽ ἄλλων ὠνῇ κλῆρον, μὴ τὸν τεὸν ἄλλος.
Τὸν φιλέοντ᾽ ἐπὶ δαῖτα καλεῖν, τὸν δ᾽ ἐχθρὸν ἐᾶσαι·
τὸν δὲ μάλιστα καλεῖν, ὅς τις σέθεν ἐγγύθι ναίει·
εἰ γάρ τοι καὶ χρῆμ᾽ ἐγχώριον ἄλλο γένηται,
γείτονες ἄζωστοι ἔκιον, ζώσαντο δὲ πηοί.
πῆμα κακὸς γείτων, ὅσσον τ᾽ ἀγαθὸς μέγ᾽ ὄνειαρ.
ἔμμορέ τοι τιμῆς, ὅς τ᾽ ἔμμορε γείτονος ἐσθλοῦ.
οὐδ᾽ ἂν βοῦς ἀπόλοιτ᾽, εἰ μὴ γείτων κακὸς εἴη.
εὖ μὲν μετρεῖσθαι παρὰ γείτονος, εὖ δ᾽ ἀποδοῦναι,
αὐτῷ τῷ μέτρῳ, καὶ λώιον, αἴ κε δύνηαι,
ὡς ἂν χρηίζων καὶ ἐς ὕστερον ἄρκιον εὕρῃς.
Μὴ κακὰ κερδαίνειν· κακὰ κέρδεα ἶσ᾽ ἀάτῃσιν.[1]
τὸν φιλέοντα φιλεῖν, καὶ τῷ προσιόντι προσεῖναι.
καὶ δόμεν, ὅς κεν δῷ, καὶ μὴ δόμεν, ὅς κεν μὴ δῷ.
δώτῃ μέν τις ἔδωκεν, ἀδώτῃ δ᾽ οὔτις ἔδωκεν.
δὼς ἀγαθή, ἅρπαξ δὲ κακή, θανάτοιο δότειρα.
ὃς μὲν γάρ κεν ἀνὴρ ἐθέλων, ὅ γε, κεἰ[2] μέγα δοίῃ,
χαίρει τῷ δώρῳ καὶ τέρπεται ὃν κατὰ θυμόν·
ὃς δέ κεν αὐτὸς ἕληται ἀναιδείηφι πιθήσας,
καί τε σμικρὸν ἐόν, τό γ᾽ ἐπάχνωσεν φίλον ἦτορ.
ὃς δ᾽ ἐπ᾽ ἐόντι φέρει, ὃ δ᾽ ἀλέξεται αἴθοπα λιμόν· 363
εἰ γάρ κεν καὶ σμικρὸν ἐπὶ σμικρῷ καταθεῖο 361
καὶ θαμὰ τοῦτ᾽ ἔρδοις, τάχα κεν μέγα καὶ τὸ γένοιτο.[3] 362

[1] ἶσα ἄτῃσι, ACDE, etc.
[2] Schoemann, Paley: καί, A and all MSS.
[3] Line 363 seems to be misplaced in the MSS.

less gods purely and cleanly, and burn rich meats also, and at other times propitiate them with libations and incense, both when you go to bed and when the holy light has come back, that they may be gracious to you in heart and spirit, and so you may buy another's holding and not another yours.

Call your friend to a feast; but leave your enemy alone; and especially call him who lives near you: for if any mischief happen in the place, neighbours come ungirt, but kinsmen stay to gird themselves.[1] A bad neighbour is as great a plague as a good one is a great blessing; he who enjoys a good neighbour, enjoys honour. Not even an ox would die but for a bad neighbour. Take fair measure from your neighbour and pay him back fairly with the same measure, or better, if you can; so that if you are in need afterwards, you may find him sure.

Do not get base gain: base gain is as bad as ruin. Be friends with the friendly, and visit him who visits you. Give to one who gives, but do not give to one who does not give. A man gives to the free-handed, but no one gives to the close-fisted. Give is a good girl, but Take is bad and she brings death. For the man who gives willingly, even though he gives a great thing, rejoices in his gift and is glad in heart; but whoever gives way to shamelessness and takes something himself, even though it be a small thing, it freezes his heart. He who adds to what he has, will keep off bright-eyed hunger; for if you add only a little to a little and do this often, soon that little will become great. What

[1] *i.e.* neighbours come at once and without making preparations, but kinsmen by marriage (who live at a distance) have to prepare, and so are long in coming.

οὐδὲ τό γ' ἐν οἴκῳ κατακείμενον ἀνέρα κήδει.
οἴκοι βέλτερον εἶναι, ἐπεὶ βλαβερὸν τὸ θύρηφιν.
ἐσθλὸν μὲν παρεόντος ἑλέσθαι, πῆμα δὲ θυμῷ
χρηίζειν ἀπεόντος, ἅ σε φράζεσθαι ἄνωγα.
ἀρχομένου δὲ πίθου καὶ λήγοντος κορέσασθαι,
μεσσόθι φείδεσθαι· δειλὴ δ' ἐνὶ πυθμένι φειδώ.
Μισθὸς δ' ἀνδρὶ φίλῳ εἰρημένος ἄρκιος ἔστω.
καί τε κασιγνήτῳ γελάσας ἐπὶ μάρτυρα θέσθαι.
πίστεις γάρ[1] τοι ὁμῶς καὶ ἀπιστίαι ὤλεσαν ἄνδρας.
Μὴ δὲ γυνή σε νόον πυγοστόλος ἐξαπατάτω
αἱμύλα κωτίλλουσα, τεὴν διφῶσα καλιήν.
ὃς δὲ γυναικὶ πέποιθε, πέποιθ' ὅ γε φηλήτῃσιν.
Μουνογενὴς δὲ πάις εἴη πατρώιον οἶκον
φερβέμεν· ὣς γὰρ πλοῦτος ἀέξεται ἐν μεγάροισιν.
γηραιὸς δὲ θάνοις ἕτερον παῖδ' ἐγκαταλείπων.
ῥεῖα δέ κεν πλεόνεσσι πόροι Ζεὺς ἄσπετον ὄλβον.
πλείων μὲν πλεόνων μελέτη, μείζων δ' ἐπιθήκη.
Σοὶ δ' εἰ πλούτου θυμὸς ἐέλδεται ἐν φρεσὶν ᾗσιν,
ὧδ' ἔρδειν, καὶ ἔργον ἐπ' ἔργῳ ἐργάζεσθαι.

Πληιάδων Ἀτλαγενέων ἐπιτελλομενάων
ἄρχεσθ' ἀμήτου, ἀρότοιο δὲ δυσομενάων.
αἳ δή τοι νύκτας τε καὶ ἤματα τεσσαράκοντα
κεκρύφαται, αὖτις δὲ περιπλομένου ἐνιαυτοῦ
φαίνονται τὰ πρῶτα χαρασσομένοιο σιδήρου.
οὗτός τοι πεδίων πέλεται νόμος, οἵ τε θαλάσσης
ἐγγύθι ναιετάουσ', οἵ τ' ἄγκεα βησσήεντα,
πόντου κυμαίνοντος ἀπόπροθι, πίονα χῶρον
ναίουσιν· γυμνὸν σπείρειν, γυμνὸν δὲ βοωτεῖν,
γυμνὸν δ' ἀμάειν, εἴ χ' ὥρια πάντ' ἐθέλῃσθα

[1] Bentley : δ' ἄρα, G.

a man has by him at home does not trouble him: it is better to have your stuff at home, for whatever is abroad may mean loss. It is a good thing to draw on what you have; but it grieves your heart to need something and not to have it, and I bid you mark this. Take your fill when the cask is first opened and when it is nearly spent, but midways be sparing: it is poor saving when you come to the lees.

Let the wage promised to a friend be fixed; even with your brother smile—and get a witness; for trust and mistrust, alike ruin men.

Do not let a flaunting woman coax and cozen and deceive you: she is after your barn. The man who trusts womankind trusts deceivers.

There should be an only son, to feed his father's house, for so wealth will increase in the home; but if you leave a second son you should die old. Yet Zeus can easily give great wealth to a greater number. More hands mean more work and more increase.

If your heart within you desires wealth, do these things and work with work upon work.

When the Pleiades, daughters of Atlas, are rising[1] begin your harvest, and your ploughing when they are going to set.[2] Forty nights and days they are hidden and appear again as the year moves round, when first you sharpen your sickle. This is the law of the plains, and of those who live near the sea, and who inhabit rich country, the glens and dingles far from the tossing sea,—strip to sow and strip to plough and strip to reap, if you wish to get in all Demeter's fruits in due season, and that each kind may grow in

[1] Early in May. [2] In November.

ἔργα κομίζεσθαι Δημήτερος· ὥς τοι ἕκαστα
ὥρι᾽ ἀέξηται, μή πως τὰ μέταζε[1] χατίζων
πτώσσῃς ἀλλοτρίους οἴκους καὶ μηδὲν ἀνύσσῃς.
ὡς καὶ νῦν ἐπ᾽ ἔμ᾽ ἦλθες· ἐγὼ δέ τοι οὐκ ἐπιδώσω
οὐδ᾽ ἐπιμετρήσω· ἐργάζευ, νήπιε Πέρση,
ἔργα, τά τ᾽ ἀνθρώποισι θεοὶ διετεκμήραντο,
μή ποτε σὺν παίδεσσι γυναικί τε θυμὸν ἀχεύων
ζητεύῃς βίοτον κατὰ γείτονας, οἳ δ᾽ ἀμελῶσιν.
δὶς μὲν γὰρ καὶ τρὶς τάχα τεύξεαι· ἢν δ᾽ ἔτι λυπῇς,
χρῆμα μὲν οὐ πρήξεις, σὺ δ᾽ ἐτώσια πόλλ᾽ ἀγορεύσεις·
ἀχρεῖος δ᾽ ἔσται ἐπέων νομός. ἀλλά σ᾽ ἄνωγα
φράζεσθαι χρειῶν τε λύσιν λιμοῦ τ᾽ ἀλεωρήν.
Οἶκον μὲν πρώτιστα γυναῖκά τε βοῦν τ᾽ ἀροτῆρα,
κτητήν, οὐ γαμετήν, ἥτις καὶ βουσὶν ἕποιτο,
χρήματα δ᾽ ἐν οἴκῳ πάντ᾽ ἄρμενα ποιήσασθαι,
μὴ σὺ μὲν αἰτῇς ἄλλον, ὁ δ᾽ ἀρνῆται, σὺ δὲ τητᾷ,
ἡ δ᾽ ὥρη παραμείβηται, μινύθῃ δὲ τὸ ἔργον.
μηδ᾽ ἀναβάλλεσθαι ἔς τ᾽ αὔριον ἔς τε ἔνηφιν·
οὐ γὰρ ἐτωσιοεργὸς ἀνὴρ πίμπλησι καλιὴν
οὐδ᾽ ἀναβαλλόμενος· μελέτη δὲ τὸ ἔργον ὀφέλλει·
αἰεὶ δ᾽ ἀμβολιεργὸς ἀνὴρ ἄτῃσι παλαίει.
Ἦμος δὴ λήγει μένος ὀξέος ἠελίοιο
καύματος ἰδαλίμου, μετοπωρινὸν ὀμβρήσαντος
Ζηνὸς ἐρισθενέος, μετὰ δὲ τρέπεται βρότεος χρὼς
πολλὸν ἐλαφρότερος· δὴ γὰρ τότε Σείριος ἀστὴρ
βαιὸν ὑπὲρ κεφαλῆς κηριτρεφέων ἀνθρώπων
ἔρχεται ἠμάτιος, πλεῖον δέ τε νυκτὸς ἐπαυρεῖ·
τῆμος ἀδηκτοτάτη πέλεται τμηθεῖσα σιδήρῳ

[1] Herodian: μεταξὺ, MSS.

its season. Else, afterwards, you may chance to be in want, and go begging to other men's houses, but without avail; as you have already come to me. But I will give you no more nor give you further measure. Foolish Perses! Work the work which the gods ordained for men, lest in bitter anguish of spirit you with your wife and children seek your livelihood amongst your neighbours, and they do not heed you. Two or three times, may be, you will succeed, but if you trouble them further, it will not avail you, and all your talk will be in vain, and your word-play unprofitable. Nay, I bid you find a way to pay your debts and avoid hunger.

First of all, get a house, and a woman and an ox for the plough—a slave woman and not a wife, to follow the oxen as well—and make everything ready at home, so that you may not have to ask of another, and he refuse you, and so, because you are in lack, the season pass by and your work come to nothing. Do not put your work off till to-morrow and the day after; for a sluggish worker does not fill his barn, nor one who puts off his work: industry makes work go well, but a man who puts off work is always at hand-grips with ruin.

When the piercing power and sultry heat of the sun abate, and almighty Zeus sends the autumn rains,[1] and men's flesh comes to feel far easier,—for then the star Sirius passes over the heads of men, who are born to misery, only a little while by day and takes greater share of night—, then, when it showers its leaves to the ground and stops sprouting,

[1] In October.

ὕλη, φύλλα δ' ἔραζε χέει, πτόρθοιό τε λήγει·
τῆμος ἄρ' ὑλοτομεῖν μεμνημένος ὥρια ἔργα.
ὅλμον μὲν τριπόδην τάμνειν, ὕπερον δὲ τρίπηχυν,
ἄξονα δ' ἑπταπόδην· μάλα γάρ νύ τοι ἄρμενον οὕτω·
εἰ δέ κεν ὀκταπόδην, ἀπὸ καὶ σφῦράν κε τάμοιο.
τρισπίθαμον δ' ἄψιν τάμνειν δεκαδώρῳ ἁμάξῃ.
πόλλ' ἐπικαμπύλα κᾶλα· φέρειν δὲ γύην, ὅτ' ἂν εὕρῃς,
ἐς οἶκον, κατ' ὄρος διζήμενος ἢ κατ' ἄρουραν,
πρίνινον· ὃς γὰρ βουσὶν ἀροῦν ὀχυρώτατός ἐστιν,
εὖτ' ἂν Ἀθηναίης δμῷος ἐν ἐλύματι πήξας
γόμφοισιν πελάσας προσαρήρεται ἱστοβοῆι.
δοιὰ δὲ θέσθαι ἄροτρα, πονησάμενος κατὰ οἶκον,
αὐτόγυον καὶ πηκτόν, ἐπεὶ πολὺ λώιον οὕτω·
εἴ χ' ἕτερον ἄξαις, ἕτερόν κ' ἐπὶ βουσὶ βάλοιο.
δάφνης δ' ἢ πτελέης ἀκιώτατοι ἱστοβοῆες,
δρυὸς ἔλυμα, γύης πρίνου· βόε δ' ἐνναετήρω
ἄρσενε κεκτῆσθαι, τῶν γὰρ σθένος οὐκ ἀλαπαδνόν,
ἥβης μέτρον ἔχοντε· τὼ ἐργάζεσθαι ἀρίστω.
οὐκ ἂν τώ γ' ἐρίσαντε ἐν αὔλακι κὰμ μὲν ἄροτρον
ἄξειαν, τὸ δὲ ἔργον ἐτώσιον αὖθι λίποιεν.
τοῖς δ' ἅμα τεσσαρακονταετὴς αἰζηὸς ἕποιτο
ἄρτον δειπνήσας τετράτρυφον, ὀκτάβλωμον,
ὃς ἔργου μελετῶν ἰθεῖάν κ' αὔλακ' ἐλαύνοι,
μηκέτι παπταίνων μεθ' ὁμήλικας, ἀλλ' ἐπὶ ἔργῳ

the wood you cut with your axe is least liable to worm. Then remember to hew your timber: it is the season for that work. Cut a mortar[1] three feet wide and a pestle three cubits long, and an axle of seven feet, for it will do very well so; but if you make it eight feet long, you can cut a beetle[2] from it as well. Cut a felloe three spans across for a waggon of ten palms' width. Hew also many bent timbers, and bring home a plough-tree when you have found it, and look out on the mountain or in the field for one of holm-oak; for this is the strongest for oxen to plough with when one of Athena's handmen has fixed in the share-beam and fastened it to the pole with dowels. Get two ploughs ready and work on them at home, one all of a piece, and the other jointed. It is far better to do this, for if you should break one of them, you can put the oxen to the other. Poles of laurel or elm are most free from worms, and a share-beam of oak and a plough-tree of holm-oak. Get two oxen, bulls of nine years; for their strength is unspent and they are in the prime of their age: they are best for work. They will not fight in the furrow and break the plough and then leave the work undone. Let a brisk fellow of forty years follow them, with a loaf of four quarters[3] and eight slices[4] for his dinner, one who will attend to his work and drive a straight furrow and is past the age for gaping after his fellows, but will keep his mind

[1] For pounding corn.
[2] A mallet for breaking clods after ploughing.
[3] The loaf is a flattish cake with two intersecting lines scored on its upper surface which divide it into four equal parts.
[4] The meaning is obscure. A scholiast renders "giving eight mouthfuls"; but the elder Philostratus uses the word in contrast to "leavened."

*θυμὸν ἔχων· τοῦ δ' οὔτι νεώτερος ἄλλος ἀμείνων
σπέρματα δάσσασθαι καὶ ἐπισπορίην ἀλέασθαι.
κουρότερος γὰρ ἀνὴρ μεθ' ὁμήλικας ἐπτοίηται.*

*Φράζεσθαι δ', εὖτ' ἂν γεράνου φωνὴν ἐπακούσῃς
ὑψόθεν ἐκ νεφέων ἐνιαύσια κεκληγυίης·
ἥτ' ἀρότοιό τε σῆμα φέρει καὶ χείματος ὥρην
δεικνύει ὀμβρηροῦ· κραδίην δ' ἔδακ' ἀνδρὸς ἀβούτεω·
δὴ τότε χορτάζειν ἕλικας βόας ἔνδον ἐόντας·
ῥηίδιον γὰρ ἔπος εἰπεῖν· βόε δὸς καὶ ἅμαξαν·
ῥηίδιον δ' ἀπανήνασθαι· πάρα ἔργα βόεσσιν.
φησὶ δ' ἀνὴρ φρένας ἀφνειὸς πήξασθαι ἅμαξαν,
νήπιος, οὐδὲ τὸ οἶδ'· ἑκατὸν δέ τε δούρατ' ἀμάξης.
τῶν πρόσθεν μελέτην ἐχέμεν οἰκήια θέσθαι.*

*Εὖτ' ἂν δὲ πρώτιστ' ἄροτος θνητοῖσι φανείῃ,
δὴ τότ' ἐφορμηθῆναι ὁμῶς δμῶές τε καὶ αὐτὸς
αὔην καὶ διερὴν ἀρόων ἀρότοιο καθ' ὥρην,
πρωὶ μάλα σπεύδων, ἵνα τοι πλήθωσιν ἄρουραι.
ἦρι πολεῖν· θέρεος δὲ νεωμένη οὔ σ' ἀπατήσει.
νειὸν δὲ σπείρειν ἔτι κουφίζουσαν ἄρουραν·
νειὸς ἀλεξιάρη παίδων εὐκηλήτειρα.*

*Εὔχεσθαι δὲ Διὶ χθονίῳ Δημήτερί θ' ἁγνῇ,
ἐκτελέα βρίθειν Δημήτερος ἱερὸν ἀκτήν,
ἀρχόμενος τὰ πρῶτ' ἀρότου, ὅτ' ἂν ἄκρον ἐχέτλης
χειρὶ λαβὼν ὅρπηκα βοῶν ἐπὶ νῶτον ἵκηαι
ἔνδρυον ἑλκόντων μεσάβων. ὁ δὲ τυτθὸς ὄπισθε
δμῷος ἔχων μακέλην πόνον ὀρνίθεσσι τιθείη
σπέρμα κατακρύπτων· εὐθημοσύνη γὰρ ἀρίστη*

on his work. No younger man will be better than he at scattering the seed and avoiding double-sowing; for a man less staid gets disturbed, hankering after his fellows.

Mark, when you hear the voice of the crane[1] who cries year by year from the clouds above, for she gives the signal for ploughing and shows the season of rainy winter; but she vexes the heart of the man who has no oxen. Then is the time to feed up your horned oxen in the byre; for it is easy to say: "Give me a yoke of oxen and a waggon," and it is easy to refuse: "I have work for my oxen." The man who is rich in fancy thinks his waggon as good as built already—the fool! he does not know that there are a hundred timbers to a waggon. Take care to lay these up beforehand at home.

So soon as the time for ploughing is proclaimed to men, then make haste, you and your slaves alike, in wet and in dry, to plough in the season for ploughing, and bestir yourself early in the morning so that your fields may be full. Plough in the spring; but fallow broken up in the summer will not belie your hopes. Sow fallow land when the soil is still getting light: fallow land is a defender from harm and a soother of children.

Pray to Zeus of the Earth and to pure Demeter to make Demeter's holy grain sound and heavy, when first you begin ploughing, when you hold in your hand the end of the plough-tail and bring down your stick on the backs of the oxen as they draw on the pole-bar by the yoke-straps. Let a slave follow a little behind with a mattock and make trouble for the birds by hiding the seed; for good management

[1] About the middle of November.

θνητοῖς ἀνθρώποις, κακοθημοσύνη δὲ κακίστη.
ὧδέ κεν ἁδροσύνῃ στάχυες νεύοιεν ἔραζε,
εἰ τέλος αὐτὸς ὄπισθεν Ὀλύμπιος ἐσθλὸν ὀπάζοι,
ἐκ δ' ἀγγέων ἐλάσειας ἀράχνια· καί σε ἔολπα
γηθήσειν βιότου αἱρεύμενον ἔνδον ἐόντος.
εὐοχθέων δ' ἵξεαι πολιὸν ἔαρ, οὐδὲ πρὸς ἄλλους
αὐγάσεαι· σέο δ' ἄλλος ἀνὴρ κεχρημένος ἔσται.
Εἰ δέ κεν ἠελίοιο τροπῇς ἀρόῳς χθόνα δῖαν,
ἥμενος ἀμήσεις ὀλίγον περὶ χειρὸς ἐέργων,
ἀντία δεσμεύων κεκονιμένος, οὐ μάλα χαίρων,
οἴσεις δ' ἐν φορμῷ· παῦροι δέ σε θηήσονται.
ἄλλοτε δ' ἀλλοῖος Ζηνὸς νόος αἰγιόχοιο,
ἀργαλέος δ' ἄνδρεσσι καταθνητοῖσι νοῆσαι.
εἰ δέ κεν ὄψ' ἀρόσῃς, τόδε κέν τοι φάρμακον εἴη·
ἦμος κόκκυξ κοκκύζει δρυὸς ἐν πετάλοισι
τὸ πρῶτον, τέρπει δὲ βροτοὺς ἐπ' ἀπείρονα γαῖαν,
τῆμος Ζεὺς ὕοι τρίτῳ ἤματι μηδ' ἀπολήγοι,
μήτ' ἄρ' ὑπερβάλλων βοὸς ὁπλὴν μήτ' ἀπολείπων·
οὕτω κ' ὀψαρότης πρῳηρότῃ[1] ἰσοφαρίζοι.
ἐν θυμῷ δ' εὖ πάντα φυλάσσεο· μηδέ σε λήθοι
μήτ' ἔαρ γιγνόμενον πολιὸν μήθ' ὥριος ὄμβρος.
Πὰρ δ' ἴθι χάλκειον θῶκον καὶ ἐπαλέα λέσχην
ὥρῃ χειμερίῃ, ὁπότε κρύος ἀνέρα ἔργων
ἰσχάνει, ἔνθα κ' ἄοκνος ἀνὴρ μέγα οἶκον ὀφέλλοι,
μή σε κακοῦ χειμῶνος ἀμηχανίη καταμάρψῃ
σὺν πενίῃ, λεπτῇ δὲ παχὺν πόδα χειρὶ πιέζῃς.
πολλὰ δ' ἀεργὸς ἀνήρ, κενεὴν ἐπὶ ἐλπίδα μίμνων,
χρηίζων βιότοιο, κακὰ προσελέξατο θυμῷ.

[1] Kirchoff: προηρότη, CD: πρωτηρότῃ, GIKL.

is the best for mortal men as bad management is the worst. In this way your corn-ears will bow to the ground with fullness if the Olympian himself gives a good result at the last, and you will sweep the cobwebs from your bins and you will be glad, I ween, as you take of your garnered substance. And so you will have plenty till you come to grey [1] springtime, and will not look wistfully to others, but another shall be in need of your help.

But if you plough the good ground at the solstice,[2] you will reap sitting, grasping a thin crop in your hand, binding the sheaves awry, dust-covered, not glad at all; so you will bring all home in a basket and not many will admire you. Yet the will of Zeus who holds the aegis is different at different times; and it is hard for mortal men to tell it; for if you should plough late, you may find this remedy—when the cuckoo first calls [3] in the leaves of the oak and makes men glad all over the boundless earth, if Zeus should send rain on the third day and not cease until it rises neither above an ox's hoof nor falls short of it, then the late-plougher will vie with the early. Keep all this well in mind, and fail not to mark grey spring as it comes and the season of rain.

Pass by the smithy and its crowded lounge in winter time when the cold keeps men from field work,—for then an industrious man can greatly prosper his house—lest bitter winter catch you helpless and poor and you chafe a swollen foot with a shrunk hand. The idle man who waits on empty hope, lacking a livelihood, reaps a full harvest of trouble in his heart;

[1] Spring is so described because the buds have not yet cast their iron-grey husks.

[2] In December.

[3] In March.

ἐλπὶς δ' οὐκ ἀγαθὴ κεχρημένον ἄνδρα κομίζει,
ἥμενον ἐν λέσχῃ, τῷ μὴ βίος ἄρκιος εἴη.
Δείκνυε δὲ δμώεσσι θέρευς ἔτι μέσσου ἐόντος·
οὐκ αἰεὶ θέρος ἐσσεῖται, ποιεῖσθε καλιάς.

Μῆνα δὲ Ληναιῶνα, κάκ' ἤματα, βουδόρα πάντα,
τοῦτον ἀλεύασθαι, καὶ πηγάδας, αἵτ' ἐπὶ γαῖαν
πνεύσαντος Βορέαο δυσηλεγέες τελέθουσιν,
ὅστε διὰ Θρῄκης ἱπποτρόφου εὐρέι πόντῳ
ἐμπνεύσας ὤρινε· μέμυκε δὲ γαῖα καὶ ὕλη·
πολλὰς δὲ δρῦς ὑψικόμους ἐλάτας τε παχείας
οὔρεος ἐν βήσσῃς πιλνᾷ χθονὶ πουλυβοτείρῃ
ἐμπίπτων, καὶ πᾶσα βοᾷ τότε νήριτος ὕλη.
θῆρες δὲ φρίσσουσ', οὐρὰς δ' ὑπὸ μέζε' ἔθεντο,
τῶν καὶ λάχνῃ δέρμα κατάσκιον· ἀλλά νυ καὶ τῶν
ψυχρὸς ἐὼν διάησι δασυστέρνων περ ἐόντων.
καί τε διὰ ῥινοῦ βοὸς ἔρχεται, οὐδέ μιν ἴσχει·
καί τε δι' αἶγα ἄησι τανύτριχα· πώεα δ' οὔ τι,
οὕνεκ' ἐπηεταναὶ τρίχες αὐτῶν, οὐ διάησιν
ἲς ἀνέμου Βορέου· τροχαλὸν δὲ γέροντα τίθησιν.
καὶ διὰ παρθενικῆς ἁπαλόχροος οὐ διάησιν,
ἥτε δόμων ἔντοσθε φίλῃ παρὰ μητέρι μίμνει
οὔ πω ἔργα ἰδυῖα πολυχρύσου Ἀφροδίτης·
εὖ τε λοεσσαμένη τέρενα χρόα καὶ λίπ' ἐλαίῳ
χρισαμένη μυχίη καταλέξεται ἔνδοθι οἴκου
ἤματι χειμερίῳ, ὅτ' ἀνόστεος ὃν πόδα τένδει
ἔν τ' ἀπύρῳ οἴκῳ καὶ ἤθεσι λευγαλέοισιν.
οὐδέ οἱ [1] ἠέλιος δείκνυ νομὸν ὁρμηθῆναι·

[1] Hermann: *οὐ γάρ οἱ*, MSS.

it is not an wholesome hope that accompanies a needy man who lolls at ease while he has no sure livelihood.

While it is yet midsummer command your slaves: "It will not always be summer, build barns."

Avoid the month Lenaeon,[1] wretched days, all of them fit to skin an ox, and the frosts which are cruel when Boreas blows over the earth. He blows across horse-breeding Thrace upon the wide sea and stirs it up, while earth and the forest howl. On many a high-leafed oak and thick pine he falls and brings them to the bounteous earth in mountain glens: then all the immense wood roars and the beasts shudder and put their tails between their legs, even those whose hide is covered with fur; for with his bitter blast he blows even through them although they are shaggy-breasted. He goes even through an ox's hide; it does not stop him. Also he blows through the goat's fine hair. But through the fleeces of sheep, because their wool is abundant, the keen wind Boreas pierces not at all; but it makes the old man curved as a wheel. And it does not blow through the tender maiden who stays indoors with her dear mother, unlearned as yet in the works of golden Aphrodite, and who washes her soft body and anoints herself with oil and lies down in an inner room within the house, on a winter's day when the Boneless One[2] gnaws his foot in his fireless house and wretched home; for the sun shows him no pastures to make

[1] The latter part of January and earlier part of February.
[2] *i.e.* the octopus or cuttle.

ἀλλ' ἐπὶ κυανέων ἀνδρῶν δῆμόν τε πόλιν τε
στρωφᾶται, βράδιον δὲ Πανελλήνεσσι φαείνει.
καὶ τότε δὴ κεραοὶ καὶ νήκεροι ὑληκοῖται
λυγρὸν μυλιόωντες ἀνὰ δρία βησσήεντα
φεύγουσιν· καὶ πᾶσιν ἐνὶ φρεσὶ τοῦτο μέμηλεν,
ὡς σκέπα μαιόμενοι πυκινοὺς κευθμῶνας ἔχωσι[1]
καὶ γλάφυ πετρῆεν· τότε δὴ τρίποδι βροτῷ ἶσοι,
οὗ τ' ἐπὶ νῶτα ἔαγε, κάρη δ' εἰς οὖδας ὁρᾶται,
τῷ ἴκελοι φοιτῶσιν, ἀλευόμενοι νίφα λευκήν.
Καὶ τότε ἕσσασθαι ἔρυμα χροός, ὥς σε κελεύω,
χλαῖνάν τε μαλακὴν καὶ τερμιόεντα χιτῶνα·
στήμονι δ' ἐν παύρῳ πολλὴν κρόκα μηρύσασθαι·
τὴν περιέσσασθαι, ἵνα τοι τρίχες ἀτρεμέωσι,
μηδ' ὀρθαὶ φρίσσωσιν ἀειρόμεναι κατὰ σῶμα.
ἀμφὶ δὲ ποσσὶ πέδιλα βοὸς ἶφι κταμένοιο
ἄρμενα δήσασθαι, πίλοις ἔντοσθε πυκάσσας.
πρωτογόνων δ' ἐρίφων, ὁπότ' ἂν κρύος ὥριον ἔλθῃ,
δέρματα συρράπτειν νεύρῳ βοός, ὄφρ' ἐπὶ νώτῳ
ὑετοῦ ἀμφιβάλῃ ἀλέην· κεφαλῆφι δ' ὕπερθεν
πῖλον ἔχειν ἀσκητόν, ἵν' οὔατα μὴ καταδεύῃ·
ψυχρὴ γάρ τ' ἠὼς πέλεται Βορέαο πεσόντος·
ἠῴιος δ' ἐπὶ γαῖαν ἀπ' οὐρανοῦ ἀστερόεντος
ἀὴρ πυροφόρος τέταται μακάρων ἐπὶ ἔργοις·
ὅστε ἀρυσσάμενος ποταμῶν ἄπο αἰεναόντων,
ὑψοῦ ὑπὲρ γαίης ἀρθεὶς ἀνέμοιο θυέλλῃ
ἄλλοτε μέν θ' ὕει ποτὶ ἕσπερον, ἄλλοτ' ἄησι
πυκνὰ Θρηικίου Βορέου νέφεα κλονέοντος.
τὸν φθάμενος ἔργον τελέσας οἶκόνδε νέεσθαι,

[1] Peppmuller: οἳ . . . ἔχουσι, MSS.

for, but goes to and fro over the land and city of dusky men,[1] and shines more sluggishly upon the whole race of the Hellenes. Then the horned and unhorned denizens of the wood, with teeth chattering pitifully, flee through the copses and glades, and all, as they seek shelter, have this one care, to gain thick coverts or some hollow rock. Then, like the Three-legged One[2] whose back is broken and whose head looks down upon the ground, like him, I say, they wander to escape the white snow.

Then put on, as I bid you, a soft coat and a tunic to the feet to shield your body,—and you should weave thick woof on thin warp. In this clothe yourself so that your hair may keep still and not bristle and stand upon end all over your body. Lace on your feet close-fitting boots of the hide of a slaughtered ox, thickly lined with felt inside. And when the season of frost comes on, stitch together skins of firstling kids with ox-sinew, to put over your back and to keep off the rain. On your head above wear a shaped cap of felt to keep your ears from getting wet, for the dawn is chill when Boreas has once made his onslaught, and at dawn a fruitful mist is spread over the earth from starry heaven upon the fields of blessed men: it is drawn from the ever flowing rivers and is raised high above the earth by windstorm, and sometimes it turns to rain towards evening, and sometimes to wind when Thracian Boreas huddles the thick clouds. Finish your work and return home ahead of him, and do not let the

[1] *i.e.* the dark-skinned people of Africa, the Egyptians or Aethiopians.

[2] *i.e.* an old man walking with a staff (the "third leg"—as in the riddle of the Sphinx).

μή ποτέ σ' οὐρανόθεν σκοτόεν νέφος ἀμφικαλύψῃ,
χρῶτα δὲ μυδαλέον θήῃ κατά θ' εἵματα δεύσῃ.
ἀλλ' ὑπαλεύασθαι· μεὶς γὰρ χαλεπώτατος οὗτος,
χειμέριος, χαλεπὸς προβάτοις, χαλεπὸς δ' ἀνθρώποις.
τῆμος τὤμισυ βουσίν, ἐπ' ἀνέρι δὲ πλέον εἴη
ἁρμαλιῆς· μακραὶ γὰρ ἐπίρροθοι εὐφρόναι εἰσίν.
ταῦτα φυλασσόμενος τετελεσμένον εἰς ἐνιαυτὸν
ἰσοῦσθαι νύκτας τε καὶ ἤματα, εἰσόκεν αὖτις
γῆ πάντων μήτηρ καρπὸν σύμμικτον ἐνείκῃ.

Εὖτ' ἂν δ' ἑξήκοντα μετὰ τροπὰς ἠελίοιο
χειμέρι' ἐκτελέσῃ Ζεὺς ἤματα, δή ῥα τότ' ἀστὴρ
Ἀρκτοῦρος προλιπὼν ἱερὸν ῥόον Ὠκεανοῖο
πρῶτον παμφαίνων ἐπιτέλλεται ἀκροκνέφαιος.
τὸν δὲ μέτ' ὀρθογόη Πανδιονὶς ὦρτο χελιδὼν
ἐς φάος ἀνθρώποις, ἔαρος νέον ἱσταμένοιο.
τὴν φθάμενος οἴνας περιταμνέμεν· ὣς γὰρ ἄμεινον.
Ἀλλ' ὁπότ' ἂν φερέοικος ἀπὸ χθονὸς ἂμ φυτὰ βαίνῃ
Πληιάδας φεύγων, τότε δὴ σκάφος οὐκέτι οἰνέων·
ἀλλ' ἅρπας τε χαρασσέμεναι καὶ δμῶας ἐγείρειν·
φεύγειν δὲ σκιεροὺς θώκους καὶ ἐπ' ἠόα[1] κοῖτον
ὥρῃ ἐν ἀμήτου, ὅτε τ' ἠέλιος χρόα κάρφει.
τημοῦτος σπεύδειν καὶ οἴκαδε καρπὸν ἀγινεῖν
ὄρθρου ἀνιστάμενος, ἵνα τοι βίος ἄρκιος εἴη.
ἠὼς γὰρ ἔργοιο τρίτην ἀπομείρεται αἶσαν,
ἠώς τοι προφέρει μὲν ὁδοῦ, προφέρει δὲ καὶ ἔργου,
ἠώς, ἥτε φανεῖσα πολέας ἐπέβησε κελεύθου
ἀνθρώπους πολλοῖσί τ' ἐπὶ ζυγὰ βουσὶ τίθησιν.

[1] Gerhard: ἠῶ, MSS.

dark cloud from heaven wrap round you and make your body clammy and soak your clothes. Avoid it; for this is the hardest month, wintry, hard for sheep and hard for men. In this season let your oxen have half their usual food, but let your man have more; for the helpful nights are long. Observe all this until the year is ended and you have nights and days of equal length, and Earth, the mother of all, bears again her various fruit.

When Zeus has finished sixty wintry days after the solstice, then the star Arcturus[1] leaves the holy stream of Ocean and first rises brilliant at dusk. After him the shrilly wailing daughter of Pandion, the swallow, appears to men when spring is just beginning. Before she comes, prune the vines, for it is best so.

But when the House-carrier[2] climbs up the plants from the earth to escape the Pleiades, then it is no longer the season for digging vineyards, but to whet your sickles and rouse up your slaves. Avoid shady seats and sleeping until dawn in the harvest season, when the sun scorches the body. Then be busy, and bring home your fruits, getting up early to make your livelihood sure. For dawn takes away a third part of your work, dawn advances a man on his journey and advances him in his work,—dawn which appears and sets many men on their road, and puts yokes on many oxen.

[1] February to March.
[2] *i.e.* the snail. The season is the middle of May.

Ἦμος δὲ σκόλυμός τ' ἀνθεῖ καὶ ἠχέτα τέττιξ
δενδρέῳ ἐφεζόμενος λιγυρὴν καταχεύετ' ἀοιδὴν
πυκνὸν ὑπὸ πτερύγων, θέρεος καματώδεος ὥρῃ,
τῆμος πιόταταί τ' αἶγες καὶ οἶνος ἄριστος,
μαχλόταται δὲ γυναῖκες, ἀφαυρότατοι δέ τοι ἄνδρες
εἰσίν, ἐπεὶ κεφαλὴν καὶ γούνατα Σείριος ἄζει,
αὐαλέος δέ τε χρὼς ὑπὸ καύματος· ἀλλὰ τότ' ἤδη
εἴη πετραίη τε σκιὴ καὶ βίβλινος οἶνος,
μάζα τ' ἀμολγαίη γάλα τ' αἰγῶν σβεννυμενάων,
καὶ βοὸς ὑλοφάγοιο κρέας μή πω τετοκυίης
πρωτογόνων τ' ἐρίφων· ἐπὶ δ' αἴθοπα πινέμεν οἶνον,
ἐν σκιῇ ἑζόμενον, κεκορημένον ἦτορ ἐδωδῆς,
ἀντίον ἀκραέος Ζεφύρου τρέψαντα πρόσωπα,
κρήνης τ' αἰενάου καὶ ἀπορρύτου, ἥτ' ἀθόλωτος,
τρὶς ὕδατος προχέειν, τὸ δὲ τέτρατον ἱέμεν οἴνου.

Δμωσὶ δ' ἐποτρύνειν Δημήτερος ἱερὸν ἀκτὴν
δινέμεν, εὖτ' ἂν πρῶτα φανῇ σθένος Ὠαρίωνος,
χώρῳ ἐν εὐαέι καὶ ἐυτροχάλῳ ἐν ἀλωῇ.
μέτρῳ δ' εὖ κομίσασθαι ἐν ἄγγεσιν· αὐτὰρ ἐπὴν δὴ
πάντα βίον κατάθηαι ἐπάρμενον ἔνδοθι οἴκου,
θῆτά τ' ἄοικον ποιεῖσθαι καὶ ἄτεκνον ἔριθον
δίζησθαι κέλομαι· χαλεπὴ δ' ὑπόπορτις ἔριθος·
καὶ κύνα καρχαρόδοντα κομεῖν, μὴ φείδεο σίτου,
μή ποτέ σ' ἡμερόκοιτος ἀνὴρ ἀπὸ χρήμαθ' ἕληται.
χόρτον δ' ἐσκομίσαι καὶ συρφετόν, ὄφρα τοι εἴη
βουσὶ καὶ ἡμιόνοισιν ἐπηετανόν. αὐτὰρ ἔπειτα
δμῶας ἀναψῦξαι φίλα γούνατα καὶ βόε λῦσαι.

But when the artichoke flowers,[1] and the chirping grass-hopper sits in a tree and pours down his shrill song continually from under his wings in the season of wearisome heat, then goats are plumpest and wine sweetest; women are most wanton, but men are feeblest, because Sirius parches head and knees and the skin is dry through heat. But at that time let me have a shady rock and wine of Biblis, a clot of curds and milk of drained goats with the flesh of an heifer fed in the woods, that has never calved, and of firstling kids; then also let me drink bright wine, sitting in the shade, when my heart is satisfied with food, and so, turning my head to face the fresh Zephyr, from the everflowing spring which pours down unfouled thrice pour an offering of water, but make a fourth libation of wine.

Set your slaves to winnow Demeter's holy grain, when strong Orion[2] first appears, on a smooth threshing-floor in an airy place. Then measure it and store it in jars. And so soon as you have safely stored all your stuff indoors, I bid you put your bondman out of doors and look out a servant-girl with no children;—for a servant with a child to nurse is troublesome. And look after the dog with jagged teeth; do not grudge him his food, or some time the Day-sleeper[3] may take your stuff. Bring in fodder and litter so as to have enough for your oxen and mules. After that, let your men rest their poor knees and unyoke your pair of oxen.

[1] In June. [2] July. [3] *i.e.* a robber.

Εὖτ᾿ ἂν δ᾿ Ὠαρίων καὶ Σείριος ἐς μέσον ἔλθῃ
οὐρανόν, Ἀρκτοῦρον δ᾿ ἐσίδῃ ῥοδοδάκτυλος Ἠώς,
ὦ Πέρση, τότε πάντας ἀποδρέπεν οἴκαδε βότρυς·
δεῖξαι δ᾿ ἠελίῳ δέκα τ᾿ ἤματα καὶ δέκα νύκτας,
πέντε δὲ συσκιάσαι, ἕκτῳ δ᾿ εἰς ἄγγε᾿ ἀφύσσαι
δῶρα Διωνύσου πολυγηθέος. αὐτὰρ ἐπὴν δὴ
Πληιάδες θ᾿ Ὑάδες τε τό τε σθένος Ὠαρίωνος
δύνωσιν, τότ᾿ ἔπειτ᾿ ἀρότου μεμνημένος εἶναι
ὡραίου· πλειὼν δὲ κατὰ χθονὸς ἄρμενος εἴσιν.

Εἰ δέ σε ναυτιλίης δυσπεμφέλου ἵμερος αἱρεῖ,
εὖτ᾿ ἂν Πληιάδες σθένος ὄβριμον Ὠαρίωνος
φεύγουσαι πίπτωσιν ἐς ἠεροειδέα πόντον,
δὴ τότε παντοίων ἀνέμων θυίουσιν[1] ἀῆται·
καὶ τότε μηκέτι νῆας ἔχειν ἐνὶ οἴνοπι πόντῳ,
γῆν ἐργάζεσθαι μεμνημένος, ὥς σε κελεύω.
νῆα δ᾿ ἐπ᾿ ἠπείρου ἐρύσαι πυκάσαι τε λίθοισι
πάντοθεν, ὄφρ᾿ ἴσχωσ᾿ ἀνέμων μένος ὑγρὸν ἀέντων,
χείμαρον ἐξερύσας, ἵνα μὴ πύθῃ Διὸς ὄμβρος.
ὅπλα δ᾿ ἐπάρμενα πάντα τεῷ ἐγκάτθεο οἴκῳ
εὐκόσμως στολίσας νηὸς πτερὰ ποντοπόροιο·
πηδάλιον δ᾿ ἐυεργὲς ὑπὲρ καπνοῦ κρεμάσασθαι.
αὐτὸς δ᾿ ὡραῖον μίμνειν πλόον, εἰσόκεν ἔλθῃ·
καὶ τότε νῆα θοὴν ἅλαδ᾿ ἑλκέμεν, ἐν δέ τε φόρτον
ἄρμενον ἐντύνασθαι, ἵν᾿ οἴκαδε κέρδος ἄρηαι,
ὥς περ ἐμός τε πατὴρ καὶ σός, μέγα νήπιε Πέρση,
πλωίζεσκ᾿ ἐν νηυσί, βίου κεχρημένος ἐσθλοῦ·
ὅς ποτε καὶ τῇδ᾿ ἦλθε, πολὺν διὰ πόντον ἀνύσσας,
Κύμην Αἰολίδα προλιπών, ἐν νηὶ μελαίνῃ·
οὐκ ἄφενος φεύγων οὐδὲ πλοῦτόν τε καὶ ὄλβον,

[1] Rzach: θυουσιν, MSS.

But when Orion and Sirius are come into mid-heaven, and rosy-fingered Dawn sees Arcturus,[1] then cut off all the grape-clusters, Perses, and bring them home. Show them to the sun ten days and ten nights: then cover them over for five, and on the sixth day draw off into vessels the gifts of joyful Dionysus. But when the Pleiades and Hyades and strong Orion begin to set,[2] then remember to plough in season: and so the completed year [3] will fitly pass beneath the earth.

But if desire for uncomfortable sea-faring seize you; when the Pleiades plunge into the misty sea [4] to escape Orion's rude strength, then truly gales of all kinds rage. Then keep ships no longer on the sparkling sea, but bethink you to till the land as I bid you. Haul up your ship upon the land and pack it closely with stones all round to keep off the power of the winds which blow damply, and draw out the bilge-plug so that the rain of heaven may not rot it. Put away all the tackle and fittings in your house, and stow the wings of the sea-going ship neatly, and hang up the well-shaped rudder over the smoke. You yourself wait until the season for sailing is come, and then haul your swift ship down to the sea and stow a convenient cargo in it, so that you may bring home profit, even as your father and mine, foolish Perses, used to sail on shipboard because he lacked sufficient livelihood. And one day he came to this very place crossing over a great stretch of sea; he left Aeolian Cyme and fled, not from riches and substance, but from wretched

[1] September. [2] The end of October.
[3] That is, the succession of stars which make up the full year.
[4] The end of October or beginning of November.

ἀλλὰ κακὴν πενίην, τὴν Ζεὺς ἄνδρεσσι δίδωσιν·
νάσσατο δ' ἄγχ' Ἑλικῶνος ὀιζυρῇ ἐνὶ κώμῃ,
Ἄσκρῃ, χεῖμα κακῇ, θέρει ἀργαλέῃ, οὐδέ ποτ'
ἐσθλῇ.
Τύνη δ', ὦ Πέρση, ἔργων μεμνημένος εἶναι
ὡραίων πάντων, περὶ ναυτιλίης δὲ μάλιστα.
νῆ' ὀλίγην αἰνεῖν, μεγάλῃ δ' ἐνὶ φορτία θέσθαι.
μείζων μὲν φόρτος, μεῖζον δ' ἐπὶ κέρδεϊ κέρδος
ἔσσεται, εἴ κ' ἄνεμοί γε κακὰς ἀπέχωσιν ἀήτας.
Εὖτ' ἂν ἐπ' ἐμπορίην τρέψας ἀεσίφρονα θυμὸν
βούληαι χρέα τε προφυγεῖν καὶ λιμὸν ἀτερπέα,
δείξω δή τοι μέτρα πολυφλοίσβοιο θαλάσσης,
οὔτε τι ναυτιλίης σεσοφισμένος οὔτε τι νηῶν.
οὐ γάρ πώ ποτε νηί γ' ἐπέπλων εὐρέα πόντον,
εἰ μὴ ἐς Εὔβοιαν ἐξ Αὐλίδος, ᾗ ποτ' Ἀχαιοὶ
μείναντες χειμῶνα πολὺν σὺν λαὸν ἄγειραν
Ἑλλάδος ἐξ ἱερῆς Τροίην ἐς καλλιγύναικα.
ἔνθα δ' ἐγὼν ἐπ' ἄεθλα δαΐφρονος Ἀμφιδάμαντος
Χαλκίδα τ' εἰς ἐπέρησα· τὰ δὲ προπεφραδμένα
πολλὰ
ἄεθλ' ἔθεσαν παῖδες μεγαλήτορος· ἔνθα μέ φημι
ὕμνῳ νικήσαντα φέρειν τρίποδ' ὠτώεντα.
τὸν μὲν ἐγὼ Μούσῃς Ἑλικωνιάδεσσ' ἀνέθηκα,
ἔνθα με τὸ πρῶτον λιγυρῆς ἐπέβησαν ἀοιδῆς.
τόσσον τοι νηῶν γε πεπείρημαι πολυγόμφων·
ἀλλὰ καὶ ὣς ἐρέω Ζηνὸς νόον αἰγιόχοιο·
Μοῦσαι γάρ μ' ἐδίδαξαν ἀθέσφατον ὕμνον ἀείδειν.
Ἤματα πεντήκοντα μετὰ τροπὰς ἠελίοιο,
ἐς τέλος ἐλθόντος θέρεος καματώδεος ὥρης,
ὡραῖος πέλεται θνητοῖς πλόος· οὔτε κε νῆα
καυάξαις οὔτ' ἄνδρας ἀποφθείσειε θάλασσα,

poverty which Zeus lays upon men, and he settled near Helicon in a miserable hamlet, Ascra, which is bad in winter, sultry in summer, and good at no time.

But you, Perses, remember all works in their season but sailing especially. Admire a small ship, but put your freight in a large one; for the greater the lading, the greater will be your piled gain, if only the winds will keep back their harmful gales.

If ever you turn your misguided heart to trading and wish to escape from debt and joyless hunger, I will show you the measures of the loud-roaring sea, though I have no skill in sea-faring nor in ships; for never yet have I sailed by ship over the wide sea, but only to Euboea from Aulis where the Achaeans once stayed through much storm when they had gathered a great host from divine Hellas for Troy, the land of fair women. Then I crossed over to Chalcis, to the games of wise Amphidamas where the sons of the great-hearted hero proclaimed and appointed prizes. And there I boast that I gained the victory with a song and carried off an handled tripod which I dedicated to the Muses of Helicon, in the place where they first set me in the way of clear song. Such is all my experience of many-pegged ships; nevertheless I will tell you the will of Zeus who holds the aegis; for the Muses have taught me to sing in marvellous song.

Fifty days after the solstice,[1] when the season of wearisome heat is come to an end, is the right time for men to go sailing. Then you will not wreck your ship, nor will the sea destroy the sailors, unless

[1] July–August.

εἰ δὴ μὴ πρόφρων γε Ποσειδάων ἐνοσίχθων
ἢ Ζεὺς ἀθανάτων βασιλεὺς ἐθέλῃσιν ὀλέσσαι·
ἐν τοῖς γὰρ τέλος ἐστὶν ὁμῶς ἀγαθῶν τε κακῶν τε.
τῆμος δ' εὐκρινέες τ' αὖραι καὶ πόντος ἀπήμων·
εὔκηλος τότε νῆα θοὴν ἀνέμοισι πιθήσας
ἑλκέμεν ἐς πόντον φόρτον τ' ἐς πάντα τίθεσθαι,
σπεύδειν δ' ὅττι τάχιστα πάλιν οἶκόνδε νέεσθαι·
μηδὲ μένειν οἶνόν τε νέον καὶ ὀπωρινὸν ὄμβρον
καὶ χειμῶν' ἐπιόντα Νότοιό τε δεινὰς ἀήτας,
ὅστ' ὤρινε θάλασσαν ὁμαρτήσας Διὸς ὄμβρῳ
πολλῷ ὀπωρινῷ, χαλεπὸν δέ τε πόντον ἔθηκεν.
Ἄλλος δ' εἰαρινὸς πέλεται πλόος ἀνθρώποισιν·
ἦμος δὴ τὸ πρῶτον, ὅσον τ' ἐπιβᾶσα κορώνη
ἴχνος ἐποίησεν, τόσσον πέταλ' ἀνδρὶ φανείῃ
ἐν κράδῃ ἀκροτάτῃ, τότε δ' ἄμβατός ἐστι θάλασσα·
εἰαρινὸς δ' οὗτος πέλεται πλόος. οὔ μιν ἔγωγε
αἴνημ'· οὐ γὰρ ἐμῷ θυμῷ κεχαρισμένος ἐστίν·
ἁρπακτός· χαλεπῶς κε φύγοις κακόν· ἀλλά νυ καὶ τὰ
ἄνθρωποι ῥέζουσιν ἀιδρείῃσι νόοιο·
χρήματα γὰρ ψυχὴ πέλεται δειλοῖσι βροτοῖσιν.
δεινὸν δ' ἐστὶ θανεῖν μετὰ κύμασιν. ἀλλά σ' ἄνωγα
φράζεσθαι τάδε πάντα μετὰ φρεσίν, ὡς ἀγορεύω.
μηδ' ἐν νηυσὶν ἅπαντα βίον κοΐλῃσι τίθεσθαι·
ἀλλὰ πλέω λείπειν, τὰ δὲ μείονα φορτίζεσθαι.
δεινὸν γὰρ πόντου μετὰ κύμασι πήματι κύρσαι.
δεινὸν δ', εἴ κ' ἐπ' ἄμαξαν ὑπέρβιον ἄχθος ἀείρας
ἄξονα καυάξαις καὶ φορτία μαυρωθείη.
μέτρα φυλάσσεσθαι· καιρὸς δ' ἐπὶ πᾶσιν ἄριστος.

Ὡραῖος δὲ γυναῖκα τεὸν ποτὶ οἶκον ἄγεσθαι,
μήτε τριηκόντων ἐτέων μάλα πόλλ' ἀπολείπων

Poseidon the Earth-Shaker be set upon it, or Zeus, the king of the deathless gods, wish to slay them; for the issues of good and evil alike are with them. At that time the winds are steady, and the sea is harmless. Then trust in the winds without care, and haul your swift ship down to the sea and put all the freight on board; but make all haste you can to return home again and do not wait till the time of the new wine and autumn rain and oncoming storms with the fierce gales of Notus who accompanies the heavy autumn rain of Zeus and stirs up the sea and makes the deep dangerous.

Another time for men to go sailing is in spring when a man first sees leaves on the topmost shoot of a fig-tree as large as the foot-print that a crow makes; then the sea is passable, and this is the spring sailing time. For my part I do not praise it, for my heart does not like it. Such a sailing is snatched, and you will hardly avoid mischief. Yet in their ignorance men do even this, for wealth means life to poor mortals; but it is fearful to die among the waves. But I bid you consider all these things in your heart as I say. Do not put all your goods in hollow ships; leave the greater part behind, and put the lesser part on board; for it is a bad business to meet with disaster among the waves of the sea, as it is bad if you put too great a load on your waggon and break the axle, and your goods are spoiled. Observe due measure: and proportion is best in all things.

Bring home a wife to your house when you are of the right age, while you are not far short of thirty

μήτ᾽ ἐπιθεὶς μάλα πολλά· γάμος δέ τοι ὥριος οὗτος·
ἡ δὲ γυνὴ τέτορ᾽ ἡβώοι, πέμπτῳ δὲ γαμοῖτο.
παρθενικὴν δὲ γαμεῖν, ὥς κ᾽ ἤθεα κεδνὰ διδάξῃς.
τὴν δὲ μάλιστα γαμεῖν, ἥ τις σέθεν ἐγγύθι ναίει,
πάντα μάλ᾽ ἀμφιιδών,[1] μὴ γείτοσι χάρματα γήμῃς.
οὐ μὲν γάρ τι γυναικὸς ἀνὴρ ληίζετ᾽ ἄμεινον
τῆς ἀγαθῆς, τῆς δ᾽ αὖτε κακῆς οὐ ῥίγιον ἄλλο,
δειπνολόχης· ἥτ᾽ ἄνδρα καὶ ἴφθιμόν περ ἐόντα
εὕει ἄτερ δαλοῖο καὶ ὠμῷ γήραϊ δῶκεν.[2]

Εὖ δ᾽ ὄπιν ἀθανάτων μακάρων πεφυλαγμένος εἶναι.
μηδὲ κασιγνήτῳ ἶσον ποιεῖσθαι ἑταῖρον·
εἰ δέ κε ποιήσῃς, μή μιν πρότερος κακὸν ἔρξῃς.
μηδὲ ψεύδεσθαι γλώσσης χάριν· εἰ δὲ σέ γ᾽ ἄρχῃ
ἤ τι ἔπος εἰπὼν ἀποθύμιον ἠὲ καὶ ἔρξας,
δὶς τόσα τίνυσθαι μεμνημένος· εἰ δὲ σέ γ᾽ αὖτις
ἡγῆτ᾽ ἐς φιλότητα, δίκην δ᾽ ἐθέλῃσι παρασχεῖν,
δέξασθαι· δειλός τοι ἀνὴρ φίλον ἄλλοτε ἄλλον
ποιεῖται, σὲ δὲ μή τι νόον κατελεγχέτω εἶδος.
Μηδὲ πολύξεινον μηδ᾽ ἄξεινον καλέεσθαι,
μηδὲ κακῶν ἕταρον μηδ᾽ ἐσθλῶν νεικεστῆρα.
Μηδέ ποτ᾽ οὐλομένην πενίην θυμοφθόρον ἀνδρὶ
τέτλαθ᾽ ὀνειδίζειν, μακάρων δόσιν αἰὲν ἐόντων.
γλώσσης τοι θησαυρὸς ἐν ἀνθρώποισιν ἄριστος
φειδωλῆς, πλείστη δὲ χάρις κατὰ μέτρον ἰούσης.
εἰ δὲ κακὸν εἴποις, τάχα κ᾽ αὐτὸς μεῖζον ἀκούσαις.

[1] Heyne: ἀμφὶς ἰδών, MSS.
[2] Another recension has δαλοῦ καὶ ἐν ὠμῷ γήραϊ θῆκεν: so AENOPQ, Plutarch, Stobaeus.

years nor much above; this is the right age for marriage. Let your wife have been grown up four years, and marry her in the fifth. Marry a maiden, so that you can teach her careful ways, and especially marry one who lives near you, but look well about you and see that your marriage will not be a joke to your neighbours. For a man wins nothing better than a good wife, and, again, nothing worse than a bad one, a greedy soul who roasts her man without fire, strong though he may be, and brings him to a raw [1] old age.

Be careful to avoid the anger of the deathless gods. Do not make a friend equal to a brother; but if you do, do not wrong him first, and do not lie to please the tongue. But if he wrong you first, offending either in word or in deed, remember to repay him double; but if he ask you to be his friend again and be ready to give you satisfaction, welcome him. He is a worthless man who makes now one and now another his friend; but as for you, do not let your face put your heart to shame.[2]

Do not get a name either as lavish or as churlish; as a friend of rogues or as a slanderer of good men.

Never dare to taunt a man with deadly poverty which eats out the heart; it is sent by the deathless gods. The best treasure a man can have is a sparing tongue, and the greatest pleasure, one that moves orderly; for if you speak evil, you yourself will soon be worse spoken of.

[1] *i.e.* untimely, premature. Juvenal similarly speaks of "cruda senectus" (caused by gluttony).

[2] The thought is parallel to that of "O, what a goodly outside falsehood hath."

Μηδὲ πολυξείνου δαιτὸς δυσπέμφελος εἶναι
ἐκ κοινοῦ· πλείστη δὲ χάρις, δαπάνη τ᾽ ὀλιγίστη.
Μηδέ ποτ᾽ ἐξ ἠοῦς Διὶ λειβέμεν αἴθοπα οἶνον
χερσὶν ἀνίπτοισιν μηδ᾽ ἄλλοις ἀθανάτοισιν·
οὐ γὰρ τοί γε κλύουσιν, ἀποπτύουσι δέ τ᾽ ἀράς.
Μηδ᾽ ἄντ᾽ ἠελίου τετραμμένος ὀρθὸς ὀμιχεῖν·
αὐτὰρ ἐπεί κε δύῃ, μεμνημένος, ἔς τ᾽ ἀνιόντα·
μήτ᾽ ἐν ὁδῷ μήτ᾽ ἐκτὸς ὁδοῦ προβάδην οὐρήσῃς
μηδ᾽ ἀπογυμνωθείς· μακάρων τοι νύκτες ἔασιν·
ἑζόμενος δ᾽ ὅ γε θεῖος ἀνήρ, πεπνυμένα εἰδώς,
ἢ ὅ γε πρὸς τοῖχον πελάσας ἐυερκέος αὐλῆς.
Μηδ᾽ αἰδοῖα γονῇ πεπαλαγμένος ἔνδοθι οἴκου
ἱστίῃ ἐμπελαδὸν παραφαινέμεν, ἀλλ᾽ ἀλέασθαι.
μηδ᾽ ἀπὸ δυσφήμοιο τάφου ἀπονοστήσαντα
σπερμαίνειν γενεήν, ἀλλ᾽ ἀθανάτων ἀπὸ δαιτός.
Μηδέ ποτ᾽ αἰενάων ποταμῶν καλλίρροον ὕδωρ
ποσσὶ περᾶν, πρίν γ᾽ εὔξῃ ἰδὼν ἐς καλὰ ῥέεθρα,
χεῖρας νιψάμενος πολυηράτῳ ὕδατι λευκῷ.
ὃς ποταμὸν διαβῇ κακότητ᾽ ἰδὲ χεῖρας ἄνιπτος,
τῷ δὲ θεοὶ νεμεσῶσι καὶ ἄλγεα δῶκαν ὀπίσσω.
Μηδ᾽ ἀπὸ πεντόζοιο θεῶν ἐν δαιτὶ θαλείῃ
αὖον ἀπὸ χλωροῦ τάμνειν αἴθωνι σιδήρῳ.
Μηδέ ποτ᾽ οἰνοχόην τιθέμεν κρητῆρος ὕπερθε
πινόντων· ὀλοὴ γὰρ ἐπ᾽ αὐτῷ μοῖρα τέτυκται.

Do not be boorish at a common feast where there are many guests; the pleasure is greatest and the expense is least.[1]

Never pour a libation of sparkling wine to Zeus after dawn with unwashen hands, nor to others of the deathless gods; else they do not hear your prayers but spit them back.

Do not stand upright facing the sun when you make water, but remember to do this when he has set and towards his rising. And do not make water as you go, whether on the road or off the road, and do not uncover yourself: the nights belong to the blessed gods. A scrupulous man who has a wise heart sits down or goes to the wall of an enclosed court.

Do not expose yourself befouled by the fireside in your house, but avoid this. Do not beget children when you are come back from ill-omened burial, but after a festival of the gods.

Never cross the sweet-flowing water of ever-rolling rivers afoot until you have prayed, gazing into the soft flood, and washed your hands in the clear, lovely water. Whoever crosses a river with hands unwashed of wickedness, the gods are angry with him and bring trouble upon him afterwards.

At a cheerful festival of the gods do not cut the withered from the quick upon that which has five branches[2] with bright steel.

Never put the ladle upon the mixing-bowl at a wine party, for malignant ill-luck is attached to that.

[1] The "common feast" is one to which all present subscribe. Theognis (line 495) says that one of the chief pleasures of a banquet is the general conversation. Hence the present passage means that such a feast naturally costs little, while the many present will make pleasurable conversation.

[2] *i.e.* "do not cut your finger-nails."

Μηδὲ δόμον ποιῶν ἀνεπίξεστον καταλείπειν,
μή τοι ἐφεζομένη κρώξῃ λακέρυζα κορώνη.
Μηδ᾽ ἀπὸ χυτροπόδων ἀνεπιρρέκτων ἀνελόντα
ἔσθειν μηδὲ λόεσθαι· ἐπεὶ καὶ τοῖς ἔνι ποινή.
Μηδ᾽ ἐπ᾽ ἀκινήτοισι καθιζέμεν, οὐ γὰρ ἄμεινον,
παῖδα δυωδεκαταῖον, ὅτ᾽ ἀνέρ᾽ ἀνήνορα ποιεῖ,
μηδὲ δυωδεκάμηνον· ἴσον καὶ τοῦτο τέτυκται.
μηδὲ γυναικείῳ λουτρῷ χρόα φαιδρύνεσθαι
ἀνέρα· λευγαλέη γὰρ ἐπὶ χρόνον ἔστ᾽ ἐπὶ καὶ τῷ
ποινή. μηδ᾽ ἱεροῖσιν ἐπ᾽ αἰθομένοισι κυρήσας
μωμεύειν ἀίδηλα· θεός νύ τι καὶ τὰ νεμεσσᾷ.
μηδέ ποτ᾽ ἐν προχοῇς ποταμῶν ἅλαδε προρεόντων
μηδ᾽ ἐπὶ κρηνάων οὐρεῖν, μάλα δ᾽ ἐξαλέασθαι·
μηδ᾽ ἐναποψύχειν· τὸ γὰρ οὔ τοι λώιόν ἐστιν.
Ὧδ᾽ ἔρδειν· δεινὴν δὲ βροτῶν ὑπαλεύεο φήμην.
φήμη γάρ τε κακὴ πέλεται, κούφη μὲν ἀεῖραι
ῥεῖα μάλ᾽, ἀργαλέη δὲ φέρειν, χαλεπὴ δ᾽ ἀπο-
θέσθαι.
φήμη δ᾽ οὔτις πάμπαν ἀπόλλυται, ἥν τινα πολλοὶ
λαοὶ φημίξωσι· θεός νύ τίς ἐστι καὶ αὐτή.

Ἤματα δ᾽ ἐκ Διόθεν πεφυλαγμένος εὖ κατὰ
μοῖραν
πεφραδέμεν δμώεσσι· τριηκάδα μηνὸς ἀρίστην
ἔργα τ᾽ ἐποπτεύειν ἠδ᾽ ἁρμαλιὴν δατέασθαι.
Αἵδε γὰρ ἡμέραι εἰσὶ Διὸς πάρα μητιόεντος,
εὖτ᾽ ἂν ἀληθείην λαοὶ κρίνοντες ἄγωσιν.
Πρῶτον ἔνη τετράς τε καὶ ἑβδόμη ἱερὸν ἦμαρ·
τῇ γὰρ Ἀπόλλωνα χρυσάορα γείνατο Λητώ·
ὀγδοάτη δ᾽ ἐνάτη τε, δύω γε μὲν ἤματα μηνὸς

When you are building a house, do not leave it rough-hewn, or a cawing crow may settle on it and croak.

Take nothing to eat or to wash with from uncharmed pots, for in them there is mischief.

Do not let a boy of twelve years sit on things which may not be moved,[1] for that is bad, and makes a man unmanly; nor yet a child of twelve months, for that has the same effect. A man should not clean his body with water in which a woman has washed, for there is bitter mischief in that also for a time. When you come upon a burning sacrifice, do not make a mock of mysteries, for Heaven is angry at this also. Never make water in the mouths of rivers which flow to the sea, nor yet in springs; but be careful to avoid this. And do not ease yourself in them: it is not well to do this.

So do: and avoid the talk of men. For Talk is mischievous, light, and easily raised, but hard to bear and difficult to be rid of. Talk never wholly dies away when many people voice her: even Talk is in some ways divine.

Mark the days which come from Zeus, duly telling your slaves of them, and that the thirtieth day of the month is best for one to look over the work and to deal out supplies.

For these are days which come from Zeus the all-wise, when men discern aright.

To begin with, the first, the fourth, and the seventh—on which Leto bare Apollo with the blade of gold—each is a holy day. The eighth and

[1] *i.e.* things which it would be sacrilege to disturb, such as tombs.

ἔξοχ' ἀεξομένοιο βροτήσια ἔργα πένεσθαι·
ἑνδεκάτη δὲ δυωδεκάτη τ', ἄμφω γε μὲν ἐσθλαί,
ἡμὲν ὄις πείκειν ἠδ' εὔφρονα καρπὸν ἀμᾶσθαι·
ἡ δὲ δυωδεκάτη τῆς ἑνδεκάτης μέγ' ἀμείνων·
τῇ γάρ τοι νῇ νήματ' ἀερσιπότητος ἀράχνης
ἤματος ἐκ πλείου, ὅτε ἴδρις σωρὸν ἀμᾶται·
τῇ δ' ἱστὸν στήσαιτο γυνὴ προβάλοιτό τε ἔργον.
Μηνὸς δ' ἱσταμένου τρισκαιδεκάτην ἀλέασθαι
σπέρματος ἄρξασθαι· φυτὰ δ' ἐνθρέψασθαι ἀρίστη.
Ἕκτη δ' ἡ μέσση μάλ' ἀσύμφορός ἐστι φυτοῖσιν,
ἀνδρογόνος δ' ἀγαθή· κούρῃ δ' οὐ σύμφορός ἐστιν,
οὔτε γενέσθαι πρῶτ' οὔτ' ἄρ γάμου ἀντιβολῆσαι.
οὐδὲ μὲν ἡ πρώτη ἕκτη κούρῃ γε [1] γενέσθαι
ἄρμενος, ἀλλ' ἐρίφους τάμνειν καὶ πώεα μήλων
σηκόν τ' ἀμφιβαλεῖν ποιμνήιον ἤπιον ἦμαρ·
ἐσθλὴ δ' ἀνδρογόνος· φιλέοι δ' ὅ γε [2] κέρτομα βάζειν
ψεύδεά θ' αἱμυλίους τε λόγους κρυφίους τ' ὀαρισμούς.
Μηνὸς δ' ὀγδοάτῃ κάπρον καὶ βοῦν ἐρίμυκον
ταμνέμεν, οὐρῆας δὲ δυωδεκάτῃ ταλαεργούς.
Εἰκάδι δ' ἐν μεγάλῃ, πλέῳ ἤματι, ἵστορα φῶτα
γείνασθαι· μάλα γάρ τε νόον πεπυκασμένος ἐστίν.
ἐσθλὴ δ' ἀνδρογόνος δεκάτη, κούρῃ δέ τε τετρὰς
μέσση· τῇ δέ τε μῆλα καὶ εἰλίποδας ἕλικας βοῦς
καὶ κύνα καρχαρόδοντα καὶ οὐρῆας ταλαεργοὺς
πρηΰνειν ἐπὶ χεῖρα τιθείς. πεφύλαξο δὲ θυμῷ

[1] Rzach: κούρῃ τε, AFGH etc.: κούρῃσι τε, KL: κουρῇσι, C.
[2] A: φιλέοι or φιλέει δέ κε, MSS.

the ninth, two days at least of the waxing month,[1] are specially good for the works of man. Also the eleventh and twelfth are both excellent, alike for shearing sheep and for reaping the kindly fruits; but the twelfth is much better than the eleventh, for on it the airy-swinging spider spins its web in full day, and then the Wise One,[2] gathers her pile. On that day a woman should set up her loom and get forward with her work.

Avoid the thirteenth of the waxing month for beginning to sow: yet it is the best day for setting plants.

The sixth of the mid-month is very unfavourable for plants, but is good for the birth of males, though unfavourable for a girl either to be born at all or to be married. Nor is the first sixth a fit day for a girl to be born, but a kindly for gelding kids and sheep and for fencing in a sheep-cote. It is favourable for the birth of a boy, but such will be fond of sharp speech, lies, and cunning words, and stealthy converse.

On the eighth of the month geld the boar and loud-bellowing bull, but hard-working mules on the twelfth.

On the great twentieth, in full day, a wise man should be born. Such an one is very sound-witted. The tenth is favourable for a male to be born; but, for a girl, the fourth day of the mid-month. On that day tame sheep and shambling, horned oxen, and the sharp-fanged dog and hardy mules to the touch of the hand. But take care to avoid troubles which

[1] The month is divided into three periods, the waxing, the mid-month, and the waning, which answer to the phases of the moon.

[2] *i.e.* the ant.

τετράδ' ἀλεύασθαι φθίνοντός θ' ἱσταμένου τε
ἄλγεα θυμοβορῆ·[1] μάλα γὰρ[2] τετελεσμένον ἦμαρ.
'Εν δὲ τετάρτῃ μηνὸς ἄγεσθαι[3] οἶκον ἄκοιτιν
οἰωνοὺς κρίνας, οἳ ἐπ' ἔργματι τούτῳ ἄριστοι.
Πέμπτας δ' ἐξαλέασθαι, ἐπεὶ χαλεπαί τε καὶ αἰναί·
ἐν πέμπτῃ γάρ φασιν 'Ερινύας ἀμφιπολεύειν
"Ορκον γεινόμενον, τὸν "Ερις τέκε πῆμ' ἐπιόρκοις.
Μέσσῃ δ' ἑβδομάτῃ Δημήτερος ἱερὸν ἀκτὴν
εὖ μάλ' ὀπιπεύοντα ἐυτροχάλῳ ἐν ἀλωῇ
βαλλέμεν, ὑλοτόμον τε ταμεῖν θαλαμήια δοῦρα
νήιά τε ξύλα πολλά, τά τ' ἄρμενα νηυσὶ πέλονται.
τετράδι δ' ἄρχεσθαι νῆας πήγνυσθαι ἀραιάς.
Εἰνὰς δ' ἡ μέσση ἐπὶ δείελα λώιον ἦμαρ,
πρωτίστη δ' εἰνὰς παναπήμων ἀνθρώποισιν·
ἐσθλὴ μὲν γάρ θ' ἥ γε[4] φυτευέμεν ἠδὲ γενέσθαι
ἀνέρι τ' ἠδὲ γυναικί· καὶ οὔποτε πάγκακον ἦμαρ.
Παῦροι δ' αὖτε ἴσασι τρισεινάδα μηνὸς ἀρίστην
ἄρξασθαί τε πίθου καὶ ἐπὶ ζυγὸν αὐχένι θεῖναι
βουσὶ καὶ ἡμιόνοισι καὶ ἵπποις ὠκυπόδεσσι,
νῆα πολυκλήιδα θοὴν εἰς οἴνοπα πόντον
εἰρύμεναι· παῦροι δέ τ' ἀληθέα κικλήσκουσιν.
Τετράδι δ' οἶγε πίθον· περὶ πάντων ἱερὸν ἦμαρ
μέσσῃ· παῦροι δ' αὖτε μετ' εἰκάδα μηνὸς ἀρίστην
ἠοῦς γιγνομένης· ἐπὶ δείελα δ' ἐστὶ χερείων.

[1] Guyet: θυμοβορεῖν, MSS.
[2] A: τοι, MSS.
[3] Sittl: ἄγεσθ' εἰς, MSS.
[4] AM: ἤδε, most MSS.

eat out the heart on the fourth of the beginning and ending of the month; it is a day very fraught with fate.

On the fourth of the month bring home your bride, but choose the omens which are best for this business.

Avoid fifth days: they are unkindly and terrible. On a fifth, they say, the Erinyes assisted at the birth of Horcus (Oath) whom Eris (Strife) bare to trouble the forsworn.

Look about you very carefully and throw out Demeter's holy grain upon the well-rolled [1] threshing floor on the seventh of the mid-month. Let the woodman cut beams for house building and plenty of ships' timbers, such as are suitable for ships. On the fourth day begin to build narrow ships.

The ninth of the mid-month improves towards evening; but the first ninth of all is quite harmless for men. It is a good day on which to beget or to be born both for a male and a female: it is never an wholly evil day.

Again, few know that the twenty-seventh of the month is best for opening a wine-jar, and putting yokes on the necks of oxen and mules and swift-footed horses, and for hauling a swift ship of many thwarts down to the sparkling sea; few call it by its right name.

On the fourth day open a jar. The fourth of the mid-month is a day holy above all. And again, few men know that the fourth day after the twentieth is best while it is morning: towards evening it is less good.

[1] Such seems to be the meaning here, though the epithet is otherwise rendered "well-rounded." Corn was threshed by means of a sleigh with two runners having three or four rollers between them, like the modern Egyptian *nurag*.

Αἵδε μὲν ἡμέραι εἰσὶν ἐπιχθονίοις μέγ' ὄνειαρ,
αἱ δ' ἄλλαι μετάδουποι, ἀκήριοι, οὔ τι φέρουσαι.
ἄλλος δ' ἀλλοίην αἰνεῖ, παῦροι δὲ ἴσασιν.
ἄλλοτε μητρυιὴ πέλει ἡμέρη, ἄλλοτε μήτηρ.
τάων εὐδαίμων τε καὶ ὄλβιος, ὃς τάδε πάντα
εἰδὼς ἐργάζηται ἀναίτιος ἀθανάτοισιν,
ὄρνιθας κρίνων καὶ ὑπερβασίας ἀλεείνων.

ΟΡΝΙΘΟΜΑΝΤΕΙΑ

Proclus on Works and Days, 828. Τούτοις δὲ ἐπάγουσί τινες τὴν Ὀρνιθομαντείαν ἅτινα Ἀπολλώνιος ὁ Ῥόδιος ἀθετεῖ.

WORKS AND DAYS

These days are a great blessing to men on earth; but the rest are changeable, luckless, and bring nothing. Everyone praises a different day but few know their nature. Sometimes a day is a stepmother, sometimes a mother. That man is happy and lucky in them who knows all these things and does his work without offending the deathless gods, who discerns the omens of birds and avoids transgression.

THE DIVINATION BY BIRDS

Some make the *Divination by Birds,* which Apollonius of Rhodes rejects as spurious, follow this verse (*Works and Days,* 828).

ΑΣΤΡΟΝΟΜΙΑ

1.

Athenaeus xi. p. 491 d. καὶ ὁ τὴν εἰς Ἡσίοδον δὴ ἀναφερομένην ποιήσας Ἀστρονομίαν αἰεὶ Πελειάδας αὐτὰς λέγει·

τὰς δὲ βροτοὶ καλέουσι Πελειάδας.

καὶ πάλιν·

χειμέριαι δύνουσι Πελειάδες.

καὶ πάλιν·

τῆμος ἀποκρύπτουσι Πελειάδες . . . .

Scholiast on Pindar, Nem. ii. 16. Πλειάδας . . . ὧν οἱ ἀστέρες οὗτοι·

Τηϋγέτη τ' ἐρόεσσα καὶ Ἠλέκτρη κυανῶπις
Ἀλκυόνη τε καὶ Ἀστερόπη δίη τε Κελαινὼ
Μαῖά τε καὶ Μερόπη, τὰς γείνατο φαίδιμος Ἄτλας.

* * * *

Κυλλήνης ἐν ὄρεσσι θεῶν κήρυκα τέχ' Ἑρμῆν.

2.

Scholiast on Aratus 254. Ζεὺς δὲ ἀστέρας αὐτὰς (τὰς Ὕαντος ἀδελφὰς) πεποίηκε, τὰς

THE ASTRONOMY

1.

And the author of the Astronomy, which is attributed forsooth to Hesiod, always calls them (the Pleiades) Peleiades: "but mortals call them Peleiades"; and again, "the stormy Peleiades go down"; and again, "then the Peleiades hide away . . . ."

The Pleiades . . . whose stars are these:—"Lovely Teÿgeta, and dark-faced Electra, and Alcyone, and bright Asterope, and Celaeno, and Maia, and Merope, whom glorious Atlas begot . . . . In the mountains of Cyllene she (Maia) bare Hermes, the herald of the gods."

2.

But Zeus made them (the sisters of Hyas) into the stars which are called Hyades. Hesiod καλουμένας Ὑάδας. ὧν τὰ ὀνόματα Ἡσίοδος ἐν τῇ Ἀστρικῇ αὐτοῦ βίβλῳ διδάσκει λέγων·

Νύμφαι Χαρίτεσσιν ὁμοῖαι,[1]
Φαισύλη ἠδὲ Κορωνὶς ἐυστέφανός τε Κλέεια
Φαιώ θ' ἱμερόεσσα ἰδ' Εὐδώρη τανύπεπλος,
ἃς Ὑάδας καλέουσιν ἐπὶ χθονὶ φῦλ' ἀνθρώπων.

3.

Pseudo-Eratosthenes Catast. frag. 1.[2] Ἄρκτος ἡ μεγάλη] ταύτην Ἡσίοδός φησι Λυκάονος θυγατέρα ἐν Ἀρκαδίᾳ οἰκεῖν, ἑλέσθαι δὲ μετὰ Ἀρτέμιδος τὴν περὶ τὰς θήρας ἀγωγὴν ἐν τοῖς ὄρεσι ποιεῖσθαι· φθαρεῖσαν δὲ ὑπὸ Διὸς ἐμμεῖναι λανθάνουσαν τὴν θεόν· φωραθῆναι δὲ ὕστερον ἐπίτοκον ἤδη οὖσαν ὀφθεῖσαν ὑπ' αὐτῆς λουομένην· ἐφ' ᾧ ὀργισθεῖσαν τὴν θεὸν ἀποθηριῶσαι αὐτήν· καὶ οὕτως τεκεῖν ἄρκτον γενομένην τὸν κληθέντα Ἀρκάδα. οὖσαν δ' ἐν τῷ ὄρει θηρευθῆναι ὑπὸ αἰπόλων τινῶν καὶ παραδοθῆναι μετὰ τοῦ βρέφους τῷ Λυκάονι· μετὰ χρόνον δέ τινα δόξαι εἰσελθεῖν εἰς τὸ τοῦ Διὸς ἄβατον [ἱερὸν] ἀγνοήσασαν τὸν νόμον. ὑπὸ δὲ τοῦ ἰδίου υἱοῦ διωκομένην καὶ τῶν Ἀρκάδων, καὶ ἀναιρεῖσθαι μέλλουσαν διὰ τὸν εἰρημένον νόμον, ὁ Ζεὺς διὰ τὴν συγγένειαν αὐτὴν ἐξείλετο καὶ ἐν τοῖς ἄστροις αὐτὴν ἔθηκεν. Ἄρκτον δὲ αὐτὴν ὠνόμασε διὰ τὸ συμβεβηκὸς αὐτῇ σύμπτωμα.

Comm. Supplem. on Aratus, p. 547 M. 8. περὶ τοῦ Βοώτου τοῦ καὶ Ἀρκτοφύλακος. περὶ τούτου

[1] This half verse is added by the Scholiast on Aratus, 172.
[2] The *Catasterismi* ("Placings among the Stars") is a collection of legends relating to the various constellations.

in his Book about Stars tells us their names as follows: "Nymphs like the Graces, Phaesyle and Coronis and rich-crowned Cleeia and lovely Phaeo and long-robed Eudora, whom the tribes of men upon the earth call Hyades."

3.

The Great Bear.]—Hesiod says she (Callisto) was the daughter of Lycaon and lived in Arcadia. She chose to occupy herself with wild-beasts in the mountains together with Artemis, and, when she was seduced by Zeus, continued some time undetected by the goddess, but afterwards, when she was already with child, was seen by her bathing and so discovered. Upon this, the goddess was enraged and changed her into a beast. Thus she became a bear and gave birth to a son called Arcas. But while she was in the mountain, she was hunted by some goat-herds and given up with her babe to Lycaon. Some while after, she thought fit to go into the forbidden precinct of Zeus, not knowing the law, and being pursued by her own son and the Arcadians, was about to be killed because of the said law; but Zeus delivered her because of her connection with him and put her among the stars, giving her the name Bear because of the misfortune which had befallen her.

Of Boötes, also called the Bear-warden. The story goes that he is Arcas the son of Callisto and λέγεται, ὅτι Ἀρκάς ἐστιν ὁ Καλλιστοῦς καὶ Διὸς γεγονώς· ᾤκησε δὲ περὶ τὸ Λύκαιον. φθείραντος αὐτὴν Διός, οὐ προσποιησάμενος ὁ Λυκάων, τὸν Δία ἐξένιζεν, ὥς φησιν Ἡσίοδος, καὶ τὸ βρέφος κατακόψας παρέθηκεν ἐπὶ τὴν τράπεζαν.

4.

Pseudo-Eratosthenes, Catast. fr. xxxii. Ὠρίων] τοῦτον Ἡσίοδός φησιν Εὐρυάλης τῆς Μίνωος καὶ Ποσειδῶνος εἶναι, δοθῆναι δὲ αὐτῷ δωρεὰν ὥστε ἐπὶ τῶν κυμάτων πορεύεσθαι καθάπερ ἐπὶ τῆς γῆς. ἐλθόντα δὲ αὐτὸν εἰς Χίον Μερόπην τὴν Οἰνοπίωνος βιάσασθαι οἰνωθέντα, γνόντα δὲ τὸν Οἰνοπίωνα καὶ χαλεπῶς ἐνεγκόντα τὴν ὕβριν ἐκτυφλῶσαι αὐτὸν καὶ ἐκ τῆς χώρας ἐκβαλεῖν· ἐλθόντα δὲ εἰς Λῆμνον ἀλητεύοντα Ἡφαίστῳ συμμῖξαι· ὃς αὐτὸν ἐλεήσας δίδωσιν αὐτῷ Κηδαλίωνα τὸν αὐτοῦ [οἰκεῖον] οἰκέτην, ὅπως ὁδηγῇ· ὃν λαβὼν ἐπὶ τῶν ὤμων ἔφερε σημαίνοντα τὰς ὁδούς. ἐλθὼν δ' ἐπὶ τὰς ἀνατολὰς καὶ Ἡλίῳ συμμίξας δοκεῖ ὑγιασθῆναι καὶ οὕτως ἐπὶ τὸν Οἰνοπίωνα ἐλθεῖν πάλιν τιμωρίαν αὐτῷ ἐπιθήσων. ὁ δὲ ὑπὸ τῶν πολιτῶν ὑπὸ γῆν ἐκέκρυπτο. ἀπελπίσας δὲ τὴν ἐκείνου ζήτησιν ἀπῆλθεν εἰς Κρήτην καὶ περὶ τὰς θήρας διῆγε κυνηγετῶν τῆς Ἀρτέμιδος παρούσης καὶ τῆς Λητοῦς, καὶ δοκεῖ ἀπειλήσασθαι ὡς πᾶν θηρίον ἀνελεῖν τῶν ἐπὶ τῆς γῆς γινομένων. θυμωθεῖσα δὲ αὐτῷ Γῆ ἀνῆκε σκορπίον εὐμεγέθη, ἐφ' οὗ τῷ κέντρῳ πληγεὶς ἀπώλετο. ὅθεν διὰ τὴν αὐτοῦ ἀνδρίαν ἐν τοῖς ἄστροις αὐτὸν ἔθηκεν ὁ Ζεὺς ὑπὸ Ἀρτέ-

Zeus, and he lived in the country about Lycaeum. After Zeus had seduced Callisto, Lycaon, pretending not to know of the matter, entertained Zeus, as Hesiod says, and set before him on the table the babe which he had cut up.

4.

Orion.]—Hesiod says that he was the son of Euryale, the daughter of Minos, and of Poseidon, and that there was given him as a gift the power of walking upon the waves as though upon land. When he was come to Chios, he outraged Merope, the daughter of Oenopion, being drunken; but Oenopion when he learned of it was greatly vexed at the outrage and blinded him and cast him out of the country. Then he came to Lemnos as a beggar and there met Hephaestus who took pity on him and gave him Cedalion his own servant to guide him. So Orion took Cedalion upon his shoulders and used to carry him about while he pointed out the roads. Then he came to the east and appears to have met Helius (the Sun) and to have been healed, and so returned back again to Oenopion to punish him; but Oenopion was hidden away by his people underground. Being disappointed, then, in his search for the king, Orion went away to Crete and spent his time hunting in company with Artemis and Leto. It seems that he threatened to kill every beast there was on earth; whereupon, in her anger, Earth sent up against him a scorpion of very great size by which he was stung and so perished. After this Zeus, at the prayer of Artemis and Leto, put him among the μιδος καὶ Λητοῦς ἀξιωθείς, ὁμοίως καὶ τὸ θηρίον τοῦ εἶναι μνημόσυνον καὶ τῆς πράξεως.

5.

Diodorus iv. 85. ἔνιοι δὲ λέγουσι σεισμῶν μεγάλων γενομένων διαρραγῆναι τὸν αὐχένα τῆς ἠπείρου καὶ γενέσθαι τὸν πορθμόν, διειργούσης τῆς θαλάσσης τὴν ἤπειρον ἀπὸ τῆς νήσου. Ἡσίοδος δὲ ὁ ποιητής φησι τοὐναντίον, ἀναπεπταμένου τοῦ πελάγους Ὠρίωνα προσχῶσαι τὸ κατὰ τὴν Πελωρίδα κείμενον ἀκρωτήριον καὶ τὸ τέμενος τοῦ Ποσειδῶνος κατασκευάσαι, τιμώμενον ὑπὸ τῶν ἐγχωρίων διαφερόντως· ταῦτα δὲ διαπραξάμενον εἰς Εὔβοιαν μεταναστῆσαι κἀκεῖ κατοικῆσαι· διὰ δὲ τὴν δόξαν ἐν τοῖς κατ᾽ οὐρανὸν ἄστροις καταριθμηθέντα τυχεῖν ἀθανάτου μνήμης.

ΧΕΙΡΩΝΟΣ ΥΠΟΘΗΚΑΙ

1.

Scholiast on Pindar, Pyth. vi. 19.

Εὖ νῦν μοι τὰ ἕκαστα μετὰ φρεσὶ πευκαλίμῃσι
φράζεσθαι· πρῶτον μέν, ὅτ᾽ ἂν δόμον εἰσαφίκηαι,
ἐρδέμεν ἱερὰ καλὰ θεοῖς αἰειγενέτῃσιν.

2.

Plutarch Mor. 1034 E.

μηδὲ δίκην δικάσῃς, πρὶν ἂν ἀμφοῖν μῦθον ἀκούσῃς.

stars, because of his manliness, and the scorpion also as a memorial of him and of what had occurred.

5.

Some say that great earthquakes occurred, which broke through the neck of land and formed the straits,[1] the sea parting the mainland from the island. But Hesiod, the poet, says just the opposite: that the sea was open, but Orion piled up the promontory by Peloris, and founded the close of Poseidon which is especially esteemed by the people thereabouts. When he had finished this, he went away to Euboea and settled there, and because of his renown was taken into the number of the stars in heaven, and won undying remembrance.

THE PRECEPTS OF CHIRON

1.

"And now, pray, mark all these things well in a wise heart. First, whenever you come to your house, offer good sacrifices to the eternal gods."

2.

"Decide no suit until you have heard both sides speak."

[1] The Straits of Messina.

3.

Plutarch de Orac. defectu ii. 415 c.
ἐννέα τοι ζώει γενεὰς λακέρυζα κορώνη
ἀνδρῶν γηράντων· ἔλαφος δέ τε τετρακόρωνος·
τρεῖς δ' ἐλάφους ὁ κόραξ γηράσκεται· αὐτὰρ ὁ φοῖνιξ
ἐννέα μὲν κόρακας, δέκα φοίνικας δέ τοι ἡμεῖς
Νύμφαι εὐπλόκαμοι, κοῦραι Διὸς αἰγιόχοιο.

4.

Quintilian, i. 1. 15. Quidam litteris instituendos, qui minores septem annis essent, non putaverunt . . . in qua sententia Hesiodum esse plurimi tradunt, qui ante Grammaticum Aristophanem fuerunt, nam is primus Ὑποθήκας, in quo libro scriptum hoc invenitur, negavit esse huius poetae.

ΜΕΓΑΛΑ ΕΡΓΑ

1.

Comm. on Aristotle, Nicomachean Ethics. v. 8. τὸ μέντοι ἔπος (τὸ τοῦ Ῥαδαμάνθυος) ἐστὶ παρ' Ἡσιόδῳ ἐν τοῖς Μεγάλοις Ἔργοις οὕτως ἔχον·

εἰ κακά τις σπείραι, κακὰ κέρδεά κ' ἀμήσειεν·
εἴ κε πάθοι τά τ' ἔρεξε, δίκη κ' ἰθεῖα γένοιτο.

2.

Proclus on Hesiod, Works and Days, 126. τὸ δὲ ἀργύρεον ἔνιοι τῇ γῇ ἀκούουσι λέγοντες ὅτι ἐν τοῖς Μεγάλοις Ἔργοις τὸ ἀργύριον τῆς γῆς γενεαλογεῖ.

3.

"A chattering crow lives out nine generations of aged men, but a stag's life is four times a crow's, and a raven's life makes three stags old, while the phoenix outlives nine ravens, but we, the rich-haired Nymphs, daughters of Zeus the aegis-holder, outlive ten phoenixes."

4.

Some consider that children under the age of seven should not receive a literary education . . . That Hesiod was of this opinion very many writers affirm who were earlier than the critic Aristophanes ; for he was the first to reject the *Precepts,* in which book this maxim occurs, as a work of that poet.

THE GREAT WORKS

1.

THE verse, however (the saying of Rhadamanthys), is in Hesiod in the Great Works and is as follows: "If a man sow evil, he shall reap evil increase; if men do to him as he has done, it will be true justice."

2.

Some believe that the Silver Race (is to be attributed to) the earth, declaring that in the Great Works Hesiod makes silver to be of the family of Earth.

ΙΔΑΙΟΙ ΔΑΚΤΥΛΟΙ

Pliny, Natural History vii. 56, 197. . . . Ferrum conflare et temperare Hesiodus in Creta eos (monstrasse) qui vocati sunt Dactyli Idaei.

Clement, Stromateis i. 16. 75. Κέλμις τε αὖ καὶ Δαμναμενεύς, οἱ τῶν Ἰδαίων Δακτύλων πρῶτοι, σίδηρον εὗρον ἐν Κύπρῳ, Δέλας δὲ ἄλλος Ἰδαῖος εὗρε χαλκοῦ κρᾶσιν, ὡς δὲ Ἡσίοδος, Σκύθης.

THE IDAEAN DACTYLS

Hesiod says that those who are called the Idaean Dactyls taught the smelting and tempering of iron in Crete.

Celmis, again, and Damnameneus, the first of the Idaean Dactyls, discovered iron in Cyprus; but bronze-smelting was discovered by Delas, another Idaean, though Hesiod calls him Scythes.[1]

[1] Or perhaps "a Scythian."

ΗΣΙΟΔΟΥ ΘΕΟΓΟΝΙΑ

Μουσάων Ἑλικωνιάδων ἀρχώμεθ' ἀείδειν,
αἵθ' Ἑλικῶνος ἔχουσιν ὄρος μέγα τε ζάθεόν τε
καί τε περὶ κρήνην ἰοειδέα πόσσ' ἁπαλοῖσιν
ὀρχεῦνται καὶ βωμὸν ἐρισθενέος Κρονίωνος.
καί τε λοεσσάμεναι τέρενα χρόα Περμησσοῖο
ἢ Ἵππου κρήνης ἢ Ὀλμειοῦ ζαθέοιο
ἀκροτάτῳ Ἑλικῶνι χοροὺς ἐνεποιήσαντο
καλούς, ἱμερόεντας· ἐπερρώσαντο δὲ ποσσίν.
ἔνθεν ἀπορνύμεναι, κεκαλυμμέναι ἠέρι πολλῇ,
ἐννύχιαι στεῖχον περικαλλέα ὄσσαν ἱεῖσαι,
ὑμνεῦσαι Δία τ' αἰγίοχον καὶ πότνιαν Ἥρην
Ἀργείην, χρυσέοισι πεδίλοις ἐμβεβαυῖαν,
κούρην τ' αἰγιόχοιο Διὸς γλαυκῶπιν Ἀθήνην
Φοῖβόν τ' Ἀπόλλωνα καὶ Ἄρτεμιν ἰοχέαιραν
ἠδὲ Ποσειδάωνα γεήοχον, ἐννοσίγαιον,
καὶ Θέμιν αἰδοίην ἑλικοβλέφαρόν τ' Ἀφροδίτην
Ἥβην τε χρυσοστέφανον καλήν τε Διώνην
Λητώ τ' Ἰαπετόν τε ἰδὲ Κρόνον ἀγκυλομήτην
Ἠῶ τ' Ἠέλιόν τε μέγαν λαμπράν τε Σελήνην
Γαῖάν τ' Ὠκεανόν τε μέγαν καὶ Νύκτα μέλαιναν
ἄλλων τ' ἀθανάτων ἱερὸν γένος αἰὲν ἐόντων.
αἵ νύ ποθ' Ἡσίοδον καλὴν ἐδίδαξαν ἀοιδήν,

THE THEOGONY OF HESIOD

From the Heliconian Muses let us begin to sing, who hold the great and holy mount of Helicon, and dance on soft feet about the deep-blue spring and the altar of the almighty son of Cronos, and, when they have washed their tender bodies in Permessus or in the Horse's Spring or Olmeius, make their fair, lovely dances upon highest Helicon and move with vigorous feet. Thence they arise and go abroad by night, veiled in thick mist, and utter their song with lovely voice, praising Zeus the aegis-holder and queenly Hera of Argos who walks on golden sandals and the daughter of Zeus the aegis-holder bright-eyed Athene, and Phoebus Apollo, and Artemis who delights in arrows, and Poseidon the earth-holder who shakes the earth, and reverend Themis and quick-glancing[1] Aphrodite, and Hebe with the crown of gold, and fair Dione, Leto, Iapetus, and Cronos the crafty counsellor, Eos and great Helius and bright Selene, Earth too, and great Oceanus, and dark Night, and the holy race of all the other deathless ones that are for ever. And one day they taught Hesiod glorious song while he was shepherding his lambs under holy

[1] The epithet probably indicates coquettishness.

ἄρνας ποιμαίνονθ' Ἑλικῶνος ὕπο ζαθέοιο.
τόνδε δέ με πρώτιστα θεαὶ πρὸς μῦθον ἔειπον,
Μοῦσαι Ὀλυμπιάδες, κοῦραι Διὸς αἰγιόχοιο·
Ποιμένες ἄγραυλοι, κάκ' ἐλέγχεα, γαστέρες οἶον,
ἴδμεν ψεύδεα πολλὰ λέγειν ἐτύμοισιν ὁμοῖα,
ἴδμεν δ', εὖτ' ἐθέλωμεν, ἀληθέα γηρύσασθαι.
Ὣς ἔφασαν κοῦραι μεγάλου Διὸς ἀρτιέπειαι·
καί μοι σκῆπτρον ἔδον δάφνης ἐριθηλέος ὄζον
δρέψασαι, θηητόν· ἐνέπνευσαν δέ μοι αὐδὴν
θέσπιν, ἵνα κλείοιμι τά τ' ἐσσόμενα πρό τ' ἐόντα.
καί μ' ἐκέλονθ' ὑμνεῖν μακάρων γένος αἰὲν ἐόντων,
σφᾶς δ' αὐτὰς πρῶτόν τε καὶ ὕστατον αἰὲν ἀείδειν.
ἀλλὰ τί ἦ μοι ταῦτα περὶ δρῦν ἢ περὶ πέτρην;

Τύνη, Μουσάων ἀρχώμεθα, ταὶ Διὶ πατρὶ
ὑμνεῦσαι τέρπουσι μέγαν νόον ἐντὸς Ὀλύμπου,
εἰρεῦσαι τά τ' ἐόντα τά τ' ἐσσόμενα πρό τ' ἐόντα,
φωνῇ ὁμηρεῦσαι· τῶν δ' ἀκάματος ῥέει αὐδὴ
ἐκ στομάτων ἡδεῖα· γελᾷ δέ τε δώματα πατρὸς
Ζηνὸς ἐριγδούποιο θεᾶν ὀπὶ λειριοέσσῃ
σκιδναμένῃ· ἠχεῖ δὲ κάρη νιφόεντος Ὀλύμπου
δώματά τ' ἀθανάτων. αἳ δ' ἄμβροτον ὄσσαν ἱεῖσαι
θεῶν γένος αἰδοῖον πρῶτον κλείουσιν ἀοιδῇ
ἐξ ἀρχῆς, οὓς Γαῖα καὶ Οὐρανὸς εὐρὺς ἔτικτεν,
οἵ τ' ἐκ τῶν ἐγένοντο θεοί, δωτῆρες ἐάων.
δεύτερον αὖτε Ζῆνα, θεῶν πατέρ' ἠδὲ καὶ ἀνδρῶν,
ἀρχόμεναί θ' ὑμνεῦσι καὶ ἐκλήγουσαι[1] ἀοιδῆς,

[1] Ludwich: θεαὶ λήγουσαί τ', MSS.

Helicon, and this word first the goddesses said to me—the Muses of Olympus, daughters of Zeus who holds the aegis :

"Shepherds of the wilderness, wretched things of shame, mere bellies, we know how to speak many false things as though they were true; but we know, when we will, to utter true things."

So said the ready-voiced daughters of great Zeus, and they plucked and gave me a rod, a shoot of sturdy olive, a marvellous thing, and breathed into me a divine voice to celebrate things that shall be and things that were aforetime; and they bade me sing of the race of the blessed gods that are eternally, but ever to sing of themselves both first and last. But why all this about oak or stone? [1]

Come thou, let us begin with the Muses who gladden the great spirit of their father Zeus in Olympus with their songs, telling of things that are and that shall be and that were aforetime with consenting voice. Unwearying flows the sweet sound from their lips, and the house of their father Zeus the loud-thunderer is glad at the lily-like voice of the goddesses as it spreads abroad, and the peaks of snowy Olympus resound, and the homes of the immortals. And they uttering their immortal voice, celebrate in song first of all the reverend race of the gods from the beginning, those whom Earth and wide Heaven begot, and the gods sprung of these, givers of good things. Then, next, the goddesses sing of Zeus, the father of gods and men, as they begin and end their strain, how much he is the most excellent among the

[1] A proverbial saying meaning, "why enlarge on irrelevant topics?"

ὅσσον φέρτατός ἐστι θεῶν κράτεΐ τε μέγιστος.
αὖτις δ' ἀνθρώπων τε γένος κρατερῶν τε Γιγάντων
ὑμνεῦσαι τέρπουσι Διὸς νόον ἐντὸς Ὀλύμπου
Μοῦσαι Ὀλυμπιάδες, κοῦραι Διὸς αἰγιόχοιο.
Τὰς ἐν Πιερίῃ Κρονίδῃ τέκε πατρὶ μιγεῖσα
Μνημοσύνη, γουνοῖσιν Ἐλευθῆρος μεδέουσα,
λησμοσύνην τε κακῶν ἄμπαυμά τε μερμηράων.
ἐννέα γάρ οἱ νύκτος ἐμίσγετο μητίετα Ζεὺς
νόσφιν ἀπ' ἀθανάτων ἱερὸν λέχος εἰσαναβαίνων·
ἀλλ' ὅτε δή ῥ' ἐνιαυτὸς ἔην, περὶ δ' ἔτραπον ὧραι
μηνῶν φθινόντων, περὶ δ' ἤματα πόλλ' ἐτελέσθη,
ἣ δ' ἔτεκ' ἐννέα κούρας ὁμόφρονας, ᾗσιν ἀοιδὴ
μέμβλεται ἐν στήθεσσιν, ἀκηδέα θυμὸν ἐχούσαις,
τυτθὸν ἀπ' ἀκροτάτης κορυφῆς νιφόεντος Ὀλύμπου.
ἔνθα σφιν λιπαροί τε χοροὶ καὶ δώματα καλά.
πὰρ δ' αὐτῇς Χάριτές τε καὶ Ἵμερος οἰκί' ἔχουσιν
ἐν θαλίῃς· ἐρατὴν δὲ διὰ στόμα ὄσσαν ἱεῖσαι
μέλπονται πάντων τε νόμους καὶ ἤθεα κεδνὰ
ἀθανάτων κλείουσιν, ἐπήρατον ὄσσαν ἱεῖσαι.
αἳ τότ' ἴσαν πρὸς Ὄλυμπον ἀγαλλόμεναι ὀπὶ καλῇ,
ἀμβροσίῃ μολπῇ· περὶ δ' ἴαχε γαῖα μέλαινα
ὑμνεύσαις, ἐρατὸς δὲ ποδῶν ὕπο δοῦπος ὀρώρει
νισσομένων πατέρ' εἰς ὅν· ὃ δ' οὐρανῷ ἐμβασιλεύει,
αὐτὸς ἔχων βροντὴν ἠδ' αἰθαλόεντα κεραυνόν,
κάρτεϊ νικήσας πατέρα Κρόνον· εὖ δὲ ἕκαστα
ἀθανάτοις διέταξεν ὁμῶς καὶ ἐπέφραδε τιμάς.
Ταῦτ' ἄρα Μοῦσαι ἄειδον, Ὀλύμπια δώματ' ἔχουσαι,
ἐννέα θυγατέρες μεγάλου Διὸς ἐκγεγαυῖαι,
Κλειώ τ' Εὐτέρπη τε Θάλειά τε Μελπομένη τε
Τερψιχόρη τ' Ἐρατώ τε Πολύμνιά τ' Οὐρανίη τε

gods and supreme in power. And again, they chant the race of men and strong giants, and gladden the heart of Zeus within Olympus,—the Olympian Muses, daughters of Zeus the aegis-holder.

Them in Pieria did Mnemosyne (Memory), who reigns over the hills of Eleuther, bear of union with the father, the son of Cronos, a forgetting of ills and a rest from sorrow. For nine nights did wise Zeus lie with her, entering her holy bed remote from the immortals. And when a year was passed and the seasons came round as the months waned, and many days were accomplished, she bare nine daughters, all of one mind, whose hearts are set upon song and their spirit free from care, a little way from the topmost peak of snowy Olympus. There are their bright dancing-places and beautiful homes, and beside them the Graces and Himerus (Desire) live in delight. And they, uttering through their lips a lovely voice, sing the laws of all and the goodly ways of the immortals, uttering their lovely voice. Then went they to Olympus, delighting in their sweet voice, with heavenly song, and the dark earth resounded about them as they chanted, and a lovely sound rose up beneath their feet as they went to their father. And he was reigning in heaven, himself holding the lightning and glowing thunderbolt, when he had overcome by might his father Cronos; and he distributed fairly to the immortals their portions and declared their privileges.

These things, then, the Muses sang who dwell on Olympus, nine daughters begotten by great Zeus, Cleio and Euterpe, Thaleia, Melpomene and Terpsichore, and Erato and Polyhymnia and Urania

Καλλιόπη θ'· ἣ δὲ προφερεστάτη ἐστὶν ἁπασέων.
ἣ γὰρ καὶ βασιλεῦσιν ἅμ' αἰδοίοισιν ὀπηδεῖ.
ὅν τινα τιμήσωσι Διὸς κοῦραι μεγάλοιο
γεινόμενόν τε ἴδωσι[1] διοτρεφέων βασιλήων,
τῷ μὲν ἐπὶ γλώσσῃ γλυκερὴν χείουσιν ἐέρσην,
τοῦ δ' ἔπε' ἐκ στόματος ῥεῖ μείλιχα· οἱ δέ τε λαοὶ
πάντες ἐς αὐτὸν ὁρῶσι διακρίνοντα θέμιστας
ἰθείῃσι δίκῃσιν· ὁ δ' ἀσφαλέως ἀγορεύων
αἶψά κε[2] καὶ μέγα νεῖκος ἐπισταμένως κατέπαυσεν·
τοὔνεκα γὰρ βασιλῆες ἐχέφρονες, οὕνεκα λαοῖς
βλαπτομένοις ἀγορῆφι μετάτροπα ἔργα τελεῦσι
ῥηιδίως, μαλακοῖσι παραιφάμενοι ἐπέεσσιν.
ἐρχόμενον δ' ἀν' ἀγῶνα[3] θεὸν ὣς ἱλάσκονται
αἰδοῖ μειλιχίῃ, μετὰ δὲ πρέπει ἀγρομένοισιν·
τοίη[4] Μουσάων ἱερὴ δόσις ἀνθρώποισιν.
ἐκ γάρ τοι Μουσέων καὶ ἑκηβόλου Ἀπόλλωνος
ἄνδρες ἀοιδοὶ ἔασιν ἐπὶ χθόνα καὶ κιθαρισταί,
ἐκ δὲ Διὸς βασιλῆες· ὁ δ' ὄλβιος, ὅν τινα Μοῦσαι
φίλωνται· γλυκερή οἱ ἀπὸ στόματος ῥέει αὐδή.
εἰ γάρ τις καὶ πένθος ἔχων νεοκηδέι θυμῷ
ἄζηται κραδίην ἀκαχήμενος, αὐτὰρ ἀοιδὸς
Μουσάων θεράπων κλέεα[5] προτέρων ἀνθρώπων
ὑμνήσῃ μάκαράς τε θεούς, οἳ Ὄλυμπον ἔχουσιν,
αἶψ' ὅ γε δυσφροσυνέων ἐπιλήθεται οὐδέ τι κηδέων
μέμνηται· ταχέως δὲ παρέτραπε δῶρα θεάων.

Χαίρετε, τέκνα Διός, δότε δ' ἱμερόεσσαν ἀοιδήν.

[1] Themistius, Stobaeus : τ' ἐσίδωσι or ἐπίδωσι, MSS.
[2] A : τε, MSS.
[3] A and Scholiasts : ἀνὰ ἄστυ, MSS.
[4] A : οἷά τε, MSS.
[5] Nauck : κλεῖα, MSS.

and Calliope,[1] who is the chiefest of them all, for she attends on worshipful princes: whomsoever of heaven-nourished princes the daughters of great Zeus honour, and behold him at his birth, they pour sweet dew upon his tongue, and from his lips flow gracious words. All the people look towards him while he settles causes with true judgements: and he, speaking surely, would soon make wise end even of a great quarrel; for therefore are there princes wise in heart, because when the people are being misguided in their assembly, they set right the matter again with ease, persuading them with gentle words. And when he passes through a gathering, they greet him as a god with gentle reverence, and he is conspicuous amongst the assembled: such is the holy gift of the Muses to men. For it is through the Muses and far-shooting Apollo that there are singers and harpers upon the earth; but princes are of Zeus, and happy is he whom the Muses love: sweet flows speech from his mouth. For though a man have sorrow and grief in his newly-troubled soul and live in dread because his heart is distressed, yet, when a singer, the servant of the Muses, chants the glorious deeds of men of old and the blessed gods who inhabit Olympus, at once he forgets his heaviness and remembers not his sorrows at all; but the gifts of the goddesses soon turn him away from these.

Hail, children of Zeus! Grant lovely song and

[1] "She of the noble voice": Calliope is queen of Epic poetry.

κλείετε δ' ἀθανάτων ἱερὸν γένος αἰὲν ἐόντων,
οἳ Γῆς τ' ἐξεγένοντο καὶ Οὐρανοῦ ἀστερόεντος,
Νυκτός τε δνοφερῆς, οὕς θ' ἁλμυρὸς ἔτρεφε Πόντος.
εἴπατε δ', ὡς τὰ πρῶτα θεοὶ καὶ γαῖα γένοντο
καὶ ποταμοὶ καὶ πόντος ἀπείριτος, οἴδματι θυίων,[1]
ἄστρα τε λαμπετόωντα καὶ οὐρανὸς εὐρὺς ὕπερθεν
[οἵ τ' ἐκ τῶν ἐγένοντο θεοί, δωτῆρες ἐάων [2]]
ὥς τ' ἄφενος δάσσαντο καὶ ὡς τιμὰς διέλοντο
ἠδὲ καὶ ὡς τὰ πρῶτα πολύπτυχον ἔσχον Ὄλυμπον.
ταῦτά μοι ἔσπετε Μοῦσαι, Ὀλύμπια δώματ' ἔχουσαι
ἐξ ἀρχῆς, καὶ εἴπαθ', ὅ τι πρῶτον γένετ' αὐτῶν.
Ἤ τοι μὲν πρώτιστα Χάος γένετ', αὐτὰρ ἔπειτα
Γαῖ' εὐρύστερνος, πάντων ἕδος ἀσφαλὲς αἰεὶ
[ἀθανάτων, οἳ ἔχουσι κάρη νιφόεντος Ὀλύμπου,[3]]
Τάρταρά τ' ἠερόεντα μυχῷ χθονὸς εὐρυοδείης,
ἠδ' Ἔρος, ὃς κάλλιστος ἐν ἀθανάτοισι θεοῖσι,
λυσιμελής, πάντων δὲ θεῶν πάντων τ' ἀνθρώπων
δάμναται ἐν στήθεσσι νόον καὶ ἐπίφρονα βουλήν.
ἐκ Χάεος δ' Ἔρεβός τε μέλαινά τε Νὺξ ἐγένοντο·
Νυκτὸς δ' αὖτ' Αἰθήρ τε καὶ Ἡμέρη ἐξεγένοντο,
οὓς τέκε κυσαμένη Ἐρέβει φιλότητι μιγεῖσα.
Γαῖα δέ τοι πρῶτον μὲν ἐγείνατο ἶσον ἑαυτῇ[4]
Οὐρανὸν ἀστερόενθ', ἵνα μιν περὶ πάντα καλύπτοι,

[1] Rzach (cf. l. 131) : θύων, MSS.
[2] Omitted by A, Theophilus, Hippolytus.
[3] Theophilus, Hippolytus, and all MSS. Plato, Aristotle and others do not know the line, which is clearly spurious.
[4] MSS. : ἑωυτῇ, A, Theophilus.

celebrate the holy race of the deathless gods who are for ever, those that were born of Earth and starry Heaven and gloomy Night and them that briny Sea did rear. Tell how at the first gods and earth came to be, and rivers, and the boundless sea with its raging swell, and the gleaming stars, and the wide heaven above, and the gods who were born of them, givers of good things, and how they divided their wealth, and how they shared their honours amongst them, and also how at the first they took many-folded Olympus. These things declare to me from the beginning, ye Muses who dwell in the house of Olympus, and tell me which of them first came to be.

Verily at the first Chaos came to be, but next wide-bosomed Earth, the ever-sure foundation of all[1] the deathless ones who hold the peaks of snowy Olympus, and dim Tartarus in the depth of the wide-pathed Earth, and Eros (Love), fairest among the deathless gods, who unnerves the limbs and overcomes the mind and wise counsels of all gods and all men within them. From Chaos came forth Erebus and black Night; but of Night were born Aether[2] and Day, whom she conceived and bare from union in love with Erebus. And Earth first bare starry Heaven, equal to herself, to cover her on every

[1] Earth, in the cosmology of Hesiod, is a disk surrounded by the river Oceanus and floating upon a waste of waters. It is called the foundation of all (the qualification "the deathless ones . . ." etc. is an interpolation), because not only trees, men, and animals, but even the hills and seas (ll. 129, 131) are supported by it.

[2] Aether is the bright, untainted upper atmosphere, as distinguished from Aër, the lower atmosphere of the earth.

ὄφρ᾽ εἴη μακάρεσσι θεοῖς ἕδος ἀσφαλὲς αἰεί.
γείνατο δ᾽ Οὔρεα μακρά, θεῶν χαρίεντας ἐναύλους,
Νυμφέων, αἳ ναίουσιν ἀν᾽ οὔρεα βησσήεντα.
ἣ δὲ καὶ ἀτρύγετον πέλαγος τέκεν, οἴδματι θυῖον,[1]
Πόντον, ἄτερ φιλότητος ἐφιμέρου· αὐτὰρ ἔπειτα
Οὐρανῷ εὐνηθεῖσα τέκ᾽ Ὠκεανὸν βαθυδίνην,
Κοῖόν τε Κρῖόν θ᾽ Ὑπερίονά τ᾽ Ἰαπετόν τε
Θείαν τε Ῥείαν τε Θέμιν τε Μνημοσύνην τε
Φοίβην τε χρυσοστέφανον Τηθύν τ᾽ ἐρατεινήν.
τοὺς δὲ μέθ᾽ ὁπλότατος γένετο Κρόνος ἀγκυλομήτης,
δεινότατος παίδων· θαλερὸν δ᾽ ἤχθηρε τοκῆα.
Γείνατο δ᾽ αὖ Κύκλωπας ὑπέρβιον ἦτορ ἔχοντας,
Βρόντην τε Στερόπην τε καὶ Ἄργην ὀβριμόθυμον,
οἳ Ζηνὶ βροντήν τε δόσαν τεῦξάν τε κεραυνόν.
οἳ δή τοι τὰ μὲν ἄλλα θεοῖς ἐναλίγκιοι ἦσαν,[2]
μοῦνος δ᾽ ὀφθαλμὸς μέσσῳ ἐνέκειτο μετώπῳ.
Κύκλωπες δ᾽ ὄνομ᾽ ἦσαν ἐπώνυμον, οὕνεκ᾽ ἄρα σφέων
κυκλοτερὴς ὀφθαλμὸς ἕεις ἐνέκειτο μετώπῳ·
ἰσχὺς δ᾽ ἠδὲ βίη καὶ μηχαναὶ ἦσαν ἐπ᾽ ἔργοις.
Ἄλλοι δ᾽ αὖ Γαίης τε καὶ Οὐρανοῦ ἐξεγένοντο
τρεῖς παῖδες μεγάλοι τε καὶ ὄβριμοι, οὐκ ὀνομαστοί,
Κόττος τε Βριάρεώς τε Γύης θ᾽, ὑπερήφανα τέκνα.
τῶν ἑκατὸν μὲν χεῖρες ἀπ᾽ ὤμων ἀίσσοντο
ἄπλαστοι, κεφαλαὶ δὲ ἑκάστῳ πεντήκοντα
ἐξ ὤμων ἐπέφυκον ἐπὶ στιβαροῖσι μέλεσσιν·

[1] A: θῦον, MSS.
[2] In place of this line Crates read—
οἳ δ᾽ ἐξ ἀθανάτων θνητοὶ τράφεν αὐδήεντες.

side, and to be an ever-sure abiding-place for the blessed gods. And she brought forth long Hills, graceful haunts of the goddess-Nymphs who dwell amongst the glens of the hills. She bare also the fruitless deep with his raging swell, Pontus, without sweet union of love. But afterwards she lay with Heaven and bare deep-swirling Oceanus, Coeus and Crius and Hyperion and Iapetus, Theia and Rhea, Themis and Mnemosyne and gold-crowned Phoebe and lovely Tethys. After them was born Cronos the wily, youngest and most terrible of her children, and he hated his lusty sire.

And again, she bare the Cyclopes, overbearing in spirit, Brontes, and Steropes and stubborn-hearted Arges,[1] who gave Zeus the thunder and made the thunderbolt: in all else they were like the gods, but one eye only was set in the midst of their foreheads. And they were surnamed Cyclopes (Orb-eyed) because one orbed eye was set in their foreheads. Strength and might and craft were in their works.

And again, three other sons were born of Earth and Heaven, great and doughty beyond telling, Cottus and Briareos and Gyes, presumptuous children. From their shoulders sprang an hundred arms, not to be approached, and each had fifty heads upon his shoulders on their strong limbs, and

[1] Brontes is the Thunderer; Steropes, the Lightener; and Arges, the Vivid One.

ἰσχὺς δ' ἄπλητος κρατερὴ μεγάλῳ ἐπὶ εἴδει.
ὅσσοι γὰρ Γαίης τε καὶ Οὐρανοῦ ἐξεγένοντο,
δεινότατοι παίδων, σφετέρῳ δ' ἤχθοντο τοκῆι
ἐξ ἀρχῆς· καὶ τῶν μὲν ὅπως τις πρῶτα γένοιτο,
πάντας ἀποκρύπτασκε, καὶ ἐς φάος οὐκ ἀνίεσκε,
Γαίης ἐν κευθμῶνι, κακῷ δ' ἐπετέρπετο ἔργῳ
Οὐρανός. ἡ δ' ἐντὸς στοναχίζετο Γαῖα πελώρη
στεινομένη· δολίην δὲ κακήν τ' ἐφράσσατο τέχνην.
αἶψα δὲ ποιήσασα γένος πολιοῦ ἀδάμαντος
τεῦξε μέγα δρέπανον καὶ ἐπέφραδε παισὶ φίλοισιν·
εἶπε δὲ θαρσύνουσα, φίλον τετιημένη ἦτορ·
Παῖδες ἐμοὶ καὶ πατρὸς ἀτασθάλου, αἴ κ' ἐθέλητε
πείθεσθαι, πατρός κε κακὴν τισαίμεθα λώβην
ὑμετέρου· πρότερος γὰρ ἀεικέα μήσατο ἔργα.
Ὣς φάτο· τοὺς δ' ἄρα πάντας ἕλεν δέος, οὐδέ τις αὐτῶν
φθέγξατο. θαρσήσας δὲ μέγας Κρόνος ἀγκυλομήτης
ἂψ αὖτις μύθοισι προσηύδα μητέρα κεδνήν·
Μῆτερ, ἐγώ κεν τοῦτό γ' ὑποσχόμενος τελέσαιμι
ἔργον, ἐπεὶ πατρός γε δυσωνύμου οὐκ ἀλεγίζω
ἡμετέρου· πρότερος γὰρ ἀεικέα μήσατο ἔργα.
Ὣς φάτο· γήθησεν δὲ μέγα φρεσὶ Γαῖα πελώρη.
εἷσε δέ μιν κρύψασα λόχῳ· ἐνέθηκε δὲ χερσὶν
ἅρπην καρχαρόδοντα· δόλον δ' ὑπεθήκατο πάντα.
Ἦλθε δὲ νύκτ' ἐπάγων μέγας Οὐρανός, ἀμφὶ δὲ Γαίῃ
ἱμείρων φιλότητος ἐπέσχετο καί ῥ' ἐτανύσθη

irresistible was the stubborn strength that was in their great forms. For of all the children that were born of Earth and Heaven, these were the most terrible, and they were hated by their own father from the first. And he used to hide them all away in a secret place of Earth so soon as each was born, and would not suffer them to come up into the light: and Heaven rejoiced in his evil doing. But vast Earth groaned within, being straitened, and she thought a crafty and an evil wile. Forthwith she made the element of grey flint and shaped a great sickle, and told her plan to her dear sons. And she spoke, cheering them, while she was vexed in her dear heart:

"My children, gotten of a sinful father, if you will obey me, we should punish the vile outrage of your father; for he first thought of doing shameful things."

So she said; but fear seized them all, and none of them uttered a word. But great Cronos the wily took courage and answered his dear mother:

"Mother, I will undertake to do this deed, for I reverence not our father of evil name, for he first thought of doing shameful things."

So he said: and vast Earth rejoiced greatly in spirit, and set and hid him in an ambush, and put in his hands a jagged sickle, and revealed to him the whole plot.

And Heaven came, bringing on night and longing for love, and he lay about Earth spreading himself full

πάντῃ· ὁ δ' ἐκ λοχεοῖο πάις ὠρέξατο χειρὶ
σκαιῇ, δεξιτερῇ δὲ πελώριον ἔλλαβεν ἅρπην
μακρὴν καρχαρόδοντα, φίλου δ' ἀπὸ μήδεα πατρὸς
ἐσσυμένως ἤμησε, πάλιν δ' ἔρριψε φέρεσθαι
ἐξοπίσω· τὰ μὲν οὔ τι ἐτώσια ἔκφυγε χειρός·
ὅσσαι γὰρ ῥαθάμιγγες ἀπέσσυθεν αἱματόεσσαι,
πάσας δέξατο Γαῖα· περιπλομένων δ' ἐνιαυτῶν
γείνατ' Ἐρινῦς τε κρατερὰς μεγάλους τε Γίγαντας,
τεύχεσι λαμπομένους, δολίχ' ἔγχεα χερσὶν ἔχοντας,
Νύμφας θ' ἃς Μελίας καλέουσ' ἐπ' ἀπείρονα γαῖαν.
μήδεα δ' ὡς τὸ πρῶτον ἀποτμήξας ἀδάμαντι
κάββαλ' ἀπ' ἠπείροιο πολυκλύστῳ ἐνὶ πόντῳ,
ὣς φέρετ' ἂμ πέλαγος πουλὺν χρόνον, ἀμφὶ δὲ λευκὸς
ἀφρὸς ἀπ' ἀθανάτου χροὸς ὤρνυτο· τῷ δ' ἔνι κούρη
ἐθρέφθη· πρῶτον δὲ Κυθήροισιν ζαθέοισιν
ἔπλητ', ἔνθεν ἔπειτα περίρρυτον ἵκετο Κύπρον.
ἐκ δ' ἔβη αἰδοίη καλὴ θεός, ἀμφὶ δὲ ποίη
ποσσὶν ὕπο ῥαδινοῖσιν ἀέξετο· τὴν δ' Ἀφροδίτην
[ἀφρογενέα τε θεὰν καὶ ἐυστέφανον Κυθέρειαν[1]]
κικλήσκουσι θεοί τε καὶ ἀνέρες, οὕνεκ' ἐν ἀφρῷ
θρέφθη· ἀτὰρ Κυθέρειαν, ὅτι προσέκυρσε Κυθήροις·
Κυπρογενέα δ', ὅτι γέντο πολυκλύστῳ ἐνὶ Κύπρῳ·
ἠδὲ φιλομμηδέα, ὅτι μηδέων ἐξεφαάνθη.

[1] The line possibly belongs to another recension: it was rejected by Heyne as interrupting the sense.

upon her.[1] Then the son from his ambush stretched forth his left hand and in his right took the great long sickle with jagged teeth, and swiftly lopped off his own father's members and cast them away to fall behind him. And not vainly did they fall from his hand ; for all the bloody drops that gushed forth Earth received, and as the seasons moved round she bare the strong Erinyes and the great Giants with gleaming armour, holding long spears in their hands, and the Nymphs whom they call Meliae[2] all over the boundless earth. And so soon as he had cut off the members with flint and cast them from the land into the surging sea, they were swept away over the main a long time : and a white foam spread around them from the immortal flesh, and in it there grew a maiden. First she drew near holy Cythera, and from there, afterwards, she came to sea-girt Cyprus, and came forth an awful and lovely goddess, and grass grew up about her beneath her shapely feet. Her gods and men call Aphrodite, and the foam-born goddess and rich-crowned Cytherea, because she grew amid the foam, and Cytherea because she reached Cythera, and Cyprogenes because she was born in billowy Cyprus, and Philommedes[3] because

[1] The myth accounts for the separation of Heaven and Earth. In Egyptian cosmology Nut (the Sky) is thrust and held apart from her brother Geb (the Earth) by their father Shu, who corresponds to the Greek Atlas.

[2] Nymphs of the ash-trees (μέλιαι), as Dryads are nymphs of the oak-trees. Cp. note on *Works and Days*, l. 145.

[3] "Member-loving": the title is perhaps only a perversion of the regular φιλομειδής (laughter-loving).

τῇ δ' Ἔρος ὡμάρτησε καὶ Ἵμερος ἕσπετο καλὸς
γεινομένῃ τὰ πρῶτα θεῶν τ' ἐς φῦλον ἰούσῃ.
ταύτην δ' ἐξ ἀρχῆς τιμὴν ἔχει ἠδὲ λέλογχε
μοῖραν ἐν ἀνθρώποισι καὶ ἀθανάτοισι θεοῖσι,
παρθενίους τ' ὀάρους μειδήματά τ' ἐξαπάτας τε
τέρψιν τε γλυκερὴν φιλότητά τε μειλιχίην τε.
Τοὺς δὲ πατὴρ Τιτῆνας ἐπίκλησιν καλέεσκε
παῖδας νεικείων μέγας Οὐρανός, οὓς τέκεν αὐτός·
φάσκε δὲ τιταίνοντας ἀτασθαλίῃ μέγα ῥέξαι
ἔργον, τοῖο δ' ἔπειτα τίσιν μετόπισθεν ἔσεσθαι.

Νὺξ δ' ἔτεκεν στυγερόν τε Μόρον καὶ Κῆρα μέλαιναν
καὶ Θάνατον, τέκε δ' Ὕπνον, ἔτικτε δὲ φῦλον Ὀνείρων·
δεύτερον αὖ Μῶμον καὶ Ὀιζὺν ἀλγινόεσσαν 214
οὔ τινι κοιμηθεῖσα θεὰ τέκε Νὺξ ἐρεβεννή,[1] 213
Ἑσπερίδας θ', ᾗς[2] μῆλα πέρην κλυτοῦ Ὠκεανοῖο
χρύσεα καλὰ μέλουσι φέροντά τε δένδρεα καρπόν.
καὶ Μοίρας καὶ Κῆρας ἐγείνατο νηλεοποίνους,
Κλωθώ τε Λάχεσίν τε καὶ Ἄτροπον, αἵτε βροτοῖσι
γεινομένοισι διδοῦσιν ἔχειν ἀγαθόν τε κακόν τε,
αἵτ' ἀνδρῶν τε θεῶν τε παραιβασίας ἐφέπουσιν·
οὐδέ ποτε λήγουσι θεαὶ δεινοῖο χόλοιο,
πρίν γ' ἀπὸ τῷ δώωσι κακὴν ὄπιν, ὅς τις ἁμάρτῃ.
τίκτε δὲ καὶ Νέμεσιν, πῆμα θνητοῖσι βροτοῖσι,
Νὺξ ὀλοή· μετὰ τὴν δ' Ἀπάτην τέκε καὶ Φιλότητα
Γῆράς τ' οὐλόμενον, καὶ Ἔριν τέκε καρτερόθυμον.

1 Schoemann's order.
2 Rzach: αἷς, MSS.

she sprang from the members. And with her went Eros, and comely Desire followed her at her birth at the first and as she went into the assembly of the gods. This honour she has from the beginning, and this is the portion allotted to her amongst men and undying gods,—the whisperings of maidens and smiles and deceits with sweet delight and love and graciousness.

But these sons whom he begot himself great Heaven used to call Titans (Strainers) in reproach, for he said that they strained and did presumptuously a fearful deed, and that vengeance for it would come afterwards.

And Night bare hateful Doom and black Fate and Death, and she bare Sleep and the tribe of Dreams. And again the goddess murky Night, though she lay with none, bare Blame and painful Woe, and the Hesperides who guard the rich, golden apples and the trees bearing fruit beyond glorious Ocean. Also she bare the Destinies and ruthless avenging Fates, Clotho and Lachesis and Atropos,[1] who give men at their birth both evil and good to have, and they pursue the transgressions of men and of gods: and these goddesses never cease from their dread anger until they punish the sinner with a sore penalty. Also deadly Night bare Nemesis (Indignation) to afflict mortal men, and after her, Deceit and Friendship and hateful Age and hard-hearted Strife.

[1] Clotho (the Spinner) is she who spins the thread of man's life; Lachesis (the Disposer of Lots) assigns to each man his destiny; Atropos (She who cannot be turned) is the "Fury with the abhorrèd shears."

Αὐτὰρ Ἔρις στυγερὴ τέκε μὲν Πόνον ἀλγινόεντα
Λήθην τε Λιμόν τε καὶ Ἄλγεα δακρυόεντα
Ὑσμίνας τε Μάχας τε Φόνους τ' Ἀνδροκτασίας τε
Νείκεά τε ψευδέας τε Λόγους Ἀμφιλλογίας τε
Δυσνομίην τ' Ἄτην τε, συνήθεας ἀλλήλῃσιν,
Ὅρκον θ', ὃς δὴ πλεῖστον ἐπιχθονίους ἀνθρώπους
πημαίνει, ὅτε κέν τις ἑκὼν ἐπίορκον ὀμόσσῃ.
Νηρέα δ' ἀψευδέα καὶ ἀληθέα γείνατο Πόντος,
πρεσβύτατον παίδων· αὐτὰρ καλέουσι γέροντα,
οὕνεκα νημερτής τε καὶ ἤπιος, οὐδὲ θεμιστέων
λήθεται, ἀλλὰ δίκαια καὶ ἤπια δήνεα οἶδεν·
αὖτις δ' αὖ Θαύμαντα μέγαν καὶ ἀγήνορα Φόρκυν
Γαίῃ μισγόμενος καὶ Κητὼ καλλιπάρῃον
Εὐρυβίην τ' ἀδάμαντος ἐνὶ φρεσὶ θυμὸν ἔχουσαν.
Νηρῆος δ' ἐγένοντο μεγήρατα τέκνα θεάων
πόντῳ ἐν ἀτρυγέτῳ καὶ Δωρίδος ἠυκόμοιο,
κούρης Ὠκεανοῖο, τελήεντος ποταμοῖο,
Πλωτώ[1] τ' Εὐκράντη τε Σαώ τ' Ἀμφιτρίτη τε
Εὐδώρη τε Θέτις τε Γαλήνη τε Γλαύκη τε
Κυμοθόη Σπειώ τε Θόη θ' Ἁλίη τ' ἐρόεσσα
Πασιθέη τ' Ἐρατώ τε καὶ Εὐνίκη ῥοδόπηχυς
καὶ Μελίτη χαρίεσσα καὶ Εὐλιμένη καὶ Ἀγαυὴ
Δωτώ τε Πρωτώ τε Φέρουσά τε Δυναμένη τε
Νησαίη τε καὶ Ἀκταίη καὶ Πρωτομέδεια
Δωρὶς καὶ Πανόπεια[2] καὶ εὐειδὴς Γαλάτεια
Ἱπποθόη τ' ἐρόεσσα καὶ Ἱππονόη ῥοδόπηχυς

[1] Rzach: Πρωτώ, MSS.
[2] Hermann: Πανόπη, MSS.

But abhorred Strife bare painful Toil and Forgetfulness and Famine and tearful Sorrows, Fightings also, Battles, Murders, Manslaughters, Quarrels, Lying Words, Disputes, Lawlessness and Ruin, all of one nature, and Oath who most troubles men upon earth when anyone wilfully swears a false oath.

And Sea begat Nereus, the eldest of his children, who is true and lies not: and men call him the Old Man because he is trusty and gentle and does not forget the laws of righteousness, but thinks just and kindly thoughts. And yet again he got great Thaumas and proud Phorcys, being mated with Earth, and fair-cheeked Ceto and Eurybia who has a heart of flint within her.

And of Nereus and rich-haired Doris, daughter of Ocean the perfect river, were born children,[1] passing lovely amongst goddesses, Ploto, Eucrante, Sao, and Amphitrite, and Eudora, and Thetis, Galene and Glauce, Cymothoë, Speo, Thoë and lovely Halie, and Pasithea, and Erato, and rosy-armed Eunice, and gracious Melite, and Eulimene, and Agaue, Doto, Proto, Pherusa, and Dynamene, and Nisaea, and Actaea, and Protomedea, Doris, Panopea, and comely Galatea, and lovely Hippothoë, and rosy-armed

[1] Many of the names which follow express various qualities or aspects of the sea: thus Galene is "Calm," Cymothoë is the "Wave-swift," Pherusa and Dynamene are "She who speeds (ships)" and "She who has power."

Κυμοδόκη θ', ἣ κυματ' ἐν ἠεροειδέι πόντῳ
πνοιάς τε ζαέων[1] ἀνέμων σὺν Κυματολήγῃ
ῥεῖα πρηΰνει καὶ ἐυσφύρῳ Ἀμφιτρίτῃ,
Κυμώ τ' Ἠιόνη τε ἐυστέφανός θ' Ἁλιμήδη
Γλαυκονόμη τε φιλομμειδὴς καὶ Ποντοπόρεια
Ληαγόρη τε καὶ Εὐαγόρη καὶ Λαομέδεια
Πουλυνόη[2] τε καὶ Αὐτονόη καὶ Λυσιάνασσα
Εὐάρνη τε φυήν τ' ἐρατὴ καὶ εἶδος ἄμωμος
καὶ Ψαμάθη χαρίεσσα δέμας δίη τε Μενίππη
Νησώ τ' Εὐπόμπη τε Θεμιστώ τε Προνόη τε
Νημερτής θ', ἣ πατρὸς ἔχει νόον ἀθανάτοιο.
αὗται μὲν Νηρῆος ἀμύμονος ἐξεγένοντο
κοῦραι πεντήκοντα, ἀμύμονα ἔργα ἰδυῖαι.
Θαύμας δ' Ὠκεανοῖο βαθυρρείταο θύγατρα
ἠγάγετ' Ἠλέκτρην· ἣ δ' ὠκεῖαν τέκεν Ἶριν
ἠυκόμους θ' Ἁρπυίας Ἀελλώ τ' Ὠκυπέτην τε,
αἵ ῥ' ἀνέμων πνοιῇσι καὶ οἰωνοῖς ἅμ' ἕπονται
ὠκείῃς πτερύγεσσι· μεταχρόνιαι γὰρ ἴαλλον.
Φόρκυϊ δ' αὖ Κητὼ Γραίας τέκε καλλιπαρῄους
ἐκ γενετῆς πολιάς, τὰς δὴ Γραίας καλέουσιν
ἀθάνατοί τε θεοὶ χαμαὶ ἐρχόμενοί τ' ἄνθρωποι,
Πεμφρηδώ τ' ἐύπεπλον Ἐνυώ τε κροκόπεπλον,
Γοργούς θ', αἳ ναίουσι πέρην κλυτοῦ Ὠκεανοῖο
ἐσχατιῇ πρὸς Νυκτός, ἵν' Ἑσπερίδες λιγύφωνοι,
Σθεννώ τ' Εὐρυάλη τε Μέδουσά τε λυγρὰ παθοῦσα.
ἣ μὲν ἔην θνητή, αἳ δ' ἀθάνατοι καὶ ἀγήρῳ,
αἱ δύο· τῇ δὲ μιῇ παρελέξατο Κυανοχαίτης
ἐν μαλακῷ λειμῶνι καὶ ἄνθεσιν εἰαρινοῖσιν.
τῆς δ' ὅτε δὴ Περσεὺς κεφαλὴν ἀπεδειροτόμησεν,

[1] Bergk : ζαθέων, MSS.
[2] Peppmüller : Πουλυνόμη, MSS.

Hipponoë, and Cymodoce who with Cymatolege[1] and Amphitrite easily calms the waves upon the misty sea and the blasts of raging winds, and Cymo, and Eïone, and rich-crowned Alimede, and Glauconome, fond of laughter, and Pontoporea, Leagore, Euagore, and Laomedea, and Polynoë, and Autonoë, and Lysianassa, and Euarne, lovely of shape and without blemish of form, and Psamathe of charming figure and divine Menippe, Neso, Eupompe, Themisto, Pronoë, and Nemertes[2] who has the nature of her deathless father. These fifty daughters sprang from blameless Nereus, skilled in excellent crafts.

And Thaumas wedded Electra the daughter of deep-flowing Ocean, and she bare him swift Iris and the long-haired Harpies, Aëllo (Storm-swift) and Ocypetes (Swift-flier) who on their swift wings keep pace with the blasts of the winds and the birds; for quick as time they dart along.

And again, Ceto bare to Phorcys the fair-cheeked Graiae, sisters grey from their birth: and both deathless gods and men who walk on earth call them Graiae, Pemphredo well-clad, and saffron-robed Enyo, and the Gorgons who dwell beyond glorious Ocean in the frontier land towards Night where are the clear-voiced Hesperides, Sthenno, and Euryale, and Medusa who suffered a woeful fate: she was mortal, but the two were undying and grew not old. With her lay the Dark-haired One[3] in a soft meadow amid spring flowers. And when Perseus cut off her

[1] The "Wave-receiver" and the "Wave-stiller."
[2] "The Unerring" or "Truthful"; cp. l. 235.
[3] *i.e.* Poseidon.

ἔκθορε Χρυσάωρ τε μέγας καὶ Πήγασος ἵππος.
τῷ μὲν ἐπώνυμον ἦεν, ὅτ᾽ Ὠκεανοῦ περὶ πηγὰς
γένθ᾽, ὁ δ᾽ ἄορ χρύσειον ἔχων μετὰ χερσὶ φίλῃσιν.
χὠ μὲν ἀποπτάμενος προλιπὼν χθόνα, μητέρα μήλων,
ἵκετ᾽ ἐς ἀθανάτους· Ζηνὸς δ᾽ ἐν δώμασι ναίει
βροντήν τε στεροπήν τε φέρων Διὶ μητιόεντι.
Χρυσάωρ δ᾽ ἔτεκεν τρικέφαλον Γηρυονῆα
μιχθεὶς Καλλιρόῃ κούρῃ κλυτοῦ Ὠκεανοῖο.
τὸν μὲν ἄρ᾽ ἐξενάριξε βίη Ἡρακληείη
βουσὶ παρ᾽ εἰλιπόδεσσι περιρρύτῳ εἰν Ἐρυθείῃ
ἤματι τῷ ὅτε περ βοῦς ἤλασεν εὐρυμετώπους
Τίρυνθ᾽ εἰς ἱερὴν διαβὰς πόρον Ὠκεανοῖο
Ὄρθον τε κτείνας καὶ βουκόλον Εὐρυτίωνα
σταθμῷ ἐν ἠερόεντι πέρην κλυτοῦ Ὠκεανοῖο.
Ἣ δ᾽ ἔτεκ᾽ ἄλλο πέλωρον ἀμήχανον, οὐδὲν ἐοικὸς
θνητοῖς ἀνθρώποις οὐδ᾽ ἀθανάτοισι θεοῖσιν,
σπῆι ἔνι γλαφυρῷ θείην κρατερόφρον᾽ Ἔχιδναν,
ἥμισυ μὲν νύμφην ἑλικώπιδα καλλιπάρῃον,
ἥμισυ δ᾽ αὖτε πέλωρον ὄφιν δεινόν τε μέγαν τε
αἰόλον ὠμηστὴν ζαθέης ὑπὸ κεύθεσι γαίης.
ἔνθα δέ οἱ σπέος ἐστὶ κάτω κοίλῃ ὑπὸ πέτρῃ
τηλοῦ ἀπ᾽ ἀθανάτων τε θεῶν θνητῶν τ᾽ ἀνθρώπων·
ἔνθ᾽ ἄρα οἱ δάσσαντο θεοὶ κλυτὰ δώματα ναίειν.
ἣ δ᾽ ἔρυτ᾽ εἰν Ἀρίμοισιν ὑπὸ χθόνι λυγρὴ Ἔχιδνα,
ἀθάνατος νύμφη καὶ ἀγήραος ἤματα πάντα.
Τῇ δὲ Τυφάονά φασι μιγήμεναι ἐν φιλότητι
δεινόν θ᾽ ὑβριστήν τ᾽ ἄνομόν θ᾽ ἑλικώπιδι κούρῃ·
ἣ δ᾽ ὑποκυσαμένη τέκετο κρατερόφρονα τέκνα.
Ὄρθον μὲν πρῶτον κύνα γείνατο Γηρυονῆι·
δεύτερον αὖτις ἔτικτεν ἀμήχανον, οὔ τι φατειὸν
Κέρβερον ὠμηστήν, Ἀίδεω κύνα χαλκεόφωνον,

head, there sprang forth great Chrysaor and the horse Pegasus who is so called because he was born near the springs (*pegae*) of Ocean; and that other, because he held a golden blade (*aor*) in his hands. Now Pegasus flew away and left the earth, the mother of flocks, and came to the deathless gods: and he dwells in the house of Zeus and brings to wise Zeus the thunder and lightning. But Chrysaor was joined in love to Callirrhoë, the daughter of glorious Ocean, and begot three-headed Geryones. Him mighty Heracles slew in sea-girt Erythea by his shambling oxen on that day when he drove the wide-browed oxen to holy Tiryns, and had crossed the ford of Ocean and killed Orthus and Eurytion the herdsman in the dim stead out beyond glorious Ocean.

And in a hollow cave she bare another monster, irresistible, in no wise like either to mortal men or to the undying gods, even the goddess fierce Echidna who is half a nymph with glancing eyes and fair cheeks, and half again a huge snake, great and awful, with speckled skin, eating raw flesh beneath the secret parts of the holy earth. And there she has a cave deep down under a hollow rock far from the deathless gods and mortal men. There, then, did the gods appoint her a glorious house to dwell in: and she keeps guard in Arima beneath the earth, grim Echidna, a nymph who dies not nor grows old all her days.

Men say that Typhaon the terrible, outrageous and lawless, was joined in love to her, the maid with glancing eyes. So she conceived and brought forth fierce offspring; first she bare Orthus the hound of Geryones, and then again she bare a second, a monster not to be overcome and that may not be described, Cerberus who eats raw flesh, the brazen-

πεντηκοντακέφαλον, ἀναιδέα τε κρατερόν τε·
τὸ τρίτον Ὕδρην αὖτις ἐγείνατο λυγρὰ ἰδυῖαν
Λερναίην, ἣν θρέψε θεὰ λευκώλενος Ἥρη
ἄπλητον κοτέουσα βίῃ Ἡρακληείῃ.
καὶ τὴν μὲν Διὸς υἱὸς ἐνήρατο νηλέι χαλκῷ
Ἀμφιτρυωνιάδης σὺν ἀρηιφίλῳ Ἰολάῳ
Ἡρακλέης βουλῇσιν Ἀθηναίης ἀγελείης.
ἣ δὲ Χίμαιραν ἔτικτε πνέουσαν ἀμαιμάκετον πῦρ,
δεινήν τε μεγάλην τε ποδώκεά τε κρατερήν τε·
τῆς δ' ἦν τρεῖς κεφαλαί· μία μὲν χαροποῖο λέοντος,
ἡ δὲ χιμαίρης, ἡ δ' ὄφιος, κρατεροῖο δράκοντος,
[πρόσθε λέων, ὄπιθεν δὲ δράκων, μέσση δὲ χίμαιρα,
δεινὸν ἀποπνείουσα πυρὸς μένος αἰθομένοιο.[1]]
τὴν μὲν Πήγασος εἷλε καὶ ἐσθλὸς Βελλεροφόντης.
ἣ δ' ἄρα Φῖκ' ὀλοὴν τέκε Καδμείοισιν ὄλεθρον
Ὄρθῳ ὑποδμηθεῖσα Νεμειαῖόν τε λέοντα,
τόν ῥ' Ἥρη θρέψασα Διὸς κυδρὴ παράκοιτις
γουνοῖσιν κατένασσε Νεμείης, πῆμ' ἀνθρώποις.
ἔνθ' ἄρ' ὃ οἰκείων ἐλεφαίρετο φῦλ' ἀνθρώπων,
κοιρανέων Τρητοῖο Νεμείης ἠδ' Ἀπέσαντος·
ἀλλά ἑ ἶς ἐδάμασσε βίης Ἡρακληείης.
Κητὼ δ' ὁπλότατον Φόρκυι φιλότητι μιγεῖσα
γείνατο δεινὸν ὄφιν, ὃς ἐρεμνῆς κεύθεσι γαίης
πείρασιν ἐν μεγάλοις παγχρύσεα μῆλα φυλάσσει.
τοῦτο μὲν ἐκ Κητοῦς καὶ Φόρκυνος γένος ἐστίν.
Τηθὺς δ' Ὠκεανῷ Ποταμοὺς τέκε δινήεντας,
Νεῖλόν τ' Ἀλφειόν τε καὶ Ἠριδανὸν βαθυδίνην
Στρυμόνα Μαίανδρόν τε καὶ Ἴστρον καλλιρέεθρον

[1] Rejected by Wolf as superfluous here and borrowed from Homer, *Iliad* vi. 181–2.

voiced hound of Hades, fifty-headed, relentless and strong. And again she bore a third, the evil-minded Hydra of Lerna, whom the goddess, white-armed Hera nourished, being angry beyond measure with the mighty Heracles. And her Heracles, the son of Zeus, of the house of Amphitryon, together with warlike Iolaus, destroyed with the unpitying sword through the plans of Athene the spoil-driver. She was the mother of Chimaera who breathed raging fire, a creature fearful, great, swift-footed and strong, who had three heads, one of a grim-eyed lion, another of a goat, and another of a snake, a fierce dragon; in her forepart she was a lion; in her hinderpart, a dragon; and in her middle, a goat, breathing forth a fearful blast of blazing fire. Her did Pegasus and noble Bellerophon slay; but Echidna was subject in love to Orthus and brought forth the deadly Sphinx which destroyed the Cadmeans, and the Nemean lion, which Hera, the good wife of Zeus, brought up and made to haunt the hills of Nemea, a plague to men. There he preyed upon the tribes of her own people and had power over Tretus of Nemea and Apesas: yet the strength of stout Heracles overcame him.

And Ceto was joined in love to Phorcys and bare her youngest, the awful snake who guards the apples all of gold in the secret places of the dark earth at its great bounds. This is the offspring of Ceto and Phorcys.

And Tethys bare to Ocean eddying rivers, Nilus, and Alpheus, and deep-swirling Eridanus, Strymon, and Meander, and the fair stream of Ister, and

Φᾶσίν τε Ῥῆσόν τ' Ἀχελώϊόν τ' ἀργυροδίνην
Νέσσον τε Ῥοδίον θ' Ἁλιάκμονά θ' Ἑπτάπορόν τε
Γρήνικόν τε καὶ Αἴσηπον θεῖόν τε Σιμοῦντα
Πηνειόν τε καὶ Ἕρμον ἐυρρείτην τε Κάικον
Σαγγάριόν τε μέγαν Λάδωνά τε Παρθένιόν τε
Εὔηνόν τε καὶ Ἄρδησκον θεῖόν τε Σκάμανδρον.
Τίκτε δὲ θυγατέρων ἱερὸν γένος, αἳ κατὰ γαῖαν
ἄνδρας κουρίζουσι σὺν Ἀπόλλωνι ἄνακτι
καὶ Ποταμοῖς, ταύτην δὲ Διὸς πάρα μοῖραν ἔχουσι,
Πειθώ τ' Ἀδμήτη τε Ἰάνθη τ' Ἠλέκτρη τε
Δωρίς τε Πρυμνώ τε καὶ Οὐρανίη θεοειδὴς
Ἱππώ τε Κλυμένη τε Ῥόδειά τε Καλλιρόη τε
Ζευξώ τε Κλυτίη τε Ἰδυῖά τε Πασιθόη τε
Πληξαύρη τε Γαλαξαύρη τ' ἐρατή τε Διώνη
Μηλόβοσίς τε Θόη τε καὶ εὐειδὴς Πολυδώρη
Κερκηίς τε φυὴν ἐρατὴ Πλουτώ τε βοῶπις
Περσηίς τ' Ἰάνειρά τ' Ἀκάστη τε Ξάνθη τε
Πετραίη τ' ἐρόεσσα Μενεσθώ τ' Εὐρώπη τε
Μῆτίς τ' Εὐρυνόμη τε Τελεστώ τε κροκόπεπλος
Χρυσηίς τ' Ἀσίη τε καὶ ἱμερόεσσα Καλυψὼ
Εὐδώρη τε Τύχη τε καὶ Ἀμφιρὼ Ὠκυρόη τε
καὶ Στύξ, ἣ δή σφεων προφερεστάτη ἐστὶν ἁπασέων.
αὗται δ' Ὠκεανοῦ καὶ Τηθύος ἐξεγένοντο
πρεσβύταται κοῦραι· πολλαί γε μέν εἰσι καὶ ἄλλαι.
τρὶς γὰρ χίλιαί εἰσι τανύσφυροι Ὠκεανῖναι,
αἵ ῥα πολυσπερέες γαῖαν καὶ βένθεα λίμνης

Phasis, and Rhesus, and the silver eddies of Achelous, Nessus, and Rhodius, Haliacmon, and Heptaporus, Granicus, and Aesepus, and holy Simoïs, and Peneüs, and Hermus, and Caicus' fair stream, and great Sangarius, Ladon, Parthenius, Euenus, Ardescus, and divine Scamander.

Also she brought forth a holy company of daughters[1] who with the lord Apollo and the Rivers have youths in their keeping—to this charge Zeus appointed them—Peitho, and Admete, and Ianthe, and Electra, and Doris, and Prymno, and Urania divine in form, Hippo, Clymene, Rhodea, and Callirrhoë, Zeuxo and Clytie, and Idyia, and Pasithoë, Plexaura, and Galaxaura, and lovely Dione, Melobosis and Thoë and handsome Polydora, Cerceïs lovely of form, and soft eyed Pluto, Perseïs, Ianeira, Acaste, Xanthe, Petraea the fair, Menestho, and Europa, Metis, and Eurynome, and Telesto saffron-clad, Chryseis and Asia and charming Calypso, Eudora, and Tyche, Amphirho, and Ocyrrhoë, and Styx who is the chiefest of them all. These are the eldest daughters that sprang from Ocean and Tethys; but there are many besides. For there are three thousand neat-ankled daughters of Ocean who are dispersed far and wide, and in every place alike serve the earth and the deep waters, children who

[1] Goettling notes that some of these nymphs derive their names from lands over which they preside, as Europa, Asia, Doris, Ianeira ("Lady of the Ionians"), but that most are called after some quality which their streams possessed: thus Xanthe is the "Brown" or "Turbid," Amphirho is the "Surrounding" river, Ianthe is "She who delights," and Ocyrrhoë is the "Swift-flowing."

πάντη ὁμῶς ἐφέπουσι, θεάων ἀγλαὰ τέκνα.
τόσσοι δ' αὖθ' ἕτεροι ποταμοὶ καναχηδὰ ῥέοντες,
υἱέες Ὠκεανοῦ, τοὺς γείνατο πότνια Τηθύς·
τῶν ὄνομ' ἀργαλέον πάντων βροτὸν ἀνέρ' ἐνισπεῖν,
οἳ δὲ ἕκαστοι ἴσασιν, οἳ ἂν περιναιετάωσιν.
  Θεία δ' Ἠέλιόν τε μέγαν λαμπράν τε Σελήνην
Ἠῶ θ', ἣ πάντεσσιν ἐπιχθονίοισι φαείνει
ἀθανάτοις τε θεοῖσι, τοὶ οὐρανὸν εὐρὺν ἔχουσι,
γείναθ' ὑποδμηθεῖσ' Ὑπερίονος ἐν φιλότητι.
  Κρίῳ δ' Εὐρυβίη τέκεν ἐν φιλότητι μιγεῖσα
Ἀστραῖόν τε μέγαν Πάλλαντά τε δῖα θεάων
Πέρσην θ', ὃς καὶ πᾶσι μετέπρεπεν ἰδμοσύνῃσιν.
  Ἀστραίῳ δ' Ἠὼς ἀνέμους τέκε καρτεροθύμους,
ἀργέστην Ζέφυρον Βορέην τ' αἰψηροκέλευθον
καὶ Νότον, ἐν φιλότητι θεὰ θεῷ εὐνηθεῖσα.
τοὺς δὲ μέτ' ἀστέρα τίκτεν Ἑωσφόρον Ἠριγένεια
ἄστρα τε λαμπετόωντα, τά τ' οὐρανὸς ἐστεφάνωται.
  Στὺξ δ' ἔτεκ' Ὠκεανοῦ θυγάτηρ Πάλλαντι μιγεῖσα
Ζῆλον καὶ Νίκην καλλίσφυρον ἐν μεγάροισιν·
καὶ Κράτος ἠδὲ Βίην ἀριδείκετα γείνατο τέκνα,
τῶν οὐκ ἔστ' ἀπάνευθε Διὸς δόμος, οὐδέ τις ἕδρη,
οὐδ' ὁδός, ὅππη μὴ κείνοις θεὸς ἡγεμονεύῃ,
ἀλλ' αἰεὶ πὰρ Ζηνὶ βαρυκτύπῳ ἑδριόωνται.
ὣς γὰρ ἐβούλευσεν Στὺξ ἄφθιτος Ὠκεανίνη
ἤματι τῷ, ὅτε πάντας Ὀλύμπιος ἀστεροπητὴς
ἀθανάτους ἐκάλεσσε θεοὺς ἐς μακρὸν Ὄλυμπον,
εἶπε δ', ὃς ἂν μετὰ εἷο θεῶν Τιτῆσι μάχοιτο,

are glorious among goddesses. And as many other rivers are there, babbling as they flow, sons of Ocean, whom queenly Tethys bare, but their names it is hard for a mortal man to tell, but people know those by which they severally dwell.

And Theia was subject in love to Hyperion and bare great Helius (Sun) and clear Selene (Moon) and Eos (Dawn) who shines upon all that are on earth and upon the deathless Gods who live in the wide heaven.

And Eurybia, bright goddess, was joined in love to Crius and bare great Astraeus, and Pallas, and Perses who also was eminent among all men in wisdom.

And Eos bare to Astraeus the strong-hearted winds, brightening Zephyrus, and Boreas, headlong in his course, and Notus,—a goddess mating in love with a god. And after these Erigeneia [1] bare the star Eosphorus (Dawn-bringer), and the gleaming stars with which heaven is crowned.

And Styx the daughter of Ocean was joined to Pallas and bare Zelus (Emulation) and trim-ankled Nike (Victory) in the house. Also she brought forth Cratos (Strength) and Bia (Force), wonderful children. These have no house apart from Zeus, nor any dwelling nor path except that wherein God leads them, but they dwell always with Zeus the loud-thunderer. For so did Styx the deathless daughter of Ocean plan on that day when the Olympian Lightener called all the deathless gods to great Olympus, and said that whosoever of the gods would fight with him against the Titans, he would

[1] *i.e.* Eos, the "Early-born."

μή τιν' ἀπορραίσειν γεράων, τιμὴν δὲ ἕκαστον
ἑξέμεν, ἣν τὸ πάρος γε μετ' ἀθανάτοισι θεοῖσιν.
τὸν δ' ἔφαθ', ὅστις ἄτιμος ὑπὸ Κρόνου ἠδ' ἀγέραστος,
τιμῆς καὶ γεράων ἐπιβησέμεν, ἣ θέμις ἐστίν.
ἦλθε δ' ἄρα πρώτη Στὺξ ἄφθιτος Οὔλυμπόνδε
σὺν σφοῖσιν παίδεσσι φίλου διὰ μήδεα πατρός.
τὴν δὲ Ζεὺς τίμησε, περισσὰ δὲ δῶρα δέδωκεν.
αὐτὴν μὲν γὰρ ἔθηκε θεῶν μέγαν ἔμμεναι ὅρκον,
παῖδας δ' ἤματα πάντα ἑοῦ μεταναιέτας εἶναι.
ὣς δ' αὔτως πάντεσσι διαμπερές, ὥς περ ὑπέστη,
ἐξετέλεσσ'· αὐτὸς δὲ μέγα κρατεῖ ἠδὲ ἀνάσσει.
Φοίβη δ' αὖ Κοίου πολυήρατον ἦλθεν ἐς εὐνήν·
κυσαμένη δὴ ἔπειτα θεὰ θεοῦ ἐν φιλότητι
Λητὼ κυανόπεπλον ἐγείνατο, μείλιχον αἰεί,
ἤπιον ἀνθρώποισι καὶ ἀθανάτοισι θεοῖσιν,
μείλιχον ἐξ ἀρχῆς, ἀγανώτατον ἐντὸς Ὀλύμπου.
γείνατο δ' Ἀστερίην εὐώνυμον, ἥν ποτε Πέρσης
ἠγάγετ' ἐς μέγα δῶμα φίλην κεκλῆσθαι ἄκοιτιν.
ἣ δ' ὑποκυσαμένη Ἑκάτην τέκε, τὴν περὶ πάντων
Ζεὺς Κρονίδης τίμησε· πόρεν δέ οἱ ἀγλαὰ δῶρα,
μοῖραν ἔχειν γαίης τε καὶ ἀτρυγέτοιο θαλάσσης.
ἣ δὲ καὶ ἀστερόεντος ἀπ' οὐρανοῦ ἔμμορε τιμῆς
ἀθανάτοις τε θεοῖσι τετιμένη ἐστὶ μάλιστα.
καὶ γὰρ νῦν, ὅτε πού τις ἐπιχθονίων ἀνθρώπων
ἔρδων ἱερὰ καλὰ κατὰ νόμον ἱλάσκηται,
κικλήσκει Ἑκάτην. πολλή τέ οἱ ἕσπετο τιμὴ
ῥεῖα μάλ', ᾧ πρόφρων γε θεὰ ὑποδέξεται εὐχάς,
καί τέ οἱ ὄλβον ὀπάζει, ἐπεὶ δύναμίς γε πάρεστιν.
ὅσσοι γὰρ Γαίης τε καὶ Οὐρανοῦ ἐξεγένοντο

not cast him out from his rights, but each should have the office which he had before amongst the deathless gods. And he declared that he who was without office or right under Cronos, should be raised to both office and rights as is just. So deathless Styx came first to Olympus with her children through the wit of her dear father. And Zeus honoured her, and gave her very great gifts, for her he appointed to be the great oath of the gods, and her children to live with him always. And as he promised, so he performed fully unto them all.

Again, Phoebe came to the desired embrace of Coeus. Then the goddess through the love of the god conceived and brought forth dark-gowned Leto, always mild, kind to men and to the deathless gods, mild from the beginning, gentlest in all Olympus. Also she bare Asteria of happy name, whom Perses once led to his great house to be called his dear wife. And she conceived and bare Hecate whom Zeus the son of Cronos honoured above all. He gave her splendid gifts, to have a share of the earth and the unfruitful sea. She received honour also in starry heaven, and is honoured exceedingly by the deathless gods. For to this day, whenever any one of men on earth offers rich sacrifices and prays for favour according to custom, he calls upon Hecate. Great honour comes full easily to him whose prayers the goddess receives favourably, and she bestows wealth upon him; for the power surely is with her. For she has authority over all those who were born of Earth and Ocean

καὶ τιμὴν ἔλαχον, τούτων ἔχει αἶσαν ἁπάντων.
οὐδέ τί μιν Κρονίδης ἐβιήσατο οὐδέ τ' ἀπηύρα,
ὅσσ' ἔλαχεν Τιτῆσι μετὰ προτέροισι θεοῖσιν,
ἀλλ' ἔχει, ὡς τὸ πρῶτον ἀπ' ἀρχῆς ἔπλετο δασμός, 425
καὶ γέρας ἐν γαίῃ τε καὶ οὐρανῷ ἠδὲ θαλάσσῃ·[1] 427
οὐδ', ὅτι μουνογενής, ἧσσον θεὰ ἔμμορε τιμῆς, 426
ἀλλ' ἔτι καὶ πολὺ μᾶλλον, ἐπεὶ Ζεὺς τίεται αὐτήν. 428
ᾧ δ' ἐθέλει, μεγάλως παραγίγνεται ἠδ' ὀνίνησιν·
ἔν τε δίκῃ βασιλεῦσι παρ' αἰδοίοισι καθίζει,[2] 434
ἔν τ' ἀγορῇ λαοῖσι μεταπρέπει, ὅν κ' ἐθέλῃσιν· 430
ἠδ' ὁπότ' ἐς πόλεμον φθεισήνορα θωρήσσωνται
ἀνέρες, ἔνθα θεὰ παραγίγνεται, οἷς κ' ἐθέλῃσι
νίκην προφρονέως ὀπάσαι καὶ κῦδος ὀρέξαι. 433
ἐσθλὴ δ' αὖθ' ὁπότ' ἄνδρες ἀεθλεύωσιν ἀγῶνι,[3] 435
ἔνθα θεὰ καὶ τοῖς παραγίγνεται ἠδ' ὀνίνησιν·
νικήσας δὲ βίῃ καὶ κάρτεϊ καλὸν ἄεθλον
ῥεῖα φέρει χαίρων τε, τοκεῦσι δὲ κῦδος ὀπάζει.
ἐσθλὴ δ' ἱππήεσσι παρεστάμεν, οἷς κ' ἐθέλῃσιν.
καὶ τοῖς, οἳ γλαυκὴν δυσπέμφελον ἐργάζονται, 440
εὔχονται δ' Ἑκάτῃ καὶ ἐρικτύπῳ Ἐννοσιγαίῳ,
ῥηιδίως ἄγρην κυδρὴ θεὸς ὤπασε πολλήν,
ῥεῖα δ' ἀφείλετο φαινομένην, ἐθέλουσά γε θυμῷ.
ἐσθλὴ δ' ἐν σταθμοῖσι σὺν Ἑρμῇ ληίδ' ἀέξειν·
βουκολίας δ' ἀγέλας τε καὶ αἰπόλια πλατέ' αἰγῶν 445
ποίμνας τ' εἰροπόκων ὀίων, θυμῷ γ' ἐθέλουσα,
ἐξ ὀλίγων βριάει καὶ ἐκ πολλῶν μείονα θῆκεν.
οὕτω τοι καὶ μουνογενὴς ἐκ μητρὸς ἐοῦσα

[1] Goettling's order.
[2] Schoemann's order.
[3] Koechly: ἀγῶνι ἀεθλεύωσιν, DGHI: ἀθλεύωσιν, other MSS.

and received an office. The son of Cronos did her no wrong nor took anything away of all that was her portion among the former Titan gods : but she holds, as the division was at the first from the beginning, privilege both in earth, and in heaven, and in sea. Also, because she is an only child, the goddess receives not less honour, but much more still, for Zeus honours her. Whom she will she greatly aids and advances : she sits by worshipful kings in judgement, and in the assembly whom she will is distinguished among the people. And when men arm themselves for the battle that destroys men, then the goddess is at hand to give victory and grant glory readily to whom she will. Good is she also when men contend at the games, for there too the goddess is with them and profits them : and he who by might and strength gets the victory wins the rich prize easily with joy, and brings glory to his parents. And she is good to stand by horsemen, whom she will : and to those whose business is in the grey discomfortable sea, and who pray to Hecate and the loud-crashing Earth-Shaker, easily the glorious goddess gives great catch, and easily she takes it away as soon as seen, if so she will. She is good in the byre with Hermes to increase the stock. The droves of kine and wide herds of goats and flocks of fleecy sheep, if she will, she increases from a few, or makes many to be less. So, then, albeit her mother's only child,[1] she is honoured amongst all the deathless

[1] Van Lennep explains that Hecate, having no brothers to support her claim, might have been slighted.

πᾶσι μετ' ἀθανάτοισι τετίμηται γεράεσσιν.
θῆκε δέ μιν Κρονίδης κουροτρόφον, οἳ μετ' ἐκείνην
ὀφθαλμοῖσιν ἴδοντο φάος πολυδερκέος Ἠοῦς.
οὕτως ἐξ ἀρχῆς κουροτρόφος, αἱ δέ τε τιμαί.

Ῥείη δὲ δμηθεῖσα Κρόνῳ τέκε φαίδιμα τέκνα,
Ἱστίην Δήμητρα καὶ Ἥρην χρυσοπέδιλον
ἴφθιμόν τ' Ἀίδην, ὃς ὑπὸ χθονὶ δώματα ναίει
νηλεὲς ἦτορ ἔχων, καὶ ἐρίκτυπον Ἐννοσίγαιον
Ζῆνά τε μητιόεντα, θεῶν πατέρ' ἠδὲ καὶ ἀνδρῶν,
τοῦ καὶ ὑπὸ βροντῆς πελεμίζεται εὐρεῖα χθών.
καὶ τοὺς μὲν κατέπινε μέγας Κρόνος, ὥς τις ἕκαστος
νηδύος ἐξ ἱερῆς μητρὸς πρὸς γούναθ' ἵκοιτο,
τὰ φρονέων, ἵνα μή τις ἀγαυῶν Οὐρανιώνων
ἄλλος ἐν ἀθανάτοισιν ἔχοι βασιληίδα τιμήν.
πεύθετο γὰρ Γαίης τε καὶ Οὐρανοῦ ἀστερόεντος,
οὕνεκά οἱ πέπρωτο ἑῷ ὑπὸ παιδὶ δαμῆναι
καὶ κρατερῷ περ ἐόντι, Διὸς[1] μεγάλου διὰ βουλάς·
τῷ ὅ γ' ἄρ' οὐκ ἀλαὸς σκοπιὴν ἔχεν, ἀλλὰ δοκεύων
παῖδας ἑοὺς κατέπινε· Ῥέην δ' ἔχε πένθος ἄλαστον.
ἀλλ' ὅτε δὴ Δί' ἔμελλε θεῶν πατέρ' ἠδὲ καὶ ἀνδρῶν
τέξεσθαι, τότ' ἔπειτα φίλους λιτάνευε τοκῆας
τοὺς αὐτῆς, Γαῖάν τε καὶ Οὐρανὸν ἀστερόεντα,
μῆτιν συμφράσσασθαι, ὅπως λελάθοιτο τεκοῦσα
παῖδα φίλον, τίσαιτο δ' ἐρινῦς πατρὸς ἑοῖο
παίδων θ', οὓς κατέπινε μέγας Κρόνος ἀγκυλομήτης.

[1] E (later hand) GHI and a Scholiast read πατρός.

gods. And the son of Cronos made her a nurse of the young who after her saw with their eyes the light of all-seeing Dawn. So from the beginning she is a nurse of the young, and these are her honours.

But Rhea was subject in love to Cronos and bare splendid children, Hestia,[1] Demeter, and gold-shod Hera and strong Hades, pitiless in heart, who dwells under the earth, and the loud-crashing Earth-Shaker, and wise Zeus, father of gods and men, by whose thunder the wide earth is shaken. These great Cronos swallowed as each came forth from the womb to his mother's knees with this intent, that no other of the proud sons of Heaven should hold the kingly office amongst the deathless gods. For he learned from Earth and starry Heaven that he was destined to be overcome by his own son, strong though he was, through the contriving of great Zeus.[2] Therefore he kept no blind outlook, but watched and swallowed down his children: and unceasing grief seized Rhea. But when she was about to bear Zeus, the father of gods and men, then she besought her own dear parents, Earth and starry Heaven, to devise some plan with her that the birth of her dear child might be concealed, and that retribution might overtake great, crafty Cronos for his own father and also for the

[1] The goddess of the *hearth* (the Roman *Vesta*), and so of the house. Cp. *Homeric Hymns* v. 22 ff.; xxix. 1 ff.

[2] The variant reading "of his father" (*sc.* Heaven) rests on inferior MS. authority and is probably an alteration due to the difficulty stated by a Scholiast: "How could Zeus, being not yet begotten, plot against his father?" The phrase is, however, part of the prophecy. The whole line may well be spurious, and is rejected by Heyne, Wolf, Gaisford and Guyet.

οἱ δὲ θυγατρὶ φίλῃ μάλα μὲν κλύον ἠδ' ἐπίθοντο,
καί οἱ πεφραδέτην, ὅσα περ πέπρωτο γενέσθαι
ἀμφὶ Κρόνῳ βασιλῆι καὶ υἱέι καρτεροθύμῳ.
πέμψαν δ' ἐς Λύκτον, Κρήτης ἐς πίονα δῆμον,
ὁππότ' ἄρ' ὁπλότατον παίδων τέξεσθαι ἔμελλε,
Ζῆνα μέγαν· τὸν μέν οἱ ἐδέξατο Γαῖα πελώρη
Κρήτῃ ἐν εὐρείῃ τραφέμεν ἀτιταλλέμεναί τε.
ἔνθα μιν ἷκτο φέρουσα θοὴν διὰ νύκτα μέλαιναν
πρώτην ἐς Λύκτον· κρύψεν δέ ἑ χερσὶ λαβοῦσα
ἄντρῳ ἐν ἠλιβάτῳ, ζαθέης ὑπὸ κεύθεσι γαίης,
Αἰγαίῳ ἐν ὄρει πεπυκασμένῳ ὑλήεντι.
τῷ δὲ σπαργανίσασα μέγαν λίθον ἐγγυάλιξεν
Οὐρανίδῃ μέγ' ἄνακτι, θεῶν προτέρῳ βασιλῆι.
τὸν τόθ' ἑλὼν χείρεσσιν ἑὴν ἐσκάτθετο νηδὺν
σχέτλιος· οὐδ' ἐνόησε μετὰ φρεσίν, ὥς οἱ ὀπίσσω
ἀντὶ λίθου ἑὸς υἱὸς ἀνίκητος καὶ ἀκηδὴς
λείπεθ', ὅ μιν τάχ' ἔμελλε βίῃ καὶ χερσὶ δαμάσσας
τιμῆς ἐξελάειν, ὃ δ' ἐν ἀθανάτοισι ἀνάξειν.
Καρπαλίμως δ' ἄρ' ἔπειτα μένος καὶ φαίδιμα γυῖα
ηὔξετο τοῖο ἄνακτος· ἐπιπλομένων δ' ἐνιαυτῶν
Γαίης ἐννεσίῃσι πολυφραδέεσσι δολωθεὶς
ὃν γόνον ἂψ ἀνέηκε μέγας Κρόνος ἀγκυλομήτης
[νικηθεὶς τέχνῃσι βίηφί τε παιδὸς ἑοῖο.[1]]
πρῶτον δ' ἐξέμεσεν λίθον, ὃν πύματον κατέπινεν·[2]
τὸν μὲν Ζεὺς στήριξε κατὰ χθονὸς εὐρυοδείης
Πυθοῖ ἐν ἠγαθέῃ γυάλοις ὕπο Παρνησοῖο
σῆμ' ἔμεν ἐξοπίσω, θαῦμα θνητοῖσι βροτοῖσιν.

[1] Rejected by Heyne as interrupting and disagreeing with the context.

[2] Peppmüller: ἐξήμησε (or ἐξήμεσε) λίθον, πύματον καταπίνων, MSS.

children whom he had swallowed down. And they readily heard and obeyed their dear daughter, and told her all that was destined to happen touching Cronos the king and his stout-hearted son. So they sent her to Lyctus, to the rich land of Crete, when she was ready to bear great Zeus, the youngest of her children. Him did vast Earth receive from Rhea in wide Crete to nourish and to bring up. Thither came Earth carrying him swiftly through the black night to Lyctus first, and took him in her arms and hid him in a remote cave beneath the secret places of the holy earth on thick-wooded Mount Aegeum; but to the mightily ruling son of Heaven, the earlier king of the gods, she gave a great stone wrapped in swaddling clothes. Then he took it in his hands and thrust it down into his belly: wretch! he knew not in his heart that in place of the stone his son was left behind, unconquered and untroubled, and that he was soon to overcome him by force and might and drive him from his honours, himself to reign over the deathless gods.

After that, the strength and glorious limbs of the prince increased quickly, and as the years rolled on, great Cronos the wily was beguiled by the deep suggestions of Earth, and brought up again his offspring, vanquished by the arts and might of his own son, and he vomited up first the stone which he had swallowed last. And Zeus set it fast in the wide-pathed earth at goodly Pytho under the glens of Parnassus, to be a sign thenceforth and a marvel to mortal men.[1] And he set free from their deadly

[1] Pausanias (x. 24. 6) saw near the tomb of Neoptolemus "a stone of no great size," which the Delphians anointed every day with oil, and which he says was supposed to be the stone given to Cronos.

λῦσε δὲ πατροκασιγνήτους ὀλοῶν ὑπὸ δεσμῶν
Οὐρανίδας, οὓς δῆσε πατὴρ ἀεσιφροσύνῃσιν·
οἵ οἱ ἀπεμνήσαντο χάριν εὐεργεσιάων,
δῶκαν δὲ βροντὴν ἠδ᾽ αἰθαλόεντα κεραυνὸν
καὶ στεροπήν· τὸ πρὶν δὲ πελώρη Γαῖα κεκεύθει·
τοῖς πίσυνος θνητοῖσι καὶ ἀθανάτοισιν ἀνάσσει.

Κούρην δ᾽ Ἰαπετὸς καλλίσφυρον Ὠκεανίνην
ἠγάγετο Κλυμένην καὶ ὁμὸν λέχος εἰσανέβαινεν.
ἡ δέ οἱ Ἄτλαντα κρατερόφρονα γείνατο παῖδα·
τίκτε δ᾽ ὑπερκύδαντα Μενοίτιον ἠδὲ Προμηθέα
ποικίλον αἰολόμητιν, ἁμαρτίνοόν τ᾽ Ἐπιμηθέα,
ὃς κακὸν ἐξ ἀρχῆς γένετ᾽ ἀνδράσιν ἀλφηστῇσιν·
πρῶτος γάρ ῥα Διὸς πλαστὴν ὑπέδεκτο γυναῖκα
παρθένον. ὑβριστὴν δὲ Μενοίτιον εὐρύοπα Ζεὺς
εἰς Ἔρεβος κατέπεμψε βαλὼν ψολόεντι κεραυνῷ
εἵνεκ᾽ ἀτασθαλίης τε καὶ ἠνορέης ὑπερόπλου.
Ἄτλας δ᾽ οὐρανὸν εὐρὺν ἔχει κρατερῆς ὑπ᾽ ἀνάγκης
πείρασιν ἐν γαίης, πρόπαρ Ἑσπερίδων λιγυφώνων,
ἑστηὼς κεφαλῇ τε καὶ ἀκαμάτῃσι χέρεσσιν·
ταύτην γάρ οἱ μοῖραν ἐδάσσατο μητίετα Ζεύς.
δῆσε δ᾽ ἀλυκτοπέδῃσι Προμηθέα ποικιλόβουλον
δεσμοῖς ἀργαλέοισι μέσον διὰ κίον᾽ ἐλάσσας·
καί οἱ ἐπ᾽ αἰετὸν ὦρσε τανύπτερον· αὐτὰρ ὅ γ᾽ ἧπαρ
ἤσθιεν ἀθάνατον, τὸ δ᾽ ἀέξετο ἶσον ἁπάντῃ
νυκτός, ὅσον πρόπαν ἦμαρ ἔδοι τανυσίπτερος ὄρνις.
τὸν μὲν ἄρ᾽ Ἀλκμήνης καλλισφύρου ἄλκιμος υἱὸς
Ἡρακλέης ἔκτεινε, κακὴν δ᾽ ἀπὸ νοῦσον ἄλαλκεν
Ἰαπετιονίδῃ καὶ ἐλύσατο δυσφροσυνάων
οὐκ ἀέκητι Ζηνὸς Ὀλυμπίου ὑψιμέδοντος,

bonds the brothers of his father, sons of Heaven whom his father in his foolishness had bound. And they remembered to be grateful to him for his kindness, and gave him thunder and the glowing thunderbolt and lightning: for before that, huge Earth had hidden these. In them he trusts and rules over mortals and immortals.

Now Iapetus took to wife the neat-ankled maid Clymene, daughter of Ocean, and went up with her into one bed. And she bare him a stout-hearted son, Atlas: also she bare very glorious Menoetius and clever Prometheus, full of various wiles, and scatter-brained Epimetheus who from the first was a mischief to men who eat bread; for it was he who first took of Zeus the woman, the maiden whom he had formed. But Menoetius was outrageous, and far-seeing Zeus struck him with a lurid thunderbolt and sent him down to Erebus because of his mad presumption and exceeding pride. And Atlas through hard constraint upholds the wide heaven with unwearying head and arms, standing at the borders of the earth before the clear-voiced Hesperides; for this lot wise Zeus assigned to him. And ready-witted Prometheus he bound with inextricable bonds, cruel chains, and drove a shaft through his middle, and set on him a long-winged eagle, which used to eat his immortal liver; but by night the liver grew as much again everyway as the long-winged bird devoured in the whole day. That bird Heracles, the valiant son of shapely-ankled Alcmene, slew; and delivered the son of Iapetus from the cruel plague, and released him from his affliction—not without the will of Olympian Zeus who reigns on high, that

ὄφρ' Ἡρακλῆος Θηβαγενέος κλέος εἴη
πλεῖον ἔτ' ἢ τὸ πάροιθεν ἐπὶ χθόνα πουλυβότειραν.
ταῦτ' ἄρα ἀζόμενος τίμα ἀριδείκετον υἱόν·
καί περ χωόμενος παύθη χόλου, ὃν πρὶν ἔχεσκεν,
οὕνεκ' ἐρίζετο βουλὰς ὑπερμενέι Κρονίωνι.
καὶ γὰρ ὅτ' ἐκρίνοντο θεοὶ θνητοί τ' ἄνθρωποι
Μηκώνῃ, τότ' ἔπειτα μέγαν βοῦν πρόφρονι θυμῷ
δασσάμενος προέθηκε, Διὸς νόον ἐξαπαφίσκων.
τοῖς μὲν γὰρ σάρκας τε καὶ ἔγκατα πίονα δημῷ
ἐν ῥινῷ κατέθηκε καλύψας γαστρὶ βοείῃ,
τῷ δ' αὖτ' ὀστέα λευκὰ βοὸς δολίῃ ἐπὶ τέχνῃ
εὐθετίσας κατέθηκε καλύψας ἀργέτι δημῷ.
δὴ τότε μιν προσέειπε πατὴρ ἀνδρῶν τε θεῶν τε·
Ἰαπετιονίδη, πάντων ἀριδείκετ' ἀνάκτων,
ὦ πέπον, ὡς ἑτεροζήλως διεδάσσαο μοίρας.
Ὣς φάτο κερτομέων Ζεὺς ἄφθιτα μήδεα εἰδώς.
τὸν δ' αὖτε προσέειπε Προμηθεὺς ἀγκυλομήτης
ἦκ' ἐπιμειδήσας, δολίης δ' οὐ λήθετο τέχνης·
Ζεῦ κύδιστε μέγιστε θεῶν αἰειγενετάων,
τῶν δ' ἕλε', ὁπποτέρην σε ἐνὶ φρεσὶ θυμὸς ἀνώγει.
Φῆ ῥα δολοφρονέων· Ζεὺς δ' ἄφθιτα μήδεα εἰδὼς
γνῶ ῥ' οὐδ' ἠγνοίησε δόλον· κακὰ δ' ὄσσετο θυμῷ
θνητοῖς ἀνθρώποισι, τὰ καὶ τελέεσθαι ἔμελλεν.
χερσὶ δ' ὅ γ' ἀμφοτέρῃσιν ἀνείλετο λευκὸν ἄλειφαρ.
χώσατο δὲ φρένας ἀμφί, χόλος δέ μιν ἵκετο θυμόν,
ὡς ἴδεν ὀστέα λευκὰ βοὸς δολίῃ ἐπὶ τέχνῃ.
ἐκ τοῦ δ' ἀθανάτοισιν ἐπὶ χθονὶ φῦλ' ἀνθρώπων
καίουσ' ὀστέα λευκὰ θυηέντων ἐπὶ βωμῶν.
τὸν δὲ μέγ' ὀχθήσας προσέφη νεφεληγερέτα Ζεύς·

the glory of Heracles the Theban-born might be yet greater than it was before over the plenteous earth. This, then, he regarded, and honoured his famous son; though he was angry, he ceased from the wrath which he had before because Prometheus matched himself in wit with the almighty son of Cronos. For when the gods and mortal men were divided at Mecone, even then Prometheus was forward to cut up a great ox and set portions before them, trying to befool the mind of Zeus. Before the rest he set flesh and inner parts thick with fat upon the hide, covering them with an ox paunch; but for Zeus he put the white bones dressed up with cunning art and covered with shining fat. Then the father of men and of gods said to him:

"Son of Iapetus, most glorious of all lords, good sir, how unfairly you have divided the portions!"

So said Zeus whose wisdom is everlasting, rebuking him. But wily Prometheus answered him, smiling softly and not forgetting his cunning trick:

"Zeus, most glorious and greatest of the eternal gods, take which ever of these portions your heart within you bids." So he said, thinking trickery. But Zeus, whose wisdom is everlasting, saw and failed not to perceive the trick, and in his heart he thought mischief against mortal men which also was to be fulfilled. With both hands he took up the white fat and was angry at heart, and wrath came to his spirit when he saw the white ox-bones craftily tricked out: and because of this the tribes of men upon earth burn white bones to the deathless gods upon fragrant altars. But Zeus who drives the clouds was greatly vexed and said to him:

Ἰαπετιονίδη, πάντων πέρι μήδεα εἰδώς,
ὦ πέπον, οὐκ ἄρα πω δολίης ἐπιλήθεο τέχνης.
Ὣς φάτο χωόμενος Ζεὺς ἄφθιτα μήδεα εἰδώς·
ἐκ τούτου δὴ ἔπειτα δόλου μεμνημένος αἰεὶ
οὐκ ἐδίδου Μελίῃσι[1] πυρὸς μένος ἀκαμάτοιο
θνητοῖς ἀνθρώποις, οἳ ἐπὶ χθονὶ ναιετάουσιν.
ἀλλά μιν ἐξαπάτησεν ἐὺς πάις Ἰαπετοῖο
κλέψας ἀκαμάτοιο πυρὸς τηλέσκοπον αὐγὴν
ἐν κοΐλῳ νάρθηκι· δάκεν δέ ἑ νειόθι θυμόν,
Ζῆν' ὑψιβρεμέτην, ἐχόλωσε δέ μιν φίλον ἦτορ,
ὡς ἴδ' ἐν ἀνθρώποισι πυρὸς τηλέσκοπον αὐγήν.
αὐτίκα δ' ἀντὶ πυρὸς τεῦξεν κακὸν ἀνθρώποισιν·
γαίης γὰρ σύμπλασσε περικλυτὸς Ἀμφιγυήεις
παρθένῳ αἰδοίῃ ἴκελον Κρονίδεω διὰ βουλάς.
ζῶσε δὲ καὶ κόσμησε θεὰ γλαυκῶπις Ἀθήνη
ἀργυφέῃ ἐσθῆτι· κατὰ κρῆθεν δὲ καλύπτρην
δαιδαλέην χείρεσσι κατέσχεθε, θαῦμα ἰδέσθαι·
[ἀμφὶ δέ οἱ στεφάνους, νεοθηλέος ἄνθεα ποίης,
ἱμερτοὺς περίθηκε καρήατι Παλλὰς Ἀθήνη.[2]]
ἀμφὶ δέ οἱ στεφάνην χρυσέην κεφαλῆφιν ἔθηκε,
τὴν αὐτὸς ποίησε περικλυτὸς Ἀμφιγυήεις
ἀσκήσας παλάμῃσι, χαριζόμενος Διὶ πατρί.
τῇ δ' ἐνὶ δαίδαλα πολλὰ τετεύχατο, θαῦμα ἰδέσθαι,
κνώδαλ', ὅσ' ἤπειρος πολλὰ τρέφει ἠδὲ θάλασσα,
τῶν ὅ γε πόλλ' ἐνέθηκε,—χάρις δ' ἀπελάμπετο πολλή,—
θαυμάσια, ζῴοισιν ἐοικότα φωνήεσσιν.

[1] Bergk (after scholiast): μελῖῃσι, DEGHI: μελίοισι, FKL.
[2] ll. 576–7 appear to belong to a different recension.

"Son of Iapetus, clever above all! So, sir, you have not yet forgotten your cunning arts!"

So spake Zeus in anger, whose wisdom is everlasting; and from that time he was always mindful of the trick, and would not give the power of unwearying fire to the Melian[1] race of mortal men who live on the earth. But the noble son of Iapetus outwitted him and stole the far-seen gleam of unwearying fire in a hollow fennel stalk. And Zeus who thunders on high was stung in spirit, and his dear heart was angered when he saw amongst men the far-seen ray of fire. Forthwith he made an evil thing for men as the price of fire; for the very famous Limping God formed of earth the likeness of a shy maiden as the son of Cronos willed. And the goddess bright-eyed Athene girded and clothed her with silvery raiment, and down from her head she spread with her hands a broidered veil, a wonder to see; and she, Pallas Athene, put about her head lovely garlands, flowers of new-grown herbs. Also she put upon her head a crown of gold which the very famous Limping God made himself and worked with his own hands as a favour to Zeus his father. On it was much curious work, wonderful to see; for of the many creatures which the land and sea rear up, he put most upon it, wonderful things, like living beings with voices: and great beauty shone out from it.

[1] A Scholiast explains: "Either because they (men) sprang from the Melian nymphs (cp. l. 187); or because, when they were born (?), they cast themselves under the ash-trees (μέλιαι), that is, the trees." The reference may be to the origin of men from ash-trees: cp. *Works and Days*, 145 and note.

Αὐτὰρ ἐπεὶ δὴ τεῦξε καλὸν κακὸν ἀντ' ἀγαθοῖο,
ἐξάγαγ', ἔνθα περ ἄλλοι ἔσαν θεοὶ ἠδ' ἄνθρωποι,
κόσμῳ ἀγαλλομένην γλαυκώπιδος ὀβριμοπάτρης.
θαῦμα δ' ἔχ' ἀθανάτους τε θεοὺς θνητούς τ' ἀνθρώπους,
ὡς εἶδον δόλον αἰπύν, ἀμήχανον ἀνθρώποισιν.
'Εκ τῆς γὰρ γένος ἐστὶ γυναικῶν θηλυτεράων,[1]
[τῆς γὰρ ὀλώιόν ἐστι γένος καὶ φῦλα γυναικῶν,]
πῆμα μέγ' αἳ θνητοῖσι μετ' ἀνδράσι ναιετάουσιν
οὐλομένης πενίης οὐ σύμφοροι, ἀλλὰ κόροιο.
ὡς δ' ὁπότ' ἐν σμήνεσσι κατηρεφέεσσι μέλισσαι
κηφῆνας βόσκωσι, κακῶν ξυνήονας ἔργων—
αἳ μέν τε πρόπαν ἦμαρ ἐς ἠέλιον καταδύντα
ἠμάτιαι σπεύδουσι τιθεῖσί τε κηρία λευκά,
οἳ δ' ἔντοσθε μένοντες ἐπηρεφέας κατὰ σίμβλους
ἀλλότριον κάματον σφετέρην ἐς γαστέρ' ἀμῶνται—
ὣς δ' αὔτως ἄνδρεσσι κακὸν θνητοῖσι γυναῖκας
Ζεὺς ὑψιβρεμέτης θῆκεν, ξυνήονας ἔργων
ἀργαλέων· ἕτερον δὲ πόρεν κακὸν ἀντ' ἀγαθοῖο·
ὅς κε γάμον φεύγων καὶ μέρμερα ἔργα γυναικῶν
μὴ γῆμαι ἐθέλῃ, ὀλοὸν δ' ἐπὶ γῆρας ἵκοιτο
χήτεϊ γηροκόμοιο· ὅ γ' οὐ βιότου ἐπιδευὴς
ζώει, ἀποφθιμένου δὲ διὰ κτῆσιν δατέονται
χηρωσταί· ᾧ δ' αὖτε γάμου μετὰ μοῖρα γένηται,
κεδνὴν δ' ἔσχεν ἄκοιτιν ἀρηρυῖαν πραπίδεσσι,
τῷ δέ τ' ἀπ' αἰῶνος κακὸν ἐσθλῷ ἀντιφερίζει
ἐμμενές· ὃς δέ κε τέτμῃ ἀταρτηροῖο γενέθλης,
ζώει ἐνὶ στήθεσσιν ἔχων ἀλίαστον ἀνίην
θυμῷ καὶ κραδίῃ, καὶ ἀνήκεστον κακόν ἐστιν.
Ὣς οὐκ ἔστι Διὸς κλέψαι νόον οὐδὲ παρελθεῖν.
οὐδὲ γὰρ Ἰαπετιονίδης ἀκάκητα Προμηθεὺς

[1] ll. 590–1 belong to different recensions.

But when he had made the beautiful evil to be the price for the blessing, he brought her out, delighting in the finery which the bright-eyed daughter of a mighty father had given her, to the place where the other gods and men were. And wonder took hold of the deathless gods and mortal men when they saw that which was sheer guile, not to be withstood by men.

For from her is the race of women and female-kind: of her is the deadly race and tribe of women who live amongst mortal men to their great trouble, no helpmeets in hateful poverty, but only in wealth. And as in thatched hives bees feed the drones whose nature is to do mischief—by day and throughout the day until the sun goes down the bees are busy and lay the white combs, while the drones stay at home in the covered skeps and reap the toil of others into their own bellies—even so Zeus who thunders on high made women to be an evil to mortal men, with a nature to do evil. And he gave them a second evil to be the price for the good they had: whoever avoids marriage and the sorrows that women cause, and will not wed, reaches deadly old age without anyone to tend his years, and though he at least has no lack of livelihood while he lives, yet, when he is dead, his kinsfolk divide his possessions amongst them. And as for the man who chooses the lot of marriage and takes a good wife suited to his mind, evil continually contends with good; for whoever happens to have mischievous children, lives always with unceasing grief in his spirit and heart within him; and this evil cannot be healed.

So it is not possible to deceive or go beyond the will of Zeus; for not even the son of Iapetus, kindly

τοῖό γ' ὑπεξήλυξε βαρὺν χόλον, ἀλλ' ὑπ' ἀνάγκης
καὶ πολύιδριν ἐόντα μέγας κατὰ δεσμὸς ἐρύκει.

'Οβριάρεῳ δ' ὡς πρῶτα πατὴρ ὠδύσσατο θυμῷ
Κόττῳ τ' ἠδὲ Γύῃ, δῆσεν κρατερῷ ἐνὶ δεσμῷ
ἠνορέην ὑπέροπλον ἀγώμενος ἠδὲ καὶ εἶδος
καὶ μέγεθος· κατένασσε δ' ὑπὸ χθονὸς εὐρυοδείης.
ἔνθ' οἵ γ' ἄλγε' ἔχοντες ὑπὸ χθονὶ ναιετάοντες
εἵατ' ἐπ' ἐσχατιῇ, μεγάλης ἐν πείρασι γαίης,
δηθὰ μάλ' ἀχνύμενοι, κραδίῃ μέγα πένθος ἔχοντες.
ἀλλά σφεας Κρονίδης τε καὶ ἀθάνατοι θεοὶ ἄλλοι,
οὓς τέκεν ἠύκομος 'Ρείη Κρόνου ἐν φιλότητι,
Γαίης φραδμοσύνῃσιν ἀνήγαγον ἐς φάος αὖτις·
αὐτὴ γάρ σφιν ἅπαντα διηνεκέως κατέλεξε
σὺν κείνοις νίκην τε καὶ ἀγλαὸν εὖχος ἀρέσθαι.
δηρὸν γὰρ μάρναντο πόνον θυμαλγέ' ἔχοντες
Τιτῆνές τε θεοὶ καὶ ὅσοι Κρόνου ἐξεγένοντο,
ἀντίον ἀλλήλοισι διὰ κρατερὰς ὑσμίνας,
οἱ μὲν ἀφ' ὑψηλῆς Ὄθρυος Τιτῆνες ἀγαυοί,
οἱ δ' ἄρ' ἀπ' Οὐλύμποιο θεοί, δωτῆρες ἐάων,
οὓς τέκεν ἠύκομος 'Ρείη Κρόνῳ εὐνηθεῖσα.
οἵ ῥα τότ' ἀλλήλοισι χόλον θυμαλγέ' ἔχοντες
συνεχέως ἐμάχοντο δέκα πλείους ἐνιαυτούς·
οὐδέ τις ἦν ἔριδος χαλεπῆς λύσις οὐδὲ τελευτὴ
οὐδετέροις, ἶσον δὲ τέλος τέτατο πτολέμοιο.
ἀλλ' ὅτε δὴ κείνοισι παρέσχεθεν ἄρμενα πάντα,·
νέκταρ τ' ἀμβροσίην τε, τά περ θεοὶ αὐτοὶ ἔδουσι,
πάντων ἐν στήθεσσιν ἀέξετο θυμὸς ἀγήνωρ.
ὡς νέκταρ τ' ἐπάσαντο καὶ ἀμβροσίην ἐρατεινήν,
δὴ τότε τοῖς μετέειπε πατὴρ ἀνδρῶν τε θεῶν τε·

Prometheus, escaped his heavy anger, but of necessity strong bands confined him, although he knew many a wile.

But when first their father was vexed in his heart with Obriareus and Cottus and Gyes, he bound them in cruel bonds, because he was jealous of their exceeding manhood and comeliness and great size: and he made them live beneath the wide-pathed earth, where they were afflicted, being set to dwell under the ground, at the end of the earth, at its great borders, in bitter anguish for a long time and with great grief at heart. But the son of Cronos and the other deathless gods whom rich-haired Rhea bare from union with Cronos, brought them up again to the light at Earth's advising. For she herself recounted all things to the gods fully, how that with these they would gain victory and a glorious cause to vaunt themselves. For the Titan gods and as many as sprang from Cronos had long been fighting together in stubborn war with heart-grieving toil, the lordly Titans from high Othrys, but the gods, givers of good, whom rich-haired Rhea bare in union with Cronos, from Olympus. So they, with bitter wrath, were fighting continually with one another at that time for ten full years, and the hard strife had no close or end for either side, and the issue of the war hung evenly balanced. But when he had provided those three with all things fitting, nectar and ambrosia which the gods themselves eat, and when their proud spirit revived within them all after they had fed on nectar and delicious ambrosia, then it was that the father of men and gods spoke amongst them:

Κέκλυτέ μευ, Γαίης τε καὶ Οὐρανοῦ ἀγλαὰ τέκνα,
ὄφρ᾽ εἴπω, τά με θυμὸς ἐνὶ στήθεσσι κελεύει.
ἤδη γὰρ μάλα δηρὸν ἐναντίοι ἀλλήλοισι
νίκης καὶ κράτεος πέρι μαρνάμεθ᾽ ἤματα πάντα
Τιτῆνές τε θεοὶ καὶ ὅσοι Κρόνου ἐκγενόμεσθα.
ὑμεῖς δὲ μεγάλην τε βίην καὶ χεῖρας ἀάπτους
φαίνετε Τιτήνεσσιν ἐναντίοι ἐν δαῒ λυγρῇ
μνησάμενοι φιλότητος ἐνηέος, ὅσσα παθόντες
ἐς φάος ἂψ ἀφίκεσθε δυσηλεγέος ὑπὸ δεσμοῦ
ἡμετέρας διὰ βουλὰς ὑπὸ ζόφου ἠερόεντος.
Ὣς φάτο· τὸν δ᾽ ἐξαῦτις ἀμείβετο Κόττος ἀμύμων·
Δαιμόνι᾽, οὐκ ἀδάητα πιφαύσκεαι· ἀλλὰ καὶ αὐτοὶ
ἴδμεν, ὅ τοι περὶ μὲν πραπίδες, περὶ δ᾽ ἐστὶ νόημα,
ἀλκτὴρ δ᾽ ἀθανάτοισιν ἀρῆς γένεο κρυεροῖο.
σῇσι δ᾽ ἐπιφροσύνῃσιν ὑπὸ ζόφου ἠερόεντος
ἄψορρον δ᾽† ἐξαῦτις ἀμειλίκτων ὑπὸ δεσμῶν
ἠλύθομεν, Κρόνου υἱὲ ἄναξ, ἀνάελπτα παθόντες.
τῷ καὶ νῦν ἀτενεῖ τε νόῳ καὶ ἐπίφρονι βουλῇ
ῥυσόμεθα κράτος ὑμὸν ἐν αἰνῇ δηϊοτῆτι
μαρνάμενοι Τιτῆσιν ἀνὰ κρατερὰς ὑσμίνας.
Ὣς φάτ᾽· ἐπῄνεσσαν δὲ θεοί, δωτῆρες ἐάων,
μῦθον ἀκούσαντες· πολέμου δ᾽ ἐλιλαίετο θυμὸς
μᾶλλον ἔτ᾽ ἢ τὸ πάροιθε· μάχην δ᾽ ἀμέγαρτον ἔγειραν
πάντες, θήλειαί τε καὶ ἄρσενες, ἤματι κείνῳ,
Τιτῆνές τε θεοὶ καὶ ὅσοι Κρόνου ἐξεγένοντο,
οὕς τε Ζεὺς Ἐρέβευσφιν [1] ὑπὸ χθονὸς ἧκε φόωσδε
δεινοί τε κρατεροί τε, βίην ὑπέροπλον ἔχοντες.

[1] DEFKLR : Ἐρέβεσφιν, GHI.

"Hear me, bright children of Earth and Heaven, that I may say what my heart within me bids. A long while now have we, who are sprung from Cronos and the Titan gods, fought with each other every day to get victory and to prevail. But do you show your great might and unconquerable strength, and face the Titans in bitter strife; for remember our friendly kindness, and from what sufferings you are come back to the light from your cruel bondage under misty gloom through our counsels."

So he said. And blameless Cottus answered him again: "Divine one, you speak that which we know well: nay, even of ourselves we know that your wisdom and understanding is exceeding, and that you became a defender of the deathless ones from chill doom. And through your devising we are come back again from the murky gloom and from our merciless bonds, enjoying what we looked not for, O lord, son of Cronos. And so now with fixed purpose and deliberate counsel we will aid your power in dreadful strife and will fight against the Titans in hard battle."

So he said: and the gods, givers of good things, applauded when they heard his word, and their spirit longed for war even more than before, and they all, both male and female, stirred up hated battle that day, the Titan gods, and all that were born of Cronos together with those dread, mighty ones of overwhelming strength whom Zeus brought up to the light from Erebus beneath the earth. An

τῶν ἑκατὸν μὲν χεῖρες ἀπ᾽ ὤμων ἀίσσοντο
πᾶσιν ὁμῶς, κεφαλαὶ δὲ ἑκάστῳ πεντήκοντα
ἐξ ὤμων ἐπέφυκον ἐπὶ στιβαροῖσι μέλεσσιν.
οἳ τότε Τιτήνεσσι κατέσταθεν ἐν δαῒ λυγρῇ
πέτρας ἠλιβάτους στιβαρῇς ἐν χερσὶν ἔχοντες.
Τιτῆνες δ᾽ ἑτέρωθεν ἐκαρτύναντο φάλαγγας
προφρονέως, χειρῶν τε βίης θ᾽ ἅμα ἔργον ἔφαινον
ἀμφότεροι· δεινὸν δὲ περίαχε πόντος ἀπείρων,
γῆ δὲ μέγ᾽ ἐσμαράγησεν, ἐπέστενε δ᾽ οὐρανὸς εὐρὺς
σειόμενος, πεδόθεν δὲ τινάσσετο μακρὸς Ὄλυμπος
ῥιπῇ ὕπ᾽ ἀθανάτων, ἔνοσις δ᾽ ἵκανε βαρεῖα
Τάρταρον ἠερόεντα, ποδῶν τ᾽ αἰπεῖα ἰωὴ
ἀσπέτου ἰωχμοῖο βολάων τε κρατεράων·
ὣς ἄρ᾽ ἐπ᾽ ἀλλήλοις ἵεσαν βέλεα στονόεντα.
φωνὴ δ᾽ ἀμφοτέρων ἵκετ᾽ οὐρανὸν ἀστερόεντα
κεκλομένων· οἳ δὲ ξύνισαν μεγάλῳ ἀλαλητῷ.
Οὐδ᾽ ἄρ᾽ ἔτι Ζεὺς ἴσχεν ἑὸν μένος, ἀλλά νυ τοῦ γε
εἶθαρ μὲν μένεος πλῆντο φρένες, ἐκ δέ τε πᾶσαν
φαῖνε βίην· ἄμυδις δ᾽ ἄρ᾽ ἀπ᾽ οὐρανοῦ ἠδ᾽ ἀπ᾽ Ὀλύμπου
ἀστράπτων ἔστειχε συνωχαδόν· οἱ δὲ κεραυνοὶ
ἴκταρ ἅμα βροντῇ τε καὶ ἀστεροπῇ ποτέοντο
χειρὸς ἄπο στιβαρῆς, ἱερὴν φλόγα εἰλυφόωντες
ταρφέες· ἀμφὶ δὲ γαῖα φερέσβιος ἐσμαράγιζε
καιομένη, λάκε δ᾽ ἀμφὶ πυρὶ μεγάλ᾽ ἄσπετος ὕλη.
ἔζεε δὲ χθὼν πᾶσα καὶ Ὠκεανοῖο ῥέεθρα
πόντος τ᾽ ἀτρύγετος· τοὺς δ᾽ ἄμφεπε θερμὸς ἀυτμὴ
Τιτῆνας χθονίους, φλὸξ δ᾽ αἰθέρα [1] δῖαν ἵκανεν

[1] Naber: ἠέρα, MSS.

hundred arms sprang from the shoulders of all alike, and each had fifty heads growing upon his shoulders upon stout limbs. These, then, stood against the Titans in grim strife, holding huge rocks in their strong hands. And on the other part the Titans eagerly strengthened their ranks, and both sides at one time showed the work of their hands and their might. The boundless sea rang terribly around, and the earth crashed loudly: wide Heaven was shaken and groaned, and high Olympus reeled from its foundation under the charge of the undying gods, and a heavy quaking reached dim Tartarus and the deep sound of their feet in the fearful onset and of their hard missiles. So, then, they launched their grievous shafts upon one another, and the cry of both armies as they shouted reached to starry heaven; and they met together with a great battle-cry.

Then Zeus no longer held back his might; but straight his heart was filled with fury and he showed forth all his strength. From Heaven and from Olympus he came forthwith, hurling his lightning: the bolts flew thick and fast from his strong hand together with thunder and lightning, whirling an awesome flame. The life-giving earth crashed around in burning, and the vast wood crackled loud with fire all about. All the land seethed, and Ocean's streams and the unfruitful sea. The hot vapour lapped round the earthborn Titans: flame unspeakable rose to the

ἄσπετος, ὄσσε δ' ἄμερδε καὶ ἰφθίμων περ ἐόντων
αὐγὴ μαρμαίρουσα κεραυνοῦ τε στεροπῆς τε.
καῦμα δὲ θεσπέσιον κάτεχεν Χάος· εἴσατο δ' ἄντα
ὀφθαλμοῖσιν ἰδεῖν ἠδ' οὔασι ὄσσαν ἀκοῦσαι
αὔτως, ὡς εἰ Γαῖα καὶ Οὐρανὸς εὐρὺς ὕπερθε
πίλνατο· τοῖος γάρ κε μέγας ὑπὸ δοῦπος ὀρώρει
τῆς μὲν ἐρειπομένης, τοῦ δ' ὑψόθεν ἐξεριπόντος·
τόσσος δοῦπος ἔγεντο θεῶν ἔριδι ξυνιόντων.
σὺν δ' ἄνεμοι ἔνοσίν τε κονίην τ' ἐσφαράγιζον
βροντήν τε στεροπήν τε καὶ αἰθαλόεντα κεραυνόν,
κῆλα Διὸς μεγάλοιο, φέρον δ' ἰαχήν τ' ἐνοπήν τε
ἐς μέσον ἀμφοτέρων· ὄτοβος δ' ἄπλητος ὀρώρει
σμερδαλέης ἔριδος, κάρτος δ' ἀνεφαίνετο ἔργων.
ἐκλίνθη δὲ μάχη· πρὶν δ' ἀλλήλοις ἐπέχοντες
ἐμμενέως ἐμάχοντο διὰ κρατερὰς ὑσμίνας.
Οἳ δ' ἄρ' ἐνὶ πρώτοισι μάχην δριμεῖαν ἔγειραν
Κόττος τε Βριάρεώς τε Γύης τ' ἄατος πολέμοιο,
οἵ ῥα τριηκοσίας πέτρας στιβαρῶν ἀπὸ χειρῶν
πέμπον ἐπασσυτέρας, κατὰ δ' ἐσκίασαν βελέεσσι
Τιτῆνας, καὶ τοὺς μὲν ὑπὸ χθονὸς εὐρυοδείης
πέμψαν καὶ δεσμοῖσιν ἐν ἀργαλέοισιν ἔδησαν
χερσὶν νικήσαντες ὑπερθύμους περ ἐόντας,
τόσσον ἔνερθ' ὑπὸ γῆς, ὅσον οὐρανός ἐστ' ἀπὸ γαίης·
τόσσον γάρ τ' ἀπὸ γῆς ἐς Τάρταρον ἠερόεντα.
ἐννέα γὰρ νύκτας τε καὶ ἤματα χάλκεος ἄκμων
οὐρανόθεν κατιὼν δεκάτῃ κ' ἐς γαῖαν ἵκοιτο·
ἐννέα δ' αὖ νύκτας τε καὶ ἤματα χάλκεος ἄκμων
ἐκ γαίης κατιὼν δεκάτῃ κ' ἐς Τάρταρον ἵκοι.
τὸν πέρι χάλκεον ἕρκος ἐλήλαται· ἀμφὶ δέ μιν νὺξ
τριστοιχεὶ κέχυται περὶ δειρήν· αὐτὰρ ὕπερθεν

bright upper air: the flashing glare of the thunder stone and lightning blinded their eyes for all that they were strong. Astounding heat seized Chaos: and to see with eyes and to hear the sound with ears it seemed even as if Earth and wide Heaven above came together; for such a mighty crash would have arisen if Earth were being hurled to ruin, and Heaven from on high were hurling her down; so great a crash was there while the gods were meeting together in strife. Also the winds brought rumbling earthquake and duststorm, thunder and lightning and the lurid thunderbolt, which are the shafts of great Zeus, and carried the clangour and the warcry into the midst of the two hosts. An horrible uproar of terrible strife arose: mighty deeds were shown and the battle inclined. But until then, they kept at one another and fought continually in cruel war.

And amongst the foremost Cottus and Briareos and Gyes insatiate for war raised fierce fighting: three hundred rocks, one upon another, they launched from their strong hands and overshadowed the Titans with their missiles, and hurled them beneath the wide-pathed earth, and bound them in bitter chains when they had conquered them by their strength for all their great spirit, as far beneath the earth as heaven is above earth; for so far is it from earth to Tartarus. For a brazen anvil falling down from heaven nine nights and days would reach the earth upon the tenth: and again, a brazen anvil falling from earth nine nights and days would reach Tartarus upon the tenth. Round it runs a fence of bronze, and night spreads in triple line all about it

γῆς ῥίζαι πεφύασι καὶ ἀτρυγέτοιο θαλάσσης.
ἔνθα θεοὶ Τιτῆνες ὑπὸ ζόφῳ ἠερόεντι
κεκρύφαται βουλῇσι Διὸς νεφεληγερέταο
χώρῳ ἐν εὐρώεντι, πελώρης ἔσχατα γαίης.
τοῖς οὐκ ἐξιτόν ἐστι. θύρας δ' ἐπέθηκε Ποσειδέων
χαλκείας, τεῖχος δὲ περοίχεται ἀμφοτέρωθεν.
ἔνθα Γύης Κόττος τε καὶ Ὀβριάρεως μεγάθυμος
ναίουσιν, φύλακες πιστοὶ Διὸς αἰγιόχοιο.
Ἔνθα δὲ γῆς δνοφερῆς καὶ Ταρτάρου ἠερόεντος
πόντου τ' ἀτρυγέτοιο καὶ οὐρανοῦ ἀστερόεντος
ἑξείης πάντων πηγαὶ καὶ πείρατ' ἔασιν
ἀργαλέ' εὐρώεντα, τά τε στυγέουσι θεοί περ,
χάσμα μέγ', οὐδέ κε πάντα τελεσφόρον εἰς ἐνιαυτὸν
οὖδας ἵκοιτ', εἰ πρῶτα πυλέων ἔντοσθε γένοιτο,
ἀλλά κεν ἔνθα καὶ ἔνθα φέροι πρὸ θύελλα θυέλλῃ
ἀργαλέη· δεινὸν δὲ καὶ ἀθανάτοισι θεοῖσι
τοῦτο τέρας.· Νυκτὸς δ' ἐρεβεννῆς οἰκία δεινὰ
ἕστηκεν νεφέλῃς κεκαλυμμένα κυανέῃσιν.
τῶν πρόσθ' Ἰαπετοῖο πάις ἔχει οὐρανὸν εὐρὺν
ἑστηὼς κεφαλῇ τε καὶ ἀκαμάτῃσι χέρεσσιν
ἀστεμφέως, ὅθι Νύξ τε καὶ Ἡμέρη ἆσσον ἰοῦσαι
ἀλλήλας προσέειπον, ἀμειβόμεναι μέγαν οὐδὸν
χάλκεον· ἣ μὲν ἔσω καταβήσεται, ἣ δὲ θύραζε
ἔρχεται, οὐδέ ποτ' ἀμφοτέρας δόμος ἐντὸς ἐέργει,
ἀλλ' αἰεὶ ἑτέρη γε δόμων ἔκτοσθεν ἐοῦσα
γαῖαν ἐπιστρέφεται, ἣ δ' αὖ δόμου ἐντὸς ἐοῦσα
μίμνει τὴν αὐτῆς ὥρην ὁδοῦ, ἔστ' ἂν ἵκηται,
ἣ μὲν ἐπιχθονίοισι φάος πολυδερκὲς ἔχουσα,

like a neck-circlet, while above grow the roots of the earth and unfruitful sea. There by the counsel of Zeus who drives the clouds the Titan gods are hidden under misty gloom, in a dank place where are the ends of the huge earth. And they may not go out; for Poseidon fixed gates of bronze upon it, and a wall runs all round it on every side. There Gyes and Cottus and great-souled Obriareus live, trusty warders of Zeus who holds the aegis.

And there, all in their order, are the sources and ends of gloomy earth and misty Tartarus and the unfruitful sea and starry heaven, loathsome and dank, which even the gods abhor. It is a great gulf, and if once a man were within the gates, he would not reach the floor until a whole year had reached its end, but cruel blast upon blast would carry him this way and that. And this marvel is awful even to the deathless gods.

There stands the awful home of murky Night wrapped in dark clouds. In front of it the son of Iapetus[1] stands immovably upholding the wide heaven upon his head and unwearying hands, where Night and Day draw near and greet one another as they pass the great threshold of bronze: and while the one is about to go down into the house, the other comes out at the door. And the house never holds them both within; but always one is without the house passing over the earth, while the other stays at home and waits until the time for her journeying come; and the one holds all-seeing light for them on earth, but the other holds in her arms Sleep the

[1] *sc.* Atlas, the Shu of Egyptian mythology: cp. note on line 177.

ἡ δ' Ὕπνον μετὰ χερσί, κασίγνητον Θανάτοιο,
Νὺξ ὀλοή, νεφέλῃ κεκαλυμμένη ἠεροειδεῖ.
Ἔνθα δὲ Νυκτὸς παῖδες ἐρεμνῆς οἰκί' ἔχουσιν,
Ὕπνος καὶ Θάνατος, δεινοὶ θεοί· οὐδέ ποτ' αὐτοὺς
Ἠέλιος φαέθων ἐπιδέρκεται ἀκτίνεσσιν
οὐρανὸν εἰς ἀνιὼν οὐδ' οὐρανόθεν καταβαίνων.
τῶν δ' ἕτερος γαῖάν τε καὶ εὐρέα νῶτα θαλάσσης
ἥσυχος ἀνστρέφεται καὶ μείλιχος ἀνθρώποισι,
τοῦ δὲ σιδηρέη μὲν κραδίη, χάλκεον δέ οἱ ἦτορ
νηλεὲς ἐν στήθεσσιν· ἔχει δ' ὃν πρῶτα λάβῃσιν
ἀνθρώπων· ἐχθρὸς δὲ καὶ ἀθανάτοισι θεοῖσιν.
Ἔνθα θεοῦ χθονίου πρόσθεν δόμοι ἠχήεντες
ἰφθίμου τ' Ἀίδεω καὶ ἐπαινῆς Περσεφονείης
ἑστᾶσιν, δεινὸς δὲ κύων προπάροιθε φυλάσσει
νηλειής, τέχνην δὲ κακὴν ἔχει· ἐς μὲν ἰόντας
σαίνει ὁμῶς οὐρῇ τε καὶ οὔασιν ἀμφοτέροισιν,
ἐξελθεῖν δ' οὐκ αὖτις ἐᾷ πάλιν, ἀλλὰ δοκεύων
ἐσθίει, ὅν κε λάβῃσι πυλέων ἔκτοσθεν ἰόντα.
[ἰφθίμου τ' Ἀίδεω καὶ ἐπαινῆς Περσεφονείης.[1]]
Ἔνθα δὲ ναιετάει στυγερὴ θεὸς ἀθανάτοισι,
δεινὴ Στύξ, θυγάτηρ ἀψορρόου Ὠκεανοῖο
πρεσβυτάτη· νόσφιν δὲ θεῶν κλυτὰ δώματα ναίει
μακρῇσιν πέτρῃσι κατηρεφέ'· ἀμφὶ δὲ πάντη
κίοσιν ἀργυρέοισι πρὸς οὐρανὸν ἐστήρικται.
παῦρα δὲ Θαύμαντος θυγάτηρ πόδας ὠκέα Ἶρις
ἀγγελίην πωλεῖται ἐπ' εὐρέα νῶτα θαλάσσης.
ὁππότ' ἔρις καὶ νεῖκος ἐν ἀθανάτοισιν ὄρηται
καί ῥ' ὅστις ψεύδηται Ὀλύμπια δώματ' ἐχόντων,
Ζεὺς δέ τε Ἶριν ἔπεμψε θεῶν μέγαν ὅρκον ἐνεῖκαι
τηλόθεν ἐν χρυσέῃ προχόῳ πολυώνυμον ὕδωρ

[1] This line (a repetition of 768) is not found in the better MSS.

brother of Death, even evil Night, wrapped in a vaporous cloud.

And there the children of dark Night have their dwellings, Sleep and Death, awful gods. The glowing Sun never looks upon them with his beams, neither as he goes up into heaven, nor as he comes down from heaven. And the former of them roams peacefully over the earth and the sea's broad back and is kindly to men; but the other has a heart of iron, and his spirit within him is pitiless as bronze: whomsoever of men he has once seized he holds fast: and he is hateful even to the deathless gods.

There, in front, stand the echoing halls of the god of the lower-world, strong Hades, and of awful Persephone. A fearful hound guards the house in front, pitiless, and he has a cruel trick. On those who go in he fawns with his tail and both his ears, but suffers them not to go out back again, but keeps watch and devours whomsoever he catches going out of the gates of strong Hades and awful Persephone.

And there dwells the goddess loathed by the deathless gods, terrible Styx, eldest daughter of back-flowing[1] Ocean. She lives apart from the gods in her glorious house vaulted over with great rocks and propped up to heaven all round with silver pillars. Rarely does the daughter of Thaumas, swift-footed Iris, come to her with a message over the sea's wide back. But when strife and quarrel arise among the deathless gods, and when any one of them who live in the house of Olympus lies, then Zeus sends Iris to bring in a golden jug the great oath of the gods

[1] Oceanus is here regarded as a continuous stream enclosing the earth and the seas, and so as flowing back upon himself.

ψυχρόν, ὅτ᾽ ἐκ πέτρης καταλείβεται ἠλιβάτοιο
ὑψηλῆς· πολλὸν δὲ ὑπὸ χθονὸς εὐρυοδείης
ἐξ ἱεροῦ ποταμοῖο ῥέει διὰ νύκτα μέλαιναν
Ὠκεανοῖο κέρας· δεκάτη δ᾽ ἐπὶ μοῖρα δέδασται·
ἐννέα μὲν περὶ γῆν τε καὶ εὐρέα νῶτα θαλάσσης
δίνῃς ἀργυρέῃς εἱλιγμένος εἰς ἅλα πίπτει,
ἡ δὲ μί᾽ ἐκ πέτρης προρέει μέγα πῆμα θεοῖσιν.
ὅς κεν τὴν ἐπίορκον ἀπολλείψας ἐπομόσσῃ
ἀθανάτων, οἳ ἔχουσι κάρη νιφόεντος Ὀλύμπου,
κεῖται νήυτμος τετελεσμένον εἰς ἐνιαυτόν·
οὐδέ ποτ᾽ ἀμβροσίης καὶ νέκταρος ἔρχεται ἆσσον
βρώσιος, ἀλλά τε κεῖται ἀνάπνευστος καὶ ἄναυδος
στρωτοῖς ἐν λεχέεσσι, κακὸν δέ ἑ κῶμα καλύπτει.
αὐτὰρ ἐπεὶ νοῦσον τελέσῃ μέγαν εἰς ἐνιαυτόν,
ἄλλος γ᾽ ἐξ ἄλλου δέχεται χαλεπώτερος ἄεθλος.
εἰνάετες δὲ θεῶν ἀπαμείρεται αἰὲν ἐόντων,
οὐδέ ποτ᾽ ἐς βουλὴν ἐπιμίσγεται οὐδ᾽ ἐπὶ δαῖτας
ἐννέα πάντα ἔτεα· δεκάτῳ δ᾽ ἐπιμίσγεται αὖτις
εἴρας ἐς ἀθανάτων, οἳ Ὀλύμπια δώματ᾽ ἔχουσιν.
τοῖον ἄρ᾽ ὅρκον ἔθεντο θεοὶ Στυγὸς ἄφθιτον ὕδωρ
ὠγύγιον, τὸ δ᾽ ἵησι καταστυφέλου διὰ χώρου.
  Ἔνθα δὲ γῆς δνοφερῆς καὶ Ταρτάρου ἠερόεντος
πόντου τ᾽ ἀτρυγέτοιο καὶ οὐρανοῦ ἀστερόεντος
ἑξείης πάντων πηγαὶ καὶ πείρατ᾽ ἔασιν
ἀργαλέ᾽ εὐρώεντα, τάτε στυγέουσι θεοί περ.
ἔνθα δὲ μαρμάρεαί τε πύλαι καὶ χάλκεος οὐδὸς
ἀστεμφής, ῥίζῃσι διηνεκέεσσιν ἀρηρώς,

from far away, the famous cold water which trickles down from a high and beetling rock. Far under the wide-pathed earth a branch of Oceanus flows through the dark night out of the holy stream, and a tenth part of his water is allotted to her. With nine silver-swirling streams he winds about the earth and the sea's wide back, and then falls into the main[1]; but the tenth flows out from a rock, a sore trouble to the gods. For whoever of the deathless gods that hold the peaks of snowy Olympus pours a libation of her water and is forsworn, lies breathless until a full year is completed, and never comes near to taste ambrosia and nectar, but lies spiritless and voiceless on a strewn bed: and a heavy trance overshadows him. But when he has spent a long year in his sickness, another penance and an harder follows after the first. For nine years he is cut off from the eternal gods and never joins their councils or their feasts, nine full years. But in the tenth year he comes again to join the assemblies of the deathless gods who live in the house of Olympus. Such an oath, then, did the gods appoint the eternal and primaeval water of Styx to be: and it spouts through a rugged place.

And there, all in their order, are the sources and ends of the dark earth and misty Tartarus and the unfruitful sea and starry heaven, loathsome and dank, which even the gods abhor. And there are shining gates and an immoveable threshold of bronze having unending roots and it is grown of itself.[2] And

[1] The conception of Oceanus is here different: he has nine streams which encircle the earth and the flow out into the "main" which appears to be the waste of waters on which, according to early Greek and Hebrew cosmology, the disk-like earth floated.

[2] *i.e.* the threshold is of "native" metal, and not artificial.

αὐτοφυής· πρόσθεν δὲ θεῶν ἔκτοσθεν ἀπάντων
Τιτῆνες *ναίουσι, πέρην* Χάεος *ζοφεροῖο.*
αὐτὰρ ἐρισμαράγοιο Διὸς *κλειτοὶ ἐπίκουροι*
δώματα ναιετάουσιν ἐπ' Ὠκεανοῖο *θεμέθλοις,*
Κόττος *τ' ἠδὲ* Γύης· Βριάρεών *γε μὲν ἠὺν ἐόντα*
γαμβρὸν ἑὸν ποίησε βαρύκτυπος Ἐννοσίγαιος,
δῶκε δὲ Κυμοπόλειαν *ὀπυίειν, θυγατέρα ἥν.*

Αὐτὰρ *ἐπεὶ* Τιτῆνας *ἀπ' οὐρανοῦ ἐξέλασεν* Ζεύς,
ὁπλότατον τέκε παῖδα Τυφωέα Γαῖα *πελώρη*
Ταρτάρου *ἐν φιλότητι διὰ χρυσέην* Ἀφροδίτην·
οὗ χεῖρες μὲν ἔασιν ἐπ' ἰσχύι, ἔργματ' ἔχουσαι,
καὶ πόδες ἀκάματοι κρατεροῦ θεοῦ· ἐκ δέ οἱ ὤμων
ἦν ἑκατὸν κεφαλαὶ ὄφιος, δεινοῖο δράκοντος,
γλώσσῃσιν δνοφερῇσι λελιχμότες, ἐκ δέ οἱ ὄσσων
θεσπεσίῃς κεφαλῇσιν ὑπ' ὀφρύσι πῦρ ἀμάρυσσεν·
πασέων δ' ἐκ κεφαλέων πῦρ καίετο δερκομένοιο·
φωναὶ δ' ἐν πάσῃσιν ἔσαν δεινῇς κεφαλῇσι
παντοίην ὄπ' ἰεῖσαι ἀθέσφατον· ἄλλοτε μὲν γὰρ
φθέγγονθ' ὥστε θεοῖσι συνιέμεν, ἄλλοτε δ' αὖτε
ταύρου ἐριβρύχεω, μένος ἀσχέτου, ὄσσαν ἀγαύρου,
ἄλλοτε δ' αὖτε λέοντος ἀναιδέα θυμὸν ἔχοντος,
ἄλλοτε δ' αὖ σκυλάκεσσιν ἐοικότα, θαύματ' ἀκοῦσαι,
ἄλλοτε δ' αὖ ῥοίζεσχ', ὑπὸ δ' ἤχεεν οὔρεα μακρά.
καί νύ κεν ἔπλετο ἔργον ἀμήχανον ἤματι κείνῳ
καί κεν ὅ γε θνητοῖσι καὶ ἀθανάτοισιν ἄναξεν,
εἰ μὴ ἄρ' ὀξὺ νόησε πατὴρ ἀνδρῶν τε θεῶν τε.
σκληρὸν δ' ἐβρόντησε καὶ ὄβριμον, ἀμφὶ δὲ γαῖα
σμερδαλέον κονάβησε καὶ οὐρανὸς εὐρὺς ὕπερθε
πόντος τ' Ὠκεανοῦ *τε ῥοαὶ καὶ τάρταρα γαίης.*

beyond, away from all the gods, live the Titans, beyond gloomy Chaos. But the glorious allies of loud-crashing Zeus have their dwelling upon Ocean's foundations, even Cottus and Gyes; but Briareos, being goodly, the deep-roaring Earth-Shaker made his son-in-law, giving him Cymopolea his daughter to wed.

But when Zeus had driven the Titans from heaven, huge Earth bare her youngest child Typhoeus of the love of Tartarus, by the aid of golden Aphrodite. Strength was with his hands in all that he did and the feet of the strong god were untiring. From his shoulders grew an hundred heads of a snake, a fearful dragon, with dark, flickering tongues, and from under the brows of his eyes in his marvellous heads flashed fire, and fire burned from his heads as he glared. And there were voices in all his dreadful heads which uttered every kind of sound unspeakable; for at one time they made sounds such that the gods understood, but at another, the noise of a bull bellowing aloud in proud ungovernable fury; and at another, the sound of a lion, relentless of heart; and at another, sounds like whelps, wonderful to hear; and again, at another, he would hiss, so that the high mountains re-echoed. (And truly a thing past help would have happened on that day, and he would have come to reign over mortals and immortals, had not the father of men and gods been quick to perceive it. But he thundered hard and mightily: and the earth around resounded terribly and the wide heaven above, and the sea and Ocean's streams and the nether parts of the earth. Great Olympus

ποσσὶ δ᾽ ὕπ᾽ ἀθανάτοισι μέγας πελεμίζετ᾽ Ὄλυμπος
ὀρνυμένοιο ἄνακτος· ἐπεστενάχιζε δὲ γαῖα.
καῦμα δ᾽ ὑπ᾽ ἀμφοτέρων κάτεχεν ἰοειδέα πόντον
βροντῆς τε στεροπῆς τε; πυρός τ᾽ ἀπὸ τοῖο πελώρου,
πρηστήρων ἀνέμων τε κεραυνοῦ τε φλεγέθοντος.
ἔζεε δὲ χθὼν πᾶσα καὶ οὐρανὸς ἠδὲ θάλασσα·
θυῖε[1] *δ᾽ ἄρ᾽ ἀμφ᾽ ἀκτὰς περί τ᾽ ἀμφί τε κύματα μακρὰ*
ῥιπῇ ὕπ᾽ ἀθανάτων, ἔνοσις δ᾽ ἄσβεστος ὀρώρει·
τρέε[2] *δ᾽ Ἀίδης, ἐνέροισι καταφθιμένοισιν ἀνάσσων,*
Τιτῆνές θ᾽ ὑποταρτάριοι, Κρόνον ἀμφὶς ἐόντες,
ἀσβέστου κελάδοιο καὶ αἰνῆς δηιοτῆτος.
Ζεὺς δ᾽ ἐπεὶ οὖν κόρθυνεν ἑὸν μένος, εἵλετο δ᾽ ὅπλα,
βροντήν τε στεροπήν τε καὶ αἰθαλόεντα κεραυνόν,
πλῆξεν ἀπ᾽ Οὐλύμποιο ἐπάλμενος· ἀμφὶ δὲ πάσας
ἔπρεσε θεσπεσίας κεφαλὰς δεινοῖο πελώρου.
αὐτὰρ ἐπεὶ δή μιν δάμασεν πληγῇσιν ἱμάσσας,
ἤριπε γυιωθείς, στενάχιζε δὲ γαῖα πελώρη.
φλὸξ δὲ κεραυνωθέντος ἀπέσσυτο τοῖο ἄνακτος
οὔρεος ἐν βήσσῃσιν ἀιδνῆς[3] *παιπαλοέσσῃς,*
πληγέντος. πολλὴ δὲ πελώρη καίετο γαῖα
ἀτμῇ θεσπεσίῃ καὶ ἐτήκετο κασσίτερος ὣς
τέχνῃ ὕπ᾽ αἰζηῶν ἐν ἐυτρήτοις χοάνοισι
θαλφθείς, ἠὲ σίδηρος, ὅ περ κρατερώτατός ἐστιν,
οὔρεος ἐν βήσσῃσι δαμαζόμενος πυρὶ κηλέῳ

[1] R: *θῦε*, MSS.
[2] Schol.: *τρέσσε*, MSS.
[3] MSS. and schol.: *Ἄιτνης*, Tzetzes.

reeled beneath the divine feet of the king as he arose and earth groaned thereat. And through the two of them heat took hold on the dark-blue sea, through the thunder and lightning, and through the fire from the monster, and the scorching winds and blazing thunderbolt. The whole earth seethed, and sky and sea: and the long waves raged along the beaches round and about, at the rush of the deathless gods: and there arose an endless shaking. Hades trembled where he rules over the dead below, and the Titans under Tartarus who live with Cronos, because of the unending clamour and the fearful strife. So when Zeus had raised up his might and seized his arms, thunder and lightning and lurid thunderbolt, he leaped from Olympus and struck him, and burned all the marvellous heads of the monster about him. But when Zeus had conquered him and lashed him with strokes, Typhoeus was hurled down, a maimed wreck, so that the huge earth groaned. And flame shot forth from the thunder-stricken lord in the dim rugged glens of the mount,[1] when he was smitten. A great part of huge earth was scorched by the terrible vapour and melted as tin melts when heated by men's art in channelled[2] crucibles; or as iron, which is hardest of all things, is sortened by glowing fire in mountain glens and

[1] According to Homer Typhoeus was overwhelmed by Zeus amongst the Arimi in Cilicia. Pindar represents him as buried under Aetna, and Tzetzes read Aetna in this passage.

[2] The epithet (which means literally *well-bored*) seems to refer to the spout of the crucible.

τήκεται ἐν χθονὶ δίῃ ὑφ' Ἡφαίστου παλάμῃσιν.
ὣς ἄρα τήκετο γαῖα σέλαι πυρὸς αἰθομένοιο.
ῥῖψε δέ μιν θυμῷ ἀκαχὼν ἐς Τάρταρον εὐρύν.
'Εκ δὲ Τυφωέος ἔστ' ἀνέμων μένος ὑγρὸν ἀέντων,
νόσφι Νότου Βορέω τε καὶ ἀργέστεω Ζεφύροιο·
οἵ γε μὲν ἐκ θεόφιν γενεή, θνητοῖς μέγ' ὄνειαρ·
οἱ δ' ἄλλοι μαψαῦραι ἐπιπνείουσι θάλασσαν·
αἳ δή τοι πίπτουσαι ἐς ἠεροειδέα πόντον,
πῆμα μέγα θνητοῖσι, κακῇ θυίουσιν ἀέλλῃ·
ἄλλοτε δ' ἄλλαι ἄεισι διασκιδνᾶσί τε νῆας
ναύτας τε φθείρουσι· κακοῦ δ' οὐ γίγνεται ἀλκὴ
ἀνδράσιν, οἳ κείνῃσι συνάντωνται κατὰ πόντον·
αἳ δ' αὖ καὶ κατὰ γαῖαν ἀπείριτον ἀνθεμόεσσαν
ἔργ' ἐρατὰ φθείρουσι χαμαιγενέων ἀνθρώπων
πιμπλεῖσαι κόνιός τε καὶ ἀργαλέου κολοσυρτοῦ.
Αὐτὰρ ἐπεί ῥα πόνον μάκαρες θεοὶ ἐξετέλεσσαν,
Τιτήνεσσι δὲ τιμάων κρίναντο βίηφι,
δή ῥα τότ' ὤτρυνον βασιλευέμεν ἠδὲ ἀνάσσειν
Γαίης φραδμοσύνῃσιν Ὀλύμπιον εὐρύοπα Ζῆν
ἀθανάτων· ὃ δὲ τοῖσιν ἑὰς διεδάσσατο τιμάς.

Ζεὺς δὲ θεῶν βασιλεὺς πρώτην ἄλοχον θέτο Μῆτιν
πλεῖστα θεῶν εἰδυῖαν ἰδὲ θνητῶν ἀνθρώπων.
ἀλλ' ὅτε δὴ ἄρ'[1] ἔμελλε θεὰν γλαυκῶπιν Ἀθήνην
τέξεσθαι, τότ' ἔπειτα δόλῳ φρένας ἐξαπατήσας
αἱμυλίοισι λόγοισιν ἑὴν ἐσκάτθετο νηδὺν
Γαίης φραδμοσύνῃσι καὶ Οὐρανοῦ ἀστερόεντος.

[1] Fick: δή ῥα, DGHI: δή ῥ', EF: δή ῥ' ἤμελλε, KL.

melts in the divine earth through the strength of Hephaestus.[1] Even so, then, the earth melted in the glow of the blazing fire. And in the bitterness of his anger Zeus cast him into wide Tartarus.

And from Typhoeus come boisterous winds which blow damply, except Notus and Boreas and clear Zephyr. These are a god-sent kind, and a great blessing to men; but the others blow fitfully upon the sea. Some rush upon the misty sea and work great havoc among men with their evil, raging blasts; for varying with the season they blow, scattering ships and destroying sailors. And men who meet these upon the sea have no help against the mischief. Others again over the boundless, flowering earth spoil the fair fields of men who dwell below, filling them with dust and cruel uproar.

But when the blessed gods had finished their toil, and settled by force their struggle for honours with the Titans, they pressed far-seeing Olympian Zeus to reign and to rule over them, by Earth's prompting. So he divided their dignities amongst them.

Now Zeus, king of the gods, made Metis his wife first, and she was wisest among gods and mortal men. But when she was about to bring forth the goddess bright-eyed Athene, Zeus craftily deceived her with cunning words and put her in his own belly, as Earth and starry Heaven advised. For they advised him

[1] The fire god. There is no reference to volcanic action: iron was smelted on Mount Ida; cp. *Epigrams of Homer*, ix. 2–4.

τως γάρ οἱ φρασάτην, ἵνα μὴ βασιληίδα τιμὴν
ἄλλος ἔχοι Διὸς ἀντὶ θεῶν αἰειγενετάων.
ἐκ γὰρ τῆς εἵμαρτο περίφρονα τέκνα γενέσθαι·
πρώτην μὲν κούρην γλαυκώπιδα Τριτογένειαν
ἶσον ἔχουσαν πατρὶ μένος καὶ ἐπίφρονα βουλήν.
αὐτὰρ ἔπειτ' ἄρα παῖδα θεῶν βασιλῆα καὶ ἀνδρῶν
ἤμελλεν τέξεσθαι, ὑπέρβιον ἦτορ ἔχοντα·
ἀλλ' ἄρα μιν Ζεὺς πρόσθεν ἑὴν ἐσκάτθετο νηδύν,
ὡς δή οἱ φράσσαιτο θεὰ ἀγαθόν τε κακόν τε.
  Δεύτερον ἠγάγετο λιπαρὴν Θέμιν, ἣ τέκεν Ὥρας,
Εὐνομίην τε Δίκην τε καὶ Εἰρήνην τεθαλυῖαν,
αἳ ἔργ' ὠρεύουσι καταθνητοῖσι βροτοῖσι,
Μοίρας θ', ᾗς πλείστην τιμὴν πόρε μητίετα Ζεύς,
Κλωθώ τε Λάχεσίν τε καὶ Ἄτροπον, αἵτε διδοῦσι
θνητοῖς ἀνθρώποισιν ἔχειν ἀγαθόν τε κακόν τε.
  Τρεῖς δέ οἱ Εὐρυνόμη Χάριτας τέκε καλλιπαρῄους,
Ὠκεανοῦ κούρη, πολυήρατον εἶδος ἔχουσα,
Ἀγλαΐην τε καὶ Εὐφροσύνην Θαλίην τ' ἐρατεινήν·
τῶν καὶ ἀπὸ βλεφάρων ἔρος εἴβετο δερκομενάων
λυσιμελής· καλὸν δέ θ' ὑπ' ὀφρύσι δερκιόωνται.
  Αὐτὰρ ὁ Δήμητρος πολυφόρβης ἐς λέχος ἦλθεν,
ἣ τέκε Περσεφόνην λευκώλενον, ἣν Ἀιδωνεὺς
ἥρπασε ἧς παρὰ μητρός· ἔδωκε δὲ μητίετα Ζεύς.
  Μνημοσύνης δ' ἐξαῦτις ἐράσσατο καλλικόμοιο,
ἐξ ἧς οἱ Μοῦσαι χρυσάμπυκες ἐξεγένοντο
ἐννέα, τῇσιν ἅδον θαλίαι καὶ τέρψις ἀοιδῆς.
  Λητὼ δ' Ἀπόλλωνα καὶ Ἄρτεμιν ἰοχέαιραν,
ἱμερόεντα γόνον περὶ πάντων Οὐρανιώνων,
γείνατ' ἄρ' αἰγιόχοιο Διὸς φιλότητι μιγεῖσα.

so, to the end that no other should hold royal sway over the eternal gods in place of Zeus; for very wise children were destined to be born of her, first the maiden bright-eyed Tritogeneia, equal to her father in strength and in wise understanding; but afterwards she was to bear a son of overbearing spirit, king of gods and men. But Zeus put her into his own belly first, that the goddess might devise for him both good and evil.

Next he married bright Themis who bare the Horae (Hours), and Eunomia (Order), Diké (Justice), and blooming Eirene (Peace), who mind the works of mortal men, and the Moerae (Fates) to whom wise Zeus gave the greatest honour, Clotho, and Lachesis, and Atropos who give mortal men evil and good to have.

And Eurynome, the daughter of Ocean, beautiful in form, bare him three fair-cheeked Charites (Graces), Aglaea, and Euphrosyne, and lovely Thaleia, from whose eyes as they glanced flowed love that unnerves the limbs: and beautiful is their glance beneath their brows.

Also he came to the bed of all-nourishing Demeter, and she bare white-armed Persephone whom Aïdoneus carried off from her mother; but wise Zeus gave her to him.

And again, he loved Mnemosyne with the beautiful hair: and of her the nine gold-crowned Muses were born who delight in feasts and the pleasures of song.

And Leto was joined in love with Zeus who holds the aegis, and bare Apollo and Artemis delighting in arrows, children lovely above all the sons of Heaven.

Λοισθοτάτην δ' Ἥρην θαλερὴν ποιήσατ' ἄκοι-
τιν·
ἡ δ' Ἥβην καὶ Ἄρηα καὶ Εἰλείθυιαν ἔτικτε
μιχθεῖσ' ἐν φιλότητι θεῶν βασιλῆι καὶ ἀνδρῶν.
Αὐτὸς δ' ἐκ κεφαλῆς γλαυκώπιδα Τριτογένειαν
δεινὴν ἐγρεκύδοιμον ἀγέστρατον ἀτρυτώνην
πότνιαν, ᾗ κέλαδοί τε ἅδον πόλεμοί τε μάχαι τε,
Ἥρη δ' Ἥφαιστον κλυτὸν οὐ φιλότητι μιγεῖσα
γείνατο, καὶ ζαμένησε καὶ ἤρισε ᾧ παρακοίτῃ,
ἐκ πάντων τέχνῃσι κεκασμένον Οὐρανιώνων.
<Ἥρη δὲ ζαμένησε καὶ ἤρισε ᾧ παρακοίτῃ.[1] 929[a]
ἐκ ταύτης δ' ἔριδος ἣ μὲν τέκε φαίδιμον υἱὸν
Ἥφαιστον, φιλότητος ἄτερ[2] Διὸς αἰγιόχοιο,
ἐκ πάντων παλάμῃσι κεκασμένον Οὐρανιώνων·
αὐτὰρ ὅ γ' Ὠκεανοῦ καὶ Τηθύος ἠυκόμοιο
κούρῃ νοσφ' Ἥρης παρελέξατο καλλιπαρήῳ,

* * * *

ἐξαπαφὼν Μῆτιν καίπερ πολυδήνε' ἐοῦσαν.
συμμάρψας δ' ὅ γε χερσὶν ἑὴν ἐγκάτθετο νηδὺν
δείσας, μὴ τέξῃ κρατερώτερον ἄλλο κεραυνοῦ.
τοὔνεκά μιν Κρονίδης ὑψίζυγος αἰθέρι ναίων
κάππιεν ἐξαπίνης· ἡ δ' αὐτίκα Παλλάδ' Ἀθήνην
κύσατο· τὴν μὲν ἔτικτε πατὴρ ἀνδρῶν τε θεῶν τε
πὰρ κορυφὴν Τρίτωνος ἐπ' ὄχθῃσιν ποταμοῖο.
Μῆτις δ' αὖτε Ζηνὸς ὑπὸ σπλάγχνοις λελαθυῖα
ἧστο, Ἀθηναίης μήτηρ, τέκταινα δικαίων
πλεῖστα θεῶν τε ἰδυῖα καταθνητῶν τ' ἀνθρώπων,
ἔνθα θεὰ παρέδεκτο ὅθεν[3] παλάμαις περὶ πάντων

[1] Restored by Peppmüller. The nineteen following lines from another recension of lines 889–900, 924–9 are quoted by Chrysippus (in Galen).
[2] Rzach: τέχνῃσιν ἄνευ, MSS.
[3] Hermann: παρέλεκτο Θέμις, MSS.

Lastly, he made Hera his blooming wife: and she was joined in love with the king of gods and men, and brought forth Hebe and Ares and Eileithyia.

But Zeus himself gave birth from his own head to bright-eyed Tritogeneia,[1] the awful, the strife-stirring, the host-leader, the unwearying, the queen, who delights in tumults and wars and battles. But Hera without union with Zeus—for she was very angry and quarrelled with her mate—bare famous Hephaestus, who is skilled in crafts more than all the sons of Heaven.

But Hera was very angry and quarrelled with her mate. And because of this strife she bare without union with Zeus who holds the aegis a glorious son, Hephaestus, who excelled all the sons of Heaven in crafts. But Zeus lay with the fair-cheeked daughter of Ocean and Tethys apart from Hera . . . deceiving Metis (Thought) although she was full wise. But he seized her with his hands and put her in his belly, for fear that she might bring forth something stronger than his thunderbolt: therefore did Zeus, who sits on high and dwells in the aether, swallow her down suddenly. But she straightway conceived Pallas Athene: and the father of men and gods gave her birth by way of his head on the banks of the river Trito. And she remained hidden beneath the inward parts of Zeus, even Metis, Athena's mother, worker of righteousness, who was wiser than gods and mortal men. There the goddess (Athena) received that[2] whereby she excelled in strength all the death-

[1] *i.e.* Athena, who was born "on the banks of the river Trito" (cp. l. 929[l]).

[2] *sc.* the aegis. Line 929[s] is probably spurious, since it disagrees with 929[q] and contains a suspicious reference to Athens.

ἀθανάτων ἐκέκασθ' οἳ Ὀλύμπια δώματ' ἔχουσιν,
[αἰγίδα ποιήσασα φοβέστρατον ἔντος Ἀθήνης·]
σὺν τῇ ἐγείνατό μιν πολεμήια τεύχε' ἔχουσαν.>

Ἐκ δ' Ἀμφιτρίτης καὶ ἐρικτύπου Ἐννοσιγαίου
Τρίτων εὐρυβίης γένετο μέγας, ὅστε θαλάσσης
πυθμέν' ἔχων παρὰ μητρὶ φίλῃ καὶ πατρὶ ἄνακτι
ναίει χρύσεα δῶ, δεινὸς θεός. αὐτὰρ Ἄρηι
ῥινοτόρῳ Κυθέρεια Φόβον καὶ Δεῖμον ἔτικτε
δεινούς, οἵτ' ἀνδρῶν πυκινὰς κλονέουσι φάλαγγας
ἐν πολέμῳ κρυόεντι σὺν Ἄρηι πτολιπόρθῳ,
Ἁρμονίην θ', ἣν Κάδμος ὑπέρθυμος θέτ' ἄκοιτιν.
Ζηνὶ δ' ἄρ' Ἀτλαντὶς Μαίη τέκε κύδιμον Ἑρμῆν,
κήρυκ' ἀθανάτων, ἱερὸν λέχος εἰσαναβᾶσα.
Καδμείη δ' ἄρα οἱ Σεμέλη τέκε φαίδιμον υἱὸν
μιχθεῖσ' ἐν φιλότητι, Διώνυσον πολυγηθέα,
ἀθάνατον θνητή· νῦν δ' ἀμφότεροι θεοί εἰσιν.
Ἀλκμήνη δ' ἄρ' ἔτικτε βίην Ἡρακληείην
μιχθεῖσ' ἐν φιλότητι Διὸς νεφεληγερέταο.
Ἀγλαΐην δ' Ἥφαιστος, ἀγακλυτὸς ἀμφιγυήεις,
ὁπλοτάτην Χαρίτων θαλερὴν ποιήσατ' ἄκοιτιν.
Χρυσοκόμης δὲ Διώνυσος ξανθὴν Ἀριάδνην,
κούρην Μίνωος, θαλερὴν ποιήσατ' ἄκοιτιν.
τὴν δέ οἱ ἀθάνατον καὶ ἀγήρω θῆκε Κρονίων.
Ἥβην δ' Ἀλκμήνης καλλισφύρου ἄλκιμος υἱός,
ἲς Ἡρακλῆος, τελέσας στονόεντας ἀέθλους,
παῖδα Διὸς μεγάλοιο καὶ Ἥρης χρυσοπεδίλου,
αἰδοίην θέτ' ἄκοιτιν ἐν Οὐλύμπῳ νιφόεντι,

less ones who dwell in Olympus, she who made the host-scaring weapon of Athena. And with it (Zeus) gave her birth, arrayed in arms of war.

And of Amphitrite and the loud-roaring Earth-Shaker was born great, wide-ruling Triton, and he owns the depths of the sea, living with his dear mother and the lord his father in their golden house, an awful god.

Also Cytherea bare to Ares the shield-piercer Panic and Fear, terrible gods who drive in disorder the close ranks of men in numbing war, with the help of Ares, sacker of towns; and Harmonia whom high-spirited Cadmus made his wife.

And Maia, the daughter of Atlas, bare to Zeus glorious Hermes, the herald of the deathless gods, for she went up into his holy bed.

And Semele, daughter of Cadmus was joined with him in love and bare him a splendid son, joyous Dionysus,—a mortal woman an immortal son. And now they both are gods.

And Alcmena was joined in love with Zeus who drives the clouds and bare mighty Heracles.

And Hephaestus, the famous Lame One, made Aglaea, youngest of the Graces, his buxom wife.

And golden-haired Dionysus made brown-haired Ariadne, the daughter of Minos, his buxom wife: and the son of Cronos made her deathless and unageing for him.

And mighty Heracles, the valiant son of neat-ankled Alcmena, when he had finished his grievous toils, made Hebe the child of great Zeus and gold-shod Hera his shy wife in snowy Olympus. Happy he! For he has finished his great work and lives

ὄλβιος, ὃς μέγα ἔργον ἐν ἀθανάτοισιν ἀνύσσας
ναίει ἀπήμαντος καὶ ἀγήραος ἤματα πάντα.
Ἠελίῳ δ' ἀκάμαντι τέκεν κλυτὸς Ὠκεανίνη
Περσηὶς Κίρκην τε καὶ Αἰήτην βασιλῆα.
Αἰήτης δ' υἱὸς φαεσιμβρότου Ἠελίοιο
κούρην Ὠκεανοῖο τελήεντος ποταμοῖο
γῆμε θεῶν βουλῇσιν Ἰδυῖαν καλλιπάρῃον.
ἡ δέ οἱ Μήδειαν ἐύσφυρον ἐν φιλότητι
γείναθ' ὑποδμηθεῖσα διὰ χρυσέην Ἀφροδίτην.

Ὑμεῖς μὲν νῦν χαίρετ', Ὀλύμπια δώματ' ἔχοντες,
νῆσοί τ' ἤπειροί τε καὶ ἁλμυρὸς ἔνδοθι πόντος.
νῦν δὲ θεάων φῦλον ἀείσατε, ἡδυέπειαι
Μοῦσαι Ὀλυμπιάδες, κοῦραι Διὸς αἰγιόχοιο,
ὅσσαι δὴ θνητοῖσι παρ' ἀνδράσιν εὐνηθεῖσαι
ἀθάναται γείναντο θεοῖς ἐπιείκελα τέκνα.
Δημήτηρ μὲν Πλοῦτον ἐγείνατο, δῖα θεάων,
Ἰασίων' ἥρωι μιγεῖσ' ἐρατῇ φιλότητι
νειῷ ἔνι τριπόλῳ, Κρήτης ἐν πίονι δήμῳ,
ἐσθλόν, ὃς εἶσ' ἐπὶ γῆν τε καὶ εὐρέα νῶτα θαλάσσης
πάντῃ· τῷ δὲ τυχόντι καὶ οὗ κ' ἐς χεῖρας ἵκηται,
τὸν δ' ἀφνειὸν ἔθηκε, πολὺν δέ οἱ ὤπασεν ὄλβον.
Κάδμῳ δ' Ἁρμονίη, θυγάτηρ χρυσέης Ἀφρο-
δίτης,
Ἰνὼ καὶ Σεμέλην καὶ Ἀγαυὴν καλλιπάρῃον
Αὐτονόην θ', ἣν γῆμεν Ἀρισταῖος βαθυχαίτης,
γείνατο καὶ Πολύδωρον ἐυστεφάνῳ ἐνὶ Θήβῃ.
Κούρη δ' Ὠκεανοῦ, Χρυσάορι καρτεροθύμῳ
μιχθεῖσ' ἐν φιλότητι πολυχρύσου Ἀφροδίτης,
Καλλιρόη τέκε παῖδα βροτῶν κάρτιστον ἁπάντων,
Γηρυονέα, τὸν κτεῖνε βίη Ἡρακληείη
βοῶν ἕνεκ' εἰλιπόδων ἀμφιρρύτῳ εἰν Ἐρυθείῃ.

amongst the undying gods, untroubled and unageing all his days.

And Perseïs, the daughter of Ocean, bare to unwearying Helios Circe and Aeëtes the king. And Aeëtes, the son of Helios who shows light to men, took to wife fair-cheeked Idyia, daughter of Ocean the perfect stream, by the will of the gods: and she was subject to him in love through golden Aphrodite and bare him neat-ankled Medea.

And now farewell, you dwellers on Olympus and you islands and continents and thou briny sea within. Now sing the company of goddesses, sweet-voiced Muses of Olympus, daughter of Zeus who holds the aegis,—even those deathless ones who lay with mortal men and bare children like unto gods.

Demeter, bright goddess, was joined in sweet love with the hero Iasion in a thrice-ploughed fallow in the rich land of Crete, and bare Plutus, a kindly god who goes everywhere over land and the sea's wide back, and him who finds him and into whose hands he comes he makes rich, bestowing great wealth upon him.

And Harmonia, the daughter of golden Aphrodite, bare to Cadmus Ino and Semele and fair-cheeked Agave and Autonoë whom long haired Aristaeus wedded, and Polydorus also in rich-crowned Thebe.

And the daughter of Ocean, Callirrhoë was joined in the love of rich Aphrodite with stout hearted Chrysaor and bare a son who was the strongest of all men, Geryones, whom mighty Heracles killed in sea-girt Erythea for the sake of his shambling oxen.

Τιθωνῷ δ' Ἠὼς τέκε Μέμνονα χαλκοκορυστήν,
Αἰθιόπων βασιλῆα, καὶ Ἠμαθίωνα ἄνακτα.
αὐτὰρ ὑπαὶ Κεφάλῳ φιτύσατο φαίδιμον υἱόν,
ἴφθιμον Φαέθοντα, θεοῖς ἐπιείκελον ἄνδρα.
τόν ῥα νέον τέρεν ἄνθος ἔχοντ' ἐρικυδέος ἥβης
παῖδ' ἀταλὰ φρονέοντα φιλομμειδὴς Ἀφροδίτη
ὦρτ' ἀναρεψαμένη, καί μιν ζαθέοις ἐνὶ νηοῖς
νηοπόλον νύχιον ποιήσατο, δαίμονα δῖον.
Κούρην δ' Αἰήταο διοτρεφέος βασιλῆος
Αἰσονίδης βουλῇσι θεῶν αἰειγενετάων
ἦγε παρ' Αἰήτεω, τελέσας στονόεντας ἀέθλους,
τοὺς πολλοὺς ἐπέτελλε μέγας βασιλεὺς ὑπερ-
ήνωρ,
ὑβριστὴς Πελίης καὶ ἀτάσθαλος, ὀβριμοεργός.
τοὺς τελέσας Ἰαωλκὸν ἀφίκετο, πολλὰ μογήσας,
ὠκείης ἐπὶ νηὸς ἄγων ἑλικώπιδα κούρην
Αἰσονίδης, καί μιν θαλερὴν ποιήσατ' ἄκοιτιν.
καί ῥ' ἥ γε δμηθεῖσ' ὑπ' Ἰήσονι, ποιμένι λαῶν,
Μήδειον τέκε παῖδα, τὸν οὔρεσιν ἔτρεφε Χείρων
Φιλυρίδης· μεγάλου δὲ Διὸς νόος ἐξετελεῖτο.
Αὐτὰρ Νηρῆος κοῦραι, ἁλίοιο γέροντος,
ἦ τοι μὲν Φῶκον Ψαμάθη τέκε δῖα θεάων
Αἰακοῦ ἐν φιλότητι διὰ χρυσέην Ἀφροδίτην,
Πηλέι δὲ δμηθεῖσα θεὰ Θέτις ἀργυρόπεζα
γείνατ' Ἀχιλλῆα ῥηξήνορα θυμολέοντα.
Αἰνείαν δ' ἄρ' ἔτικτεν ἐυστέφανος Κυθέρεια
Ἀγχίσῃ ἥρωι μιγεῖσ' ἐρατῇ φιλότητι
Ἴδης ἐν κορυφῇσι πολυπτύχου ὑληέσσης.
Κίρκη δ', Ἠελίου θυγάτηρ Ὑπεριονίδαο,
γείνατ' Ὀδυσσῆος ταλασίφρονος ἐν φιλότητι
Ἄγριον ἠδὲ Λατῖνον ἀμύμονά τε κρατερόν τε·

And Eos bare to Tithonus brazen-crested Memnon, king of the Ethiopians, and the Lord Emathion. And to Cephalus she bare a splendid son, strong Phaëthon, a man like the gods, whom, when he was a young boy in the tender flower of glorious youth with childish thoughts, laughter-loving Aphrodite seized and caught up and made a keeper of her shrine by night, a divine spirit.

And the son of Aeson by the will of the gods led away from Aeëtes the daughter of Aeëtes the heaven-nurtured king, when he had finished the many grievous labours which the great king, overbearing Pelias, that outrageous and presumptuous doer of violence, put upon him. But when the son of Aeson had finished them, he came to Iolcus after long toil bringing the coy-eyed girl with him on his swift ship, and made her his buxom wife. And she was subject to Iason, shepherd of the people, and bare a son Medeus whom Cheiron the son of Philyra brought up in the mountains. And the will of great Zeus was fulfilled.

But of the daughters of Nereus, the Old man of the Sea, Psamathe the fair goddess, was loved by Aeacus through golden Aphrodite and bare Phocus. And the silver-shod goddess Thetis was subject to Peleus and brought forth lion-hearted Achilles, the destroyer of men.

And Cytherea with the beautiful crown was joined in sweet love with the hero Anchises and bare Aeneas on the peaks of Ida with its many wooded glens.

And Circe the daughter of Helius, Hyperion's son, loved steadfast Odysseus and bare Agrius and Latinus who was faultless and strong: also she brought forth

[Τηλέγονον δ' ἄρ' ἔτικτε διὰ χρυσέην Ἀφροδίτην.[1]]
οἳ δή τοι μάλα τῆλε μυχῷ νήσων ἱεράων
πᾶσιν Τυρσηνοῖσιν ἀγακλειτοῖσιν ἄνασσον.
Ναυσίθοον δ' Ὀδυσῆι Καλυψὼ δῖα θεάων
γείνατο Ναυσίνοόν τε μιγεῖσ' ἐρατῇ φιλότητι.
Αὗται μὲν θνητοῖσι παρ' ἀνδράσιν εὐνηθεῖσαι
ἀθάναται γείναντο θεοῖς ἐπιείκελα τέκνα.

Νῦν δὲ γυναικῶν φῦλον ἀείσατε, ἡδυέπειαι
Μοῦσαι Ὀλυμπιάδες, κοῦραι Διὸς αἰγιόχοιο.

* * * *

ΚΑΤΑΛΟΓΟΙ ΓΥΝΑΙΚΩΝ. ΗΟΙΑΙ

1.

Scholiast on Apollonius Rhodius Arg. iii. 1086. ὅτι Προμηθέως καὶ Προνοίης[2] υἱὸς Δευκαλίων Ἡσίοδος ἐν πρώτῳ Καταλόγῳ φησί, καὶ ὅτι Δευκαλίωνος καὶ Πύρρας Ἕλλην.

2.

Ioannes Lydus,[3] *de Mens.* i. 13. Λατίνους μὲν τοὺς ἐπιχωριάζοντας, Γραικοὺς δὲ τοὺς ἑλληνίζοντας ἐκάλουν ἀπὸ Λατίνου . . . καὶ Γραίκου τῶν ἀδελφῶν, ὥς φησιν Ἡσίοδος ἐν Καταλόγοις·

[1] Omitted by D, Eustathius, and Laurentian Scholiast on Apollonius Rhodius iii. 200. [2] Sittl: Πανδώρας, scholiast.
[3] An antiquarian writer of Byzantium, c. 490–570 A.D.

Telegonus by the will of golden Aphrodite. And they ruled over the famous Tyrsenians, very far off in a recess of the holy islands.

And the bright goddess Calypso was joined to Odysseus in sweet love, and bare him Nausithoüs and Nausinoüs.

These are the immortal goddesses who lay with mortal men and bare them children like unto gods.

But now, sweet-voiced Muses of Olympus, daughters of Zeus who holds the aegis, sing of the company of women.

THE CATALOGUES OF WOMEN AND EOIAE[1]

1.

That Deucalion was the son of Prometheus and Pronoea, Hesiod states in the first *Catalogue*, as also that Hellen was the son of Deucalion and Pyrrha.

2.

They came to call those who followed local manners Latins, but those who followed Hellenic customs Greeks, after the brothers Latinus and Graecus; as Hesiod says:

[1] A catalogue of heroines each of whom was introduced with the words ἢ οἵη, "Or like her."

κούρη δ' ἐν μεγάροισιν ἀγαυοῦ Δευκαλίωνος
Πανδώρη Διὶ πατρί, θεῶν σημάντορι πάντων,
μιχθεῖσ' ἐν φιλότητι τέκεν Γραῖκον μενεχάρμην.

3.

Constantinus Porphyrogenitus,[1] *de Them*. 2 p. 48 B. Μακεδονία ἡ χώρα (ὠνομάσθη) ἀπὸ Μακεδόνος τοῦ Διὸς καὶ Θυίας τῆς Δευκαλίωνος, ὥς φησιν Ἡσίοδος·

ἡ δ' ὑποκυσαμένη Διὶ γείνατο τερπικεραύνῳ
υἷε δύω Μάγνητα Μακηδόνα θ' ἱππιοχάρμην,
οἳ περὶ Πιερίην καὶ Ὄλυμπον δώματ' ἔναιον.

* * * *

Μάγνης δ' αὖ Δίκτυν τε καὶ ἀντίθεον Πολυδεκτεα.

4.

Plutarch, *Mor*. p. 747 ; *Schol. on Pindar Pyth*. iv. 263.

Ἕλληνος δ' ἐγένοντο φιλοπτολέμου βασιλῆος
Δῶρός τε Ξοῦθός τε καὶ Αἴολος ἱππιοχάρμης.
Αἰολίδαι δ' ἐγένοντο θεμιστοπόλοι βασιλῆες
Κρηθεὺς ἠδ' Ἀθάμας καὶ Σίσυφος αἰολόμητις
Σαλμωνεύς τ' ἄδικος καὶ ὑπέρθυμος Περιήρης.

5.

Scholiast on Apollonius Rhodius, *Arg*. iv. 266. οἱ ἀπὸ Δευκαλίωνος τὸ γένος ἔχοντες ἐβασίλευον Θεσσαλίας, ὥς φησιν Ἑκαταῖος καὶ Ἡσίοδος.

6.

Idem, i. 482. Ἀλωιάδας . . . . Ἡσίοδος δὲ Ἀλωέως καὶ Ἰφιμεδείας κατ' ἐπίκλησιν, ταῖς δὲ ἀλη-

"And in the palace Pandora the daughter of noble Deucalion was joined in love with father Zeus, leader of all the gods, and bare Graecus, staunch in battle."

3.

The district Macedonia took its name from Macedon the son of Zeus and Thyia, Deucalion's daughter, as Hesiod says:

"And she conceived and bare to Zeus who delights in the thunderbolt two sons, Magnes and Macedon, rejoicing in horses, who dwell round about Pieria and Olympus. . . . And Magnes again (begot) Dictys and godlike Polydectes.

4.

"And from Hellen the war-loving king sprang Dorus and Xuthus and Aeolus delighting in horses. And the sons of Aeolus, kings dealing justice, were Cretheus, and Athamas, and clever Sisyphus, and wicked Salmoneus and overbold Perieres."

5.

Those who were descended from Deucalion used to rule over Thessaly as Hecataeus and Hesiod say.

6.

Aloïadae. Hesiod said they were sons of Aloëus,—called so after him,—and of Iphimedea, but in

[1] Constantine VII. "Born in the Porphyry Chamber," 905–959 A.D.

θείαις Ποσειδῶνος καὶ Ἰφιμεδείας ἔφη, καὶ Ἄλόν πόλιν Αἰτωλίας ὑπὸ τοῦ πατρὸς αὐτῶν ἐκτίσθαι.

7.

Berlin Papyri 7497 *and Oxyrhynchus Papyri*, 421.[1]

[Εὐρυνόμη Νίσου θυγάτηρ Παν]διονίδαο,
[τὴν πᾶσαν τέχνην ἐδιδ]άξατο Παλλὰς Ἀθήνη,
[μήδεα ἰδμοσύνην τ' ἐπί· οἶδ]ε [2] γαρ ἶσα θεοῖσι.
[θεσπεσίη δ' ὀδμὴ παρὰ εἵ]ματος ἀργυφεοῖο
[ὄρνυτο κινυμένης· βλεφάρων] δ' ἀπὸ εἶδος ἄητο.
[τῆς δ' ἄρ Γλαῦκος Ἀθηναί]ης πειρήσατο βουλαῖς,
βοῦς ἐλάσα[ς· ἀλλ' οὔ τι Διὸ]ς νόον αἰγιόχοιο
ἔγνω· ὁ μ[ὲν δώροις διζ]ήμενος ἦλθε γυναῖκα
βουλῇ Ἀθ[ηναίης· ὁ δ' ἄναξ] νεφεληγερέτα Ζεὺ[ς
ἀθανάτων [ἀνένευε κ]αρήατι μήποτ' ὀπάτ[ρους [3]
ἔσσεσθαι π[αῖδας . . .]ντου Σισυφίδαο.
ἡ δὲ Ποσε[ιδαῶνος ἐν] ἀγκοίνῃσι μιγεῖσα
Γλαύκου ἐν [4] [οἴκῳ ἔτικτεν] ἀμυμόνα Βελλ[εροφόντην
ἔξοχον ἀνθ[ρώπων . .]κτηι ἐπ' ἀπείρονα π[όντον.
τῷ δὲ καὶ ἠ[λάσκοντι πα]τὴρ πόρε Πήγασο[ν, ὃς δὴ
ὠκύτατον [πτερύγεσσι φέρων γέ] μιν ἔπτε[τ' ἀτειρὴς
πάντη ἀν[ὰ χθονὰ . . . ἐπεὶ ἠύτ' ἀ]ῆται ἴαλ[λε
σὺν τῷ πῦ[ρ πνείουσαν ἑλὼν κατέπεφνε Χίμειραν,
γῆμε δὲ π[αῖδα φίλην μεγαλητόρος Ἰοβάταο
αἰδοίου βασ[ιλῆος
κοίρανος α . . .
ἣ τέ[κε . . .

[1] *Berlin Papyri*, 7497 (left-hand fragment) and *Oxyrhynchus Papyri*, 421 (right-hand fragment). For the restoration see *Class. Quart.* vii. 217–8.

[2] οἶδ]ε :]τε, *Ox. Pap.* [3] ὄπα[τρους, ὀπασ]σαι, *Ox. Pap.*

[4] Γλαυκω εν (not ετ), *Berl. Pap.*

reality, sons of Poseidon and Iphimedea, and that Alus a city of Aetolia was founded by their father.

7.

"... Eurynome the daughter of Nisus, Pandion's son, to whom Pallas Athena taught all her art, both wit and wisdom too; for she was as wise as the gods. A marvellous scent rose from her silvern raiment as she moved, and beauty was wafted from her eyes. Her, then, Glaucus sought to win by Athena's advising, and he drove oxen[1] for her. But he knew not at all the intent of Zeus who holds the aegis. So Glaucus came seeking her to wife with gifts; but cloud-driving Zeus, king of the deathless gods, bent his head in oath that the ... son of Sisyphus should never have children born of one father.[2] So she lay in the arms of Poseidon and bare in the house of Glaucus blameless Bellerophon, surpassing all men in ... over the boundless sea. And when he began to roam, his father gave him Pegasus who would bear him most swiftly on his wings, and flew unwearying everywhere over the earth, for like the gales he would course along. With him Bellerophon caught and slew the fire-breathing Chimera. And he wedded the dear child of the great-hearted Iobates, the worshipful king ... lord (of) ... and she bare...."

[1] As the price to be given to her father for her: so in *Iliad* xviii. 593 maidens are called "earners of oxen." Possibly Glaucus, like Aias (fr. 68, ll. 55 ff.), raided (*βοῦς ἐλάσας*) the cattle of others.

[2] *i.e.* Glaucus should father the children of others. The curse of Aphrodite on the daughters of Tyndareus (fr. 67) may be compared.

8.

Scholiast on Apollonius Rhodius Arg. iv. 57. τὸν δὲ Ἐνδυμίωνα Ἡσίοδος μὲν Ἀεθλίου τοῦ Διὸς καὶ Καλύκης, παρὰ Διὸς εἰληφότα τὸ δῶρον

ἶν δ' αὐτῷ θανάτου ταμίης ὅτε μέλλοι ὀλέσθαι.

9.

Scholiast Ven. on Homer, Il. xi. 750. Ἀκτορίωνε Μολίονε. . . . Ἡσίοδος Ἄκτορος κατ' ἐπίκλησιν καὶ Μολιόνης αὐτοὺς γεγενεαλόγηκεν, γόνῳ δὲ Ποσειδῶνος.

Porphyrius, Quaest. Hom. ad Iliad. pert., 265. Ἀρίσταρχος δὲ διδύμους ἀκούει οὐχ . . . οἷοι ἦσαν καὶ οἱ Διόσκοροι, ἀλλὰ τοὺς διφυεῖς, δύω ἔχοντας σώματα, Ἡσιόδῳ μάρτυρι χρώμενος, καὶ τοὺς συμπεφυκότας ἀλλήλοις.

10.

Scholiast on Apollonius Rhodius, Arg. i. 156. Ἡσίοδος δὲ μεταβληθέντα εἴς τινα τῶν συνήθων μορφῶν ἐπικαθεσθῆναι τῷ ὀμφαλῷ τοῦ ζυγοῦ τῶν Ἡρακλέους ἵππων, βουλόμενον εἰς μάχην καταστῆναι τῷ ἥρωι, τὸν δὲ Ἡρακλέα καιρίως αὐτὸν κατατοξεῦσαι τῆς Ἀθηνᾶς ὑποδειξάσης. φησὶ δὲ οὕτως·

. . Περικλύμενόν τ' ἀγέρωχον
ὄλβιον, ᾧ πόρε δῶρα Ποσειδάων ἐνοσίχθων
παντοῖ'· ἄλλοτε μὲν γὰρ ἐν ὀρνίθεσσι φάνεσκεν
αἰετός, ἄλλοτε δ' αὖτε πέλέσκετο, θαῦμα ἰδέσθαι,
μύρμηξ, ἄλλοτε δ' αὖτε μελισσέων ἀγλαὰ φῦλα,
ἄλλοτε δ' αἰνὸς ὄφις καὶ ἀμείλιχος. εἶχε δὲ δῶρα

8.

Hesiod says that Endymion was the son of Aethlius the son of Zeus and Calyce, and received the gift from Zeus: "(To be) keeper of death for his own self when he was ready to die."

9.

The two sons of Actor and Molione. . . . Hesiod has given their descent by calling them after Actor and Molione; but their father was Poseidon.

But Aristarchus is informed that they were twins, not . . . such as were the Dioscuri, but, on Hesiod's testimony, double in form and with two bodies and joined to one another.

10.

But Hesiod says that he changed himself in one of his wonted shapes and perched on the yoke-boss of Heracles' horses, meaning to fight with the hero; but that Heracles, secretly instructed by Athena, wounded him mortally with an arrow. And he says as follows:

". . . and lordly Periclymenus. Happy he! For earth-shaking Poseidon gave him all manner of gifts. At one time he would appear among birds, an eagle; and again at another he would be an ant, a marvel to see; and again at another time a dread relentless snake. And he possessed all manner of

παντοῖ', οὐκ ὀνομαστά, τά μιν καὶ ἔπειτα δόλωσε
βουλῇ 'Αθηναίης.

11.

Stephanus of Byzantium, s.v. Γερηνία.

κτεῖνε δὲ Νηλῆος ταλασίφρονος υἱέας ἐσθλοὺς
ἕνδεκα, δωδέκατος δὲ Γερήνιος ἱππότα Νέστωρ
ξεῖνος ἐὼν ἐτύχησε παρ' ἱπποδάμοισι Γερηνοῖς.

* * * *

Νέστωρ οἶος ἄλυξεν ἐν ἀνθεμόεντι Γερήνῳ.

12.

Eustathius, Hom. 1796. 39.

Τηλεμάχῳ δ' ἄρ' ἔτικτεν ἐύζωνος Πολυκάστη,
Νέστορος ὁπλοτάτη κούρη Νηληιάδαο,
Περσέπολιν μιχθεῖσα διὰ χρυσέην 'Αφροδίτην.

13.

Scholiast on Homer, Od. xii. 69. Τυρὼ ἡ Σαλμωνέως ἔχουσα δύο παῖδας ἐκ Ποσειδῶνος, Νηλέα τε καὶ Πελίαν, ἔγημε Κρηθέα, καὶ ἴσχει παῖδας ἐξ αὐτοῦ τρεῖς, Αἴσονα καὶ Φέρητα καὶ 'Αμυθάονα. Αἴσονος δὲ καὶ Πολυμήδης καθ' Ἡσίοδον γίνεται 'Ιάσων.

Αἴσων, ὃς τέκεθ' υἱὸν 'Ιήσονα, ποιμένα λαῶν,
ὃν Χίρων ἔθρεψ' ἐνὶ Πηλίῳ ὑλήεντι.

14.

Petrie Papyri (ed. Mahaffy), Pl. III. 3.

ἀγακλε]ιτοῖο ἄνακτος
]ποδώκης δῖ' 'Αταλάντη
Σχοινῆος θυγάτηρ,] Χαρίτων ἀμαρύγματ' ἔχουσα,
ὡραίη περ ἐοῦσ' ἀπ]αναίνετο φῦλον ὁμοῖον
ἀνδρῶν βουλομένη φεύγε]ιν γάμον ἀλφηστάων.

gifts which cannot be told, and these then ensnared him through the devising of Athene."

11.

"(Heracles) slew the noble sons of steadfast Neleus, eleven of them; but the twelfth, the horseman Gerenian Nestor chanced to be staying with the horse-taming Gerenians. . . Nestor alone escaped in flowery Gerenon."

12.

"So well-girded Polycaste, the youngest daughter of Nestor, Neleus' son, was joined in love with Telemachus through golden Aphrodite and bare Persepolis."

13.

Tyro the daughter of Salmoneus, having two sons by Poseidon, Neleus and Pelias, married Cretheus, and had by him three sons, Aeson, Pheres and Amythaon. And of Aeson and Polymede, according to Hesiod, Iason was born.

"Aeson, who begot a son Iason, shepherd of the people, whom Chiron brought up in woody Pelion."

14.

". . . of the glorious lord . . . fair Atalanta, swift of foot, the daughter of Schoeneus, who had the beaming eyes of the Graces, though she was ripe for wedlock rejected the company of her equals and sought to avoid marriage with men who eat bread."

Scholiast on Homer, Iliad xxiii. 683. νεώτερος οὖν Ἡσίοδος γυμνὸν εἰσάγων Ἱππομένη ἀγωνιζόμενον Ἀταλάντῃ.

Papiri greci e latini, ii. No. 130 (2nd–3rd century).

Τῷ δ' ἄρ' ἐπ' αὐτίκ' ἔπειτα τ]ανίσφυρ[ος] ὤρνυτο κούρη[1]
ἔξοχον εἶδος ἔχουσ]α· πολὺς δ' ἀμφίσταθ' ὅμιλος
δεινὸν δερκομένη· θ]άμβος δ' ἔχε πάντας ὁρῶντας.
τῆς μὲν κινυμένης πν]οίη ζεφύροιο χιτῶνα
σιγαλόεντ' ἐλέλιξε πε]ρὶ στήθεσσ' ἁπαλοῖσι.
στῆ δ' αὖθ' Ἱππομένης· πολ]λὸς δ' ἐπεγείρετο λαός.
τοὶ δὴ ἀκὴν ἦσαν Σχ]οινεὺς δὲ γέγωνε βοήσας·
Κέκλυτέ μευ πάντες ἠμ]ὲν ν[έ]οι ἠδὲ γέροντες,
ὄφρ' εἴπω τά με θυμὸς] ἐνὶ στήθεσσι κελεύει.
Ἱππομένης μνηστεύει] ἐμὴν ἑλικώπιδα κούρην.
μῦθος δ' ὅσθ' ὑγιὴς νῦν] οἱ εἰρημένος ἔστω·
οὔ μιν ἀέθλου ἄτερ κεκτ]ήσεται. εἰ δέ κεν οὗτος
νικήσας θάνατόν τε φύγῃ καὶ] κῦδος ἀρέσθαι
ἀθάνατοι δώωσ' οἳ Ὀλύμ]πια δώματ' ἔχουσιν,
ἦ τοι νοστήσοντι φί]λην ἐς πατρίδα γαῖαν
παῖδα φίλην δώσω, ἔτι δ' ὠκυ]πόδων σθένος ἵππων,
τούς ῥα δόμονδ' ἄξει κει]μήλια· καί νύ κε θυμῷ
τερφθείη μὲν ἔχων, αἰεὶ] δ' ἀνιηρὸν ἄεθλον
μεμνέωτ' εὐφροσύνῃσι. πατὴρ] δ' ἀνδρῶν τε θεῶν τε

* * * *

[1] Slight remains of five lines precede line 1 in the original: after line 20 an unknown number of lines have been lost, and traces of a verse preceding line 21 are here omitted. Between lines 29 and 30 are fragments of six verses which do not suggest any definite restoration. The numbering of the original publication is given in brackets.

Hesiod is therefore later in date than Homer since he represents Hippomenes as stripped when contending with Atalanta.[1]

"Then straightway there rose up against him the trim-ankled maiden (Atalanta), peerless in beauty: a great throng stood round about her as she gazed fiercely, and wonder held all men as they looked upon her. As she moved, the breath of the west wind stirred the shining garment about her tender bosom; but Hippomenes stood where he was: and much people was gathered together. All these kept silence; but Schoeneus cried and said:

"'Hear me all, both young and old, while I speak as my spirit within my breast bids me. Hippomenes seeks my coy-eyed daughter to wife; but let him now hear my wholesome speech. He shall not win her without contest; yet, if he be victorious and escape death, and if the deathless gods who dwell on Olympus grant him to win renown, verily he shall return to his dear native land, and I will give him my dear child and strong, swift-footed horses besides which he shall lead home to be cherished possessions; and may he rejoice in heart possessing these, and ever remember with gladness the painful contest. May the father of men and of gods (grant that splendid children may be born to him[2])'

* * * *

[1] In the earliest times a loin-cloth was worn by athletes, but was discarded after the 14th Olympiad.

[2] The end of Schoeneus' speech, the preparations and the beginning of the race are lost.

δεξιτερῇ δ[. . . . .
κ]αί μιν ἐπαίσσων ἐπ[. . . . .
ἦχ' ὑποχωρήσας [ἐπ'] ἀριστερά. [τοῖς δ' ἀμέγαρτον
ἆθλον ἔκειθ'· ἡ μέν ῥα π[οδώκης δῖ' Ἀταλάντη
ἵετ' ἀναινομένη δῶρα [χρυσέης Ἀφροδίτης,
τῷ δὲ περὶ ψυχῆς πέλε[το δρόμος, ἠ μόρον εὑρεῖν
ἠ]ὲ φυγεῖν· τῷ καί ῥα δολ[οφρονέων προσέειπε·
Ὦ θύγατερ Σχοινῆος, ἀμ[είλιχον ἦτορ ἔχουσα,
δ]έξο τάδ' ἀγλαὰ δῶρα θε[ᾶς, χρυσέης Ἀφροδίτης

* * * *

αὐτὰρ ὁ [ῥίμφα πό]δεσσι μ[ετελθὼν ἧκε τὸ πρῶτον,
ἡ δ' αἶψ' ὥσθ' Ἅρπυια μετ[αστρεφθεῖσα τὸ μῆλον
ἔμμαρψ'· αὐτὰρ ὁ χειρὶ τὸ δεύτερον ἧ[κε χαμᾶζε.
καὶ δὴ ἔχεν δύο μῆλα ποδώκης δῖ' Ἀτ[αλάντη,
ἐγγὺς δ' ἦν τέλεος· ὁ δὲ τὸ τρίτον ἧκε [χαμᾶζε,
σὺν τῷ δ' ἐξέφυγεν θάνατον καὶ κ[ῆρα μέλαιναν
ἔστη δ' ἀμπνείων καὶ . . . .

15.

Strabo, i. p. 42.

καὶ κούρην Ἀράβοιο, τὸν Ἑρμάων ἀκάκητα
γείνατο καὶ Θρονίη, κούρη Βήλοιο ἄνακτος.

16.

Eustathius, Hom. 461. 2.

Ἄργος ἄνυδρον ἐὸν Δαναὸς ποίησεν ἔνυδρον.

17.

Hecataeus[1] *in Scholiast on Euripides, Orestes,* 872.

ὁ δὲ Αἴγυπτος αὐτὸς μὲν οὐκ ἦλθεν εἰς Ἄργος, παῖδας δὲ [ἀπέστειλεν], ὡς μὲν Ἡσίοδος ἐποίησε, πεντήκοντα.

[1] Of Miletus, flourished about 520 B.C. His work, a mixture of history and geography, was used by Herodotus.

"on the right . . . and he, rushing upon her, . . . drawing back slightly towards the left. And on them was laid an unenviable struggle: for she, even fair, swift-footed Atalanta, ran scorning the gifts of golden Aphrodite; but with him the race was for his life, either to find his doom, or to escape it. Therefore with thoughts of guile he said to her:

"'O daughter of Schoeneus, pitiless in heart, receive these glorious gifts of the goddess, golden Aphrodite . . .'

* * * *

"But he, following lightly on his feet, cast the first apple[1]: and, swiftly as a Harpy, she turned back and snatched it. Then he cast the second to the ground with his hand. And now fair, swift-footed Atalanta had two apples and was near the goal; but Hippomenes cast the third apple to the ground, and therewith escaped death and black fate. And he stood panting and . . ."

15.

"And the daughter of Arabus, whom worthy Hermaon begat with Thronia, daughter of the lord Belus."

16.

"Argos which was waterless Danaus made well-watered."

17.

Aegyptus himself did not go to Argos, but sent his sons, fifty in number, as Hesiod represented.

[1] Of the three which Aphrodite gave him to enable him to overcome Atalanta.

18.

Strabo,[1] viii. p. 370. καὶ Ἀπολλόδωρος . . . φησὶν . . . Ἡσίοδον μέντοι καὶ Ἀρχίλοχον ἤδη εἰδέναι καὶ Ἕλληνας λεγομένους τοὺς σύμπαντας καὶ Πανέλληνας, . . . περὶ τῶν Προιτίδων λέγοντα ὡς Πανέλληνες ἐμνήστευον αὐτάς.

Apollodorus, ii. 2. 1. 4. Ἀκρίσιος μὲν Ἄργους βασιλεύει, Προῖτος δὲ Τίρυνθος. καὶ γίνεται Ἀκρισίῳ μὲν ἐξ Εὐρυδίκης τῆς Λακεδαίμονος Δανάη, Προίτῳ δὲ ἐκ Σθενεβοίας

Λυσίππη [τε] καὶ Ἰφινόη καὶ Ἰφιάνασσα

αὗται δὲ . . . ἐμάνησαν, ὡς μὲν Ἡσίοδός φησιν, ὅτι τὰς Διονύσου τελετὰς οὐ κατεδέχοντο.

Probus[2] *on Vergil, Eclogue* vi. 48. Has, quod Iunonis contempserant numen, insania exterritas, quae crederent se boves factas, patriam Argos reliquisse, postea a Melampode Amythaonis filio sanatas.

Suidas s.v. μαχλοσύνη.

εἵνεκα μαχλοσύνης στυγερῆς τέρεν ὤλεσαν ἄνθος.

Eustathius, Hom. 1746. 7.

καὶ γάρ σφιν κεφαλῆσι κατὰ κνύος αἰνὸν ἔχευεν·
ἀλφὸς γὰρ χρόα πάντα κατέσχεθεν, ἐκ δέ νυ χαῖται
ἔρρεον ἐκ κεφαλέων, ψιλοῦτο δὲ καλὰ κάρηνα.

[1] The geographer ; fl. c. 24 B.C.
[2] Fl. 56–88 A.D.: he is best known for his work on Vergil.

18.[1]

And Apollodorus says that Hesiod already knew that the whole people were called both Hellenes and Panhellenes, as when he says of the daughters of Proetus that the Panhellenes sought them in marriage.

Acrisius was king of Argos and Proetus of Tiryns. And Acrisius had by Eurydice the daughter of Lacedemon, Danae; and Proetus by Stheneboea "Lysippe and Iphinoë and Iphianassa." And these fell mad, as Hesiod states, because they would not receive the rites of Dionysus.

These (the daughters of Proetus), because they had scorned the divinity of Juno, were overcome with madness, such that they believed they had been turned into cows, and left Argos their own country. Afterwards they were cured by Melampus, the son of Amythaon.

"Because of their hideous wantonness they lost their tender beauty . . . For he shed upon their heads a fearful itch: and leprosy covered all their flesh, and their hair dropped from their heads, and their fair scalps were made bare."

[1] The Hesiodic story of the daughters of Proetus can be reconstructed from these notices. They were sought in marriage by all the Greeks (Panhellenes), but having offended Dionysus (or, according to Servius, Juno), were afflicted with a disease which destroyed their beauty (or were turned into cows). They were finally healed by Melampus.

19.

Scholiast on Homer, Il. xii. 292. Εὐρώπην τὴν Φοίνικος Ζεὺς θεασάμενος ἔν τινι λειμῶνι μετὰ νυμφῶν ἄνθη ἀναλέγουσαν ἠράσθη καὶ κατελθὼν ἤλλαξεν ἑαυτὸν εἰς ταῦρον καὶ ἀπὸ τοῦ στόματος κρόκον ἔπνει· οὕτως τε τὴν Εὐρώπην ἀπατήσας ἐβάστασε καὶ διαπορθμεύσας εἰς Κρήτην ἐμίγη αὐτῇ· εἶθ' οὕτως συνῴκισεν αὐτὴν Ἀστερίωνι τῷ Κρητῶν βασιλεῖ· γενομένη δὲ ἔγκυος ἐκείνη τρεῖς παῖδας ἐγέννησε, Μίνωα, Σαρπηδόνα καὶ Ῥαδάμανθυν. ἡ ἱστορία παρ' Ἡσιόδῳ καὶ Βακχυλίδῃ.

20.

Scholiast on Apollonius Rhodius, Arg. ii. 178. ὡς δὲ Ἡσίοδός φησιν, (Φινεὺς) Φοίνικος τοῦ Ἀγήνορος καὶ Κασσιεπείας.

21.

Apollodorus,[1] iii. 14. 4. 1. Ἡσίοδος δὲ αὐτὸν (Ἄδωνιν) Φοίνικος καὶ Ἀλφεσιβοίας λέγει.

22.

Porphyrius,[2] *Quaest. Hom. ad Iliad. pert.* p. 189. ὡς παρ' Ἡσιόδῳ ἐν Γυναικῶν Καταλόγῳ ἐπὶ τῆς Ἀγήνορος παιδὸς Δημοδόκης

[Δημοδόκη] τὴν πλεῖστοι ἐπιχθονίων ἀνθρώπων
μνήστευον καὶ πολλὰ καὶ ἀγλαὰ δῶρ' ὀνόμηναν
ἴφθιμοι βασιλῆες, ἀπειρέσιον κατὰ εἶδος.

[1] Apollodorus of Athens (fl. 144 B.C.) was a pupil of Aristarchus. He wrote a Handbook of Mythology, from which the extant work bearing his name is derived.

[2] Porphyry, scholar, mathematician, philosopher and historian, lived 233–305 (?) A.D. He was a pupil of the neo-Platonist Plotinus.

19.

Zeus saw Europa the daughter of Phoenix gathering flowers in a meadow with some nymphs and fell in love with her. So he came down and changed himself into a bull and breathed from his mouth a crocus.[1] In this way he deceived Europa, carried her off and crossed the sea to Crete where he had intercourse with her. Then in this condition he made her live with Asterion the king of the Cretans. There she conceived and bore three sons, Minos, Sarpedon and Rhadamanthys. The tale is in Hesiod and Bacchylides.

20.

But according to Hesiod (Phineus) was the son of Phoenix, Agenor's son and Cassiopea.

21.

But Hesiod says that he (Adonis) was the son of Phoenix and Alphesiboea.

22.

As it is said in Hesiod in the Catalogue of Women concerning Demodoce the daughter of Agenor:

"Demodoce whom very many of men on earth, mighty princes, wooed, promising splendid gifts, because of her exceeding beauty."

[1] The crocus was to attract Europa, as in the very similar story of Persephone: cp. *Homeric Hymns* ii. lines 8 ff.

23.

Apollodorus, iii. 5. 6. 2. Ἡσίοδος δὲ δέκα μὲν υἱούς, δέκα δὲ θυγατερὰς (Ἀμφίονος καὶ Νιόβης).

Aelian,[1] *Var. Hist.* xii. 36. Ἡσίοδος δὲ (λέγει) ἐννέα (ἄρρενας) καὶ δέκα (κόρας), εἰ μὴ ἄρα οὐκ ἐστὶν Ἡσιόδου τὰ ἔπη, ἀλλ' ὡς πολλὰ καὶ ἄλλα κατέψευσται αὐτοῦ.

24.

Scholiast on Homer, Il. xxiii. 679. καὶ Ἡσίοδος δέ φησιν ἐν Θήβαις αὐτοῦ (Οἰδίποδος) ἀποθανόντος, Ἀργείαν τὴν Ἀδράστου σὺν ἄλλοις ἐλθεῖν ἐπὶ τὴν κηδείαν τοῦ Οἰδίποδος.

25.

Herodian[2] *in Etymologicum Magnum*, p. 60, 40. Εἰλαρίδην Τιτυόν.

26.

Argument: Pindar, Ol. xiv. Κηφισὸς δὲ ποταμὸς ἐν Ὀρχομενῷ, ἔνθα καὶ αἱ Χάριτες τιμῶνται· ταύταις Ἐτέοκλος ὁ Κηφισοῦ τοῦ ποταμοῦ πρῶτος ἔθυσεν, ὥς φησιν Ἡσίοδος·

Schol. on Homer, Il. ii. 522.
ὅστε Λιλαίηθεν προΐει καλλίρροον ὕδωρ.

Strabo, ix. 424.
ὅστε παρὲκ Πανοπῆα διὰ Γλήχωνά τ' ἐρυμνὴν
καί τε δι' Ἐρχομενοῦ εἱλιγμένος εἶσι δράκων ὥς.

27.

Scholiast on Homer, Il. vii. 9. ὁ γὰρ τοῦ Μενεσθίου πατὴρ Ἀρηίθοος Βοιωτὸς ἦν κατοικῶν Ἄρνην· ἔστι δὲ αὕτη Βοιωτίας, ὡς καὶ Ἡσίοδός φησιν·

23.

Hesiod says that (the children of Amphion and Niobe) were ten sons and ten daughters.

But Hesiod says they were nine boys and ten girls;—unless after all the verses are not Hesiod's but are falsely ascribed to him as are many others.

24.

And Hesiod says that when Oedipus had died at Thebes, Argea the daughter of Adrastus came with others to the funeral of Oedipus.

25.

Tityos the son of Elara.

26.

Cephisus is a river in Orchomenus where also the Graces are worshipped. Eteoclus the son of the river Cephisus first sacrificed to them, as Hesiod says: "which from Lilaea spouts forth its sweet-flowing water . . . And which flows on by Panopeus and through fenced Glechon and through Orchomenus, winding like a snake."

27.

For the father of Menesthius, Areïthoüs was a Boeotian living at Arnae: and this is in Boeotia, as also Hesiod says.

---

[1] Priest at Praeneste. He lived *c.* 170–230 A.D.

[2] Son of Apollonius Dyscolus, lived in Rome under Marcus Aurelius. His chief work was on accentuation.

28.

Stephanus of Byzantium.[1] Ὀγχηστός· ἄλσος· . . . κεῖται δὲ ἐν τῇ Ἁλιαρτίων χώρᾳ, ἱδρυθὲν δὲ ὑπὸ Ὀγχηστοῦ τοῦ Βοιωτοῦ, ὥς φησιν Ἡσίοδος.

29.

Stephanus of Byzantium. Αἰγά . . . ἔστι καὶ Αἰγαῖον πεδίον συνάπτον τῇ Κίρρᾳ, ὡς Ἡσίοδος.

30.

Apollodorus, ii. 1. 1. 5. Ἡσίοδος δὲ τὸν Πελασγὸν αὐτόχθονά φησιν εἶναι.

31.

Strabo, v. p. 221. τῷ δ' Ἐφόρῳ τοῦ ἐξ Ἀρκαδίας εἶναι τὸ φῦλον τοῦτο (τοὺς Πελασγούς) ἦρξεν Ἡσίοδος· φησὶ γάρ·

υἱέες ἐξεγένοντο Λυκάονος ἀντιθέοιο
ὅν ποτε τίκτε Πελασγός.

32.

Stephanus of Byzantium. Παλλάντιον· πόλις Ἀρκαδίας, ἀπὸ Πάλλαντος, ἑνὸς τῶν Λυκάονος παίδων, ὡς Ἡσίοδος.

33.

Φέλλον ἐυμμελίην τέκετο κλειτὴ Μελίβοια.

34.

Herodian, On Peculiar Diction, p. 18. παρ' Ἡσιόδῳ ἐν δευτέρῳ (Καταλόγῳ)

οἳ πρόσθε φανὴν ἔντοσθεν ἔκευθον.

[1] Author of a geographical lexicon, produced after 400 A.D., and abridged under Justinian.

28.

Onchestus: a grove.[1] It is situate in the country of Haliartus and was founded by Onchestus the Boeotian, as Hesiod says.

29.

There is also a plain of Aega bordering on Cirrha, according to Hesiod.

30.

But Hesiod says that Pelasgus was autochthonous.

31.

That this tribe (the Pelasgi) were from Arcadia, Ephorus states on the authority of Hesiod; for he says:

"Sons were born to god-like Lycaon whom Pelasgus once begot."

32.

Pallantium. A city of Arcadia, so named after Pallas, one of Lycaon's sons, according to Hesiod.

33.

"Famous Meliboea bare Phellus the good spearman."

34.

In Hesiod in the second Catalogue:

"Who once hid the torch[2] within."

[1] Sacred to Poseidon. For the custom observed there, cp. *Homeric Hymns* iii. 231 ff. [2] The allusion is obscure.

35.

Herodian, On Peculiar Diction, p. 42. Ἡσίοδος ἐν τρίτῳ (Καταλόγῳ)

νοῦθος δὲ ποδῶν ὑπόδουπος ὀρώρει.

36.

Apollonius Dyscolus,[1] *On the Pronoun*, p. 125.

σφὶν δ' αὐτοῖς μέγα πῆμα.

37.

Scholiast on Apollonius Rhodius, Arg. i. 45. οὔτε Ὅμηρος οὔτε Ἡσίοδος . . . λέγουσι τὸν Ἴφικλον σὺν τοῖς Ἀργοναύταις.

38.

"*Eratosthenes*,"[2] *Catast.* xix. p. 124. Κριός] οὗτος ὁ Φρίξον διακομίσας καὶ Ἕλλην· ἄφθιτος δὲ ὢν ἐδόθη αὐτοῖς ὑπὸ Νεφέλης τῆς μητρός· εἶχε δὲ χρυσῆν δοράν, ὡς Ἡσίοδος καὶ Φερεκύδης εἰρήκασιν.

39.

Scholiast on Apollonius Rhodius, Arg. ii. 181. πεπηρῶσθαι δὲ Φινέα φησὶν Ἡσίοδος ἐν μεγάλαις Ἠοίαις, ὅτι Φρίξῳ τὴν ὁδὸν ἐμήνυσεν, ἐν δὲ τῷ γ' Καταλόγῳ, ἐπειδὴ τὸν μακρὸν χρόνον τῆς ὄψεως προέκρινεν.

Ib. παῖδας δέ φησιν αὐτῷ γενέσθαι Ἡσίοδος δύο, Θυνὸν καὶ Μαριανδυνόν.

[1] Apollonius "the Crabbed" was a grammarian of Alexandria under Hadrian. He wrote largely on Grammar and Syntax.

35.

Hesiod in the third Catalogue writes:

"And a resounding thud of feet rose up."

36.

"And a great trouble to themselves."

37.

Neither Homer nor Hesiod speak of Iphiclus as amongst the Argonauts.

38.

The Ram. This it was that transported Phrixus and Helle. It was immortal and was given them by their mother Nephele, and had a golden fleece, as Hesiod and Pherecydes say.

39.

Hesiod in the Great Eoiae says that Phineus was blinded because he revealed to Phrixus the road; but in the third Catalogue, because he preferred long life to sight.

Hesiod says he had two sons, Thynus and Mariandynus.

---

[2] 275–195 (?) B.C., mathematician, astronomer, scholar, and head of the Library at Alexandria.

Ephorus[1] *in Strabo*, vii. 302. Ἡσίοδον δ' ἐν τῇ καλουμένῃ γῆς περιόδῳ τὸν Φινέα ὑπὸ τῶν Ἁρπυιῶν ἄγεσθαι—

γλακτοφάγων ἐς γαῖαν ἀπήνας οἰκί' ἐχόντων.

40.

Strabo, vii. p. 300.
Αἰθίοπάς τε Λίγυς τε ἰδὲ Σκύθας ἱππημολγούς.

41.

Apollodorus, i. 9. 21. 6. διωκομένων δὲ τῶν Ἁρπυιῶν ἡ μὲν κατὰ Πελοπόννησον εἰς τὸν Τίγρην ποταμὸν ἐμπίπτει, ὃς νῦν ἀπ' ἐκείνης Ἅρπυς καλεῖται· ταύτην δὲ οἱ μὲν Νικοθόην, οἱ δὲ Ἀελλόπουν καλοῦσιν. ἡ δὲ ἑτέρα καλουμένη Ὠκυπέτη, ὡς δὲ ἔνιοι Ὠκυθόη (Ἡσίοδος δὲ λέγει αὐτὴν Ὠκυπόδην), αὕτη κατὰ τὴν Προποντίδα φεύγουσα μέχρι Ἐχινάδων ἦλθε νήσων, αἳ νῦν ἀπ' ἐκείνης Στροφάδες καλοῦνται.

42.

Scholiast on Apollonius Rhodius, Arg. ii. 297, 296. ὅτι δὲ ηὔξαντο οἱ περὶ Ζήτην τῷ Διί στραφέντες λέγει καὶ Ἡσίοδος·

ἔνθ' οἵ γ' εὐχέσθην Αἰνηίῳ ὑψιμέδοντι.

Ἀπολλώνιος μὲν οὖν τὴν ἀποστρέψασαν τοὺς περὶ Ζήτην Ἶριν λέγει, Ἡσίοδος δὲ Ἑρμῆν.

οἱ δὲ Στροφάδας φασὶν αὐτὰς κεκλῆσθαι, καθὸ ἐπιστραφέντες αὐτόθι ηὔξαντο τῷ Διὶ καταλαβεῖν

[1] Of Cyme. He wrote a universal history covering the period between the Dorian Migration and 340 B.C.

Hesiod, in the so-called Journey round the Earth, says that Phineus was brought by the Harpies "to the land of milk-feeders[1] who have waggons for houses."

40.

"The Aethiopians and Ligurians and mare-milking Scythians."

41.

As they were being pursued, one of the Harpies fell into the river Tigres, in Peloponnesus which is now called Harpys after her. Some call this one Nicothoë, and others Aëllopus. The other who was called Ocypete, or as some say Ocythoë (though Hesiod calls her Ocypus), fled down the Propontis and reached as far as to the Echinades islands which are now called because of her, Strophades (Turning Islands).

42.

Hesiod also says that those with Zetes[2] turned and prayed to Zeus:

"There they prayed to the lord of Aenos who reigns on high."

Apollonius indeed says it was Iris who made Zetes and his following turn away, but Hesiod says Hermes.

Others say (the islands) were called Strophades, because they turned there and prayed Zeus to seize

[1] *i.e.* the nomad Scythians, who are described by Herodotus as feeding on mares' milk and living in caravans.

[2] Zetes and Calais, sons of Boreas, who were amongst the Argonauts, delivered Phineus from the Harpies. The Strophades ("Islands of Turning") are here supposed to have been so called because the sons of Boreas were there turned back by Iris from pursuing the Harpies.

τὰς Ἁρπυίας. κατὰ δὲ Ἡσίοδον . . . οὐ κτείνονται.

43.

Philodemus,[1] *On Piety*, 10. οὐδ' Ἡσιόδῳ μή τις ἐγγελᾷ, ὃς . . . ἢ καὶ τῶν Κατουδαίων καὶ τῶν Πυγμαίων μνημονεύει.

44.

Strabo, i. p. 43. Ἡσιόδου δ' οὐκ ἄν τις αἰτιάσαιτο ἄγνοιαν Ἡμίκυνας λέγοντος καὶ Μακροκεφάλους καὶ Πυγμαίους.

45.

Scholiast on Apollonius Rhodius, Arg. iv. 284. Ἡσίοδος δὲ διὰ Φάσιδος αὐτοὺς (τοὺς Ἀργοναύτας) εἰσπεπλευκέναι λέγει.

Id. iv. 259. Ἡσίοδος δὲ . . . διὰ τοῦ Ὠκεανοῦ . . . ἐλθεῖν αὐτοὺς εἰς Λιβύην καὶ βαστάσαντες τὴν Ἀργὼ εἰς τὸ ἡμέτερον πέλαγος γενέσθαι.

46.

Id. iii. 311. φησὶ δὲ Ἀπολλώνιος Ἡσιόδῳ ἑπόμενος ἐπὶ τοῦ ἅρματος τοῦ Ἡλίου εἰς τὴν κατὰ Τυρρηνίαν κειμένην νῆσον τὴν Κίρκην ἐλθεῖν· Ἑσπερίαν δὲ αὐτὴν εἶπεν, ἐπεὶ πρὸς δυσμὰς κεῖται.

47.

Scholiast on Apollonius Rhodius, Arg. iv. 892. ἠκολούθησεν Ἡσιόδῳ οὕτως ὀνομάζοντι τὴν νῆσον τῶν Σειρήνων—

νῆσον ἐς Ἀνθεμόεσσαν, ἵνα σφίσι δῶκε Κρονίων.

ὀνόματα δὲ αὐτῶν, Θελξιόπη ἢ Θελξινόη, Μολπή, Ἀγλαόφωνος.

[1] An Epicurean philosopher, fl. 50 B.C.

the Harpies. But according to Hesiod . . . they were not killed.

43.

Nor let anyone mock at Hesiod who mentions . . . or even the Troglodytes and the Pygmies.

44.

No one would accuse Hesiod of ignorance though he speaks of the Half-dog people and the Great-Headed people and the Pygmies.

45.

But Hesiod says they (the Argonauts) had sailed in through the Phasis.

But Hesiod (says) . . . they came through the Ocean to Libya, and so, carrying the Argo, reached our sea.

46.

Apollonius, following Hesiod, says that Circe came to the island over against Tyrrhenia on the chariot of the Sun. And he called it Hesperian, because it lies towards the west.

47.

He (Apollonius) followed Hesiod who thus names the island of the Sirens:

"To the island Anthemoessa (Flowery) which the son of Cronos gave them."

And their names are Thelxiope or Thelxinoe, Molpe and Aglaophonus.[1]

[1] "Charming-with-her-voice" (or "Charming-the-mind"), "Song," and "Lovely-sounding."

Scholiast on Homer, Od. xii. 168. ἐντεῦθεν Ἡσίοδος καὶ τοὺς ἀνέμους θέλγειν αὐτὰς ἔφη.

48.

Scholiast on Homer, Od. i. 85. τὴν μὲν γὰρ Ὠγυγίαν ἐντὸς εἶναι πρὸς ἑσπέραν, τὴν δὲ Ὠγυλίαν κατὰ Κρήτην Ἡσίοδός φησι κεῖσθαι·

[πόν]τον δ' Ὠγύλιον ἠδ' Ὠγυλίην . . . . νῆσον.

49.

Id. Od. vii. 54. Ἡσίοδος δὲ ἀδελφὴν Ἀλκινόου τὴν Ἀρήτην ὑπέλαβεν.

50.

Schol. on Pindar, Ol. x. 46.

τὴν δ' Ἀμαρυγκείδης Ἱππόστρατος, ὄζος Ἄρηος,
Φυκτέος ἀγλαὸς υἱός, Ἐπειῶν ὄρχαμος ἀνδρῶν . . .

51.

Apollodorus i. 8. 4. 1. Ἀλθαίας δὲ ἀποθανούσης ἔγημεν Οἰνεὺς Περίβοιαν τὴν Ἱππονόου. ταύτην δὲ . . . Ἡσίοδος . . . ἐξ Ὠλένου τῆς Ἀχαίας, ἐφθαρμένην ὑπὸ Ἱπποστράτου τοῦ Ἀμαρυγκέως, Ἱππόνουν τὸν πατέρα πέμψαι πρὸς Οἰνέα πόρρω τῆς Ἑλλάδος ὄντα ἐντειλάμενον ἀποκτεῖναι.

ᾤκεε δ' Ὠλενίην πέτρην ποταμοῖο παρ' ὄχθας
εὐρῆος Πείροιο.

52.

Diodorus[1] v. 81. ἦν δ' ὁ Μακαρεὺς υἱὸς μὲν Κρινάκου τοῦ Διός, ὥς φησιν Ἡσίοδος . . ., κατοικῶν δ' ἐν Ὠλένῳ τῆς τότε μὲν Ἰάδος, νῦν δ' Ἀχαίας καλουμένης.

[1] Diodorus Siculus, fl. 8 B.C., author of an universal history ending with Caesar's Gallic Wars.

Hence Hesiod said that they charmed even the winds.

8.

Hesiod says that Ogygia is within towards the west, but Ogylia lies over against Crete: ". . . the Ogylian sea and . . . the island Ogylia."

49.

Hesiod regarded Arete as the sister of Alcinous.

50.

Her Hippostratus (did wed), a scion of Ares, the splendid son of Phyctes, of the line of Amarynces, leader of the Epeians.

51.

When Althea was dead, Oeneus married Periboea, the daughter of Hipponoüs. Hesiod says that she was seduced by Hippostratus the son of Amarynces and that her father Hipponoüs sent her from Olenus in Achaea to Oeneus because he was far away from Hellas, bidding him kill her.

"She used to dwell on the cliff of Olenus by the banks of wide Peirus."

52.

Macareus was a son of Crinacus the son of Zeus as Hesiod says . . . and dwelt in Olenus in the country then called Ionian, but now Achaean.

53.

Scholiast on Pindar, Nem. iii. 21. περὶ τῶν Μυρμιδόνων Ἡσίοδος μὲν οὕτω φησίν·

ἡ δ' ὑποκυσαμένη τέκεν Αἰακὸν ἱππιοχάρμην.
αὐτὰρ ἐπεί ῥ' ἥβης πολυηράτου ἵκετο μέτρον,
μοῦνος ἐὼν ἤσχαλλε· πατὴρ δ' ἀνδρῶν τε θεῶν τε,
ὅσσοι ἔσαν μύρμηκες ἐπηράτου ἔνδοθι νήσου,
τοὺς ἄνδρας ποίησε βαθυζώνους τε γυναῖκας.
οἳ δή τοι πρῶτοι ζεῦξαν νέας ἀμφιελίσσας,
πρῶτοι δ' ἱστί' ἔθεν νηὸς πτερὰ ποντοπόροιο.

54.

Polybius v. 2.

Αἰακίδας πολέμῳ κεχαρηότας ἠύτε δαιτί.

55.

Porphyrius, Quaest. Hom. ad Iliad. pertin. p. 93. συντόμως δὲ τὰ αἰσχρὰ δεδήλωκε μιγῆναι οὐκ ἐθελούσῃ, ἀλλ' οὐχ ὥσπερ Ἡσίοδος τὰ περὶ τοῦ Πηλέως καὶ τῆς Ἀκάστου γυναικὸς διὰ μακρῶν ἐπεξελθών.

56.

Schol. on Pindar, Nem. iv. 95.

ἥδε δέ οἱ κατὰ θυμὸν ἀρίστη φαίνετο βουλή,
αὐτὸν μὲν σχέσθαι, κρύψαι δ' ἀδόκητα μάχαιραν
καλήν, ἥν οἱ ἔτευξε περικλυτὸς Ἀμφιγυήεις,
ὡς τὴν μαστεύων οἶος κατὰ Πήλιον αἰπὺ
αἶψ' ὑπὸ Κενταύροισιν ὀρεσκῴοισι δαμείη

57.

Voll. Herculan. (Papyri from Herculaneum), 2nd Collection, viii. 105. ὁ δὲ τὰ Κύπρια ποιήσας Ἥρᾳ

53.

Concerning the Myrmidons Hesiod speaks thus: "And she conceived and bare Aeacus, delighting in horses. Now when he came to the full measure of desired youth, he chafed at being alone. And the father of men and gods made all the ants that were in the lovely isle into men and wide-girdled women. These were the first who fitted with thwarts ships with curved sides, and the first who used sails, the wings of a sea-going ship."

54.

"The sons of Aeacus who rejoiced in battle as though a feast."

55.

He has indicated the shameful deed briefly by the phrase "to lie with her against her will," and not like Hesiod who recounts at length the story of Peleus and the wife of Acastus.

56.

"And this seemed to him (Acastus) in his mind the best plan; to keep back himself, but to hide beyond guessing the beautiful knife which the very famous Lame One had made for him, that in seeking it alone over steep Pelion, he (Peleus) might be slain forthwith by the mountain-bred Centaurs.

57.

The author of the *Cypria*[1] says that Thetis avoided

[1] The first epic in the "Trojan Cycle": like all ancient epics it was ascribed to Homer, but also, with more probability, to Stasinus of Cyprus.

χαριζομένην (Θέτιν) φεύγειν αὐτοῦ (Διὸς) τὸν γάμον· Δία δὲ ὀμόσαι χολωθέντα διότι θνητῷ συνοικίσει. καὶ παρ' Ἡσιόδῳ δὲ κεῖται τὸ παραπλήσιον.

58.

Strassburg Greek Papyri 55 (2nd cent. A.D.).

Φθίην ἐξίκετο, μητέρα μήλων,
πολλὰ κ]τήματ' ἄγων ἐξ εὐρυχόρου Ἰαωλκοῦ
Πηλεὺς] Αἰακίδης, φίλος ἀθανάτοισι θεοῖσιν,
λαοῖσιν] δὲ ἰδοῦσιν ἀγαίετο θυμὸς ἅπασιν,
ὥς τε πό]λιν ἀλάπαξεν ἐύκτιτον ὥς τ' ἐτέλεσσεν
ἱμερόεντα γά]μον· καὶ τοῦτ' ἔπος εἶπαν ἅπαντες·
Τρὶς μάκαρ Αἰακίδη καὶ τετράκις, ὄλβιε Πηλεῦ,
ᾧ τ' ἄλοχον πολύ]δωρον Ὀλύμπιος εὐρύοπα Ζεὺς
ὤπασεν ἠδὲ γάμον μ]άκαρες θεοὶ ἐξετέλεσσαν,
ὃς τοῖσδ' ἐν μεγάροις ἱερὸν λέχος εἰσαναβαίνεις[1]
Νηρεΐδος· μάλα δή σε πα]τὴρ ποίησε Κρονίων
ἔξοχον ἡρώων περί] τ' ἄλλων ἀλφηστάων
τιμήεντ' ἀνδρῶν, χθονὸ]ς ὅ[σσοι καρ]πὸν ἔδουσιν.

59.

Origen, Against Celsus, iv. 79.

ξυναὶ γὰρ τότε δαῖτες ἔσαν, ξυνοὶ δὲ θόωκοι
ἀθανάτοισι θεοῖσι καταθνητοῖς τ' ἀνθρώποις.

60.

Scholiast on Homer Il. xvi. 175. . . . Ἡσιόδου καὶ τῶν ἄλλων Πολυδώρην αὐτὴν (τὴν θυγατέρα τοῦ Πηλέως) καλούντων.

61.

Eustathius,[2] *Hom.* 112. 44 sq. ἰστέον δὲ ὅτι τὸν

[1] Tzetzes: εἰσαναβαίνων, Strassburg papyrus.

[2] Archbishop of Thessalonica 1175–1192 (?) A.D., author of commentaries on Pindar and on the *Iliad* and *Odyssey*.

wedlock with Zeus to please Hera; but that Zeus was angry and swore that she should mate with a mortal. Hesiod also has the like account.

58.

"Peleus the son of Aeacus, dear to the deathless gods, came to Phthia the mother of flocks, bringing great possessions from spacious Iolcus. And all the people envied him in their hearts seeing how he had sacked the well-built city, and accomplished his joyous marriage; and they all spake this word: 'Thrice, yea, four times blessed son of Aeacus, happy Peleus! For far-seeing Olympian Zeus has given you a wife with many gifts and the blessed gods have brought your marriage fully to pass, and in these halls you go up to the holy bed of a daughter of Nereus. Truly the father, the son of Cronos, made you very pre-eminent among heroes and honoured above other men who eat bread and consume the fruit of the ground.'"

59.[1]

"For in common then were the banquets, and in common the seats of deathless gods and mortal men."

60.

. . . whereas Hesiod and the rest call her (Peleus' daughter) Polydora.

61.

It should be observed that the ancient narrative

[1] This fragment is placed by Spohn after *Works and Days* 120.

Πάτροκλον ἡ παλαιὰ ἱστορία καὶ συγγενῆ τῷ Ἀχιλλεῖ παραδίδωσι λέγουσα, ὅτι Ἡσίοδός φησι Μενοίτιον, τὸν Πατρόκλου πατέρα, Πηλέως εἶναι ἀδελφόν, ὡς εἶναι αὐτανεψίους οὕτως ἀμφοτέρους ἀλλήλοις.

62.

Scholiast on Pindar, Ol. x. 83. τινὲς γράφουσι Σῆρος Ἁλιρροθίου, οὗ μέμνηται Ἡσίοδος—

ἦ τοι ὃ μὲν Σῆρον καὶ Ἀλάζυγον, υἱέας ἐσθλούς.

ἦν δὲ ὁ Σῆρος τοῦ Ἁλιρροθίου τοῦ Περιήρους καὶ Ἀλκυόνης.

63.

Pausanias[1] ii. 26. 7. οὗτος ὁ χρησμὸς δηλοῖ μάλιστα οὐκ ὄντα Ἀσκληπιὸν Ἀρσινόης, ἀλλὰ Ἡσίοδον, ἢ τῶν τινὰ ἐμπεποιηκότων εἰς τὰ Ἡσιόδου, τὰ ἔπη συνθέντα εἰς τὴν Μεσσηνίων χάριν.

Scholiast on Pindar, Pyth. iii. 14. οἱ μὲν Ἀρσινόης, οἱ δὲ Κορωνίδος φασὶν αὐτὸν εἶναι. Ἀσκληπιάδης δέ φησι τὴν Ἀρσινόην Λευκίππου εἶναι τοῦ Περιήρους, ἧς καὶ Ἀπόλλωνος Ἀσκληπιὸς καὶ θυγάτηρ Ἐριῶπις·

ἣ δ' ἔτεκ' ἐν μεγάροις Ἀσκληπιόν, ὄρχαμον ἀνδρῶν,
Φοίβῳ ὑποδμηθεῖσα, ἐυπλόκαμόν τ' Ἐριῶπιν.[2]

καὶ †Ἀρσινόης ὁμοίως.

Ἀρσινόη δὲ μιγεῖσα Διὸς καὶ Λητόος υἱῷ
τίκτ' Ἀσκληπιὸν υἱὸν ἀμύμονά τε κρατερόν τε.[2]

[1] A Greek of Asia Minor, author of the *Description of Greece* (on which he was still engaged in 173 A.D.).

[2] Wilamowitz thinks one or other of these citations belongs to the Catalogue.

hands down the account that Patroclus was even a kinsman of Achilles; for Hesiod says that Menoetius the father of Patroclus, was a brother of Peleus, so that in that case they were first cousins.

62.

Some write "Serus the son of Halirrhothius," whom Hesiod mentions: "He (begot) Serus and Alazygus, goodly sons." And Serus was the son of Halirrhothius Perieres' son, and of Alcyone.

63.

This oracle most clearly proves that Asclepius was not the son of Arsinoë, but that Hesiod or one of Hesiod's interpolators composed the verses to please the Messenians.

Some say (Asclepius) was the son of Arsinoë, others of Coronis. But Asclepiades says that Arsinoë was the daughter of Leucippus, Perieres' son, and that to her and Apollo Asclepius and a daughter, Eriopis, were born:

"And she bare in the palace Asclepius, leader of men, and Eriopis with the lovely hair, being subject in love to Phoebus"

And of Arsinoë likewise:

"And Arsinoë was joined with the son of Zeus and Leto and bare a son Asclepius, blameless and strong."

64.

Scholiast on Hesiod, Theogony, 142. πῶς γὰρ τοὺς αὐτοὺς (Κύκλωπας) θεοῖς ἐναλιγκίους λέγει καὶ ἐν τῷ τῶν Λευκιππίδων Καταλόγῳ ὑπὸ Ἀπόλλωνος ἀνῃρῆσθαι ποιεῖ;

65.

Scholiast on Pindar, Ol. xi. 79.
Τιμάνδρην Ἔχεμος θαλερὴν ποιήσατ' ἄκοιτιν.

66.

Scholiast on Pindar, Nem. x. 150. ὁ μὲν Ἡσίοδος ἀμφοτέρους (Κάστορα καὶ Πολυδεύκη) Διὸς εἶναι γενεαλογεῖ.

Ib. ὁ μέντοι Ἡσίοδος οὔτε Λήδας οὔτε Νεμεσέως δίδωσι τὴν Ἑλένην, ἀλλὰ θυγατρὸς Ὠκεανοῦ καὶ Διός.

67.

Scholiast on Euripides, Orestes 249. Στησίχορός φησιν, ὡς θύων τοῖς θεοῖς Τυνδάρεως Ἀφροδίτης ἐπελάθετο, διὸ ὀργισθεῖσαν τὴν θεὸν διγάμους τε καὶ τριγάμους καὶ λειψάνδρους αὐτοῦ τὰς θυγατέρας ποιῆσαι . . . καὶ Ἡσίοδος δέ·

Τῇσιν δὲ φιλομμειδὴς Ἀφροδίτη
ἠγάσθη προσιδοῦσα, κακῇ δέ σφ' ἔμβαλε φήμη.
Τιμάνδρη μὲν ἔπειτ' Ἔχεμον προλιποῦσ' ἐβεβήκει,
ἵκετο δ' ἐς Φυλῆα, φίλον μακάρεσσι θεοῖσιν·
ὡς δὲ Κλυταιμνήστρη προλιποῦσ' Ἀγαμέμνονα δῖον
Αἰγίσθῳ παρέλεκτο καὶ εἵλετο χείρον' ἀκοίτην·
ὡς δ' Ἑλένη ᾔσχυνε λέχος ξανθοῦ Μενελάου.

64.

For how does he say that the same persons (the Cyclopes) were like the gods, and yet represent them as being destroyed by Apollo in the *Catalogue of the Daughters of Leucippus ?*

65.

"Echemus made Timandra his buxom wife."

66.

Hesiod in giving their descent makes them (Castor and Polydeuces) both sons of Zeus.

Hesiod, however, makes Helen the child neither of Leda nor Nemesis, but of a daughter of Ocean and Zeus.

67.

Stesichorus says that while sacrificing to the gods Tyndareus forgot Aphrodite and that the goddess was angry and made his daughters twice and thrice wed and deserters of their husbands. . . . . And Hesiod also says :

"And laughter-loving Aphrodite felt jealous when she looked on them and cast them into evil report. Then Timandra deserted Echemus and went and came to Phyleus, dear to the deathless gods ; and even so Clytaemnestra deserted god-like Agamemnon and lay with Aegisthus and chose a worse mate ; and even so Helen dishonoured the couch of golden-haired Menelaus."

68.

Μνᾶτο Φιλοκτή]της ἀγὸς ἀνδρῶν [αἰχμ]ητάων
. . . . .]ης, πάντων ἀριδε[ίκετ]ος ἀνδρῶν
τοξάζεσθαι ἑκ]άς τε καὶ ἔγχεϊ ὀξ[υόε]ντι.
βῆ δ' ἐς Τυνδαρέ]ου λιπαρὴν πόλι[ν ε]ἵνεκα κούρη[ς]
Ἀργεΐης ἣ εἶ]δος ἔχεν χρυσέης Ἀφ[ροδί]της
τὴν δ' . . . ἔτεκε]ν Χαρίτων ἀμαρ[ύγμ]ατ' ἔχουσαν
Ζηνὸς ἐν ἀγκοίνῃς καὶ] Τυνδάρεω βασ[ιλῆ]ος
μιχθεῖσ' ἐν λαμπ]ροῖσι δόμοις [κούρη] κυανῶπις
Ὠκεανοῦ θυγάτηρ] μέν' ἐ[πήρατον εἶδος ἔχουσα

* * * *

τοσσαύτας δὲ γυναῖκας ἀμύμονα ἔργα ἰδυίας
πάσας χρυσείας φιάλας ἐν χερσὶν ἐχούσας.
καί νύ κε δὴ Κάστωρ τε καὶ ὁ κρατερὸς Πολυδεύκης
γαμβρὸν ποιήσαντο κατὰ κράτος· ἀλλ' Ἀγαμέμνων
γαμβρὸς ἐὼν ἐμνᾶτο κασιγνήτῳ Μενελάῳ.
Υἱὼ δ' Ἀμφιαράου Ὀικλεΐδαο ἄνακτος
ἐξ] Ἄρ[γ]εος ἐμνῶντο μά[λ' ἐγ]γύθεν· ἀλλ' ἄρα καὶ τοὺς
βλάψ]ε θεῶν [αἴδως μακάρων νέ]μεσίς τ' ἀ[νθρώπων

* * * *

ἀλλ' οὐκ ἦν ἀπάτης ἔργον παρὰ Τυνδαρίδῃσιν.

68.[1]

"... Philoctetes sought her, a leader of spearmen, ...', most famous of all men at shooting from afar and with the sharp spear. And he came to Tyndareus' bright city for the sake of the Argive maid who had the beauty of golden Aphrodite, and the sparkling eyes of the Graces; and the dark-faced daughter of Ocean, very lovely of form, bare her when she had shared the embraces of Zeus and the king Tyndareus in the bright palace . . . . . .

(And . . . . sought her to wife offering as gifts) . . . . and as many woman skilled in blameless arts, each holding a golden bowl in her hands. And truly Castor and strong Polydeuces would have made him[2] their brother perforce, but Agamemnon, being son-in-law to Tyndareus, wooed her for his brother Menelaus.

And the two sons of Amphiaraus the lord, Oecleus' son, sought her to wife from Argos very near at hand; yet . . . fear of the blessed gods and the indignation of men caused them also to fail.

* * * *

but there was no deceitful dealing in the sons of Tyndareus.

[1] Lines 1–51 are from Berlin Papyri, 9739; lines 52–106 with B. 1–50 (and following fragments) are from Berlin Papyri 10560. A reference by Pausanias (iii. 24. 10) to ll. 100 ff. proves that the two fragments together come from the *Catalogue of Women.* The second book (the beginning of which is indicated after l. 106) can hardly be the second book of the *Catalogue* proper: possibly it should be assigned to the 'Hoῖαι, which were sometimes treated as part of the *Catalogue*, and sometimes separated from it.

The remains of the thirty-seven lines following B. 50 in the Papyrus are too slight to admit of restoration.

[2] *sc.* the Suitor whose name is lost.

Ἐκ δ' Ἰθάκης ἐμνᾶτο Ὀδυσσῆος ἱερὴ ἲς,
υἱὸς Λαέρταο πολύκροτα μήδεα εἰδώς.
δῶρα μὲν οὔ ποτ' ἔπεμπε τανυσφύρου εἵνεκα κούρης·
ᾔδεε γὰρ κατὰ θυμὸν ὅτι ξανθὸς Μενέλαος
νικήσει· κτήνει γὰρ Ἀχαιῶν φέρτατος ἦεν·
ἀγγελίην δ' αἰεὶ Λακεδαιμονάδε προΐαλλε
Κάσ[τ]ορ[ι θ' ἱ]πποδάμῳ καὶ ἀεθλοφόρῳ Πολυδεύκει.
μνᾶτο δ' [. . . . . ο]νος υἱός
. . . . ἔε]δνα
. . . .]λ[έ]βητας

* * * *

Κάστορι θ' ἱπποδάμῳ καὶ ἀεθλοφόρῳ Πολυδεύκει
ἱμείρων Ἑλένης πόσις ἔμμεναι ἠυκόμοιο
εἶδος οὔτι ἰδών, ἀλλ' ἄλλων μῦθον ἀκούων.
Ἐκ Φυλάκης δ' ἐμνῶντο δυ' ἀνέρες ἔξοχ' ἄριστοι,
υἱός τ' Ἰφίκλοιο Ποδάρκης Φυλακίδαο,
ἠύς τ' Ἀκτορίδης ὑπερήνωρ Πρωτεσίλαος·
ἄμφω δ' ἀγγελίην Λακεδαιμονάδε προΐαλλον
Τυνδαρέου π[οτ]ὶ δῶμα δαΐφρονος Οἰβαλίδαο
πολλὰ δ' ἔεδν[α δίδον], μέγα γὰρ κλέος [ἔσκε γυ]ναικός,
χαλκ
χρυ[σ

* * * *

Ἀργείης Ἑλένης πόσις ἔμμενα[ι ἠυκόμοιο.
Ἐκ δ' ἀρ' Ἀθηνέων μνᾶθ' υἱὸς Π[ετεῶο Μενεσθεύς,
πολλὰ δ' ἔεδνα δίδου· κειμήλια γ[ὰρ μάλα πολλὰ

And from Ithaca the sacred might of Odysseus, Laërtes' son, who knew many-fashioned wiles, sought her to wife. He never sent gifts for the sake of the neat-ankled maid, for he knew in his heart that golden-haired Menelaus would win, since he was greatest of the Achaeans in possessions and was ever sending messages[1] to horse-taming Castor and prize-winning Polydeuces.

And . . . on's son sought her to wife (and brought) . . . bridal-gifts . . . cauldrons . . . .

* * * *

to horse-taming Castor and prize-winning Polydeuces, desiring to be the husband of rich-haired Helen, though he had never seen her beauty, but because he heard the report of others.

And from Phylace two men of exceeding worth sought her to wife, Podarces son of Iphiclus, Phylacus' son, and Actor's noble son, overbearing Protesilaus. Both of them kept sending messages to Lacedaemon, to the house of wise Tyndareus, Oebalus' son, and they offered many bridal-gifts, for great was the girl's renown, brazen . . . golden . . .

* * * *

(desiring) to be the husband of rich-haired Helen.

From Athens the son of Peteöus, Menestheus, sought her to wife, and offered many bridal-gifts; for he possessed very many stored treasures, gold and

[1] Wooing was by proxy; so Agamemnon wooed Helen for his brother Menelaus (ll. 14–15), and Idomeneus, who came in person and sent no deputy, is specially mentioned as an exception, and the reason for this—if the restoration printed in the text be right—is stated (ll. 69 ff.).

ἔκτητο, χρυσόν τε λέβητάς τ[ε τρίποδας τε,
καλά, τά ῥ' ἔνδοθι κεῦθε δόμος [Πετεῶο ἄνακτος
οἷς μιν θυμὸς ἀνῆκεν ἐεδνώσ[ασθαι ἄκοιτιν
πλεῖστα πορόντ'· ἐπεὶ ο[ὔ] τιν' ἐέλπε[το φέρτερον εἶναι
πάντω]ν ἡρώων κτήνεσσί τε δω[τίναις τε.
"Ικετο δ' Οἰβα]λιδάο[1] δόμους κρατερὸς [Λυκομήδης
νησοὶν ἐκ Κρήτης Ἑλένη]ς ἕνεκ' ἠυ[κόμοιο.

* * * *

* * * *

μνᾶτο· πλεῖστα δὲ δῶρα μετὰ ξανθὸν Μενέλαον
μνηστήρων ἐδίδου· μάλα δ' ἤθελε ὃν κατὰ θυμὸν
Ἀργείης Ἑλένης πόσις ἔμμεναι ἠυκόμοιο.
Αἴας δ' ἐκ Σαλαμῖνος ἀμώμητος πολεμιστὴς
μνᾶτο· δίδου δ' ἄρ' ἔεδνα ἔ[οι]κότα, θαυματὰ ἔργα·
οἳ γὰρ ἔχον Τροιζῆνα καὶ ἀγχίαλον Ἐπίδαυρον
νῆσόν τ' Αἴγιναν Μάσητά τε κοῦροι Ἀχαιῶν
καὶ Μέγαρα σκιόεντα καὶ ὀφρυόεντα Κόρινθον
Ἑρμιόνην Ἀσίνην τε παρὲξ ἅλα ναιεταώσας,
τῶν ἔφατ' εἰλίποδάς τε βόας καὶ ἴφια μῆλα
συνελάσας δώσειν, ἐκέκαστο γὰρ ἔγχεϊ μακρῷ.
Αὐτὰρ ἀπ' Εὐβοίης Ἐλεφήνωρ, ὄρχαμος ἀνδρῶν,
Χαλκωδοντιάδης, μεγαθύμων ἀρ[χὸς Ἀβάντων
μνᾶτο· πλεῖστα δὲ δῶρα δίδου· μάλα δ' [ἤθελε θυμῷ
Ἀργεΐης Ἑλένης πόσις ἔμμενα[ι ἠυκόμοιο.
Ἐκ Κρήτης δ' ἐμνᾶτο μέγα σθένο[ς Ἰ]δομ[ενῆος,
Δευκαλίδης Μίνωος ἀγακλειτοῖο γ[εν]έ[θλη,
οὐδέ τινα μνηστῆρα μετάγγελον ἄλλ[ον ἔπεμψεν,
ἀλλ' αὐτὸς σὺν νηὶ πολυκλήιδι μελαίνῃ

[1]]γειδαο, Berlin Papyrus.

cauldrons and tripods, fine things which lay hid in the house of the lord Peteöus, and with them his heart urged him to win his bride by giving more gifts than any other; for he thought that no one of all the heroes would surpass him in possessions and gifts.

There came also by ship from Crete to the house of the son of Oebalus strong Lycomedes for rich-haired Helen's sake. * * *

* * * *

sought her to wife. And after golden-haired Menelaus he offered the greatest gifts of all the suitors, and very much he desired in his heart to be the husband of Argive Helen with the rich hair.

And from Salamis Aias, blameless warrior, sought her to wife, and offered fitting gifts, even wonderful deeds; for he said that he would drive together and give the shambling oxen and strong sheep of all those who lived in Troezen and Epidaurus near the sea, and in the island of Aegina and in Mases, sons of the Achaeans, and shadowy Megara and frowning Corinthus, and Hermione and Asine which lie along the sea: for he was famous with the long spear.

But from Euboea Elephenor, leader of men, the son of Chalcodon, prince of the bold Abantes, sought her to wife. And he offered very many gifts, and greatly he desired in his heart to be the husband of rich-haired Helen.

And from Crete the mighty Idomeneus sought her to wife, Deucalion's son, offspring of renowned Minos. He sent no one to woo her in his place, but came himself in his black ship of many thwarts over the

βῆ ὑπὲρ Ὠγυλίου πόντου διὰ κῦμα κελαι[νὸν
Τυνδαρέου ποτὶ δῶμα δαΐφρονος, ὄφρα [ἴδοιτο
Ἀ]ρ[γείην] Ἑλένην, μηδ' ἄλλος [1] οἷ κατά[γοιτο
κούρην, τῆς κ]λέα πᾶσαν ἐπὶ χθόνα δῖαν ἵκανεν.
Ἵκετο δ' ἐνν]εσίῃ Ζηνὸς μέγα [μηδομένοιο

(Thirteen lines lost.)

Τυνδάρεος δὲ ἄναξ, ὅποσοι] κ[ίον] εἵνεκα κούρης,
οὔτ' ἀπέπεμψεν ἑκὼν] οὔτ' [αὖθ'] ἕλε [δῶρο]ν ἑκά[στου·
πάντας δὲ μνηστῆρας ἀπῄτεεν ὅρκ[ια πιστὰ
ὀμνύμεναί τ' ἐκέλευσε καὶ [ἀκρή]τῳ ἀ[ρά]ασθαι
σπονδῇ, μή τιν' ἔτ' ἄλλον ἄνευ ἕθεν ἄλλα π[ένεσθαι
ἀμφὶ γάμῳ κούρης εὐ[ω]λ[ένου· ὅ]ς δέ κεν ἀνδρῶν
αὐτὸς ἕλοιτο βίῃ νέμεσίν τ' ἀποθεῖτο καὶ αἰδῶ,
τὸν μέτα πάντας ἄνωγεν ἀολλέας ὁρμηθῆναι
ποινὴν τισόμενους. τοὶ δ' ἀπτερέως ἐπίθοντο
ἐλπόμενοι τελέειν πάντες γάμον· ἀλλ' ἅ[μα πάντας
Ἀτρείδης [νίκησε]ν ἀρηΐφιλος Μενέλαος .
πλεῖστα πορών· Χείρων δ' ἐνὶ Πηλίῳ ὑλήεντι
Πηλείδην ἐκόμιζε πόδας ταχὺν ἔξοχον ἀνδρῶν,
παῖδ' ἔτ' ἐόντ'· οὐ γάρ κεν ἀρηΐφιλος Μενέλαος
νίκησ' οὐδέ τις ἄλλος ἐπιχθονίων ἀνθρώπων
μνηστεύων Ἑλένην, εἴ μιν κίχε παρθένον οὖσαν
οἴκαδε νοστήσας ἐκ Πηλίου ὠκὺς Ἀχιλλεύς.
ἀλλ' ἄρα τὴν πρίν γ' ἔσχεν ἀρηΐφιλος Μενέλαος.

B

Ἡ τέκεν Ἑρμιόνην καλλίσφυρον ἐν μεγάροισιν
ἄελπτον. πάντες δὲ θεοὶ δίχα θυμὸν ἔθεντο
ἐξ ἔριδος· δὴ γὰρ τότε μήδετο θέσκελα ἔργα

[1] αλλος οιον ακ . . . . . Papyrus.

Ogylian sea across the dark wave to the home of wise Tyndareus, to see Argive Helen and that no one else should bring back for him the girl wnose renown spread all over the holy earth.

And at the prompting of Zeus the all-wise came.

* * * *

But of all who came for the maid's sake, the lord Tyndareus sent none away, nor yet received the gift of any, but asked of all the suitors sure oaths, and bade them swear and vow with unmixed libations that no one else henceforth should do aught apart from him as touching the marriage of the maid with shapely arms; but if any man should cast off fear and reverence and take her by force, he bade all the others together follow after and make him pay the penalty. And they, each of them hoping to accomplish his marriage, obeyed him without wavering. But warlike Menelaus, the son of Atreus, prevailed against them all together, because he gave the greatest gifts.

But Chiron was tending the son of Peleus, swift-footed Achilles, pre-eminent among men, on woody Pelion; for he was still a boy. For neither warlike Menelaus nor any other of men on earth would have prevailed in suit for Helen, if fleet Achilles had found her unwed. But, as it was, warlike Menelaus won her before.

II.[1]

And she (Helen) bare neat-ankled Hermione in the palace, a child unlooked for.

Now all the gods were divided through strife; for

[1] The Papyrus here marks the beginning of a second book, possibly of the *Eoiae*. The passage (ll. 2–50) probably led up to an account of the Trojan (and Theban ?) war, in which,

Ζεὺς ὑψιβρεμέτης, μεῖξαι κατ' ἀπείρονα γαῖαν
τυρβασίας, ἤδη δὲ γένος μερόπων ἀνθρώπων
πολλὸν ἀιστῶσαι σπεῦδε, πρόφασιν μὲν ὀλέσσαι
ψυχὰς ἡμιθέω[ν ἵνα μὴ δειλ]οῖσι βροτοῖσιν
τέκνα θεῶν μι[γέῃ, μόρον ὀφ]θαλμοῖσιν ὁρῶντα,
ἀλλ' οἱ μὲν μάκαρες [καὶ ἐς ὕστερο]ν ὡς τὸ πάρος περ
χωρὶς ἀπ' ἀνθρώπων [βίοτον κα]ὶ ἤθε' ἔχωσιν.
τ[οῖς δὲ] μάλ' [ἀθα]νάτ[ων τε καὶ ἐκ] θνητῶν ἀνθρώπων
[γειναμένοις ἐπέθηκε πόνον τε κ]αὶ ἄλγος ἐπ' ἄλγει
Ζεὺ[ς . . . . ἥρ]ωας ἔκερσε

(Two lines missing.)

. . . . μηδέ τις ἀνδρῶν
. . . . νηῶν τε] μελαινάων ἔπι βαίη
. . . . . χερσίν τε β]ίηφι τε φέρτατος εἶναι
. . . .]ε καταθνητῶν ἀνθρώπων
ὅσσα τ' ἔῃν ὅσα τ' ἔ[στὶ καὶ ὁππόσα μέλλει ἔσεσθαι
πᾶσι θεμιστεύων μέγ]α μήδεται ἠδὲ γεραίρει
βουλὰς πατρὸς ἑοῖο], Διὸς νεφεληγερέταο·
οὐ γάρ τις σάφα ᾔδε'] ὅττι φράσσασθαι ἔμελλεν
οὔτε θ]εῶν μακάρων οὔτε θνητῶν ἀνθρώπων
παμπ]όλλας Ἀίδῃ κεφαλὰς ἀπὸ χαλκῷ ἰάψειν
ἀνδρῶν ἡρώων ἐνὶ δηιοτῆτι πεσόντων.
ἀλλ' οὔπω τότε πατρὸς ἐπῃσθάνετο φρενὸς ὁρμήν,
οἷα τε κῆρ' ἀλεείνοντες σφετέροισι τέκεσσι
τέρποντ' ἄνθρωποι· πραπίδων [δ'] ἐπετέρπετ' ἐρωῇ
πατρὸς ἐρισθενέος μεγάλ' ἀνδράσι μηδομένοιο.
Πολλὰ δ' ἀπὸ βλωθρῶν δένδρων ἀμύοντα χαμᾶζε

at that very time Zeus who thunders on high was meditating marvellous deeds, even to mingle storm and tempest over the boundless earth, and already he was hastening to make an utter end of the race of mortal men, declaring that he would destroy the lives of the demi-gods, that the children of the gods should not mate with wretched mortals, seeing their fate with their own eyes; but that the blessed gods henceforth even as aforetime should have their living and their habitations apart from men. But on those who were born of immortals and of mankind verily Zeus laid toil and sorrow upon sorrow.

* * * *

nor any one of men . . . should go upon black ships . . . to be strongest in the might of his hands . . . of mortal men declaring to all those things that were, and those that are, and those that shall be, he brings to pass and glorifies the counsels of his father Zeus who drives the clouds. For no one, either of the blessed gods or of mortal men, knew surely that he would contrive through the sword to send to Hades full many a one of heroes fallen in strife. But at that time he knew not as yet the intent of his father's mind, and how men delight in protecting their children from doom. And he delighted in the desire of his mighty father's heart who rules powerfully over men.

From stately trees the fair leaves fell in abun-

according to *Works and Days* 161–166, the Race of Heroes perished. The opening of the *Cypria* is somewhat similar. Somewhere in the fragmentary lines 13–19 a son of Zeus—almost certainly Apollo—was introduced, though for what purpose is not clear. With l. 31 the destruction of man (cp. ll. 4–5) by storms which spoil his crops begins: the remaining verses are parenthetical, describing the snake "which bears its young in the spring season."

χεύετο καλὰ πέτηλα, ῥέεσκε δὲ καρπὸς ἔραζε
πνείοντος Βορέαο περιζαμενὲς Διὸς αἴσῃ·
ἔζεσκεν δὲ θάλασσα, τρόμεεσκε δὲ πάντ' ἀπ̣ὸ τοῖο,
τρύζεσκεν δὲ μένος βρ̣ότεον, μινύθεσκε δὲ καρπὸς
ὥρῃ ἐν εἰαριν̣ῇ, ὅτε τ' ἄτριχος οὔρεσι τίκτει
γαίης ἐν κευθμῶνι τρίτῳ ἔτεϊ τρία τέκνα.
ἔαρο]ς μὲν κατ' ὄρος καὶ ἀνὰ δρυμὰ πυκνὰ καὶ ὕλην
νόσφι]ν ἀλυσκάζων καὶ ἀπεχθαίρων πάτον ἀνδρῶν
ἄγκεα καὶ κνημοὺς κατα[ναίεται ὑληέντας·
χειμῶνος δ' ἐπιόντος ὑπὸ [χθονὶ πυκνῷ ἐν ἄντρῳ
κεῖται πόλλ' ἐπιεσσάμενος ἐ[ριθηλέα (?) φύλλα,
δεινὸς ὄφις κατὰ νῶτα δα[φοινὸς στίγμασιν αἰνοῖς.
ἀλλά μιν ὑβριστήν τε καὶ [ἄγριον, οὔ τι φατείον,
κῆλα Διὸς δαμνᾷ· φῆ [. . . . .
ψυχὴ τοῦ γ' οἴη καταλείπε[ται ἐν χθονὶ δίῃ.
ἡ δ' ἀμφ' αὐτόχυτον θαλάμ[ην τρίζουσα ποτᾶται
ἠβαιήν· ἐπί θ' ἱρὰ κατὰ χθ[ονὸς εὐρυοδείης
εἶσιν ἀμαυρωθεῖσα ποθ[
κεῖται δὲ

(Traces of 37 following lines.)

69.

Tzetzes,[1] *Exeg. Iliad.* 68. 19 H. ὁ Ἀγαμέμνων, ὁμοίως δὲ καὶ Μενέλαος καθ' Ἡσίοδον καὶ Αἰσχύλον Πλεισθένους υἱοῦ Ἀτρέως παῖδες νομίζονται . . . κατὰ δὲ Ἡσίοδον . . . Ἀτρέως καὶ Ἀερόπης Πλεισθένης. Πλεισθένους δὲ καὶ Κλεόλλας .τῆς Δίαντος Ἀγαμέμνων, Μενέλαος καὶ Ἀναξιβία.

[1] c. 1110–1180 A.D. His chief work was a poem, *Chiliades*, in accentual verse of nearly 13,000 lines.

dance fluttering down to the ground, and the fruit fell to the ground because Boreas blew very fiercely at the behest of Zeus; the deep seethed and all things trembled at his blast: the strength of mankind consumed away and the fruit failed in the season of spring, at that time when the Hairless One[1] in a secret place in the mountains gets three young every three years. In spring he dwells upon the mountain among tangled thickets and brushwood, keeping afar from and hating the path of men, in the glens and wooded glades. But when winter comes on, he lies in a close cave beneath the earth and covers himself with piles of luxuriant leaves, a dread serpent whose back is speckled with awful spots.

But when he becomes violent and fierce unspeakably, the arrows of Zeus lay him low. . . . Only his soul is left on the holy earth, and that flits gibbering about a small unformed den. And it comes enfeebled to sacrifices beneath the broad-pathed earth . . . . and it lies . . . ."

69.

Agamemnon and Menelaus likewise according to Hesiod and Aeschylus are regarded as the sons of Pleisthenes, Atreus' son. And according to Hesiod, Pleisthenes was a son of Atreus and Aërope, and Agamemnon, Menelaus and Anaxibia were the children of Pleisthenes and Cleolla the daughter of Dias.

[1] *i.e.* the snake; as in *Works and Days* 524, the "Boneless One" is the cuttle-fish.

70.

Laurentian Scholiast on Sophocles' Electra 539.

ἣ τέκεθ' Ἑρμιόνην δουρικλειτῷ Μενελάῳ·
ὁπλότατον δ' ἔτεκεν Νικόστρατον ὄζον Ἄρηος.

71.

Pausanias, i. 43. 1. οἶδα δὲ Ἡσίοδον ποιήσαντα ἐν Καταλόγῳ γυναικῶν Ἰφιγένειαν οὐκ ἀποθανεῖν, γνώμῃ δὲ Ἀρτέμιδος Ἑκάτην εἶναι.

72.

Eustathius, Hom. 13. 44. sq. ἦν δέ, φασι, Βούτης υἱὸς Ποσειδῶνος, ὡς Ἡσίοδος ἐν Καταλόγῳ.

73.

Pausanias, ii. 6. 5. . . . Ἡσίοδος . . . ἐποίησεν ὡς Ἐρεχθέως εἴη Σικυών.

74.

Plato, Minos, p. 320. D.

ὃς βασιλεύτατος ἔσκε καταθνητῶν βασιλήων
καὶ πλείστων ἤνασσε περικτιόνων ἀνθρώπων
Ζηνὸς ἔχων σκῆπτρον· τῷ καὶ πολέων βασίλευεν.

75.

Hesychius,[1] ἐπ' Εὐρυγύῃ ἀγών. Μελησαγόρας τὸν Ἀνδρόγεων Εὐρυγύην εἰρῆσθαί φησι τὸν Μίνωος, ἐφ' ᾧ τὸν ἀγῶνα τίθεσθαι ἐπιτάφιον Ἀθήνησιν ἐν τῷ Κεραμεικῷ. καὶ Ἡσίοδος·

Εὐρυγύης δ' ἔτι κοῦρος Ἀθηνάων ἱεράων.

[1] Of Alexandria. He lived in the 5th century, and compiled a Greek Lexicon.

70.

"And she (Helen) bare to Menelaus, famous with the spear, Hermione and her youngest-born, Nicostratus, a scion of Ares."

71.

I know that Hesiod in the *Catalogue of Women* represented that Iphigeneia was not killed but, by the will of Artemis, became Hecate.[1]

72.

Butes, it is said, was a son ot Poseidon: so Hesiod in the *Catalogue.*

73.

Hesiod represented Sicyon as the son of Erechtheus.

74.

"(Minos) who was most kingly of mortal kings and reigned over very many people dwelling round about, holding the sceptre of Zeus wherewith he ruled many."

75.

The athletic contest in memory of Eurygyes. Melesagoras says that Androgeos the son of Minos was called Eurygyes, and that a contest in his honour is held near his tomb at Athens in the Ceramicus. And Hesiod writes:

"And Eurygyes,[2] while yet a lad in holy Athens. . . ."

[1] According to this account Iphigeneia was carried by Artemis to the Tauric Chersonnese (the Crimea). The Tauri (Herodotus iv. 103) identified their maiden-goddess with Iphigeneia; but Euripides (*Iph. in Tauris*) makes her merely priestess of the goddess.

[2] For his murder Minos exacted a yearly tribute of boys and girls, to be devoured by the Minotaur, from the Athenians.

76.

Plutarch, Theseus 20. πολλοὶ δὲ λόγοι . . . περὶ τῆς Ἀριάδνης . . . ἀπολειφθῆναι δὲ τοῦ Θησέως ἐρῶντος ἑτέρας·—

δεινὸς γάρ μιν ἔτειρεν ἔρος Πανοπηΐδος Αἴγλης.

τοῦτο γὰρ τὸ ἔπος ἐκ τῶν Ἡσιόδου Πεισίστρατον ἐξελεῖν φησιν Ἡρέας ὁ Μεγαρεύς.

Athenaeus,[1] xiii. 557 A. Ἡσίοδος δέ φησιν καὶ Ἵππην καὶ Αἴγλην (τὸν Θησέα νομίμως γῆμαι).

77.

Strabo, ix. p. 393. Κυχρείδης ὄφις· ὅν φησιν Ἡσίοδος τραφέντα ὑπὸ Κυχρέως ἐξελαθῆναι ὑπὸ Εὐρυλόχου λυμαινόμενον τὴν νῆσον, ὑποδέξασθαι δὲ αὐτὸν τὴν Δήμητρα εἰς Ἐλευσῖνα καὶ γενέσθαι ταύτης ἀμφίπολον.

78.

Argument I. to the Shield of Heracles. Ἀπολλώνιος δὲ ὁ Ῥόδιος . . . φησὶν αὐτοῦ (Ἡσιόδου) εἶναι ἔκ τε τοῦ χαρακτῆρος καὶ ἐκ τοῦ πάλιν τὸν Ἰόλαον ἐν τῷ Καταλόγῳ εὑρίσκειν ἡνιοχοῦντα Ἡρακλεῖ.

79.

Schol. on Soph. Trach. 266.

ἣ δ' ὑποκυσαμένη καλλίζωνος Στρατονίκη
Εὔρυτον ἐν μεγάροισιν ἐγείνατο φίλτατον υἱόν·
τοῦ δ' υἱεῖς ἐγένοντο Διδαίων τε Κλυτίος τε
Τοξεύς τ' ἀντίθεος ἰδὲ Ἴφιτος, ὄζος Ἄρηος·
τοὺς δὲ μεθ' ὁπλοτάτην τέκετο ξανθὴν Ἰόλειαν
Ἀντιόπη κρείουσα παλαιοῦ Ναυβολίδαο.

[1] Of Naucratis. His *Deipnosophistae* ("Dons at Dinner") is an encyclopædia of miscellaneous topics in the form of a dialogue. His date is *c.* 230 A.D.

76.

There are many tales . . . about Ariadne . . ., how that she was deserted by Theseus for love of another woman :

"For strong love for Aegle the daughter of Panopeus overpowered him."

For Hereas of Megara says that Peisistratus removed this verse from the works of Hesiod.

But Hesiod says that Theseus wedded both Hippe and Aegle lawfully.

77.

The snake of Cychreus : Hesiod says that it was brought up by Cychreus, and was driven out by Eurylochus as defiling the island, but that Demeter received it into Eleusis, and that it became her attendant.

78.

But Apollonius of Rhodes says that it (the *Shield of Heracles*) is Hesiod's both from the general character of the work and from the fact that in the *Catalogue* we again find Iolaus as charioteer of Heracles.

79.

"And fair-girdled Stratonica conceived and bare in the palace Eurytus her well-loved son. Of him sprang sons, Didaeon and Clytius and god-like Toxeus and Iphitus, a scion of Ares. And after these Antiope the queen, daughter of the aged son of Naubolus, bare her youngest child, golden-haired Iolea."

80.

Herodian.
ᾗ τέκεν Αὐτόλυκόν τε Φιλάμμονά τε κλυτὸν αὐδήν

Etymologicum Magnum.
ὅττι κε χερσὶ λάβεσκεν, ἀείδελα πάντα τίθεσκεν.

81.

Apollonius, Hom. Lexicon.
Αἴπυτος αὖ τέκετο Τλησήνορα Πειρίθοόν τε.

82.

Strabo vii. p. 322.
ἦ τοι γὰρ Λοκρὸς Λελέγων ἡγήσατο λαῶν,
τούς ῥά ποτε Κρονίδης Ζεὺς ἄφθιτα μήδεα εἰδὼς
λεκτοὺς ἐκ γαίης λᾶας[1] πόρε Δευκαλίωνι.
ἐκ δὲ λίθων ἐγένοντο βροτοὶ λαοὶ δὲ καλεῦντο.

83.

Tzetzes, Schol. in Exeg. Iliad. 126.
Ἰλέα, τὸν ῥ' ἐφίλησε ἄναξ Διὸς υἱὸς Ἀπόλλων·
καί οἱ τοῦτ' ὀνόμην' ὄνομ' ἔμμεναι, οὕνεκα νύμφην
εὑρόμενος ἵλεων μίχθη ἐρατῇ φιλότητι
ἤματι τῷ ὅτε τεῖχος ἐυδμήτοιο πόληος
ὑψηλὸν ποίησε Ποσειδάων καὶ Ἀπόλλων.

84.

Scholiast on Homer, Od. xi. 326. Κλυμένη Μινύου τοῦ Ποσειδῶνος καὶ Εὐρυανάσσης τῆς Ὑπέρφαντος γαμηθεῖσα Φυλάκῳ τῷ Δηίονος Ἴφικλον τίκτει ποδώκη παῖδα. τοῦτον λέγεται διὰ τὴν τῶν

[1] Heyne: ἀλέας, Villebrun: ἀλέους, Strabo. Line 4 (quoted by Scholiast on Pindar, *Ol.* ix. 68) was added by Bergk to Strabo's citation.

80.

"Who bare Autolycus and Philammon, famous in speech . . . All things that he (Autolycus) took in his hands, he made to disappear."

81.

"Aepytus again, begot Tlesenor and Peirithöus."

82.

"For Locrus truly was leader of the Lelegian people, whom Zeus the Son of Cronos, whose wisdom is unfailing, gave to Deucalion, stones gathered out of the earth. So out of stones mortal men were made, and they were called people." [1]

83.

" . . . Ileus whom the lord Apollo, son of Zeus, loved. And he named him by this name, because he found a nymph complaisant [2] and was joined with her in sweet love, on that day when Poseidon and Apollo raised high the wall of the well-built city."

84.

Clymene the daughter of Minyas the son of Poseidon and of Euryanassa, Hyperphas' daughter, was wedded to Phylacus the son of Deïon, and bare Iphiclus, a boy fleet of foot. It is said of him that

[1] There is a fancied connection between λᾶας (stone) and λαός (people). The reference is to the stones which Deucalion and Pyrrha transformed into men and women after the Flood.

[2] Eustathius identifies Ileus with Oïleus, father of Aias. Here again there is fanciful etymology, Ἰλεύς being similar to ἵλεως (complaisant, gracious).

ποδῶν ἀρετὴν συναμιλλᾶσθαι τοῖς ἀνέμοις, ἐπί τε τῶν ἀσταχύων διέρχεσθαι . . . ἡ δὲ ἱστορία παρ' Ἡσιόδῳ

ἄκρον ἐπ' ἀνθερίκων καρπὸν θέεν οὐδὲ κατέκλα,
ἀλλ' ἐπὶ πυραμίνων ἀθέρων δρομάασκε πόδεσσι
καὶ οὐ σινέσκετο καρπόν.

85.

Choeroboscus,[1] i. 123, 22 H.

ἣ δὲ Θόαν τέκεν υἱόν.

86.

Eustathius, *Hom.* 1623. 44. τὸν δὲ Μάρωνα . . . οὗ τὸν πατέρα Εὐάνθην Ἡσίοδος Οἰνοπίωνός, φασιν, ἱστορεῖ υἱοῦ Διονύσου.

87.

Athenaeus x. 428 B, C.

οἷα Διώνυσος δῶκ' ἀνδράσι χάρμα καὶ ἄχθος.
ὅστις ἄδην πίνῃ, οἶνος δέ οἱ ἔπλετο μάργος,
σὺν δὲ πόδας χεῖράς τε δέει γλῶσσάν τε νόον τε
δεσμοῖς ἀφράστοισι· φιλεῖ δέ ἑ μαλθακὸς ὕπνος.

88.

Strabo ix. p. 442.

Ἢ οἴη Διδύμους ἱεροὺς ναίουσα κολωνοὺς
Δωτίῳ ἐν πεδίῳ πολυβότρυος ἄντ' Ἀμύροιο
νίψατο Βοιβιάδος λίμνης πόδα παρθένος ἀδμής.

89.

Schol. on Pindar, *Pyth.* iii. 48.

τῷ μὲν ἄρ' ἄγγελος ἦλθε κόραξ ἱερῆς ἀπὸ δαιτὸς
Πυθὼ ἐς ἠγαθέην, φράσσεν δ' ἄρα ἔργ' ἀίδηλα

[1] c. 600 A.D., a lecturer and grammarian of Constantinople.

through his power of running he could race the winds and could move along upon the ears of corn[1] . . . The tale is in Hesiod:

"He would run over the fruit of the asphodel and not break it; nay, he would run with his feet upon wheaten ears and not hurt the fruit."

85.

"And she bare a son Thoas."

86.

Maro,[2] whose father, it is said, Hesiod relates to have been Euanthes the son of Oenopion, the son of Dionysus.

87.

"Such gifts as Dionysus gave to men, a joy and a sorrow both. Who ever drinks to fullness, in him wine becomes violent and binds together his hands and feet, his tongue also and his wits with fetters unspeakable: and soft sleep embraces him."

88.

"Or like her (Coronis) who lived by the holy Twin Hills in the plain of Dotium over against Amyrus rich in grapes, and washed her feet in the Boebian lake, a maid unwed."

89.

"To him, then, there came a messenger from the sacred feast to goodly Pytho, a crow,[3] and he told

[1] Imitated by Vergil, *Aen.* vii. 808, describing Camilla.

[2] Priest of Apollo, and, according to Homer, discoverer of wine. Maronea in Thrace is said to have been called after him.

[3] The crow was originally white, but was turned black by Apollo in his anger at the news brought by the bird.

Φοίβῳ ἀκερσοκόμῃ ὅτι Ἴσχυς ἔγημε Κόρωνιν
Εἰλατίδης, Φλεγύαο διογνήτοιο θύγατρα.

90.

Athenagoras,[1] *Petition for the Christians*, 29. περὶ δὲ Ἀσκληπιοῦ Ἡσίοδος μέν—

πατὴρ δ' ἀνδρῶν τε θεῶν τε
χώσατ', ἀπ' Οὐλύμπου δὲ βαλὼν ψολόεντι κεραυνῷ
ἔκτανε Λητοΐδην, Φοίβῳ σὺν θυμὸν ὀρίνων.

91.

Philodemus, On Piety, 34. Ἡσίοδος δέ (λέγει τὸν Ἀπόλλωνα) . . . μέλλειν μὲν εἰς τὸν Τάρταρον ὑπὸ τοῦ Διὸς ἐμβληθῆναι, τῆς Λητοῦς δ' ἱκετευσάσης, ἀνδρὶ θητεῦσαι.

92.

Schol. on Pindar, Pyth. ix. 6.

Ἢ οἵη Φθίῃ Χαρίτων ἄπο κάλλος ἔχουσα
Πηνειοῦ παρ' ὕδωρ καλὴ ναίεσκε Κυρήνη.

93.

Servius on Vergil, Georg. i. 14. Aristaeum invocat, id est, Apollinis et Cyrenes filium, quem Hesiodus dicit Apollinem pastoralem.

94.

Scholiast on Vergil, Georg. iv. 361.

at illum
Curvata in montis faciem circumstetit unda.

Hunc versum ex Hesiodi Gynaecon transtulit.

[1] A philosopher of Athens under Hadrian and Antoninus. He became a Christian and wrote a defence of the Christians addressed to Antoninus Pius.

unshorn Phoebus of secret deeds, that Ischys son of Elatus had wedded Coronis the daughter of Phlegyas of birth divine.

90.

Concerning Asclepius Hesiod says: "And the father of men and gods was wrath, and from Olympus he smote the son of Leto with a lurid thunderbolt and killed him, arousing the anger of Phoebus."

91.

But Hesiod (says that Apollo) would have been cast by Zeus into Tartarus [1]; but Leto interceded for him, and he became bondman to a mortal.

92.

"Or like her, beautiful Cyrene, who dwelt in Phthia by the water of Peneus and had the beauty of the Graces."

93.

He invokes Aristaeus, that is, the son of Apollo and Cyrene, whom Hesiod calls "the shepherd Apollo." [2]

94.

"But the water stood all round him, bowed into the semblance of a mountain."

This verse he has taken over from Hesiod's *Catalogue of Women.*

[1] Zeus slew Asclepius (fr. 90) because of his success as a healer, and Apollo in revenge killed the Cyclopes (fr. 64). In punishment Apollo was forced to serve Admetus as herdsman. (Cp. Euripides, *Alcestis*, 1–8.)

[2] For Cyrene and Aristaeus, cp. Vergil, *Georgics*, iv. 315 ff.

95.

Schol. on Homer, Iliad ii. 469.

Ἢ οἵην Ὑρίη Βοιωτίη ἔτρεφε κούρην.

96.

Palaephatus,[1] c. 42. περὶ Ζήθου καὶ Ἀμφίονος· ἱστοροῦσιν ἄλλοι τε καὶ Ἡσίοδος, ὅτι κιθάρᾳ τὸ τεῖχος τῶν Θηβῶν ἐτείχισαν.

97.

Schol. on Soph. Trach. 1167.

Ἔστι τις Ἑλλοπίη πολυλήιος ἠδ' εὐλείμων,
ἀφνειὴ μήλοισι καὶ εἰλιπόδεσσι βόεσσιν·
ἐν δ' ἄνδρες ναίουσι πολύρρηνες πολυβοῦται
πολλοὶ ἀπειρέσιοι, φῦλα θνητῶν ἀνθρώπων·
ἔνθα δὲ Δωδώνη τις ἐπ' ἐσχατιῇ πεπόλισται·
τὴν δὲ Ζεὺς ἐφίλησε καὶ ὃν χρηστήριον εἶναι
τίμιον ἀνθρώποις . . .
. . . ναῖον δ' ἐν πυθμένι φηγοῦ·
ἔνθεν ἐπιχθόνιοι μαντήια πάντα φέρονται,
ὃς δὴ κεῖθι μολὼν θεὸν ἄμβροτον ἐξερεείνῃ
δῶρα φέρων τ' ἔλθῃσι σὺν οἰωνοῖς ἀγαθοῖσιν.

98.

Berlin Papyri, No. 9777.[2]

ὑσμίν[η . . . θνητῶν δέ γε τίς κεν ἀνέτλη
ἔγχεϊ μάρνασθα[ι καὶ·ἐναντίον ὁρμηθῆναι,
πλήν γ' Ἡρακλῆ[ος μεγαλήτορος Ἀλκαίοιο;
αὐτεοιατ'† ἀρηίφ[ιλος κρατερὸς Μελέαγρος
ξανθοκόμης [Οἰνῆος ἴδ' Ἀλθαίης φίλος υἱός·
τοῦ καὶ ἀπ' ὀφθ[αλμῶν ἀπελάμπετο θεσπιδαὲς πῦρ
γοργῶν· ὑψηλ[ῷ δέ ποτ' ἐν Καλυδῶνι δάμασσε

[1] A writer on mythology of uncertain date.

[2] The fragment is part of a leaf from a papyrus book of the 4th century A.D.

95.

"Or like her (Antiope) whom Boeotian Hyria nurtured as a maid."

96.

Of Zethus and Amphion. Hesiod and some others relate that they built the walls of Thebes by playing on the lyre.

97.

"There is a land Ellopia with much glebe and rich meadows, and rich in flocks and shambling kine. There dwell men who have many sheep and many oxen, and they are in number past telling, tribes of mortal men. And there upon its border is built a city, Dodona[1]; and Zeus loved it and (appointed) it to be his oracle, reverenced by men . . . And they (the doves) lived in the hollow of an oak. From them men of earth carry away all kinds of prophecy,—whosoever fares to that spot and questions the deathless god, and comes bringing gifts with good omens."

98.

". . . strife . . . Of mortals who would have dared to fight him with the spear and charge against him, save only Heracles, the great-hearted offspring of Alcaeus? Such an one was (?) strong Meleager loved of Ares, the golden-haired, dear son of Oeneus and Althaea. From his fierce eyes there shone forth portentous fire: and once in high Calydon he slew the destroying beast, the fierce wild

[1] In Epirus. The oracle was first consulted by Deucalion and Pyrrha after the Flood. Later writers say that the god responded in the rustling of leaves in the oaks for which the place was famous.

θῆρ' ὀ[λοὸν χλούνην σῦν ἄγριον ἀργιόδοντα.
οὔτε τις ἐν πολέμῳ [οὔτ' αἰνῇ δηιοτῆτι
ἔτλη ἐς ἄντα ἰδ[ὼν σχεδὸν ἐλθέμεν οὐδὲ μάχεσθαι
ἀνδρῶν ἡρώων, ὁπότ' [ἐν προμάχοισι φανείη
ἀλλ' ὑπ' Ἀπόλλωνος χερ[σὶν βέλεσίν τ' ἐδαμάσθη
μαρνάμενος Κού[ρησιν ὑπὲρ Καλυδῶνος ἐραννῆς.
τοὺς δ' ἄλλους Οἰνῆ[ι τέκεν, Πορθάονος υἱῷ,
Φηρέα θ' ἱππόδαμ[ον Ἀγέλαόν τ' ἔξοχον ἄλλων
Τοξέα τε Κλύμεν[όν τε καὶ ἀντίθεον Περίφαντα
Γόργην τ' ἠύκομον [καὶ ἐπίφρονα Δηιάνειραν,
ἣ τέχ' ὑποδμηθεῖ[σα βίῃ Ἡρακληείῃ
Ὕλλον καὶ Γλῆνον καὶ [Κτήσιππον καὶ Ὀδίτην·
τοὺς τέκε, καὶ δειν[ὸν ἐν ἀϊδρείῃσιν ἔρεξε
ὁππότε φαρμακό[εν. . . . .
λῶπ[ος] κῆ[ρα μέλαιναν ἔχον . . . . .

99A.

Schol. on Homer, Iliad. xxiii. 679. καὶ Ἡσίοδος δέ φησιν ἐν Θήβαις αὐτοῦ ἀποθανόντος, Ἀργείαν τὴν Ἀδράστου σὺν ἄλλοις ἐλθεῖν ἐπὶ τὴν κηδείαν τοῦ Οἰδιπόδος.

99.

Papyri greci e latine, No. 131 (2nd–3rd century).[1]

τῷ δ' ἔτεκ' ἐν μεγάροις] Ἀλκμάονα π[οιμέ]να λα[ῶν.
τόν ῥ' ὑπὲρ Ἀργεί]ους Καδμηίδες ἑλκεσίπε[πλοι,

[1] Most of the smaller restorations appear in the original publication, but the larger are new: these last are highly conjectural, there being no definite clue to the general sense.

boar with gleaming tusks. In war and in dread strife no man of the heroes dared to face him and to approach and fight with him when he appeared in the forefront. But he was slain by the hands and arrows of Apollo,[1] while he was fighting with the Curetes for pleasant Calydon. And these others (Althaea) bare to Oeneus, Porthaon's son; horse-taming Pheres, and Agelaus surpassing all others, Toxeus and Clymenus and godlike Periphas, and rich-haired Gorga and wise Deianeira, who was subject in love to mighty Heracles and bare him Hyllus and Glenus and Ctesippus and Odites. These she bare and in ignorance she did a fearful thing: when (she had received) . . . the poisoned robe that held black doom . . . ."

99A.

And yet Hesiod says that after he had died in Thebes, Argeia the daughter of Adrastus together with others (cp. frag. 99) came to the lamentation over Oedipus.

99.[2]

And (Eriphyle) bare in the palace Alcmaon,[3] shepherd of the people, to Amphiaraus. Him (Am-

[1] According to Homer and later writers Meleager wasted away when his mother Althea burned the brand on which his life depended, because he had slain her brothers in the dispute for the hide of the Calydonian boar. (Cp. Bacchylides, *Ode* v. 136 ff.)

[2] The fragment probably belongs to the *Catalogues* proper rather than to the *Eoiae*; but, as its position is uncertain, it may conveniently be associated with Frags. 99A and the *Shield of Heracles*.

[3] Alcmaon (who took part in the second of the two heroic Theban expeditions) is perhaps mentioned only incidentally as the son of Amphiaraus, who seems to be clearly indicated in ll. 7–8, and whose story occupies ll. 5–10. At l. 11 the subject changes and Electryon is introduced as father of Alcmena.

ὄμματα τ' εὐμεγε]θές τε δέμας εἰσάντα ἰδοῦ[σαι,
ἀμφιέποντα] ταφὰς πολυκηδέος Οἰδιπό[δαο,
θαύμασαν . . .] . . ενουκ . τινουπ̣ο [. . .]ρι[. . . .
τῷ δὲ ποτ' εἰς Θῆβα]ς Δαναοὶ θεράποντες Ἄρη[ος
ἔσπονθ' ὥς κε . . .] Πολυνείκεϊ κ̣ῦ̣δ̣ο̣ς [1] [ἄροιντο.
εὖ δὲ καὶ εἰδότα περ] Ζηνὸς παρὰ θέσφατα [πάντα
γαῖα χανοῦσά ἑ τηλοῦ] ἀπ' Ἀλφειοῦ βαθυδί[νεω
κάππιε σύν θ' ἵππ]οισι καὶ ἅρμασι κολλητ[οῖσι.
Γῆμεν δ' Ἠλεκτρύων] Πέλοπος περικαλλέα [κούρην·
γείνατο δ' ἐν μεγάροισιν] ὁμὸν λέχος εἰσαναβ[αίνων
Περσείδης] ἥρωα καὶ αἰχμητήν περ [ἐόντα
. . .] Φυλόνομόν τε Κελαινέα τ' Ἀμ]φίμαχόν τε
. . . . .] τε καὶ Εὐρύβιον κλειτόν τε [. . .
τοὺς πάντας] Τάφιοι ναυσίκλυτοι ἐξενά[ριξαν
βοῦσιν ἐπ' εἰλι]πόδεσσιν, ἑλεῖν α[.]να[. . .
. . . ν]ήεσσιν ἐπ' εὐρέα νῶτα θα[λάσσης
Ἀλκμήνη δ' ἄρα] μούνη [ἐλείπ]ετο χάρμα γο[νεῦσιν
. . . .] . . κα[ὶ Ἠλ]εκτρυών[η [2] . . .

* * * *

ἣ τέχ' ὑποδμηθεῖσα] κ[ελαι]νεφέϊ Κρο[νίωνι

* * * *

100.

Argument to the Shield of Heracles, i. τῆς Ἀσπίδος ἡ ἀρχὴ ἐν τῷ τετάρτῳ Καταλόγῳ φέρεται μέχρι στίχων ν' καὶ ϛ'.

[1] ητ̣αφο[ν (?), original publication.
[2] For scansion cf. *Shield*, ll. 16, 82.

phiaraus) did the Cadmean (Theban) women with trailing robes admire when they saw face to face his eyes and well-grown frame, as he was busied about the burying of Oedipus, the man of many woes. . . . Once the Danaï, servants of Ares, followed him to Thebes, to win renown . . . for Polynices. But, though well he knew from Zeus all things ordained, the earth yawned and swallowed him up with his horses and jointed chariot, far from deep-eddying Alpheus.

But Electryon married the all-beauteous daughter of Pelops and, going up into one bed with her, the son of Perses begat . . . and Phylonomus and Celaeneus and Amphimachus and . . . and Eurybius and famous . . . All these the Taphians, famous shipmen, slew in fight for oxen with shambling hoofs, . . . in ships across the sea's wide back. So Alcmena alone was left to delight her parents . . . and the daughter of Electryon . . . who was subject in love to the dark-clouded son of Cronos and bare (famous Heracles).

100.

The beginning of the *Shield* as far as the 56th verse is current in the fourth *Catalogue*.

ΗΣΙΟΔΟΥ ΑΣΠΙΣ

Ἠ οἵη προλιποῦσα δόμους καὶ πατρίδα γαῖαν
ἤλυθεν ἐς Θήβας μετ' ἀρήιον Ἀμφιτρύωνα
Ἀλκμήνη, θυγάτηρ λαοσσόου Ἠλεκτρύωνος·
ἥ ῥα γυναικῶν φῦλον ἐκαίνυτο θηλυτεράων
εἴδεΐ τε μεγέθει τε· νόον γε μὲν οὔ τις ἔριζε
τάων, ἃς θνηταὶ θνητοῖς τέκον εὐνηθεῖσαι.
τῆς καὶ ἀπὸ κρῆθεν βλεφάρων τ' ἄπο κυανεάων
τοῖον ἄηθ' οἷόν τε πολυχρύσου Ἀφροδίτης.
ἣ δὲ καὶ ὣς κατὰ θυμὸν ἑὸν τίεσκεν ἀκοίτην,
ὡς οὔ πώ τις ἔτισε γυναικῶν θηλυτεράων·
ἦ μέν οἱ πατέρ' ἐσθλὸν ἀπέκτανε ἶφι δαμάσσας,
χωσάμενος περὶ βουσί· λιπὼν δ' ὅ γε πατρίδα γαῖαν
ἐς Θήβας ἱκέτευσε φερεσσακέας Καδμείους.
ἔνθ' ὅ γε δώματ' ἔναιε σὺν αἰδοίῃ παρακοίτι
νόσφιν ἄτερ φιλότητος ἐφιμέρου, οὐδέ οἱ ἦεν
πρὶν λεχέων ἐπιβῆναι ἐυσφύρου Ἠλεκτρυώνης,
πρίν γε φόνον τίσαιτο κασιγνήτων μεγαθύμων
ἧς ἀλόχου, μαλερῷ δὲ καταφλέξαι πυρὶ κώμας
ἀνδρῶν ἡρώων Ταφίων ἰδὲ Τηλεβοάων.
τὼς [1] γάρ οἱ διέκειτο, θεοὶ δ' ἐπὶ μάρτυροι ἦσαν·
τῶν ὅ γ' ὀπίζετο μῆνιν, ἐπείγετο δ' ὅττι τάχιστα
ἐκτελέσαι μέγα ἔργον, ὅ οἱ Διόθεν θέμις ἦεν.
τῷ δ' ἅμα ἱέμενοι πολέμοιό τε φυλόπιδός τε
Βοιωτοὶ πλήξιπποι, ὑπὲρ σακέων πνείοντες,
Λοκροί τ' ἀγχέμαχοι καὶ Φωκῆες μεγάθυμοι
ἕσποντ'· ἦρχε δὲ τοῖσιν ἐὺς πάις Ἀλκαίοιο
κυδιόων λαοῖσι. πατὴρ δ' ἀνδρῶν τε θεῶν τε

[1] A: ὡς, MSS.

HESIOD'S SHIELD OF HERACLES

Or like her who left home and country and came to Thebes, following warlike Amphitryon,—even Alcmena, the daughter of Electryon, gatherer of the people. She surpassed the tribe of womankind in beauty and in height; and in wisdom none vied with her of those whom mortal women bare of union with mortal men. Her face and her dark eyes wafted such charm as comes from golden Aphrodite. And she so honoured her husband in her heart as none of womankind did before her. Verily he had slain her noble father violently when he was angry about oxen; so he left his own country and came to Thebes and was suppliant to the shield-carrying men of Cadmus. There he dwelt with his modest wife without the joys of love, nor might he go in unto the neat-ankled daughter of Electryon until he had avenged the death of his wife's great-hearted brothers and utterly burned with blazing fire the villages of the heroes, the Taphians and Teleboans; for this thing was laid upon him, and the gods were witnesses to it. And he feared their anger, and hastened to perform the great task to which Zeus had bound him. With him went the horse-driving Boeotians, breathing above their shields, and the Locrians who fight hand to hand, and the gallant Phocians eager for war and battle. And the noble son of Alcaeus led them, rejoicing in his host.

But the father of men and gods was forming

ἄλλην μῆτιν ὕφαινε μετὰ φρεσίν, ὥς ῥα θεοῖσιν
ἀνδράσι τ' ἀλφηστῇσιν ἀρῆς ἀλκτῆρα φυτεύσαι.
ὦρτο δ' ἀπ' Οὐλύμποιο δόλον φρεσὶ βυσσοδομεύων,
ἱμείρων φιλότητος ἐυζώνοιο γυναικός,
ἐννύχιος· τάχα δ' ἷξε Τυφαόνιον· τόθεν αὖτις
Φίκιον ἀκρότατον προσεβήσατο μητίετα Ζεύς.
ἔνθα καθεζόμενος φρεσὶ μήδετο θέσκελα ἔργα·
αὐτῇ μὲν γὰρ νυκτὶ τανυσφύρου Ἠλεκτρυώνης
εὐνῇ καὶ φιλότητι μίγη, τέλεσεν δ' ἄρ' ἐέλδωρ·
αὐτῇ δ' Ἀμφιτρύων λαοσσόος, ἀγλαὸς ἥρως,
ἐκτελέσας μέγα ἔργον ἀφίκετο ὅνδε δόμονδε.
οὐδ' ὅ γ' ἐπὶ δμῶας καὶ ποιμένας ἀγροιώτας
ὦρτ' ἰέναι, πρίν γ' ἧς ἀλόχου ἐπιβήμεναι εὐνῆς·
τοῖος γὰρ κραδίην πόθος αἴνυτο ποιμένα λαῶν.
ὡς δ' ὅτ' ἀνὴρ ἀσπαστὸν ὑπεκπροφύγῃ κακότητα
νούσου ὕπ' ἀργαλέης ἢ καὶ κρατεροῦ ὑπὸ δεσμοῦ,
ὥς ῥα τότ' Ἀμφιτρύων χαλεπὸν πόνον ἐκτολυπεύσας
ἀσπασίως τε φίλως τε ἑὸν δόμον εἰσαφίκανεν.
παννύχιος δ' ἄρ' ἔλεκτο σὺν αἰδοίῃ παρακοίτι
τερπόμενος δώροισι πολυχρύσου Ἀφροδίτης.
ἡ δὲ θεῷ δμηθεῖσα καὶ ἀνέρι πολλὸν ἀρίστῳ
Θήβῃ ἐν ἑπταπύλῳ διδυμάονε γείνατο παῖδε,
οὐ καθ' ὁμὰ φρονέοντε· κασιγνήτω γε μὲν ἤστην·
τὸν μὲν χειρότερον, τὸν δ' αὖ μέγ' ἀμείνονα φῶτα,
δεινόν τε κρατερόν τε, βίην Ἡρακληείην·
τὸν μὲν ὑποδμηθεῖσα κελαινεφέι Κρονίωνι,
τὸν δ' ἄρα Ἰφικλῆα δορυσσόῳ[1] Ἀμφιτρύωνι,
κεκριμένην γενεήν· τὸν μὲν βροτῷ ἀνδρὶ μιγεῖσα,
τὸν δὲ Διὶ Κρονίωνι, θεῶν σημάντορι πάντων.

[1] λαοσσόῳ, KLM.

another scheme in his heart, to beget one to defend against destruction gods and men who eat bread. So he arose from Olympus by night pondering guile in the deep of his heart, and yearned for the love of the well-girded woman. Quickly he came to Typhaonium, and from there again wise Zeus went on and trod the highest peak of Phicium[1]: there he sat and planned marvellous things in his heart. So in one night Zeus shared the bed and love of the neat-ankled daughter of Electryon and fulfilled his desire; and in the same night Amphitryon, gatherer of the people, the glorious hero, came to his house when he had ended his great task. He hastened not to go to his bondmen and shepherds afield, but first went in unto his wife: such desire took hold on the shepherd of the people. And as a man who has escaped joyfully from misery, whether of sore disease or cruel bondage, so then did Amphitryon, when he had wound up all his heavy task, come glad and welcome to his home. And all night long he lay with his modest wife, delighting in the gifts of golden Aphrodite. And she, being subject in love to a god and to a man exceeding goodly, brought forth twin sons in seven-gated Thebe. Though they were brothers, these were not of one spirit; for one was weaker but the other a far better man, one terrible and strong, the mighty Heracles. Him she bare through the embrace of the son of Cronos lord of dark clouds and the other, Iphicles, of Amphitryon the spear-wielder—offspring distinct, this one of union with a mortal man, but that other of union with Zeus, leader of all the gods.

[1] A mountain peak near Thebes which took its name from the Sphinx (called in *Theog.* 326 Φῖξ).

Ὃς καὶ Κύκνον ἔπεφνεν, Ἀρητιάδην μεγάθυμον.
εὗρε γὰρ ἐν τεμένει ἑκατηβόλου Ἀπόλλωνος
αὐτὸν καὶ πατέρα ὃν Ἄρην, ἄατον πολέμοιο,
τεύχεσι λαμπομένους σέλας ὣς πυρὸς αἰθομένοιο,
ἑσταότ᾿ ἐν δίφρῳ· χθόνα δ᾿ ἔκτυπον ὠκέες ἵπποι
νύσσοντες χηλῇσι, κόνις δέ σφ᾿ ἀμφιδεδήει
κοπτομένη πλεκτοῖσιν ὑφ᾿ ἅρμασι καὶ ποσὶν ἵππων.
ἅρματα δ᾿ εὐποίητα καὶ ἄντυγες ἀμφαράβιζον
ἵππων ἱεμένων· κεχάρητο δὲ Κύκνος ἀμύμων,
ἐλπόμενος Διὸς υἱὸν ἀρήιον ἡνίοχόν τε
χαλκῷ δηιώσειν καὶ ἀπὸ κλυτὰ τεύχεα δύσειν.
ἀλλά οἱ εὐχωλέων οὐκ ἔκλυε Φοῖβος Ἀπόλλων·
αὐτὸς γάρ οἱ ἐπῶρσε βίην Ἡρακληείην.
πᾶν δ᾿ ἄλσος καὶ βωμὸς Ἀπόλλωνος Παγασαίου
λάμπεν ὑπὸ δεινοῖο θεοῦ τευχέων τε καὶ αὐτοῦ·
πῦρ δ᾿ ὣς ὀφθαλμῶν ἀπελάμπετο. τίς κεν ἐκείνου
ἔτλη θνητὸς ἐὼν κατεναντίον ὁρμηθῆναι
πλήν γ᾿ Ἡρακλῆος καὶ κυδαλίμου Ἰολάου;
κείνων γὰρ μεγάλη τε βίη καὶ χεῖρες ἄαπτοι
ἐξ ὤμων ἐπέφυκον ἐπὶ στιβαροῖσι μέλεσσιν.
ὅς ῥα τόθ᾿ ἡνίοχον προσέφη κρατερὸν Ἰόλαον·
Ἥρως ὦ Ἰόλαε, βροτῶν πολὺ φίλτατε πάντων,
ἦ τε μέγ᾿ ἀθανάτους μάκαρας, τοὶ Ὄλυμπον ἔχουσιν,
ἤλιτεν Ἀμφιτρύων, ὅτ᾿ ἐυστέφανον ποτὶ Θήβην
ἦλθε λιπὼν Τίρυνθα,[1] ἐυκτίμενον πτολίεθρον,
κτείνας Ἠλεκτρύωνα βοῶν ἕνεκ᾿ εὐρυμετώπων·
ἵκετο δ᾿ ἐς Κρείοντα καὶ Ἡνιόχην τανύπεπλον,
οἵ ῥά μιν ἠσπάζοντο καὶ ἄρμενα πάντα παρεῖχον,
ἣ δίκη ἔσθ᾿ ἱκέτῃσι, τίον δέ ἑ [2] κηρόθι μᾶλλον.

[1] M : τίρυνθ᾿, GHI : Τίρυνθον, most MSS. : τήρνυθον, B.
[2] Ranke : δέ γε, GHI : δ᾿ ἄρα, other MSS.

And he slew Cycnus, the gallant son of Ares. For he found him in the close of far-shooting Apollo, him and his father Ares, never sated with war. Their armour shone like a flame of blazing fire as they two stood in their car: their swift horses struck the earth and pawed it with their hoofs, and the dust rose like smoke about them, pounded by the chariot wheels and the horses' hoofs, while the well-made chariot and its rails rattled around them as the horses plunged. And blameless Cycnus was glad, for he looked to slay the warlike son of Zeus and his charioteer with the sword, and to strip off their splendid armour. But Phoebus Apollo would not listen to his vaunts, for he himself had stirred up mighty Heracles against him. And all the grove and altar of Pagasaean Apollo flamed because of the dread god and because of his arms; for his eyes flashed as with fire. What mortal man would have dared to meet him face to face save Heracles and glorious Iolaus? For great was their strength and unconquerable were the arms which grew from their shoulders on their strong limbs. Then Heracles spake to his charioteer strong Iolaus:

"O hero Iolaus, best beloved of all men, truly Amphitryon sinned deeply against the blessed gods who dwell on Olympus when he came to sweet-crowned Thebe and left Tiryns, the well-built citadel, because he slew Electryon for the sake of his wide-browed oxen. Then he came to Creon and long-robed Eniocha, who received him kindly and gave him all fitting things, as is due to suppliants, and honoured him in their hearts even more. And he

ζῶε δ' ἀγαλλόμενος σὺν ἐυσφύρῳ Ἠλεκτρυώνῃ,
ᾗ ἀλόχῳ· τάχα δ' ἄμμες ἐπιπλομένων ἐνιαυτῶν
γεινόμεθ' οὔτε φυὴν ἐναλίγκιοι οὔτε νόημα,
σός τε πατὴρ καὶ ἐγώ· τοῦ μὲν φρένας ἐξέλετο Ζεύς,
ὃς προλιπὼν σφέτερόν τε δόμον σφετέρους τε τοκῆας
ᾤχετο, τιμήσων ἀλιτήμενον Εὐρυσθῆα,
σχέτλιος· ἦ που πολλὰ μετεστεναχίζετ' ὀπίσσω
ἣν ἄτην ὀχέων·[1] ἣ δ' οὐ παλινάγρετός ἐστιν.
αὐτὰρ ἐμοὶ δαίμων χαλεποὺς ἐπετέλλετ' ἀέθλους.
Ὦ φίλος, ἀλλὰ σὺ θᾶσσον ἔχ' ἡνία φοινικόεντα
ἵππων ὠκυπόδων· μέγα δὲ φρεσὶ θάρσος ἀέξων
ἰθὺς ἔχειν θοὸν ἅρμα καὶ ὠκυπόδων σθένος ἵππων,
μηδὲν ὑποδδείσας κτύπον Ἄρεος ἀνδροφόνοιο,
ὃς νῦν κεκληγὼς περιμαίνεται ἱερὸν ἄλσος
Φοίβου Ἀπόλλωνος, ἑκατηβελέταο ἄνακτος·
ἦ μὴν καὶ κρατερός περ ἐὼν ἄαται πολέμοιο.
Τὸν δ' αὖτε προσέειπεν ἀμώμητος Ἰόλαος·
ἠθεῖ', ἦ μάλα δή τι πατὴρ ἀνδρῶν τε θεῶν τε
τιμᾷ σὴν κεφαλὴν καὶ ταύρεος Ἐννοσίγαιος,
ὃς Θήβης κρήδεμνον ἔχει ῥύεταί τε πόληα·
οἷον δὴ καὶ τόνδε βροτὸν κρατερόν τε μέγαν τε
σὰς ἐς χεῖρας ἄγουσιν, ἵνα κλέος ἐσθλὸν ἄρηαι.
ἀλλ' ἄγε δύσεο τεύχε' ἀρήια, ὄφρα τάχιστα
δίφρους ἐμπελάσαντες Ἄρηός θ' ἡμέτερόν τε
μαρνώμεσθ', ἐπεὶ οὔ τοι ἀτάρβητον Διὸς υἱὸν
οὐδ' Ἰφικλεΐδην δειδίξεται, ἀλλά μιν οἴω
φεύξεσθαι δύο παῖδας ἀμύμονος Ἀλκεΐδαο,
οἳ δή σφι σχεδόν εἰσι, λιλαιόμενοι πολέμοιο
φυλόπιδα στῆσαι, τά σφιν πολὺ φίλτερα θοίνης.

[1] BCDF: ἀχέων, other MSS.

lived joyfully with his wife the neat-ankled daughter of Electryon : and presently, while the years rolled on, we were born, unlike in body as in mind, even your father and I. From him Zeus took away sense, so that he left his home and his parents and went to do honour to the wicked Eurystheus—unhappy man! Deeply indeed did he grieve afterwards in bearing the burden of his own mad folly; but that cannot be taken back. But on me fate laid heavy tasks.

"Yet, come, friend, quickly take the red-dyed reins of the swift horses and raise high courage in your heart and guide the swift chariot and strong fleet-footed horses straight on. Have no secret fear at the noise of man-slaying Ares who now rages shouting about the holy grove of Phoebus Apollo, the lord who shoots from afar. Surely, strong though he be, he shall have enough of war."

And blameless Iolaus answered him again: "Good friend, truly the father of men and gods greatly honours your head and the bull-like Earth-Shaker also, who keeps Thebe's veil of walls and guards the city,—so great and strong is this fellow they bring into your hands that you may win great glory. But come, put on your arms of war that with all speed we may bring the car of Ares and our own together and fight; for he shall not frighten the dauntless son of Zeus, nor yet the son of Iphiclus: rather I think he will flee before the two sons of blameless Alcides who are near him and eager to raise the war cry for battle; for this they love better than a feast."

Ὣς φάτο· μείδησεν δὲ βίη Ἡρακληείη
θυμῷ γηθήσας· μάλα γάρ νύ οἱ ἄρμενα εἶπεν·
καί μιν ἀμειβόμενος ἔπεα πτερόεντα προσηύδα·
Ἥρως ὦ Ἰόλαε, διοτρεφές, οὐκέτι τηλοῦ
ὑσμίνη τρηχεῖα· σὺ δ' ὡς πάρος ἦσθα δαΐφρων,
ὣς καὶ νῦν μέγαν ἵππον Ἀρίονα κυανοχαίτην
πάντῃ ἀναστρωφᾶν καὶ ἀρηγέμεν, ὥς κε δύνηαι.
Ὣς εἰπὼν κνημῖδας ὀρειχάλκοιο φαεινοῦ,
Ἡφαίστου κλυτὰ δῶρα, περὶ κνήμῃσιν ἔθηκεν·
δεύτερον αὖ θώρηκα περὶ στήθεσσιν ἔδυνε
καλὸν χρύσειον πολυδαίδαλον, ὅν οἱ ἔδωκε
Παλλὰς Ἀθηναίη, κούρη Διός, ὁππότ' ἔμελλε
τὸ πρῶτον στονόεντας ἐφορμήσεσθαι ἀέθλους.
θήκατο δ' ἀμφ' ὤμοισιν ἀρῆς ἀλκτῆρα σίδηρον
δεινὸς ἀνήρ· κοΐλην δὲ περὶ στήθεσσι φαρέτρην
καββάλετ' ἐξόπιθεν· πολλοὶ δ' ἔντοσθεν ὀιστοὶ
ῥιγηλοί, θανάτοιο λαθιφθόγγοιο δοτῆρες.
πρόσθεν μὲν θάνατόν τ' εἶχον καὶ δάκρυσι μῦρον,
μέσσοι δὲ ξεστοί, περιμήκεες, αὐτὰρ ὄπισθε
μόρφνοιο φλεγύαο καλυπτόμενοι πτερύγεσσιν.
εἵλετο δ'[1] ὄβριμον ἔγχος, ἀκαχμένον αἴθοπι χαλκῷ,
κρατὶ δ' ἔπ' ἰφθίμῳ κυνέην εὔτυκτον ἔθηκε,
δαιδαλέην ἀδάμαντος, ἐπὶ κροτάφοις ἀραρυῖαν,
ἥτ' εἴρυτο κάρη Ἡρακλῆος θείοιο.
Χερσί γε μὴν σάκος εἷλε παναίολον, οὐδέ τις αὐτὸ
οὔτ' ἔρρηξε βαλὼν οὔτ' ἔθλασε, θαῦμα ἰδέσθαι.
πᾶν μὲν γὰρ κύκλῳ τιτάνῳ λευκῷ τ' ἐλέφαντι
ἠλέκτρῳ θ' ὑπολαμπὲς ἔην χρυσῷ τε φαεινῷ

[1] Hermann: ἦσαν· ὃ δ', MSS.

So he said. And mighty Heracles was glad in heart and smiled, for the other's words pleased him well, and he answered him with winged words:

"O hero Iolaus, heaven-sprung, now is rough battle hard at hand. But, as you have shown your skill at other times, so now also wheel the great black-maned horse Arion about every way, and help me as you may be able."

So he said, and put upon his legs greaves of shining bronze, the splendid gift of Hephaestus. Next he fastened about his breast a fine golden breast-plate, curiously wrought, which Pallas Athene the daughter of Zeus had given him when first he was about to set out upon his grievous labours. Over his shoulders the fierce warrior put the steel that saves men from doom, and across his breast he slung behind him a hollow quiver. Within it were many chilling arrows, dealers of death which makes speech forgotten: in front they had death, and trickled with tears; their shafts were smooth and very long; and their butts were covered with feathers of a brown eagle. And he took his strong spear, pointed with shining bronze, and on his valiant head set a well-made helm of adamant, cunningly wrought, which fitted closely on the temples; and that guarded the head of god-like Heracles.

In his hands he took his shield, all glittering: no one ever broke it with a blow or crushed it. And a wonder it was to see; for its whole orb was a-shimmer with enamel and white ivory and electrum, and it glowed with shining gold; and there were

λαμπόμενον, κυάνου δὲ διὰ πτύχες ἠλήλαντο.
ἐν μέσσῳ δ' ἀδάμαντος[1] ἔην Φόβος οὔ τι φατειός,
ἔμπαλιν ὄσσοισιν πυρὶ λαμπομένοισι δεδορκώς·
τοῦ καὶ ὀδόντων μὲν πλῆτο στόμα λευκὰ θεόντων,
δεινῶν ἀπλήτων, ἐπὶ δὲ βλοσυροῖο μετώπου
δεινὴ Ἔρις πεπότητο κορύσσουσα κλόνον ἀνδρῶν,
σχετλίη, ἥ ῥα νόον τε καὶ ἐκ φρένας εἵλετο φωτῶν,
οἵτινες ἀντιβίην πόλεμον Διὸς υἷι φέροιεν.
τῶν καὶ ψυχαὶ μὲν χθόνα δύμεναι Ἄιδος εἴσω
κάκκιον,[2] ὀστέα δέ σφι περὶ ῥινοῖο σαπείσης
Σειρίου ἀζαλέοιο μελαίνῃ πύθεται αἴῃ.
Ἐν δὲ Προΐωξίς τε Παλίωξίς τε τέτυκτο,
ἐν δ' Ὅμαδός τε Φόβος τ' Ἀνδροκτασίη τε δεδήει,
ἐν δ' Ἔρις, ἐν δὲ Κυδοιμὸς ἐθύνεον, ἐν δ' ὀλοὴ Κὴρ
ἄλλον ζωὸν ἔχουσα νεούτατον, ἄλλον ἄουτον,
ἄλλον τεθνηῶτα κατὰ μόθον ἕλκε ποδοῖιν.
εἷμα δ' ἔχ' ἀμφ' ὤμοισι δαφοινεὸν αἵματι φωτῶν,
δεινὸν δερκομένη καναχῇσί τε βεβρυχυῖα.
Ἐν δ' ὀφίων κεφαλαὶ δεινῶν ἔσαν, οὔ τι φατειῶν,
δώδεκα, ταὶ φοβέεσκον ἐπὶ χθονὶ φῦλ' ἀνθρώπων,
οἵ τινες ἀντιβίην πόλεμον Διὸς υἷι φέροιεν·
τῶν καὶ ὀδόντων μὲν καναχὴ πέλεν, εὖτε μάχοιτο
Ἀμφιτρυωνιάδης, τὰ δ' ἐδαίετο θαυματὰ ἔργα.
στίγματα δ' ὡς ἐπέφαντο ἰδεῖν δεινοῖσι δράκουσιν·
κυάνεοι κατὰ νῶτα, μελάνθησαν δὲ γένεια.

[1] Schol. : δὲ δράκοντος, MSS.
[2] (=κατέκιον : cp. l. 254), Tr.: αὐτῶν, MSS.

zones of cyanus[1] drawn upon it. In the centre was Fear worked in adamant, unspeakable, staring backwards with eyes that glowed with fire. His mouth was full of teeth in a white row, fearful and daunting, and upon his grim brow hovered frightful Strife who arrays the throng of men: pitiless she, for she took away the mind and senses of poor wretches who made war against the son of Zeus. Their souls passed beneath the earth and went down into the house of Hades; but their bones, when the skin is rotted about them, crumble away on the dark earth under parching Sirius.

Upon the shield Pursuit and Flight were wrought, and Tumult, and Panic, and Slaughter. Strife also, and Uproar were hurrying about, and deadly Fate was there holding one man newly wounded, and another unwounded; and one, who was dead, she was dragging by the feet through the tumult. She had on her shoulders a garment red with the blood of men, and terribly she glared and gnashed her teeth.

And there were heads of snakes unspeakably frightful, twelve of them; and they used to frighten the tribes of men on earth whosoever made war against the son of Zeus; for they would clash their teeth when Amphitryon's son was fighting: and brightly shone these wonderful works. And it was as though there were spots upon the frightful snakes: and their backs were dark blue and their jaws were black.

[1] Cyanus was a glass-paste of deep blue colour: the "zones" were concentric bands in which were the scenes described by the poet. The figure of Fear (l. 44) occupied the centre of the shield, and Oceanus (l. 314) enclosed the whole.

Ἐν δὲ συῶν ἀγέλαι χλούνων ἔσαν ἠδὲ λεόντων
ἐς σφέας δερκομένων, κοτεόντων θ' ἱεμένων τε.
τῶν καὶ ὁμιληδὸν στίχες ἤισαν· οὐδέ νυ τώ γε
οὐδέτεροι τρεέτην· φρῖσσόν γε μὲν αὐχένας ἄμφω.
ἤδη γάρ σφιν ἔκειτο μέγας λῖς, ἀμφὶ δὲ κάπροι
δοιοί, ἀπουράμενοι ψυχάς, κατὰ δέ σφι κελαινὸν
αἷμ' ἀπελείβετ' ἔραζ'· οἳ δ' αὐχένας ἐξεριπόντες
κείατο τεθνηῶτες ὑπὸ βλοσυροῖσι λέουσιν.
τοὶ δ' ἔτι μᾶλλον ἐγειρέσθην κοτέοντε μάχεσθαι,
ἀμφότεροι, χλοῦναί τε σύες χαροποί τε λέοντες.
Ἐν δ' ἦν ὑσμίνη Λαπιθάων αἰχμητάων
Καινέα τ' ἀμφὶ ἄνακτα Δρύαντά τε Πειρίθοόν τε
Ὁπλέα τ' Ἐξάδιόν τε Φάληρόν τε Πρόλοχόν τε
Μόψον τ' Ἀμπυκίδην, Τιταρήσιον, ὄζον Ἄρηος,
Θησέα τ' Αἰγεΐδην, ἐπιείκελον ἀθανάτοισιν·
ἀργύρεοι, χρύσεια περὶ χροῒ τεύχε' ἔχοντες.
Κένταυροι δ' ἑτέρωθεν ἐναντίοι ἠγερέθοντο
ἀμφὶ μέγαν Πετραῖον ἰδ' Ἄσβολον οἰωνιστὴν
Ἄρκτον τ' Οὔρειόν τε μελαγχαίτην τε Μίμαντα
καὶ δύο Πευκεΐδας, Περιμήδεά τε Δρύαλόν τε,
ἀργύρεοι, χρυσέας ἐλάτας ἐν χερσὶν ἔχοντες.
καί τε συναΐγδην ὡς εἰ ζωοί περ ἐόντες
ἔγχεσιν ἠδ' ἐλάτῃς αὐτοσχεδὸν ὠριγνῶντο.
Ἐν δ' Ἄρεος βλοσυροῖο ποδώκεες ἕστασαν ἵπποι
χρύσεοι, ἐν δὲ καὶ αὐτὸς ἐναρσφόρος οὔλιος Ἄρης
αἰχμὴν ἐν χείρεσσιν ἔχων, πρυλέεσσι κελεύων,
αἵματι φοινικόεις, ὡς εἰ ζωοὺς ἐναρίζων
δίφρου ἐπεμβεβαώς· παρὰ δὲ Δεῖμός τε Φόβος τε
ἕστασαν ἱέμενοι πόλεμον καταδύμεναι ἀνδρῶν.
Ἐν δὲ Διὸς θυγάτηρ ἀγελείη Τριτογένεια,

Also there were upon the shield droves of boars and lions who glared at each other, being furious and eager : the rows of them moved on together, and neither side trembled but both bristled up their manes. For already a great lion lay between them and two boars, one on either side, bereft of life, and their dark blood was dripping down upon the ground ; they lay dead with necks outstretched beneath the grim lions. And both sides were roused still more to fight because they were angry, the fierce boars and the bright-eyed lions.

And there was the strife of the Lapith spearmen gathered round the prince Caeneus and Dryas and Peirithöus, with Hopleus, Exadius, Phalereus, and Prolochus, Mopsus the son of Ampyce of Titaresia, a scion of Ares, and Theseus, the son of Aegeus, like unto the deathless gods. These were of silver, and had armour of gold upon their bodies. And the Centaurs were gathered against them on the other side with Petraeus and Asbolus the diviner, Arctus, and Ureus, and black-haired Mimas, and the two sons of Peuceus, Perimedes and Dryalus : these were of silver, and they had pinetrees of gold in their hands. and they were rushing together as though they were alive and striking at one another hand to hand with spears and with pines.

And on the shield stood the fleet-footed horses of grim Ares made of gold, and deadly Ares the spoil-winner himself. He held a spear in his hands and was urging on the footmen : he was red with blood as if he were slaying living men, and he stood in his chariot. Beside him stood Fear and Flight, eager to plunge amidst the fighting men.

There, too, was the daughter of Zeus, Tritogeneia

τῇ ἰκέλη ὡς εἴ τε μάχην ἐθέλουσα κορύσσειν,
ἔγχος ἔχουσ' ἐν χερσὶν ἰδὲ χρυσέην τρυφάλειαν
αἰγίδα τ' ἀμφ' ὤμοις· ἐπὶ δ' ᾤχετο φύλοπιν αἰνήν.
'Εν δ' ἦν ἀθανάτων ἱερὸς χορός· ἐν δ' ἄρα μέσσῳ
ἱμερόεν κιθάριζε Διὸς καὶ Λητοῦς υἱὸς
χρυσείῃ φόρμιγγι· [θεῶν δ' ἕδος ἁγνὸς Ὄλυμπος·
ἐν δ' ἀγορή, περὶ δ' ὄλβος ἀπείριτος ἐστεφάνωτο
ἀθανάτων ἐν ἀγῶνι·[1]] θεαὶ δ' ἐξῆρχον ἀοιδῆς
Μοῦσαι Πιερίδες, λιγὺ μελπομένῃς ἐικυῖαι.
'Εν δὲ λιμὴν εὔορμος ἀμαιμακέτοιο θαλάσσης
κυκλοτερὴς ἐτέτυκτο πανέφθου κασσιτέροιο
κλυζομένῳ ἴκελος· [πολλοί γε μὲν ἂμ μέσον αὐτοῦ
δελφῖνες τῇ καὶ τῇ ἐθύνεον ἰχθυάοντες
νηχομένοις ἴκελοι·[2]] δοιὼ δ' ἀναφυσιόωντες
ἀργύρεοι δελφῖνες ἐθοινῶντ'[3] ἔλλοπας ἰχθῦς.
τῶν δ' ὕπο χάλκειοι τρέον ἰχθύες· αὐτὰρ ἐπ' ἀκταῖς
ἧστο ἀνὴρ ἁλιεὺς δεδοκημένος· εἶχε δὲ χερσὶν
ἰχθύσιν ἀμφίβληστρον ἀπορρίψοντι ἐοικώς.
'Εν δ' ἦν ἠυκόμου Δανάης τέκος, ἱππότα Περσεύς,
οὔτ' ἄρ' ἐπιψαύων σάκεος ποσὶν οὔθ' ἑκὰς αὐτοῦ,
θαῦμα μέγα φράσσασθ', ἐπεὶ οὐδαμῇ ἐστήρικτο.
τὼς γάρ μιν παλάμαις τεῦξεν κλυτὸς Ἀμφιγυήεις
χρύσεον· ἀμφὶ δὲ ποσσὶν ἔχεν πτερόεντα πέδιλα.
ὤμοισιν δέ μιν ἀμφὶ μελάνδετον ἆορ ἔκειτο
χαλκέου ἐκ τελαμῶνος· ὃ δ' ὥς τε νόημ' ἐποτᾶτο·

[1] ll. 203–5 are clearly intrusive and are rejected by Baumeister.
[2] ll. 209–11 are not found in Q, and are rejected by Peppmüller. They appear to be an alternative version of ll. 211–212.
[3] Ranke: ἐφοίνεον, Q: ἔφοιβον, F: ἐφοίτων, other MSS.

who drives the spoil.[1] She was like as if she would array a battle, with a spear in her hand, and a golden helmet, and the aegis about her shoulders. And she was going towards the awful strife.

And there was the holy company of the deathless gods: and in the midst the son of Zeus and Leto played sweetly on a golden lyre. There also was the abode of the gods, pure Olympus, and their assembly, and infinite riches were spread around in the gathering of the deathless gods. Also the goddesses, the Muses of Pieria were beginning a song like clear-voiced singers.

And on the shield was a harbour with a safe haven from the irresistible sea, made of refined tin wrought in a circle, and it seemed to heave with waves. In the middle of it were many dolphins rushing this way and that, fishing: and they seemed to be swimming. Two dolphins of silver were spouting and devouring the mute fishes. And beneath them fishes of bronze were trembling. And on the shore sat a fisherman watching: in his hands he held a casting net for fish, and seemed as if about to cast it forth.

There, too, was the son of rich-haired Danaë, the horseman Perseus: his feet did not touch the shield and yet were not far from it—very marvellous to remark, since he was not supported anywhere; for so did the famous Lame One fashion him of gold with his hands. On his feet he had winged sandals, and his black-sheathed sword was slung across his shoulders by a cross-belt of bronze. He was flying

[1] "She who drives herds," *i.e.* "The Victorious," since herds were the chief spoil gained by the victor in ancient warfare.

πᾶν δὲ μετάφρενον εἶχε κάρη δεινοῖο πελώρου,
Γοργοῦς· ἀμφὶ δέ μιν κίβισις θέε, θαῦμα ἰδέσθαι,
ἀργυρέη· θύσανοι δὲ κατηωρεῦντο φαεινοὶ
χρύσειοι· δεινὴ δὲ περὶ κροτάφοισιν ἄνακτος
κεῖτ' Ἄιδος κυνέη νυκτὸς ζόφον αἰνὸν ἔχουσα.
αὐτὸς δὲ σπεύδοντι καὶ ἐρρίγοντι ἐοικὼς
Περσεὺς Δαναΐδης ἐτιταίνετο. ταὶ δὲ μετ' αὐτὸν
Γοργόνες ἄπλητοί τε καὶ οὐ φαταὶ ἐρρώοντο
ἱέμεναι μαπέειν. ἐπὶ δὲ χλωροῦ ἀδάμαντος
βαινουσέων ἰάχεσκε σάκος μεγάλῳ ὀρυμαγδῷ
ὀξέα καὶ λιγέως· ἐπὶ δὲ ζώνῃσι δράκοντε
δοιὼ ἀπῃωρεῦντ' ἐπικυρτώοντε κάρηνα.
λίχμαζον δ' ἄρα τώ γε· μένει δ' ἐχάρασσον ὀδόντας
ἄγρια δερκομένω. ἐπὶ δὲ δεινοῖσι καρήνοις
Γοργείοις ἐδονεῖτο μέγας Φόβος. οἳ δ' ὑπὲρ αὐτέων
ἄνδρες ἐμαρνάσθην πολεμήια τεύχε' ἔχοντες,
τοὶ μὲν ὑπὲρ σφετέρης πόλιος σφετέρων τε τοκήων
λοιγὸν ἀμύνοντες, τοὶ δὲ πραθέειν μεμαῶτες.
πολλοὶ μὲν κέατο, πλέονες δ' ἔτι δῆριν ἔχοντες
μάρνανθ'· αἱ δὲ γυναῖκες ἐυδμήτων ἐπὶ πύργων
χαλκέων ὀξὺ βόων, κατὰ δ' ἐδρύπτοντο παρειάς,
ζωῇσιν ἴκελαι, ἔργα κλυτοῦ Ἡφαίστοιο.
ἄνδρες δ', οἳ πρεσβῆες ἔσαν γῆράς τε μέμαρπεν,
ἀθρόοι ἔκτοσθεν πυλέων ἔσαν, ἂν δὲ θεοῖσι
χεῖρας ἔχον μακάρεσσι, περὶ σφετέροισι τέκεσσι
δειδιότες· τοὶ δ' αὖτε μάχην ἔχον. αἳ δὲ μετ' αὐτοὺς
Κῆρες κυάνεαι, λευκοὺς ἀραβεῦσαι ὀδόντας,
δεινωπαὶ βλοσυραί τε δαφοιναί τ' ἄπληταί τε
δῆριν ἔχον περὶ πιπτόντων· πᾶσαι δ' ἄρ' ἵεντο
αἷμα μέλαν πιέειν· ὃν δὲ πρῶτον μεμάποιεν

swift as thought. The head of a dreadful monster, the Gorgon, covered the broad of his back, and a bag of silver—a marvel to see—contained it: and from the bag bright tassels of gold hung down. Upon the head of the hero lay the dread cap[1] of Hades which had the awful gloom of night. Perseus himself, the son of Danaë, was at full stretch, like one who hurries and shudders with horror. And after him rushed the Gorgons, unapproachable and unspeakable, longing to seize him: as they trod upon the pale adamant, the shield rang sharp and clear with a loud clanging. Two serpents hung down at their girdles with heads curved forward: their tongues were flickering, and their teeth gnashing with fury, and their eyes glaring fiercely. And upon the awful heads of the Gorgons great Fear was quaking.

237 And beyond these there were men fighting in warlike harness, some defending their own town and parents from destruction, and others eager to sack it; many lay dead, but the greater number still strove and fought. The women on well-built towers of bronze were crying shrilly and tearing their cheeks like living beings—the work of famous Hephaestus. And the men who were elders and on whom age had laid hold were all together outside the gates, and were holding up their hands to the blessed gods, fearing for their own sons. But these again were engaged in battle: and behind them the dusky Fates, gnashing their white fangs, lowering, grim, bloody, and unapproachable, struggled for those who were falling, for they all were longing to drink dark blood. So soon as they caught a man

[1] The cap of darkness which made its wearer invisible.

κείμενον ἢ πίπτοντα νεούτατον, ἀμφὶ μὲν αὐτῷ
βάλλ' ὄνυχας μεγάλους, ψυχὴ δ' Ἄιδόσδε κατῇεν
Τάρταρον ἐς κρυόενθ'. αἳ δὲ φρένας εὖτ' ἀρέσαντο
αἵματος ἀνδρομέου, τὸν μὲν ῥίπτασκον ὀπίσσω,
ἂψ δ' ὅμαδον καὶ μῶλον ἐθύνεον αὖτις ἰοῦσαι.
Κλωθὼ καὶ Λάχεσίς σφιν ἐφέστασαν· ἣ μὲν ὑφήσσων
Ἄτροπος οὔ τι πέλεν μεγάλη θεός, ἀλλ' ἄρα ἥ γε
τῶν γε μὲν ἀλλάων προφερής τ' ἦν πρεσβυτάτη τε.
πᾶσαι δ' ἀμφ' ἑνὶ φωτὶ μάχην δριμεῖαν ἔθεντο.
δεινὰ δ' ἐς ἀλλήλας δράκον ὄμμασι θυμήνασαι,
ἐν δ' ὄνυχας χεῖράς τε θρασείας ἰσώσαντο.
πὰρ δ' Ἀχλὺς εἱστήκει ἐπισμυγερή τε καὶ αἰνή,
χλωρὴ ἀυσταλέη λιμῷ καταπεπτηυῖα,
γουνοπαχής, μακροὶ δ' ὄνυχες χείρεσσιν ὑπῆσαν.
τῆς ἐκ μὲν ῥινῶν μύξαι ῥέον, ἐκ δὲ παρειῶν
αἷμ' ἀπελείβετ' ἔραζ'· ἣ δ' ἄπλητον σεσαρυῖα
εἱστήκει, πολλὴ δὲ κόνις κατενήνοθεν ὤμους,
δάκρυσι μυδαλέη. παρὰ δ' εὔπυργος πόλις ἀνδρῶν·
χρύσειαι δέ μιν εἶχον ὑπερθυρίοις ἀραρυῖαι
ἑπτὰ πύλαι· τοὶ δ' ἄνδρες ἐν ἀγλαΐῃς τε χοροῖς τε
τέρψιν ἔχον· τοὶ μὲν γὰρ ἐυσσώτρου ἐπ' ἀπήνης
ἤγοντ' ἀνδρὶ γυναῖκα, πολὺς δ' ὑμέναιος ὀρώρει·
τῆλε δ' ἀπ' αἰθομένων δαΐδων σέλας εἱλύφαζε
χερσὶν ἔνι δμῳῶν· ταὶ δ' ἀγλαΐῃ τεθαλυῖαι
πρόσθ' ἔκιον· τῇσιν δὲ χοροὶ παίζοντες ἕποντο.
τοὶ μὲν ὑπὸ λιγυρῶν συρίγγων ἵεσαν αὐδὴν
ἐξ ἁπαλῶν στομάτων, περὶ δέ σφισιν ἄγνυτο ἠχώ.
αἳ δ' ὑπὸ φορμίγγων ἄναγον χορὸν ἱμερόεντα.
ἔνθεν δ' αὖθ' ἑτέρωθε νέοι κώμαζον ὑπ' αὐλοῦ,

overthrown or falling newly wounded, one of them would clasp her great claws about him, and his soul would go down to Hades to chilly Tartarus. And when they had satisfied their souls with human blood, they would cast that one behind them, and rush back again into the tumult and the fray. Clotho and Lachesis were over them and Atropos less tall than they, a goddess of no great frame, yet superior to the others and the eldest of them. And they all made a fierce fight over one poor wretch, glaring evilly at one another with furious eyes and fighting equally with claws and hands. By them stood Darkness of Death, mournful and fearful, pale, shrivelled, shrunk with hunger, swollen-kneed. Long nails tipped her hands, and she dribbled at the nose, and from her cheeks blood dripped down to the ground. She stood leering hideously, and much dust sodden with tears lay upon her shoulders.

Next, there was a city of men with goodly towers; and seven gates of gold, fitted to the lintels, guarded it. The men were making merry with festivities and dances; some were bringing home a bride to her husband on a well-wheeled car, while the bridal-song swelled high, and the glow of blazing torches held by handmaidens rolled in waves afar. And these maidens went before, delighting in the festival; and after them came frolicsome choirs, the youths singing soft-mouthed to the sound of shrill pipes, while the echo was shivered around them, and the girls leading on the lovely dance to the sound of lyres. Then again on the other side was a rout of young men revelling, with flutes playing; some

τοί γε μὲν αὖ παίζοντες ὑπ' ὀρχηθμῷ καὶ ἀοιδῇ
τοί γε μὲν αὖ γελόωντες ὑπ' αὐλητῆρι ἕκαστος
πρόσθ' ἔκιον· πᾶσαν δὲ πόλιν θαλίαι τε χοροί τε
ἀγλαΐαι τ' εἶχον. τοὶ δ' αὖ προπάροιθε πόληος
νῶθ' ἵππων ἐπιβάντες ἐθύνεον. οἱ δ' ἀροτῆρες
ἤρεικον χθόνα δῖαν, ἐπιστολάδην δὲ χιτῶνας
ἐστάλατ'. αὐτὰρ ἔην βαθὺ λήιον· οἵ γε μὲν ἤμων
αἰχμῇς ὀξείῃσι κορωνιόωντα πέτηλα,
βριθόμενα σταχύων, ὡς εἰ Δημήτερος ἀκτήν·
οἳ δ' ἄρ' ἐν ἐλλεδανοῖσι δέον καὶ ἔπιτνον ἀλωήν,[1]
οἳ δ' ἐτρύγων οἴνας δρεπάνας ἐν χερσὶν ἔχοντες,
οἳ δ' αὖτ' ἐς ταλάρους ἐφόρευν ὑπὸ τρυγητήρων
λευκοὺς καὶ μέλανας βότρυας μεγάλων ἀπὸ ὄρχων,
βριθομένων φύλλοισι καὶ ἀργυρέῃς ἑλίκεσσιν.
οἳ δ' αὖτ' ἐς ταλάρους ἐφόρευν. παρὰ δέ σφισιν ὄρχος
χρύσεος ἦν, κλυτὰ ἔργα περίφρονος Ἡφαίστοιο,
σειόμενος φύλλοισι καὶ ἀργυρέῃσι κάμαξι,
βριθόμενος σταφυλῇσι· μελάνθησάν γε μὲν αἵδε.
οἵ γε μὲν ἐτράπεον, τοὶ δ' ἤρυον· οἳ δ' ἐμάχοντο
πύξ τε καὶ ἑλκηδόν· τοὶ δ' ὠκύποδας λαγὸς ᾕρευν
ἄνδρες θηρευταί, καὶ καρχαρόδοντε κύνε πρό,
ἱέμενοι μαπέειν, οἳ δ' ἱέμενοι ὑπαλύξαι.
Πὰρ δ' αὐτοῖς ἱππῆες ἔχον πόνον, ἀμφὶ δ' ἀέθλῳ
δῆριν ἔχον καὶ μόχθον. ἐυπλεκέων δ' ἐπὶ δίφρων
ἡνίοχοι βεβαῶτες ἐφίεσαν ὠκέας ἵππους
ῥυτὰ χαλαίνοντες, τὰ δ' ἐπικροτέοντα πέτοντο

[1] GH have the alternative reading ἔπιπλον.

---

298 τοί γε μὲν αὖ παίζοντες ὑπ' αὐλητῆρι ἕκαστος

This line, which is perhaps an alternative for ll. 282–3 and may have once stood at the foot of a MS. page, is omitted by many MSS.

frolicking with dance and song, and others laughing all in time with the flute player as they went along. And the whole town was filled with mirth and dance and festivity.

285 Others again were mounted on horseback and galloping before the town. And there were ploughmen breaking up the good soil, clothed in tunics girt up. Also there was a wide cornland and some men were reaping with sharp hooks the stalks which bended with the weight of the ears—as if they were reaping Demeter's grain: others were binding the sheaves with bands and were spreading the threshing floor. And some held reaping hooks and were gathering the vintage, while others were taking from the reapers into baskets white and black clusters from the long rows of vines which were heavy with leaves and tendrils of silver. Others again were gathering them into baskets. Beside them was a row of vines in gold, the splendid work of cunning Hephaestus: it had shivering leaves and stakes of silver and was laden with grapes which turned black.[1] And there were men treading out the grapes and others drawing off the liquor. Also there were men boxing and wrestling, and huntsmen chasing swift hares with a leash of sharp-toothed dogs before them, they eager to catch the hares, and the hares eager to escape.

Next to them were horsemen hard set, and they contended and laboured for a prize. The charioteers standing on their well-woven cars, urged on their swift horses with loose rein; the jointed cars flew

[1] The existing text of the vineyard scene is a compound of two different versions, clumsily adapted, and eked out with some makeshift additions.

ἅρματα κολλήεντ', ἐπὶ δὲ πλῆμναι μέγ' ἀύτευν.
οἳ μὲν ἄρ' ἀίδιον εἶχον πόνον οὐδέ ποτέ σφιν
νίκη ἐπηνύσθη, ἀλλ' ἄκριτον εἶχον ἄεθλον.
τοῖσιν δὲ προέκειτο μέγας τρίπος ἐντὸς ἀγῶνος,
χρύσειος, κλυτὰ ἔργα περίφρονος Ἡφαίστοιο.
Ἀμφὶ δ' ἴτυν ῥέεν Ὠκεανὸς πλήθοντι ἐοικώς,
πᾶν δὲ συνεῖχε σάκος πολυδαίδαλον, οἳ δὲ κατ' αὐτὸν
κύκνοι ἀερσιπόται μεγάλ' ἤπυον, οἵ ῥά τε πολλοὶ
νῆχον ἐπ' ἄκρον ὕδωρ· παρὰ δ' ἰχθύες ἐκλονέοντο.
Θαῦμα ἰδεῖν καὶ Ζηνὶ βαρυκτύπῳ, οὗ διὰ βουλὰς
Ἥφαιστος ποίησε σάκος μέγα τε στιβαρόν τε,
ἀρσάμενος παλάμῃσι. τὸ μὲν Διὸς ἄλκιμος υἱὸς
πάλλεν ἐπικρατέως· ἐπὶ δ' ἱππείου θόρε δίφρου,
εἴκελος ἀστεροπῇ πατρὸς Διὸς αἰγιόχοιο,
κοῦφα βιβάς· τῷ δ' ἡνίοχος κρατερὸς Ἰόλαος
δίφρου ἐπεμβεβαὼς ἰθύνετο καμπύλον ἅρμα.
ἀγχίμολον δέ σφ' ἦλθε θεὰ γλαυκῶπις Ἀθήνη,
καί σφεας θαρσύνουσα ἔπεα πτερόεντα προσηύδα·
Χαίρετε, Λυγκῆος γενεὴ τηλεκλειτοῖο·
νῦν δὴ Ζεὺς κράτος ὔμμι διδοῖ μακάρεσσιν ἀνάσσων
Κύκνον τ' ἐξεναρεῖν καὶ ἀπὸ κλυτὰ τεύχεα δῦσαι.
ἄλλο δέ τοί τι ἔπος ἐρέω, μέγα φέρτατε λαῶν·
εὖτ' ἂν δὴ Κύκνον γλυκερῆς αἰῶνος ἀμέρσῃς,
τὸν μὲν ἔπειτ' αὐτοῦ λιπέειν καὶ τεύχεα τοῖο,
αὐτὸς δὲ βροτολοιγὸν Ἄρην ἐπιόντα δοκεύσας,
ἔνθα κε γυμνωθέντα σάκευς ὕπο δαιδαλέοιο
ὀφθαλμοῖσιν ἴδῃς, ἔνθ' οὐτάμεν ὀξέι χαλκῷ·
ἂψ δ' ἀναχάσσασθαι· ἐπεὶ οὔ νύ τοι αἴσιμόν ἐστιν
οὔθ' ἵππους ἑλέειν οὔτε κλυτὰ τεύχεα τοῖο.

along clattering and the naves of the wheels shrieked loudly. So they were engaged in an unending toil, and the end with victory came never to them, and the contest was ever unwon. And there was set out for them within the course a great tripod of gold, the splendid work of cunning Hephaestus.

And round the rim Ocean was flowing, with a full stream as it seemed, and enclosed all the cunning work of the shield. Over it swans were soaring and calling loudly, and many others were swimming upon the surface of the water; and near them were shoals of fish.

A wonderful thing the great strong shield was to see—even for Zeus the loud-thunderer, by whose will Hephaestus made it and fitted it with his hands. This shield the valiant son of Zeus wielded masterly, and leaped upon his horse-chariot like the lightning of his father Zeus who holds the aegis, moving lithely. And his charioteer, strong Iolaus, standing upon the car, guided the curved chariot.

Then the goddess grey-eyed Athene came near them and spoke winged words, encouraging them: "Hail, offspring of far-famed Lynceus! Even now Zeus who reigns over the blessed gods gives you power to slay Cycnus and to strip off his splendid armour. Yet I will tell you something besides, mightiest of the people. When you have robbed Cycnus of sweet life, then leave him there and his armour also, and you yourself watch man-slaying Ares narrowly as he attacks, and wherever you shall see him uncovered below his cunningly-wrought shield, there wound him with your sharp spear. Then draw back; for it is not ordained that you should take his horses or his splendid armour."

Ὣς εἰποῦσ' ἐς δίφρον ἐβήσατο δῖα θεάων,
νίκην ἀθανάτῃς χερσὶν καὶ κῦδος ἔχουσα,
ἐσσυμένως. τότε δή ῥα διόγνητος Ἰόλαος
σμερδαλέον ἵπποισιν ἐκέκλετο· τοὶ δ' ὑπ' ὁμοκλῆς
ῥίμφ' ἔφερον θοὸν ἅρμα κονίοντες πεδίοιο.
ἐν γάρ σφιν μένος ἧκε θεὰ γλαυκῶπις Ἀθήνη
αἰγίδ' ἀνασσείσασα· περιστονάχησε δὲ γαῖα.
τοὶ δ' ἅμυδις προγένοντ' ἴκελοι πυρὶ ἠὲ θυέλλῃ,
Κύκνος θ' ἱππόδαμος καὶ Ἄρης ἀκόρητος ἀυτῆς.
τῶν ἵπποι μὲν ἔπειθ' ὑπεναντίοι ἀλλήλοισιν
ὀξεῖα χρέμισαν, περὶ δέ σφισιν ἄγνυτο ἠχώ.
τὸν πρότερος προσέειπε βίη Ἡρακληείη·
Κύκνε πέπον, τί νυ νῶιν ἐπίσχετον ὠκέας ἵππους
ἀνδράσιν, οἵ τε πόνου καὶ ὀιζύος ἴδριές εἰμεν;
ἀλλὰ παρὲξ ἔχε δίφρον ἐύξοον ἠδὲ κελεύθου
εἶκε παρὲξ ἰέναι. Τρηχῖνα δέ τοι παρελαύνω
ἐς Κήυκα ἄνακτα· ὃ γὰρ δυνάμι τε καὶ αἰδοῖ
Τρηχῖνος προβέβηκε, σὺ δ' εὖ μάλα οἶσθα καὶ αὐτός·
τοῦ γὰρ ὀπυίεις παῖδα Θεμιστονόην κυανῶπιν.
ὦ πέπον, οὐ μὲν γάρ τοι Ἄρης θανάτοιο τελευτὴν
ἀρκέσει, εἰ δὴ νῶι συνοισόμεθα πτολεμίζειν
ἤδη μέν τέ ἕ φημι καὶ ἄλλοτε πειρηθῆναι
ἔγχεος ἡμετέρου, ὅθ' ὑπὲρ Πύλου ἠμαθόεντος
ἀντίος ἔστη ἐμεῖο, μάχης ἄμοτον μενεαίνων.
τρὶς μὲν ἐμῷ ὑπὸ δουρὶ τυπεὶς ἠρείσατο γαίῃ
οὐταμένου σάκεος, τὸ δὲ τέτρατον ἤλασα μηρὸν
παντὶ μένει σπεύδων, διὰ δὲ μέγα σαρκὸς ἄραξα.
πρηνὴς δ' ἐν κονίῃσι χαμαὶ πέσεν ἔγχεος ὁρμῇ.
ἔνθα κε δὴ λωβητὸς ἐν ἀθανάτοισιν ἐτύχθη
χερσὶν ὑφ' ἡμετέρῃσι λιπὼν ἔναρα βροτόεντα.

So said the bright-eyed goddess and swiftly got up into the car with victory and renown in her hands. Then heaven-nurtured Iolaus called terribly to the horses, and at his cry they swiftly whirled the fleet chariot along, raising dust from the plain; for the goddess bright-eyed Athene put mettle into them by shaking her aegis. And the earth groaned all round them. And they, horse-taming Cycnus and Ares, insatiable in war, came on together like fire or whirlwind. Then their horses neighed shrilly, face to face; and the echo was shivered all round them. And mighty Heracles spoke first and said to that other:

"Cycnus, good sir! Why, pray, do you set your swift horses at us, men who are tried in labour and pain? Nay, guide your fleet car aside and yield and go out of the path. It is to Trachis I am driving on, to Ceyx the king, who is the first in Trachis for power and for honour, and that you yourself know well, for you have his daughter dark-eyed Themistinoë to wife. Fool! For Ares shall not deliver you from the end of death, if we two meet together in battle. Another time ere this I declare he has made trial of my spear, when he defended sandy Pylos and stood against me, fiercely longing for fight. Thrice was he stricken by my spear and dashed to earth, and his shield was pierced; but the fourth time I struck his thigh, laying on with all my strength, and tare deep into his flesh. And he fell headlong in the dust upon the ground through the force of my spear-thrust; then truly he would have been disgraced among the deathless gods, if by my hands he had left behind his bloody spoils."

Ὣς ἔφατ᾽· οὐδ᾽ ἄρα Κύκνος ἐυμμελίης ἐμενοίνα
τῷ ἐπιπειθόμενος ἐχέμεν ἐρυσάρματας ἵππους.
δὴ τότ᾽ ἀπ᾽ εὐπλεκέων δίφρων θόρον αἶψ᾽ ἐπὶ γαῖαν
παῖς τε Διὸς μεγάλου καὶ Ἐνυαλίοιο ἄνακτος.
ἡνίοχοι δ᾽ ἔμπλην ἔλασαν καλλίτριχας ἵππους·
τῶν δ᾽ ὕπο σευομένων κανάχιζε πόσ᾽ εὐρεῖα χθών.
ὡς δ᾽ ὅτ᾽ ἀφ᾽ ὑψηλῆς κορυφῆς ὄρεος μεγάλοιο
πέτραι ἀποθρῴσκωσιν, ἐπ᾽ ἀλλήλῃς δὲ πέσωσι,
πολλαὶ δὲ δρῦς ὑψίκομοι, πολλαὶ δέ τε πεῦκαι
αἴγειροί τε τανύρριζοι ῥήγνυνται ὑπ᾽ αὐτέων
ῥίμφα κυλινδομένων, εἵως πεδίονδ᾽ ἀφίκωνται,
ὣς οἳ ἐπ᾽ ἀλλήλοισι πέσον μέγα κεκλήγοντες.
πᾶσα δὲ Μυρμιδόνων τε πόλις κλειτή τ᾽ Ἰαωλκὸς
Ἄρνη τ᾽ ἠδ᾽ Ἑλίκη Ἄνθειά τε ποιήεσσα
φωνῇ ὕπ᾽ ἀμφοτέρων μεγάλ᾽ ἴαχον· οἱ δ᾽ ἀλαλητῷ
θεσπεσίῳ σύνισαν· μέγα δ᾽ ἔκτυπε μητίετα Ζεύς.
κὰδ δ᾽ ἄρ᾽ ἀπ᾽ οὐρανόθεν ψιάδας βάλεν αἱματοέσσας,
σῆμα τιθεὶς πολέμοιο ἑῷ μεγαθαρσέι παιδί.
Οἷος δ᾽ ἐν βήσσῃς ὄρεος χαλεπὸς προϊδέσθαι
κάπρος χαυλιόδων φρονέει θυμῷ μαχέσασθαι
ἀνδράσι θηρευτῇς, θήγει δέ τε λευκὸν ὀδόντα
δοχμωθείς, ἀφρὸς δὲ περὶ στόμα μαστιχόωντι
λείβεται, ὄσσε δέ οἱ πυρὶ λαμπετόωντι ἔικτον,
ὀρθὰς δ᾽ ἐν λοφιῇ φρίσσει τρίχας ἀμφί τε δειρήν·
τῷ ἴκελος Διὸς υἱὸς ἀφ᾽ ἱππείου θόρε δίφρου.
ἦμος δὲ χλοερῷ κυανόπτερος ἠχέτα τέττιξ
ὄζῳ ἐφεζόμενος θέρος ἀνθρώποισιν ἀείδειν
ἄρχεται, ᾧ τε πόσις καὶ βρῶσις θῆλυς ἐέρση,
καί τε πανημέριός τε καὶ ἠώιος χέει αὐδὴν
ἴδει ἐν αἰνοτάτῳ, ὅτε τε χρόα Σείριος ἄζει,

So said he. But Cycnus the stout spearman cared not to obey him and to pull up the horses that drew his chariot. Then it was that from their well-woven cars they both leaped straight to the ground, the son of Zeus and the son of the Lord of War. The charioteers drove near by their horses with beautiful manes, and the wide earth rang with the beat of their hoofs as they rushed along. As when rocks leap forth from the high peak of a great mountain, and fall on one another, and many towering oaks and pines and long-rooted poplars are broken by them as they whirl swiftly down until they reach the plain; so did they fall on one another with a great shout: and all the town of the Myrmidons, and famous Iolcus, and Arne, and Helice, and grassy Anthea echoed loudly at the voice of the two. With an awful cry they closed: and wise Zeus thundered loudly and rained down drops of blood, giving the signal for battle to his dauntless son.

As a tusked boar, that is fearful for a man to see before him in the glens of a mountain, resolves to fight with the huntsmen and whets his white tusks, turning sideways, while foam flows all round his mouth as he gnashes, and his eyes are like glowing fire, and he bristles the hair on his mane and around his neck—, like him the son of Zeus leaped from his horse-chariot. And when the dark-winged whirring grasshopper, perched on a green shoot, begins to sing of summer to men—his food and drink is the dainty dew—and all day long from dawn pours forth his voice in the deadliest heat, when Sirius scorches the flesh (then the beard grows upon the millet

τῆμος δὴ κέγχροισι πέρι γλῶχες τελέθουσι
τούς τε θέρει σπείρουσιν, ὅτ' ὄμφακες αἰόλλονται,
οἷα Διώνυσος δῶκ' ἀνδράσι χάρμα καὶ ἄχθος·
τὴν ὥρην μάρναντο, πολὺς δ' ὀρυμαγδὸς ὀρώρει.
ὡς δὲ λέοντε δύω ἀμφὶ κταμένης ἐλάφοιο
ἀλλήλοις κοτέοντες ἐπὶ σφέας ὁρμήσωσι,
δεινὴ δέ σφ' ἰαχὴ ἄραβός θ' ἅμα γίγνετ' ὀδόντων·
οἱ δ' ὥς τ' αἰγυπιοὶ γαμψώνυχες, ἀγκυλοχεῖλαι,
πέτρῃ ἔφ' ὑψηλῇ μεγάλα κλάζοντε μάχονται
αἰγὸς ὀρεσσινόμου ἢ ἀγροτέρης ἐλάφοιο
πίονος, ἥν τ' ἐδάμασσε βαλὼν αἰζήιος ἀνὴρ
ἰῷ ἀπὸ νευρῆς, αὐτὸς δ' ἀπαλήσεται ἄλλῃ
χώρου ἄιδρις ἐών· οἱ δ' ὀτραλέως ἐνόησαν,
ἐσσυμένως δέ οἱ ἀμφὶ μάχην δριμεῖαν ἔθεντο·
ὣς οἱ κεκλήγοντες ἐπ' ἀλλήλοισιν ὄρουσαν.
　Ἔνθ' ἤ τοι Κύκνος μὲν ὑπερμενέος Διὸς υἱὸν
κτεινέμεναι μεμαὼς σάκει ἔμβαλε χάλκεον ἔγχος,
οὐδ' ἔρρηξεν χαλκόν· ἔρυτο δὲ δῶρα θεοῖο.
Ἀμφιτρυωνιάδης δέ, βίη Ἡρακληείη,
μεσσηγὺς κόρυθός τε καὶ ἀσπίδος ἔγχεϊ μακρῷ
αὐχένα γυμνωθέντα θοῶς ὑπένερθε γενείου
ἤλασ' ἐπικρατέως· ἀπὸ δ' ἄμφω κέρσε τένοντε
ἀνδροφόνος μελίη· μέγα γὰρ σθένος ἔμπεσε φωτός.
ἤριπε δ', ὡς ὅτε τις δρῦς ἤριπεν ἢ ὅτε πεύκη
ἠλίβατος, πληγεῖσα Διὸς ψολόεντι κεραυνῷ·
ὣς ἔριπ'· ἀμφὶ δέ οἱ βράχε τεύχεα ποικίλα χαλκῷ.
　Τὸν μὲν ἔπειτ' εἴασε Διὸς ταλακάρδιος υἱός,
αὐτὸς δὲ βροτολοιγὸν Ἄρην προσιόντα δοκεύσας,
δεινὸν ὁρῶν ὄσσοισι, λέων ὣς σώματι κύρσας,

which men sow in summer), when the crude grapes which Dionysus gave to men—a joy and a sorrow both—begin to colour, in that season they fought and loud rose the clamour.

As two lions[1] on either side of a slain deer spring at one another in fury, and there is a fearful snarling and a clashing also of teeth—, like vultures with crooked talons and hooked beak that fight and scream aloud on a high rock over a mountain goat or fat wild-deer which some active man has shot with an arrow from the string, and himself has wandered away elsewhere, not knowing the place; but they quickly mark it and vehemently do keen battle about it—, like these they two rushed upon one another with a shout.

Then Cycnus, eager to kill the son of almighty Zeus, struck upon his shield with a brazen spear, but did not break the bronze; and the gift of the god saved his foe. But the son of Amphitryon, mighty Heracles, with his long spear struck Cycnus violently in the neck beneath the chin, where it was unguarded between helm and shield. And the deadly spear cut through the two sinews; for the hero's full strength lighted on his foe. And Cycnus fell as an oak falls or a lofty pine that is stricken by the lurid thunderbolt of Zeus; even so he fell, and his armour adorned with bronze clashed about him.

Then the stout hearted son of Zeus let him be, and himself watched for the onset of manslaying Ares: fiercely he stared, like a lion who has come upon a

[1] The conception is similar to that of the sculptured group at Athens of Two Lions devouring a Bull (Dickens, *Cat. of the Acropolis Museum*, No. 3).

ὅς τε μάλ' ἐνδυκέως ῥινὸν κρατεροῖς ὀνύχεσσι
σχίσσας ὅττι τάχιστα μελίφρονα θυμὸν ἀπηύρα·
ἐμ μένεος[1] δ' ἄρα τοῦ γε κελαινὸν πίμπλαται ἦτορ·
γλαυκιόων δ' ὄσσοις δεινὸν πλευράς τε καὶ ὤμους
οὐρῇ μαστιόων ποσσὶν γλάφει, οὐδέ τις αὐτὸν
ἔτλη ἐς ἄντα ἰδὼν σχεδὸν ἐλθέμεν[2] οὐδὲ μάχεσθαι·
τοῖος ἄρ' Ἀμφιτρυωνιάδης, ἀκόρητος ἀυτῆς,
ἀντίος ἔστη Ἄρηος, ἐνὶ φρεσὶ θάρσος ἀέξων,
ἐσσυμένως· ὃ δέ οἱ σχεδὸν ἤλυθεν ἀχνύμενος κῆρ·
ἀμφότεροι δ' ἰάχοντες ἐπ' ἀλλήλοισιν ὄρουσαν.
ὡς δ' ὅτ' ἀπὸ μεγάλου πέτρη πρηῶνος ὀρούσῃ,
μακρὰ δ' ἐπιθρῴσκουσα κυλίνδεται, ἣ δέ τε ἠχῇ
ἔρχεται ἐμμεμαυῖα, πάγος δέ οἱ ἀντεβόλησεν
ὑψηλός· τῷ δὴ συνενείκεται, ἔνθα μιν ἴσχει·
τόσσῃ ὃ μὲν ἰαχῇ βρισάρματος οὔλιος Ἄρης
κεκληγὼς ἐπόρουσεν· ὃ δ' ἐμμαπέως ὑπέδεκτο.
Αὐτὰρ Ἀθηναίη, κούρη Διὸς αἰγιόχοιο,
ἀντίη ἦλθεν Ἄρηος ἐρεμνὴν αἰγίδ' ἔχουσα·
δεινὰ δ' ὑπόδρα ἰδοῦσα ἔπεα πτερόεντα προσηύδα·
Ἄρες, ἔπισχε μένος κρατερὸν καὶ χεῖρας ἀάπτους·
οὐ γάρ τοι θέμις ἐστὶν ἀπὸ κλυτὰ τεύχεα δῦσαι
Ἡρακλέα κτείναντα, Διὸς θρασυκάρδιον υἱόν·
ἀλλ' ἄγε παῦε μάχην, μηδ' ἀντίος ἵστασ' ἐμεῖο.
Ὣς ἔφατ'· ἀλλ' οὐ πεῖθ' Ἄρεος μεγαλήτορα θυμόν,
ἀλλὰ μέγα ἰάχων φλογὶ εἴκελά τ' ἔγχεα πάλλων
καρπαλίμως ἐπόρουσε βίῃ Ἡρακληείῃ
κακτάμεναι μεμαώς· καί ῥ' ἔμβαλε χάλκεον ἔγχος,

[1] Dindorf, Meyer: ἐμμενέως, MSS.
[2] A: ἐλθεῖν, MSS.

body and full eagerly rips the hide with his strong claws and takes away the sweet life with all speed: his dark heart is filled with rage and his eyes glare fiercely, while he tears up the earth with his paws and lashes his flanks and shoulders with his tail so that no one dares to face him and go near to give battle. Even so, the son of Amphitryon, unsated of battle, stood eagerly face to face with Ares, nursing courage in his heart. And Ares drew near him with grief in his heart; and they both sprang at one another with a cry. As it is when a rock shoots out from a great cliff and whirls down with long bounds, careering eagerly with a roar, and a high crag clashes with it and keeps it there where they strike together; with no less clamour did deadly Ares, the chariot-borne, rush shouting at Heracles. And he quickly received the attack.

But Athene the daughter of aegis-bearing Zeus came to meet Ares, wearing the dark aegis, and she looked at him with an angry frown and spoke winged words to him. "Ares, check your fierce anger and matchless hands; for it is not ordained that you should kill Heracles, the bold-hearted son of Zeus, and strip off his rich armour. Come, then, cease fighting and do not withstand me."

So said she, but did not move the courageous spirit of Ares. But he uttered a great shout and waving his spears like fire, he rushed headlong at strong Heracles, longing to kill him, and hurled a brazen spear upon the great shield, for he was furiously

σπερχνὸν παιδὸς ἑοῦ κοτέων πέρι τεθνηῶτος,
ἐν σάκεϊ μεγάλῳ. ἀπὸ δὲ γλαυκῶπις Ἀθήνη
ἔγχεος ὁρμὴν ἔτραπ' ὀρεξαμένη ἀπὸ δίφρου.
δριμὺ δ' Ἄρην ἄχος εἷλε· ἐρυσσάμενος δ' ἄορ ὀξὺ
ἔσσυτ' ἐφ' Ἡρακλέα κρατερόφρονα· τὸν δ' ἐπιόντα
Ἀμφιτρυωνιάδης, δεινῆς ἀκόρητος ἀυτῆς,
μηρὸν γυμνωθέντα σάκευς ὕπο δαιδαλέοιο
οὔτασ' ἐπικρατέως· διὰ δὲ μέγα σαρκὸς ἄραξε
δούρατι νωμήσας, ἐπὶ δὲ χθονὶ κάββαλε μέσσῃ.
τῷ δὲ Φόβος καὶ Δεῖμος ἐύτροχον ἅρμα καὶ ἵππους
ἤλασαν αἶψ' ἐγγύς, καὶ ἀπὸ χθονὸς εὐρυοδείης
ἐς δίφρον θῆκαν πολυδαίδαλον· αἶψα δ' ἔπειτα
ἵππους μαστιέτην· ἵκοντο δὲ μακρὸν Ὄλυμπον.
Υἱὸς δ' Ἀλκμήνης καὶ κυδάλιμος Ἰόλαος
Κύκνον σκυλεύσαντες ἀπ' ὤμων τεύχεα καλὰ
νίσσοντ'· αἶψα δ' ἔπειτα πόλιν Τρηχῖνος ἵκοντο
ἵπποις ὠκυπόδεσσιν. ἀτὰρ γλαυκῶπις Ἀθήνη
ἐξίκετ' Οὔλυμπόν τε μέγαν καὶ δώματα πατρός.
Κύκνον δ' αὖ Κῆυξ θάπτεν καὶ λαὸς ἀπείρων,
οἵ ῥ' ἐγγὺς ναῖον πόλιας κλειτοῦ βασιλῆος
Ἄνθην Μυρμιδόνων τε πόλιν κλειτήν τ' Ἰαωλκὸν
Ἄρνην τ' ἠδ' Ἑλίκην· πολλὸς δ' ἠγείρετο λαός,
τιμῶντες Κήυκα, φίλον μακάρεσσι θεοῖσιν.
τοῦ δὲ τάφον καὶ σῆμ' ἀιδὲς ποίησεν Ἄναυρος
ὄμβρῳ χειμερίῳ πλήθων· τὼς γάρ μιν Ἀπόλλων
Λητοΐδης ἤνωξ', ὅτι ῥα κλειτὰς ἑκατόμβας
ὅστις ἄγοι Πυθοῖδε βίῃ σύλασκε δοκεύων.

angry because of his dead son; but bright-eyed Athene reached out from the car and turned aside the force of the spear. Then bitter grief seized Ares and he drew his keen sword and leaped upon bold-hearted Heracles. But as he came on, the son of Amphitryon, unsated of fierce battle, shrewdly wounded his thigh where it was exposed under his richly-wrought shield, and tare deep into his flesh with the spear-thrust and cast him flat upon the ground. And Panic and Dread quickly drove his smooth-wheeled chariot and horses near him and lifted him from the wide-pathed earth into his richly-wrought car, and then straight lashed the horses and came to high Olympus.

But the son of Alcmena and glorious Iolaus stripped the fine armour off Cycnus' shoulders and went, and their swift horses carried them straight to the city of Trachis. And bright-eyed Athene went thence to great Olympus and her father's house.

As for Cycnus, Ceyx buried him and the countless people who lived near the city of the glorious king, in Anthe and the city of the Myrmidons, and famous Iolcus, and Arne, and Helice: and much people were gathered doing honour to Ceyx, the friend of the blessed gods. But Anaurus, swelled by a rain-storm, blotted out the grave and memorial of Cycnus; for so Apollo, Leto's son, commanded him, because he used to watch for and violently despoil the rich hecatombs that any might bring to Pytho.

ΚΗΥΚΟΣ ΓΑΜΟΣ

1.

Scholiast on Apollonius Rhodius, Arg. i. 1289. Ἡσίοδος ἐν τῷ Κήυκος γάμῳ ἐκβάντα φησὶν αὐτὸν ἐφ᾽ ὕδατος ζήτησιν τῆς Μαγνησίας περὶ τὰς ἀπὸ τῆς ἀφέσεως αὐτοῦ Ἀφετὰς καλουμένας ἀπολειφθῆναι.

2.

Zenobius,[1] ii. 19. οὕτως Ἡσίοδος ἐχρήσατο τῇ παροιμίᾳ, ὡς Ἡρακλέους ἐπιφοιτήσαντος ἐπὶ τὴν οἰκίαν Κήυκος τοῦ Τραχινίου καὶ οὕτως εἰπόντος·

αὐτόματοι δ᾽ ἀγαθοὶ ἀγαθῶν ἐπὶ δαῖτας ἵενται.

3.

Schol. on Homer, Il. xiv. 119.

ἰδὼν δ᾽ ἱππηλάτα Κῆυξ.

4.

Athenaeus, ii. p. 49 *b*. Ἡσίοδος ἐν Κήυκος γάμῳ—κἂν γὰρ γραμματικῶν παῖδες ἀποξενῶσι τοῦ ποιητοῦ τὰ ἔπη ταῦτα, ἀλλ᾽ ἐμοὶ δοκεῖ ἀρχαῖα εἶναι—τρίποδας τὰς τραπέζας φησί.

5.

Gregory of Corinth, On Forms of Speech (*Rhett. Gr.* vii. 776).

αὐτὰρ ἐπεὶ δαιτὸς μὲν ἐίσης ἐξ ἔρον ἕντο,
[δὴ τόθ᾽ οἱ ἐξ ὕλης τὴν] μητέρα μητρὸς ἄγοντο
αὐαλέην τε καὶ ὀπταλέην σφετέροισι τέκεσσι
τεθνάμεναι.

[1] A Greek sophist who taught rhetoric at Rome in the time of Hadrian. He is the author of a collection of proverbs in three books.

THE MARRIAGE OF CEYX

1.

Hesiod in the Marriage of Ceyx says that he (Heracles) landed (from the Argo) to look for water and was left behind in Magnesia near the place called Aphetae because of his desertion there.

2.

Hesiod used the proverb in the following way: Heracles is represented as having constantly visited the house of Ceyx of Trachis and spoken thus:
"Of their own selves the good make for the feasts of the good."

3.

"And horse-driving Ceyx beholding . . . ."

4.

Hesiod in the Marriage of Ceyx—for though grammar-school boys alienate it from the poet, yet I consider the poem ancient—calls the tables tripods.

5.

"But when they had done with desire for the equal-shared feast, even then they brought from the forest the mother of a mother (*sc.* wood), dry and parched, to be slain by her own children" (*sc.* to be burnt in the flames).

ΜΕΓΑΛΑΙ ΗΟΙΑΙ

1.

Pausanias, ii. 26. 3. Ἐπίδαυρος δὲ ἀφ᾽ οὗ τὸ ὄνομα τῇ γῇ ἐτέθη . . . κατὰ δὲ Ἀργείων δόξαν καὶ τὰ ἔπη τὰς Μεγάλας Ἠοίας ἦν Ἐπιδαύρῳ πατὴρ Ἄργος ὁ Διός.

2.

Anonymous Comment. on Aristotle, Nicomachean Ethics, iii. 7. καὶ ὅτι, φασί, τὸ πονηρὸς ἐπὶ τοῦ ἐπιπόνου τάττεται καὶ δυστυχοῦς, ἱκανὸς Ἡσίοδος παραστῆσαι ἐν ταῖς Μεγάλαις Ἠοίαις τὴν Ἀλκμήνην ποιῶν πρὸς τὸν Ἡρακλέα λέγουσαν

ὦ τέκος, ἦ μάλα δή σε πονηρότατον καὶ ἄριστον
Ζεὺς τέκνωσε πατήρ.

καὶ πάλιν

αἱ Μοῖραί σε πονηρότατον καὶ ἄριστον.

3.

Scholiast on Pindar, Isthm. v. 53. εἴληπται δὲ ἐκ τῶν Μεγάλων Ἠοιῶν ἡ ἱστορία· ἐκεῖ γὰρ εὑρίσκεται ἐπιξενούμενος ὁ Ἡρακλῆς τῷ Τελαμῶνι καὶ ἐμβαίνων τῇ δορᾷ. καὶ εὐχόμενος καὶ οὕτως ὁ διόπομπος αἰετός, ἀφ᾽ οὗ τὴν προσωνυμίαν ἔλαβεν Αἴας.

THE GREAT EOIAE

1.

Epidaurus. According to the opinion of the Argives and the epic poem, the *Great Eoiae,* Argos the son of Zeus was father of Epidaurus.

2.

And, they say, Hesiod is sufficient to prove that the word *ponēros* (bad) has the same sense as "laborious" or "ill-fated"; for in the *Great Eoiae* he represents Alcmene as saying to Heracles:

"My son, truly Zeus your father begot you to be the most toilful as the most excellent . . .";

and again:

"The Fates (made) you the most toilful and the most excellent . . ."

3.

The story has been taken from the *Great Eoiae*; for there we find Heracles entertained by Telamon, standing dressed in his lion-skin and praying, and there also we find the eagle sent by Zeus, from which Aias took his name.[1]

[1] When Heracles prayed that a son might be born to Telamon and Eriboea, Zeus sent forth an eagle in token that the prayer would be granted. Heracles then bade the parents call their son Aias after the eagle (*aietos*).

4.

Pausanias, iv. 2. 1. . . . ἀλλὰ Ὕλλου μὲν τοῦ Ἡρακλέους θυγατρὶ Εὐαίχμῃ συνοικῆσαι Πολυάονα υἱὸν Βούτου λεγούσας τὰς Μεγάλας οἶδα Ἠοίας.

5.

Pausanias, ix. 40. 6.

Φύλας δ' ὤπυιεν κούρην κλειτοῦ Ἰολάου
Λειπεφίλην, ἣ εἶδος Ὀλυμπιάδεσσιν ὁμοίη,
Ἱπποτάδην τέ οἱ υἱὸν ἐνὶ μεγάροισιν ἔτικτε
Θηρώ τ' εὐειδέα, ἰκέλην φαέεσσι σελήνης.
Θηρὼ δ' Ἀπόλλωνος ἐν ἀγκοίνῃσι πεσοῦσα
γείνατο Χαίρωνος κρατερὸν μένος ἱπποδάμοιο.

6.

Schol. on Pindar, Pyth. iv. 35.

Ἢ οἵη Ὑρίῃ πυκινόφρων Μηκιονίκη,
ἣ τέκεν Εὔφημον γαιηόχῳ Ἐννοσιγαίῳ
μιχθεῖσ' ἐν φιλότητι πολυχρύσου Ἀφροδίτης.

7.

Pausanias, ix. 36. 7.

Ὕηττος δὲ Μόλουρον Ἀρίσβαντος φίλον υἱὸν
κτείνας ἐν μεγάροις εὐνῆς ἕνεχ' ἧς ἀλόχοιο
οἶκον ἀποπρολιπὼν φεῦγ' Ἄργεος ἱπποβότοιο,
ἷξεν δ' Ὀρχόμενον Μινυήιον· καί μιν ὅ γ' ἥρως
δέξατο καὶ κτεάνων μοῖραν πόρεν, ὡς ἐπιεικές.

8.

Pausanias, ii. 2. 3. πεποίηται δὲ ἐν Ἠοίαις Μεγάλαις Οἰβάλου θυγατέρα εἶναι Πειρήνην.

9.

Pausanias, ii. 16. 4. ταύτην (Μυκήνην) εἶναι θυγατέρα Ἰνάχου, γυναῖκα δὲ Ἀρέστορος τὰ ἔπη

4.

But I know that the so-called *Great Eoiae* say that Polycaon the son of Butes married Euaechme, daughter of Hyllus, Heracles' son.

5.

"And Phylas wedded Leipephile the daughter of famous Iolaus: and she was like the Olympians in beauty. She bare him a son Hippotades in the palace, and comely Thero who was like the beams of the moon. And Thero lay in the embrace of Apollo and bare horse-taming Chaeron of hardy strength."

6.

"Or like her in Hyria, careful-minded Mecionice, who was joined in the love of golden Aphrodite with the Earth-holder and Earth-Shaker, and bare Euphemus."

7.

"And Hyettus killed Molurus the dear son of Aristas in his house because he lay with his wife. Then he left his home and fled from horse-rearing Argos and came to Minyan Orchomenus. And the hero received him and gave him a portion of his goods, as was fitting."

8.

But in the *Great Eoiae* Peirene is represented to be the daughter of Oebalus.

9.

The epic poem, which the Greek call the *Great Eoiae*, says that she (Mycene) was the daughter of λέγει ἃ δὴ Ἕλληνες καλοῦσιν Ἠοίας Μεγάλας· ἀπὸ ταύτης οὖν γεγονέναι καὶ τὸ ὄνομα τῇ πόλει φασίν.

10.

Pausanias, vi. 21. 10 *sq*. ἀπέθανον δὲ ὑπὸ τοῦ Οἰνομάου κατὰ τὰ ἔπη τὰς Μεγάλας Ἠοίας Ἀλκάθους ὁ Πορθάονος, δεύτερος οὗτος ἐπὶ τῷ Μάρμακι, μετὰ δὲ Ἀλκάθουν Εὐρύαλος καὶ Εὐρύμαχός τε καὶ Κρόταλος. . . . τὸν δὲ ἀποθανόντα ἐπ' αὐτοῖς Ἀκρίαν τεκμαίροιτο ἄν τις Λακεδαιμόνιόν τε εἶναι καὶ οἰκιστὴν Ἀκριῶν. ἐπὶ δὲ τῷ Ἀκρίᾳ Κάπετόν φασιν ὑπὸ τοῦ Οἰνομάου φονευθῆναι καὶ Λυκοῦργον Λάσιόν τε καὶ Χαλκώδοντα καὶ Τρικόλωνον . . . Τρικολώνου δὲ ὕστερον ἐπέλαβεν ἐν τῷ δρόμῳ τὸ χρεὼν Ἀριστόμαχόν τε καὶ Πρίαντα, ἔτι δὲ Πελάγοντα καὶ Αἰόλιόν τε καὶ Κρόνιον.

11.

Scholiast on Apollonius Rhodius, Arg. iv. 57. ἐν δὲ ταῖς Μεγάλαις Ἠοίαις λέγεται τὸν Ἐνδυμίωνα ἀνενεχθῆναι ὑπὸ τοῦ Διὸς εἰς οὐρανόν· ἐρασθέντα δὲ Ἥρας εἰδώλῳ παραλογισθῆναι νεφέλης καὶ ἐκβληθέντα κατελθεῖν εἰς Ἅιδου.

12.

Scholiast on Apollonius Rhodius, Arg. i. 118. ἐν δὲ ταῖς Μεγάλαις Ἠοίαις λέγεται ὡς ἄρα Μελάμπους φίλτατος ὢν τῷ Ἀπόλλωνι ἀποδημήσας κατέλυσε παρὰ Πολυφάντῃ. βοὸς δὲ αὐτῷ τεθυμένου δράκοντος ἀνερπύσαντος παρὰ τὸ θῦμα διαφθεῖραι

Inachus and wife of Arestor: from her, then, it is said, the city received its name.

10.

According to the poem the *Great Eoiae*, these were killed by Oenomäus[1]: Alcathöus the son of Porthaon next after Marmax, and after Alcathöus, Euryalus, Eurymachus and Crotalus. The man killed next after them, Acrias, we should judge to have been a Lacedemonian and founder of Acria. And after Acrias, they say, Capetus was done to death by Oenomäus, and Lycurgus, Lasius, Chalcodon and Tricolonus. . . . And after Tricolonus fate overtook Aristomachus and Prias on the course, as also Pelagon and Aeolius and Cronius.

11.

In the *Great Eoiae* it is said that Endymion was transported by Zeus into heaven, but when he fell in love with Hera, was befooled with a shape of cloud, and was cast out and went down into Hades.

12.

In the *Great Eoiae* it is related that Melampus, who was very dear to Apollo, went abroad and stayed with Polyphantes. But when the king had sacrificed an ox, a serpent crept up to the sacrifice and

[1] Oenomäus, king of Pisa in Elis, warned by an oracle that he should be killed by his son-in-law, offered his daughter Hippodamia to the man who could defeat him in a chariot race, on condition that the defeated suitors should be slain by him. Ultimately Pelops, through the treachery of the charioteer of Oenomäus, became victorious.

αὐτὸν τοὺς θεράποντας τοῦ βασιλέως. τοῦ δὲ βασιλέως χαλεπήναντος [καὶ ἀποκτείναντος], τὸν Μελάμποδα λαβεῖν καὶ θάψαι. τὰ δὲ τούτου ἔγγονα τραφέντα ὑπὸ τούτου λείχειν τὰ ὦτα καὶ ἐμπνεῦσαι αὐτῷ τὴν μαντικήν. διόπερ κλέπτοντα αὐτὸν τὰς βόας τοῦ Ἰφίκλου εἰς Αἴγιναν τὴν πόλιν περιληφθέντα δεθῆναι καὶ τοῦ οἴκου μέλλοντος πεσεῖν ἐν ᾧ ἦν ὁ Ἴφικλος, τῇ διακόνων πρεσβύτιδι μηνῦσαι τοῦ Ἰφίκλου καὶ τούτου χάριν ἀφεθῆναι.

13.

Scholiast on Apollonius Rhodius, Arg. iv. 828. ἐν δὲ ταῖς Μεγάλαις Ἠοίαις Φόρβαντος καὶ Ἑκατης ἡ Σκύλλα.

14.

Scholiast on Apollonius Rhodius, Arg. ii. 181. πεπηρῶσθαι δὲ Φινέα φησὶν Ἡσίοδος ἐν Μεγάλαις Ἠοίαις, ὅτι Φρίξῳ τὴν ὁδὸν ἐμήνυσεν.

15.

Scholiast on Apollonius Rhodius, Arg. ii. 1122. Ἄργος] εἷς τῶν Φρίξου παίδων οὗτος. τούτους δὲ . . . Ἡσίοδος ἐν ταῖς Μεγάλαις Ἠοίαις φασὶν ἐξ Ἰοφώσσης τῆς Αἰήτου. καὶ οὗτος μέν φησιν αὐτοὺς τέσσαρας, Ἄργον Φρόντιν Μέλανα Κυτίσωρον.

16.

Antoninus Liberalis, xxiii. Βάττος· ἱστορεῖ . . . Ἡσίοδος ἐν Μεγάλαις Ἠοίαις. . . .

Ἄργου τοῦ Φρίξου καὶ Περιμήλης τῆς Ἀδμήτου θυγατρὸς ἐγένετο Μάγνης. οὗτος ᾤκησεν destroyed his servants. At this the king was angry and killed the serpent, but Melampus took and buried it. And its offspring, brought up by him, used to lick his ears and inspire him with prophecy. And so, when he was caught while trying to steal the cows of Iphiclus and taken bound to the city of Aegina, and when the house, in which Iphiclus was, was about to fall, he told an old woman, one of the servants of Iphiclus, and in return was released.

13.

In the *Great Eoiae* Scylla is the daughter of Phoebus and Hecate.

14.

Hesiod in the *Great Eoiae* says that Phineus was blinded because he told Phrixus the way.[1]

15.

Argus. This is one of the children of Phrixus. These . . . Hesiod in the *Great Eoiae* says were born of Iophossa the daughter of Aeëtes. And he says there were four of them, Argus, Phrontis, Melas, and Cytisorus.

16.

Battus. Hesiod tells the story in the *Great Eoiae*. . . . Magnes was the son of Argus, the son of Phrixus and Perimele, Admetus' daughter, and

[1] *sc.* to Scythia.

ἐγγὺς Θεσσαλίας καὶ τὴν γῆν ταύτην ἀπ' αὐτοῦ Μαγνησίαν προσηγόρευσαν οἱ ἄνθρωποι. ἐγένετο δ' αὐτῷ παῖς περίβλεπτος τὴν ὄψιν Ὑμέναιος. ἐπεὶ δὲ Ἀπόλλωνα ἰδόντα ἔρως ἔλαβε τοῦ παιδὸς καὶ οὐκ ἐξελίμπανε τὰ οἰκία τοῦ Μάγνητος, Ἑρμῆς ἐπιβουλεύει τῇ ἀγέλῃ τῶν βοῶν τοῦ Ἀπόλλωνος. αἱ δὲ ἐνέμοντο, ἵνα περ ἦσαν αἱ Ἀδμήτου βόες. καὶ πρῶτα μὲν ἐμβάλλει ταῖς κυσίν, αἳ ἐφύλαττον αὐτάς, λήθαργον καὶ κυνάγχην· αἱ δὲ ἐξελάθοντο τῶν βοῶν καὶ τὴν ὑλακὴν ἀπώλεσαν· εἶτα δ' ἀπελαύνει πόρτιας δώδεκα καὶ ἑκατὸν βοῦς ἄζυγας καὶ ταῦρον, ὃς ταῖς βουσὶν ἐπέβαινεν. ἐξῆπτε δὲ ἐκ τῆς οὐρᾶς πρὸς ἕκαστον ὕλην, ὡς ἂν τὰ ἴχνη τῶν βοῶν ἀφανίσῃ. καὶ ἦγεν αὐτὰς ἐλαύνων διά τε Πελασγῶν καὶ δι' Ἀχαΐας τῆς Φθιώτιδος καὶ διὰ Λοκρίδος καὶ Βοιωτίας καὶ Μεγαρίδος καὶ ἐντεῦθεν εἰς Πελοπόννησον διὰ Κορίνθου καὶ Λαρίσσης ἄχρι Τεγέας. καὶ ἐντεῦθεν παρὰ τὸ Λύκαιον ὄρος ἐπορεύετο καὶ παρὰ τὸ Μαινάλιον καὶ τὰς λεγομένας Βάττου σκοπιάς. ᾤκει δὲ ὁ Βάττος οὗτος ἐπ' ἄκρῳ τῷ σκοπέλῳ καὶ ἐπεὶ τῆς φωνῆς ἤκουσε παρελαυνομένων τῶν μόσχων, προελθὼν ἐκ τῶν οἰκίων ἔγνω περὶ τῶν βοῶν ὅτι κλοπιμαίας ἄγει· καὶ μισθὸν ᾔτησεν, ἵνα πρὸς μηδένα φράσῃ περὶ αὐτῶν. Ἑρμῆς δὲ δώσειν ἐπὶ τούτοις ὑπέσχετο, καὶ ὁ Βάττος ὤμοσε περὶ τῶν βοῶν πρὸς μηδένα κατερεῖν. ἐπεὶ δὲ αὐτὰς Ἑρμῆς ἔκρυψεν ἐν τῷ πρηῶνι παρὰ τὸ Κορυφάσιον εἰς τὸ σπήλαιον εἰσελάσας ἄντικρυς Ἰταλίας καὶ Σικελίας, αὖθις ἀφίκετο πρὸς τὸν Βάττον ἀλλάξας ἑαυτὸν καὶ πειρώμενος, εἰ αὐτῷ συμμένειν ἐπὶ τοῖς ὁρκίοις lived in the region of Thessaly, in the land which men called after him Magnesia. He had a son of remarkable beauty, Hymenaeus. And when Apollo saw the boy, he was seized with love for him, and would not leave the house of Magnes. Then Hermes made designs on Apollo's herd of cattle which were grazing in the same place as the cattle of Admetus. First he cast upon the dogs which were guarding them a stupor and strangles, so that the dogs forgot the cows and lost the power of barking. Then he drove away twelve heifers and a hundred cows never yoked, and the bull who mounted the cows, fastening to the tail of each one brushwood to wipe out the footmarks of the cows. He drove them through the country of the Pelasgi, and Achaea in the land of Phthia, and through Locris, and Boeotia and Megaris, and thence into Peloponnesus by way of Corinth and Larissa, until he brought them to Tegea. From there he went on by the Lycaean mountains, and past Maenalus and what are called the watch-posts of Battus. Now this Battus used to live on the top of the rock and when he heard the voice of the heifers as they were being driven past, he came out from his own place, and knew that the cattle were stolen. So he asked for a reward to tell no one about them. Hermes promised to give it him on these terms, and Battus swore to say nothing to anyone about the cattle. But when Hermes had hidden them in the cliff by Coryphasium, and had driven them into a cave facing towards Italy and Sicily, he changed himself and came again to Battus and tried whether he would be true to him as he had vowed. So, offering ἐθέλει. διδοὺς δὲ μισθὸν χλαῖναν ἐπυνθάνετο παρ' αὐτοῦ, εἰ μὴ κλοπιμαίας βοῦς ἔγνω παρελαθείσας. ὁ δὲ Βάττος ἔλαβε τὴν χλαμύδα καὶ ἐμήνυσε περὶ τῶν βοῶν. Ἑρμῆς δὲ χαλεπήνας, ὅτι διχόμυθος ἦν, ἐρράπισεν αὐτὸν τῇ ῥάβδῳ καὶ μετέβαλεν εἰς πέτρον. καὶ αὐτὸν οὐκ ἐκλείπει κρύος οὐδὲ καῦμα.

ΜΕΛΑΜΠΟΔΕΙΑ

1.

Strabo, xiv. p. 642. λέγεται δὲ ὁ Κάλχας ὁ μάντις μετ' Ἀμφιλόχου τοῦ Ἀμφιαράου κατὰ τὴν ἐκ Τροίας ἐπάνοδον πεζῇ δεῦρο ἀφικέσθαι, περιτυχὼν δ' ἑαυτοῦ κρείττονι μάντει κατὰ τὴν Κλάρον Μόψῳ τῷ Μαντοῦς τῆς Τειρεσίου θυγατρός, διὰ λύπην ἀποθανεῖν. Ἡσίοδος μὲν οὖν οὕτω πως διασκευάζει τὸν μῦθον· προτεῖναι γάρ τι τοιοῦτο τῷ Μόψῳ τὸν Κάλχαντα·

Θαῦμά μ' ἔχει κατὰ θυμόν, ἐρινεὸς ὅσσον ὀλύνθων
οὗτος ἔχει μικρός περ ἐών· εἴποις ἂν ἀριθμόν;

τὸν δὲ ἀποκρίνασθαι·

Μύριοί εἰσιν ἀριθμόν, ἀτὰρ μέτρον γε μέδιμνος·
εἷς δὲ περισσεύει, τὸν ἐπενθέμεν οὔ κε δύναιο.
Ὣς φάτο· καί σφιν ἀριθμὸς ἐτήτυμος εἴδετο μέτρου·
καὶ τότε δὴ Κάλχαντα τέλος θανάτοιο κάλυψεν.

him a robe as a reward, he asked of him whether he had noticed stolen cattle being driven past. And Battus took the robe and told him about the cattle. But Hermes was angry because he was double-tongued, and struck him with his staff and changed him into a rock. And either frost or heat never leaves him.[1]

THE MELAMPODIA

1.

It is said that Calchas the seer returned from Troy with Amphilochus the son of Amphiaraus and came on foot to this place.[2] But happening to find near Clarus a seer greater than himself, Mopsus, the son of Manto, Teiresias' daughter, he died of vexation, Hesiod, indeed, works up the story in some such form as this: Calchas set Mopsus the following problem:

"I am filled with wonder at the quantity of figs this wild fig-tree bears though it is so small. Can you tell their number?"

And Mopsus answered: "Ten thousand is their number, and their measure is a bushel: one fig is left over, which you would not be able to put into the measure."

So said he; and they found the reckoning of the measure true. Then did the end of death shroud Calchas.

[1] In the Homeric *Hymn to Hermes* Battus almost disappears from the story, and a somewhat different account of the stealing of the cattle is given.

[2] *sc.* Colophon. Proclus in his abstract of the *Returns* (*sc.* of the heroes from Troy) says Calchas and his party were present at the death of Teiresias at Colophon, perhaps indicating another version of this story.

2.

Tzetzes on Lycophron, 682. . . . νῦν δὲ τὸν Τειρεσίαν λέγει, ἐπειδή φασιν αὐτὸν ἑπτὰ γενεὰς ζῆσαι· ἄλλοι δὲ ἐννέα· ἀπὸ γὰρ Κάδμου ἦν καὶ κατωτέρω Ἐτεοκλέους καὶ Πολυνείκους, ὥς φησι καὶ ὁ τῆς Μελαμποδίας ποιητής· παρεισάγει γὰρ τὸν Τειρεσίαν λέγοντα·

Ζεῦ πάτερ, εἴθε μοι ἥσσον' ἔχειν αἰῶνα βίοιο
ὤφελλες δοῦναι καὶ ἴσα [φρεσὶ] μήδεα ἴδμεν
θνητοῖς ἀνθρώποις· νῦν δ' οὐδέ με τυτθὸν ἔτισας,
ὅς γέ με μακρὸν ἔθηκας ἔχειν αἰῶνα βίοιο
ἑπτά τ' ἐπὶ ζώειν γενεὰς μερόπων ἀνθρώπων.

3.

Scholiast on Homer, Odyssey, x. 494. φασὶν ὡς δράκοντας δύο ἐν Κιθαιρῶνι μιγνυμένους ἰδὼν (Τειρεσίας) ἀνεῖλε τὴν θήλειαν καὶ οὕτως μεταβέβληται εἰς γυναῖκα, καὶ πάλιν τὸν ἄρρενα καὶ ἀπέλαβε τὴν ἰδίαν φύσιν. τοῦτον Ζεὺς καὶ Ἥρα κριτὴν εἵλοντο, τίς μᾶλλον ἥδεται τῇ συνουσίᾳ, τὸ ἄρρεν ἢ τὸ θῆλυ· ὁ δὲ εἶπεν·

οἴην μὲν μοῖραν δέκα μοιρέων τέρπεται ἀνήρ,
τὰς δέκα δ' ἐμπίπλησι γυνὴ τέρπουσα νόημα.

διόπερ ἡ μὲν Ἥρα ὀργισθεῖσα ἐπήρωσεν, ὁ δὲ Ζεὺς τὴν μαντείαν δωρεῖται.

4.

ἡδὺ [μέν] ἐστ' ἐν δαιτὶ καὶ εἰλαπίνῃ τεθαλυίῃ
τέρπεσθαι μύθοισιν, ἐπὴν δαιτὸς κορέσωνται,
ἡδὺ δὲ καὶ τὸ πυθέσθαι, ὅσα θνητοῖσιν ἔνειμαν
ἀθάνατοι, δειλῶν τε καὶ ἐσθλῶν τέκμαρ ἐναργές.

2.

But now he is speaking of Teiresias, since it is said that he lived seven generations—though others say nine. He lived from the times of Cadmus down to those of Eteocles and Polyneices, as the author of Melampodia also says: for he introduces Teiresias speaking thus:

"Father Zeus, would that you had given me a shorter span of life to be mine and wisdom of heart like that of mortal men! But now you have honoured me not even a little, though you ordained me to have a long span of life, and to live through seven generations of mortal kind."

3.

They say that Teiresias saw two snakes mating on Cithaeron and that, when he killed the female, he was changed into a woman, and again, when he killed the male, took again his own nature. This same Teiresias was chosen by Zeus and Hera to decide the question whether the male or the female has most pleasure in intercourse. And he said:

"Of ten parts a man enjoys one only; but a woman's sense enjoys all ten in full."

For this Hera was angry and blinded him, but Zeus gave him the seer's power.

4.[1]

"For pleasant it is at a feast and rich banquet to tell delightful tales, when men have had enough of feasting; and pleasant also it is to know a clear token of ill or good amid all the signs that the deathless ones have given to mortal men."

[1] ll. 1–2 are quoted by Athenaeus ii. p. 40; ll. 3–4 by Clement of Alexandria, *Stromateis* vi. 2. 26. Buttmann saw that the two fragments should be joined.

5.

Athenaeus, xi. 498. A.

. . . τῷ δὲ Μάρης θοὸς ἄγγελος ἦλθε δι' οἴκου
πλήσας δ' ἀργύρεον σκύπφον φέρε, δῶκε δ' ἄνακτι.

6.

Ib. B.

καὶ τότε Μάντης μὲν δεσμον ροος αινυτο χερσίν,
Ἴφικλος δ' ἐπὶ νῶτ' ἐπεμαίετο. τῷ δ' ἐπ' ὄπισθεν
σκύπφον ἔχων ἑτέρῃ, ἑτέρῃ δὲ σκῆπτρον ἀείρας
ἔστειχεν Φύλακος καὶ ἐνὶ δμώεσσιν ἔειπεν.

7.

Athenaeus, xiii. p. 609 *e*. Ἡσίοδος δ' ἐν τρίτῳ Μελαμποδίας τὴν ἐν Εὐβοίᾳ Χαλκίδα καλλιγύναικα εἶπεν.

8.

Strabo, xiv. p. 676. Ἡσίοδος δ' ἐν Σόλοις ὑπὸ Ἀπόλλωνος ἀναιρεθῆναι τὸν Ἀμφίλοχόν φησιν.

9.

Clement of Alexandria, Stromateis, v. p. 259.

μάντις δ' οὐδείς ἐστιν ἐπιχθονίων ἀνθρώπων
ὅστις ἂν εἰδείη Ζηνὸς νόον αἰγιόχοιο.

ΑΙΓΙΜΙΟΣ

1.

Scholiast on Apollonius Rhodius, Arg. iii. 587. ὁ δὲ τὸν Αἰγίμιον ποιήσας διὰ [τὸ] δέρας αὐτὸν αὐθαιρέτως φησὶ προσδεχθῆναι. λέγει δὲ ὅτι μετὰ τὴν θυσίαν ἁγνίσας τὸ δέρας οὕτως

κῶας ἔχων ἔστειχεν ἐς Αἰήταο μέλαθρα.[1]

[1] Restored by Schenkl.

5.

"And Mares, swift messenger, came to him through the house and brought a silver goblet which he had filled, and gave it to the lord."

6.

"And then Mantes took in his hands the ox's halter and Iphiclus lashed him upon the back. And behind him, with a cup in one hand and a raised sceptre in the other, walked Phylacus and spake amongst the bondmen."

7.

Hesiod in the third book of the Melampodia called Chalcis in Euboea "the land of fair women."

8.

But Hesiod says that Amphilochus was killed by Apollo at Soli.

9.

"And now there is no seer among mortal men such as would know the mind of Zeus who holds the aegis."

AEGIMIUS

1.

But the author of the Aegimius says that he (Phrixus) was received without intermediary because of the fleece.[1] He says that after the sacrifice he purified the fleece and so

"Holding the fleece he walked into the halls of Aeëtes."

[1] *sc.* the golden fleece of the ram which carried Phrixus and Helle away from Athamas and Ino. When he reached Colchis Phrixus sacrificed the ram to Zeus.

2.

Scholiast on Apollonius Rhodius, Arg. iv. 816. ὁ τὸν Αἰγίμιον ποιήσας ἐν δευτέρῳ φησὶν ὅτι ἡ Θέτις εἰς λέβητα ὕδατος ἔβαλλεν τοὺς ἐκ Πηλέως γεννωμένους, γνῶναι βουλομένη εἰ θνητοί εἰσιν . . . καὶ δὴ πολλῶν διαφθαρέντων ἀγανακτῆσαι τὸν Πηλέα καὶ κωλῦσαι τὸν Ἀχιλλέα ἐμβληθῆναι εἰς λέβητα.

3.

Apollodorus, ii. 1. 3. 1. Ἡσίοδος δὲ καὶ Ἀκουσίλαος Πειρῆνος αὐτήν (Ἰώ) φασιν εἶναι. ταύτην ἱερωσύνην τῆς Ἥρας ἔχουσαν Ζεὺς ἔφθειρε. φωραθεὶς δὲ ὑφ' Ἥρας τῆς μὲν κόρης ἁψάμενος εἰς βοῦν μετεμόρφωσε λευκήν, ἀπωμόσατο δὲ ταύτῃ μὴ συνελθεῖν. διό φησιν Ἡσίοδος οὐκ ἐπισπᾶσθαι τὴν ἀπὸ τῶν θεῶν ὀργὴν τοὺς γινομένους ὅρκους ὑπὲρ ἔρωτος.

ἐκ τοῦ δ' ὅρκον ἔθηκεν ἀποίνιμον ἀνθρώποισι
νοσφιδίων ἔργων πέρι Κύπριδος.

4.

Herodian in Stephanus of Byzantium.

νήσῳ ἐν Ἀβαντίδι δίῃ,
τὴν πρὶν Ἀβαντίδα κίκλησκον θεοὶ αἰὲν ἐόντες,
Εὔβοιαν δὲ βοὸς τότ' ἐπώνυμον ὠνόμασεν Ζεύς.

5.

Schol. on Euripides Phoen. 1116.

καί οἱ ἐπίσκοπον Ἄργον ἵει κρατερόν τε μέγαν τε,
τέτρασιν ὀφθαλμοῖσιν ὁρώμενον ἔνθα καὶ ἔνθα·
ἀκάματον δέ οἱ ὦρσε θεὰ μένος, οὐδέ οἱ ὕπνος
πίπτεν ἐπὶ βλεφάροις, φυλακὴν δ' ἔχεν ἔμπεδον
αἰεί.

2.

The author of the Aegimius says in the second book that Thetis used to throw the children she had by Peleus into a cauldron of water, because she wished to learn whether they were mortal. . . . And that after many had perished Peleus was annoyed, and prevented her from throwing Achilles into the cauldron.

3.

Hesiod and Acusilaus say that she (Io) was the daughter of Peiren. While she was holding the office of priestess of Hera, Zeus seduced her, and being discovered by Hera, touched the girl and changed her into a white cow, while he swore that he had no intercourse with her. And so Hesiod says that oaths touching the matter of love do not draw down anger from the gods.

"And thereafter he ordained that an oath concerning the secret deeds of the Cyprian should be without penalty for men."

4.

"(Zeus changed Io) in the fair island Abantis, which the gods, who are eternally, used to call Abantis aforetime, but Zeus then called it Euboea after the cow."[1]

5.

"And (Hera) set a watcher upon her (Io), great and strong Argus, who with four eyes looks every way. And the goddess stirred in him unwearying strength: sleep never fell upon his eyes; but he kept sure watch always."

[1] Euboea properly means the "Island of fine Cattle (or Cows)."

6.

Scholiast on Homer, Il. xxiv. 24. Ἀργειφόντην . . . κατὰ τοὺς Ἡσιόδου μύθους τὸν βουκόλον Ἰοῦς ἐφόνευσεν (Ἑρμῆς).

7.

Athenaeus, xi. p. 503 *d.* καὶ ὁ τὸν Αἰγίμιον ποιήσας, εἴθ' Ἡσίοδός ἐστιν ἢ Κέρκωψ ὁ Μιλήσιος,

ἔνθα ποτ' ἔσται ἐμὸν ψυκτήριον, ὄρχαμε λαῶν.

8.

Etym. Gen. Ἡσίοδος δὲ διὰ τὸ τριχῇ αὐτοὺς οἰκῆσαι,

πάντες δὲ τριχαίκες καλέονται,
τρισσὴν οὕνεκα γαῖαν ἑκὰς πάτρης ἐδάσαντο.

τρία γὰρ Ἑλληνικὰ ἔθνη τῆς Κρήτης ἐποικῆσαι, Πελασγούς, Ἀχαιούς, Δωριεῖς. οὓς τριχαίκας κεκλήκασι.

INCERTAE SEDIS FRAGMENTA

1.

Diogenes Laertius, viii. 1. 25.

Οὐρανίη δ' ἄρ' ἔτικτε Λίνον πολυήρατον υἱόν,
ὃν δή, ὅσοι βροτοί εἰσιν ἀοιδοὶ καὶ κιθαρισταί,
πάντες μὲν θρηνεῦσιν ἐν εἰλαπίναις τε χοροῖς τε,
ἀρχόμενοι δὲ Λίνον καὶ λήγοντες καλέουσιν

Clement of Alexandria, Strom. i. p. 121.

παντοίης σοφίης δεδαηκότα.

2.

Schol. on Homer, Odyssey, iv. 232.

εἰ μὴ Ἀπόλλων Φοῖβος ὑπὲκ θανάτοιο σαώσαι
ἢ αὐτὸς Παιήων, ὃς ἁπάντων φάρμακα οἶδεν.

6.

"Slayer of Argus." According to Hesiod's tale he (Hermes) slew (Argus) the herdsman of Io.

7.

And the author of the Aegimius, whether he is Hesiod or Cercops of Miletus (says)

"There, some day, shall be my place of refreshment, O leader of the people."

8.

Hesiod (says they were so called) because they settled in three groups: "And they all were called the Three-fold people, because they divided in three the land far from their country." For (he says) that three Hellenic tribes settled in Crete, the Pelasgi, Achaeans and Dorians. And these have been called Three-fold People.

FRAGMENTS OF UNKNOWN POSITION

1.

"So Urania bare Linus, a very lovely son: and him all men who are singers and harpers do bewail at feasts and dances, and as they begin and as they end they call on Linus * * * who was skilled in all manner of wisdom."

2:

"Unless Phoebus Apollo should save him from death, or Paean himself who knows the remedies for all things."

3.

Clement of Alexandria, Protrept, c. vii. p. 21.

αὐτὸς γὰρ πάντων βασιλεὺς καὶ κοίρανός ἐστιν
ἀθανάτων τέ οἱ οὔ τις ἐρήρισται κράτος ἄλλος.

4.

Anecd. Oxon (Cramer), i. p. 148.

δῶρα θεῶν μακάρων πλῆσθαι χθονί.

5.

Clement of Alexandria, Strom. i. p. 123.

Μουσάων, αἵτ' ἄνδρα πολυφραδέοντα τιθεῖσι
θέσπιον αὐδήεντα.

6.

Strabo, x. p. 471.

[τάων δ'] οὔρειαι Νύμφαι θεαὶ ἐξεγένοντο
καὶ γένος οὐτιδανῶν Σατύρων καὶ ἀμηχανοεργῶν
Κουρῆτές τε θεοὶ φιλοπαίγμονες ὀρχηστῆρες.

7.

Schol. on Apoll. Rhod. Arg. i. 824.

θεσσάμενος γενεὴν Κλεοδαίου κυδαλίμοιο.

8.

Suidas, s.v. ἀλκή.

ἀλκὴν μὲν γὰρ ἔδωκεν Ὀλύμπιος Αἰακίδῃσι,
νοῦν δ' Ἀμυθαονίδαις, πλοῦτον δ' ἔπορ' Ἀτρείδῃσιν.

9.

Schol. on Homer, Iliad, xiii. 155.

τῇδε γὰρ ἀξυλίῃ κατεπύθετο κήλεα νηῶν.

10.

Etymologicum Magnum.

οὐκέτι δὴ βαίνουσι λαροῖς ποσίν.

11.

Schol. on Homer, Iliad, xxiv. 624.

ὤπτησαν μὲν πρῶτα, περιφραδέως δ' ἐρύσαντο.

3.

"For he alone is king and lord of all the undying gods, and no other vies with him in power."

4.

"(To cause ?) the gifts of the blessed gods to come near to earth."

5.

"Of the Muses who make a man very wise, marvellous in utterance."

6.

"But of them (*sc.* the daughters of Hecaterus) were born the divine mountain Nymphs and the tribe of worthless, helpless Satyrs, and the divine Curetes, sportive dancers."

7.

"Beseeching the offspring of glorious Cleodaeus."

8.

"For the Olympian gave might to the sons of Aeacus, and wisdom to the sons of Amythaon, and wealth to the sons of Atreus."

9.

"For through this lack of wood the timber of the ships rotted."

10.

"No longer do they walk with delicate feet."

11.

"First of all they roasted (pieces of meat), and drew them carefully off the spits."

12.

Chrysippus, Fragg. ii. 254. 11.

τοῦ γὰρ ἀέξετο θυμὸς ἐνὶ στήθεσσι φίλοισιν.

13.

Ib. 15.

οἷον ἐνὶ στήθεσσι χόλον θυμαλγέ' ἔχουσα.

14.

Strabo, vii. p. 327.

Δωδώνην φηγόν τε, Πελασγῶν ἕδρανον, ᾖεν.

15.

Anecd. Oxon (Cramer), iii. p. 318. *not.*

πίσσης τε δνοφερῆς καὶ κέδρου νηλέι καπνῷ.

16.

Schol. on Apoll. Rhod. Arg. i. 757.

αὐτὸς δ' ἐν πλήσμῃσι διιπετέος ποταμοῖο.

17.

Stephanus of Byzantium, Παρθένιος.

ὡς ἀκαλὰ προρέων ὡς ἁβρὴ παρθένος εἶσιν.

18.

Schol. on Theocritus, xi. 75.

νήπιος, ὅστις ἕτοιμα λιπὼν ἀνέτοιμα διώκει.

19.

Harpocration.

ἔργα νέων, βουλαὶ δὲ μέσων, εὐχαὶ δὲ γερόντων.

20.

Porphyr, On Abstinence, ii. 18. p. 134.

ὥς κε πόλις ῥέζῃσι, νόμος δ' ἀρχαῖος ἄριστος.

21.

Schol. on Nicander, Theriaca, 452.

χρὴ δέ σε πατρὶ . . . κτίλον ἔμμεναι.

12.

"For his spirit increased in his dear breast."

13.

"With such heart-grieving anger in her breast."

14.

"He went to Dodona and the oak-grove, the dwelling place of the Pelasgi."

15.

"With the pitiless smoke of black pitch and of cedar."

16.

"But he himself in the swelling tide of the rain-swollen river."

17.

(The river) Parthenius

"Flowing as softly as a dainty maiden goes."

18.

"Foolish the man who leaves what he has, and follows after what he has not."

19.

"The deeds of the young, the counsels of the middle-aged, and the prayers of the aged."

20.

"Howsoever the city does sacrifice, the ancient custom is best."

21.

"But you should be gentle towards your father."

22.

Plato, Epist. xi. 358.

ὃ εἰπόντος μὲν ἐμεῖο
φαῦλόν κεν δόξειεν ἔμεν, χαλεπὸν δὲ νοῆσαι.

23.

Bacchylides, v. 191–3. Βοιωτὸς ἀνὴρ τᾷδε φών[ησεν γλυκειᾶν] | Ἡσίοδος πρόπολος | Μουσᾶν, ὃν <ἂν> ἀθάνατοι τιμῶσι, τούτῳ | καὶ βροτῶν φήμαν ἕπ[εσθαι.

FRAGMENTA DUBIA

1.

Galen, de plac. Hipp. et Plat. i. 266. 7.

καὶ τότε δὴ στηθέων Ἀθάμα φρένας ἐξέλετο Ζεύς.

2.

Schol. on Homer, Od. vii. 104.

ἀλετρεύουσι μύλης ἔπι μήλοπα καρπόν.

3.

Schol. on Pindar, Nem. ii. 1.

ἐν Δήλῳ τότε πρῶτον ἐγὼ καὶ Ὅμηρος ἀοιδοὶ
μέλπομεν, ἐν νεαροῖς ὕμνοις ῥάψαντες ἀοιδήν,
Φοῖβον Ἀπόλλωνα χρυσάορον, ὃν τέκε Λητώ.

4.

Julian, Misopogon, p. 369 B.

χαλεπὸς δ' ἐπὶ δράγματι λιμός.

5.

Servius on Vergil, Aen. iv. 484. Hesiodus has Hesperidas . . . Noctis filias ultra Oceanum mala aurea habuisse dicit.

Αἴγλη τ' ἠδ' Ἐρύθεια καὶ Ἑσπερέθουσα βοῶπις.[1]

[1] Cf. Scholion on Clement, *Protrept.* i. p. 302.

22.

"And if I said this, it would seem a poor thing and hard to understand."

23.

Thus spake the Boeotian, even Hesiod,[1] servant of the sweet Muses: "whomsoever the immortals honour, the good report of mortals also followeth him."

DOUBTFUL FRAGMENTS

1.

"And then it was Zeus took away sense from the heart of Athamas."

2.

"They grind the yellow grain at the mill."

3.

"Then first in Delos did I and Homer, singers both, raise our strain—stitching song in new hymns—Phoebus Apollo with the golden sword, whom Leto bare."

4.

"But starvation on a handful is a cruel thing."

5.

Hesiod says that these Hesperides . . . , daughters of Night, guarded the golden apples beyond Ocean.

"Aegle and Erythea and ox-eyed Hesperethusa."

[1] cp. Hes. *Theog.* 81 ff. But Theognis 169, "Whomso the gods honour, even a man inclined to blame praiseth him," is much nearer.

6.

Plato, Republic, iii. 390 E.

δῶρα θεοὺς πείθει, δῶρ' αἰδοίους βασιλῆας.

7.[1]

Clement of Alexandria, Strom. v. p. 256.

ἑβδομάτῃ δ' αὖτις λαμπρὸν φάος ἠελίοιο.

8.

Apollonius, Lex. Hom. Φοῖβος.

φοῖβον ὕδωρ ἐπάγων κέρασ' Ὠκεανοῖο ῥοῇσι.

9.

Stephanus of Byzantium.

Ασπληδὼν Κλύμενός τε καὶ Ἀμφίδοκος θεοειδής.

10.

Schol. on Pindar, Nem. iii. 64.

Τελαμὼν ἀκόρητος αὐτῆς
ἡμετέροις ἑτάροισι φόως πρώτιστος ἔθηκε
κτείνας ἀνδρολέτειραν ἀμώμητον Μελανίππην,
αὐτοκασιγνήτην χρυσοζώνοιο ἀνάσσης.

[1] This line may once have been read in the text of *Works and Days* after l. 771.

6.

"Gifts move the gods, gifts move worshipful princes."

7.

"On the seventh day again the bright light of the sun . . . ."

8.

"He brought pure water and mixed it with Ocean's streams."

9.

"Aspledon and Clymenus and god-like Amphidocus" (sons of Orchomenus).

10.

"Telamon never sated with battle first brought light to our comrades by slaying blameless Melanippe, destroyer of men, own sister of the golden-girdled queen.

THE HOMERIC HYMNS

I

ΕΙΣ ΔΙΩΝΥΣΟΝ[1]

* * * *

οἱ μὲν γὰρ Δρακάνῳ σ', οἱ δ' Ἰκάρῳ ἠνεμοέσσῃ
φάσ', οἱ δ' ἐν Νάξῳ, δῖον γένος, εἰραφιῶτα,
οἱ δέ σ' ἐπ' Ἀλφειῷ ποταμῷ βαθυδινήεντι
κυσαμένην Σεμέλην τεκέειν Διὶ τερπικεραύνῳ·
ἄλλοι δ' ἐν Θήβῃσιν, ἄναξ, σε λέγουσι γενέσθαι,
ψευδόμενοι· σὲ δ' ἔτικτε πατὴρ ἀνδρῶν τε θεῶν τε
πολλὸν ἀπ' ἀνθρώπων, κρύπτων λευκώλενον Ἥρην.
ἔστι δέ τις Νύση, ὕπατον ὄρος, ἀνθέον ὕλῃ,
τηλοῦ Φοινίκης, σχεδὸν Αἰγύπτοιο ῥοάων,

* * * *

καί οἱ ἀναστήσουσιν ἀγάλματα πόλλ' ἐνὶ νηοῖς.
ὡς δὲ τὰ μὲν τρία, σοὶ πάντως τριετηρίσιν αἰεὶ
ἄνθρωποι ῥέξουσι τεληέσσας ἑκατόμβας.
Ἦ καὶ κυανέῃσιν ἐπ' ὀφρύσι νεῦσε Κρονίων·
ἀμβρόσιαι δ' ἄρα χαῖται ἐπερρώσαντο ἄνακτος
κρατὸς ἀπ' ἀθανάτοιο· μέγαν δ' ἐλέλιξεν Ὄλυμπον.

[1] ll. 1–9 are preserved by Diodorus Siculus iii. 66. 3; ll. 10–21 are extant only in M.

I

TO DIONYSUS

*　　　*　　　*　　　*

For some say, at Dracanum; and some, on windy Icarus; and some, in Naxos, O Heaven-born, Insewn[1]; and others by the deep-eddying river Alpheus that pregnant Semele bare you to Zeus the thunder-lover. And others yet, lord, say you were born in Thebes; but all these lie. The Father of men and gods gave you birth remote from men and secretly from white-armed Hera. There is a certain Nysa, a mountain most high and richly grown with woods, far off in Phoenice, near the streams of Aegyptus

*　　　*　　　*　　　*

"and men will lay up for her[2] many offerings in her shrines. And as these things are three,[3] so shall mortals ever sacrifice perfect hecatombs to you at your feasts each three years."

The Son of Cronos spoke and nodded with his dark brows. And the divine locks of the king flowed forward from his immortal head, and he made great

[1] Dionysus, after his untimely birth from Semele, was sewn into the thigh of Zeus.

[2] *sc.* Semele. Zeus is here speaking.

[3] The reference is apparently to something in the body of the hymn, now lost.

ὣς εἰπὼν ἐπένευσε καρήατι μητίετα Ζεύς.
"Ἵληθ', εἰραφιῶτα, γυναιμανές· οἱ δέ σ' ἀοιδοὶ
ᾄδομεν ἀρχόμενοι λήγοντές τ'· οὐδέ πῃ ἔστι
σεῖ' ἐπιληθομένῳ[1] ἱερῆς μεμνῆσθαι ἀοιδῆς.
καὶ σὺ μὲν οὕτω χαῖρε, Διώνυσ' εἰραφιῶτα,
σὺν μητρὶ Σεμέλῃ, ἥν περ καλέουσι Θυώνην.

II

ΕΙΣ ΔΗΜΗΤΡΑΝ

Δήμητρ' ἠύκομον, σεμνὴν θεόν, ἄρχομ' ἀείδειν,
αὐτὴν ἠδὲ θύγατρα τανύσφυρον, ἣν Ἀιδωνεὺς
ἥρπαξεν, δῶκεν δὲ βαρύκτυπος εὐρύοπα Ζεύς,
νόσφιν Δήμητρος χρυσαόρου, ἀγλαοκάρπου,
παίζουσαν κούρῃσι σὺν Ὠκεανοῦ βαθυκόλποις
ἄνθεά τ' αἰνυμένην, ῥόδα καὶ κρόκον ἠδ' ἴα καλὰ
λειμῶν' ἂμ μαλακὸν καὶ ἀγαλλίδας ἠδ' ὑάκινθον
νάρκισσόν θ', ὃν φῦσε δόλον καλυκώπιδι κούρῃ
Γαῖα Διὸς βουλῇσι χαριζομένη Πολυδέκτῃ,
θαυμαστὸν γανόωντα· σέβας τό γε πᾶσιν ἰδέσθαι
ἀθανάτοις τε θεοῖς ἠδὲ θνητοῖς ἀνθρώποις·
τοῦ καὶ ἀπὸ ῥίζης ἑκατὸν κάρα ἐξεπεφύκει·
κῶζ' ἥδιστ' ὀδμή,[2] πᾶς τ' οὐρανὸς εὐρὺς ὕπερθεν
γαῖά τε πᾶσ' ἐγέλασσε καὶ ἁλμυρὸν οἶδμα θαλάσσης.
ἡ δ' ἄρα θαμβήσασ' ὠρέξατο χερσὶν ἅμ' ἄμφω
καλὸν ἄθυρμα λαβεῖν· χάνε δὲ χθὼν εὐρυάγυια

[1] Allen: ἐπιλαθόμενοι, M. [2] Tyrrell: κῶδις τ' ὀδμῇ, M.

Olympus reel. So spake wise Zeus and ordained it with a nod.

Be favourable, O Insewn, Inspirer of frenzied women! we singers sing of you as we begin and as we end a strain, and none forgetting you may call holy song to mind. And so, farewell, Dionysus, Insewn, with your mother Semele whom men call Thyone.

II

TO DEMETER

I BEGIN to sing of rich-haired Demeter, awful goddess—of her and her trim-ankled daughter whom Aïdoneus rapt away, given to him by all-seeing Zeus the loud-thunderer.

Apart from Demeter, lady of the golden sword and glorious fruits, she was playing with the deep-bosomed daughters of Oceanus and gathering flowers over a soft meadow, roses and crocuses and beautiful violets, irises also and hyacinths and the narcissus, which Earth made to grow at the will of Zeus and to please the Host of Many, to be a snare for the bloom-like girl—a marvellous, radiant flower. It was a thing of awe whether for deathless gods or mortal men to see: from its root grew a hundred blooms and it smelled most sweetly, so that all wide heaven above and the whole earth and the sea's salt swell laughed for joy. And the girl was amazed and reached out with both hands to take the lovely toy; but the wide-pathed earth yawned there in the plain

Νύσιον ἂμ πεδίον, τῇ ὄρουσεν ἄναξ Πολυδέγμων
ἵπποις ἀθανάτοισι, Κρόνου πολυώνυμος υἱός.
Ἁρπάξας δ' ἀέκουσαν ἐπὶ χρυσέοισιν ὄχοισιν
ἦγ' ὀλοφυρομένην· ἰάχησε δ' ἄρ' ὄρθια φωνῇ,
κεκλομένη πατέρα Κρονίδην ὕπατον καὶ ἄριστον.
οὐδέ τις ἀθανάτων οὐδὲ θνητῶν ἀνθρώπων
ἤκουσεν φωνῆς, οὐδ' ἀγλαόκαρποι ἐλαῖαι†
εἰ μὴ Περσαίου θυγάτηρ ἀταλὰ φρονέουσα
ἄιεν ἐξ ἄντρου, Ἑκάτη λιπαροκρήδεμνος,
Ἠέλιός τε ἄναξ, Ὑπερίονος ἀγλαὸς υἱός,
κούρης κεκλομένης πατέρα Κρονίδην· ὁ δὲ νόσφιν
ἧστο θεῶν ἀπάνευθε πολυλλίστῳ ἐνὶ νηῷ,
δέγμενος ἱερὰ καλὰ παρὰ θνητῶν ἀνθρώπων.
τὴν δ' ἀεκαζομένην ἦγεν Διὸς ἐννεσίῃσι
πατροκασίγνητος, Πολυσημάντωρ Πολυδέγμων,
ἵπποις ἀθανάτοισι, Κρόνου πολυώνυμος υἱός.
Ὄφρα μὲν οὖν γαῖάν τε καὶ οὐρανὸν ἀστερόεντα
λεῦσσε θεὰ καὶ πόντον ἀγάρροον ἰχθυόεντα
αὐγάς τ' ἠελίου, ἔτι δ' ἤλπετο μητέρα κεδνὴν
ὄψεσθαι καὶ φῦλα θεῶν αἰειγενετάων,
τόφρα οἱ ἐλπὶς ἔθελγε μέγαν νόον ἀχνυμένης περ·

* * * *

ἤχησαν δ' ὀρέων κορυφαὶ καὶ βένθεα πόντου
φωνῇ ὑπ' ἀθανάτῃ· τῆς δ' ἔκλυε πότνια μήτηρ.
Ὀξὺ δέ μιν κραδίην ἄχος ἔλλαβεν, ἀμφὶ δὲ χαίταις
ἀμβροσίαις κρήδεμνα δαΐζετο χερσὶ φίλῃσι,

of Nysa, and the lord, Host of Many, with his immortal horses sprang out upon her—the Son of Cronos, He who has many names.[1]

He caught her up reluctant on his golden car and bare her away lamenting. Then she cried out shrilly with her voice, calling upon her father, the Son of Cronos, who is most high and excellent. But no one, either of the deathless gods or of mortal men, heard her voice, nor yet the olive-trees bearing rich fruit: only tender-hearted Hecate, bright-coiffed, the daughter of Persaeus, heard the girl from her cave, and the lord Helios, Hyperion's bright son, as she cried to her father, the Son of Cronos. But he was sitting aloof, apart from the gods, in his temple where many pray, and receiving sweet offerings from mortal men. So he, that Son of Cronos, of many names, who is Ruler of Many and Host of Many, was bearing her away by leave of Zeus on his immortal chariot—his own brother's child and all unwilling.

And so long as she, the goddess, yet beheld earth and starry heaven and the strong-flowing sea where fishes shoal, and the rays of the sun, and still hoped to see her dear mother and the tribes of the eternal gods, so long hope calmed her great heart for all her trouble. . . . and the heights of the mountains and the depths of the sea rang with her immortal voice: and her queenly mother heard her.

Bitter pain seized her heart, and she rent the covering upon her divine hair with her dear hands:

[1] The Greeks feared to name Pluto directly and mentioned him by one of many descriptive titles, such as "Host of Many": compare the Christian use of ὁ διάβολος or our "Evil One."

κυάνεον δὲ κάλυμμα κατ᾽ ἀμφοτέρων βάλετ᾽ ὤμων,
σεύατο δ᾽ ὥστ᾽ οἰωνός, ἐπὶ τραφερήν τε καὶ ὑγρὴν
μαιομένη· τῇ δ᾽ οὔτις ἐτήτυμα μυθήσασθαι
ἤθελεν οὔτε θεῶν οὔτε θνητῶν ἀνθρώπων,
οὔτ᾽ οἰωνῶν τις τῇ ἐτήτυμος ἄγγελος ἦλθεν.
ἐννῆμαρ μὲν ἔπειτα κατὰ χθόνα πότνια Δηὼ
στρωφᾶτ᾽ αἰθομένας δαΐδας μετὰ χερσὶν ἔχουσα,
οὐδέ ποτ᾽ ἀμβροσίης καὶ νέκταρος ἡδυπότοιο
πάσσατ᾽ ἀκηχεμένη, οὐδὲ χρόα βάλλετο λουτροῖς.
ἀλλ᾽ ὅτε δὴ δεκάτη οἱ ἐπήλυθε φαινολὶς ἠώς,
ἤντετό οἱ Ἑκάτη, σέλας ἐν χείρεσσιν ἔχουσα
καί ῥά οἱ ἀγγελέουσα ἔπος φάτο φώνησέν τε·
Πότνια Δημήτηρ, ὡρηφόρε, ἀγλαόδωρε,
τίς θεῶν οὐρανίων ἠὲ θνητῶν ἀνθρώπων
ἥρπασε Περσεφόνην καὶ σὸν φίλον ἤκαχε θυμόν;
φωνῆς γὰρ ἤκουσ᾽, ἀτὰρ οὐκ ἴδον ὀφθαλμοῖσιν,
ὅστις ἔην· σοὶ δ᾽ ὦκα λέγω νημερτέα πάντα.
Ὣς ἄρ᾽ ἔφη Ἑκάτη· τὴν δ᾽ οὐκ ἠμείβετο μύθῳ
Ῥείης ἠυκόμου θυγάτηρ, ἀλλ᾽ ὦκα σὺν αὐτῇ
ἤιξ᾽ αἰθομένας δαΐδας μετὰ χερσὶν ἔχουσα.
Ἠέλιον δ᾽ ἵκοντο, θεῶν σκοπὸν ἠδὲ καὶ ἀνδρῶν,
στὰν δ᾽ ἵππων προπάροιθε καὶ εἴρετο δῖα θεάων·
Ἠέλι᾽, αἴδεσσαί με θεὰν σύ περ,[1] εἴ ποτε δή σευ
ἢ ἔπει ἢ ἔργῳ κραδίην καὶ θυμὸν ἴηνα·
κούρην τὴν ἔτεκον, γλυκερὸν θάλος, εἴδεϊ κυδρήν,
τῆς ἀδινὴν ὄπ᾽ ἄκουσα δι᾽ αἰθέρος ἀτρυγέτοιο
ὥστε βιαζομένης, ἀτὰρ οὐκ ἴδον ὀφθαλμοῖσιν.
ἀλλά, σὺ γὰρ δὴ πᾶσαν ἐπὶ χθόνα καὶ κατὰ πόντον
αἰθέρος ἐκ δίης καταδέρκεαι ἀκτίνεσσι,
νημερτέως μοι ἔνισπε φίλον τέκος, εἴ που ὄπωπας,

[1] Ludwich: θέας ὕπερ, M.

her dark cloak she cast down from both her shoulders and sped, like a wild-bird, over the firm land and yielding sea, seeking her child. But no one would tell her the truth, neither god nor mortal man; and of the birds of omen none came with true news for her. Then for nine days queenly Deo wandered over the earth with flaming torches in her hands, so grieved that she never tasted ambrosia and the sweet draught of nectar, nor sprinkled her body with water. But when the tenth enlightening dawn had come, Hecate, with a torch in her hands, met her, and spoke to her and told her news:

"Queenly Demeter, bringer of seasons and giver of good gifts, what god of heaven or what mortal man has rapt away Persephone and pierced with sorrow your dear heart? For I heard her voice, yet saw not with my eyes who it was. But I tell you truly and shortly all I know."

So, then, said Hecate. And the daughter of rich-haired Rhea answered her not, but sped swiftly with her, holding flaming torches in her hands. So they came to Helios, who is watchman of both gods and men, and stood in front of his horses: and the bright goddess enquired of him: "Helios, do you at least regard me, goddess as I am, if ever by word or deed of mine I have cheered your heart and spirit. Through the fruitless air I heard the thrilling cry of my daughter whom I bare, sweet scion of my body and lovely in form, as of one seized violently; though with my eyes I saw nothing. But you—for with your beams you look down from the bright upper air over all the earth and sea—tell me truly of my dear

ὅστις νόσφιν ἐμεῖο λαβὼν ἀέκουσαν ἀνάγκῃ
οἴχεται ἠὲ θεῶν ἢ καὶ θνητῶν ἀνθρώπων.
Ὣς φάτο· τὴν δ' Ὑπεριονίδης ἠμείβετο μύθῳ·
Ῥείης ἠυκόμου θύγατερ, Δήμητερ ἄνασσα,
εἰδήσεις· δὴ γὰρ μέγα σ' ἅζομαι ἠδ' ἐλεαίρω
ἀχνυμένην περὶ παιδὶ τανυσφύρῳ· οὐδέ τις ἄλλος
αἴτιος ἀθανάτων, εἰ μὴ νεφεληγερέτα Ζεύς,
ὅς μιν ἔδωκ' Ἀίδῃ θαλερὴν κεκλῆσθαι ἄκοιτιν
αὐτοκασιγνήτῳ· ὃ δ' ὑπὸ ζόφον ἠερόεντα
ἁρπάξας ἵπποισιν ἄγεν μεγάλα ἰάχουσαν.
ἀλλά, θεά, κατάπαυε μέγαν γόον· οὐδέ τί σε χρὴ
μὰψ αὔτως ἄπλητον ἔχειν χόλον· οὔ τοι ἀεικὴς
γαμβρὸς ἐν ἀθανάτοις Πολυσημάντωρ Ἀιδωνεύς,
αὐτοκασίγνητος καὶ ὁμόσπορος· ἀμφὶ δὲ τιμὴν
ἔλλαχεν ὡς τὰ πρῶτα διάτριχα δασμὸς ἐτύχθη,
τοῖς μεταναιετάειν,[1] τῶν ἔλλαχε κοίρανος εἶναι.
Ὣς εἰπὼν ἵπποισιν ἐκέκλετο· τοὶ δ' ὑπ' ὀμοκλῆς
ῥίμφα φέρον θοὸν ἅρμα τανύπτεροι ὥστ' οἰωνοί.
Τὴν δ' ἄχος αἰνότερον καὶ κύντερον ἵκετο θυμόν·
χωσαμένη δὴ ἔπειτα κελαινεφέι Κρονίωνι
νοσφισθεῖσα θεῶν ἀγορὴν καὶ μακρὸν Ὄλυμπον
ᾤχετ' ἐπ' ἀνθρώπων πόλιας καὶ πίονα ἔργα
εἶδος ἀμαλδύνουσα πολὺν χρόνον· οὐδέ τις ἀνδρῶν
εἰσορόων γίγνωσκε βαθυζώνων τε γυναικῶν,
πρίν γ' ὅτε δὴ Κελεοῖο δαΐφρονος ἵκετο δῶμα,
ὃς τότ' Ἐλευσῖνος θυοέσσης κοίρανος ἦεν.
ἕζετο δ' ἐγγὺς ὁδοῖο φίλον τετιημένη ἦτορ,
Παρθενίῳ φρέατι, ὅθεν ὑδρεύοντο πολῖται,

[1] Puntoni: μετὰ ναίεται, M.

child, if you have seen her anywhere, what god or mortal man has violently seized her against her will and mine, and so made off."

So said she. And the Son of Hyperion answered her: "Queen Demeter, daughter of rich-haired Rhea, I will tell you the truth; for I greatly reverence and pity you in your grief for your trim-ankled daughter. None other of the deathless gods is to blame, but only cloud-gathering Zeus who gave her to Hades, her father's brother, to be called his buxom wife. And Hades seized her and took her loudly crying in his chariot down to his realm of mist and gloom. Yet, goddess, cease your loud lament and keep not vain anger unrelentingly: Aïdoneus, the Ruler of Many, is no unfitting husband among the deathless gods for your child, being your own brother and born of the same stock: also, for honour, he has that third share which he received when division was made at the first, and is appointed lord of those among whom he dwells."

So he spake, and called to his horses: and at his chiding they quickly whirled the swift chariot along, like long-winged birds.

But grief yet more terrible and savage came into the heart of Demeter, and thereafter she was so angered with the dark-clouded Son of Cronos that she avoided the gathering of the gods and high Olympus, and went to the towns and rich fields of men, disfiguring her form a long while. And no one of men or deep-bosomed women knew her when they saw her, until she came to the house of wise Celeus who then was lord of fragrant Eleusis. Vexed in her dear heart, she sat near the wayside by the Maiden Well, from which the women of the place were used to

ἐν σκιῇ, αὐτὰρ ὕπερθε πεφύκει θάμνος ἐλαίης,
γρηὶ παλαιγενέι ἐναλίγκιος, ἥτε τόκοιο
εἴργηται δώρων τε φιλοστεφάνου Ἀφροδίτης,
οἷαί τε τροφοί εἰσι θεμιστοπόλων βασιλήων
παίδων καὶ ταμίαι κατὰ δώματα ἠχήεντα.
τὴν δὲ ἴδον Κελεοῖο Ἐλευσινίδαο θύγατρες
ἐρχόμεναι μεθ' ὕδωρ εὐήρυτον, ὄφρα φέροιεν
κάλπισι χαλκείῃσι φίλα πρὸς δώματα πατρός,
τέσσαρες, ὥστε θεαί, κουρήιον ἄνθος ἔχουσαι,
Καλλιδίκη καὶ Κλεισιδίκη Δημώ τ' ἐρόεσσα
Καλλιθόη θ', ἣ τῶν προγενεστάτη ἦεν ἁπασῶν·
οὐδ' ἔγνον·[1] χαλεποὶ δὲ θεοὶ θνητοῖσιν ὁρᾶσθαι.
ἀγχοῦ δ' ἱστάμεναι ἔπεα πτερόεντα προσηύδων·
Τίς πόθεν ἐσσί, γρηῦ, παλαιγενέων ἀνθρώπων;
τίπτε δὲ νόσφι πόληος ἀπέστιχες, οὐδὲ δόμοισι
πίλνασαι; ἔνθα γυναῖκες ἀνὰ μέγαρα σκιόεντα
τηλίκαι, ὡς σύ περ ὧδε καὶ ὁπλότεραι γεγάασιν,
αἵ κέ σε φίλωνται ἠμὲν ἔπει ἠδὲ καὶ ἔργῳ.
Ὣς ἔφαν· ἡ δ' ἐπέεσσιν ἀμείβετο πότνα θεάων·
τέκνα φίλ', αἵ τινές ἐστε γυναικῶν θηλυτεράων,
χαίρετ'· ἐγὼ δ' ὑμῖν μυθήσομαι· οὔ τοι ἀεικὲς
ὑμῖν εἰρομένῃσιν ἀληθέα μυθήσασθαι.
Δωσὼ[2] ἐμοί γ' ὄνομ' ἐστί· τὸ γὰρ θέτο πότνια μήτηρ.
νῦν αὖτε Κρήτηθεν ἐπ' εὐρέα νῶτα θαλάσσης
ἤλυθον οὐκ ἐθέλουσα, βίῃ δ' ἀέκουσαν ἀνάγκῃ
ἄνδρες ληιστῆρες ἀπήγαγον. οἱ μὲν ἔπειτα
νηὶ θοῇ Θόρικόνδε κατέσχεθον, ἔνθα γυναῖκες
ἠπείρου ἐπέβησαν ἀολλέες ἠδὲ καὶ αὐτοί,
δεῖπνόν τ' ἐπηρτύνοντο παρὰ πρυμνήσια νηός·
ἀλλ' ἐμοὶ οὐ δόρποιο μελίφρονος ἤρατο θυμός·

[1] Cobet: ἔγνων, M. [2] Passow: Δώς, M.

draw water, in a shady place over which grew an olive shrub. And she was like an ancient woman who is cut off from childbearing and the gifts of garland-loving Aphrodite, like the nurses of king's children who deal justice, or like the house-keepers in their echoing halls. There the daughters of Celeus, son of Eleusis, saw her, as they were coming for easy-drawn water, to carry it in pitchers of bronze to their dear father's house: four were they and like goddesses in the flower of their girlhood, Callidice and Cleisidice and lovely Demo and Callithoë who was the eldest of them all. They knew her not, —for the gods are not easily discerned by mortals—, but standing near by her spoke winged words:

"Old mother, whence and who are you of folk born long ago? Why are you gone away from the city and do not draw near the houses? For there in the shady halls are women of just such age as you, and others younger; and they would welcome you both by word and by deed."

Thus they said. And she, that queen among goddesses answered them saying: "Hail, dear children, whosoever you are of woman-kind. I will tell you my story; for it is not unseemly that I should tell you truly what you ask. Doso is my name, for my stately mother gave it me. And now I am come from Crete over the sea's wide back,—not willingly; but pirates brought me thence by force of strength against my liking. Afterwards they put in with their swift craft to Thoricus, and there the women landed on the shore in full throng and the men likewise, and they began to make ready a meal by the stern-cables of the ship. But my heart craved not pleasant food, and I fled secretly across

λάθρῃ δ᾽ ὁρμηθεῖσα δι᾽ ἠπείροιο μελαίνης
φεῦγον ὑπερφιάλους σημάντορας, ὄφρα κε μή με
ἀπριάτην περάσαντες ἐμῆς ἀποναίατο τιμῆς.
οὕτω δεῦρ᾽ ἱκόμην ἀλαλημένη, οὐδέ τι οἶδα,
ἥ τις δὴ γαῖ᾽ ἐστι καὶ οἵ τινες ἐγγεγάασιν.
ἀλλ᾽ ὑμῖν μὲν πάντες Ὀλύμπια δώματ᾽ ἔχοντες
δοῖεν κουριδίους ἄνδρας, καὶ τέκνα τεκέσθαι,
ὡς ἐθέλουσι τοκῆες· ἐμὲ δ᾽ αὖτ᾽ οἰκτείρατε, κοῦραι.
[τοῦτο δέ μοι σαφέως ὑποθήκατε, ὄφρα πύθωμαι,[1]] 137a
προφρονέως, φίλα τέκνα, τέων πρὸς δώμαθ᾽ ἵκωμαι
ἀνέρος ἠδὲ γυναικός, ἵνα σφίσιν ἐργάζωμαι
πρόφρων, οἷα γυναικὸς ἀφήλικος ἔργα τέτυκται·
καί κεν παῖδα νεογνὸν ἐν ἀγκοίνῃσιν ἔχουσα
καλὰ τιθηνοίμην καὶ δώματα τηρήσαιμι
καί κε λέχος στορέσαιμι μυχῷ θαλάμων εὐπήκτων
δεσπόσυνόν καί κ᾽ ἔργα διδασκήσαιμι γυναῖκας.
Φῆ ῥα θεά· τὴν δ᾽ αὐτίκ᾽ ἀμείβετο παρθένος ἀδμής,
Καλλιδίκη, Κελεοῖο θυγατρῶν εἶδος ἀρίστη·
Μαῖα, θεῶν μὲν δῶρα καὶ ἀχνύμενοί περ ἀνάγκῃ
τέτλαμεν ἄνθρωποι· δὴ γὰρ πολὺ φέρτεροί εἰσι.
ταῦτα δέ τοι σαφέως ὑποθήσομαι ἠδ᾽ ὀνομήνω
ἀνέρας οἷσιν ἔπεστι μέγα κράτος ἐνθάδε τιμῆς
δήμου τε προὔχουσιν ἰδὲ κρήδεμνα πόληος
εἰρύαται βουλῇσι καὶ ἰθείῃσι δίκῃσιν·
ἠμὲν Τριπτολέμου πυκιμήδεος ἠδὲ Διόκλου
ἠδὲ Πολυξείνου καὶ ἀμύμονος Εὐμόλποιο
καὶ Δολίχου καὶ πατρὸς ἀγήνορος ἡμετέροιο,
τῶν πάντων ἄλοχοι κατὰ δώματα πορσαίνουσι·
τάων οὐκ ἄν τίς σε κατὰ πρώτιστον ὀπωπὴν

[1] Allen.

the dark country and escaped my masters, that they should not take me unpurchased across the sea, there to win a price for me. And so I wandered and am come here: and I know not at all what land this is or what people are in it. But may all those who dwell on Olympus give you husbands and birth of children as parents desire, so you take pity on me, maidens, and show me this clearly that I may learn, dear children, to the house of what man and woman I may go, to work for them cheerfully at such tasks as belong to a woman of my age. Well could I nurse a new born child, holding him in my arms, or keep house, or spread my masters' bed in a recess of the well-built chamber, or teach the women their work."

So said the goddess. And straightway the unwed maiden Callidice, goodliest in form of the daughters of Celeus, answered her and said:

"Mother, what the gods send us, we mortals bear perforce, although we suffer; for they are much stronger than we. But now I will teach you clearly, telling you the names of men who have great power and honour here and are chief among the people, guarding our city's coif of towers by their wisdom and true judgements: there is wise Triptolemus and Dioclus and Polyxeinus and blameless Eumolpus and Dolichus and our own brave father. All these have wives who manage in the house, and no one of them, so soon as she

εἶδος ἀτιμήσασα δόμων ἀπονοσφίσσειεν,
ἀλλά σε δέξονται· δὴ γὰρ θεοείκελός ἐσσι.
εἰ δ' ἐθέλεις, ἐπίμεινον, ἵνα πρὸς δώματα πατρὸς
ἔλθωμεν καὶ μητρὶ βαθυζώνῳ Μετανείρῃ
εἴπωμεν τάδε πάντα διαμπερές, αἴ κέ σ' ἀνώγῃ
ἡμέτερόνδ' ἰέναι μηδ' ἄλλων δώματ' ἐρευνᾶν.
τηλύγετος δέ οἱ υἱὸς ἐνὶ μεγάρῳ εὐπήκτῳ
ὀψίγονος τρέφεται, πολυεύχετος ἀσπάσιός τε.
εἰ τόν γ' ἐκθρέψαιο καὶ ἥβης μέτρον ἵκοιτο,
ῥεῖά κέ τίς σε ἰδοῦσα γυναικῶν θηλυτεράων
ζηλώσαι· τόσα κέν τοι ἀπὸ θρεπτήρια δοίη.
  Ὣς ἔφαθ'· ἣ δ' ἐπένευσε καρήατι· ταὶ δὲ φαεινὰ
πλησάμεναι ὕδατος φέρον ἄγγεα κυδιάουσαι.
ῥίμφα δὲ πατρὸς ἵκοντο μέγαν δόμον, ὦκα δὲ μητρὶ
ἔννεπον, ὡς εἶδόν τε καὶ ἔκλυον. ἣ δὲ μάλ' ὦκα
ἐλθούσας ἐκέλευε καλεῖν ἐπ' ἀπείρονι μισθῷ.
αἳ δ' ὥστ' ἢ ἔλαφοι ἢ πόρτιες εἴαρος ὥρῃ
ἅλλοντ' ἂν λειμῶνα κορεσσάμεναι φρένα φορβῇ,
ὣς αἳ ἐπισχόμεναι ἑανῶν πτύχας ἱμεροέντων
ἤιξαν κοίλην κατ' ἀμαξιτόν· ἀμφὶ δὲ χαῖται
ὤμοις ἀίσσοντο κροκηίῳ ἄνθει ὁμοῖαι.
τέτμον δ' ἐγγὺς ὁδοῦ κυδρὴν θεόν, ἔνθα πάρος περ
κάλλιπον· αὐτὰρ ἔπειτα φίλου [1] πρὸς δώματα πατρὸς
ἡγεῦνθ'· ἣ δ' ἄρ' ὄπισθε φίλον τετιημένη ἦτορ
στεῖχε κατὰ κρῆθεν κεκαλυμμένη· ἀμφὶ δὲ πέπλος
κυάνεος ῥαδινοῖσι θεᾶς ἐλελίζετο ποσσίν.
  Αἶψα δὲ δώμαθ' ἵκοντο διοτρεφέος Κελεοῖο,
βὰν δὲ δι' αἰθούσης, ἔνθα σφίσι πότνια μήτηρ

[1] Matthiae: φίλα, M.

had seen you, would dishonour you and turn you from the house, but they will welcome you; for indeed you are godlike. But if you will, stay here; and we will go to our father's house and tell Metaneira, our deep-bosomed mother, all this matter fully, that she may bid you rather come to our home than search after the houses of others. She has an only son, late-born, who is being nursed in our well-built house, a child of many prayers and welcome: if you could bring him up until he reached the full measure of youth, any one of womankind who should see you would straightway envy you, such gifts would our mother give for his upbringing."

So she spake: and the goddess bowed her head in assent. And they filled their shining vessels with water and carried them off rejoicing. Quickly they came to their father's great house and straightway told their mother according as they had heard and seen. Then she bade them go with all speed and invite the stranger to come for a measureless hire. As hinds or heifers in spring time, when sated with pasture, bound about a meadow, so they, holding up the folds of their lovely garments, darted down the hollow path, and their hair like a crocus flower streamed about their shoulders. And they found the good goddess near the wayside where they had left her before, and led her to the house of their dear father. And she walked behind, distressed in her dear heart, with her head veiled and wearing a dark cloak which waved about the slender feet of the goddess.

Soon they came to the house of heaven-nurtured Celeus and went through the portico to where their

ἧστο παρὰ σταθμὸν τέγεος πύκα ποιητοῖο
παῖδ' ὑπὸ κόλπῳ ἔχουσα, νέον θάλος· αἳ δὲ παρ αὐτὴν
ἔδραμον· ἣ δ' ἄρ' ἐπ' οὐδὸν ἔβη ποσὶ καί ῥα μελάθρου
κῦρε κάρη, πλῆσεν δὲ θύρας σέλαος θείοιο.
τὴν δ' αἰδώς τε σέβας τε ἰδὲ χλωρὸν δέος εἷλεν·
εἶξε δέ οἱ κλισμοῖο καὶ ἑδριάασθαι ἄνωγεν.
ἀλλ' οὐ Δημήτηρ ὡρηφόρος, ἀγλαόδωρος,
ἤθελεν ἑδριάασθαι ἐπὶ κλισμοῖο φαεινοῦ,
ἀλλ' ἀκέουσ' ἀνέμιμνε κατ' ὄμματα καλὰ βαλοῦσα,
πρίν γ' ὅτε δή οἱ ἔθηκεν Ἰάμβη κέδν' εἰδυῖα
πηκτὸν ἕδος, καθύπερθε δ' ἐπ' ἀργύφεον βάλε κῶας.
ἔνθα καθεζομένη προκατέσχετο χερσὶ καλύπτρην·
δηρὸν δ' ἄφθογγος τετιημένη ἧστ' ἐπὶ δίφρου,
οὐδέ τιν' οὔτ' ἔπεϊ προσπτύσσετο οὔτε τι ἔργῳ,
ἀλλ' ἀγέλαστος, ἄπαστος ἐδητύος ἠδὲ ποτῆτος
ἧστο πόθῳ μινύθουσα βαθυζώνοιο θυγατρός,
πρίν γ' ὅτε δὴ χλεύῃς μιν Ἰάμβη κέδν' εἰδυῖα
πολλὰ παρασκώπτουσ' ἐτρέψατο πότνιαν ἁγνήν,
μειδῆσαι γελάσαι τε καὶ ἵλαον σχεῖν θυμόν·
ἣ δή οἱ καὶ ἔπειτα μεθύστερον εὔαδεν ὀργαῖς.
τῇ δὲ δέπας Μετάνειρα δίδου μελιηδέος οἴνου
πλήσασ'· ἣ δ' ἀνένευσ'· οὐ γὰρ θεμιτόν οἱ ἔφασκε
πίνειν οἶνον ἐρυθρόν· ἄνωγε δ' ἄρ' ἄλφι καὶ ὕδωρ
δοῦναι μίξασαν πιέμεν γλήχωνι τερείνῃ.
ἣ δὲ κυκεῶ τεύξασα θεᾷ πόρεν, ὡς ἐκέλευε·
δεξαμένη δ' ὁσίης ἕνεκεν πολυπότνια Δηώ

* * * *

queenly mother sat by a pillar of the close-fitted roof, holding her son, a tender scion, in her bosom. And the girls ran to her. But the goddess walked to the threshold: and her head reached the roof and she filled the doorway with a heavenly radiance. Then awe and reverence and pale fear took hold of Metaneira, and she rose up from her couch before Demeter, and bade her be seated. But Demeter, bringer of seasons and giver of perfect gifts, would not sit upon the bright couch, but stayed silent with lovely eyes cast down until careful Iambe placed a jointed seat for her and threw over it a silvery fleece. Then she sat down and held her veil in her hands before her face. A long time she sat upon the stool[1] without speaking because of her sorrow, and greeted no one by word or by sign, but rested, never smiling, and tasting neither food nor drink, because she pined with longing for her deep-bosomed daughter, until careful Iambe—who pleased her moods in aftertime also—moved the holy lady with many a quip and jest to smile and laugh and cheer her heart. Then Metaneira filled a cup with sweet wine and offered it to her; but she refused it, for she said it was not lawful for her to drink red wine, but bade them mix meal and water with soft mint and give her to drink. And Metaneira mixed the draught and gave it to the goddess as she bade. So the great queen Deo received it to observe the sacrament[2] * * * *

[1] Demeter chooses the lowlier seat, supposedly as being more suitable to her assumed condition, but really because in her sorrow she refuses all comforts.

[2] An act of communion—the drinking of the potion (κυκεών) here described—was one of the most important pieces of ritual in the Eleusinian mysteries, as commemorating the sorrows of the goddess.

τῇσι δὲ μύθων ἦρχεν ἐύζωνος Μετάνειρα·
  Χαῖρε, γύναι, ἐπεὶ οὔ σε κακῶν ἄπ᾽ ἔολπα τοκήων
ἔμμεναι, ἀλλ᾽ ἀγαθῶν· ἐπί τοι πρέπει ὄμμασιν αἰδὼς
καὶ χάρις, ὡς εἴ πέρ τε θεμιστοπόλων βασιλήων.
ἀλλὰ θεῶν μὲν δῶρα καὶ ἀχνύμενοί περ ἀνάγκῃ
τέτλαμεν ἄνθρωποι· ἐπὶ γὰρ ζυγὸς αὐχένι κεῖται.
νῦν δ᾽, ἐπεὶ ἵκεο δεῦρο, παρέσσεται ὅσσα τ᾽ ἐμοί περ.
παῖδα δέ μοι τρέφε τόνδε, τὸν ὀψίγονον καὶ ἄελπτον
ὤπασαν ἀθάνατοι, πολυάρητος δέ μοί ἐστιν.
εἰ τόν γε θρέψαιο καὶ ἥβης μέτρον ἵκοιτο,
ῥεῖά κέ τίς σε ἰδοῦσα γυναικῶν θηλυτεράων
ζηλώσαι· τόσα κέν τοι ἀπὸ θρεπτήρια δοίην.
  Τὴν δ᾽ αὖτε προσέειπεν ἐυστέφανος Δημήτηρ·
καὶ σύ, γύναι, μάλα χαῖρε, θεοὶ δέ τοι ἐσθλὰ πόροιεν·
παῖδα δέ τοι πρόφρων ὑποδέξομαι, ὥς με κελεύεις,
θρέψω κοὔ μιν, ἔολπα, κακοφραδίῃσι τιθήνης
οὔτ᾽ ἄρ᾽ ἐπηλυσίη δηλήσεται οὔθ᾽ ὑποτάμνον·
οἶδα γὰρ ἀντίτομον μέγα·φέρτερον ὑλοτόμοιο,
οἶδα δ᾽ ἐπηλυσίης πολυπήμονος ἐσθλὸν ἐρυσμόν.
  Ὣς ἄρα φωνήσασα θυώδεϊ δέξατο κόλπῳ
χείρεσσ᾽ ἀθανάτῃσι· γεγήθει δὲ φρένα μήτηρ.
ὣς ὁ μὲν Κελεοῖο δαΐφρονος ἀγλαὸν υἱὸν
Δημοφόωνθ᾽, ὃν ἔτικτεν ἐύζωνος Μετάνειρα,
ἔτρεφεν ἐν μεγάροις· ὁ δ᾽ ἀέξετο δαίμονι ἶσος,
οὔτ᾽ οὖν σῖτον ἔδων, οὐ θησάμενος [γάλα μητρὸς[1]
ἡματίη μὲν γὰρ καλλιστέφανος[2]] Δημήτηρ 236a

[1] Hermann's restoration. [2] Voss' restoration.

And of them all, well-girded Metaneira first began to speak: "Hail, lady! For I think you are not meanly but nobly born; truly dignity and grace are conspicuous upon your eyes as in the eyes of kings that deal justice. Yet we mortals bear perforce what the gods send us, though we be grieved; for a yoke is set upon our necks. But now, since you are come here, you shall have what I can bestow: and nurse me this child whom the gods gave me in my old age and beyond my hope, a son much prayed for. If you should bring him up until he reach the full measure of youth, any one of womankind that sees you will straightway envy you, so great reward would I give for his upbringing."

Then rich-haired Demeter answered her: "And to you, also, lady, all hail, and may the gods give you good! Gladly will I take the boy to my breast, as you bid me, and will nurse him. Never, I ween, through any heedlessness of his nurse shall witchcraft hurt him nor yet the Undercutter:[1] for I know a charm far stronger than the Woodcutter, and I know an excellent safeguard against woeful witchcraft."

When she had so spoken, she took the child in her fragrant bosom with her divine hands: and his mother was glad in her heart. So the goddess nursed in the palace Demophoön, wise Celeus' goodly son whom well-girded Metaneira bare. And the child grew like some immortal being, not fed with food nor nourished at the breast: for by day rich-crowned Demeter would anoint him with

[1] Undercutter and Woodcutter are probably popular names (after the style of Hesiod's "Boneless One") for the worm thought to be the cause of teething and toothache.

χρίεσκ᾽ ἀμβροσίῃ ὡσεὶ θεοῦ ἐκγεγαῶτα
ἡδὺ καταπνείουσα καὶ ἐν κόλποισιν ἔχουσα·
νύκτας δὲ κρυπτεσκε πυρὸς μένει ἠύτε δαλὸν
λάθρα φίλων γονέων· τοῖς δὲ μέγα θαῦμ᾽ ἐτέτυκτο,
ὡς προθαλὴς τελέθεσκε· θεοῖσι γὰρ ἄντα ἐῴκει.
καί κέν μιν ποίησεν ἀγήρων τ᾽ ἀθάνατόν τε,
εἰ μὴ ἄρ᾽ ἀφραδίῃσιν ἐύζωνος Μετάνειρα
νύκτ᾽ ἐπιτηρήσασα θυώδεος ἐκ θαλάμοιο
σκέψατο· κώκυσεν δὲ καὶ ἄμφω πλήξατο μηρὼ
δείσασ᾽ ᾧ περὶ παιδὶ καὶ ἀάσθη μέγα θυμῷ
καί ῥ᾽ ὀλοφυρομένη ἔπεα πτερόεντα προσηύδα·
Τέκνον Δημοφόων, ξείνη σε πυρὶ ἔνι πολλῷ [1]
κρύπτει, ἐμοὶ δὲ γόον καὶ κήδεα λυγρὰ τίθησιν.
Ὣς φάτ᾽ ὀδυρομένη· τῆς δ᾽ ἄιε δῖα θεάων.
τῇ δὲ χολωσαμένη καλλιστέφανος Δημήτηρ
παῖδα φίλον, τὸν ἄελπτον ἐνὶ μεγάροισιν ἔτικτε,
χείρεσσ᾽ ἀθανάτῃσιν ἀπὸ ἕθεν ἧκε [2] πέδονδε,
ἐξανελοῦσα πυρός, θυμῷ κοτέσασα μάλ᾽ αἰνῶς,
καί ῥ᾽ ἄμυδις προσέειπεν ἐύζωνον Μετάνειραν·
Νήιδες ἄνθρωποι καὶ ἀφράδμονες οὔτ᾽ ἀγαθοῖο
αἶσαν ἐπερχομένου προγνώμεναι οὔτε κακοῖο·
καὶ σὺ γὰρ ἀφραδίῃσι τεῇς νήκεστον ἀάσθης.
ἴστω γὰρ θεῶν ὅρκος, ἀμείλικτον Στυγὸς ὕδωρ,
ἀθάνατόν κέν τοι καὶ ἀγήραον ἤματα πάντα
παῖδα φίλον ποίησα καὶ ἄφθιτον ὤπασα τιμήν·
νῦν δ᾽ οὐκ ἔσθ᾽ ὥς κεν θάνατον καὶ κῆρας ἀλύξαι·
τιμὴ δ᾽ ἄφθιτος αἰὲν ἐπέσσεται, οὕνεκα γούνων

[1] M : πυρῇ ἔνι πολλῇ, *Berlin Papyrus* 44.
[2] Cobet : ἕο θῆκε, M.

ambrosia as if he were the offspring of a god and breathe sweetly upon him as she held him in her bosom. But at night she would hide him like a brand in the heart of the fire, unknown to his dear parents. And it wrought great wonder in these that he grew beyond his age; for he was like the gods face to face. And she would have made him deathless and unageing, had not well-girded Metaneira in her heedlessness kept watch by night from her sweet-smelling chamber and spied. But she wailed and smote her two hips, because she feared for her son and was greatly distraught in her heart; so she lamented and uttered winged words:

"Demophoön, my son, the strange woman buries you deep in fire and works grief and bitter sorrow for me"

Thus she spoke, mourning. And the bright goddess, lovely-crowned Demeter, heard her, and was wroth with her. So with her divine hands she snatched from the fire the dear son whom Metaneira had born unhoped-for in the palace, and cast him from her to the ground; for she was terribly angry in her heart. Forthwith she said to well-girded Metaneira:

"Witless are you mortals and dull to foresee your lot, whether of good or evil, that comes upon you. For now in your heedlessness you have wrought folly past healing; for—be witness the oath of the gods, the relentless water of Styx—I would have made your dear son deathless and unageing all his days and would have bestowed on him everlasting honour, but now he can in no way escape death and the fates. Yet shall unfailing honour

ἡμετέρων ἐπέβη καὶ ἐν ἀγκοίνῃσιν ἴαυσεν.
ὥρῃσιν δ' ἄρα τῷ γε περιπλομένων ἐνιαυτῶν
παῖδες Ἐλευσινίων πόλεμον καὶ φύλοπιν αἰνὴν
αἰὲν ἐν ἀλλήλοισιν συνάξουσ' ἤματα πάντα.
εἰμὶ δὲ Δημήτηρ τιμάοχος, ἥτε μέγιστον
ἀθανάτοις θνητοῖς τ' ὄνεαρ καὶ χάρμα τέτυκται.
ἀλλ' ἄγε μοι νηόν τε μέγαν καὶ βωμὸν ὑπ' αὐτῷ
τευχόντων πᾶς δῆμος ὑπαὶ πόλιν αἰπύ τε τεῖχος
Καλλιχόρου καθύπερθεν ἐπὶ προὔχοντι κολωνῷ.
ὄργια δ' αὐτὴ ἐγὼν ὑποθήσομαι, ὡς ἂν ἔπειτα
εὐαγέως ἔρδοντες ἐμὸν νόον ἱλάσκοισθε.
  Ὣς εἰποῦσα θεὰ μέγεθος καὶ εἶδος ἄμειψε
γῆρας ἀπωσαμένη· περί τ' ἀμφί τε κάλλος ἄητο·
ὀδμὴ δ' ἱμερόεσσα θυηέντων ἀπὸ πέπλων
σκίδνατο, τῆλε δὲ φέγγος ἀπὸ χροὸς ἀθανάτοιο
λάμπε θεᾶς, ξανθαὶ δὲ κόμαι κατενήνοθεν ὤμους,
αὐγῆς δ' ἐπλήσθη πυκινὸς δόμος ἀστεροπῆς ὥς·
βῆ δὲ διὲκ μεγάρων· τῆς δ' αὐτίκα γούνατ' ἔλυντο,
δηρὸν δ' ἄφθογγος γένετο χρόνον, οὐδέ τι παιδὸς
μνήσατο τηλυγέτοιο ἀπὸ δαπέδου ἀνελέσθαι.
τοῦ δὲ κασίγνηται φωνὴν ἐσάκουσαν ἐλεινήν,
κὰδ δ' ἄρ' ἀπ' εὐστρώτων λεχέων θόρον· ἡ μὲν ἔπειτα
παῖδ' ἀνὰ χερσὶν ἑλοῦσα ἑῷ ἐγκάτθετο κόλπῳ·
ἡ δ' ἄρα πῦρ ἀνέκαι'· ἡ δ' ἔσσυτο πόσσ' ἁπαλοῖσι
μητέρ' ἀναστήσουσα θυώδεος ἐκ θαλάμοιο.
ἀγρόμεναι δέ μιν ἀμφὶς ἐλούεον ἀσπαίροντα
ἀμφαγαπαζόμεναι· τοῦ δ' οὐ μειλίσσετο θυμός·
χειρότεραι γὰρ δή μιν ἔχον τροφοὶ ἠδὲ τιθῆναι.

always rest upon him, because he lay upon my knees and slept in my arms. But, as the years move round and when he is in his prime, the sons of the Eleusinians shall ever wage war and dread strife with one another continually. Lo! I am that Demeter who has share of honour and is the greatest help and cause of joy to the undying gods and mortal men. But now, let all the people build me a great temple and an altar below it and beneath the city and its sheer wall upon a rising hillock above Callichorus. And I myself will teach my rites, that hereafter you may reverently perform them and so win the favour of my heart."

When she had so said, the goddess changed her stature and her looks, thrusting old age away from her: beauty spread round about her and a lovely fragrance was wafted from her sweet-smelling robes, and from the divine body of the goddess a light shone afar, while golden tresses spread down over her shoulders, so that the strong house was filled with brightness as with lightning. And so she went out from the palace.

And straightway Metaneira's knees were loosed and she remained speechless for a long while and did not remember to take up her late-born son from the ground. But his sisters heard his pitiful wailing and sprang down from their well-spread beds: one of them took up the child in her arms and laid him in her bosom, while another revived the fire, and a third rushed with soft feet to bring their mother from her fragrant chamber. And they gathered about the struggling child and washed him, embracing him lovingly; but he was not comforted, because nurses and handmaids much less skilful were holding him now.

Αἱ μὲν παννύχιαι κυδρὴν θεὸν ἱλάσκοντο
δείματι παλλόμεναι, ἅμα δ' ἠοῖ φαινομένηφιν
εὐρυβίῃ Κελεῷ νημερτέα μυθήσαντο,
ὡς ἐπέτελλε θεά, καλλιστέφανος Δημήτηρ.
αὐτὰρ ὅ γ' εἰς ἀγορὴν καλέσας πολυπείρονα λαὸν
ἤνωγ' ἠυκόμῳ Δημήτερι πίονα νηὸν
ποιῆσαι καὶ βωμὸν ἐπὶ προὔχοντι κολωνῷ.
οἱ δὲ μάλ' αἶψ' ἐπίθοντο καὶ ἔκλυον αὐδήσαντος,
τεῦχον δ', ὡς ἐπέτελλ'. ὃ δ' ἀέξετο δαίμονι ἶσος.[1]
Αὐτὰρ ἐπεὶ τέλεσαν καὶ ἐρώησαν καμάτοιο,
βάν ῥ' ἴμεν οἶκαδ' ἕκαστος· ἀτὰρ ξανθὴ Δημήτηρ
ἔνθα καθεζομένη μακάρων ἀπὸ νόσφιν ἁπάντων
μίμνε πόθῳ μινύθουσα βαθυζώνοιο θυγατρός.
αἰνότατον δ' ἐνιαυτὸν ἐπὶ χθόνα πουλυβότειραν
ποίησ' ἀνθρώποις καὶ κύντατον· οὐδέ τι γαῖα
σπέρμ' ἀνίει, κρύπτεν γὰρ ἐυστέφανος Δημήτηρ·
πολλὰ δὲ καμπύλ' ἄροτρα μάτην βόες εἷλκον ἀρούραις·
πολλὸν δὲ κρῖ λευκὸν ἐτώσιον ἔμπεσε γαίῃ·
καί νύ κε πάμπαν ὄλεσσε γένος μερόπων ἀνθρώπων
λιμοῦ ὑπ' ἀργαλέης, γεράων τ' ἐρικυδέα τιμὴν
καὶ θυσιῶν ἤμερσεν Ὀλύμπια δώματ' ἔχοντας,
εἰ μὴ Ζεὺς ἐνόησεν ἑῷ τ' ἐφράσσατο θυμῷ.
Ἶριν δὲ πρῶτον χρυσόπτερον ὦρσε καλέσσαι
Δήμητρ' ἠύκομον, πολυήρατον εἶδος ἔχουσαν.
ὣς ἔφαθ'· ἣ δὲ Ζηνὶ κελαινεφέι Κρονίωνι
πείθετο καὶ τὸ μεσηγὺ διέδραμεν ὦκα πόδεσσιν.
ἵκετο δὲ πτολίεθρον Ἐλευσῖνος θυοέσσης,
εὗρεν δ' ἐν νηῷ Δημήτερα κυανόπεπλον
καί μιν φωνήσασ' ἔπεα πτερόεντα προσηύδα·

[1] Tr. (cp. 235): δαίμονος αἴσῃ, MSS.

All night long they sought to appease the glorious goddess, quaking with fear. But, as soon as dawn began to show, they told powerful Celeus all things without fail, as the lovely-crowned goddess Demeter charged them. So Celeus called the countless people to an assembly and bade them make a goodly temple for rich-haired Demeter and an altar upon the rising hillock. And they obeyed him right speedily and harkened to his voice, doing as he commanded. As for the child, he grew like an immortal being.

Now when they had finished building and had drawn back from their toil, they went every man to his house. But golden-haired Demeter sat there apart from all the blessed gods and stayed, wasting with yearning for her deep-bosomed daughter. Then she caused a most dreadful and cruel year for mankind over the all-nourishing earth: the ground would not make the seed sprout, for rich-crowned Demeter kept it hid. In the fields the oxen drew many a curved plough in vain, and much white barley was cast upon the land without avail. So she would have destroyed the whole race of man with cruel famine and have robbed them who dwell on Olympus of their glorious right of gifts and sacrifices, had not Zeus perceived and marked this in his heart. First he sent golden-winged Iris to call rich-haired Demeter, lovely in form. So he commanded. And she obeyed the dark-clouded Son of Cronos, and sped with swift feet across the space between. She came to the stronghold of fragrant Eleusis, and there finding dark-cloaked Demeter in her temple, spake to her and uttered winged words:

Δήμητερ, καλέει σε πατὴρ Ζεὺς ἄφθιτα εἰδὼς
ἐλθέμεναι μετὰ φῦλα θεῶν αἰειγενετάων.
ἀλλ' ἴθι, μηδ' ἀτέλεστον ἐμὸν ἔπος ἐκ Διὸς ἔστω.
  Ὣς φάτο λισσομένη· τῇ δ' οὐκ ἐπεπείθετο θυμός.
αὖτις ἔπειτα πατὴρ μάκαρας θεοὺς αἰὲν ἐόντας
πάντας ἐπιπροΐαλλεν· ἀμοιβηδὶς δὲ κιόντες
κίκλησκον καὶ πολλὰ δίδον περικαλλέα δῶρα
τιμάς θ', †ἅς κ' ἐθέλοιτο† μετ' ἀθανάτοισιν ἑλέσθαι.
ἀλλ' οὔτις πεῖσαι δύνατο φρένας οὐδὲ νόημα
θυμῷ χωομένης· στερεῶς δ' ἠναίνετο μύθους.
οὐ μὲν γάρ ποτ' ἔφασκε θυώδεος Οὐλύμποιο
πρίν γ' ἐπιβήσεσθαι, οὐ πρὶν γῆς καρπὸν ἀνήσειν,
πρὶν ἴδοι ὀφθαλμοῖσιν ἑὴν εὐώπιδα κούρην.
  Αὐτὰρ ἐπεὶ τό γ' ἄκουσε βαρύκτυπος εὐρύοπα Ζεύς,
εἰς Ἔρεβος πέμψε χρυσόρραπιν Ἀργειφόντην,
ὄφρ' Ἀίδην μαλακοῖσι παραιφάμενος ἐπέεσσιν
ἁγνὴν Περσεφόνειαν ὑπὸ ζόφου ἠερόεντος
ἐς φάος ἐξαγάγοι μετὰ δαίμονας, ὄφρα ἑ μήτηρ
ὀφθαλμοῖσιν ἰδοῦσα μεταλήξειε χόλοιο.
Ἑρμῆς δ' οὐκ ἀπίθησεν, ἄφαρ δ' ὑπὸ κεύθεα γαίης
ἐσσυμένως κατόρουσε λιπὼν ἕδος Οὐλύμποιο.
τέτμε δὲ τόν γε ἄνακτα δόμων ἔντοσθεν ἐόντα,
ἥμενον ἐν λεχέεσσι σὺν αἰδοίῃ παρακοίτι,
πόλλ' ἀεκαζομένῃ μητρὸς πόθῳ· ἣ δ' ἀποτηλοῦ [1]
ἔργοις θεῶν μακάρων [δεινὴν] μητίσετο βουλήν.[2]
ἀγχοῦ δ' ἱστάμενος προσέφη κρατὺς Ἀργειφόντης·

[1] Ilgen: ἐπ' ἀτλήτων, M. [2] Voss: βουλῇ, M.

"Demeter, father Zeus, whose wisdom is everlasting, calls you to come join the tribes of the eternal gods: come therefore, and let not the message I bring from Zeus pass unobeyed."

Thus said Iris imploring her. But Demeter's heart was not moved. Then again the father sent forth all the blessed and eternal gods besides: and they came, one after the other, and kept calling her and offering many very beautiful gifts and whatever rights she might be pleased to choose among the deathless gods. Yet no one was able to persuade her mind and will, so wrath was she in her heart; but she stubbornly rejected all their words: for she vowed that she would never set foot on fragrant Olympus nor let fruit spring out of the ground, until she beheld with her eyes her own fair-faced daughter.

Now when all-seeing Zeus the loud-thunderer heard this, he sent the Slayer of Argus whose wand is of gold to Erebus, so that having won over Hades with soft words, he might lead forth chaste Persephone to the light from the misty gloom to join the gods, and that her mother might see her with her eyes and cease from her anger. And Hermes obeyed, and leaving the house of Olympus, straightway sprang down with speed to the hidden places of the earth. And he found the lord Hades in his house seated upon a couch, and his shy mate with him, much reluctant, because she yearned for her mother. But she was afar off, brooding on her fell design because of the deeds of the blessed gods. And the strong Slayer of Argus drew near and said:

Ἅιδη κυανοχαῖτα, καταφθιμένοισιν ἀνάσσων,
Ζεύς με πατὴρ ἤνωγεν ἀγαυὴν Περσεφόνειαν
ἐξαγαγεῖν Ἐρέβευσφι μετὰ σφέας, ὄφρα ἑ μήτηρ
ὀφθαλμοῖσιν ἰδοῦσα χόλου καὶ μήνιος αἰνῆς
ἀθανάτοις λήξειεν· ἐπεὶ μέγα μήδεται ἔργον,
φθῖσαι φῦλ' ἀμενηνὰ χαμαιγενέων ἀνθρώπων,
σπέρμ' ὑπὸ γῆς κρύπτουσα, καταφθινύθουσα δὲ τιμὰς
ἀθανάτων· ἡ δ' αἰνὸν ἔχει χόλον, οὐδὲ θεοῖσι
μίσγεται, ἀλλ' ἀπάνευθε θυώδεος ἔνδοθι νηοῦ
ἧσται Ἐλευσῖνος κραναὸν πτολίεθρον ἔχουσα.
Ὣς φάτο· μείδησεν δὲ ἄναξ ἐνέρων Ἀιδωνεὺς
ὀφρύσιν, οὐδ' ἀπίθησε Διὸς βασιλῆος ἐφετμῆς·
ἐσσυμένως δ' ἐκέλευσε δαΐφρονι Περσεφονείῃ·
Ἔρχεο, Περσεφόνη, παρὰ μητέρα κυανόπεπλον
ἤπιον ἐν στήθεσσι μένος καὶ θυμὸν ἔχουσα,
μηδέ τι δυσθύμαινε λίην περιώσιον ἄλλων·
οὔ τοι ἐν ἀθανάτοισιν ἀεικὴς ἔσσομ' ἀκοίτης,
αὐτοκασίγνητος πατρὸς Διός· ἔνθα δ' ἐοῦσα
δεσπόσσεις πάντων ὁπόσα ζώει τε καὶ ἕρπει,
τιμὰς δὲ σχήσησθα μετ' ἀθανάτοισι μεγίστας.
τῶν δ' ἀδικησάντων τίσις ἔσσεται ἤματα πάντα,
οἳ κεν μὴ θυσίῃσι τεὸν μένος ἱλάσκωνται
εὐαγέως ἔρδοντες, ἐναίσιμα δῶρα τελοῦντες.
Ὣς φάτο· γήθησεν δὲ περίφρων Περσεφόνεια,
καρπαλίμως δ' ἀνόρουσ' ὑπὸ χάρματος· αὐτὰρ ὅ γ' αὐτὸς
ῥοιῆς κόκκον ἔδωκε φαγεῖν μελιηδέα λάθρῃ,
ἀμφὶ ἓ νωμήσας, ἵνα μὴ μένοι ἤματα πάντα
αὖθι παρ' αἰδοίῃ Δημήτερι κυανοπέπλῳ.
ἵππους δὲ προπάροιθεν ὑπὸ χρυσέοισιν ὄχεσφιν
ἔντυεν ἀθανάτους Πολυσημάντωρ Ἀιδωνεύς.

"Dark-haired Hades, ruler over the departed, father Zeus bids me bring noble Persephone forth from Erebus unto the gods, that her mother may see her with her eyes and cease from her dread anger with the immortals; for now she plans an awful deed, to destroy the weakly tribes of earth-born men by keeping seed hidden beneath the earth, and so she makes an end of the honours of the undying gods. For she keeps fearful anger and does not consort with the gods, but sits aloof in her fragrant temple, dwelling in the rocky hold of Eleusis."

So he said. And Aïdoneus, ruler over the dead, smiled grimly and obeyed the behest of Zeus the king. For he straightway urged wise Persephone, saying:—

"Go now, Persephone, to your dark-robed mother, go, and feel kindly in your heart towards me: be not so exceedingly cast down; for I shall be no unfitting husband for you among the deathless gods, that am own brother to father Zeus. And while you are here, you shall rule all that lives and moves and shall have the greatest rights among the deathless gods: those who defraud you and do not appease your power with offerings, reverently performing rites and paying fit gifts, shall be punished for evermore."

When he said this, wise Persephone was filled with joy and hastily sprang up for gladness. But he on his part secretly gave her sweet pomegranate seed to eat, taking care for himself that she might not remain continually with grave, dark-robed Demeter. Then Aïdoneus the Ruler of Many openly got ready his deathless horses beneath the golden chariot. And she mounted on the chariot,

ἣ δ' ὀχέων ἐπέβη, πάρα δὲ κρατὺς Ἀργειφόντης
ἡνία καὶ μάστιγα λαβὼν μετὰ χερσὶ φίλῃσι
σεῦε διὲκ μεγάρων· τὼ δ' οὐκ ἀέκοντε πετέσθην.
ῥίμφα δὲ μακρὰ κέλευθα διήνυσαν· οὐδὲ θάλασσα
οὔθ' ὕδωρ ποταμῶν οὔτ' ἄγκεα ποιήεντα
ἵππων ἀθανάτων οὔτ' ἄκριες ἔσχεθον ὁρμήν,
ἀλλ' ὑπὲρ αὐτάων βαθὺν ἠέρα τέμνον ἰόντες.
στῆσε δ' ἄγων, ὅθι μίμνεν ἐυστέφανος Δημήτηρ,
νηοῖο προπάροιθε θυώδεος· ἣ δὲ ἰδοῦσα
ἤιξ', ἠύτε μαινὰς ὄρος κάτα δάσκιον ὕλῃ.
Περσεφόνη δ' ἑτέρ[ωθὲν ἐπεὶ ἴδεν ὄμματα καλὰ[1]]
μητρὸς ἑῆς κατ' [ἄρ' ἥ γ' ὄχεα προλιποῦσα καὶ ἵππους]
ἆλτο θέει[ν, δειρῇ δέ οἱ ἔμπεσε ἀμφιχυθεῖσα·]
τῇ δὲ [φίλην ἔτι παῖδα ἑῆς μετὰ χερσὶν ἐχούσῃ]
α[ἶψα δόλον θυμός τιν' ὀίσατο, τρέσσε δ' ἄρ' αἰνῶς]
παυομ[ένη φιλότητος, ἄφαρ δ' ἐρεείνετο μύθῳ·]
τέκνον, μή ῥά τι μοι σ[ύ γε πάσσαο νέρθεν ἐοῦσα]
βρώμης; ἐξαύδα, μ[ὴ κεῦθ', ἵνα εἴδομεν ἄμφω·]
ὣς μὲν γάρ κεν ἐοῦσα π[αρὰ στυγεροῦ Ἀίδαο]
καὶ παρ' ἐμοὶ καὶ πατρὶ κελ[αινεφέϊ Κρονίωνι]
ναιετάοις πάντεσσι τετιμ[ένη ἀθανάτοι]σιν.
εἰ δ' ἐπάσω, πάλιν αὖτις ἰοῦσ' ὑπ[ὸ κεύθεσι γαίης]
οἰκήσεις ὡρέων τρίτατον μέρ[ος εἰς ἐνιαυτόν,]
τὰς δὲ δύω παρ' ἐμοί τε καὶ [ἄλλοις ἀθανά]τοισιν.
ὁππότε δ' ἄνθεσι γαῖ' εὐώδε[σιν] εἰαρινο[ῖσι]
παντοδαποῖς θάλλῃ, τόθ' ὑπὸ ζόφου ἠερόεντος
αὖτις ἄνει μέγα θαῦμα θεοῖς θνητοῖς τ' ἀνθρώποις.
[εἶπε δὲ πῶς σ' ἥρπαξεν ὑπὸ ζόφον ἠερόεντα[2]] 403a
καὶ τίνι σ' ἐξαπάτησε δόλῳ κρατερὸς Πολυδέγμων;

[1] The restorations of this and the following lines are those printed in the Oxford (1911) text.

[2] Allen.

and the strong Slayer of Argus took reins and whip in his dear hands and drove forth from the hall, the horses speeding readily. Swiftly they traversed their long course, and neither the sea nor river-waters nor grassy glens nor mountain-peaks checked the career of the immortal horses, but they clave the deep air above them as they went. And Hermes brought them to the place where rich-crowned Demeter was staying and checked them before her fragrant temple.

And when Demeter saw them, she rushed forth as does a Maenad down some thick-wooded mountain, while Persephone on the other side, when she saw her mother's sweet eyes, left the chariot and horses, and leaped down to run to her, and falling upon her neck, embraced her. But while Demeter was still holding her dear child in her arms, her heart suddenly misgave her for some snare, so that she feared greatly and ceased fondling her daughter and asked of her at once: "My child, tell me, surely you have not tasted any food while you were below? Speak out and hide nothing, but let us both know. For if you have not, you shall come back from loathly Hades and live with me and your father, the dark-clouded Son of Cronos and be honoured by all the deathless gods; but if you have tasted food, you must go back again beneath the secret places of the earth, there to dwell a third part of the seasons every year: yet for the two parts you shall be with me and the other deathless gods. But when the earth shall bloom with the fragrant flowers of spring in every kind, then from the realm of darkness and gloom thou shalt come up once more to be a wonder for gods and mortal men. And now tell me how he rapt you away to the realm of darkness and gloom, and by what trick did the strong Host of Many beguile you?"

Τὴν δ᾽ αὖ Περσεφόνη περικαλλὴς ἀντίον ηὔδα·
τοιγὰρ ἐγώ τοι, μῆτερ, ἐρέω νημερτέα πάντα·
εὖτέ μοι Ἑρμῆς ἦλθ᾽ ἐριούνιος ἄγγελος ὠκὺς
πὰρ πατέρος Κρονίδαο καὶ ἄλλων Οὐρανιώνων,
ἐλθεῖν ἐξ Ἐρέβευς, ἵνα μ᾽ ὀφθαλμοῖσιν ἰδοῦσα
λήξαις ἀθανάτοισι χόλου καὶ μήνιος αἰνῆς,
αὐτίκ᾽ ἐγὼν ἀνόρουσ᾽ ὑπὸ χάρματος· αὐτὰρ ὃ λάθρῃ
ἔμβαλέ μοι ῥοιῆς κόκκον, μελιηδέ᾽ ἐδωδήν,
ἄκουσαν δὲ βίῃ με προσηνάγκασσε πάσασθαι.
ὡς δέ μ᾽ ἀναρπάξας Κρονίδεω πυκινὴν διὰ μῆτιν
ᾤχετο πατρὸς ἐμοῖο, φέρων ὑπὸ κεύθεα γαίης,
ἐξερέω, καὶ πάντα διίξομαι; ὡς ἐρεείνεις.
ἡμεῖς μὲν μάλα πᾶσαι ἀν᾽ ἱμερτὸν λειμῶνα,
Λευκίππη Φαινώ τε καὶ Ἠλέκτρη καὶ Ἰάνθη
καὶ Μελίτη Ἰάχη τε Ῥόδειά τε Καλλιρόη τε
Μηλόβοσίς τε Τύχη τε καὶ Ὠκυρόη καλυκῶπις
Χρυσηίς τ᾽ Ἰάνειρά τ᾽ Ἀκάστη τ᾽ Ἀδμήτη τε
καὶ Ῥοδόπη Πλουτώ τε καὶ ἱμερόεσσα Καλυψὼ
καὶ Στὺξ Οὐρανίη τε Γαλαξαύρη τ᾽ ἐρατεινὴ
Παλλάς τ᾽ ἐγρεμάχη καὶ Ἄρτεμις ἰοχέαιρα,
παίζομεν ἠδ᾽ ἄνθεα δρέπομεν χείρεσσ᾽ ἐρόεντα,
μίγδα κρόκον τ᾽ ἀγανὸν καὶ ἀγαλλίδας ἠδ᾽ ὑάκινθον
καὶ ῥοδέας κάλυκας καὶ λείρια, θαῦμα ἰδέσθαι,
νάρκισσόν θ᾽, ὃν ἔφυσ᾽ ὥς περ κρόκον εὐρεῖα χθών.
αὐτὰρ ἐγὼ δρεπόμην περὶ χάρματι· γαῖα δ᾽ ἔνερθε
χώρησεν· τῇ δ᾽ ἔκθορ᾽ ἄναξ κρατερὸς Πολυδέγμων·
βῆ δὲ φέρων ὑπὸ γαῖαν ἐν ἅρμασι χρυσείοισι
πόλλ᾽ ἀεκαζομένην· ἐβόησα δ᾽ ἄρ᾽ ὄρθια φωνῇ.
ταῦτά τοι ἀχνυμένη περ ἀληθέα πάντ᾽ ἀγορεύω.

Then beautiful Persephone answered her thus: "Mother, I will tell you all without error. When luck-bringing Hermes came, swift messenger from my father the Son of Cronos and the other Sons of Heaven, bidding me come back from Erebus that you might see me with your eyes and so cease from your anger and fearful wrath against the gods, I sprang up at once for joy; but he secretly put in my mouth sweet food, a pomegranate seed, and forced me to taste against my will. Also I will tell how he rapt me away by the deep plan of my father the Son of Cronos and carried me off beneath the depths of the earth, and will relate the whole matter as you ask. All we were playing in a lovely meadow, Leucippe[1] and Phaeno and Electra and Ianthe, Melita also and Iache with Rhodea and Callirhoë and Melobosis and Tyche and Ocyrhoë, fair as a flower, Chryseïs, Ianeira, Acaste and Admete and Rhodope and Pluto and charming Calypso; Styx too was there and Urania and lovely Galaxaura with Pallas who rouses battles and Artemis delighting in arrows: we were playing and gathering sweet flowers in our hands, soft crocuses mingled with irises and hyacinths, and rose-blooms and lilies, marvellous to see, and the narcissus which the wide earth caused to grow yellow as a crocus. That I plucked in my joy; but the earth parted beneath, and there the strong lord, the Host of Many, sprang forth and in his golden chariot he bore me away, all unwilling, beneath the earth: then I cried with a shrill cry. All this is true, sore though it grieves me to tell the tale."

[1] The list of names is taken—with five additions—from Hesiod, *Theogony* 349 ff.: for their general significance see note on that passage.

Ὣς τότε μὲν πρόπαν ἦμαρ ὁμόφρονα θυμὸν ἔχουσαι
πολλὰ μάλ᾽ ἀλλήλων κραδίην καὶ θυμὸν ἴαινον
ἀμφαγαπαζόμεναι· ἀχέων δ᾽ ἀπεπαύετο θυμός.
γηθοσύνας δ᾽ ἐδέχοντο παρ᾽ ἀλλήλων ἔδιδόν τε.
τῇσιν δ᾽ ἐγγύθεν ἦλθ᾽ Ἑκάτη λιπαροκρήδεμνος·
πολλὰ δ᾽ ἄρ᾽ ἀμφαγάπησε κόρην Δημήτερος ἁγνήν·
ἐκ τοῦ οἱ πρόπολος καὶ ὀπάων ἔπλετ᾽ ἄνασσα.
Ταῖς δὲ μέτ᾽ ἄγγελον ἧκε βαρύκτυπος εὐρύοπα Ζεὺς
Ῥείην ἠύκομον, Δημήτερα κυανόπεπλον
ἀξέμεναι μετὰ φῦλα θεῶν, ὑπέδεκτο δὲ τιμὰς
δωσέμεν, ἅς κεν ἕλοιτο μετ᾽ ἀθανάτοισι θεοῖσι·
νεῦσε δέ οἱ κούρην ἔτεος περιτελλομένοιο
τὴν τριτάτην μὲν μοῖραν ὑπὸ ζόφον ἠερόεντα,
τὰς δὲ δύω παρὰ μητρὶ καὶ ἄλλοις ἀθανάτοισιν.
ὣς ἔφατ᾽· οὐδ᾽ ἀπίθησε θεὰ Διὸς ἀγγελιάων.
ἐσσυμένως δ᾽ ἤιξε κατ᾽ Οὐλύμποιο καρήνων,
ἐς δ᾽ ἄρα Ῥάριον ἷξε, φερέσβιον οὖθαρ ἀρούρης
τὸ πρίν, ἀτὰρ τότε γ᾽ οὔτι φερέσβιον, ἀλλὰ ἕκηλον
ἑστήκει πανάφυλλον· ἔκευθε δ᾽ ἄρα κρῖ λευκὸν
μήδεσι Δήμητρος καλλισφύρου· αὐτὰρ ἔπειτα
μέλλεν ἄφαρ ταναοῖσι κομήσειν ἀσταχύεσσιν
ἦρος ἀεξομένοιο, πέδῳ δ᾽ ἄρα πίονες ὄγμοι
βρισέμεν ἀσταχύων, τὰ δ᾽ ἐν ἐλλεδανοῖσι δεδέσθαι.
ἔνθ᾽ ἐπέβη πρώτιστον ἀπ᾽ αἰθέρος ἀτρυγέτοιο·
ἀσπασίως δ᾽ ἴδον ἀλλήλας, κεχάρηντο δὲ θυμῷ.
τὴν δ᾽ ὧδε προσέειπε Ῥέη λιπαροκρήδεμνος·
Δεῦρο τέκος, καλέει σε βαρύκτυπος εὐρύοπα Ζεὺς
ἐλθέμεναι μετὰ φῦλα θεῶν, ὑπέδεκτο δὲ τιμὰς

So did they then, with hearts at one, greatly cheer each the other's soul and spirit with many an embrace: their hearts had relief from their griefs while each took and gave back joyousness.

Then bright-coiffed Hecate came near to them, and often did she embrace the daughter of holy Demeter: and from that time the lady Hecate was minister and companion to Persephone.

And all-seeing Zeus sent a messenger to them, rich-haired Rhea, to bring dark-cloaked Demeter to join the families of the gods: and he promised to give her what rights she should choose among the deathless gods and agreed that her daughter should go down for the third part of the circling year to darkness and gloom, but for the two parts should live with her mother and the other deathless gods. Thus he commanded. And the goddess did not disobey the message of Zeus; swiftly she rushed down from the peaks of Olympus and came to the plain of Rharus, rich, fertile corn-land once, but then in nowise fruitful, for it lay idle and utterly leafless, because the white grain was hidden by design of trim-ankled Demeter. But afterwards, as springtime waxed, it was soon to be waving with long ears of corn, and its rich furrows to be loaded with grain upon the ground, while others would already be bound in sheaves. There first she landed from the fruitless upper air: and glad were the goddesses to see each other and cheered in heart. Then bright-coiffed Rhea said to Demeter:

"Come, my daughter; for far-seeing Zeus the loud-thunderer calls you to join the families of the gods, and has promised to give you what rights you please

[δωσέμεν, ἅς κ' ἐθέλῃσθα] μετ' ἀθανάτοισι θεοῖσι.[1]
[νεῦσε δέ σοι κούρην ἔτεος π]εριτελλομένοιο
[τὴν τριτάτην μὲν μοῖραν ὑπὸ ζόφον ἠ]ερόεντα,
[τὰς δὲ δύω παρὰ σοί τε καὶ ἄλλοις] ἀθανάτοισιν.
[ὣς ἄρ' ἔφη τελέ]εσθαι· ἐῷ δ' ἐπένευσε κάρητι.
[ἀλλ' ἴθι, τέκνον] ἐμόν, καὶ πείθεο, μηδέ τι λίην
ἀ[ζηχὲς μεν]έαινε κελαινεφέι Κρονίωνι.
α[ἶψα δὲ κα]ρπὸν ἄεξε φερέσβιον ἀνθρώποισιν.
  Ὧ[ς ἔφατ'. οὐ]δ' ἀπίθησεν ἐυστέφανος Δημήτηρ·
αἶψα δὲ καρπὸν ἀνῆκεν ἀρουράων ἐριβώλων·
πᾶσα δὲ φύλλοισίν τε καὶ ἄνθεσιν εὐρεῖα χθὼν
ἔβρισ'· ἣ δὲ κιοῦσα θεμιστοπόλοις βασιλεῦσι
δεῖξεν Τριπτολέμῳ τε Διοκλεῖ τε πληξίππῳ
Εὐμόλπου τε βίῃ Κελεῷ θ' ἡγήτορι λαῶν
δρησμοσύνην θ' ἱερῶν καὶ ἐπέφραδεν ὄργια πᾶσι,
Τριπτολέμῳ τε Πολυξείνῳ, ἐπὶ τοῖς δὲ Διοκλεῖ
σεμνά, τά τ' οὔπως ἔστι παρεξίμεν οὔτε πυθέσθαι
οὔτ' ἀχέειν· μέγα γάρ τι θεῶν σέβας ἰσχάνει αὐδήν.
ὄλβιος, ὃς τάδ' ὄπωπεν ἐπιχθονίων ἀνθρώπων·
ὃς δ' ἀτελὴς ἱερῶν ὅς τ' ἄμμορος, οὔποθ' ὁμοίων
αἶσαν ἔχει φθίμενός περ ὑπὸ ζόφῳ ἠερόεντι.
  Αὐτὰρ ἐπειδὴ πάνθ' ὑπεθήκατο δῖα θεάων,
βάν ῥ' ἴμεν Οὔλυμπόνδε θεῶν μεθ' ὁμήγυριν ἄλλων.
ἔνθα δὲ ναιετάουσι παραὶ Διὶ τερπικεραύνῳ
σεμναί τ' αἰδοῖαί τε· μέγ' ὄλβιος, ὅν τιν' ἐκεῖναι
προφρονέως φίλωνται ἐπιχθονίων ἀνθρώπων·
αἶψα δέ οἱ πέμπουσιν ἐφέστιον ἐς μέγα δῶμα
Πλοῦτον, ὃς ἀνθρώποις ἄφενος θνητοῖσι δίδωσιν.

[1] The restorations of this and the following lines are those printed in the Oxford (1911) text.

among the deathless gods, and has agreed that for a third part of the circling year your daughter shall go down to darkness and gloom, but for the two parts shall be with you and the other deathless gods: so has he declared it shall be and has bowed his head in token. But come, my child, obey, and be not too angry unrelentingly with the dark-clouded Son of Cronos; but rather increase forthwith for men the fruit that gives them life."

So spake Rhea. And rich-crowned Demeter did not refuse but straightway made fruit to spring up from the rich lands, so that the whole wide earth was laden with leaves and flowers. Then she went, and to the kings who deal justice, Triptolemus and Diocles, the horse-driver, and to doughty Eumolpus and Celeus, leader of the people, she showed the conduct of her rites and taught them all her mysteries, to Triptolemus and Polyxeinus and Diocles also,—awful mysteries which no one may in any way transgress or pry into or utter, for deep awe of the gods checks the voice. Happy is he among men upon earth who has seen these mysteries; but he who is uninitiate and who has no part in them, never has lot of like good things once he is dead, down in the darkness and gloom.

But when the bright goddess had taught them all, they went to Olympus to the gathering of the other gods. And there they dwell beside Zeus who delights in thunder, awful and reverend goddesses. Right blessed is he among men on earth whom they freely love: soon they do send Plutus as guest to his great house, Plutus who gives wealth to mortal men.

Ἀλλ' ἄγ'[1] Ἐλευσῖνος θυοέσσης δῆμον ἔχουσα
καὶ Πάρον ἀμφιρύτην Ἀντρῶνά τε πετρήεντα,
πότνια, ἀγλαόδωρ', ὡρηφόρε, Δηοῖ ἄνασσα,
αὐτὴ καὶ κούρη περικαλλὴς Περσεφόνεια·
πρόφρονες ἀντ' ᾠδῆς βίοτον θυμήρε' ὄπαζε.
αὐτὰρ ἐγὼ καὶ σεῖο καὶ ἄλλης μνήσομ' ἀοιδῆς.

III

ΕΙΣ ΑΠΟΛΛΩΝΑ [ΔΗΛΙΟΝ]

Μνήσομαι οὐδὲ λάθωμαι Ἀπόλλωνος ἑκάτοιο,
ὅντε θεοὶ κατὰ δῶμα Διὸς τρομέουσιν ἰόντα·
καί ῥά τ' ἀναΐσσουσιν ἐπὶ σχεδὸν ἐρχομένοιο
πάντες ἀφ' ἑδράων, ὅτε φαίδιμα τόξα τιταίνει.
Λητὼ δ' οἴη μίμνε παραὶ Διὶ τερπικεραύνῳ,
ἥ ῥα βιόν τ' ἐχάλασσε καὶ ἐκλήισσε φαρέτρην,
καί οἱ ἀπ' ἰφθίμων ὤμων χείρεσσιν ἑλοῦσα
τόξα κατεκρέμασε πρὸς κίονα πατρὸς ἑοῖο
πασσάλου ἐκ χρυσέου· τὸν δ' ἐς θρόνον εἷσεν ἄγουσα.
τῷ δ' ἄρα νέκταρ ἔδωκε πατὴρ δέπαϊ χρυσείῳ
δεικνύμενος φίλον υἱόν· ἔπειτα δὲ δαίμονες ἄλλοι
ἔνθα καθίζουσιν· χαίρει δέ τε πότνια Λητώ,
οὕνεκα τοξοφόρον καὶ καρτερὸν υἱὸν ἔτικτε.
χαῖρε, μάκαιρ' ὦ Λητοῖ, ἐπεὶ τέκες ἀγλαὰ τέκνα,
Ἀπόλλωνά τ' ἄνακτα καὶ Ἄρτεμιν ἰοχέαιραν,
τὴν μὲν ἐν Ὀρτυγίῃ, τὸν δὲ κραναῇ ἐνὶ Δήλῳ,
κεκλιμένη πρὸς μακρὸν ὄρος καὶ Κύνθιον ὄχθον,
ἀγχοτάτω φοίνικος, ἐπ' Ἰνωποῖο ῥεέθροις.

[1] Ruhnken: ἀλλὰ θελευσῖνος, M.

And now, queen of the land of sweet Eleusis and sea-girt Paros and rocky Antron, lady, giver of good gifts, bringer of seasons, queen Deo, be gracions, you and your daughter all beauteous Persephone, and for my song grant me heart-cheering substance. And now I will remember you and another song also.

III

TO DELIAN APOLLO

I WILL remember and not be unmindful of Apollo who shoots afar. As he goes through the house of Zeus, the gods tremble before him and all spring up from their seats when he draws near, as he bends his bright bow. But Leto alone stays by the side of Zeus who delights in thunder; and then she unstrings his bow, and closes his quiver, and takes his archery from his strong shoulders in her hands and hangs them on a golden peg against a pillar of his father's house. Then she leads him to a seat and makes him sit: and the Father gives him nectar in a golden cup welcoming his dear son, while the other gods make him sit down there, and queenly Leto rejoices because she bare a mighty son and an archer. Rejoice, blessed Leto, for you bare glorious children, the lord Apollo and Artemis who delights in arrows; her in Ortygia, and him in rocky Delos, as you rested against the great mass of the Cynthian hill hard by a palm-tree by the streams of Inopus.

Πῶς τ' ἄρ σ' ὑμνήσω πάντως εὔυμνον ἐόντα;
πάντη γάρ τοι, Φοῖβε, νόμοι βεβλήατ' ἀοιδοῖς,
ἠμὲν ἀν' ἤπειρον πορτιτρόφον ἠδ' ἀνὰ νήσους·
πᾶσαι δὲ σκοπιαί τοι ἅδον καὶ πρώονες ἄκροι
ὑψηλῶν ὀρέων ποταμοί θ' ἅλαδε προρέοντες
ἀκταί τ' εἰς ἅλα κεκλιμέναι λιμένες τε θαλάσσης.
ἢ ὥς σε πρῶτον Λητὼ τέκε, χάρμα βροτοῖσι,
κλινθεῖσα πρὸς Κύνθου ὄρος κραναῇ ἐνὶ νήσῳ,
Δήλῳ ἐν ἀμφιρύτῃ; ἑκάτερθε δὲ κῦμα κελαινὸν
ἐξῄει χέρσονδε λιγυπνοίοις ἀνέμοισιν,
ἔνθεν ἀπορνύμενος πᾶσι θνητοῖσιν ἀνάσσεις.
ὅσσους Κρήτη τ' ἐντὸς ἔχει καὶ δῆμος Ἀθηνῶν
νῆσός τ' Αἰγίνη ναυσικλειτή τ' Εὔβοια,
Αἰγαί, Πειρεσίαι[1] τε καὶ ἀγχιάλη Πεπάρηθος
Θρηΐκιός τ' Ἀθόως καὶ Πηλίου ἄκρα κάρηνα
Θρηϊκίη τε Σάμος Ἴδης τ' ὄρεα σκιόεντα,
Σκῦρος καὶ Φώκαια καὶ Αὐτοκάνης ὄρος αἰπύ,
Ἴμβρος τ' εὐκτιμένη καὶ Λῆμνος ἀμιχθαλόεσσα
Λέσβος τ' ἠγαθέη, Μάκαρος ἕδος Αἰολίωνος,
καὶ Χίος, ἣ νήσων λιπαρωτάτη εἰν ἁλὶ κεῖται,
παιπαλόεις τε Μίμας καὶ Κωρύκου ἄκρα κάρηνα
καὶ Κλάρος αἰγλήεσσα καὶ Αἰσαγέης ὄρος αἰπὺ
καὶ Σάμος ὑδρηλὴ Μυκάλης τ' αἰπεινὰ κάρηνα
Μίλητός τε Κόως τε, πόλις Μερόπων ἀνθρώπων,
καὶ Κνίδος αἰπεινὴ καὶ Κάρπαθος ἠνεμόεσσα
Νάξος τ' ἠδὲ Πάρος Ῥήναιά τε πετρήεσσα,
τόσσον ἔπ' ὠδίνουσα Ἑκηβόλον ἵκετο Λητώ,
εἴ τίς οἱ γαιέων υἱεῖ θέλοι οἰκία θέσθαι.
αἱ δὲ μάλ' ἐτρόμεον καὶ ἐδείδισαν, οὐδέ τις ἔτλη
Φοῖβον δέξασθαι, καὶ πιοτέρη περ ἐοῦσα·

[1] Ruhnken: τ' Εἰρεσίαι, MSS.

How, then, shall I sing of you who in all ways are a worthy theme of song? For everywhere, O Phoebus, the whole range of song is fallen to you, both over the mainland that rears heifers and over the isles. All mountain-peaks and high headlands of lofty hills and rivers flowing out to the deep and beaches sloping seawards and havens of the sea are your delight. Shall I sing how at the first Leto bare you to be the joy of men, as she rested against Mount Cynthus in that rocky isle, in sea-girt Delos—while on either hand a dark wave rolled on landwards driven by shrill winds—whence arising you rule over all mortal men?

Among those who are in Crete, and in the township of Athens, and in the isle of Aegina and Euboea, famous for ships, in Aegae and Eiresiae and Peparethus near the sea, in Thracian Athos and Pelion's towering heights and Thracian Samos and the shady hills of Ida, in Scyros and Phocaea and the high hill of Autocane and fair-lying Imbros and smouldering Lemnos and rich Lesbos, home of Macar, the son of Aeolus, and Chios, brightest of all the isles that lie in the sea, and craggy Mimas and the heights of Corycus and gleaming Claros and the sheer hill of Aesagea and watered Samos and the steep heights of Mycale, in Miletus and Cos, the city of Meropian men, and steep Cnidos and windy Carpathos, in Naxos and Paros and rocky Rhenaea—so far roamed Leto in travail with the god who shoots afar, to see if any land would be willing to make a dwelling for her son. But they greatly trembled and feared, and none, not even the richest of them, dared receive

πρίν γ' ὅτε δή ῥ' ἐπὶ Δήλου ἐβήσατο πότνια Λητώ
καί μιν ἀνειρομένη ἔπεα πτερόεντα προσηύδα·
Δῆλ', εἰ γάρ κ' ἐθέλοις ἕδος ἔμμεναι υἷος ἐμοῖο,
Φοίβου Ἀπόλλωνος, θέσθαι τ' ἔνι πίονα νηόν,—
ἄλλος δ' οὔτις σεῖό ποθ' ἅψεται, οὐδέ σε λήσει·
οὐδ' εὔβων σέ γ' ἔσεσθαι ὀίομαι οὔτ' εὔμηλον,
οὐδὲ τρύγην οἴσεις οὔτ' ἂρ φυτὰ μυρία φύσεις.
εἰ δέ κ' Ἀπόλλωνος ἑκαέργου νηὸν ἔχῃσθα,
ἄνθρωποί τοι πάντες ἀγινήσουσ' ἑκατόμβας
ἐνθάδ' ἀγειρόμενοι, κνίσση δέ τοι ἄσπετος αἰεὶ
δημοῦ ἀναΐξει βοσκήσεις θ' οἵ κέ σ' ἔχωσι
χειρὸς ἀπ' ἀλλοτρίης, ἐπεὶ οὔ τοι πῖαρ ὑπ' οὖδας.
ὣς φάτο· χαῖρε δὲ Δῆλος, ἀμειβομένη δὲ προσηύδα·
Λητοῖ, κυδίστη θύγατερ μεγάλου Κοίοιο,
ἀσπασίη κεν ἐγώ γε γονὴν ἑκάτοιο ἄνακτος
δεξαίμην· αἰνῶς γὰρ ἐτήτυμόν εἰμι δυσηχὴς
ἀνδράσιν· ὧδε δέ κεν περιτιμήεσσα γενοίμην.
ἀλλὰ τόδε τρομέω, Λητοῖ, ἔπος, οὐδέ σε κεύσω·
λίην γάρ τινά φασιν ἀτάσθαλον Ἀπόλλωνα
ἔσσεσθαι, μέγα δὲ πρυτανευσέμεν ἀθανάτοισι
καὶ θνητοῖσι βροτοῖσιν ἐπὶ ζείδωρον ἄρουραν.
τῷ ῥ' αἰνῶς δείδοικα κατὰ φρένα καὶ κατὰ θυμόν,
μή, ὁπότ' ἂν τὸ πρῶτον ἴδῃ φάος ἠελίοιο,
νῆσον ἀτιμήσας, ἐπεὶ ἦ κραναήπεδός εἰμι,
ποσσὶ καταστρέψας ὤσῃ ἁλὸς ἐν πελάγεσσιν,
ἔνθ' ἐμὲ μὲν μέγα κῦμα κατὰ κρατὸς ἅλις αἰεὶ
κλύσσει· ὁ δ' ἄλλην γαῖαν ἀφίξεται, ἥ κεν ἅδῃ οἱ,
τεύξασθαι νηόν τε καὶ ἄλσεα δενδρήεντα·
πουλύποδες δ' ἐν ἐμοὶ θαλάμας φῶκαί τε μέλαιναι
οἰκία ποιήσονται ἀκηδέα, χήτεϊ λαῶν.

Phoebus, until queenly Leto set foot on Delos and uttered winged words and asked her:

"Delos, if you would be willing to be the abode of my son Phoebus Apollo and make him a rich temple—; for no other will touch you, as you will find: and I think you will never be rich in oxen and sheep, nor bear vintage nor yet produce plants abundantly. But if you have the temple of far-shooting Apollo, all men will bring you hecatombs and gather here, and incessant savour of rich sacrifice will always arise, and you will feed those who dwell in you from the hand of strangers; for truly your own soil is not rich."

So spake Leto. And Delos rejoiced and answered and said: "Leto, most glorious daughter of great Coeus, joyfully would I receive your child the far-shooting lord; for it is all too true that I am ill-spoken of among men, whereas thus I should become very greatly honoured. But this saying I fear, and I will not hide it from you, Leto. They say that Apollo will be one that is very haughty and will greatly lord it among gods and men all over the fruitful earth. Therefore, I greatly fear in heart and spirit that as soon as he sees the light of the sun, he will scorn this island—for truly I have but a hard, rocky soil—and overturn me and thrust me down with his feet in the depths of the sea; then will the great ocean wash deep above my head for ever, and he will go to another land such as will please him, there to make his temple and wooded groves. So, many-footed creatures of the sea will make their lairs in me and black seals their dwellings undisturbed, because I lack people. Yet if

ἀλλ᾽ εἴ μοι τλαίης γε, θεά, μέγαν ὅρκον ὀμόσσαι,
ἐνθάδε μιν πρῶτον τεύξειν περικαλλέα νηὸν
ἔμμεναι ἀνθρώπων χρηστήριον, αὐτὰρ ἔπειτα
[τεύξασθαι νηούς τε καὶ ἄλσεα δενδρήεντα [1]]
πάντας ἐπ᾽ ἀνθρώπους, ἐπεὶ ἦ πολυώνυμος ἔσται.
  Ὣς ἄρ᾽ ἔφη· Λητὼ δὲ θεῶν μέγαν ὅρκον ὄμοσσε·
ἴστω νῦν τάδε Γαῖα καὶ Οὐρανὸς εὐρὺς ὕπερθεν
καὶ τὸ κατειβόμενον Στυγὸς ὕδωρ, ὅστε μέγιστος
ὅρκος δεινότατός τε πέλει μακάρεσσι θεοῖσιν·
ἦ μὴν Φοίβου τῇδε θυώδης ἔσσεται αἰεὶ
βωμὸς καὶ τέμενος, τίσει δέ σέ γ᾽ ἔξοχα πάντων.
  Αὐτὰρ ἐπεί ῥ᾽ ὄμοσέν τε τελεύτησέν τε τὸν ὅρκον,
Δῆλος μὲν μάλα χαῖρε γονῇ [2] ἑκάτοιο ἄνακτος·
Λητὼ δ᾽ ἐννῆμάρ τε καὶ ἐννέα νύκτας ἀέλπτοις
ὠδίνεσσι πέπαρτο. θεαὶ δ᾽ ἔσαν ἔνδοθι πᾶσαι,
ὅσσαι ἄρισται ἔασι, Διώνη τε Ῥείη τε
Ἰχναίη τε Θέμις καὶ ἀγάστονος Ἀμφιτρίτη
ἄλλαι τ᾽ ἀθάναται νόσφιν λευκωλένου Ἥρης·
ἧστο γὰρ ἐν μεγάροισι Διὸς νεφεληγερέταο·
μούνη δ᾽ οὐκ ἐπέπυστο μογοστόκος Εἰλείθυια·
ἧστο γὰρ ἄκρῳ Ὀλύμπῳ ὑπὸ χρυσέοισι νέφεσσιν,
Ἥρης φραδμοσύνῃς λευκωλένου, ἥ μιν ἔρυκε
ζηλοσύνῃ, ὅτ᾽ ἄρ᾽ υἱὸν ἀμύμονά τε κρατερόν τε
Λητὼ τέξεσθαι καλλιπλόκαμος τότ᾽ ἔμελλεν.
  Αἳ δ᾽ Ἶριν προὔπεμψαν ἐυκτιμένης ἀπὸ νήσου,
ἀξέμεν Εἰλείθυιαν, ὑποσχόμεναι μέγαν ὅρμον,
χρυσείοισι λίνοισιν ἐερμένον, ἐννεάπηχυν·
νόσφιν δ᾽ ἤνωγον καλέειν λευκωλένου Ἥρης,
μή μιν ἔπειτ᾽ ἐπέεσσιν ἀποστρέψειεν ἰοῦσαν.
αὐτὰρ ἐπεὶ τό γ᾽ ἄκουσε ποδήνεμος ὠκέα Ἶρις,

[1] Allen. [2] Franke: γόνῳ, MSS.

you will but dare to sware a great oath, goddess, that here first he will build a glorious temple to be an oracle for men, then let him afterwards make temples and wooded groves amongst all men; for surely he will be greatly renowned.

So said Delos. And Leto sware the great oath of the gods: "Now hear this, Earth and wide Heaven above, and dropping water of Styx (this is the strongest and most awful oath for the blessed gods), surely Phoebus shall have here his fragrant altar and precinct, and you he shall honour above all."

Now when Leto had sworn and ended her oath, Delos was very glad at the birth of the far-shooting lord. But Leto was racked nine days and nine nights with pangs beyond wont. And there were with her all the chiefest of the goddesses, Dione and Rhea and Ichnaea and Themis and loud-moaning Amphitrite and the other deathless goddesses save white-armed Hera, who sat in the halls of cloud-gathering Zeus. Only Eilithyia, goddess of sore travail, had not heard of Leto's trouble, for she sat on the top of Olympus beneath golden clouds by white-armed Hera's contriving, who kept her close through envy, because Leto with the lovely tresses was soon to bear a son faultless and strong.

But the goddesses sent out Iris from the well-set isle to bring Eilithyia, promising her a great necklace strung with golden threads, nine cubits long. And they bade Iris call her aside from white-armed Hera, lest she might afterwards turn her from coming with her words. When swift Iris, fleet of foot as the wind, had heard all this, she set to run; and

βῆ ῥα θέειν, ταχέως δὲ διήνυσε πᾶν τὸ μεσηγύ.
αὐτὰρ ἐπεί ῥ' ἵκανε θεῶν ἕδος, αἰπὺν Ὄλυμπον,
αὐτίκ' ἄρ' Εἰλείθυιαν ἀπὲκ μεγάροιο θύραζε
ἐκπροκαλεσσαμένη ἔπεα πτερόεντα προσηύδα,
πάντα μάλ', ὡς ἐπέτελλον Ὀλύμπια δώματ' ἔχουσαι.
τῇ δ' ἄρα θυμὸν ἔπειθεν ἐνὶ στήθεσσι φίλοισι·
βὰν δὲ ποσὶ τρήρωσι πελειάσιν ἴθμαθ' ὁμοῖαι.
εὖτ' ἐπὶ Δήλου ἔβαινε μογοστόκος Εἰλείθυια,
δὴ τότε τὴν τόκος εἷλε, μενοίνησεν δὲ τεκέσθαι.
ἀμφὶ δὲ φοίνικι βάλε πήχεε, γοῦνα δ' ἔρεισε
λειμῶνι μαλακῷ· μείδησε δὲ γαῖ' ὑπένερθεν·
ἐκ δ' ἔθορε πρὸ φόωσδε· θεαὶ δ' ὀλόλυξαν ἅπασαι.
Ἔνθα σέ, ἤιε Φοῖβε, θεαὶ λόον ὕδατι καλῷ
ἁγνῶς καὶ καθαρῶς, σπάρξαν δ' ἐν φάρεϊ λευκῷ,
λεπτῷ, νηγατέῳ· περὶ δὲ χρύσεον στρόφον ἧκαν.
Οὐδ' ἄρ' Ἀπόλλωνα χρυσάορα θήσατο μήτηρ,
ἀλλὰ Θέμις νέκταρ τε καὶ ἀμβροσίην ἐρατεινὴν
ἀθανάτῃσιν χερσὶν ἐπήρξατο· χαῖρε δὲ Λητώ,
οὕνεκα τοξοφόρον καὶ καρτερὸν υἱὸν ἔτικτεν.
αὐτὰρ ἐπεὶ δή, Φοῖβε, κατέβρως ἄμβροτον εἶδαρ,
οὔ σέ γ' ἔπειτ' ἴσχον χρύσεοι στρόφοι ἀσπαίροντα,
οὐδ' ἔτι δέσματ' ἔρυκε, λύοντο δὲ πείρατα πάντα.
αὐτίκα δ' ἀθανάτῃσι μετηύδα Φοῖβος Ἀπόλλων·
Εἴη μοι κίθαρίς τε φίλη καὶ καμπύλα τόξα,
χρήσω δ' ἀνθρώποισι Διὸς νημερτέα βουλήν.
Ὣς εἰπὼν ἐβίβασκεν ἐπὶ χθονὸς εὐρυοδείης
Φοῖβος ἀκερσεκόμης, ἑκατηβόλος· αἱ δ' ἄρα πᾶσαι

quickly finishing all the distance she came to the home of the gods, sheer Olympus, and forthwith called Eilithyia out from the hall to the door and spoke winged words to her, telling her all as the goddesses who dwell on Olympus had bidden her. So she moved the heart of Eilithyia in her dear breast; and they went their way, like shy wild-doves in their going.

And as soon as Eilithyia the goddess of sore travail set foot on Delos, the pains of birth seized Leto, and she longed to bring forth; so she cast her arms about a palm tree and kneeled on the soft meadow while the earth laughed for joy beneath. Then the child leaped forth to the light, and all the goddesses raised a cry. Straightway, great Phoebus, the goddesses washed you purely and cleanly with sweet water, and swathed you in a white garment of fine texture, new-woven, and fastened a golden band about you.

Now Leto did not give Apollo, bearer of the golden blade, her breast; but Themis duly poured nectar and ambrosia with her divine hands: and Leto was glad because she had borne a strong son and an archer. But as soon as you had tasted that divine heavenly food, O Phoebus, you could no longer then be held by golden cords nor confined with bands, but all their ends were undone. Forthwith Phoebus Apollo spoke out among the deathless goddesses:

"The lyre and the curved bow shall ever be dear to me, and I will declare to men the unfailing will of Zeus."

So said Phoebus, the long-haired god who shoots afar and began to walk upon the wide-pathed earth;

θάμβεον ἀθάναται· χρυσῷ δ' ἄρα Δῆλος ἅπασα
[βεβρίθει, καθορῶσα Διὸς Λητοῦς τε γενέθλην,
γηθοσύνῃ, ὅτι μιν θεὸς εἵλετο οἰκία θέσθαι
νήσων ἠπείρου τε, φίλησε δὲ κηρόθι μᾶλλον[1].]
ἤνθησ', ὡς ὅτε τε ῥίον οὔρεος ἄνθεσιν ὕλης.
Αὐτὸς δ', ἀργυρότοξε, ἄναξ ἑκατηβόλ' Ἄπολλον,
ἄλλοτε μέν τ' ἐπὶ Κύνθου ἐβήσαο παιπαλόεντος,
ἄλλοτε δ' ἂν νήσους τε καὶ ἀνέρας ἠλάσκαζες.
πολλοί τοι νηοί τε καὶ ἄλσεα δενδρήεντα·
πᾶσαι δὲ σκοπιαί τε φίλαι καὶ πρώονες ἄκροι
ὑψηλῶν ὀρέων ποταμοί θ' ἅλαδε προρέοντες·
ἀλλὰ σὺ Δήλῳ, Φοῖβε, μάλιστ' ἐπιτέρπεαι ἦτορ,
ἔνθα τοι ἑλκεχίτωνες Ἰάονες ἠγερέθονται
αὐτοῖς σὺν παίδεσσι καὶ αἰδοίῃς ἀλόχοισιν.
οἱ δέ σε πυγμαχίῃ τε καὶ ὀρχηθμῷ καὶ ἀοιδῇ
μνησάμενοι τέρπουσιν, ὅτ' ἂν στήσωνται ἀγῶνα.
φαίη κ' ἀθανάτους καὶ ἀγήρως ἔμμεναι αἰεί,
ὃς τόθ' ὑπαντιάσει', ὅτ' Ἰάονες ἀθρόοι εἶεν·
πάντων γάρ κεν ἴδοιτο χάριν, τέρψαιτο δὲ θυμὸν
ἄνδρας τ' εἰσορόων καλλιζώνους τε γυναῖκας
νῆάς τ' ὠκείας ἠδ' αὐτῶν κτήματα πολλά.
πρὸς δὲ τόδε μέγα θαῦμα, ὅου κλέος οὔποτ' ὀλεῖται,
κοῦραι Δηλιάδες, ἑκατηβελέταο θεράπναι·
αἵ τ' ἐπεὶ ἂρ πρῶτον μὲν Ἀπόλλων' ὑμνήσωσιν,
αὖτις δ' αὖ Λητώ τε καὶ Ἄρτεμιν ἰοχέαιραν,
μνησάμεναι ἀνδρῶν τε παλαιῶν ἠδὲ γυναικῶν
ὕμνον ἀείδουσιν, θέλγουσι δὲ φῦλ' ἀνθρώπων.

[1] ll. 136-8 are intrusive, being alternative for l. 139. They are found in Π and the edition of Stephanus (in text), and in the margin of ETL (with the note "in another copy these verses also are extant"). In D they are added by a second hand.

and all the goddesses were amazed at him. Then with gold all Delos [was laden, beholding the child of Zeus and Leto, for joy because the god chose her above the islands and shore to make his dwelling in her: and she loved him yet more in her heart.] blossomed as does a mountain-top with woodland flowers.

And you, O lord Apollo, god of the silver bow, shooting afar, now walked on craggy Cynthus, and now kept wandering about the islands and the people in them. Many are your temples and wooded groves, and all peaks and towering bluffs of lofty mountains and rivers flowing to the sea are dear to you, Phoebus, yet in Delos do you most delight your heart; for there the long robed Ionians gather in your honour with their children and shy wives: mindful, they delight you with boxing and dancing and song, so often as they hold their gathering. A man would say that they were deathless and unageing if he should then come upon the Ionians so met together. For he would see the graces of them all, and would be pleased in heart gazing at the men and well-girded women with their swift ships and great wealth. And there is this great wonder besides—and its renown shall never perish—, the girls of Delos, hand-maidens of the Far-shooter; for when they have praised Apollo first, and also Leto and Artemis who delights in arrows, they sing a strain telling of men and women of past days, and charm the tribes of men. Also they can imitate the

πάντων δ' ἀνθρώπων φωνὰς καὶ βαμβαλιαστὺν[1]
μιμεῖσθ' ἴσασιν· φαίη δέ κεν αὐτὸς ἕκαστος
φθέγγεσθ'· οὕτω σφιν καλὴ συνάρηρεν ἀοιδή.
'Αλλ' ἄγεθ' ἱλήκοι μὲν 'Απόλλων 'Αρτέμιδι ξύν,
χαίρετε δ' ὑμεῖς πᾶσαι· ἐμεῖο δὲ καὶ μετόπισθεν
μνήσασθ', ὁππότε κέν τις ἐπιχθονίων ἀνθρώπων
ἐνθάδ' ἀνείρηται ξεῖνος ταλαπείριος ἐλθών·
ὦ κοῦραι, τίς δ' ὔμμιν ἀνὴρ ἥδιστος ἀοιδῶν
ἐνθάδε πωλεῖται, καὶ τέῳ τέρπεσθε μάλιστα;
ὑμεῖς δ' εὖ μάλα πᾶσαι ὑποκρίνασθαι ἀφήμως·
τυφλὸς ἀνήρ, οἰκεῖ δὲ Χίῳ ἔνι παιπαλοέσσῃ
τοῦ πᾶσαι μετόπισθεν ἀριστεύσουσιν ἀοιδαί.
ἡμεῖς δ' ὑμέτερον κλέος οἴσομεν, ὅσσον ἐπ' αἶαν
ἀνθρώπων στρεφόμεσθα πόλεις εὖ ναιεταώσας·
οἳ δ' ἐπὶ δὴ πείσονται, ἐπεὶ καὶ ἐτήτυμόν ἐστιν.
αὐτὰρ ἐγὼν οὐ λήξω ἑκηβόλον 'Απόλλωνα
ὑμνέων ἀργυρότοξον, ὃν ἠύκομος τέκε Λητώ.

[ΕΙΣ ΑΠΟΛΛΩΝΑ ΠΥΘΙΟΝ]

Ὦ ἄνα, καὶ Λυκίην καὶ Μῃονίην ἐρατεινὴν
καὶ Μίλητον ἔχεις, ἔναλον πόλιν ἱμερόεσσαν,
αὐτὸς δ' αὖ Δήλοιο περικλύστης μέγ' ἀνάσσεις.
Εἶσι δὲ φορμίζων Λητοῦς ἐρικυδέος υἱὸς
φόρμιγγι γλαφυρῇ πρὸς Πυθὼ πετρήεσσαν,
ἄμβροτα εἵματ' ἔχων τεθυωμένα· τοῖο δὲ φόρμιγξ
χρυσέου ὑπὸ πλήκτρου καναχὴν ἔχει ἱμερόεσσαν.
ἔνθεν δὲ πρὸς Ὄλυμπον ἀπὸ χθονός, ὥστε νόημα,
εἶσι Διὸς πρὸς δῶμα θεῶν μεθ' ὁμήγυριν ἄλλων.

[1] ETLΠ : κρεμβαλιαστὺν, other MSS. The former word is connected with βαμβαίνειν = to chatter with the teeth, and is usually taken to mean "castanet-playing"; but since imita-

tongues of all men and their clattering speech: each would say that he himself were singing, so close to truth is their sweet song.

And now may Apollo be favourable and Artemis; and farewell all you maidens. Remember me in after time whenever any one of men on earth, a stranger who has seen and suffered much, comes here and asks of you: "Whom think ye, girls, is the sweetest singer that comes here, and in whom do you most delight?" Then answer, each and all, with one voice: "He is a blind man, and dwells in rocky Chios: his lays are evermore supreme." As for me, I will carry your renown as far as I roam over the earth to the well-placed cities of man, and they will believe also; for indeed this thing is true. And I will never cease to praise far-shooting Apollo, god of the silver bow, whom rich-haired Leto bare.

TO PYTHIAN APOLLO

O LORD, Lycia is yours and lovely Maeonia and Miletus, charming city by the sea, but over Delos you greatly reign your own self.

Leto's all-glorious son goes to rocky Pytho, playing upon his hollow lyre, clad in divine, perfumed garments; and at the touch of the golden key his lyre sings sweet. Thence, swift as thought, he speeds from earth to Olympus, to the house of Zeus, to join the gathering of the other gods: then straightway

tion of castanet-playing would hardly be worthy of mention as a feat of skill, it seems more likely that the stammering or harsh dental pronunciation of foreigners is to be understood.

αὐτίκα δ' ἀθανάτοισι μέλει κίθαρις καὶ ἀοιδή·
Μοῦσαι μέν θ' ἅμα πᾶσαι ἀμειβόμεναι ὀπὶ καλῇ
ὑμνεῦσίν ῥα θεῶν δῶρ' ἄμβροτα ἠδ' ἀνθρώπων
τλημοσύνας, ὅσ' ἔχοντες ὑπ' ἀθανάτοισι θεοῖσι
ζώουσ' ἀφραδέες καὶ ἀμήχανοι, οὐδὲ δύνανται
εὑρέμεναι θανάτοιό τ' ἄκος καὶ γήραος ἄλκαρ·
αὐτὰρ ἐϋπλόκαμοι Χάριτες καὶ ἐΰφρονες Ὧραι
Ἁρμονίη θ' Ἥβη τε Διὸς θυγάτηρ τ' Ἀφροδίτη
ὀρχεῦντ' ἀλλήλων ἐπὶ καρπῷ χεῖρας ἔχουσαι·
τῇσι μὲν οὔτ' αἰσχρὴ μεταμέλπεται οὔτ' ἐλάχεια,
ἀλλὰ μάλα μεγάλη τε ἰδεῖν καὶ εἶδος ἀγητή,
Ἄρτεμις ἰοχέαιρα ὁμότροφος Ἀπόλλωνι.
ἐν δ' αὖ τῇσιν Ἄρης καὶ ἐΰσκοπος Ἀργειφόντης
παίζουσ'· αὐτὰρ ὁ Φοῖβος Ἀπόλλων ἐγκιθαρίζει
καλὰ καὶ ὕψι βιβάς· αἴγλη δέ μιν ἀμφιφαείνει
μαρμαρυγαί τε ποδῶν καὶ ἐϋκλώστοιο χιτῶνος.
οἱ δ' ἐπιτέρπονται θυμὸν μέγαν εἰσορόωντες
Λητώ τε χρυσοπλόκαμος καὶ μητίετα Ζεὺς
υἷα φίλον παίζοντα μετ' ἀθανάτοισι θεοῖσι.

Πῶς τ' ἄρ σ' ὑμνήσω πάντως εὔυμνον ἐόντα;
ἠέ σ' ἐνὶ μνηστῆρσιν[1] ἀείδω καὶ φιλότητι,
ὅππως μνωόμενος[2] ἔκιες Ἀζαντίδα κούρην
Ἴσχυ' ἅμ' ἀντιθέῳ, Ἐλατιονίδῃ εὐίππῳ;
ἢ ἅμα Φόρβαντι Τριοπέῳ[3] γένος, ἢ ἅμ' Ἐρευθεῖ;
ἢ ἅμα Λευκίππῳ καὶ Λευκίπποιο δάμαρτι

* * * *

πεζός, ὁ δ' ἵπποισιν· οὐ μὴν Τρίοπός γ' ἐνέλειπεν.
ἢ ὡς τὸ πρῶτον χρηστήριον ἀνθρώποισι
ζητεύων κατὰ γαῖαν ἔβης, ἑκατηβόλ' Ἄπολλον;

[1] Martin: μνηστῇσιν, MSS.
[2] Martin: ὁππόταν ἱέμενος, M: the other MSS. are still more corrupt.
[3] Allen-Sikes: τριόπω, τριοπῷ and τριοπόω, MSS.

the undying gods think only of the lyre and song, and all the Muses together, voice sweetly answering voice, hymn the unending gifts the gods enjoy and the sufferings of men, all that they endure at the hands of the deathless gods, and how they live witless and helpless and cannot find healing for death or defence against old age. Meanwhile the rich-tressed Graces and cheerful Seasons dance with Harmonia and Hebe and Aphrodite, daughter of Zeus, holding each other by the wrist. And among them sings one, not mean nor puny, but tall to look upon and enviable in mien, Artemis who delights in arrows, sister of Apollo. Among them sport Ares and the keen-eyed Slayer of Argus, while Apollo plays his lyre stepping high and featly and a radiance shines around him, the gleaming of his feet and close-woven vest. And they, even gold-tressed Leto and wise Zeus, rejoice in their great hearts as they watch their dear son playing among the undying gods.

How then shall I sing of you—though in all ways you are a worthy theme for song? Shall I sing of you as wooer and in the fields of love, how you went wooing the daughter of Azan along with god-like Ischys the son of well-horsed Elatius, or with Phorbas sprung from Triops, or with Ereutheus, or with Leucippus and the wife of Leucippus . . . you on foot, he with his chariot, yet he fell not short of Triops. Or shall I sing how at the first you went about the earth seeking a place of oracle for men, O far-shooting Apollo? To Pieria

Πιερίην μὲν πρῶτον ἀπ' Οὐλύμποιο κατῆλθες·
Λέκτον τ' ἠμαθόεντα παρέστιχες ἠδ' Ἐνιῆνας[1]
καὶ διὰ Περραιβούς· τάχα δ' εἰς Ἰαωλκὸν ἵκανες,
Κηναίου τ' ἐπέβης ναυσικλειτῆς Εὐβοίης.
στῆς δ' ἐπὶ Ληλάντῳ πεδίῳ· τό τοι οὐχ ἅδε θυμῷ
τεύξασθαι νηόν τε καὶ ἄλσεα δενδρήεντα.
ἔνθεν δ' Εὔριπον διαβάς, ἑκατηβόλ' Ἄπολλον,
βῆς ἀν' ὄρος ζάθεον, χλωρόν· τάχα δ' ἷξες ἀπ' αὐτοῦ
ἐς Μυκαλησσὸν ἰὼν καὶ Τευμησσὸν λεχεποίην.
Θήβης δ' εἰσαφίκανες ἕδος καταειμένον ὕλῃ·
οὐ γάρ πώ τις ἔναιε βροτῶν ἱερῇ ἐνὶ Θήβῃ,
οὐδ' ἄρα πω τότε γ' ἦσαν ἀταρπιτοὶ οὐδὲ κέλευθοι
Θήβης ἂμ πεδίον πυρηφόρον, ἀλλ' ἔχεν ὕλη.
Ἔνθεν δὲ προτέρω ἔκιες, ἑκατηβόλ' Ἄπολλον,
Ὀγχηστὸν δ' ἷξες, Ποσιδήιον ἀγλαὸν ἄλσος·
ἔνθα νεοδμὴς πῶλος ἀναπνέει ἀχθόμενός περ
ἕλκων ἅρματα καλά· χαμαὶ δ' ἐλατὴρ ἀγαθός περ
ἐκ δίφροιο θορὼν ὁδὸν ἔρχεται· οἳ δὲ τέως μὲν
κείν' ὄχεα κροτέουσι ἀνακτορίην ἀφιέντες.
εἰ δέ κεν ἅρματ' ἀγῇσιν ἐν ἄλσεϊ δενδρήεντι,
ἵππους μὲν κομέουσι, τὰ δὲ κλίναντες ἐῶσιν·
ὣς γὰρ τὰ πρώτισθ' ὁσίη γένεθ'· οἳ δὲ ἄνακτι
εὔχονται, δίφρον δὲ θεοῦ τότε μοῖρα φυλάσσει.
Ἔνθεν δὲ προτέρω ἔκιες, ἑκατηβόλ' Ἄπολλον·
Κηφισσὸν δ' ἄρ' ἔπειτα κιχήσαο καλλιρέεθρον,
ὅς τε Λιλαίηθεν προχέει καλλίρροον ὕδωρ.
τὸν διαβάς, Ἑκάεργε, καὶ Ὠκαλέην πολύπυργον
ἔνθεν ἄρ' εἰς Ἁλίαρτον ἀφίκεο ποιήεντα.
Βῆς δ' ἐπὶ Τελφούσης· τόθι τοι ἅδε χῶρος ἀπήμων
τεύξασθαι νηόν τε καὶ ἄλσεα δενδρήεντα·
στῆς δὲ μάλ' ἄγχ' αὐτῆς καί μιν πρὸς μῦθον ἔειπες·

[1] Matthiae: Ἀγνιῆνας, M.

first you went down from Olympus and passed by sandy Lectus and Enienae and through the land of the Perrhaebi. Soon you came to Iolcus and set foot on Cenaeum in Euboea, famed for ships: you stood in the Lelantine plain, but it pleased not your heart to make a temple there and wooded groves. From there you crossed the Euripus, far-shooting Apollo, and went up the green, holy hills, going on to Mycalessus and grassy-bedded Teumessus, and so came to the wood-clad abode of Thebe; for as yet no man lived in holy Thebe, nor were there tracks or ways about Thebe's wheat-bearing plain as yet.

And further still you went, O far-shooting Apollo, and came to Onchestus, Poseidon's bright grove: there the new-broken colt distressed with drawing the trim chariot gets spirit again, and the skilled driver springs from his car and goes on his way. Then the horses for a while rattle the empty car, being rid of guidance; and if they break the chariot in the woody grove, men look after the horses, but tilt the chariot and leave it there; for this was the rite from the very first. And the drivers pray to the lord of the shrine; but the chariot falls to the lot of the god.

Further yet you went, O far-shooting Apollo, and reached next Cephissus' sweet stream which pours forth its sweet-flowing water from Lilaea, and crossing over it, O worker from afar, you passed many-towered Ocalea and reached grassy Haliartus.

Then you went towards Telphusa: and there the pleasant place seemed fit for making a temple and wooded grove. You came very near and spoke to

Τελφοῦσ᾽, ἐνθάδε δὴ φρονέω περικαλλέα νηὸν
ἀνθρώπων τεῦξαι χρηστήριον, οἵτε μοι αἰεὶ
ἐνθάδ᾽ ἀγινήσουσι τεληέσσας ἑκατόμβας,
ἠμὲν ὅσοι Πελοπόννησον πίειραν ἔχουσιν
ἠδ᾽ ὅσοι Εὐρώπην τε καὶ ἀμφιρύτας κατὰ νήσους,
χρησόμενοι· τοῖσιν δέ κ᾽ ἐγὼ νημερτέα βουλὴν
πᾶσι θεμιστεύοιμι χρέων ἐνὶ πίονι νηῷ.
Ὣς εἰπὼν διέθηκε θεμείλια Φοῖβος Ἀπόλλων
εὐρέα καὶ μάλα μακρὰ διηνεκές· ἡ δὲ ἰδοῦσα
Τελφοῦσα κραδίην ἐχολώσατο εἶπέ τε μῦθον·
Φοῖβε ἄναξ ἑκάεργε, ἔπος τί τοι ἐν φρεσὶ θήσω.
ἐνθάδ᾽ ἐπεὶ φρονέεις τεῦξαι περικαλλέα νηὸν
ἔμμεναι ἀνθρώποις χρηστήριον, οἵτε τοι αἰεὶ
ἐνθάδ᾽ ἀγινήσουσι τεληέσσας ἑκατόμβας·
ἀλλ᾽ ἔκ τοι ἐρέω, σὺ δ᾽ ἐνὶ φρεσὶ βάλλεο σῇσι,
πημανέει σ᾽ αἰεὶ κτύπος ἵππων ὠκειάων
ἀρδόμενοί τ᾽ οὐρῆες ἐμῶν ἱερῶν ἀπὸ πηγέων·
ἔνθα τις ἀνθρώπων βουλήσεται εἰσοράασθαι
ἅρματά τ᾽ εὐποίητα καὶ ὠκυπόδων κτύπον ἵππων
ἢ νηόν τε μέγαν καὶ κτήματα πόλλ᾽ ἐνεόντα.
ἀλλ᾽ εἰ δή τι πίθοιο, σὺ δὲ κρείσσων καὶ ἀρείων
ἐσσί, ἄναξ, ἐμέθεν, σεῦ δὲ σθένος ἐστὶ μέγιστον,
ἐν Κρίσῃ ποίησαι ὑπὸ πτυχὶ Παρνησοῖο.
ἔνθ᾽ οὔθ᾽ ἅρματα καλὰ δονήσεται οὔτε τοι ἵππων
ὠκυπόδων κτύπος ἔσται ἐΰδμητον περὶ βωμόν,
ἀλλά τοι ὣς προσάγοιεν Ἰηπαιήονι δῶρα
ἀνθρώπων κλυτὰ φῦλα· σὺ δὲ φρένας ἀμφιγεγηθὼς
δέξαι᾽ ἱερὰ καλὰ περικτιόνων ἀνθρώπων.
ὣς εἰποῦσ᾽ Ἑκάτου πέπιθε φρένας, ὄφρα οἱ αὐτῇ
Τελφούσῃ κλέος εἴη ἐπὶ χθονί, μηδ᾽ Ἑκάτοιο.
Ἔνθεν δὲ προτέρω ἔκιες, ἑκατηβόλ᾽ Ἄπολλον·

her: "Telphusa, here I am minded to make a glorious temple, an oracle for men, and hither they will always bring perfect hecatombs, both those who live in rich Peloponnesus and those of Europe and all the wave-washed isles, coming to seek oracles. And I will deliver to them all counsel that cannot fail, giving answer in my rich temple."

So said Phoebus Apollo, and laid out all the foundations throughout, wide and very long. But when Telphusa saw this, she was angry in heart and spoke, saying: "Lord Phoebus, worker from afar, I will speak a word of counsel to your heart, since you are minded to make here a glorious temple to be an oracle for men who will always bring hither perfect hecatombs for you; yet I will speak out, and do you lay up my words in your heart. The trampling of swift horses and the sound of mules watering at my sacred springs will always irk you, and men will like better to gaze at the well-made chariots and stamping, swift-footed horses than at your great temple and the many treasures that are within. But if you will be moved by me—for you, lord, are stronger and mightier than I, and your strength is very great—build at Crisa below the glades of Parnassus: there no bright chariot will clash, and there will be no noise of swift-footed horses near your well-built altar. But so the glorious tribes of men will bring gifts to you as Iepaeon ('Hail-Healer'), and you will receive with delight rich sacrifices from the people dwelling round about." So said Telphusa, that she alone, and not the Far-Shooter, should have renown there; and she persuaded the Far-Shooter.

Further yet you went, far-shooting Apollo, until

ἷξες δ' ἐς Φλεγύων ἀνδρῶν πόλιν ὑβριστάων,
οἳ Διὸς οὐκ ἀλέγοντες ἐπὶ χθονὶ ναιετάασκον
ἐν καλῇ βήσσῃ Κηφισίδος ἐγγύθι λίμνης.
ἔνθεν καρπαλίμως προσέβης πρὸς δειράδα θύων
ἵκεο δ' ἐς Κρίσην ὑπὸ Παρνησὸν νιφόεντα,
κνημὸν πρὸς Ζέφυρον τετραμμένον, αὐτὰρ ὕπερθεν
πέτρη ἐπικρέμαται, κοίλη δ' ὑποδέδρομε βῆσσα,
τρηχεῖ· ἔνθα ἄναξ τεκμήρατο Φοῖβος Ἀπόλλων
νηὸν ποιήσασθαι ἐπήρατον εἶπέ τε μῦθον·
Ἐνθάδε δὴ φρονέω τεῦξαι περικαλλέα νηὸν
ἔμμεναι ἀνθρώποις χρηστήριον, οἵτε μοι αἰεὶ
ἐνθάδ' ἀγινήσουσι τεληέσσας ἑκατόμβας,
ἠμὲν ὅσοι Πελοπόννησον πίειραν ἔχουσιν,
ἠδ' ὅσοι Εὐρώπην τε καὶ ἀμφιρύτας κατὰ νήσους,
χρησόμενοι· τοῖσιν δ' ἄρ' ἐγὼ νημερτέα βουλὴν
πᾶσι θεμιστεύοιμι χρέων ἐνὶ πίονι νηῷ.
Ὣς εἰπὼν διέθηκε θεμείλια Φοῖβος Ἀπόλλων
εὐρέα καὶ μάλα μακρὰ διηνεκές· αὐτὰρ ἐπ' αὐτοῖς
λάινον οὐδὸν ἔθηκε Τροφώνιος ἠδ' Ἀγαμήδης,
υἱέες Ἐργίνου, φίλοι ἀθανάτοισι θεοῖσιν·
ἀμφὶ δὲ νηὸν ἔνασσαν ἀθέσφατα φῦλ' ἀνθρώπων
ξεστοῖσιν λάεσσιν, ἀοίδιμον ἔμμεναι αἰεί.
Ἀγχοῦ δὲ κρήνη καλλίρροος, ἔνθα δράκαιναν
κτεῖνεν ἄναξ, Διὸς υἱός, ἀπὸ κρατεροῖο βιοῖο,
ζατρεφέα, μεγάλην, τέρας ἄγριον, ἣ κακὰ πολλὰ
ἀνθρώπους ἔρδεσκεν ἐπὶ χθονί, πολλὰ μὲν αὐτούς,
πολλὰ δὲ μῆλα ταναύποδ', ἐπεὶ πέλε πῆμα δαφοινόν.
καί ποτε δεξαμένη χρυσοθρόνου ἔτρεφεν Ἥρης
δεινόν τ' ἀργαλέον τε Τυφάονα, πῆμα βροτοῖσιν·
ὅν ποτ' ἄρ' Ἥρη ἔτικτε χολωσαμένη Διὶ πατρί,

you came to the town of the presumptuous Phlegyae who dwell on this earth in a lovely glade near the Cephisian lake, caring not for Zeus. And thence you went speeding swiftly to the mountain ridge, and came to Crisa beneath snowy Parnassus, a foothill turned towards the west: a cliff hangs over it from above, and a hollow, rugged glade runs under. There the lord Phoebus Apollo resolved to make his lovely temple, and thus he said:

"In this place I am minded to build a glorious temple to be an oracle for men, and here they will always bring perfect hecatombs, both they who dwell in rich Peloponnesus and the men of Europe and from all the wave-washed isles, coming to question me. And I will deliver to them all counsel that cannot fail, answering them in my rich temple."

When he had said this, Phoebus Apollo laid out all the foundations throughout, wide and very long; and upon these the sons of Erginus, Trophonius and Agamedes, dear to the deathless gods, laid a footing of stone. And the countless tribes of men built the whole temple of wrought stones, to be sung of for ever.

But near by was a sweet flowing spring, and there with his strong bow the lord, the son of Zeus, killed the bloated, great she-dragon, a fierce monster wont to do great mischief to men upon earth, to men themselves and to their thin-shanked sheep; for she was a very bloody plague. She it was who once received from gold-throned Hera and brought up fell, cruel Typhaon to be a plague to men. Once on a time Hera bare him because she was angry with father

ἥνικ᾽ ἄρα[1] Κρονίδης ἐρικυδέα γείνατ᾽ Ἀθήνην
ἐν κορυφῇ· ἡ δ᾽ αἶψα χολώσατο πότνια Ἥρη
ἠδὲ καὶ ἀγρομένοισι μετ᾽ ἀθανάτοισιν ἔειπε·
Κέκλυτέ μευ, πάντες τε θεοὶ πᾶσαί τε θέαιναι,
ὡς ἔμ᾽ ἀτιμάζειν ἄρχει νεφεληγερέτα Ζεὺς
πρῶτος, ἐπεί μ᾽ ἄλοχον ποιήσατο κέδν᾽ εἰδυῖαν·
καὶ νῦν νόσφιν ἐμεῖο τέκε γλαυκῶπιν Ἀθήνην,
ἣ πᾶσιν μακάρεσσι μεταπρέπει ἀθανάτοισιν·
αὐτὰρ ὅ γ᾽ ἠπεδανὸς γέγονεν μετὰ πᾶσι θεοῖσι
παῖς ἐμὸς Ἥφαιστος, ῥικνὸς πόδας, ὃν τέκον αὐτή·
[αἶσχος ἐμοὶ καὶ ὄνειδος ἐν οὐρανῷ ὄντε καὶ αὐτή[2]]
ῥῖψ᾽ ἀνὰ χερσὶν ἑλοῦσα καὶ ἔμβαλον εὐρέι πόντῳ·
ἀλλά ἑ Νηρῆος θυγάτηρ Θέτις ἀργυρόπεζα
δέξατο καὶ μετὰ ᾗσι κασιγνήτῃσι κόμισσεν.
ὡς ὄφελ᾽ ἄλλο θεοῖσι χαρίζεσθαι μακάρεσσι.
σχέτλιε, ποικιλομῆτα, τί νῦν μητίσεαι ἄλλο;
πῶς ἔτλης οἶος τεκέειν γλαυκῶπιν Ἀθήνην;
οὐκ ἂν ἐγὼ τεκόμην; καὶ σὴ κεκλημένη ἔμπης
ἦα ῥ᾽[3] ἐν ἀθανάτοισιν, οἳ οὐρανὸν εὐρὺν ἔχουσι.
φράζεο νῦν μή τοί τι κακὸν μητίσομ᾽ ὀπίσσω.
καὶ νῦν μέντοι ἐγὼ τεχνήσομαι, ὥς κε γένηται
παῖς ἐμός, ὅς κε θεοῖσι μεταπρέποι ἀθανάτοισιν,
οὔτε σὸν αἰσχύνασ᾽ ἱερὸν λέχος οὔτ᾽ ἐμὸν αὐτῆς.
οὐδέ τοι εἰς εὐνὴν πωλήσομαι, ἀλλ᾽ ἀπὸ σεῖο
τηλόθ᾽ ἐοῦσα[4] θεοῖσι μετέσσομαι ἀθανάτοισιν.
Ὣς εἰποῦσ᾽ ἀπὸ νόσφι θεῶν κίε χωομένη κῆρ.
αὐτίκ᾽ ἔπειτ᾽ ἠρᾶτο βοῶπις πότνια Ἥρη,
χειρὶ καταπρηνεῖ δ᾽ ἔλασε χθόνα καὶ φάτο μῦθον·

[1] Allen-Sikes: ἧνεκ᾽ ἄρα, M.
[2] Suggested by Allen-Sikes to fill up the lacuna.
[3] Matthiae: ἢ ῥ᾽, MSS.
[4] Hermann: τηλόθεν οὖσα, MSS.

Zeus, when the Son of Cronos bare all-glorious Athena in his head. Thereupon queenly Hera was angry and spoke thus among the assembled gods:

"Hear from me, all gods and goddesses, how cloud-gathering Zeus begins to dishonour me wantonly, when he has made me his true-hearted wife. See now, apart from me he has given birth to bright-eyed Athena who is foremost among all the blessed gods. But my son Hephaestus whom I bare was weakly among all the blessed gods and shrivelled of foot, a shame and a disgrace to me in heaven, whom I myself took in my hands and cast out so that he fell in the great sea. But silver-shod Thetis the daughter of Nereus took and cared for him with her sisters: would that she had done other service to the blessed gods! O wicked one and crafty! What else will you now devise? How dared you by yourself give birth to bright-eyed Athena? Would not I have borne you a child—I, who was at least called your wife among the undying gods who hold wide heaven. Beware now lest I devise some evil thing for you hereafter: yes, now I will contrive that a son be born me to be foremost among the undying gods—and that without casting shame on the holy bond of wedlock between you and me. And I will not come to your bed, but will consort with the blessed gods far off from you."

When she had so spoken, she went apart from the gods, being very angry. Then straightway large-eyed queenly Hera prayed, striking the ground flatwise with her hand, and speaking thus:

Κέκλυτε νῦν μευ, Γαῖα καὶ Οὐρανὸς εὐρὺς ὕπερθεν
Τιτῆνές τε θεοί, τοὶ ὑπὸ χθονὶ ναιετάοντες
Τάρταρον ἀμφὶ μέγαν, τῶν ἒξ ἄνδρες τε θεοί τε·
αὐτοὶ νῦν μευ πάντες ἀκούσατε καὶ δότε παῖδα
νόσφι Διός, μηδέν τι βίην ἐπιδευέα κείνου·
ἀλλ' ὅ γε φέρτερος ἔστω,[1] ὅσον Κρόνου εὐρύοπα Ζεύς.
ὣς ἄρα φωνήσασ' ἵμασε χθόνα χειρὶ παχείῃ·
κινήθη δ' ἄρα Γαῖα φερέσβιος· ἣ δὲ ἰδοῦσα
τέρπετο ὃν κατὰ θυμόν· ὀίετο γὰρ τελέεσθαι.
ἐκ τούτου δὴ ἔπειτα τελεσφόρον εἰς ἐνιαυτὸν
οὔτε πότ' εἰς εὐνὴν Διὸς ἤλυθε μητιόεντος,
οὔτε πότ' ἐς θῶκον πολυδαίδαλον, ὡς τὸ πάρος περ
αὐτῷ ἐφεζομένη πυκινὰς φράζεσκετο βουλάς·
ἀλλ' ἥ γ' ἐν νηοῖσι πολυλλίστοισι μένουσα
τέρπετο οἷς ἱεροῖσι βοῶπις πότνια Ἥρη.
ἀλλ' ὅτε δὴ μῆνές τε καὶ ἡμέραι ἐξετελεῦντο
ἂψ περιτελλομένου ἔτεος καὶ ἐπήλυθον ὧραι,
ἣ δ' ἔτεκ' οὔτε θεοῖς ἐναλίγκιον οὔτε βροτοῖσι,
δεινόν τ' ἀργαλέον τε Τυφάονα, πῆμα βροτοῖσιν.
αὐτίκα τόνδε λαβοῦσα βοῶπις πότνια Ἥρη
δῶκεν ἔπειτα φέρουσα κακῷ κακόν· ἣ δ' ὑπέδεκτο.
ὃς κακὰ πόλλ' ἔρδεσκεν ἀγακλυτὰ φῦλ' ἀνθρώπων·
ὃς τῇ γ' ἀντιάσειε, φέρεσκέ μιν αἴσιμον ἦμαρ,
πρίν γέ οἱ ἰὸν ἐφῆκε ἄναξ ἑκάεργος Ἀπόλλων
καρτερόν· ἣ δ' ὀδύνῃσιν ἐρεχθομένη χαλεπῇσι
κεῖτο μέγ' ἀσθμαίνουσα κυλινδομένη κατὰ χῶρον.
θεσπεσίη δ' ἐνοπὴ γένετ' ἄσπετος· ἣ δὲ καθ' ὕλην

[1] Allen-Sikes: ἔστιν, M.

"Hear now, I pray, Earth and wide Heaven above, and you Titan gods who dwell beneath the earth about great Tartarus, and from whom are sprung both gods and men! Harken you now to me, one and all, and grant that I may bear a child apart from Zeus, no wit lesser than him in strength—nay, let him be as much stronger than Zeus as all-seeing Zeus than Cronos." Thus she cried and lashed the earth with her strong hand. Then the life-giving earth was moved: and when Hera saw it she was glad in heart, for she thought her prayer would be fulfilled. And thereafter she never came to the bed of wise Zeus for a full year, nor to sit in her carved chair as aforetime to plan wise counsel for him, but stayed in her temples where many pray, and delighted in her offerings, large-eyed queenly Hera. But when the months and days were fulfilled and the seasons duly came on as the earth moved round, she bare one neither like the gods nor mortal men, fell, cruel Typhaon, to be a plague to men. Straightway large-eyed queenly Hera took him and bringing one evil thing to another such, gave him to the dragoness; and she received him. And this Typhaon used to work great mischief among the famous tribes of men. Whosoever met the dragoness, the day of doom would sweep him away, until the lord Apollo, who deals death from afar, shot a strong arrow at her. Then she, rent with bitter pangs, lay drawing great gasps for breath and rolling about that place. An awful noise swelled up unspeakable as she writhed

πυκνὰ μάλ' ἔνθα καὶ ἔνθα ἑλίσσετο, λεῖπε δὲ θυμὸν
φοινὸν ἀποπνείουσ'· ὁ δ' ἐπηύξατο Φοῖβος Ἀπόλλων·
Ἐνταυθοῖ νῦν πύθευ ἐπὶ χθονὶ βωτιανείρῃ·
οὐδὲ σύ γε ζώουσα κακὸν δήλημα βροτοῖσιν
ἔσσεαι, οἳ γαίης πολυφόρβου καρπὸν ἔδοντες
ἐνθάδ' ἀγινήσουσι τεληέσσας ἑκατόμβας·
οὐδέ τί τοι θάνατόν γε δυσηλεγέ' οὔτε Τυφωεὺς
ἀρκέσει οὔτε Χίμαιρα δυσώνυμος, ἀλλά σέ γ' αὐτοῦ
πύσει Γαῖα μέλαινα καὶ ἠλέκτωρ Ὑπερίων.
Ὣς φάτ' ἐπευχόμενος· τὴν δὲ σκότος ὄσσε κάλυψε.
τὴν δ' αὐτοῦ κατέπυσ' ἱερὸν μένος Ἠελίοιο,
ἐξ οὗ νῦν Πυθὼ κικλήσκεται· οἳ δὲ ἄνακτα
Πύθιον ἀγκαλέουσιν[1] ἐπώνυμον, οὕνεκα κεῖθι.
αὐτοῦ πῦσε πέλωρ μένος ὀξέος Ἠελίοιο.
Καὶ τότ' ἄρ' ἔγνω ᾗσιν ἐνὶ φρεσὶ Φοῖβος Ἀπόλλων,
οὕνεκά μιν κρήνη καλλίρροος ἐξαπάφησε·
βῆ δ' ἐπὶ Τελφούσῃ κεχολωμένος, αἶψα δ' ἵκανε·
στῆ δὲ μάλ' ἄγχ' αὐτῆς καί μιν πρὸς μῦθον ἔειπε·
Τελφοῦσ', οὐκ ἄρ' ἔμελλες ἐμὸν νόον ἐξαπαφοῦσα
χῶρον ἔχουσ' ἐρατὸν προρέειν καλλίρροον ὕδωρ.
ἐνθάδε δὴ καὶ ἐμὸν κλέος ἔσσεται, οὐδὲ σὸν οἴης.
Ἦ καὶ ἐπὶ ῥίον ὦσε ἄναξ ἑκάεργος Ἀπόλλων
πετραίης προχυτῇσιν, ἀπέκρυψεν δὲ ῥέεθρα
καὶ βωμὸν ποιήσατ' ἐν ἄλσεϊ δενδρήεντι,
ἄγχι μάλα κρήνης καλλιρρόου· ἔνθαδ' ἄνακτι
πάντες ἐπίκλησιν Τελφουσίῳ εὐχετόωνται,
οὕνεκα Τελφούσης ἱερῆς ᾔσχυνε ῥέεθρα.

[1] Hermann: Πύθιον καλέουσιν, MSS.

continually this way and that amid the wood: and so she left her life, breathing it forth in blood. Then Phoebus Apollo boasted over her:

"Now rot here upon the soil that feeds man! You at least shall live no more to be a fell bane to men who eat the fruit of the all-nourishing earth, and who will bring hither perfect hecatombs. Against cruel death neither Typhoeus shall avail you nor ill-famed Chimera, but here shall the Earth and shining Hyperion make you rot."

Thus said Phoebus, exulting over her: and darkness covered her eyes. And the holy strength of Helios made her rot away there; wherefore the place is now called Pytho, and men call the lord Apollo by another name, Pythian; because on that spot the power of piercing Helios made the monster rot away.

Then Phoebus Apollo saw that the sweet-flowing spring had beguiled him, and he started out in anger against Telphusa; and soon coming to her, he stood close by and spoke to her:

"Telphusa, you were not, after all, to keep to yourself this lovely place by deceiving my mind, and pour forth your clear flowing water: here my renown shall also be and not yours alone?"

Thus spoke the lord, far-working Apollo, and pushed over upon her a crag with a shower of rocks, hiding her streams: and he made himself an altar in a wooded grove very near the clear-flowing stream. In that place all men pray to the great one by the name Telphusian, because he humbled the stream of holy Telphusa.

Καὶ τότε δὴ κατὰ θυμὸν ἐφράζετο Φοῖβος Ἀπόλλων,
οὕστινας ἀνθρώπους ὀργείονας εἰσαγάγοιτο,
οἳ θεραπεύσονται Πυθοῖ ἔνι πετρηέσσῃ·
ταῦτ' ἄρα ὁρμαίνων ἐνόησ' ἐπὶ οἴνοπι πόντῳ
νῆα θοήν· ἐν δ' ἄνδρες ἔσαν πολέες τε καὶ ἐσθλοί,
Κρῆτες ἀπὸ Κνωσοῦ Μινωίου, οἵ ῥα ἄνακτι
ἱερά τε ῥέζουσι καὶ ἀγγέλλουσι θέμιστας
Φοίβου Ἀπόλλωνος χρυσαόρου, ὅττι κεν εἴπῃ
χρείων ἐκ δάφνης γυάλων ὕπο Παρνησοῖο.
οἳ μὲν ἐπὶ πρῆξιν καὶ χρήματα νηὶ μελαίνῃ
ἐς Πύλον ἠμαθόεντα Πυλοιγενέας τ' ἀνθρώπους
ἔπλεον· αὐτὰρ ὁ τοῖσι συνήντετο Φοῖβος Ἀπόλλων·
ἐν πόντῳ δ' ἐπόρουσε δέμας δελφῖνι ἐοικὼς
νηὶ θοῇ καὶ κεῖτο πέλωρ μέγα τε δεινόν τε·
τῶν δ' οὔτις κατὰ θυμὸν ἐπεφράσαθ' ὥστε νοῆσαι[1]
[ἐκβάλλειν δ' ἔθελον δελφῖν'· ὁ δὲ νῆα μέλαιναν[2]]
πάντοσ' ἀνασσείσασκε, τίνασσε δὲ νήια δοῦρα.
οἳ δ' ἀκέων ἐνὶ νηὶ καθήατο δειμαίνοντες·
οὐδ' οἵ γ' ὅπλ' ἔλυον κοίλην ἀνὰ νῆα μέλαιναν,
οὐδ' ἔλυον λαῖφος νηὸς κυανοπρώροιο,
ἀλλ' ὡς τὰ πρώτιστα κατεστήσαντο βοεῦσιν,
ὣς ἔπλεον· κραιπνὸς δὲ Νότος κατόπισθεν ἔπειγε
νῆα θοήν· πρῶτον δὲ παρημείβοντο Μάλειαν,
πὰρ δὲ Λακωνίδα γαῖαν ἁλιστέφανον πτολίεθρον
ἷξον καὶ χῶρον τερψιμβρότου Ἠελίοιο,
Ταίναρον, ἔνθα τε μῆλα βαθύτριχα βόσκεται αἰεὶ
Ἠελίοιο ἄνακτος, ἔχει δ' ἐπιτερπέα χῶρον.
οἳ μὲν ἄρ' ἔνθ' ἔθελον νῆα σχεῖν ἠδ' ἀποβάντες

[1] Tr.: ἐπεφράσατο νοῆσαι, M. For the absolute use of ἐπιφράζω cp. Herodotus iv. 200 ὧδε ἐπιφρασθείς. ὥστε νοῆσαι expresses the natural result of reflection.

[2] Allen-Sikes's supplement.

Then Phoebus Apollo pondered in his heart what men he should bring in to be his ministers in sacrifice and to serve him in rocky Pytho. And while he considered this, he became aware of a swift ship upon the wine-like sea in which were many men and goodly, Cretans from Cnossos,[1] the city of Minos, they who do sacrifice to the prince and announce his decrees, whatsoever Phoebus Apollo, bearer of the golden blade, speaks in answer from his laurel tree below the dells of Parnassus. These men were sailing in their black ship for traffic and for profit to sandy Pylos and to the men of Pylos. But Phoebus Apollo met them: in the open sea he sprang upon their swift ship, like a dolphin in shape, and lay there, a great and awesome monster, and none of them gave heed so as to understand[2]; but they sought to cast the dolphin overboard. But he kept shaking the black ship every way and making the timbers quiver. So they sat silent in their craft for fear, and did not loose the sheets throughout the black, hollow ship, nor lowered the sail of their dark-prowed vessel, but as they had set it first of all with oxhide ropes, so they kept sailing on; for a rushing south wind hurried on the swift ship from behind. First they passed by Malea, and then along the Laconian coast they came to Taenarum, sea-garlanded town and country of Helios who gladdens men, where the thick-fleeced sheep of the lord Helios feed continually and occupy a gladsome country. There they wished to put their ship

[1] Inscriptions show that there was a temple of Apollo Delphinius (cp. ll. 495-6) at Cnossus and a Cretan month bearing the same name.

[2] *sc.* that the dolphin was really Apollo.

φράσσασθαι μέγα θαῦμα καὶ ὀφθαλμοῖσιν ἰδέσθαι,
εἰ μενέει νηὸς γλαφυρῆς δαπέδοισι πέλωρον
ἢ εἰς οἶδμ' ἅλιον πολυΐχθυον αὖτις ὀρούσει.
ἀλλ' οὐ πηδαλίοισιν ἐπείθετο νηῦς εὐεργής,
ἀλλὰ παρὲκ Πελοπόννησον πίειραν ἔχουσα
ἤϊ' ὁδόν· πνοιῇ δὲ ἄναξ ἑκάεργος Ἀπόλλων
ῥηϊδίως ἴθυν'· ἡ δὲ πρήσσουσα κέλευθον
Ἀρήνην ἵκανε καὶ Ἀργυφέην ἐρατεινὴν
καὶ Θρύον, Ἀλφειοῖο πόρον, καὶ ἐύκτιτον Αἶπυ
καὶ Πύλον ἠμαθόεντα Πυλοιγενέας τ' ἀνθρώπους.
βῆ δὲ παρὰ Κρουνοὺς καὶ Χαλκίδα καὶ παρὰ Δύμην
ἠδὲ παρ' Ἤλιδα δῖαν, ὅθι κρατέουσιν Ἐπειοί.
εὖτε Φερὰς ἐπέβαλλεν, ἀγαλλομένη Διὸς οὔρῳ,
καί σφιν ὑπὲκ νεφέων Ἰθάκης τ' ὄρος αἰπὺ πέφαντο
Δουλίχιόν τε Σάμη τε καὶ ὑλήεσσα Ζάκυνθος.
ἀλλ' ὅτε δὴ Πελοπόννησον παρενίσατο πᾶσαν
καὶ δὴ ἐπὶ Κρίσης κατεφαίνετο κόλπος ἀπείρων,
ὅστε διὲκ Πελοπόννησον πίειραν ἐέργει·
ἦλθ' ἄνεμος Ζέφυρος μέγας, αἴθριος, ἐκ Διὸς αἴσης,
λάβρος ἐπαιγίζων ἐξ αἰθέρος, ὄφρα τάχιστα
νηῦς ἀνύσειε θέουσα θαλάσσης ἁλμυρὸν ὕδωρ.
ἄψορροι δὴ ἔπειτα πρὸς ἠῶ τ' ἠέλιόν τε
ἔπλεον· ἡγεμόνευε δ' ἄναξ Διὸς υἱὸς Ἀπόλλων·
ἶξον δ' ἐς Κρίσην εὐδείελον, ἀμπελόεσσαν,
ἐς λιμέν'· ἡ δ' ἀμάθοισιν ἐχρίμψατο ποντοπόρος νηῦς.

Ἔνθ' ἐκ νηὸς ὄρουσε ἄναξ ἑκάεργος Ἀπόλλων,
ἀστέρι εἰδόμενος μέσῳ ἤματι· τοῦ δ' ἀπὸ πολλαὶ
σπινθαρίδες πωτῶντο, σέλας δ' εἰς οὐρανὸν ἶκεν·
ἐς δ' ἄδυτον κατέδυσε διὰ τριπόδων ἐριτίμων.
ἔνθ' ἄρ' ὅ γε φλόγα δαῖε πιφαυσκόμενος τὰ ἃ κῆλα·

to shore, and land and comprehend the great marvel and see with their eyes whether the monster would remain upon the deck of the hollow ship, or spring back into the briny deep where fishes shoal. But the well-built ship would not obey the helm, but went on its way all along Peloponnesus: and the lord, far-working Apollo, guided it easily with the breath of the breeze. So the ship ran on its course and came to Arena and lovely Argyphea and Thryon, the ford of Alpheus, and well-placed Aepy and sandy Pylos and the men of Pylos; past Cruni it went and Chalcis and past Dyme and fair Elis, where the Epei rule. And at the time when she was making for Pherae, exulting in the breeze from Zeus, there appeared to them below the clouds the steep mountain of Ithaca, and Dulichium and Same and wooded Zacynthus. But when they were passed by all the coast of Peloponnesus, then, towards Crisa, that vast gulf began to heave in sight which through all its length cuts off the rich isle of Pelops. There came on them a strong, clear west-wind by ordinance of Zeus and blew from heaven vehemently, that with all speed the ship might finish coursing over the briny water of the sea. So they began again to voyage back towards the dawn and the sun: and the lord Apollo, son of Zeus, led them on until they reached far-seen Crisa, land of vines, and into haven: there the sea-coursing ship grounded on the sands.

Then, like a star at noonday, the lord, far-working Apollo, leaped from the ship: flashes of fire flew from him thick and their brightness reached to heaven. He entered into his shrine between priceless tripods, and there made a flame to flare up bright, showing forth the splendour of his shafts, so

πᾶσαν δὲ Κρίσην κάτεχεν σέλας· αἱ δ' ὀλόλυξαν
Κρισαίων ἄλοχοι καλλίζωνοί τε θύγατρες
Φοίβου ὑπὸ ῥιπῆς· μέγα γὰρ δέος ἔμβαλ' ἑκάστῳ.
ἔνθεν δ' αὖτ' ἐπὶ νῆα νόημ' ὣς ἆλτο πέτεσθαι,
ἀνέρι εἰδόμενος αἰζηῷ τε κρατερῷ τε,
πρωθήβῃ, χαίτης εἰλυμένος εὐρέας ὤμους·
καί σφεας φωνήσας ἔπεα πτερόεντα προσηύδα·
Ὦ ξεῖνοι, τίνες ἐστέ; πόθεν πλεῖθ' ὑγρὰ κέλευθα;
ἤ τι κατὰ πρῆξιν ἦ μαψιδίως ἀλάλησθε [1]
οἷά τε ληιστῆρες ὑπεὶρ ἅλα, τοί τ' ἀλόωνται
ψυχὰς παρθέμενοι, κακὸν ἀλλοδαποῖσι φέροντες;
τίφθ' οὕτως ἧσθον τετιηότες, οὐδ' ἐπὶ γαῖαν
ἐκβῆτ', οὐδὲ καθ' ὅπλα μελαίνης νηὸς ἔθεσθε;
αὕτη μέν γε δίκη πέλει ἀνδρῶν ἀλφηστάων,
ὁππότ' ἂν ἐκ πόντοιο ποτὶ χθονὶ νηὶ μελαίνῃ
ἔλθωσιν καμάτῳ ἀδηκότες, αὐτίκα δέ σφεας
σίτοιο γλυκεροῖο περὶ φρένας ἵμερος αἱρεῖ.
Ὣς φάτο καί σφιν θάρσος ἐνὶ στήθεσσιν ἔθηκε.
τὸν καὶ ἀμειβόμενος Κρητῶν ἀγὸς ἀντίον ηὔδα·
ξεῖν', ἐπεὶ οὐ μὲν γάρ τι καταθνητοῖσι ἔοικας,
οὐ δέμας οὐδὲ φυήν, ἀλλ' ἀθανάτοισι θεοῖσιν,
οὖλέ τε καὶ μέγα χαῖρε, θεοὶ δέ τοι ὄλβια δοῖεν.
καί μοι τοῦτ' ἀγόρευσον ἐτήτυμον, ὄφρ' εὖ εἰδῶ·
τίς δῆμος; τίς γαῖα; τίνες βροτοὶ ἐγγεγάασιν;
ἄλλῃ γὰρ φρονέοντες ἐπεπλέομεν μέγα λαῖτμα
ἐς Πύλον ἐκ Κρήτης, ἔνθεν γένος εὐχόμεθ' εἶναι·
νῦν δ' ὧδε ξὺν νηὶ κατήλθομεν οὔ τι ἑκόντες,
νόστου ἱέμενοι, ἄλλην ὁδόν, ἄλλα κέλευθα·
ἀλλά τις ἀθανάτων δεῦρ' ἤγαγεν οὐκ ἐθέλοντας.

that their radiance filled all Crisa, and the wives and well-girded daughters of the Crisaeans raised a cry at that outburst of Phoebus; for he cast great fear upon them all. From his shrine he sprang forth again, swift as a thought, to speed again to the ship, bearing the form of a man, brisk and sturdy, in the prime of his youth, while his broad shoulders were covered with his hair: and he spoke to the Cretans, uttering winged words:

"Strangers, who are you? Whence come you sailing along the paths of the sea? Are you for traffic, or do you wander at random over the sea as pirates do who put their own lives to hazard and bring mischief to men of foreign parts as they roam? Why rest you so and are afraid, and do not go ashore nor stow the gear of your black ship? For that is the custom of men who live by bread, whenever they come to land in their dark ships from the main, spent with toil: at once desire for sweet food catches them about the heart."

So speaking, he put courage in their hearts, and the master of the Cretans answered him and said: "Stranger—though you are nothing like mortal men in shape or stature, but are as the deathless gods—hail and all happiness to you, and may the gods give you good. Now tell me truly that I may surely know it: what country is this, and what land, and what men live herein? As for us, with thoughts set otherwards, we were sailing over the great sea to Pylos from Crete (for from there we declare that we are sprung), but now are come on shipboard to this place by no means willingly—another way and other paths—and gladly would we return. But one of the deathless gods brought us here against our will."

Τοὺς δ' ἀπαμειβόμενος προσέφη ἑκάεργος Ἀπόλλων·
'ξεῖνοι, τοὶ Κνωσὸν πολυδένδρεον ἀμφενέμεσθε
τὸ πρίν, ἀτὰρ νῦν οὐκ ἔθ' ὑπότροποι αὖτις ἔσεσθε
ἔς τε πόλιν ἐρατὴν καὶ δώματα καλὰ ἕκαστος
ἔς τε φίλας ἀλόχους· ἀλλ' ἐνθάδε πίονα νηὸν
ἕξετ' ἐμὸν πολλοῖσι τετιμένον ἀνθρώποισιν.
εἰμὶ δ' ἐγὼ Διὸς υἱός, Ἀπόλλων δ' εὔχομαι εἶναι·
ὑμέας δ' ἤγαγον ἐνθάδ' ὑπὲρ μέγα λαῖτμα θαλάσσης,
οὔ τι κακὰ φρονέων, ἀλλ' ἐνθάδε πίονα νηὸν
ἕξετ' ἐμὸν πᾶσιν μάλα τίμιον ἀνθρώποισι,
βουλάς τ' ἀθανάτων εἰδήσετε, τῶν ἰότητι
αἰεὶ τιμήσεσθε διαμπερὲς ἤματα πάντα.
ἀλλ' ἄγεθ', ὡς ἂν ἐγὼ εἴπω, πείθεσθε τάχιστα·
ἱστία μὲν πρῶτον κάθετον λύσαντε βοείας,
νῆα δ' ἔπειτα θοὴν μὲν ἐπ' ἠπείρου ἐρύσασθε,
ἐκ δὲ κτήμαθ' ἕλεσθε καὶ ἔντεα νηὸς ἐίσης
καὶ βωμὸν ποιήσατ' ἐπὶ ῥηγμῖνι θαλάσσης·
πῦρ δ' ἐπικαίοντες ἐπί τ' ἄλφιτα λευκὰ θύοντες
εὔχεσθαι δὴ ἔπειτα παριστάμενοι περὶ βωμόν.
ὡς μὲν ἐγὼ τὸ πρῶτον ἐν ἠεροειδέι πόντῳ
εἰδόμενος δελφῖνι θοῆς ἐπὶ νηὸς ὄρουσα,
ὣς ἐμοὶ εὔχεσθαι Δελφινίῳ· αὐτὰρ ὁ βωμὸς
αὐτὸς Δελφίνιος καὶ ἐπόψιος ἔσσεται αἰεί.
δειπνῆσαί τ' ἄρ' ἔπειτα θοῇ παρὰ νηὶ μελαίνῃ
καὶ σπεῖσαι μακάρεσσι θεοῖς, οἳ Ὄλυμπον ἔχουσιν.
αὐτὰρ ἐπὴν σίτοιο μελίφρονος ἐξ ἔρον ἧσθε,
ἔρχεσθαί θ' ἅμ' ἐμοὶ καὶ ἰηπαιήον' ἀείδειν,
εἰς ὅ κε χῶρον ἵκησθον, ἵν' ἕξετε πίονα νηόν.

Then far-working Apollo answered them and said: "Strangers who once dwelt about wooded Cnossos but now shall return no more each to his loved city and fair house and dear wife; here shall you keep my rich temple that is honoured by many men. I am the son of Zeus; Apollo is my name: but you I brought here over the wide gulf of the sea, meaning you no hurt; nay, here you shall keep my rich temple that is greatly honoured among men, and you shall know the plans of the deathless gods, and by their will you shall be honoured continually for all time. And now come, make haste and do as I say. First loose the sheets and lower the sail, and then draw the swift ship up upon the land. Take out your goods and the gear of the straight ship, and make an altar upon the beach of the sea: light fire upon it and make an offering of white meal. Next, stand side by side around the altar and pray: and in as much as at the first on the hazy sea I sprang upon the swift ship in the form of a dolphin, pray to me as Apollo Delphinius; also the altar itself shall be called Delphinius and overlooking[1] for ever. Afterwards, sup beside your dark ship and pour an offering to the blessed gods who dwell on Olympus. But when you have put away craving for sweet food, come with me singing the hymn Ie Paean (Hail, Healer!), until you come to the place where you shall keep my rich temple."

[1] The epithets are transferred from the god to his altar. "Overlooking" is especially an epithet of Zeus, as in Apollonius Rhodius ii. 1124.

Ὣς ἔφαθ'· οἱ δ' ἄρα τοῦ μάλα μὲν κλύον ἠδ' ἐπίθοντο.
ἱστία μὲν πρῶτον κάθεσαν, λῦσαν δὲ βοείας,
ἱστὸν δ' ἱστοδόκῃ πέλασαν προτόνοισιν ὑφέντες·
ἐκ δὲ καὶ αὐτοὶ βαῖνον ἐπὶ ῥηγμῖνι θαλάσσης.
ἐκ δ' ἁλὸς ἤπειρόνδε θοὴν ἀνὰ νῆ' ἐρύσαντο
ὑψοῦ ἐπὶ ψαμάθοις, ὑπὸ δ' ἕρματα μακρὰ τάνυσσαν·
καὶ βωμὸν ποίησαν ἐπὶ ῥηγμῖνι θαλάσσης·
πῦρ δ' ἐπικαίοντες ἐπί τ' ἄλφιτα λευκὰ θύοντες
εὔχονθ', ὡς ἐκέλευε, παριστάμενοι περὶ βωμόν.
δόρπον ἔπειθ' εἵλοντο θοῇ παρὰ νηὶ μελαίνῃ
καὶ σπεῖσαν μακάρεσσι θεοῖς, οἳ Ὄλυμπον ἔχουσιν.
αὐτὰρ ἐπεὶ πόσιος καὶ ἐδητύος ἐξ ἔρον ἕντο,
βάν ῥ' ἴμεν· ἦρχε δ' ἄρα σφιν ἄναξ Διὸς υἱὸς Ἀπόλλων,
φόρμιγγ' ἐν χείρεσσιν ἔχων, ἐρατὸν κιθαρίζων,
καλὰ καὶ ὕψι βιβάς· οἱ δὲ ῥήσσοντες ἕποντο
Κρῆτες πρὸς Πυθὼ καὶ ἰηπαιήον' ἄειδον,
οἷοί τε Κρητῶν παιήονες, οἷσί τε Μοῦσα
ἐν στήθεσσιν ἔθηκε θεὰ μελίγηρυν ἀοιδήν.
ἄκμητοι δὲ λόφον προσέβαν ποσίν, αἶψα δ' ἵκοντο
Παρνησὸν καὶ χῶρον ἐπήρατον, ἔνθ' ἄρ' ἔμελλον
οἰκήσειν πολλοῖσι τετιμένοι[1] ἀνθρώποισι·
δεῖξε δ' ἄγων ἄδυτον ζάθεον καὶ πίονα νηόν.
Τῶν δ' ὠρίνετο θυμὸς ἐνὶ στήθεσσι φίλοισι·
τὸν καὶ ἀνειρόμενος Κρητῶν ἀγὸς ἀντίον ηὔδα·
Ὦ ἄνα, εἰ δὴ[2] τῆλε φίλων καὶ πατρίδος αἴης
ἤγαγες· οὕτω που τῷ σῷ φίλον ἔπλετο θυμῷ·

[1] Pierson: ἔμελλεν . . . τετιμένοι, MSS.
[2] Hermann: ὦ ἄν' ἐπειδή, MSS.

So said Apollo. And they readily harkened to him and obeyed him. First they unfastened the sheets and let down the sail and lowered the mast by the forestays upon the mast-rest. Then, landing upon the beach of the sea, they hauled up the ship from the water to dry land and fixed long stays under it. Also they made an altar upon the beach of the sea, and when they had lit a fire, made an offering of white meal, and prayed standing around the altar as Apollo had bidden them. Then they took their meal by the swift, black ship, and poured an offering to the blessed gods who dwell on Olympus. And when they had put away craving for drink and food, they started out with the lord Apollo, the son of Zeus, to lead them, holding a lyre in his hands, and playing sweetly as he stepped high and featly. So the Cretans followed him to Pytho, marching in time as they chanted the Ie Paean after the manner of the Cretan paean-singers and of those in whose hearts the heavenly Muse has put sweet-voiced song. With tireless feet they approached the ridge and straightway came to Parnassus and the lovely place where they were to dwell honoured by many men. There Apollo brought them and showed them his most holy sanctuary and rich temple.

But their spirit was stirred in their dear breasts, and the master of the Cretans asked him, saying:

"Lord, since you have brought us here far from our dear ones and our fatherland,—for so it seemed

πῶς καὶ νῦν βιόμεσθα; τό σε φράζεσθαι ἄνωγμεν.
οὔτε τρυγηφόρος ἥδε γ' ἐπήρατος οὔτ' εὐλείμων,
ὥστ' ἀπό τ' εὖ ζώειν καὶ ἅμ' ἀνθρώποισιν
ὀπάζειν.
Τοὺς δ' ἐπιμειδήσας προσέφη Διὸς υἱὸς Ἀπόλλων·
Νήπιοι ἄνθρωποι, δυστλήμονες, οἳ μελεδῶνας
βούλεσθ' ἀργαλέους τε πόνους καὶ στείνεα θυμῷ·
ῥηΐδιον ἔπος ὔμμ' ἐρέω καὶ ἐπὶ φρεσὶ θήσω,
δεξιτερῇ μάλ' ἕκαστος ἔχων ἐν χειρὶ μάχαιραν,
σφάζειν αἰεὶ μῆλα· τὰ δ' ἄφθονα πάντα παρέσται,
ὅσσα τ' ἐμοί κ' ἀγάγωσι περικλυτὰ φῦλ' ἀνθρώπων·
νηὸν δὲ προφύλαχθε, δέδεχθε δὲ φῦλ' ἀνθρώπων
ἐνθάδ' ἀγειρομένων καὶ ἐμὴν ἰθύν τε μάλιστα.
[δείκνυσθε θνητοῖσι· σὺ δὲ φρεσὶ δέξο θέμιστα.
εἰ δέ τις ἀφραδίῃς οὐ πείσεται, ἀλλ' ἀλογήσει [1]]
ἠέ τι τηΰσιον ἔπος ἔσσεται ἠέ τι ἔργον
ὕβρις θ', ἣ θέμις ἐστὶ καταθνητῶν ἀνθρώπων,
ἄλλοι ἔπειθ' ὑμῖν σημάντορες ἄνδρες ἔσονται,
τῶν ὑπ' ἀναγκαίῃ δεδμήσεσθ' ἤματα πάντα.
εἴρηταί τοι πάντα· σὺ δὲ φρεσὶ σῇσι φύλαξαι.
Καὶ σὺ μὲν οὕτω χαῖρε, Διὸς καὶ Λητοῦς υἱέ·
αὐτὰρ ἐγὼ καὶ σεῖο καὶ ἄλλης μνήσομ' ἀοιδῆς.

IV

ΕΙΣ ΕΡΜΗΝ

Ἑρμῆν ὕμνει, Μοῦσα, Διὸς καὶ Μαιάδος υἱόν,
Κυλλήνης μεδέοντα καὶ Ἀρκαδίης πολυμήλου,
ἄγγελον ἀθανάτων ἐριούνιον, ὃν τέκε Μαῖα,

[1] Allen suggests these two lines to fill the lacuna.

good to your heart,—tell us now how we shall live. That we would know of you. This land is not to be desired either for vineyards or for pastures so that we can live well thereon and also minister to men."

Then Apollo, the son of Zeus, smiled upon them and said: "Foolish mortals and poor drudges are you, that you seek cares and hard toils and straits! Easily will I tell you a word and set it in your hearts. Though each one of you with knife in hand should slaughter sheep continually, yet would you always have abundant store, even all that the glorious tribes of men bring here for me. But guard you my temple and receive the tribes of men that gather to this place, and especially show mortal men my will, and do you keep righteousness in your heart. But if any shall be disobedient and pay no heed to my warning, or if there shall be any idle word or deed and outrage as is common among mortal men, then other men shall be your masters and with a strong hand shall make you subject for ever. All has been told you: do you keep it in your heart."

And so, farewell, son of Zeus and Leto; but I will remember you and another hymn also.

IV

TO HERMES

Muse, sing of Hermes, the son of Zeus and Maia, lord of Cyllene and Arcadia rich in flocks, the luck-bringing messenger of the immortals whom Maia bare, the rich-tressed nymph, when she was joined in

νύμφη ἐυπλόκαμος, Διὸς ἐν φιλότητι μιγεῖσα,
αἰδοίη· μακάρων δὲ θεῶν ἠλεύαθ' ὅμιλον,
ἄντρον ἔσω ναίουσα παλισκίον, ἔνθα Κρονίων
νύμφῃ ἐυπλοκάμῳ μισγέσκετο νυκτὸς ἀμολγῷ,
ὄφρα κατὰ γλυκὺς ὕπνος ἔχοι λευκώλενον Ἥρην,
λήθων ἀθανάτους τε θεοὺς θνητούς τ' ἀνθρώπους.
ἀλλ' ὅτε δὴ μεγάλοιο Διὸς νόος ἐξετελεῖτο,
τῇ δ' ἤδη δέκατος μεὶς οὐρανῷ ἐστήρικτο,
εἴς τε φόως ἄγαγεν ἀρίσημά τε ἔργα τέτυκτο·
καὶ τότ' ἐγείνατο παῖδα πολύτροπον, αἱμυλομήτην,
ληιστῆρ', ἐλατῆρα βοῶν, ἡγήτορ' ὀνείρων,
νυκτὸς ὀπωπητῆρα, πυληδόκον, ὃς τάχ' ἔμελλεν
ἀμφανέειν κλυτὰ ἔργα μετ' ἀθανάτοισι θεοῖσιν.
ἠῷος γεγονὼς μέσῳ ἤματι ἐγκιθάριζεν,
ἑσπέριος βοῦς κλέψεν ἑκηβόλου Ἀπόλλωνος
τετράδι τῇ προτέρῃ, τῇ μιν τέκε πότνια Μαῖα.
ὃς καί, ἐπειδὴ μητρὸς ἀπ' ἀθανάτων θόρε γυίων,
οὐκέτι δηρὸν ἔκειτο μένων ἱερῷ ἐνὶ λίκνῳ,
ἀλλ' ὅ γ' ἀναΐξας ζήτει βόας Ἀπόλλωνος
οὐδὸν ὑπερβαίνων ὑψηρεφέος ἄντροιο.
ἔνθα χέλυν εὑρὼν ἐκτήσατο μυρίον ὄλβον·
Ἑρμῆς τοι πρώτιστα χέλυν τεκτήνατ' ἀοιδόν·
ἥ ῥά οἱ ἀντεβόλησεν ἐπ' αὐλείῃσι θύρῃσι
βοσκομένη προπάροιθε δόμων ἐριθηλέα ποίην,
σαῦλα ποσὶν βαίνουσα· Διὸς δ' ἐριούνιος υἱὸς
ἀθρήσας ἐγέλασσε καὶ αὐτίκα μῦθον ἔειπε·
Σύμβολον ἤδη μοι μέγ' ὀνήσιμον· οὐκ ὀνοτάζω.
χαῖρε, φυὴν ἐρόεσσα, χοροίτυπε, δαιτὸς ἑταίρη,
ἀσπασίη προφανεῖσα· πόθεν τόδε καλὸν ἄθυρμα
αἰόλον ὄστρακον ἕσσο [1] χέλυς ὄρεσι ζώουσα;
ἀλλ' οἴσω σ' ἐς δῶμα λαβών· ὄφελός τι μοι ἔσσῃ,
οὐδ' ἀποτιμήσω· σὺ δέ με πρώτιστον ὀνήσεις

[1] Tyrrell: ἐσσί, MSS.

love with Zeus,—a shy goddess, for she avoided the company of the blessed gods, and lived within a deep, shady cave. There the son of Cronos used to lie with the rich-tressed nymph, unseen by deathless gods and mortal men, at dead of night that sweet sleep might hold white-armed Hera fast. And when the purpose of great Zeus was fulfilled, and the tenth moon with her was fixed in heaven, she was delivered and a notable thing was come to pass. For then she bare a son, of many shifts, blandly cunning, a robber, a cattle driver, a bringer of dreams, a watcher by night, a thief at the gates, one who was soon to show forth wonderful deeds among the deathless gods. Born with the dawning, at mid-day he played on the lyre, and in the evening he stole the cattle of far-shooting Apollo on the fourth day of the month; for on that day queenly Maia bare him. So soon as he had leaped from his mother's heavenly womb, he lay not long waiting in his holy cradle, but he sprang up and sought the oxen of Apollo. But as he stepped over the threshold of the high-roofed cave, he found a tortoise there and gained endless delight. For it was Hermes who first made the tortoise a singer. The creature fell in his way at the courtyard gate, where it was feeding on the rich grass before the dwelling, waddling along. When he saw it, the luck-bringing son of Zeus laughed and said:

"An omen of great luck for me so soon! I do not slight it. Hail, comrade of the feast, lovely in shape, sounding at the dance! With joy I meet you! Where got you that rich gaud for covering, that spangled shell—a tortoise living in the mountains? But I will take and carry you within: you shall help me and I will do you no disgrace, though first

οἴκοι βέλτερον εἶναι, ἐπεὶ βλαβερὸν τὸ θύρηφιν·
ἦ γὰρ ἐπηλυσίης πολυπήμονος ἔσσεαι ἔχμα
ζώουσ'· ἢν δὲ θάνῃς, τότε κεν μάλα καλὸν ἀείδοις.
῝Ως ἄρ' ἔφη· καὶ χερσὶν ἅμ' ἀμφοτέρῃσιν ἀείρας
ἂψ εἴσω κίε δῶμα φέρων ἐρατεινὸν ἄθυρμα.
ἔνθ' ἀναπηρώσας[1] γλυφάνῳ πολιοῖο σιδήρου
αἰῶν' ἐξετόρησεν ὀρεσκῴοιο χελώνης.
ὡς δ' ὁπότ' ὠκὺ νόημα διὰ στέρνοιο περήσῃ
ἀνέρος, ὅν τε θαμειαὶ ἐπιστρωφῶσι μέριμναι,
ἢ ὅτε δινηθῶσιν ἀπ' ὀφθαλμῶν ἀμαρυγαί,
ὣς ἅμ' ἔπος τε καὶ ἔργον ἐμήδετο κύδιμος Ἑρμῆς.
πῆξε δ' ἄρ' ἐν μέτροισι ταμὼν δόνακας καλάμοιο
πειρήνας διὰ νῶτα διὰ ῥίνοιο χελώνης.
ἀμφὶ δὲ δέρμα τάνυσσε βοὸς πραπίδεσσιν ἑῇσι,
καὶ πήχεις ἐνέθηκ', ἐπὶ δὲ ζυγὸν ἤραρεν ἀμφοῖν,
ἑπτὰ δὲ θηλυτέρων[2] ὀίων ἐτανύσσατο χορδάς.
αὐτὰρ ἐπεὶ δὴ τεῦξε λύρην,[3] ἐρατεινὸν ἄθυρμα,
πλήκτρῳ ἐπειρήτιζε κατὰ μέρος· ἣ δ' ὑπὸ χειρὸς
σμερδαλέον κονάβησε· θεὸς δ' ὑπὸ καλὸν ἄειδεν
ἐξ αὐτοσχεδίης πειρώμενος, ἠύτε κοῦροι
ἡβηταὶ θαλίῃσι παραιβόλα κερτομέουσιν,
ἀμφὶ Δία Κρονίδην καὶ Μαιάδα καλλιπέδιλον,
ὡς πάρος ὠρίζεσκον ἑταιρείῃ φιλότητι,
ἥν τ' αὐτοῦ γενεὴν ὀνομακλυτὸν ἐξονομάζων·
ἀμφιπόλους τε γέραιρε καὶ ἀγλαὰ δώματα νύμφης
καὶ τρίποδας κατὰ οἶκον ἐπηετανούς τε λέβητας.
Καὶ τὰ μὲν οὖν ἤειδε, τὰ δὲ φρεσὶν ἄλλα μενοίνα.
καὶ τὴν μὲν κατέθηκε φέρων ἱερῷ ἐνὶ λίκνῳ,

[1] Tr.: ἀναπηλήσας, MSS.
[2] Antigonus Carystius: συμφώνους, MSS.
[3] Guttmann: φέρων, MSS.

of all you must profit me. It is better to be at home: harm may come out of doors. Living, you shall be a spell against mischievous witchcraft [1]; but if you die, then you shall make sweetest song."

Thus speaking, he took up the tortoise in both hands and went back into the house carrying his charming toy. Then he cut off its limbs and scooped out the marrow of the mountain-tortoise with a scoop of grey iron. As a swift thought darts through the heart of a man when thronging cares haunt him, or as bright glances flash from the eye, so glorious Hermes planned both thought and deed at once. He cut stalks of reed to measure and fixed them, fastening their ends across the back and through the shell of the tortoise, and then stretched ox hide all over it by his skill. Also he put in the horns and fitted a cross-piece upon the two of them, and stretched seven strings of sheep-gut. And when he had finished the lyre, a lovely play-thing, he took it and proved each string in turn with the key. At the touch of his hand it sounded marvellously; and, as he tried it, the god sang sweet random snatches, even as youths bandy taunts at festivals. He sang of Zeus the son of Cronos and neat-shod Maia, the converse which they had before in the comradeship of love, telling all the glorious tale of his own begetting. He celebrated, too, the handmaids of the nymph, and her bright home, and the tripods all about the house, and the abundant cauldrons.

But while he was singing of all these, his heart was bent on other matters. And he took the hollow

[1] Pliny notices the efficacy of the flesh of a tortoise against witchcraft. In *Geoponica* i. 14. 8 the living tortoise is prescribed as a charm to preserve vineyards from hail.

φόρμιγγα γλαφυρήν· ὁ δ' ἄρα κρειῶν ἐρατίζων
ἆλτο κατὰ σκοπιὴν εὐώδεος ἐκ μεγάροιο
ὁρμαίνων δόλον αἰπὺν ἐνὶ φρεσίν, οἷά τε φῶτες
φηληταὶ διέπουσι μελαίνης νυκτὸς ἐν ὥρῃ.
Ἠέλιος μὲν ἔδυνε κατὰ χθονὸς Ὠκεανόνδε
αὐτοῖσίν θ' ἵπποισι καὶ ἅρμασιν· αὐτὰρ ἄρ' Ἑρμῆς
Πιερίης ἀφίκανε θέων ὄρεα σκιόεντα,
ἔνθα θεῶν μακάρων βόες ἄμβροτοι αὖλιν ἔχεσκον
βοσκόμεναι λειμῶνας ἀκηρασίους, ἐρατεινούς.
τῶν τότε Μαιάδος υἱός, ἐύσκοπος Ἀργειφόντης,
πεντήκοντ' ἀγέλης ἀπετάμνετο βοῦς ἐριμύκους.
πλανοδίας δ' ἤλαυνε διὰ ψαμαθώδεα χῶρον
ἴχνι' ἀποστρέψας· δολίης δ' οὐ λήθετο τέχνης
ἀντία ποιήσας ὁπλάς, τὰς πρόσθεν ὄπισθεν,
τὰς δ' ὄπιθεν πρόσθεν· κατὰ δ' ἔμπαλιν αὐτὸς ἔβαινε.
σάνδαλα δ' αὐτίκα ῥιψὶν[1] ἐπὶ ψαμάθοις ἁλίῃσιν,
ἄφραστ' ἠδ' ἀνόητα διέπλεκε, θαυματὰ ἔργα,
συμμίσγων μυρίκας καὶ μυρσινοειδέας ὄζους.
τῶν τότε συνδήσας νεοθηλέος ἄγκαλον ὕλης
ἀβλαβέως ὑπὸ ποσσὶν ἐδήσατο σάνδαλα κοῦφα
αὐτοῖσιν πετάλοισι τὰ κύδιμος Ἀργειφόντης
ἔσπασε Πιερίηθεν ὁδοιπορίην ἀλεγύνων,[2]
οἷά τ' ἐπειγόμενος δολιχὴν ὁδόν, αὐτοτροπήσας.†
Τὸν δὲ γέρων ἐνόησε δέμων ἀνθοῦσαν ἀλωὴν
ἱέμενον πεδίονδε δι' Ὀγχηστὸν λεχεποίην·

[1] Postgate: ἔριψεν, MSS.
[2] Windisch: ἀλεείνων, MSS

lyre and laid it in his sacred cradle, and sprang from the sweet-smelling hall to a watch-place, pondering sheer trickery in his heart—deeds such as knavish folk pursue in the dark night-time; for he longed to taste flesh.

The Sun was going down beneath the earth towards Ocean with his horses and chariot when Hermes came hurrying to the shadowy mountains of Pieria, where the divine cattle of the blessed gods had their steads and grazed the pleasant, unmown meadows. Of these the Son of Maia, the sharp-eyed slayer of Argus then cut off from the herd fifty loud-lowing kine, and drove them straggling-wise across a sandy place, turning their hoof-prints aside. Also, he bethought him of a crafty ruse and reversed the marks of their hoofs, making the front behind and the hind before, while he himself walked the other way.[1] Then he wove sandals with wicker-work by the sand of the sea, wonderful things, unthought of, unimagined; for he mixed together tamarisk and myrtle-twigs, fastening together an armful of their fresh, young wood, and tied them, leaves and all securely under his feet as light sandals. That brushwood the glorious Slayer of Argus plucked in Pieria as he was preparing for his journey, making shift[2] as one making haste for a long journey.

But an old man tilling his flowering vineyard saw him as he was hurrying down the plain through

[1] Hermes makes the cattle walk backwards way, so that they seem to be going towards the meadow instead of leaving it (cp. l. 345); he himself walks in the normal manner, relying on his sandals as a disguise.

[2] Such seems to be the meaning indicated by the context, though the verb is taken by Allen and Sikes to mean "to be like oneself," and so "to be original."

τὸν πρότερος προσέφη Μαίης ἐρικυδέος υἱός·
'Ω γέρον, ὅστε φυτὰ σκάπτεις ἐπικαμπύλος ὤμους,
ἦ πολυοινήσεις, εὖτ' ἂν τάδε πάντα φέρῃσι,
[εἴ κε πίθῃ, μάλα περ μεμνημένος ἐν φρεσὶ σῇσι [1]] 91a
καί τε ἰδὼν μὴ ἰδὼν εἶναι καὶ κωφὸς ἀκούσας,
καὶ σιγᾶν ὅτε μή τι καταβλάπτῃ τὸ σὸν αὐτοῦ.
Τόσσον φὰς συνέσευε [2] βοῶν ἴφθιμα κάρηνα.
πολλὰ δ' ὄρη σκιόεντα καὶ αὐλῶνας κελαδεινοὺς
καὶ πεδί' ἀνθεμόεντα διήλασε κύδιμος Ἑρμῆς.
ὀρφναίη δ' ἐπίκουρος ἐπαύετο δαιμονίη νύξ,
ἡ πλείων, τάχα δ' ὄρθρος ἐγίγνετο δημιοεργός·
ἡ δὲ νέον σκοπιὴν προσεβήσατο δῖα Σελήνη,
Πάλλαντος θυγάτηρ Μεγαμηδείδαο ἄνακτος.
τῆμος ἐπ' Ἀλφειὸν ποταμὸν Διὸς ἄλκιμος υἱὸς
Φοίβου Ἀπόλλωνος βοῦς ἤλασεν εὐρυμετώπους.
ἀκμῆτες δ' ἵκανον ἐπ' αὔλιον ὑψιμέλαθρον
καὶ ληνοὺς προπάροιθεν ἀριπρεπέος λειμῶνος.
ἔνθ' ἐπεὶ εὖ βοτάνης ἐπεφόρβει βοῦς ἐριμύκους
καὶ τὰς μὲν συνέλασσεν ἐς αὔλιον ἀθρόας οὔσας,
λωτὸν ἐρεπτομένας ἠδ' ἐρσήεντα κύπειρον·
σὺν δ' ἐφόρει ξύλα πολλά, πυρὸς δ' ἐπεμαίετο τέχνην.
δάφνης ἀγλαὸν ὄζον ἑλὼν ἀπέλεψε σιδήρῳ

* * * *

ἄρμενον ἐν παλάμῃ· ἄμπνυτο δὲ θερμὸς ἀυτμή·
Ἑρμῆς τοι πρώτιστα πυρήια πῦρ τ' ἀνέδωκε.
πολλὰ δὲ κάγκανα κᾶλα κατουδαίῳ ἐνὶ βόθρῳ
οὖλα λαβὼν ἐπέθηκεν ἐπηετανά· λάμπετο δὲ φλὸξ
τηλόσε φῦσαν ἱεῖσα πυρὸς μέγα δαιομένοιο.

[1] Translator. [2] Demetrius: φασὶν ἔσευε, MSS.

grassy Onchestus. So the Son of Maia began and said to him :

"Old man, digging about your vines with bowed shoulders, surely you shall have much wine when all these bear fruit, if you obey me and strictly remember not to have seen what you have seen, and not to have heard what you have heard, and to keep silent when nothing of your own is harmed."

When he had said this much, he hurried the strong cattle on together : through many shadowy mountains and echoing gorges and flowery plains glorious Hermes drove them. And now the divine night, his dark ally, was mostly passed, and dawn that sets folk to work was quickly coming on, while bright Selene, daughter of the lord Pallas, Megamedes' son, had just climbed her watch-post, when the strong Son of Zeus drove the wide-browed cattle of Phoebus Apollo to the river Alpheus. And they came unwearied to the high-roofed byres and the drinking-troughs that were before the noble meadow. Then, after he had well-fed the loud-bellowing cattle with fodder and driven them into the byre, close-packed and chewing lotus and dewy galingal, he gathered a pile of wood and began to seek the art of fire. He chose a stout laurel branch and trimmed it with the knife . . .[1] held firmly in his hand : and the hot smoke rose up. For it was Hermes who first invented fire-sticks and fire. Next he took many dried sticks and piled them thick and plenty in a sunken trench : and flame began to glow, spreading afar the blast of fierce-burning fire.

[1] Kuhn points out that there is a lacuna here. In l. 109 the borer is described, but the friction of this upon the fire-block (to which the phrase "held firmly" clearly belongs) must also have been mentioned.

Ὄφρα δὲ πῦρ ἀνέκαιε βίη κλυτοῦ Ἡφαίστοιο,
τόφρα δ' ὑποβρύχους ἕλικας βοῦς εἷλκε θύραζε
δοιὰς ἄγχι πυρός· δύναμις δέ οἱ ἔσπετο πολλή.
ἀμφοτέρας δ' ἐπὶ νῶτα χαμαὶ βάλε φυσιοώσας·
ἀγκλίνων[1] δ' ἐκύλινδε δι' αἰῶνας τετορήσας.
ἔργῳ δ' ἔργον ὄπαζε ταμὼν κρέα πίονα δημῷ·
ὤπτα δ' ἀμφ' ὀβελοῖσι πεπαρμένα δουρατέοισι
σάρκας ὁμοῦ καὶ νῶτα γεράσμια καὶ μέλαν αἷμα
ἐργμένον ἐν χολάδεσσι· τὰ δ' αὐτοῦ κεῖτ' ἐπὶ χώρης·
ῥινοὺς δ' ἐξετάνυσσε καταστυφέλῳ ἐνὶ πέτρῃ,
ὡς ἔτι νῦν τὰ μέτασσα πολυχρόνιοι πεφύασι,
δηρὸν δὴ μετὰ ταῦτα καὶ ἄκριτον· αὐτὰρ ἔπειτα
Ἑρμῆς χαρμόφρων εἰρύσατο πίονα ἔργα
λείῳ ἐπὶ πλαταμῶνι καὶ ἔσχισε δώδεκα μοίρας
κληροπαλεῖς· τέλεον δὲ γέρας προσέθηκεν ἑκάστῃ.
ἔνθ' ὁσίης κρεάων ἠράσσατο κύδιμος Ἑρμῆς·
ὀδμὴ γάρ μιν ἔτειρε καὶ ἀθάνατόν περ ἐόντα
ἡδεῖ'· ἀλλ' οὐδ' ὧς οἱ ἐπείθετο θυμὸς ἀγήνωρ,
καί τε μάλ' ἱμείροντι, περῆν† ἱερῆς κατὰ δειρῆς.
ἀλλὰ τὰ μὲν κατέθηκεν ἐς αὔλιον ὑψιμέλαθρον,
δημὸν καὶ κρέα πολλά, μετήορα δ' αἶψ' ἀνάειρε,
σῆμα νέης φωρῆς· ἐπὶ δὲ ξύλα κάγκαν' ἀγείρας[2]
οὐλόποδ', οὐλοκάρηνα πυρὸς κατεδάμνατ' ἀυτμῇ.

[1] Gemoll: ἐγκλίνων, MSS. [2] Ilgen: ἀείρας, MSS.

---

[1] The cows being on their sides on the ground, Hermes bends their heads back towards their flanks and so can reach their backbones.

[2] O. Müller thinks the "hides" were a stalactite formation in the "Cave of Nestor" near Messenian Pylos,—though the cave of Hermes is near the Alpheus (l. 139). Others

And while the strength of glorious Hephaestus was beginning to kindle the fire, he dragged out two lowing, horned cows close to the fire; for great strength was with him. He threw them both panting upon their backs on the ground, and rolled them on their sides, bending their necks over,[1] and pierced their vital chord. Then he went on from task to task: first he cut up the rich, fatted meat, and pierced it with wooden spits, and roasted flesh and the honourable chine and the paunch full of dark blood all together. He laid them there upon the ground, and spread out the hides on a rugged rock: and so they are still there many ages afterwards, a long, long time after all this, and are continually.[2] Next glad-hearted Hermes dragged the rich meats he had prepared and put them on a smooth, flat stone, and divided them into twelve portions distributed by lot, making each portion wholly honourable. Then glorious Hermes longed for the sacrificial meat, for the sweet savour wearied him, god though he was; nevertheless his proud heart was not prevailed upon to devour the flesh, although he greatly desired.[3] But he put away the fat and all the flesh in the high-roofed byre, placing them high up to be a token of his youthful theft. And after that he gathered dry sticks and utterly destroyed with fire all the hoofs and all the heads.

suggest that actual skins were shown as relics before some cave near Triphylian Pylos.

[3] Gemoll explains that Hermes, having offered all the meat as sacrifice to the Twelve Gods, remembers that he himself as one of them must be content with the savour instead of the substance of the sacrifice. Can it be that by eating he would have forfeited the position he claimed as one of the Twelve Gods?

Αὐτὰρ ἐπεί τοι πάντα κατὰ χρέος ἤνυσε δαίμων,
σάνδαλα μὲν προέηκεν ἐς Ἀλφειὸν βαθυδίνην·
ἀνθρακιὴν δ' ἐμάρανε, κόνιν δ' ἀμάθυνε μέλαιναν
παννύχιος· καλὸν δὲ φόως κατέλαμπε Σελήνης.
Κυλλήνης δ' αἶψ' αὖτις ἀφίκετο δῖα κάρηνα
ὄρθριος, οὐδέ τί οἱ δολιχῆς ὁδοῦ ἀντεβόλησεν
οὔτε θεῶν μακάρων οὔτε θνητῶν ἀνθρώπων,
οὐδὲ κύνες λελάκοντο· Διὸς δ' ἐριούνιος Ἑρμῆς
δοχμωθεὶς μεγάροιο διὰ κλήιθρον ἔδυνεν
αὔρῃ ὀπωρινῇ ἐναλίγκιος, ἠύτ' ὀμίχλη.
ἰθύσας δ' ἄντρου ἐξίκετο πίονα νηὸν
ἦκα ποσὶ προβιβῶν· οὐ γὰρ κτύπεν, ὥσπερ ἐπ' οὔδει.
ἐσσυμένως δ' ἄρα λίκνον ἐπῴχετο κύδιμος Ἑρμῆς·
σπάργανον ἀμφ' ὤμοις εἰλυμένος, ἠύτε τέκνον
νήπιον, ἐν παλάμῃσι περ' ἰγνύσι λαῖφος ἀθύρων
κεῖτο, χέλυν ἐρατὴν ἐπ' ἀριστερὰ χειρὸς ἐέργων.
μητέρα δ' οὐκ ἄρ' ἔληθε θεὰν θεὸς εἰπέ τε μῦθον·
Τίπτε σύ, ποικιλομῆτα, πόθεν τόδε νυκτὸς ἐν ὥρῃ
ἔρχῃ, ἀναιδείην ἐπιειμένε; νῦν σε μάλ' οἴω
ἢ τάχ' ἀμήχανα δεσμὰ περὶ πλευρῇσιν ἔχοντα
Λητοΐδου ὑπὸ χερσὶ διὲκ προθύροιο περήσειν
ἢ σὲ φέροντα μεταξὺ κατ' ἄγκεα φηλητεύσειν.
ἔρρε πάλιν· μεγάλην σε πατὴρ ἐφύτευσε μέριμναν
θνητοῖς ἀνθρώποισι καὶ ἀθανάτοισι θεοῖσι.
Τὴν δ' Ἑρμῆς μύθοισιν ἀμείβετο κερδαλέοισι·
μῆτερ ἐμή, τί με ταῦτα δεδίσκεαι,[1] ἠύτε τέκνον
νήπιον, ὃς μάλα παῦρα μετὰ φρεσὶν αἴσυλα οἶδε,

[1] Pierson : τιτύσκεαι, MSS.

And when the god had duly finished all, he threw his sandals into deep-eddying Alpheus, and quenched the embers, covering the black ashes with sand, and so spent the night while Selene's soft light shone down. Then the god went straight back again at dawn to the bright crests of Cyllene, and no one met him on the long journey either of the blessed gods or mortal men, nor did any dog bark. And luck-bringing Hermes, the son of Zeus, passed edgeways through the key-hole of the hall like the autumn breeze, even as mist: straight through the cave he went and came to the rich inner chamber, walking softly, and making no noise as one might upon the floor. Then glorious Hermes went hurriedly to his cradle, wrapping his swaddling clothes about his shoulders as though he were a feeble babe, and lay playing with the covering about his knees; but at his left hand he kept close his sweet lyre.

But the god did not pass unseen by the goddess his mother; but she said to him: "How now, you rogue! Whence come you back so at night-time, you that wear shamelessness as a garment? And now I surely believe the son of Leto will soon have you forth out of doors with unbreakable cords about your ribs, or you will live a rogue's life in the glens robbing by whiles. Go to, then; your father got you to be a great worry to mortal men and deathless gods."

Then Hermes answered her with crafty words: "Mother, why do you seek to frighten me like a feeble child whose heart knows few words of blame,

ταρβαλέον, καὶ μητρὸς ὑπαιδείδοικεν ἐνιπάς;
αὐτὰρ ἐγὼ τέχνης ἐπιβήσομαι, ἥ τις ἀρίστη,
βουκολέων [1] ἐμὲ καὶ σὲ διαμπερές· οὐδὲ θεοῖσι
νῶι μετ' ἀθανάτοισιν ἀδώρητοι καὶ ἄλιστοι
αὐτοῦ τῇδε μένοντες ἀνεξόμεθ', ὡς σὺ κελεύεις.
βέλτερον ἤματα πάντα μετ' ἀθανάτοις ὀαρίζειν,
πλούσιον, ἀφνειόν, πολυλήιον, ἢ κατὰ δῶμα
ἄντρῳ ἐν ἠερόεντι θαασσέμεν· ἀμφὶ δὲ τιμῆς,
κἀγὼ τῆς ὁσίης ἐπιβήσομαι, ἧς περ Ἀπόλλων.
εἰ δέ κε μὴ δώῃσι πατὴρ ἐμός, ἢ τοι ἔγωγε
πειρήσω, δύναμαι, φηλητέων ὄρχαμος εἶναι.
εἰ δέ μ' ἐρευνήσει Λητοῦς ἐρικυδέος υἱός,
ἄλλο τί οἱ καὶ μεῖζον ὀίομαι ἀντιβολήσειν.
εἶμι γὰρ ἐς Πυθῶνα μέγαν δόμον ἀντιτορήσων·
ἔνθεν ἅλις τρίποδας περικαλλέας ἠδὲ λέβητας
πορθήσω καὶ χρυσόν, ἅλις τ' αἴθωνα σίδηρον
καὶ πολλὴν ἐσθῆτα· σὺ δ' ὄψεαι, αἴ κ' ἐθέλῃσθα.
 Ὣς οἱ μέν ῥ' ἐπέεσσι πρὸς ἀλλήλους ἀγόρευον,
υἱός τ' αἰγιόχοιο Διὸς καὶ πότνια Μαῖα.
Ἠὼς δ' ἠριγένεια φόως θνητοῖσι φέρουσα
ὤρνυτ' ἀπ' Ὠκεανοῖο βαθυρρόου· αὐτὰρ Ἀπόλλων
Ὀγχηστόνδ' ἀφίκανε κιών, πολυήρατον ἄλσος
ἁγνὸν ἐρισφαράγου Γαιηόχου· ἔνθα γέροντα
κνώδαλον εὗρε νέμοντα παρ' ἔξοδον ἕρκεος αὐλῆς.[2]
τὸν πρότερος προσέφη Λητοῦς ἐρικυδέος υἱός·
 Ὦ γέρον, Ὀγχηστοῖο βατοδρόπε ποιήεντος,
βοῦς ἀπὸ Πιερίης διζήμενος ἐνθάδ' ἱκάνω,
πάσας θηλείας, πάσας κεράεσσιν ἑλικτάς,
ἐξ ἀγέλης· ὁ δὲ ταῦρος ἐβόσκετο μοῦνος ἀπ' ἄλλων

[1] Ludwich: βουλεύων, MSS.
[2] Tr.: παρὲξ ὁδοῦ ἕρκος ἀλωῆς, MSS.

a fearful babe that fears its mother's scolding? Nay, but I will try whatever plan is best, and so feed myself and you continually. We will not be content to remain here, as you bid, alone of all the gods unfee'd with offerings and prayers. Better to live in fellowship with the deathless gods continually, rich, wealthy, and enjoying stores of grain, than to sit always in a gloomy cave: and, as regards honour, I too will enter upon the rite that Apollo has. If my father will not give it me, I will seek—and I am able—to be a prince of robbers. And if Leto's most glorious son shall seek me out, I think another and a greater loss will befall him. For I will go to Pytho to break into his great house, and will plunder therefrom splendid tripods, and cauldrons, and gold, and plenty of bright iron, and much apparel; and you shall see it if you will."

With such words they spoke together, the son of Zeus who holds the aegis, and the lady Maia. Now Eros the early born was rising from deep-flowing Ocean, bringing light to men, when Apollo, as he went, came to Onchestus, the lovely grove and sacred place of the loud-roaring Holder of the Earth. There he found an old man grazing his beast along the pathway from his court-yard fence, and the all-glorious Son of Leto began and said to him.

"Old man, weeder[1] of grassy Onchestus, I am come here from Pieria seeking cattle, cows all of them, all with curving horns, from my herd. The black bull was grazing alone away from the rest,

[1] *Lit.* "thorn-plucker."

κυάνεος· χαροποὶ δὲ κύνες κατόπισθεν ἕποντο
τέσσαρες, ἠύτε φῶτες, ὁμόφρονες· οἳ μὲν ἔλειφθεν,
οἵ τε κύνες ὅ τε ταῦρος· ὃ δὴ περὶ θαῦμα τέτυκται·
ταὶ δ' ἔβαν ἠελίοιο νέον καταδυομένοιο
ἐκ μαλακοῦ λειμῶνος ἀπὸ γλυκεροῖο νομοῖο.
ταῦτά μοι εἰπέ, γεραιὲ παλαιγενές, εἴ που ὄπωπας
ἀνέρα ταῖσδ' ἐπὶ βουσὶ διαπρήσσοντα κέλευθον.
Τὸν δ' ὁ γέρων μύθοισιν ἀμειβόμενος προσέειπεν·
ὦ φίλος, ἀργαλέον μέν, ὅσ' ὀφθαλμοῖσιν ἴδοιτο,
πάντα λέγειν· πολλοὶ γὰρ ὁδὸν πρήσσουσιν ὁδῖται,
τῶν οἳ μὲν κακὰ πολλὰ μεμαότες, οἳ δὲ μάλ' ἐσθλὰ
φοιτῶσιν· χαλεπὸν δὲ δαήμεναί ἐστιν ἕκαστον·
αὐτὰρ ἐγὼ πρόπαν ἦμαρ ἐς ἠέλιον καταδύντα
ἔσκαπτον περὶ γουνὸν ἀλωῆς οἰνοπέδοιο·
παῖδα δ' ἔδοξα, φέριστε, σαφὲς δ' οὐκ οἶδα, νοῆσαι,
ὅς τις ὁ παῖς, ἅμα βουσὶν ἐυκραίρῃσιν ὀπήδει
νήπιος, εἶχε δὲ ῥάβδον· ἐπιστροφάδην δ' ἐβάδιζεν.
ἐξοπίσω δ' ἀνέεργε, κάρη δ' ἔχεν ἀντίον αὐτῷ.
Φῆ ῥ' ὁ γέρων· ὃ δὲ θᾶσσον ὁδὸν κίε μῦθον ἀκούσας·
οἰωνὸν δ' ἐνόει τανυσίπτερον, αὐτίκα δ' ἔγνω
φηλητὴν γεγαῶτα Διὸς παῖδα Κρονίωνος.
ἐσσυμένως δ' ἤιξεν ἄναξ Διὸς υἱὸς Ἀπόλλων
ἐς Πύλον ἠγαθέην διζήμενος εἰλίποδας βοῦς,
πορφυρέῃ νεφέλῃ κεκαλυμμένος εὐρέας ὤμους·
ἴχνιά τ' εἰσενόησεν Ἑκηβόλος εἶπέ τε μῦθον·
Ὢ πόποι, ἦ μέγα θαῦμα τόδ' ὀφθαλμοῖσιν ὁρῶμαι·
ἴχνια μὲν τάδε γ' ἐστὶ βοῶν ὀρθοκραιράων,
ἀλλὰ πάλιν τέτραπται ἐς ἀσφοδελὸν λειμῶνα·
βήματα δ' οὔτ' ἀνδρὸς τάδε γίγνεται οὔτε γυναικὸς

but fierce-eyed hounds followed the cows, four of them, all of one mind, like men. These were left behind, the dogs and the bull—which is a great marvel; but the cows strayed out of the soft meadow, away from the pasture when the sun was just going down. Now tell me this, old man born long ago: have you seen one passing along behind those cows?"

Then the old man answered him and said: "My son, it is hard to tell all that one's eyes see; for many wayfarers pass to and fro this way, some bent on much evil, and some on good: it is difficult to know each one. However, I was digging about my plot of vineyard all day long until the sun went down, and I thought, good sir, but I do not know for certain, that I marked a child, whoever the child was, that followed long-horned cattle—an infant who had a staff and kept walking from side to side: he was driving them backwards way, with their heads towards him."

So said the old man. And when Apollo heard this report, he went yet more quickly on his way, and presently, seeing a long-winged bird, he knew at once by that omen that the thief was the child of Zeus the son of Cronos. So the lord Apollo, son of Zeus, hurried on to goodly Pylos seeking his shambling oxen, and he had his broad shoulders covered with a dark cloud. But when the Far-Shooter perceived the tracks, he cried:

"Oh, oh! Truly this is a great marvel that my eyes behold! These are indeed the tracks of straight-horned oxen, but they are turned backwards towards the flowery meadow. But these others are not the footprints of man or woman or grey wolves or bears

οὔτε λύκων πολιῶν οὔτ' ἄρκτων οὔτε λεόντων·
οὔτε τι Κενταύρου λασιαύχενος ἔλπομαι εἶναι,
ὅς τις τοῖα πέλωρα βιβᾷ ποσὶ καρπαλίμοισιν·
αἰνὰ μὲν ἔνθεν ὁδοῖο, τὰ δ' αἰνότερ' ἔνθεν ὁδοῖο.
Ὣς εἰπὼν ἤιξεν ἄναξ Διὸς υἱὸς Ἀπόλλων·
Κυλλήνης δ' ἀφίκανεν ὄρος καταειμένον ὕλῃ,
πέτρης ἐς κευθμῶνα βαθύσκιον, ἔνθα τε νύμφη
ἀμβροσίη ἐλόχευσε Διὸς παῖδα Κρονίωνος.
ὀδμὴ δ' ἱμερόεσσα δι' οὔρεος ἠγαθέοιο
κίδνατο, πολλὰ δὲ μῆλα ταναύποδα βόσκετο ποίην.
ἔνθα τότε σπεύδων κατεβήσατο λάινον οὐδὸν
ἄντρον ἐς ἠερόεν ἑκατηβόλος αὐτὸς Ἀπόλλων.
Τὸν δ' ὡς οὖν ἐνόησε Διὸς καὶ Μαιάδος υἱὸς
χωόμενον περὶ βουσὶν ἑκηβόλον Ἀπόλλωνα,
σπάργαν' ἔσω κατέδυνε θυήεντ'· ἠύτε πολλὴν
πρέμνων ἀνθρακιὴν ὕλης σποδὸς ἀμφικαλύπτει,
ὣς Ἑρμῆς Ἑκάεργον ἰδὼν ἀνέειλεν[1] ἑαυτόν.
ἐν δ' ὀλίγῳ συνέλασσε κάρη χεῖράς τε πόδας τε,
φή ῥα νεόλλουτος, προκαλεύμενος ἥδυμον ὕπνον,
ἐγρήσσων ἐτεόν γε· χέλυν δ' ὑπὸ μασχάλῃ εἶχε.
γνῶ δ' οὐδ' ἠγνοίησε Διὸς καὶ Λητοῦς υἱὸς
νύμφην τ' οὐρείην περικαλλέα καὶ φίλον υἱόν,
παῖδ' ὀλίγον, δολίῃς εἰλυμένον ἐντροπίῃσι.
παπτήνας δ' ἀνὰ πάντα μυχὸν μεγάλοιο δόμοιο
τρεῖς ἀδύτους ἀνέῳγε λαβὼν κληῖδα φαεινὴν
νέκταρος ἐμπλείους ἠδ' ἀμβροσίης ἐρατεινῆς·
πολλὸς δὲ χρυσός τε καὶ ἄργυρος ἔνδον ἔκειτο,
πολλὰ δὲ φοινικόεντα καὶ ἄργυφα εἵματα νύμφης,
οἷα θεῶν μακάρων ἱεροὶ δόμοι ἐντὸς ἔχουσιν·
ἔνθ' ἐπεὶ ἐξερέεινε μυχοὺς μεγάλοιο δόμοιο
Λητοΐδης, μύθοισι προσηύδα κύδιμον Ἑρμῆν·

[1] Lohsee: ἀλέεινεν, MSS.

or lions, nor do I think they are the tracks of a rough-maned Centaur—whoever it be that with swift feet makes such monstrous footprints; wonderful are the tracks on this side of the way, but yet more wonderful are those on that."

When he had so said, the lord Apollo, the Son of Zeus hastened on and came to the forest-clad mountain of Cyllene and the deep-shadowed cave in the rock where the divine nymph brought forth the child of Zeus who is the son of Cronos. A sweet odour spread over the lovely hill, and many thin-shanked sheep were grazing on the grass. Then far-shooting Apollo himself stepped down in haste over the stone threshold into the dusky cave.

Now when the Son of Zeus and Maia saw Apollo in a rage about his cattle, he snuggled down in his fragrant swaddling-clothes; and as wood-ash covers over the deep embers of tree-stumps, so Hermes cuddled himself up when he saw the Far-Shooter. He squeezed head and hands and feet together in a small space, like a new born child seeking sweet sleep, though in truth he was wide awake, and he kept his lyre under his armpit. But the Son of Leto was aware and failed not to perceive the beautiful mountain-nymph and her dear son, albeit a little child and swathed so craftily. He peered in every corner of the great dwelling and, taking a bright key, he opened three closets full of nectar and lovely ambrosia. And much gold and silver was stored in them, and many garments of the nymph, some purple and some silvery white, such as are kept in the sacred houses of the blessed gods. Then, after the Son of Leto had searched out the recesses of the great house, he spake to glorious Hermes:

Ὦ παῖ, ὃς ἐν λίκνῳ κατάκειαι, μήνυέ μοι βοῦς
θᾶσσον· ἐπεὶ τάχα νῶι διοισόμεθ' οὐ κατὰ κόσμον.
ῥίψω γάρ σε λαβὼν ἐς Τάρταρον ἠερόεντα,
ἐς ζόφον αἰνόμορον καὶ ἀμήχανον· οὐδέ σε μήτηρ
ἐς φάος οὐδὲ πατὴρ ἀναλύσεται, ἀλλ' ὑπὸ γαίῃ
ἐρρήσεις ὀλίγοισι μετ' ἀνδράσιν ἡγεμονεύων.
Τὸν δ' Ἑρμῆς μύθοισιν ἀμείβετο κερδαλέοισι·
Λητοΐδη, τίνα τοῦτον ἀπηνέα μῦθον ἔειπας;
καὶ βοῦς ἀγραύλους διζήμενος ἐνθάδ' ἱκάνεις;
οὐκ ἴδον, οὐ πυθόμην, οὐκ ἄλλου μῦθον ἄκουσα·
οὐκ ἂν μηνύσαιμ', οὐκ ἂν μήνυτρον ἀροίμην·
οὐδὲ βοῶν ἐλατῆρι, κραταιῷ φωτί, ἔοικα.
οὐκ ἐμὸν ἔργον τοῦτο, πάρος δέ μοι ἄλλα μέμηλεν·
ὕπνος ἐμοί γε μέμηλε καὶ ἡμετέρης γάλα μητρὸς
σπάργανά τ' ἀμφ' ὤμοισιν ἔχειν καὶ θερμὰ λοετρά.
μή τις τοῦτο πύθοιτο, πόθεν τόδε νεῖκος ἐτύχθη·
καί κεν δὴ μέγα θαῦμα μετ' ἀθανάτοισι γένοιτο,
παῖδα νέον γεγαῶτα διὲκ προθύροιο περῆσαι
βουσὶν ἐπ'[1] ἀγραύλοισι· τὸ δ' ἀπρεπέως ἀγορεύεις.
χθὲς γενόμην, ἁπαλοὶ δὲ πόδες, τρηχεῖα δ' ὑπο χθών.
εἰ δ' ἐθέλεις, πατρὸς κεφαλὴν μέγαν ὅρκον ὀμοῦμαι·
μὴ μὲν ἐγὼ μήτ' αὐτὸς ὑπίσχομαι αἴτιος εἶναι,
μήτε τιν' ἄλλον ὄπωπα βοῶν κλοπὸν ὑμετεράων,
αἵ τινες αἱ βόες εἰσί· τὸ δὲ κλέος οἶον ἀκούω.
Ὣς ἄρ' ἔφη καὶ πυκνὸν ἀπὸ βλεφάρων ἀμαρύσσων
ὀφρῦς ῥιπτάζεσκεν ὁρώμενος ἔνθα καὶ ἔνθα,

[1] Schneidewin: μετ', MSS.

"Child, lying in the cradle, make haste and tell me of my cattle, or we two will soon fall out angrily. For I will take and cast you into dusky Tartarus and awful hopeless darkness, and neither your mother nor your father shall free you or bring you up again to the light, but you will wander under the earth and be the leader amongst little folk."[1]

Then Hermes answered him with crafty words: "Son of Leto, what harsh words are these you have spoken? And is it cattle of the field you are come here to seek? I have not seen them: I have not heard of them: no one has told me of them. I cannot give news of them, nor win the reward for news. Am I like a cattle-lifter, a stalwart person? This is no task for me: rather I care for other things: I care for sleep, and milk of my mother's breast, and wrappings round my shoulders, and warm baths. Let no one hear the cause of this dispute; for this would be a great marvel indeed among the deathless gods, that a child newly born should pass in through the forepart of the house with cattle of the field: herein you speak extravagantly. I was born yesterday, and my feet are soft and the ground beneath is rough; nevertheless, if you will have it so, I will swear a great oath by my father's head and vow that neither am I guilty myself, neither have I seen any other who stole your cows—whatever cows may be; for I know them only by hearsay."

So, then, said Hermes, shooting quick glances from his eyes: and he kept raising his brows and looking

[1] Hermes is ambitious (l. 175), but if he is cast into Hades he will have to be content with the leadership of mere babies like himself, since those in Hades retain the state of growth—whether childhood or manhood—in which they are at the moment of leaving the upper world.

μάκρ' ἀποσυρίζων, ἅλιον τὸν μῦθον ἀκούων.
Τὸν δ' ἁπαλὸν γελάσας προσέφη ἑκάεργος Ἀπόλλων·
ὦ πέπον, ἠπεροπευτά, δολοφραδές, ἦ σε μάλ' οἴω
πολλάκις ἀντιτοροῦντα δόμους εὖ ναιετάοντας
ἔννυχον οὐχ ἕνα μοῦνον ἐπ' οὔδεϊ φῶτα καθίσσαι,
σκευάζοντα κατ' οἶκον ἄτερ ψόφου, οἷ' ἀγορεύεις·
πολλοὺς δ' ἀγραύλους ἀκαχήσεις μηλοβοτῆρας
οὔρεος ἐν βήσσῃς, ὁπότ' ἂν κρειῶν ἐρατίζων
ἀντᾷς βουκολίοισι καὶ εἰροπόκοις ὀίεσσιν.
ἀλλ' ἄγε, μὴ πύματόν τε καὶ ὕστατον ὕπνον ἰαύσῃς,
ἐκ λίκνου κατάβαινε, μελαίνης νυκτὸς ἑταῖρε.
τοῦτο γὰρ οὖν καὶ ἔπειτα μετ' ἀθανάτοις γέρας ἕξεις·
ἀρχὸς φηλητέων κεκλήσεαι ἤματα πάντα.
Ὣς ἄρ' ἔφη καὶ παῖδα λαβὼν φέρε Φοῖβος Ἀπόλλων.
σὺν δ' ἄρα φρασσάμενος τότε δὴ κρατὺς Ἀργειφόντης
οἰωνὸν προέηκεν ἀειρόμενος μετὰ χερσί,
τλήμονα γαστρὸς ἔριθον, ἀτάσθαλον ἀγγελιώτην.
ἐσσυμένως δὲ μετ' αὐτὸν ἐπέπταρε· τοῖο δ' Ἀπόλλων
ἔκλυεν, ἐκ χειρῶν δὲ χαμαὶ βάλε κύδιμον Ἑρμῆν.
ἕζετο δὲ προπάροιθε καὶ ἐσσύμενός περ ὁδοῖο
Ἑρμῆν κερτομέων καί μιν πρὸς μῦθον ἔειπε·
Θάρσει, σπαργανιῶτα, Διὸς καὶ Μαιάδος υἱέ·
εὑρήσω καὶ ἔπειτα βοῶν ἴφθιμα κάρηνα
τούτοις οἰωνοῖσι· σὺ δ' αὖθ' ὁδὸν ἡγεμονεύσεις.
Ὣς φάθ'· ὁ δ' αὖτ' ἀνόρουσε θοῶς Κυλλήνιος Ἑρμῆς,

this way and that, whistling long and listening to Apollo's story as to an idle tale.

But far-working Apollo laughed softly and said to him: "O rogue, deceiver, crafty in heart, you talk so innocently that I most surely believe that you have broken into many a well-built house and stripped more than one poor wretch bare this night,[1] gathering his goods together all over the house without noise. You will plague many a lonely herdsman in mountain glades, when you come on herds and thick-fleeced sheep, and have a hankering after flesh. But come now, if you would not sleep your last and latest sleep, get out of your cradle, you comrade of dark night. Surely hereafter this shall be your title amongst the deathless gods, to be called the prince of robbers continually."

So said Phoebus Apollo, and took the child and began to carry him. But at that moment the strong Slayer of Argus had his plan, and, while Apollo held him in his hands, sent forth an omen, a hard-worked belly-serf, a rude messenger, and sneezed directly after. And when Apollo heard it, he dropped glorious Hermes out of his hands on the ground: then sitting down before him, though he was eager to go on his way, he spoke mockingly to Hermes:

"Fear not, little swaddling baby, son of Zeus and Maia. I shall find the strong cattle presently by these omens, and you shall lead the way."

When Apollo had so said, Cyllenian Hermes

[1] Literally, "you have made him sit on the floor," *i.e.* "you have stolen everything down to his last chair."

σπουδῇ ἰών· ἄμφω δὲ παρ' οὔατα χερσὶν ἐώθει
σπάργανον ἀμφ' ὤμοισιν ἐελμένος, εἶπε δὲ μῦθον·
Πῇ με φέρεις, Ἑκάεργε, θεῶν ζαμενέστατε πάντων;
ἦ με βοῶν ἕνεχ' ὧδε χολούμενος ὀρσολοπεύεις;
ὢ πόποι, εἴθ' ἀπόλοιτο βοῶν γένος· οὐ γὰρ ἐγώ γε
ὑμετέρας ἔκλεψα βόας οὐδ' ἄλλον ὄπωπα,
αἵτινες αἱ βόες εἰσί· τὸ δὲ κλέος οἶον ἀκούω.
δὸς δὲ δίκην καὶ δέξο παρὰ Ζηνὶ Κρονίωνι.
Αὐτὰρ ἐπεὶ τὰ ἕκαστα διαρρήδην ἐρίδαινον
Ἑρμῆς τ' οἰοπόλος καὶ Λητοῦς ἀγλαὸς υἱός,
ἀμφὶς θυμὸν ἔχοντες. ὃ μὲν νημερτέα φωνὴν

* * * *

οὐκ ἀδίκως ἐπὶ βουσὶν ἐλάζυτο κύδιμον Ἑρμῆν,
αὐτὰρ ὃ τέχνῃσίν τε καὶ αἱμυλίοισι λόγοισιν
ἤθελεν ἐξαπατᾶν Κυλλήνιος Ἀργυρότοξον.
αὐτὰρ ἐπεὶ πολύμητις ἐὼν πολυμήχανον εὗρεν,
ἐσσυμένως δὴ ἔπειτα διὰ ψαμάθοιο βάδιζε
πρόσθεν, ἀτὰρ κατόπισθε Διὸς καὶ Λητοῦς υἱός.
αἶψα δὲ τέρθρον ἵκοντο θυώδεος Οὐλύμποιο
ἐς πατέρα Κρονίωνα Διὸς περικαλλέα τέκνα·
κεῖθι γὰρ ἀμφοτέροισι δίκης κατέκειτο τάλαντα.
οὐμιλίη [1] δ' ἔχ' Ὄλυμπον ἀγάννιφον, ἀθάνατοι δὲ
ἄφθιτοι ἠγερέθοντο μετὰ χρυσόθρονον Ἠῶ.[2]
Ἔστησαν δ' Ἑρμῆς τε καὶ ἀργυρότοξος Ἀπόλλων
πρόσθε Διὸς γούνων· ὃ δ' ἀνείρετο φαίδιμον υἱὸν
Ζεὺς ὑψιβρεμέτης καί μιν πρὸς μῦθον ἔειπε·
Φοῖβε, πόθεν ταύτην μενοεικέα ληίδ' ἐλαύνεις,
παῖδα νέον γεγαῶτα, φυὴν κήρυκος ἔχοντα;
σπουδαῖον τόδε χρῆμα θεῶν μεθ' ὁμήγυριν ἦλθε.

[1] Allen's (Oxf. Text) suggestion: εὐμιλίη, M: εὐμυλίη, other MSS.
[2] E and L (in margin): ποτὶ πτύχας Οὐλύμποιο, other MSS.

sprang up quickly, starting in haste. With both hands he pushed up to his ears the covering that he had wrapped about his shoulders, and said:

"Where are you carrying me, Far-Worker, hastiest of all the gods? Is it because of your cattle that you are so angry and harass me? O dear, would that all the sort of oxen might perish; for it is not I who stole your cows, nor did I see another steal them—whatever cows may be, and of that I have only heard report. Nay, give right and take it before Zeus, the Son of Cronos."

So Hermes the shepherd and Leto's glorious son kept stubbornly disputing each article of their quarrel: Apollo, speaking truly . . . .
not unfairly sought to seize glorious Hermes because of the cows; but he, the Cyllenian, tried to deceive the God of the Silver Bow with tricks and cunning words. But when, though he had many wiles, he found the other had as many shifts, he began to walk across the sand, himself in front, while the Son of Zeus and Leto came behind. Soon they came, these lovely children of Zeus, to the top of fragrant Olympus, to their father, the Son of Cronos; for there were the scales of judgement set for them both. There was an assembly on snowy Olympus, and the immortals who perish not were gathering after the hour of gold-throned Dawn.

Then Hermes and Apollo of the Silver Bow stood at the knees of Zeus: and Zeus who thunders on high spoke to his glorious son and asked him:

"Phoebus, whence come you driving this great spoil, a child new born that has the look of a herald? This is a weighty matter that is come before the council of the gods."

Τὸν δ' αὖτε προσέειπεν ἄναξ ἑκάεργος Ἀπόλλων·
ὦ πάτερ, ἦ τάχα μῦθον ἀκούσεαι οὐκ ἀλαπαδνόν,
κερτομέων ὡς οἶος ἐγὼ φιλολήιός εἰμι.
παῖδά τιν' εὗρον τόνδε διαπρύσιον κεραϊστὴν
Κυλλήνης ἐν ὄρεσσι, πολὺν διὰ χῶρον ἀνύσσας,
κέρτομον, οἷον ἐγώ γε θεῶν οὐκ ἄλλον ὄπωπα
οὐδ' ἀνδρῶν, ὁπόσοι λησίμβροτοί εἰσ' ἐπὶ γαίῃ.
κλέψας δ' ἐκ λειμῶνος ἐμὰς βοῦς ᾤχετ' ἐλαύνων
ἑσπέριος παρὰ θῖνα πολυφλοίσβοιο θαλάσσης,
εὐθὺ Πύλονδ' ἐλάων· τὰ δ' ἄρ' ἴχνια δοιὰ πέλωρα,
οἷά τ' ἀγάσσασθαι, καὶ ἀγαυοῦ δαίμονος ἔργα.
τῇσιν μὲν γὰρ βουσὶν ἐς ἀσφοδελὸν λειμῶνα
ἀντία βήματ' ἔχουσα κόνις ἀνέφαινε μέλαινα·
αὐτὸς δ' ἐκτὸς ὁδοῦ, τις[1] ἀμήχανος, οὔτ' ἄρα ποσσὶν
οὔτ' ἄρα χερσὶν ἔβαινε διὰ ψαμαθώδεα χῶρον·
ἀλλ' ἄλλην τινὰ μῆτιν ἔχων διέτριβε κέλευθα
τοῖα πέλωρ' ὡς εἴ τις ἀραιῇσι δρυσὶ βαίνοι.
ὄφρα μὲν οὖν ἐδίωκε διὰ ψαμαθώδεα χῶρον,
ῥεῖα μάλ' ἴχνια πάντα διέπρεπεν ἐν κονίῃσιν·
αὐτὰρ ἐπεὶ ψαμάθοιο μέγαν στίβον ἐξεπέρησεν,
ἄφραστος γένετ' ὦκα βοῶν στίβος ἠδὲ καὶ αὐτοῦ
χῶρον ἀνὰ κρατερόν· τὸν δ' ἐφράσατο βροτὸς ἀνὴρ
ἐς Πύλον εὐθὺς ἐλῶντα βοῶν γένος εὐρυμετώπων.
αὐτὰρ ἐπεὶ δὴ τὰς μὲν ἐν ἡσυχίῃ κατέερξε
καὶ διαπυρπαλάμησεν ὁδοῦ τὸ μὲν ἔνθα, τὸ δ' ἔνθα,
ἐν λίκνῳ κατέκειτο μελαίνῃ νυκτὶ ἐοικώς,
ἄντρῳ ἐν ἠερόεντι κατὰ ζόφον· οὐδέ κεν αὐτὸν
αἰετὸς ὀξὺ λάων ἐσκέψατο· πολλὰ δὲ χερσὶν
αὐγὰς ὡμόργαζε δολοφροσύνην ἀλεγύνων.
αὐτὸς δ' αὐτίκα μῦθον ἀπηλεγέως ἀγόρευεν·

[1] Translator: οὗτος ὅδ' ἐκτός, MSS.

Then the lord, far-working Apollo, answered him: "O my father, you shall soon hear no trifling tale though you reproach me that I alone am fond of spoil. Here is a child, a burgling robber, whom I found after a long journey in the hills of Cyllene: for my part I have never seen one so pert either among the gods or all men that catch folk unawares throughout the world. He stole away my cows from their meadow and drove them off in the evening along the shore of the loud-roaring sea, making straight for Pylos. There were double tracks, and wonderful they were, such as one might marvel at, the doing of a clever sprite; for as for the cows, the dark dust kept and showed their footprints leading towards the flowery meadow; but he himself—bewildering creature—crossed the sandy ground outside the path, not on his feet nor yet on his hands; but, furnished with some other means he trudged his way—wonder of wonders!—as though one walked on slender oak-trees. Now while he followed the cattle across sandy ground, all the tracks showed quite clearly in the dust; but when he had finished the long way across the sand, presently the cows' track and his own could not be traced over the hard ground. But a mortal man noticed him as he drove the wide-browed kine straight towards Pylos. And as soon as he had shut them up quietly, and had gone home by crafty turns and twists, he lay down in his cradle in the gloom of a dim cave, as still as dark night, so that not even an eagle keenly gazing would have spied him. Much he rubbed his eyes with his hands as he prepared falsehood, and himself straightway said roundly: 'I have not seen them: I have not

οὐκ ἴδον, οὐ πυθόμην, οὐκ ἄλλου μῦθον ἄκουσα
οὐδέ κε μηνύσαιμ', οὐδ' ἂν μήνυτρον ἀροίμην.
Ἦ τοι ἄρ' ὣς εἰπὼν κατ' ἄρ' ἕζετο Φοῖβος Ἀπόλλων·
Ἑρμῆς δ' αὖθ' ἑτέρωθεν ἀμειβόμενος ἔπος ηὔδα,[1]
δείξατο δ' ἐς Κρονίωνα, θεῶν σημάντορα πάντων·
Ζεῦ πάτερ, ἦ τοι ἐγώ σοι ἀληθείην καταλέξω·
νημερτής τε γάρ εἰμι καὶ οὐκ οἶδα ψεύδεσθαι.
ἦλθεν ἐς ἡμετέρου διζήμενος εἰλίποδας βοῦς
σήμερον ἠελίοιο νέον ἐπιτελλομένοιο·
οὐδὲ θεῶν μακάρων ἄγε μάρτυρας οὐδὲ κατόπτας,
μηνύειν δ' ἐκέλευεν ἀναγκαίης ὑπὸ πολλῆς,
πολλὰ δέ μ' ἠπείλησε βαλεῖν ἐς Τάρταρον εὐρύν,
οὕνεχ' ὃ μὲν τέρεν ἄνθος ἔχει φιλοκυδέος ἥβης,
αὐτὰρ ἐγὼ χθιζὸς γενόμην, τὰ δέ τ' οἶδε καὶ αὐτός,
οὔτι βοῶν ἐλατῆρι, κραταιῷ φωτί, ἐοικώς.
πείθεο· καὶ γὰρ ἐμεῖο πατὴρ φίλος εὔχεαι εἶναι,
ὡς οὐκ οἴκαδ' ἔλασσα βόας, ὣς ὄλβιος εἴην,
οὐδ' ὑπὲρ οὐδὸν ἔβην· τὸ δέ τ' ἀτρεκέως ἀγορεύω.
Ἠέλιον δὲ μάλ' αἰδέομαι καὶ δαίμονας ἄλλους,
καί σε φιλῶ καὶ τοῦτον ὀπίζομαι· οἶσθα καὶ αὐτός,
ὡς οὐκ αἴτιός εἰμι· μέγαν δ' ἐπιδώσομαι[2] ὅρκον·
οὐ μὰ τάδ' ἀθανάτων εὐκόσμητα προθύραια.
καί που[3] ἐγὼ τούτῳ τίσω ποτὲ νηλέα φώρην,
καὶ κρατερῷ περ ἐόντι· σὺ δ' ὁπλοτέροισιν ἄρηγε.
Ὣς φάτ' ἐπιλλίζων Κυλλήνιος Ἀργειφόντης·
καὶ τὸ σπάργανον εἶχεν ἐπ' ὠλένῃ οὐδ' ἀπέβαλλε.
Ζεὺς δὲ μέγ' ἐξεγέλασσεν ἰδὼν κακομηδέα παῖδα

[1] Most MSS.: ἄλλον μῦθον ἐν ἀθανάτοισιν ἔειπεν ("told another story among the immortals"), E and L (in margin).
[2] Barnes: ἐπιδεύομαι, M: ἐπιδαίομαι, other MSS.
[3] Hermann: ποτ', MSS.

heard of them: no man has told me of them. I could not tell you of them, nor win the reward of telling.' "

When he had so spoken, Phoebus Apollo sat down. But Hermes on his part answered and said, pointing at the Son of Cronos, the lord of all the gods:

"Zeus, my father, indeed I will speak truth to you; for I am truthful and I cannot tell a lie. He came to our house to-day looking for his shambling cows, as the sun was newly rising. He brought no witnesses with him nor any of the blessed gods who had seen the theft, but with great violence ordered me to confess, threatening much to throw me into wide Tartarus. For he has the rich bloom of glorious youth, while I was born but yesterday—as he too knows—, nor am I like a cattle-lifter, a sturdy fellow. Believe my tale (for you claim to be my own father), that I did not drive his cows to my house—so may I prosper—nor crossed the threshold: this I say truly. I reverence Helios greatly and the other gods, and you I love and him I dread. You yourself know that I am not guilty: and I will swear a great oath upon it:—No! by these rich-decked porticoes of the gods. And some day I will punish him, strong as he is, for this pitiless inquisition; but now do you help the younger."

So spake the Cyllenian, the Slayer of Argus, while he kept shooting sidelong glances and kept his swaddling-clothes upon his arm, and did not cast them away. But Zeus laughed out loud to see his

εὖ καὶ ἐπισταμένως ἀρνεύμενον ἀμφὶ βόεσσιν.
ἀμφοτέρους δ' ἐκέλευσεν ὁμόφρονα θυμὸν ἔχοντας
ζητεύειν, Ἑρμῆν δὲ διάκτορον ἡγεμονεύειν
καὶ δεῖξαι τὸν χῶρον ἐπ' ἀβλαβίῃσι νόοιο,
ὅππη δὴ αὖτ' ἀπέκρυψε βοῶν ἴφθιμα κάρηνα.
νεῦσεν δὲ Κρονίδης, ἐπεπείθετο δ' ἀγλαὸς Ἑρμῆς·
ῥηιδίως γὰρ ἔπειθε Διὸς νόος αἰγιόχοιο.
Τὼ δ' ἄμφω σπεύδοντε Διὸς περικαλλέα τέκνα
ἐς Πύλον ἠμαθόεντα ἐπ' Ἀλφειοῦ πόρον ἶξον·
ἀγροὺς δ' ἐξίκοντο καὶ αὔλιον ὑψιμέλαθρον,
ἠχοῦ [1] δὴ τὰ χρήματ' ἀτάλλετο νυκτὸς ἐν ὥρῃ.
ἔνθ' Ἑρμῆς μὲν ἔπειτα κιὼν παρὰ λάινον ἄντρον
ἐς φῶς ἐξήλαυνε βοῶν ἴφθιμα κάρηνα·
Λητοΐδης δ' ἀπάτερθεν ἰδὼν ἐνόησε βοείας
πέτρῃ ἐπ' ἠλιβάτῳ, τάχα δ' εἴρετο κύδιμον Ἑρμῆν·
Πῶς ἐδύνω, δολομῆτα, δύω βόε δειροτομῆσαι,
ὧδε νεογνὸς ἐὼν καὶ νήπιος; αὐτὸς ἐγώ γε
θαυμαίνω κατόπισθε τὸ σὸν κράτος· οὐδέ τί σε χρὴ
μακρὸν ἀέξεσθαι, Κυλλήνιε, Μαιάδος υἱέ.
Ὣς ἄρ' ἔφη καὶ χερσὶ περίστρεφε καρτερὰ δεσμὰ
[ἐνδῆσαι μεμαὼς Ἑρμῆν κρατεραῖσι λύγοισι.[2]
τὸν δ' οὐκ ἴσχανε δεσμά, λύγοι δ' ἀπὸ τηλόσε
πῖπτον [3]]
ἄγνου· ταὶ δ' ὑπὸ ποσσὶ κατὰ χθονὸς αἶψα φύοντο
αὐτόθεν, ἐμβολάδην ἐστραμμέναι ἀλλήλῃσι,
ῥεῖά τε καὶ πάσῃσιν ἐπ' ἀγραύλοισι βόεσσιν,
Ἑρμέω βουλῇσι κλεψίφρονος· αὐτὰρ Ἀπόλλων
θαύμασεν ἀθρήσας. τότε δὴ κρατὺς Ἀργειφόντης
χῶρον ὑποβλήδην ἐσκέψατο, πῦρ ἀμαρύσσων,

*   *   *   *

[1] Fick : ἦχ' οὐ and ἦχ' οὗ, MSS : ὄχου, M.
[2] Allen. [3] Hymn to Dionysus, 13.

evil-plotting child well and cunningly denying guilt about the cattle. And he bade them both to be of one mind and search for the cattle, and guiding Hermes to lead the way and, without mischievousness of heart, to show the place where now he had hidden the strong cattle. Then the Son of Cronos bowed his head: and goodly Hermes obeyed him; for the will of Zeus who holds the aegis easily prevailed with him.

Then the two all-glorious children of Zeus hastened both to sandy Pylos, and reached the ford of Alpheus, and came to the fields and the high-roofed byre where the beasts were cherished at night-time. Now while Hermes went to the cave in the rock and began to drive out the strong cattle, the son of Leto, looking aside, saw the cowhides on the sheer rock. And he asked glorious Hermes at once:

"How were you able, you crafty rogue, to flay two cows, new-born and babyish as you are? For my part, I dread the strength that will be yours: there is no need you should keep growing long, Cyllenian, son of Maia!"

So saying, Apollo twisted strong withes with his hands meaning to bind Hermes with firm bands; but the bands would not hold him, and the withes of osier fell far from him and began to grow at once from the ground beneath their feet in that very place. And intertwining with one another, they quickly grew and covered all the wild-roving cattle by the will of thievish Hermes, so that Apollo was astonished as he gazed.

Then the strong slayer of Argus looked furtively upon the ground with eyes flashing fire . . . desiring to hide . . . Very easily he softened the

ἐγκρύψαι μεμαώς· Λητοῦς δ' ἐρικυδέος υἱὸν
ῥεῖα μάλ' ἐπρήυνεν ἑκηβόλον, ὡς ἔθελ' αὐτός,
καὶ κρατερόν περ ἐόντα· λαβὼν δ' ἐπ' ἀριστερὰ χειρὸς
πλήκτρῳ ἐπειρήτιζε κατὰ μέρος· ἡ δ' ὑπὸ χειρὸς
σμερδαλέον κονάβησε· γέλασσε δὲ Φοῖβος Ἀπόλλων
γηθήσας, ἐρατὴ δὲ διὰ φρένας ἤλυθ' ἰωὴ
θεσπεσίης ἐνοπῆς καί μιν γλυκὺς ἵμερος ᾕρει
θυμῷ ἀκουάζοντα· λύρῃ δ' ἐρατὸν κιθαρίζων
στῆ ῥ' ὅ γε θαρσήσας ἐπ' ἀριστερὰ Μαιάδος υἱὸς
Φοίβου Ἀπόλλωνος· τάχα δὲ λιγέως κιθαρίζων
γηρύετ' ἀμβολάδην—ἐρατὴ δέ οἱ ἕσπετο φωνή—
κραίνων ἀθανάτους τε θεοὺς καὶ γαῖαν ἐρεμνήν,
ὡς τὰ πρῶτα γένοντο καὶ ὡς λάχε μοῖραν ἕκαστος.
Μνημοσύνην μὲν πρῶτα θεῶν ἐγέραιρεν ἀοιδῇ,
μητέρα Μουσάων· ἡ γὰρ λάχε Μαιάδος υἱόν·
τοὺς δὲ κατὰ πρέσβιν τε καὶ ὡς γεγάασιν ἕκαστος
ἀθανάτους ἐγέραιρε θεοὺς Διὸς ἀγλαὸς υἱός,
πάντ' ἐνέπων κατὰ κόσμον, ἐπωλένιον κιθαρίζων.
τὸν δ' ἔρος ἐν στήθεσσιν ἀμήχανος αἴνυτο θυμόν,
καί μιν φωνήσας ἔπεα πτερόεντα προσηύδα·
Βουφόνε, μηχανιῶτα, πονεύμενε, δαιτὸς ἑταῖρε,
πεντήκοντα βοῶν ἀντάξια ταῦτα μέμηλας.
ἡσυχίως καὶ ἔπειτα διακρινέεσθαι ὀίω·
νῦν δ' ἄγε μοι τόδε εἰπέ, πολύτροπε Μαιάδος υἱέ,
ἦ σοί γ' ἐκ γενετῆς τάδ' ἅμ' ἕσπετο θαυματὰ ἔργα
ἠέ τις ἀθανάτων ἠὲ θνητῶν ἀνθρώπων
δῶρον ἀγαυὸν ἔδωκε καὶ ἔφρασε θέσπιν ἀοιδήν;
θαυμασίην γὰρ τήνδε νεήφατον ὄσσαν ἀκούω,
ἣν οὐ πώ ποτέ φημι δαήμεναι οὔτε τιν' ἀνδρῶν
οὔτε τιν' ἀθανάτων, οἳ Ὀλύμπια δώματ' ἔχουσι,
νόσφι σέθεν, φηλῆτα, Διὸς καὶ Μαιάδος υἱέ.

son of all-glorious Leto as he would, stern though the Far-shooter was. He took the lyre upon his left arm and tried each string in turn with the key, so that it sounded awesomely at his touch. And Phoebus Apollo laughed for joy; for the sweet throb of the marvellous music went to his heart, and a soft longing took hold on his soul as he listened. Then the son of Maia, harping sweetly upon his lyre, took courage and stood at the left hand of Phoebus Apollo; and soon, while he played shrilly on his lyre, he lifted up his voice and sang, and lovely was the sound of his voice that followed. He sang the story of the deathless gods and of the dark earth, how at the first they came to be, and how each one received his portion. First among the gods he honoured Mnemosyne, mother of the Muses, in his song; for the son of Maia was of her following. And next the goodly son of Zeus hymned the rest of the immortals according to their order in age, and told how each was born, mentioning all in order as he struck the lyre upon his arm. But Apollo was seized with a longing not to be allayed, and he opened his mouth and spoke winged words to Hermes:

"Slayer of oxen, trickster, busy one, comrade of the feast, this song of yours is worth fifty cows, and I believe that presently we shall settle our quarrel peacefully. But come now, tell me this, resourceful son of Maia: has this marvellous thing been with you from your birth, or did some god or mortal man give it you—a noble gift—and teach you heavenly song? For wonderful is this new-uttered sound I hear, the like of which I vow that no man nor god dwelling on Olympus ever yet has known but you, O thievish son of Maia. What skill is this? What

τίς τέχνη, τίς μοῦσα ἀμηχανέων μελεδώνων,
τίς τρίβος; ἀτρεκέως γὰρ ἅμα τρία πάντα πάρεστιν,
εὐφροσύνην καὶ ἔρωτα καὶ ἥδυμον ὕπνον ἑλέσθαι.
καὶ γὰρ ἐγὼ Μούσῃσιν Ὀλυμπιάδεσσιν ὀπηδός,
τῇσι χοροί τε μέλουσι καὶ ἀγλαὸς οἶμος[1] ἀοιδῆς
καὶ μολπὴ τεθαλυῖα καὶ ἱμερόεις βρόμος αὐλῶν·
ἀλλ' οὔ πω τί μοι ὧδε μετὰ φρεσὶν ἄλλο μέλησεν,
οἷα νέων θαλίῃς ἐνδέξια ἔργα πέλονται.
θαυμάζω, Διὸς υἱέ, τάδ', ὡς ἐρατὸν κιθαρίζεις.
νῦν δ' ἐπεὶ οὖν ὀλίγος περ ἐὼν κλυτὰ μήδεα οἶδας,
ἷζε, πέπον, καὶ μῦθον[2] ἐπαίνει πρεσβυτέροισι·
νῦν γάρ τοι κλέος ἔσται ἐν ἀθανάτοισι θεοῖσι
σοί τ' αὐτῷ καὶ μητρί· τὸ δ' ἀτρεκέως ἀγορεύσω·
ναὶ μὰ τόδε κρανέινον ἀκόντιον, ἦ μὲν ἐγώ σε
κυδρὸν ἐν ἀθανάτοισι καὶ ὄλβιον ἡγεμόν' εἴσω[3]
δώσω τ' ἀγλαὰ δῶρα καὶ ἐς τέλος οὐκ ἀπατήσω.
Τὸν δ' Ἑρμῆς μύθοισιν ἀμείβετο κερδαλέοισιν·
εἰρωτᾷς μ', Ἑκάεργε, περιφραδές· αὐτὰρ ἐγώ σοι
τέχνης ἡμετέρης ἐπιβήμεναι οὔ τι μεγαίρω.
σήμερον εἰδήσεις· ἐθέλω δέ τοι ἤπιος εἶναι
βουλῇ καὶ μύθοισι. σὺ δὲ φρεσὶ πάντ' εὖ οἶδας·
πρῶτος γάρ, Διὸς υἱέ, μετ' ἀθανάτοισι θαάσσεις,
ἠΰς τε κρατερός τε· φιλεῖ δέ σε μητίετα Ζεὺς
ἐκ πάσης ὁσίης, ἔπορεν δέ τοι ἀγλαὰ δῶρα.
καὶ τιμάς σέ γέ φασι δαήμεναι ἐκ Διὸς ὀμφῆς
μαντείας θ', Ἑκάεργε, Διὸς παρά, θέσφατα πάντα·
τῶν νῦν αὐτὸς ἐγώ σε μαλ' ἀφνειὸν[4] δεδάηκα·
σοὶ δ' αὐτάγρετόν ἐστι δαήμεναι, ὅττι μενοινᾷς.

[1] Most MSS: ὕμνος, M with E and L (margin).
[2] Ruhnken: θυμὸν, M. [3] Tyrrell: ἡγεμονεύσω, MSS.
[4] Translator: ἔγωγε παῖδ' ἀφνειόν, MSS.

song for desperate cares? What way of song? For verily here are three things to hand all at once from which to choose,—mirth, and love, and sweet sleep. And though I am a follower of the Olympian Muses who love dances and the bright path of song—the full-toned chant and ravishing thrill of flutes—yet I never cared for any of those feats of skill at young men's revels, as I do now for this: I am filled with wonder, O son of Zeus, at your sweet playing. But now, since you, though little, have such glorious skill, sit down, dear boy, and respect the words of your elders. For now you shall have renown among the deathless gods, you and your mother also. This I will declare to you exactly: by this shaft of cornel wood I will surely make you a leader renowned among the deathless gods, and fortunate, and will give you glorious gifts and will not deceive you from first to last."

Then Hermes answered him with artful words: "You question me carefully, O Far-worker; yet I am not jealous that you should enter upon my art: this day you shall know it. For I seek to be friendly with you both in thought and word. Now you well know all things in your heart, since you sit foremost among the deathless gods, O son of Zeus, and are goodly and strong. And wise Zeus loves you as all right is, and has given you splendid gifts. And they say that from the utterance of Zeus you have learned both the honours due to the gods, O Far-worker, and oracles from Zeus, even all his ordinances. Of all these I myself have already learned that you have great wealth. Now, you are free to learn whatever

ἀλλ᾽ ἐπεὶ οὖν τοι θυμὸς ἐπιθύει κιθαρίζειν,
μέλπεο καὶ κιθάριζε καὶ ἀγλαΐας ἀλέγυνε
δέγμενος ἐξ ἐμέθεν· σὺ δέ μοι, φίλε, κῦδος ὄπαζε.
εὐμόλπει μετὰ χερσὶν ἔχων λιγύφωνον ἑταίρην,
καλὰ καὶ εὖ κατὰ κόσμον ἐπιστάμενος ἀγορεύειν.
εὔκηλος μὲν ἔπειτα φέρειν ἐς δαῖτα θάλειαν
καὶ χορὸν ἱμερόεντα καὶ ἐς φιλοκυδέα κῶμον
εὐφροσύνην νυκτός τε καὶ ἤματος. ὅς τις ἂν αὐτὴν
τέχνῃ καὶ σοφίῃ δεδαημένος ἐξερεείνῃ,
φθεγγομένη παντοῖα νόῳ χαρίεντα διδάσκει
ῥεῖα συνηθείῃσιν ἀθυρομένη μαλακῇσιν,
ἐργασίην φεύγουσα δυήπαθον· ὃς δέ κεν αὐτὴν
νῆις ἐὼν τὸ πρῶτον ἐπιζαφελῶς ἐρεείνῃ,
μὰψ αὔτως κεν ἔπειτα μετήορά τε θρυλλίζοι.
σοὶ δ᾽ αὐτάγρετόν ἐστι δαήμεναι, ὅττι μενοινᾷς.
καί τοι ἐγὼ δώσω ταύτην, Διὸς ἀγλαὲ κοῦρε·
ἡμεῖς δ᾽ αὖτ᾽ ὄρεός τε καὶ ἱπποβότου πεδίοιο
βουσὶ νομούς, Ἑκάεργε, νομεύσομεν ἀγραύλοισιν.
ἔνθεν ἅλις τέξουσι βόες ταύροισι μιγεῖσαι
μίγδην θηλείας τε καὶ ἄρσενας· οὐδέ τί σε χρὴ
κερδαλέον περ ἐόντα περιζαμενῶς κεχολῶσθαι.
Ὣς εἰπὼν ὤρεξ᾽· ὁ δ᾽ ἐδέξατο Φοῖβος Ἀπόλλων,
Ἑρμῇ δ᾽ ἐγγυάλιξεν ἑκὼν[1] μάστιγα φαεινήν,
βουκολίας τ᾽ ἐπέτελλεν· ἔδεκτο δὲ Μαιάδος υἱὸς
γηθήσας· κίθαριν δὲ λαβὼν ἐπ᾽ ἀριστερὰ χειρὸς
Λητοῦς ἀγλαὸς υἱός, ἄναξ ἑκάεργος Ἀπόλλων,
πλήκτρῳ ἐπειρήτιζε κατὰ μέρος· ἣ δ᾽ ὑπένερθε
σμερδαλέον[2] κονάβησε· θεὸς δ᾽ ὑπὸ καλὸν ἄεισεν.
Ἔνθα βόας μὲν ἔπειτα ποτὶ ζάθεον λειμῶνα
ἐτραπέτην· αὐτοὶ δέ, Διὸς περικαλλέα τέκνα,

[1] Martin: ἔχων, MSS. [2] M: ἱμερόεν, other MSS.

you please; but since, as it seems, your heart is so strongly set on playing the lyre, chant, and play upon it, and give yourself to merriment, taking this as a gift from me, and do you, my friend, bestow glory on me. Sing well with this clear-voiced companion in your hands; for you are skilled in good, well-ordered utterance. From now on bring it confidently to the rich feast and lovely dance and glorious revel, a joy by night and by day. Whoso with wit and wisdom enquires of it cunningly, him it teaches through its sound all manner of things that delight the mind, being easily played with gentle familiarities, for it abhors toilsome drudgery; but whoso in ignorance enquires of it violently, to him it chatters mere vanity and foolishness. But you are able to learn whatever you please. So then, I will give you this lyre, glorious son of Zeus, while I for my part will graze down with wild-roving cattle the pastures on hill and horse-feeding plain: so shall the cows covered by the bulls calve abundantly both males and females. And now there is no need for you, bargainer though you are, to be furiously angry."

When Hermes had said this, he held out the lyre: and Phoebus Apollo took it, and readily put his shining whip in Hermes' hand, and ordained him keeper of herds. The son of Maia received it joyfully, while the glorious son of Leto, the lord far-working Apollo, took the lyre upon his left arm and tried each string with the key. Awesomely it sounded at the touch of the god, while he sang sweetly to its note.

Afterwards they two, the all-glorious sons of Zeus turned the cows back towards the sacred meadow,

ἄψορροι πρὸς Ὄλυμπον ἀγάννιφον ἐρρώσαντο
τερπόμενοι φόρμιγγι· χάρη δ' ἄρα μητιέτα Ζεύς,
ἄμφω δ' ἐς φιλότητα συνήγαγε· καὶ τὰ μὲν Ἑρμῆς
Λητοΐδην ἐφίλησε διαμπερὲς ὡς ἔτι καὶ νῦν,
σήματ' ἐπεὶ κίθαριν μὲν Ἑκηβόλῳ ἐγγυάλιξεν
ἱμερτήν, δεδαώς, ὃ δ' ἐπωλένιον κιθάριζεν·
αὐτὸς δ' αὖθ' ἑτέρης σοφίης ἐκμάσσατο τέχνην·
συρίγγων ἐνοπὴν ποιήσατο τηλόθ' ἀκουστήν.
Καὶ τότε Λητοΐδης Ἑρμῆν πρὸς μῦθον ἔειπε·
δείδια, Μαιάδος υἱέ, διάκτορε, ποικιλομῆτα,
μή μοι ἅμα κλέψῃς κίθαριν καὶ καμπύλα τόξα·
τιμὴν γὰρ πὰρ Ζηνὸς ἔχεις ἐπαμοίβια ἔργα
θήσειν ἀνθρώποισι κατὰ χθόνα πουλυβότειραν.
ἀλλ' εἴ μοι τλαίης γε θεῶν μέγαν ὅρκον ὀμόσσαι,
ἢ κεφαλῇ νεύσας ἢ ἐπὶ Στυγὸς ὄβριμον ὕδωρ,
πάντ' ἂν ἐμῷ θυμῷ κεχαρισμένα καὶ φίλα ἔρδοις.
Καὶ τότε Μαιάδος υἱὸς ὑποσχόμενος κατένευσε,
μή ποτ' ἀποκλέψειν, ὅσ' Ἑκηβόλος ἐκτεάτισται,
μηδέ ποτ' ἐμπελάσειν πυκινῷ δόμῳ· αὐτὰρ Ἀπόλλων
Λητοΐδης κατένευσεν ἐπ' ἀρθμῷ καὶ φιλότητι,
μή τινα φίλτερον ἄλλον ἐν ἀθανάτοισιν ἔσεσθαι,
μήτε θεὸν μήτ' ἄνδρα Διὸς γόνον· ἐκ δὲ τέλειον
[αἰετὸν ἧκε πατήρ· ὁ δ' ἐπώμοσεν· ἦ σε μάλ' οἶον[1]]
σύμβολον ἀθανάτων ποιήσομαι ἠδ' ἅμα πάντων,
πιστὸν ἐμῷ θυμῷ καὶ τίμιον· αὐτὰρ ἔπειτα
ὄλβου καὶ πλούτου δώσω περικαλλέα ῥάβδον,
χρυσείην, τριπέτηλον, ἀκήριον ἥ σε φυλάξει
πάντας ἐπικραίνουσ' ἄθλους[2] ἐπέων τε καὶ ἔργων
τῶν ἀγαθῶν, ὅσα φημὶ δαήμεναι ἐκ Διὸς ὀμφῆς.

[1] Allen's supplement. [2] Sikes: θεούς, MSS.

but themselves hastened back to snowy Olympus, delighting in the lyre. Then wise Zeus was glad and made them both friends. And Hermes loved the son of Leto continually, even as he does now, when he had given the lyre as token to the Far-shooter, who played it skilfully, holding it upon his arm. But for himself Hermes found out another cunning art and made himself the pipes whose sound is heard afar.

Then the son of Leto said to Hermes: "Son of Maia, guide and cunning one, I fear you may steal from me the lyre and my curved bow together; for you have an office from Zeus, to establish deeds of barter amongst men throughout the fruitful earth. Now if you would only swear me the great oath of the gods, either by nodding your head, or by the potent water of Styx, you would do all that can please and ease my heart."

Then Maia's son nodded his head and promised that he would never steal anything of all the Far-shooter possessed, and would never go near his strong house; but Apollo, son of Leto, swore to be fellow and friend to Hermes, vowing that he would love no other among the immortals, neither god nor man sprung from Zeus, better than Hermes: and the Father sent forth an eagle in confirmation. And Apollo sware also: "Verily I will make you only to be an omen for the immortals and all alike, trusted and honoured by my heart. Moreover, I will give you a splendid staff of riches and wealth: it is of gold, with three branches, and will keep you scatheless, accomplishing every task, whether of words or deeds that are good, which I claim to know through the utterance of Zeus. But as for

μαντείην δέ, φέριστε, διοτρεφές, ἣν ἐρεείνεις,
οὔτε σὲ θέσφατόν ἐστι δαήμεναι οὔτε τιν' ἄλλον
ἀθανάτων· τὸ γὰρ οἶδε Διὸς νόος· αὐτὰρ ἐγώ γε
πιστωθεὶς κατένευσα καὶ ὤμοσα καρτερὸν ὅρκον,
μή τινα νόσφιν ἐμεῖο θεῶν αἰειγενετάων
ἄλλον γ' εἴσεσθαι Ζηνὸς πυκινόφρονα βουλήν.
καὶ σύ, κασίγνητε χρυσόρραπι, μή με κέλευε
θέσφατα πιφαύσκειν, ὅσα μήδεται εὐρύοπα Ζευς.
ἀνθρώπων δ' ἄλλον δηλήσομαι, ἄλλον ὀνήσω,
πολλὰ περιτροπέων ἀμεγάρτων φῦλ' ἀνθρώπων.
καὶ μὲν ἐμῆς ὀμφῆς ἀπονήσεται, ὅς τις ἂν ἔλθῃ
φωνῇ καὶ πτερύγεσσι τεληέντων οἰωνῶν·
οὗτος ἐμῆς ὀμφῆς ἀπονήσεται, οὐδ' ἀπατήσω.
ὃς δέ κε μαψιλόγοισι πιθήσας οἰωνοῖσι
μαντείην ἐθέλῃσι παρὲκ νόον ἐξερεείνειν
ἡμετέρην, νοέειν δὲ θεῶν πλέον αἰὲν ἐόντων,
φήμ', ἁλίην ὁδὸν εἶσιν. ἐγὼ δέ κε δῶρα δεχοίμην.
Ἄλλο δέ τοι ἐρέω, Μαίης ἐρικυδέος υἱὲ
καὶ Διὸς αἰγιόχοιο, θεῶν ἐριούνιε δαῖμον·
σεμναὶ γάρ τινες εἰσί, κασίγνηται γεγαυῖαι,
παρθένοι, ὠκείῃσιν ἀγαλλόμεναι πτερύγεσσι,
τρεῖς· κατὰ δὲ κρατὸς πεπαλαγμέναι ἄλφιτα λευκά,
οἰκία ναιετάουσιν ὑπὸ πτυχὶ Παρνησοῖο,
μαντείης ἀπάνευθε διδάσκαλοι, ἣν ἐπὶ βουσὶ
παῖς ἔτ' ἐὼν μελέτησα· πατὴρ δ' ἐμὸς οὐκ ἀλέγιζεν,
ἐντεῦθεν δὴ ἔπειτα ποτώμεναι ἄλλοτε ἄλλῃ
κηρία βόσκονται καί τε κραίνουσιν ἕκαστα.

sooth-saying, noble, heaven-born child, of which you ask, it is not lawful for you to learn it, nor for any other of the deathless gods: only the mind of Zeus knows that. I am pledged and have vowed and sworn a strong oath that no other of the eternal gods save I should know the wise-hearted counsel of Zeus. And do not you, my brother, bearer of the golden wand, bid me tell those decrees which all-seeing Zeus intends. As for men, I will harm one and profit another, sorely perplexing the tribes of unenviable men. Whosoever shall come guided by the call and flight of birds of sure omen, that man shall have advantage through my voice, and I will not deceive him. But whoso shall trust to idly-chattering birds and shall seek to invoke my prophetic art contrary to my will, and to understand more than the eternal gods, I declare that he shall come on an idle journey; yet his gifts I would take.

But I will tell you another thing, Son of all-glorious Maia and Zeus who holds the aegis, luck-bringing genius of the gods. There are certain holy ones, sisters born—three virgins[1] gifted with wings: their heads are besprinkled with white meal, and they dwell under a ridge of Parnassus. These are teachers of divination apart from me, the art which I practised while yet a boy following herds, though my father paid no heed to it. From their home they fly now here, now there, feeding on honey-comb

[1] The Thriae, who practised divination by means of pebbles (also called θριαί). In this hymn they are represented as aged maidens (ll. 553–4), but are closely associated with bees (ll. 559–563) and possibly are here conceived as having human heads and breasts with the bodies and wings of bees. See the edition of Allen and Sikes, Appendix III.

αἳ δ' ὅτε μὲν θυΐωσιν ἐδηδυῖαι μέλι χλωρόν,
προφρονέως ἐθέλουσιν ἀληθείην ἀγορεύειν·
ἢν δ' ἀπονοσφισθῶσι θεῶν ἡδεῖαν ἐδωδήν,
ψεύδονται δὴ ἔπειτα δι' ἀλλήλων δονέουσαι.[1]
τάς τοι ἔπειτα δίδωμι· σὺ δ' ἀτρεκέως ἐρεείνων
σὴν αὐτοῦ φρένα τέρπε, καὶ εἰ βροτὸν ἄνδρα δαείης,
πολλάκι σῆς ὀμφῆς ἐπακούσεται, αἴ κε τύχῃσι.
ταῦτ' ἔχε, Μαιάδος υἱέ, καὶ ἀγραύλους ἕλικας βοῦς
ἵππους τ' ἀμφιπόλευε καὶ ἡμιόνους ταλαεργούς.
[ὣς ἔφατ'· οὐρανόθεν δὲ πατὴρ Ζεὺς αὐτὸς ἔπεσσι 568a
θῆκε τέλος· πᾶσιν δ' ἄρ' ὅ γ' οἰωνοῖσι κέλευσεν [2]] 568b
καὶ χαροποῖσι λέουσι καὶ ἀργιόδουσι σύεσσι
καὶ κυσὶ καὶ μήλοισιν, ὅσα τρέφει εὐρεῖα χθών,
πᾶσι δ' ἐπὶ προβάτοισιν ἀνάσσειν κύδιμον Ἑρμῆν,
οἶον δ' εἰς Ἀΐδην τετελεσμένον ἄγγελον εἶναι,
ὅς τ' ἄδοτός περ ἐὼν δώσει γέρας οὐκ ἐλάχιστον.
Οὕτω Μαιάδος υἱὸν ἄναξ ἐφίλησεν Ἀπόλλων
παντοίῃ φιλότητι· χάριν δ' ἐπέθηκε Κρονίων.
πᾶσι δ' ὅ γε θνητοῖσι καὶ ἀθανάτοισιν ὁμιλεῖ.
παῦρα μὲν οὖν ὀνίνησι, τὸ δ' ἄκριτον ἠπεροπεύει
νύκτα δι' ὀρφναίην φῦλα θνητῶν ἀνθρώπων.
Καὶ σὺ μὲν οὕτω χαῖρε, Διὸς καὶ Μαιάδος υἱέ·
αὐτὰρ ἐγὼ καὶ σεῖο καὶ ἄλλης μνήσομ' ἀοιδῆς.

[1] E and L: πειρῶνται δὴ ἔπειτα παρὲξ ὁδὸν ἡγεμονεύειν ("Then they try to lead men aside out of the way"), other MSS.
[2] Allen's supplement.

and bringing all things to pass. And when they are inspired through eating yellow honey, they are willing to speak truth; but if they be deprived of the gods' sweet food, then they speak falsely, as they swarm in and out together. These, then, I give you; enquire of them strictly and delight your heart: and if you should teach any mortal so to do, often will he hear your response—if he have good fortune. Take these, Son of Maia, and tend the wild roving, horned oxen and horses and patient mules."

So he spake. And from heaven father Zeus himself gave confirmation to his words, and commanded that glorious Hermes should be lord over all birds of omen and grim-eyed lions, and boars with gleaming tusks, and over dogs and all flocks that the wide earth nourishes, and over all sheep; also that he only should be the appointed messenger to Hades, who, though he takes no gift, shall give him no mean prize.

Thus the lord Apollo showed his kindness for the Son of Maia by all manner of friendship: and the Son of Cronos gave him grace besides. He consorts with all mortals and immortals: a little he profits, but continually throughout the dark night he cozens the tribes of mortal men.

And so, farewell, Son of Zeus and Maia; but I will remember you and another song also.

V

ΕΙΣ ΑΦΡΟΔΙΤΗΝ

Μοῦσά μοι ἔννεπε ἔργα πολυχρύσου Ἀφροδίτης,
Κύπριδος, ἥτε θεοῖσιν ἐπὶ γλυκὺν ἵμερον ὦρσε
καί τ' ἐδαμάσσατο φῦλα καταθνητῶν ἀνθρώπων
οἰωνούς τε διιπετέας καὶ θηρία πάντα,
ἠμὲν ὅσ' ἤπειρος πολλὰ τρέφει ἠδ' ὅσα πόντος·
πᾶσιν δ' ἔργα μέμηλεν ἐϋστεφάνου Κυθερείης.
Τρισσὰς δ' οὐ δύναται πεπιθεῖν φρένας οὐδ' ἀπατῆσαι·
κούρην τ' αἰγιόχοιο Διός, γλαυκῶπιν Ἀθήνην·
οὐ γάρ οἱ εὔαδεν ἔργα πολυχρύσου Ἀφροδίτης,
ἀλλ' ἄρα οἱ πόλεμοί τε ἅδον καὶ ἔργον Ἄρηος
ὑσμῖναί τε μάχαι τε καὶ ἀγλαὰ ἔργ' ἀλεγύνειν.
πρώτη τέκτονας ἄνδρας ἐπιχθονίους ἐδίδαξε
ποιῆσαι σατίνας τε καὶ ἅρματα ποικίλα χαλκῷ.
ἡ δέ τε παρθενικὰς ἁπαλόχροας ἐν μεγάροισιν
ἀγλαὰ ἔργ' ἐδίδαξεν ἐπὶ φρεσὶ θεῖσα ἑκάστῃ.
οὐδέ ποτ' Ἄρτέμιδα χρυσηλάκατον, κελαδεινὴν
δάμναται ἐν φιλότητι φιλομμειδὴς Ἀφροδίτη.
καὶ γὰρ τῇ ἅδε τόξα καὶ οὔρεσι θῆρας ἐναίρειν,
φόρμιγγές τε χοροί τε διαπρύσιοί τ' ὀλολυγαὶ
ἄλσεά τε σκιόεντα δικαίων τε πτόλις ἀνδρῶν.
οὐδὲ μὲν αἰδοίῃ κούρῃ ἅδε ἔργ' Ἀφροδίτης,
Ἱστίῃ, ἣν πρώτην τέκετο Κρόνος ἀγκυλομήτης,
αὖτις δ' ὁπλοτάτην, βουλῇ Διὸς αἰγιόχοιο,

TO APHRODITE

MUSE, tell me the deeds of golden Aphrodite the Cyprian, who stirs up sweet passion in the gods and subdues the tribes of mortal men and birds that fly in air and all the many creatures that the dry land rears, and all that the sea: all these love the deeds of rich-crowned Cytherea.

Yet there are three hearts that she cannot bend nor yet ensnare. First is the daughter of Zeus who holds the aegis, bright-eyed Athene; for she has no pleasure in the deeds of golden Aphrodite, but delights in wars and in the work of Ares, in strifes and battles and in preparing famous crafts. She first taught earthly craftsmen to make chariots of war and cars variously wrought with bronze, and she, too, teaches tender maidens in the house and puts knowledge of goodly arts in each one's mind. Nor does laughter-loving Aphrodite ever tame in love Artemis, the huntress with shafts of gold; for she loves archery and the slaying of wild beasts in the mountains, the lyre also and dancing and thrilling cries and shady woods and the cities of upright men. Nor yet does the pure maiden Hestia love Aphrodite's works. She was the first-born child of wily Cronos and youngest too,[1] by will of Zeus who holds the aegis,—a queenly maid whom both

[1] Cronos swallowed each of his children the moment that they were born, but ultimately was forced to disgorge them. Hestia, being the first to be swallowed, was the last to be disgorged, and so was at once the first and latest born of the children of Cronos. Cp. Hesiod *Theogony*, ll. 495-7.

πότνιαν, ἣν ἐμνῶντο Ποσειδάων καὶ Ἀπόλλων·
ἡ δὲ μάλ' οὐκ ἔθελεν, ἀλλὰ στερεῶς ἀπέειπεν·
ὤμοσε δὲ μέγαν ὅρκον, ὃ δὴ τετελεσμένος ἐστίν,
ἁψαμένη κεφαλῆς πατρὸς Διὸς αἰγιόχοιο,
παρθένος ἔσσεσθαι πάντ' ἤματα, δῖα θεάων.
τῇ δὲ πατὴρ Ζεὺς δῶκε καλὸν γέρας ἀντὶ γάμοιο
καί τε μέσῳ οἴκῳ κατ' ἄρ' ἕζετο πῖαρ ἑλοῦσα.
πᾶσιν δ' ἐν νηοῖσι θεῶν τιμάοχός ἐστι
καὶ παρὰ πᾶσι βροτοῖσι θεῶν πρέσβειρα τέτυκται.
  Τάων οὐ δύναται πεπιθεῖν φρένας οὐδ' ἀπατῆσαι·
τῶν δ' ἄλλων οὔ πέρ τι πεφυγμένον ἔστ' Ἀφροδίτην
οὔτε θεῶν μακάρων οὔτε θνητῶν ἀνθρώπων.
καί τε παρὲκ Ζηνὸς νόον ἤγαγε τερπικεραύνου,
ὅστε μέγιστός τ' ἐστὶ μεγίστης τ' ἔμμορε τιμῆς.
καί τε τοῦ, εὖτ' ἐθέλοι, πυκινὰς φρένας ἐξαπαφοῦσα
ῥηιδίως συνέμιξε καταθνητῇσι γυναιξίν,
Ἥρης ἐκλελαθοῦσα, κασιγνήτης ἀλόχου τε,
ἣ μέγα εἶδος ἀρίστη ἐν ἀθανάτῃσι θεῇσι.
κυδίστην δ' ἄρα μιν τέκετο Κρόνος ἀγκυλομήτης
μήτηρ τε Ῥείη· Ζεὺς δ' ἄφθιτα μήδεα εἰδὼς
αἰδοίην ἄλοχον ποιήσατο κέδν' εἰδυῖαν.
  Τῇ δὲ καὶ αὐτῇ Ζεὺς γλυκὺν ἵμερον ἔμβαλε θυμῷ
ἀνδρὶ καταθνητῷ μιχθήμεναι, ὄφρα τάχιστα
μηδ' αὐτὴ βροτέης εὐνῆς ἀποεργμένη εἴη,
καί ποτ' ἐπευξαμένη εἴπῃ μετὰ πᾶσι θεοῖσιν
ἡδὺ γελοιήσασα, φιλομμειδὴς Ἀφροδίτη,
ὥς ῥα θεοὺς συνέμιξε καταθνητῇσι γυναιξί,
καί τε καταθνητοὺς υἱεῖς τέκον ἀθανάτοισιν,
ὥς τε θεὰς ἀνέμιξε καταθνητοῖς ἀνθρώποις.

Poseidon and Apollo sought to wed. But she was wholly unwilling, nay, stubbornly refused; and touching the head of father Zeus who holds the aegis, she, that fair goddess, sware a great oath which has in truth been fulfilled, that she would be a maiden all her days. So Zeus the Father gave her an high honour instead of marriage, and she has her place in the midst of the house and has the richest portion. In all the temples of the gods she has a share of honour, and among all mortal men she is chief of the goddesses.

Of these three Aphrodite cannot bend or ensnare the hearts. But of all others there is nothing among the blessed gods or among mortal men that has escaped Aphrodite. Even the heart of Zeus, who delights in thunder, is led astray by her; though he is greatest of all and has the lot of highest majesty, she beguiles even his wise heart whensoever she pleases, and mates him with mortal women, unknown to Hera, his sister and his wife, the grandest far in beauty among the deathless goddesses—most glorious is she whom wily Cronos with her mother Rhea did beget: and Zeus, whose wisdom is everlasting, made her his chaste and careful wife.

But upon Aphrodite herself Zeus cast sweet desire to be joined in love with a mortal man, to the end that, very soon, not even she should be innocent of a mortal's love; lest laughter-loving Aphrodite should one day softly smile and say mockingly among all the gods that she had joined the gods in love with mortal women who bare sons of death to the deathless gods, and had mated the goddesses with mortal men.

Ἀγχίσεω δ' ἄρα οἱ γλυκὺν ἵμερον ἔμβαλε θυμῷ,
ὃς τότ' ἐν ἀκροπόλοις ὄρεσιν πολυπιδάκου Ἴδης
βουκολέεσκεν βοῦς δέμας ἀθανάτοισιν ἐοικώς.
τὸν δὴ ἔπειτα ἰδοῦσα φιλομμειδὴς Ἀφροδίτη
ἠράσατ', ἔκπαγλος δὲ κατὰ φρένας ἵμερος εἷλεν.
ἐς Κύπρον δ' ἐλθοῦσα θυώδεα νηὸν ἔδυνεν,
ἐς Πάφον· ἔνθα δέ οἱ τέμενος βωμός τε θυώδης.
ἔνθ' ἥ γ' εἰσελθοῦσα θύρας ἐπέθηκε φαεινάς·
ἔνθα δέ μιν Χάριτες λοῦσαν καὶ χρῖσαν ἐλαίῳ
ἀμβρότῳ, οἷα θεοὺς ἐπενήνοθεν αἰὲν ἐόντας,
ἀμβροσίῳ ἑδανῷ,[1] τό ῥά οἱ τεθυωμένον ἦεν.
ἑσσαμένη δ' εὖ πάντα περὶ χροῒ εἵματα καλὰ
χρυσῷ κοσμηθεῖσα φιλομμειδὴς Ἀφροδίτη
σεύατ' ἐπὶ Τροίης προλιποῦσ' εὐώδεα Κύπρον,
ὕψι μετὰ νέφεσιν ῥίμφα πρήσσουσα κέλευθον.
Ἴδην δ' ἵκανεν πολυπίδακα, μητέρα θηρῶν,
βῆ δ' ἰθὺς σταθμοῖο δι' οὔρεος· οἱ δὲ μετ' αὐτὴν
σαίνοντες πολιοί τε λύκοι χαροποί τε λέοντες,
ἄρκτοι παρδάλιές τε θοαὶ προκάδων ἀκόρητοι
ᾔισαν· ἡ δ' ὁρόωσα μετὰ φρεσὶ τέρπετο θυμὸν
καὶ τοῖς ἐν στήθεσσι βάλ' ἵμερον· οἱ δ' ἅμα πάντες
σύνδυο κοιμήσαντο κατὰ σκιόεντας ἐναύλους.
  Αὐτὴ δ' ἐς κλισίας εὐποιήτους ἀφίκανε·
τὸν δ' εὗρε σταθμοῖσι λελειμμένον οἶον ἀπ' ἄλλων
Ἀγχίσην ἥρωα, θεῶν ἄπο κάλλος ἔχοντα.
οἱ δ' ἅμα βουσὶν ἕποντο νομοὺς κατὰ ποιήεντας
πάντες· ὁ δὲ σταθμοῖσι λελειμμένος οἶος ἀπ' ἄλλων
πωλεῖτ' ἔνθα καὶ ἔνθα διαπρύσιον κιθαρίζων.
στῆ δ' αὐτοῦ προπάροιθε Διὸς θυγάτηρ Ἀφροδίτη
παρθένῳ ἀδμήτῃ μέγεθος καὶ εἶδος ὁμοίη,

[1] Clarke: ἑανῷ, MSS.

And so he put in her heart sweet desire for Anchises who was tending cattle at that time among the steep hills of many-fountained Ida, and in shape was like the immortal gods. Therefore, when laughter-loving Aphrodite saw him, she loved him, and terribly desire seized her in her heart. She went to Cyprus, to Paphos, where her precinct is and fragrant altar, and passed into her sweet-smelling temple. There she went in and put to the glittering doors, and there the Graces bathed her with heavenly oil such as blooms upon the bodies of the eternal gods—oil divinely sweet, which she had by her, filled with fragrance. And laughter-loving Aphrodite put on all her rich clothes, and when she had decked herself with gold, she left sweet-smelling Cyprus and went in haste towards Troy, swiftly travelling high up among the clouds. So she came to many-fountained Ida, the mother of wild creatures and went straight to the homestead across the mountains. After her came grey wolves, fawning on her, and grim-eyed lions, and bears, and fleet leopards, ravenous for deer: and she was glad in heart to see them, and put desire in their breasts, so that they all mated, two together, about the shadowy coombes.

But she herself came to the neat-built shelters, and him she found left quite alone in the homestead—the hero Anchises who was comely as the gods. All the others were following the herds over the grassy pastures, and he, left quite alone in the homestead, was roaming hither and thither and playing thrillingly upon the lyre. And Aphrodite, the daughter of Zeus stood before him, being like a pure maiden in height and mien, that he should not

μή μιν ταρβήσειεν ἐν ὀφθαλμοῖσι νοήσας.
Ἀγχίσης δ' ὁρόων ἐφράζετο θαύμαινέν τε
εἶδός τε μέγεθός τε καὶ εἵματα σιγαλόεντα.
πέπλον μὲν γὰρ ἕεστο φαεινότερον πυρὸς αὐγῆς,
καλόν,[1] χρύσειον, παμποίκιλον· ὡς δὲ σελήνη 89
στήθεσιν ἀμφ' ἁπαλοῖσιν ἐλάμπετο, θαῦμα ἰδέσθαι· 90
εἶχε δ' ἐπιγναμπτὰς ἕλικας κάλυκάς τε φαεινάς· 87
ὅρμοι δ' ἀμφ' ἁπαλῇ δειρῇ περικαλλέες ἦσαν. 88
  Ἀγχίσην δ' ἔρος εἷλεν, ἔπος δέ μιν ἀντίον ηὔδα· 91
χαῖρε, ἄνασσ', ἥ τις μακάρων τάδε δώμαθ' ἱκάνεις,
Ἄρτεμις ἢ Λητὼ ἠὲ χρυσέη Ἀφροδίτη
ἢ Θέμις ἠυγενὴς ἠὲ γλαυκῶπις Ἀθήνη,
ἤ πού τις Χαρίτων δεῦρ' ἤλυθες, αἵτε θεοῖσι
πᾶσιν ἑταιρίζουσι καὶ ἀθάνατοι καλέονται,
ἤ τις Νυμφάων, αἵτ' ἄλσεα καλὰ νέμονται
ἢ Νυμφῶν, αἳ καλὸν ὄρος τόδε ναιετάουσι
καὶ πηγὰς ποταμῶν καὶ πίσεα ποιήεντα.
σοὶ δ' ἐγὼ ἐν σκοπιῇ, περιφαινομένῳ ἐνὶ χώρῳ,
βωμὸν ποιήσω, ῥέξω δέ τοι ἱερὰ καλὰ
ὥρῃσιν πάσῃσι. σὺ δ' εὔφρονα θυμὸν ἔχουσα
δός με μετὰ Τρώεσσιν ἀριπρεπέ' ἔμμεναι ἄνδρα,
ποίει δ' ἐξοπίσω θαλερὸν γόνον, αὐτὰρ ἔμ' αὐτὸν
δηρὸν ἐὺ ζώειν καὶ ὁρᾶν φάος ἠελίοιο,
ὄλβιον ἐν λαοῖς, καὶ γήραος οὐδὸν ἱκέσθαι.
  Τὸν δ' ἠμείβετ' ἔπειτα Διὸς θυγάτηρ Ἀφροδίτη·
Ἀγχίση, κύδιστε χαμαιγενέων ἀνθρώπων,
οὔ τίς τοι θεός εἰμι· τί μ' ἀθανάτῃσιν ἐίσκεις;
ἀλλὰ καταθνητή τε, γυνὴ δέ με γείνατο μήτηρ.
Ὀτρεὺς δ' ἐστὶ πατὴρ ὀνομακλυτός, εἴ που ἀκούεις,

[1] Wakefield, καλοί etc., MSS.

be frightened when he took heed of her with his eyes. Now when Anchises saw her, he marked her well and wondered at her mien and height and shining garments. For she was clad in a robe out-shining the brightness of fire, a splendid robe of gold, enriched with all manner of needlework, which shimmered like the moon over her tender breasts, a marvel to see. Also she wore twisted brooches and shining earrings in the form of flowers; and round her soft throat were lovely necklaces.

And Anchises was seized with love, and said to her: "Hail, lady, whoever of the blessed ones you are that are come to this house, whether Artemis, or Leto, or golden Aphrodite, or high-born Themis, or bright-eyed Athene. Or, maybe, you are one of the Graces come hither, who bear the gods company and are called immortal, or else one of the Nymphs who haunt the pleasant woods, or of those who inhabit this lovely mountain and the springs of rivers and grassy meads. I will make you an altar upon a high peak in a far seen place, and will sacrifice rich offerings to you at all seasons. And do you feel kindly towards me and grant that I may become a man very eminent among the Trojans, and give me strong offspring for the time to come. As for my own self, let me live long and happily, seeing the light of the sun, and come to the threshold of old age, a man prosperous among the people."

Thereupon Aphrodite the daughter of Zeus answered him: "Anchises, most glorious of all men born on earth, know that I am no goddess: why do you liken me to the deathless ones? Nay, I am but a mortal, and a woman was the mother that bare me. Otreus of famous name is my father, if so be you

ὃς πάσης Φρυγίης εὐτειχήτοιο ἀνάσσει.
γλῶσσαν δ' ὑμετέρην τε καὶ ἡμετέρην σάφα οἶδα.
Τρῳὰς γὰρ μεγάρῳ με τροφὸς τρέφεν· ἣ δὲ διαπρὸ
σμικρὴν παῖδ' ἀτίταλλε, φίλης παρὰ μητρὸς ἑλοῦσα.
ὣς δή τοι γλῶσσάν γε καὶ ὑμετέρην εὖ οἶδα.
νῦν δέ μ' ἀνήρπαξε χρυσόρραπις Ἀργειφόντης
ἐκ χοροῦ Ἀρτέμιδος χρυσηλακάτου, κελαδεινῆς.
πολλαὶ δὲ νύμφαι καὶ παρθένοι ἀλφεσίβοιαι
παίζομεν, ἀμφὶ δ' ὅμιλος ἀπείριτος ἐστεφάνωτο.
ἔνθεν μ' ἥρπαξε χρυσόρραπις Ἀργειφόντης·
πολλὰ δ' ἔπ' ἤγαγεν ἔργα καταθνητῶν ἀνθρώπων,
πολλὴν δ' ἄκληρόν τε καὶ ἄκτιτον, ἣν διὰ θῆρες
ὠμοφάγοι φοιτῶσι κατὰ σκιόεντας ἐναύλους·
οὐδὲ ποσὶ ψαύσειν ἐδόκουν φυσιζόου αἴης·
Ἀγχίσεω δέ με φάσκε παραὶ λέχεσιν καλέεσθαι
κουριδίην ἄλοχον, σοὶ δ' ἀγλαὰ τέκνα τεκεῖσθαι.
αὐτὰρ ἐπεὶ δὴ δεῖξε καὶ ἔφρασεν, ἦ τοι ὅ γ' αὖτις
ἀθανάτων μετὰ φῦλ' ἀπέβη κρατὺς Ἀργειφόντης·
αὐτὰρ ἐγώ σ' ἱκόμην, κρατερὴ δέ μοι ἔπλετ' ἀνάγκη.
ἀλλά σε πρὸς Ζηνὸς γουνάζομαι ἠδὲ τοκήων
ἐσθλῶν· οὐ μὲν γάρ κε κακοὶ τοιόνδε τέκοιεν·
ἀδμήτην μ' ἀγαγὼν καὶ ἀπειρήτην φιλότητος
πατρί τε σῷ δεῖξον καὶ μητέρι κέδν' εἰδυίῃ
σοῖς τε κασιγνήτοις, οἵ τοι ὁμόθεν γεγάασιν.
οὔ σφιν ἀεικελίη νυὸς ἔσσομαι, ἀλλ' εἰκυῖα.[1]
πέμψαι δ' ἄγγελον ὦκα μετὰ Φρύγας αἰολοπώλους
εἰπεῖν πατρί τ' ἐμῷ καὶ μητέρι κηδομένῃ περ·

[1] MELΠT give the alternative verse:
εἴ τοι ἀεικελίη γυνὴ ἔσσομαι ἠὲ καὶ οὐκί.
("to see whether I shall be an ill-liking wife for you or no.")

have heard of him, and he reigns over all Phrygia rich in fortresses. But I know your speech well beside my own, for a Trojan nurse brought me up at home: she took me from my dear mother and reared me thenceforth when I was a little child. So comes it, then, that I well know your tongue also. And now the Slayer of Argus with the golden wand has caught me up from the dance of huntress Artemis, her with the golden arrows. For there were many of us, nymphs and marriageable[1] maidens, playing together; and an innumerable company encircled us: from these the Slayer of Argus with the golden wand rapt me away. He carried me over many fields of mortal men and over much land untilled and unpossessed, where savage wild-beasts roam through shady coombes, until I thought never again to touch the life-giving earth with my feet. And he said that I should be called the wedded wife of Anchises, and should bear you goodly children. But when he had told and advised me, he, the strong Slayer of Argos, went back to the families of the deathless gods, while I am now come to you: for unbending necessity is upon me. But I beseech you by Zeus and by your noble parents—for no base folk could get such a son as you—take me now, stainless and unproved in love, and show me to your father and careful mother and to your brothers sprung from the same stock. I shall be no ill-liking daughter for them, but a likely. Moreover, send a messenger quickly to the swift-horsed Phrygians, to tell my father and my sorrowing mother; and they will send

[1] "Cattle-earning," because an accepted suitor paid for his bride in cattle.

οἱ δέ κέ τοι χρυσόν τε ἅλις ἐσθῆτά θ' ὑφαντὴν
πέμψουσιν· σὺ δὲ πολλὰ καὶ ἀγλαὰ δέχθαι ἄποινα.
ταῦτα δὲ ποιήσας δαίνυ γάμον ἱμερόεντα,
τίμιον ἀνθρώποισι καὶ ἀθανάτοισι θεοῖσιν.
  Ὣς εἰποῦσα θεὰ γλυκὺν ἵμερον ἔμβαλε θυμῷ.
Ἀγχίσην δ' ἔρος εἷλεν ἔπος τ' ἔφατ' ἔκ τ' ὀνόμαζεν·
  Εἰ μὲν θνητή τ' ἐσσί, γυνὴ δέ σε γείνατο μήτηρ,
Ὀτρεὺς δ' ἐστὶ πατὴρ ὀνομακλυτός, ὡς ἀγορεύεις,
ἀθανάτου δὲ ἕκητι διακτόρου ἐνθάδ' ἱκάνεις
Ἑρμέω, ἐμὴ δ' ἄλοχος κεκλήσεαι ἤματα πάντα·
οὔ τις ἔπειτα θεῶν οὔτε θνητῶν ἀνθρώπων
ἐνθάδε με σχήσει, πρὶν σῇ φιλότητι μιγῆναι
αὐτίκα νῦν· οὐδ' εἴ κεν ἑκηβόλος αὐτὸς Ἀπόλλων
τόξου ἀπ' ἀργυρέου προΐῃ βέλεα στονόεντα.
βουλοίμην κεν ἔπειτα, γύναι ἐικυῖα θεῇσι,
σῆς εὐνῆς ἐπιβὰς δῦναι δόμον Ἄιδος εἴσω.
  Ὣς εἰπὼν λάβε χεῖρα· φιλομμειδὴς δ' Ἀφροδίτη
ἕρπε μεταστρεφθεῖσα κατ' ὄμματα καλὰ βαλοῦσα
ἐς λέχος εὔστρωτον, ὅθι περ πάρος ἔσκεν ἄνακτι
χλαίνῃσιν μαλακῇς ἐστρωμένον· αὐτὰρ ὕπερθεν
ἄρκτων δέρματ' ἔκειτο βαρυφθόγγων τε λεόντων,
τοὺς αὐτὸς κατέπεφνεν ἐν οὔρεσιν ὑψηλοῖσιν.
οἱ δ' ἐπεὶ οὖν λεχέων εὐποιήτων ἐπέβησαν,
κόσμον μέν οἱ πρῶτον ἀπὸ χροὸς εἷλε φαεινόν,
πόρπας τε γναμπτάς θ' ἕλικας κάλυκάς τε καὶ
    ὅρμους.
λῦσε δέ οἱ ζώνην ἰδὲ εἵματα σιγαλόεντα
ἔκδυε καὶ κατέθηκεν ἐπὶ θρόνου ἀργυροήλου
Ἀγχίσης· ὁ δ' ἔπειτα θεῶν ἰότητι καὶ αἴσῃ
ἀθανάτῃ παρέλεκτο θεᾷ βροτός, οὐ σάφα εἰδώς.
  Ἦμος δ' ἂψ εἰς αὖλιν ἀποκλίνουσι νομῆες
βοῦς τε καὶ ἴφια μῆλα νομῶν ἐξ ἀνθεμοέντων·

you gold in plenty and woven stuffs, many splendid gifts; take these as bride-piece. So do, and then prepare the sweet marriage that is honourable in the eyes of men and deathless gods."

When she had so spoken, the goddess put sweet desire in his heart. And Anchises was seized with love, so that he opened his mouth and said:

"If you are a mortal and a woman was the mother who bare you, and Otreus of famous name is your father as you say, and if you are come here by the will of Hermes the immortal Guide, and are to be called my wife always, then neither god nor mortal man shall here restrain me till I have lain with you in love right now; no, not even if far-shooting Apollo himself should launch grievous shafts from his silver bow. Willingly would I go down into the house of Hades, O lady, beautiful as the goddesses, once I had gone up to your bed."

So speaking, he caught her by the hand. And laughter-loving Aphrodite, with face turned away and lovely eyes downcast, crept to the well-spread couch which was already laid with soft coverings for the hero; and upon it lay skins of bears and deep-roaring lions which he himself had slain in the high mountains. And when they had gone up upon the well-fitted bed, first Anchises took off her bright jewelry of pins and twisted brooches and earrings and necklaces, and loosed her girdle and stripped off her bright garments and laid them down upon a silver-studded seat. Then by the will of the gods and destiny he lay with her, a mortal man with an immortal goddess, not clearly knowing what he did.

But at the time when the herdsmen drive their oxen and hardy sheep back to the fold from the

τῆμος ἄρ' Ἀγχίσῃ μὲν ἐπὶ γλυκὺν ὕπνον ἔχευε
νήδυμον, αὐτὴ δὲ χροῒ ἕννυτο εἵματα καλά.
ἑσσαμένη δ' εὖ πάντα περὶ χροῒ δῖα θεάων
ἔστη πὰρ[1] κλισίῃ, κεὐποιήτοιο[2] μελάθρου
κῦρε κάρη· κάλλος δὲ παρειάων ἀπέλαμπεν
ἄμβροτον, οἷόν τ' ἐστὶν ἐυστεφάνου Κυθερείης,
ἐξ ὕπνου τ' ἀνέγειρεν ἔπος τ' ἔφατ' ἔκ τ' ὀνόμαζεν·
  Ὄρσεο, Δαρδανίδη· τί νυ νήγρετον ὕπνον ἰαύεις ;
καὶ φράσαι, εἴ τοι ὁμοίη ἐγὼν ἰνδάλλομαι εἶναι,
οἵην δή με τὸ πρῶτον ἐν ὀφθαλμοῖσι νόησας ;
  Ὣς φάθ'· ὁ δ' ἐξ ὕπνοιο μάλ' ἐμμαπέως ὑπάκουσεν.
ὡς δὲ ἴδεν δειρήν τε καὶ ὄμματα κάλ' Ἀφροδίτης,
τάρβησέν τε καὶ ὄσσε παρακλιδὸν ἔτραπεν ἄλλῃ·
ἂψ δ' αὖτις χλαίνῃ τε καλύψατο καλὰ πρόσωπα
καί μιν λισσόμενος ἔπεα πτερόεντα προσηύδα·
  Αὐτίκα σ' ὡς τὰ πρῶτα, θεά, ἴδον ὀφθαλμοῖσιν,
ἔγνων ὡς θεὸς ἦσθα· σὺ δ' οὐ νημερτὲς ἔειπες.
ἀλλά σε πρὸς Ζηνὸς γουνάζομαι αἰγιόχοιο,
μή με ζῶντ' ἀμενηνὸν ἐν ἀνθρώποισιν ἐάσῃς
ναίειν, ἀλλ' ἐλέαιρ'· ἐπεὶ οὐ βιοθάλμιος ἀνὴρ
γίγνεται, ὅς τε θεαῖς εὐνάζεται ἀθανάτῃσι.
  Τὸν δ' ἠμείβετ' ἔπειτα Διὸς θυγάτηρ Ἀφροδίτη·
Ἀγχίση, κύδιστε καταθνητῶν ἀνθρώπων,
θάρσει, μηδέ τι σῇσι μετὰ φρεσὶ δείδιθι λίην·
οὐ γάρ τοί τι δέος παθέειν κακὸν ἐξ ἐμέθεν γε,
οὐδ' ἄλλων μακάρων· ἐπεὶ ἦ φίλος ἐσσὶ θεοῖσι.
σοὶ δ' ἔσται φίλος υἱός, ὃς ἐν Τρώεσσιν ἀνάξει
καὶ παῖδες παίδεσσι διαμπερὲς ἐκγεγάοντες·[3]
τῷ δὲ καὶ Αἰνείας ὄνομ' ἔσσεται, οὕνεκά μ' αἰνὸν

[1] Stephanus : ἄρα, MSS. [2] Sikes.
[3] Baumeister : ἐγγεγάονται, MSS.

flowery pastures, even then Aphrodite poured soft sleep upon Anchises, but herself put on her rich raiment. And when the bright goddess had fully clothed herself, she stood by the couch, and her head reached to the well-hewn roof-tree; from her cheeks shone unearthly beauty such as belongs to rich-crowned Cytherea. Then she aroused him from sleep and opened her mouth and said:

"Up, son of Dardanus!—why sleep you so heavily?—and consider whether I look as I did when first you saw me with your eyes."

So she spake. And he awoke in a moment and obeyed her. But when he saw the neck and lovely eyes of Aphrodite, he was afraid and turned his eyes aside another way, hiding his comely face with his cloak. Then he uttered winged words and entreated her:

"So soon as ever I saw you with my eyes, goddess, I knew that you were divine; but you did not tell me truly. Yet by Zeus who holds the aegis I beseech you, leave me not to lead a palsied life among men, but have pity on me; for he who lies with a deathless goddess is no hale man afterwards."

Then Aphrodite the daughter of Zeus answered him: "Anchises, most glorious of mortal men, take courage and be not too fearful in your heart. You need fear no harm from me nor from the other blessed ones, for you are dear to the gods: and you shall have a dear son who shall reign among the Trojans, and children's children after him, springing up continually. His name shall be Aeneas,[1] because

[1] The name Aeneas is here connected with the epithet *ainos* (awful): similarly the name Odysseus is derived (in *Od.* i. 62) from ὀδύσσομαι (I grieve).

ἔσχεν ἄχος, ἕνεκα βροτοῦ ἀνέρος ἔμπεσον εὐνῇ·
ἀγχίθεοι δὲ μάλιστα καταθνητῶν ἀνθρώπων
αἰεὶ ἀφ' ὑμετέρης γενεῆς εἶδός τε φυήν τε.
Ἦ τοι μὲν ξανθὸν Γανυμήδεα μητιέτα Ζεὺς
ἥρπασε ὃν διὰ κάλλος, ἵν' ἀθανάτοισι μετείη
καί τε Διὸς κατὰ δῶμα θεοῖς ἐπιοινοχοεύοι,
θαῦμα ἰδεῖν, πάντεσσι τετιμένος ἀθανάτοισι,
χρυσέου ἐκ κρητῆρος ἀφύσσων νέκταρ ἐρυθρόν.
Τρῶα δὲ πένθος ἄλαστον ἔχε φρένας, οὐδέ τι ᾔδει,
ὅππῃ οἱ φίλον υἱὸν ἀνήρπασε θέσπις ἄελλα·
τὸν δὴ ἔπειτα γόασκε διαμπερὲς ἤματα πάντα
καί μιν Ζεὺς ἐλέησε, δίδου δέ οἱ υἷος ἄποινα,
ἵππους ἀρσίποδας, τοί τ' ἀθανάτους φορέουσι.
τούς οἱ δῶρον ἔδωκεν ἔχειν· εἶπεν δὲ ἕκαστα
Ζηνὸς ἐφημοσύνῃσι διάκτορος Ἀργειφόντης,
ὡς ἔοι ἀθάνατος καὶ ἀγήρως ἶσα θεοῖσιν.
αὐτὰρ ἐπειδὴ Ζηνὸς ὅ γ' ἔκλυεν ἀγγελιάων,
οὐκέτ' ἔπειτα γόασκε, γεγήθει δὲ φρένας ἔνδον,
γηθόσυνος δ' ἵπποισιν ἀελλοπόδεσσιν ὀχεῖτο.
Ὣς δ' αὖ Τιθωνὸν χρυσόθρονος ἥρπασεν Ἠώς,
ὑμετέρης γενεῆς, ἐπιείκελον ἀθανάτοισι.
βῆ δ' ἴμεν αἰτήσουσα κελαινεφέα Κρονίωνα,
ἀθάνατόν τ' εἶναι καὶ ζώειν ἤματα πάντα·
τῇ δὲ Ζεὺς ἐπένευσε καὶ ἐκρήηνεν ἐέλδωρ.
νηπίη, οὐδ' ἐνόησε μετὰ φρεσὶ πότνια Ἠὼς
ἥβην αἰτῆσαι ξῦσαί τ' ἄπο γῆρας ὀλοιόν.
τὸν δ' ἦ τοι εἵως μὲν ἔχεν πολυήρατος ἥβη,
Ἠοῖ τερπόμενος χρυσοθρόνῳ, ἠριγενείῃ

I felt awful grief in that I laid me in the bed of a mortal man: yet are those of your race always the most like to gods of all mortal men in beauty and in stature.[1]

Verily wise Zeus carried off golden-haired Ganymedes because of his beauty, to be amongst the Deathless Ones and pour drink for the gods in the house of Zeus—a wonder to see—, honoured by all the immortals as he draws the red nectar from the golden bowl. But grief that could not be soothed filled the heart of Tros; for he knew not whither the heaven-sent whirlwind had caught up his dear son, so that he mourned him always, unceasingly, until Zeus pitied him and gave him high-stepping horses such as carry the immortals as recompense for his son. These he gave him as a gift. And at the command of Zeus, the Guide, the slayer of Argus, told him all, and how his son would be deathless and unageing, even as the gods. So when Tros heard these tidings from Zeus, he no longer kept mourning but rejoiced in his heart and rode joyfully with his storm-footed horses.

So also golden-throned Eos rapt away Tithonus who was of your race and like the deathless gods. And she went to ask the dark-clouded Son of Cronos that he should be deathless and live eternally; and Zeus bowed his head to her prayer and fulfilled her desire. Too simple was queenly Eos: she thought not in her heart to ask youth for him and to strip him of the slough of deadly age. So while he enjoyed the sweet flower of life he lived rapturously with golden-throned Eos, the early-born, by the streams

[1] Aphrodite extenuates her disgrace by claiming that the race of Anchises is almost divine, as is shown in the persons of Ganymedes and Tithonus.

ναῖε παρ' Ὠκεανοῖο ῥοῇς ἐπὶ πείρασι γαίης·
αὐτὰρ ἐπεὶ πρῶται πολιαὶ κατέχυντο ἔθειραι
καλῆς ἐκ κεφαλῆς εὐηγενέος τε γενείου,
τοῦ δ' ἦ τοι εὐνῆς μὲν ἀπείχετο πότνια Ἠώς,
αὐτὸν δ' αὖτ' ἀτίταλλεν ἐνὶ μεγάροισιν ἔχουσα,
σίτῳ τ' ἀμβροσίῃ τε καὶ εἵματα καλὰ διδοῦσα.
ἀλλ' ὅτε δὴ πάμπαν στυγερὸν κατὰ γῆρας ἔπειγεν,
οὐδέ τι κινῆσαι μελέων δύνατ' οὐδ' ἀναεῖραι,
ἥδε δέ οἱ κατὰ θυμὸν ἀρίστη φαίνετο βουλή·
ἐν θαλάμῳ κατέθηκε, θύρας δ' ἐπέθηκε φαεινάς.
τοῦ δ' ἦ τοι φωνὴ ῥέει [1] ἄσπετος, οὐδέ τι κῖκυς
ἔσθ', οἵη πάρος ἔσκεν ἐνὶ γναμπτοῖσι μέλεσσιν.
Οὐκ ἂν ἐγώ γε σὲ τοῖον ἐν ἀθανάτοισιν ἑλοίμην
ἀθάνατόν τ' εἶναι καὶ ζώειν ἤματα πάντα.
ἀλλ' εἰ μὲν τοιοῦτος ἐὼν εἶδός τε δέμας τε
ζώοις ἡμέτερός τε πόσις κεκλημένος εἴης,
οὐκ ἂν ἔπειτά μ' ἄχος πυκινὰς φρένας ἀμφικαλύπτοι.
νῦν δέ σε μὲν τάχα γῆρας ὁμοίιον ἀμφικαλύψει
νηλειές, τό τ' ἔπειτα παρίσταται ἀνθρώποισιν,
οὐλόμενον, καματηρόν, ὅτε στυγέουσι θεοί περ.
Αὐτὰρ ἐμοὶ μέγ' ὄνειδος ἐν ἀθανάτοισι θεοῖσιν
ἔσσεται ἤματα πάντα διαμπερὲς εἵνεκα σεῖο,
οἳ πρὶν ἐμοὺς ὀάρους καὶ μήτιας, αἷς ποτε πάντας
ἀθανάτους συνέμιξα καταθνητῇσι γυναιξί,
τάρβεσκον· πάντας γὰρ ἐμὸν δάμνασκε νόημα.
νῦν δὲ δὴ οὐκέτι μοι στόμα χείσεται [2] ἐξονομῆναι
τοῦτο μετ' ἀθανάτοισιν, ἐπεὶ μάλα πολλὸν ἀάσθην,
σχέτλιον, οὐκ ὀνοταστόν,[3] ἀπεπλάγχθην δὲ νόοιο,
παῖδα δ' ὑπὸ ζώνῃ ἐθέμην βροτῷ εὐνηθεῖσα.

[1] Wolf: ῥεῖ, MSS. [2] Martin: στοναχήσεται, MSS.
[3] Clarke: ὀνοτατόν, MSS.

of Ocean, at the ends of the earth; but when the first grey hairs began to ripple from his comely head and noble chin, queenly Eos kept away from his bed, though she cherished him in her house and nourished him with food and ambrosia and gave him rich clothing. But when loathsome old age pressed full upon him, and he could not move nor lift his limbs, this seemed to her in her heart the best counsel: she laid him in a room and put to the shining doors. There he babbles endlessly, and no more has strength at all, such as once he had in his supple limbs.

I would not have you be deathless among the deathless gods and live continually after such sort. Yet if you could live on such as now you are in look and in form, and be called my husband, sorrow would not then enfold my careful heart. But, as it is, harsh[1] old age will soon enshroud you—ruthless age which stands someday at the side of every man, deadly, wearying, dreaded even by the gods.

And now because of you I shall have great shame among the deathless gods henceforth, continually. For until now they feared my jibes and the wiles by which, or soon or late, I mated all the immortals with mortal women, making them all subject to my will. But now my mouth shall no more have this power among the gods; for very great has been my madness, my miserable and dreadful madness, and I went astray out of my mind who have gotten a child beneath my girdle, mating with a mortal man.

[1] So Christ connecting the word with *ὠμός*. L. and S. give = *ὁμοῖος*, "common to all."

τὸν μέν, ἐπὴν δὴ πρῶτον ἴδῃ φάος ἠελίοιο,
Νύμφαι μιν θρέψουσιν ὀρεσκῷοι βαθύκολποι,
αἳ τόδε ναιετάουσιν ὄρος μέγα τε ζάθεόν τε·
αἵ ῥ' οὔτε θνητοῖς οὔτ' ἀθανάτοισιν ἕπονται.
δηρὸν μὲν ζώουσι καὶ ἄμβροτον εἶδαρ ἔδουσι
καί τε μετ' ἀθανάτοισι καλὸν χορὸν ἐρρώσαντο.
τῇσι δὲ Σειληνοὶ καὶ ἐύσκοπος Ἀργειφόντης
μίσγοντ' ἐν φιλότητι μυχῷ σπείων ἐροέντων.
τῇσι δ' ἅμ' ἢ ἐλάται ἠὲ δρύες ὑψικάρηνοι
γεινομένῃσιν ἔφυσαν ἐπὶ χθονὶ βωτιανείρῃ,
καλαί, τηλεθάουσαι, ἐν οὔρεσιν ὑψηλοῖσιν.
ἑστᾶσ' ἠλίβατοι, τεμένη δέ ἑ κικλήσκουσιν
ἀθανάτων· τὰς δ' οὔ τι βροτοὶ κείρουσι σιδήρῳ·
ἀλλ' ὅτε κεν δὴ μοῖρα παρεστήκῃ θανάτοιο,
ἀζάνεται μὲν πρῶτον ἐπὶ χθονὶ δένδρεα καλά,
φλοιὸς δ' ἀμφιπεριφθινύθει, πίπτουσι δ' ἄπ' ὄζοι,
τῶν δέ θ' ὁμοῦ ψυχὴ λείπει φάος ἠελίοιο.
αἳ μὲν ἐμὸν θρέψουσι παρὰ σφίσιν υἱὸν ἔχουσαι.
τὸν μὲν ἐπὴν δὴ πρῶτον ἕλῃ πολυήρατος ἥβη,
ἄξουσίν σοι δεῦρο θεαὶ δείξουσί τε παῖδα.
σοὶ δ' ἐγώ, ὄφρα κε ταῦτα μετὰ φρεσὶ πάντα διέλθω,
ἐς πέμπτον ἔτος αὖτις ἐλεύσομαι υἱὸν ἄγουσα.
τὸν μὲν ἐπὴν δὴ πρῶτον ἴδῃς θάλος ὀφθαλμοῖσι,
γηθήσεις ὁρόων· μάλα γὰρ θεοείκελος ἔσται·
ἄξεις δ' αὐτίκα νιν ποτὶ Ἴλιον ἠνεμόεσσαν.
ἢν δέ τις εἴρηταί σε καταθνητῶν ἀνθρώπων,
ἥ τις σοι φίλον υἱὸν ὑπὸ ζώνῃ θέτο μήτηρ,
τῷ δὲ σὺ μυθεῖσθαι μεμνημένος, ὥς σε κελεύω·
φάσθαι[1] τοι Νύμφης καλυκώπιδος ἔκγονον εἶναι,
αἳ τόδε ναιετάουσιν ὄρος καταειμένον ὕλῃ.

[1] Matthiae: φασί, MSS.

As for the child, as soon as he sees the light of the sun, the deep-breasted mountain Nymphs who inhabit this great and holy mountain shall bring him up. They rank neither with mortals nor with immortals: long indeed do they live, eating heavenly food and treading the lovely dance among the immortals, and with them the Sileni and the sharp-eyed Slayer of Argus mate in the depths of pleasant caves; but at their birth pines or high-topped oaks spring up with them upon the fruitful earth, beautiful, flourishing trees, towering high upon the lofty mountains (and men call them holy places of the immortals, and never mortal lops them with the axe); but when the fate of death is near at hand, first those lovely trees wither where they stand, and the bark shrivels away about them, and the twigs fall down, and at last the life of the Nymph and of the tree leave the light of the sun together. These Nymphs shall keep my son with them and rear him, and, as soon as he is come to lovely boyhood, the goddesses will bring him here to you and show you your child. But, that I may tell you all that I have in mind, I will come here again towards the fifth year and bring you my son. So soon as ever you have seen him—a scion to delight the eyes—, you will rejoice in beholding him; for he shall be most godlike: then bring him once to windy Ilion. And if any mortal man ask you who got your dear son beneath her girdle, remember to tell him as I bid you: say he is the offspring of one of the flower-like Nymphs who inhabit this forest-clad hill. But if you

εἰ δέ κεν ἐξείπῃς καὶ ἐπεύξεαι ἄφρονι θυμῷ
ἐν φιλότητι μιγῆναι ἐυστεφάνῳ Κυθερείῃ,
Ζεύς σε χολωσάμενος βαλέει ψολόεντι κεραυνῷ.
εἴρηταί τοι πάντα· σὺ δὲ φρεσὶ σῇσι νοήσας,
ἴσχεο μηδ' ὀνόμαινε, θεῶν δ' ἐποπίζεο μῆνιν.
Ὣς εἰποῦσ' ἤιξε πρὸς οὐρανὸν ἠνεμόεντα.
Χαῖρε, θεά, Κύπροιο ἐυκτιμένης μεδέουσα·
σεῦ δ' ἐγὼ ἀρξάμενος μεταβήσομαι ἄλλον ἐς ὕμνον.

VI

ΕΙΣ ΑΦΡΟΔΙΤΗΝ

Αἰδοίην, χρυσοστέφανον, καλὴν Ἀφροδίτην
ᾄσομαι, ἣ πάσης Κύπρου κρήδεμνα λέλογχεν
εἰναλίης, ὅθι μιν Ζεφύρου μένος ὑγρὸν ἀέντος
ἤνεικεν κατὰ κῦμα πολυφλοίσβοιο θαλάσσης
ἀφρῷ ἔνι μαλακῷ· τὴν δὲ χρυσάμπυκες Ὧραι
δέξαντ' ἀσπασίως, περὶ δ' ἄμβροτα εἵματα ἕσσαν·
κρατὶ δ' ἐπ' ἀθανάτῳ στεφάνην εὔτυκτον ἔθηκαν
καλήν, χρυσείην· ἐν δὲ τρητοῖσι λοβοῖσιν
ἄνθεμ' ὀρειχάλκου χρυσοῖό τε τιμήεντος·
δειρῇ δ' ἀμφ' ἁπαλῇ καὶ στήθεσιν ἀργυφέοισιν
ὅρμοισι χρυσέοισιν ἐκόσμεον, οἷσί περ αὐταὶ
Ὧραι κοσμείσθην χρυσάμπυκες, ὁππότ' ἴοιεν
ἐς χορὸν ἱμερόεντα θεῶν καὶ δώματα πατρός.
αὐτὰρ ἐπειδὴ πάντα περὶ χροῒ κόσμον ἔθηκαν,
ἦγον ἐς ἀθανάτους· οἱ δ' ἠσπάζοντο ἰδόντες
χερσί τ' ἐδεξιόωντο καὶ ἠρήσαντο ἕκαστος
εἶναι κουριδίην ἄλοχον καὶ οἴκαδ' ἄγεσθαι,
εἶδος θαυμάζοντες ἰοστεφάνου Κυθερείης.

tell all and foolishly boast that you lay with rich-crowned Aphrodite, Zeus will smite you in his anger with a smoking thunderbolt. Now I have told you all. Take heed: refrain and name me not, but have regard to the anger of the gods."

When the goddess had so spoken, she soared up to windy heaven.

Hail, goddess, queen of well-builded Cyprus with you have I begun; now I will turn me to another hymn.

VI

TO APHRODITE

I WILL sing of stately Aphrodite, gold-crowned and beautiful, whose dominion is the walled cities of all sea-set Cyprus. There the moist breath of the western wind wafted her over the waves of the loud-moaning sea in soft foam, and there the gold-filleted Hours welcomed her joyously. They clothed her with heavenly garments: on her head they put a fine, well-wrought crown of gold, and in her pierced ears they hung ornaments of orichalc and precious gold, and adorned her with golden necklaces over her soft neck and snow-white breasts, jewels which the gold-filleted Hours wear themselves whenever they go to their father's house to join the lovely dances of the gods. And when they had fully decked her, they brought her to the gods, who welcomed her when they saw her, giving her their hands. Each one of them prayed that he might lead her home to be his wedded wife, so greatly were they amazed at the beauty of violet-crowned Cytherea.

Χαῖρ' ἑλικοβλέφαρε, γλυκυμείλιχε· δὸς δ' ἐν ἀγῶνι
νίκην τῷδε φέρεσθαι, ἐμὴν δ' ἔντυνον ἀοιδήν.
αὐτὰρ ἐγὼ καὶ σεῖο καὶ ἄλλης μνήσομ' ἀοιδῆς.

VII

ΕΙΣ ΔΙΟΝΥΣΟΝ

Ἀμφὶ Διώνυσον, Σεμέλης ἐρικυδέος υἱόν,
μνήσομαι, ὡς ἐφάνη παρὰ θῖν' ἁλὸς ἀτρυγέτοιο
ἀκτῇ ἔπι προβλῆτι νεηνίῃ ἀνδρὶ ἐοικώς,
πρωθήβῃ· καλαὶ δὲ περισσείοντο ἔθειραι,
κυάνεαι, φᾶρος δὲ περὶ στιβαροῖς ἔχεν ὤμοις
πορφύρεον· τάχα δ' ἄνδρες ἐυσσέλμου ἀπὸ νηὸς
λῃσταὶ προγένοντο θοῶς ἐπὶ οἴνοπα πόντον,
Τυρσηνοί· τοὺς δ' ἦγε κακὸς μόρος· οἳ δὲ ἰδόντες
νεῦσαν ἐς ἀλλήλους, τάχα δ' ἔκθορον. αἶψα δ' ἑλόντες
εἷσαν ἐπὶ σφετέρης νηὸς κεχαρημένοι ἦτορ.
υἱὸν γάρ μιν ἔφαντο διοτρεφέων βασιλήων
εἶναι καὶ δεσμοῖς ἔθελον δεῖν ἀργαλέοισι.
τὸν δ' οὐκ ἴσχανε δεσμά, λύγοι δ' ἀπὸ τηλόσε πῖπτον
χειρῶν ἠδὲ ποδῶν· ὃ δὲ μειδιάων ἐκάθητο
ὄμμασι κυανέοισι· κυβερνήτης δὲ νοήσας
αὐτίκα οἷς ἑτάροισιν ἐκέκλετο φώνησέν τε·
Δαιμόνιοι, τίνα τόνδε θεὸν δεσμεύεθ' ἑλόντες,
καρτερόν; οὐδὲ φέρειν δύναταί μιν νηῦς εὐεργής.
ἢ γὰρ Ζεὺς ὅδε γ' ἐστὶν ἢ ἀργυρότοξος Ἀπόλλων
ἠὲ Ποσειδάων· ἐπεὶ οὐ θνητοῖσι βροτοῖσιν

Hail, sweetly-winning, coy-eyed goddess! Grant that I may gain the victory in this contest, and order you my song. And now I will remember you and another song also.

VII

TO DIONYSUS

I WILL tell of Dionysus, the son of glorious Semele, how he appeared on a jutting headland by the shore of the fruitless sea, seeming like a stripling in the first flush of manhood: his rich, dark hair was waving about him, and on his strong shoulders he wore a purple robe. Presently there came swiftly over the sparkling sea Tyrsenian[1] pirates on a well-decked ship—a miserable doom led them on. When they saw him they made signs to one another and sprang out quickly, and seizing him straightway, put him on board their ship exultingly; for they thought him the son of heaven-nurtured kings. They sought to bind him with rude bonds, but the bonds would not hold him, and the withes fell far away from his hands and feet: and he sat with a smile in his dark eyes. Then the helmsman understood all and cried out at once to his fellows and said:

"Madmen! what god is this whom you have taken and bind, strong that he is? Not even the well-built ship can carry him. Surely this is either Zeus or Apollo who has the silver bow, or Poseidon, for he looks not like mortal men but like the gods

[1] Probably not Etruscans, but the non-Hellenic peoples of Thrace and (according to Thucydides) of Lemnos and Athens. Cp. Herodotus i. 57; Thucydides iv. 109.

εἴκελος, ἀλλὰ θεοῖς, οἳ Ὀλύμπια δώματ' ἔχουσιν.
ἀλλ' ἄγετ', αὐτὸν ἀφῶμεν ἐπ' ἠπείροιο μελαίνης
αὐτίκα· μηδ' ἐπὶ χεῖρας ἰάλλετε, μή τι χολωθεὶς
ὄρσῃ ἔπ' ἀργαλέους τ' ἀνέμους καὶ λαίλαπα πολλήν.
῝Ως φάτο· τὸν δ' ἀρχὸς στυγερῷ ἠνίπαπε μύθῳ·
δαιμόνι', οὖρον ὅρα, ἅμα δ' ἱστίον ἕλκεο νηὸς
σύμπανθ' ὅπλα λαβών· ὅδε δ' αὖτ' ἄνδρεσσι μελήσει.
ἔλπομαι, ἢ Αἴγυπτον ἀφίξεται ἢ ὅ γε Κύπρον
ἢ ἐς Ὑπερβορέους ἢ ἑκαστέρω· ἐς δὲ τελευτὴν
ἔκ ποτ' ἐρεῖ αὐτοῦ τε φίλους καὶ κτήματα πάντα
οὕς τε κασιγνήτους, ἐπεὶ ἡμῖν ἔμβαλε δαίμων.
῝Ως εἰπὼν ἱστόν τε καὶ ἱστίον ἕλκετο νηός.
ἔμπνευσεν δ' ἄνεμος μέσον ἱστίον· ἀμφὶ δ' ἄρ' ὅπλα
καττάνυσαν· τάχα δέ σφιν ἐφαίνετο θαυματὰ ἔργα.
οἶνος μὲν πρώτιστα θοὴν ἀνὰ νῆα μέλαιναν
ἡδύποτος κελάρυζ' εὐώδης, ὤρνυτο δ' ὀδμὴ
ἀμβροσίη· ναύτας δὲ τάφος λάβε πάντας ἰδόντας.
αὐτίκα δ' ἀκρότατον παρὰ ἱστίον ἐξετανύσθη
ἄμπελος ἔνθα καὶ ἔνθα, κατεκρημνῶντο δὲ πολλοὶ
βότρυες· ἀμφ' ἱστὸν δὲ μέλας εἱλίσσετο κισσός,
ἄνθεσι τηλεθάων, χαρίεις δ' ἐπὶ καρπὸς ὀρώρει·
πάντες δὲ σκαλμοὶ στεφάνους ἔχον· οἳ δὲ ἰδόντες,
νῆ' ἤδη[1] τότ' ἔπειτα κυβερνήτην ἐκέλευον
γῇ πελάαν· ὃ δ' ἄρα σφι λέων γένετ' ἔνδοθι νηὸς
δεινὸς ἐπ' ἀκροτάτης, μέγα δ' ἔβραχεν, ἐν δ' ἄρα μέσσῃ
ἄρκτον ἐποίησεν λασιαύχενα, σήματα φαίνων·
ἂν δ' ἔστη μεμαυῖα· λέων δ' ἐπὶ σέλματος ἄκρου
δεινὸν ὑπόδρα ἰδών· οἳ δ' ἐς πρύμνην ἐφόβηθεν,

[1] Hermann: μὴ δ' ἤδη, M (other MSS. are further corrupted).

who dwell on Olympus. Come, then, let us set him free upon the dark shore at once: do not lay hands on him, lest he grow angry and stir up dangerous winds and heavy squalls."

So said he: but the master chid him with taunting words: "Madman, mark the wind and help hoist sail on the ship: catch all the sheets. As for this fellow we men will see to him: I reckon he is bound for Egypt or for Cyprus or to the Hyperboreans or further still. But in the end he will speak out and tell us his friends and all his wealth and his brothers, now that providence has thrown him in our way."

When he had said this, he had mast and sail hoisted on the ship, and the wind filled the sail and the crew hauled taut the sheets on either side. But soon strange things were seen among them. First of all sweet, fragrant wine ran streaming throughout all the black ship and a heavenly smell arose, so that all the seamen were seized with amazement when they saw it. And all at once a vine spread out both ways along the top of the sail with many clusters hanging down from it, and a dark ivy-plant twined about the mast, blossoming with flowers, and with rich berries growing on it; and all the thole-pins were covered with garlands. When the pirates saw all this, then at last they bade the helmsman to put the ship to land. But the god changed into a dreadful lion there on the ship, in the bows, and roared loudly: amidships also he showed his wonders and created a shaggy bear which stood up ravening, while on the forepeak was the lion glaring fiercely with scowling brows. And so the sailors fled into the

ἀμφὶ κυβερνήτην δὲ σαόφρονα θυμὸν ἔχοντα
ἔσταν ἄρ' ἐκπληγέντες· ὁ δ' ἐξαπίνης ἐπορούσας
ἀρχὸν ἕλ', οἱ δὲ θύραζε κακὸν μόρον ἐξαλύοντες
πάντες ὁμῶς πήδησαν, ἐπεὶ ἴδον, εἰς ἅλα δῖαν,
δελφῖνες δ' ἐγένοντο· κυβερνήτην δ' ἐλεήσας
ἔσχεθε καί μιν ἔθηκε πανόλβιον εἶπέ τε μῦθον·
Θάρσει,†δῖε κάτωρ†, τῷ ἐμῷ κεχαρισμένε θυμῷ·
εἰμὶ δ' ἐγὼ Διόνυσος ἐρίβρομος, ὃν τέκε μήτηρ
Καδμηὶς Σεμέλη Διὸς ἐν φιλότητι μιγεῖσα.
Χαῖρε, τέκος Σεμέλης εὐώπιδος· οὐδέ πη ἔστι
σεῖό γε ληθόμενον γλυκερὴν κοσμῆσαι ἀοιδήν.

VIII

ΕΙΣ ΑΡΕΑ

Ἆρες ὑπερμενέτα, βρισάρματε, χρυσεοπήληξ,
ὀβριμόθυμε, φέρασπι, πολισσόε, χαλκοκορυστά,
καρτερόχειρ, ἀμόγητε, δορισθενές, ἕρκος Ὀλύμπου,
Νίκης εὐπολέμοιο πάτερ, συναρωγὲ Θέμιστος,
ἀντιβίοισι τύραννε, δικαιοτάτων ἀγὲ φωτῶν,
ἠνορέης σκηπτοῦχε, πυραυγέα κύκλον ἑλίσσων
αἰθέρος ἑπταπόροις ἐνὶ τείρεσιν, ἔνθα σε πῶλοι
ζαφλεγέες τριτάτης ὑπὲρ ἄντυγος αἰὲν ἔχουσι·
κλῦθι, βροτῶν ἐπίκουρε, δοτὴρ εὐθαρσέος[1] ἥβης,
πρηὺ καταστίλβων σέλας ὑψόθεν ἐς βιότητα
ἡμετέρην καὶ κάρτος ἀρήιον, ὥς κε δυναίμην
σεύασθαι κακότητα πικρὴν ἀπ' ἐμοῖο καρήνου,
καὶ ψυχῆς ἀπατηλὸν ὑπογνάμψαι φρεσὶν ὁρμήν,

[1] M: εὐθαλέος "flourishing," ET.

stern and crowded bemused about the right-minded helmsman, until suddenly the lion sprang upon the master and seized him; and when the sailors saw it they leapt out overboard one and all into the bright sea, escaping from a miserable fate, and were changed into dolphins. But on the helmsman Dionysus had mercy and held him back and made him altogether happy, saying to him:

"Take courage, good . . .; you have found favour with my heart. I am loud-crying Dionysus whom Cadmus' daughter Semele bare of union with Zeus."

Hail, child of fair-faced Semele! He who forgets you can in no wise order sweet song.

VIII

TO ARES

Ares, exceeding in strength, chariot-rider, golden-helmed, doughty in heart, shield-bearer, Saviour of cities, harnessed in bronze, strong of arm, unwearying, mighty with the spear, O defence of Olympus, father of warlike Victory, ally of Themis, stern governor of the rebellious, leader of righteous men, sceptred King of manliness, who whirl your fiery sphere among the planets in their sevenfold courses through the aether wherein your blazing steeds ever bear you above the third firmament of heaven; hear me, helper of men, giver of dauntless youth! Shed down a kindly ray from above upon my life, and strength of war, that I may be able to drive away bitter cowardice from my head and crush down the deceitful impulses of my soul. Restrain

θυμοῦ τ' αὖ μένος ὀξὺ κατισχέμεν, ὅς μ' ἐρέθῃσι
φυλόπιδος κρυερῆς ἐπιβαινέμεν· ἀλλὰ σὺ θάρσος
δός, μάκαρ, εἰρήνης τε μένειν ἐν ἀπήμοσι θεσμοῖς
δυσμενέων προφυγόντα μόθον Κῆράς τε βιαίους.

IX

ΕΙΣ ΑΡΤΕΜΙΝ

Ἄρτεμιν ὕμνει, Μοῦσα, κασιγνήτην Ἑκάτοιο,
παρθένον ἰοχέαιραν, ὁμότροφον Ἀπόλλωνος,
ἥθ' ἵππους ἄρσασα βαθυσχοίνοιο Μέλητος
ῥίμφα διὰ Σμύρνης παγχρύσεον ἅρμα διώκει
ἐς Κλάρον ἀμπελόεσσαν, ὅθ' ἀργυρότοξος Ἀπόλλων
ἧσται μιμνάζων ἑκατηβόλον ἰοχέαιραν.
Καὶ σὺ μὲν οὕτω χαῖρε θεαί θ' ἅμα πᾶσαι ἀοιδῇ·
αὐτὰρ ἐγώ σε πρῶτα καὶ ἐκ σέθεν ἄρχομ' ἀείδειν,
σεῦ δ' ἐγὼ ἀρξάμενος μεταβήσομαι ἄλλον ἐς ὕμνον.

X

ΕΙΣ ΑΦΡΟΔΙΤΗΝ

Κυπρογενῆ Κυθέρειαν ἀείσομαι, ἥτε βροτοῖσι
μείλιχα δῶρα δίδωσιν, ἐφ' ἱμερτῷ δὲ προσώπῳ
αἰεὶ μειδιάει καὶ ἐφ' ἱμερτὸν θέει ἄνθος.
Χαῖρε, θεά, Σαλαμῖνος[1] ἐυκτιμένης μεδέουσα
εἰναλίης τε Κύπρου· δὸς δ' ἱμερόεσσαν ἀοιδήν.
αὐτὰρ ἐγὼ καὶ σεῖο καὶ ἄλλης μνήσομ' ἀοιδῆς.

[1] All MSS. save M which has χαῖρε μάκαιρα, Κυθήρης, "hail, blessed one, (queen of) Cythera."

also the keen fury of my heart which provokes me to tread the ways of blood-curdling strife. Rather, O blessed one, give you me boldness to abide within the harmless laws of peace, avoiding strife and hatred and the violent fiends of death.

IX

TO ARTEMIS

Muse, sing of Artemis, sister of the Far-shooter, the virgin who delights in arrows, who was fostered with Apollo. She waters her horses from Meles deep in reeds, and swiftly drives her all-golden chariot through Smyrna to vine-clad Claros where Apollo, god of the silver bow, sits waiting for the far-shooting goddess who delights in arrows.

And so hail to you, Artemis, in my song and to all goddesses as well. Of you first I sing and with you I begin; now that I have begun with you, I will turn to another song.

X

TO APHRODITE

Of Cytherea, born in Cyprus, I will sing. She gives kindly gifts to men: smiles are ever on her lovely face, and lovely is the brightness that plays over it.

Hail, goddess, queen of well-built Salamis and sea-girt Cyprus; grant me a cheerful song. And now I will remember you and another song also.

XI

ΕΙΣ ΑΘΗΝΑΝ

Παλλάδ' Ἀθηναίην ἐρυσίπτολιν ἄρχομ' ἀείδειν,
δεινήν, ᾗ σὺν Ἄρηι μέλει πολεμήια ἔργα
περθόμεναί τε πόληες ἀϋτή τε πτόλεμοί τε,
καί τ' ἐρρύσατο λαὸν ἰόντα τε νισσόμενόν τε.
Χαῖρε, θεά, δὸς δ' ἄμμι τύχην εὐδαιμονίην τε.

XII

ΕΙΣ ΗΡΑΝ

Ἥρην ἀείδω χρυσόθρονον, ἣν τέκε Ῥείη,
ἀθανάτων[1] βασίλειαν, ὑπείροχον εἶδος ἔχουσαν,
Ζηνὸς ἐριγδούποιο κασιγνήτην ἄλοχόν τε,
κυδρήν, ἣν πάντες μάκαρες κατὰ μακρὸν Ὄλυμπον
ἁζόμενοι τίουσιν ὁμῶς Διὶ τερπικεραύνῳ.

XIII

ΕΙΣ ΔΗΜΗΤΡΑΝ

Δημήτηρ' ἠύκομον, σεμνὴν θεάν, ἄρχομ' ἀείδειν,
αὐτὴν καὶ κούρην, περικαλλέα Περσεφόνειαν.
Χαῖρε, θεά, καὶ τήνδε σάου πόλιν· ἄρχε δ' ἀοιδῆς.

[1] Matthiae: ἀθανάτην, MSS.

XI

TO ATHENA

Of Pallas Athene, guardian of the city, I begin to sing. Dread is she, and with Ares she loves deeds of war, the sack of cities and the shouting and the battle. It is she who saves the people as they go out to war and come back.

Hail, goddess, and give us good fortune with happiness!

XII

TO HERA

I sing of golden-throned Hera whom Rhea bare. Queen of the immortals is she, surpassing all in beauty: she is the sister and the wife of loud-thundering Zeus,—the glorious one whom all the blessed throughout high Olympus reverence and honour even as Zeus who delights in thunder.

XIII

'O DEMETER

I begin to sing of rich-haired Demeter, awful ɔddess, of her and of her daughter lovely ersephone.

Hail, goddess! Keep this city safe, and govern y son

XIV

ΕΙΣ ΜΗΤΕΡΑ ΘΕΩΝ

Μητέρα μοι πάντων τε θεῶν πάντων τ' ἀνθρώπων
ὕμνει, Μοῦσα λίγεια, Διὸς θυγάτηρ μεγάλοιο,
ᾗ κροτάλων τυπάνων τ' ἰαχὴ σύν τε βρόμος αὐλῶν
εὔαδεν ἠδὲ λύκων κλαγγὴ χαροπῶν τε λεόντων
οὔρεά τ' ἠχήεντα καὶ ὑλήεντες ἔναυλοι.
Καὶ σὺ μὲν οὕτω χαῖρε θεαί θ' ἅμα πᾶσαι ἀοιδῇ.

XV

ΕΙΣ ΗΡΑΚΛΕΑ ΛΕΟΝΤΟΘΥΜΟΝ

Ἡρακλέα, Διὸς υἱόν, ἀείσομαι, ὃν μέγ' ἄριστον
γείνατ' ἐπιχθονίων Θήβῃς ἔνι καλλιχόροισιν
Ἀλκμήνη μιχθεῖσα κελαινεφέι Κρονίωνι·
ὃς πρὶν μὲν κατὰ γαῖαν ἀθέσφατον ἠδὲ θάλασσαν
πλαζόμενος πομπῇσιν ὕπ' Εὐρυσθῆος ἄνακτος [1]
πολλὰ μὲν αὐτὸς ἔρεξεν ἀτάσθαλα, πολλὰ δ' ἀνέτλη·[2]
νῦν δ' ἤδη κατὰ καλὸν ἕδος νιφόεντος Ὀλύμπου
ναίει τερπόμενος καὶ ἔχει καλλίσφυρον Ἥβην.
Χαῖρε, ἄναξ, Διὸς υἱέ· δίδου δ' ἀρετήν τε καὶ ὄλβον.

[1] Most MSS. : πημαίνετ' ἀεθλεύων <δε> κραταιῶς, M.
[2] Most MSS. : ἔξοχα ἔργα, M.

XIV

TO THE MOTHER OF THE GODS

I PRITHEE, clear-voiced Muse, daughter of mighty Zeus, sing of the mother of all gods and men. She is well-pleased with the sound of rattles and of timbrels, with the voice of flutes and the outcry of wolves and bright-eyed lions, with echoing hills and wooded coombes.

And so hail to you in my song and to all goddesses as well!

XV

TO HERACLES THE LION-HEARTED

I WILL sing of Heracles, the son of Zeus and much the mightiest of men on earth. Alcmena bare him in Thebes, the city of lovely dances, when the dark-clouded Son of Cronos had lain with her. Once he used to wander over unmeasured tracts of land and sea at the bidding of King Eurystheus, and himself did many deeds of violence and endured many; but now he lives happily in the glorious home of snowy Olympus, and has neat-ankled Hebe for his wife.

Hail, lord, son of Zeus! Give me success and prosperity.

XVI

ΕΙΣ ΑΣΚΛΗΠΙΟΝ

Ἰητῆρα νόσων Ἀσκληπιὸν ἄρχομ' ἀείδειν,
υἱὸν Ἀπόλλωνος, τὸν ἐγείνατο δῖα Κορωνὶς
Δωτίῳ ἐν πεδίῳ, κούρη Φλεγύου βασιλῆος,
χάρμα μέγ' ἀνθρώποισι, κακῶν θελκτῆρ' ὀδυνάων.
Καὶ σὺ μὲν οὕτω χαῖρε, ἄναξ· λίτομαι δέ σ' ἀοιδῇ.

XVII

ΕΙΣ ΔΙΟΣΚΟΥΡΟΥΣ

Κάστορα καὶ Πολυδεύκε' ἀείσεο, Μοῦσα λίγεια,
Τυνδαρίδας, οἳ Ζηνὸς Ὀλυμπίου ἐξεγένοντο·
τοὺς ὑπὸ Τηϋγέτου κορυφῆς τέκε πότνια Λήδη
λάθρη ὑποδμηθεῖσα κελαινεφέι Κρονίωνι.
Χαίρετε, Τυνδαρίδαι, ταχέων ἐπιβήτορες ἵππων.

XVIII

ΕΙΣ ΕΡΜΗΝ

Ἑρμῆν ἀείδω Κυλλήνιον, Ἀργειφόντην,
Κυλλήνης μεδέοντα καὶ Ἀρκαδίης πολυμήλου,
ἄγγελον ἀθανάτων ἐριούνιον, ὃν τέκε Μαῖα,
Ἄτλαντος θυγάτηρ, Διὸς ἐν φιλότητι μιγεῖσα,
αἰδοίη· μακάρων δὲ θεῶν ἀλέεινεν ὅμιλον,
ἄντρῳ ναιετάουσα παλισκίῳ· ἔνθα Κρονίων
νύμφῃ ἐυπλοκάμῳ μισγέσκετο νυκτὸς ἀμολγῷ,

XVI

TO ASCLEPIUS

I BEGIN to sing of Asclepius, son of Apollo and healer of sicknesses. In the Dotian plain fair Coronis, daughter of King Phlegyas, bare him, a great joy to men, a soother of cruel pangs.

And so hail to you, lord: in my song I make my prayer to thee!

XVII

TO THE DIOSCURI

SING, clear-voiced Muse, of Castor and Polydeuces, the Tyndaridae, who sprang from Olympian Zeus. Beneath the heights of Taÿgetus stately Leda bare them, when the dark-clouded Son of Cronos had privily bent her to his will.

Hail, children of Tyndareus, riders upon swift horses!

XVIII

TO HERMES

I SING of Cyllenian Hermes, the Slayer of Argus, lord of Cyllene and Arcadia rich in flocks, luck-bringing messenger of the deathless gods. He was born of Maia, the daughter of Atlas, when she had mated with Zeus,—a shy goddess she. Ever she avoided the throng of the blessed gods and lived in a shadowy cave, and there the Son of Cronos used to lie with the rich-tressed nymph at dead

εὖτε κατὰ γλυκὺς ὕπνος ἔχοι λευκώλενον Ἥρην·
λάνθανε δ' ἀθανάτους τε θεοὺς θνητούς τ' ἀνθρώπους.
Καὶ σὺ μὲν οὕτω χαῖρε, Διὸς καὶ Μαιάδος υἱέ·
σεῦ δ' ἐγὼ ἀρξάμενος μεταβήσομαι ἄλλον ἐς ὕμνον.
[χαῖρ', Ἑρμῆ χαριδῶτα, διάκτορε, δῶτορ ἐάων.[1]]

XIX

ΕΙΣ ΠΑΝΑ

Ἀμφί μοι Ἑρμείαο φίλον γόνον ἔννεπε, Μοῦσα,
αἰγιπόδην, δικέρωτα, φιλόκροτον, ὅστ' ἀνὰ πίση
δενδρήεντ' ἄμυδις φοιτᾷ χοροηθέσι νύμφαις,
αἵ τε κατ' αἰγίλιπος πέτρης στείβουσι κάρηνα
Πᾶν' ἀνακεκλόμεναι, νόμιον θεόν, ἀγλαέθειρον,
αὐχμήενθ', ὃς πάντα λόφον νιφόεντα λέλογχε
καὶ κορυφὰς ὀρέων καὶ πετρήεντα κάρηνα.
φοιτᾷ δ' ἔνθα καὶ ἔνθα διὰ ῥωπήια πυκνά,
ἄλλοτε μὲν ῥείθροισιν ἐφελκόμενος μαλακοῖσιν,
ἄλλοτε δ' αὖ πέτρῃσιν ἐν ἠλιβάτοισι διοιχνεῖ,
ἀκροτάτην κορυφὴν μηλοσκόπον εἰσαναβαίνων.
πολλάκι δ' ἀργινόεντα διέδραμεν οὔρεα μακρά,
πολλάκι δ' ἐν κνημοῖσι διήλασε θῆρας ἐναίρων,
ὀξέα δερκόμενος· τότε δ' ἕσπερος ἔκλαγεν οἶον
ἄγρης ἐξανιών, δονάκων ὕπο μοῦσαν ἀθύρων
νήδυμον· οὐκ ἂν τόν γε παραδράμοι ἐν μελέεσσιν
ὄρνις, ἥτ' ἔαρος πολυανθέος ἐν πετάλοισι
θρῆνον ἐπιπροχέουσ' ἀχέει[2] μελίγηρυν ἀοιδήν.
σὺν δέ σφιν τότε Νύμφαι ὀρεστιάδες λιγύμολποι

[1] This line appears to be an alternative to ll. 10–11.
[2] Ilgen: ἐπιπροχέουσα χέει, MSS.

of night, while white-armed Hera lay bound in sweet sleep: and neither deathless god nor mortal man knew it.

And so hail to you, Son of Zeus and Maia; with you I have begun: now I will turn to another song!

Hail, Hermes, giver of grace, guide, and giver of good things!

XIX

TO PAN

Muse, tell me about Pan, the dear son of Hermes, with his goat's feet and two horns—a lover of merry noise. Through wooded glades he wanders with dancing nymphs who foot it on some sheer cliff's edge, calling upon Pan, the shepherd-god, long-haired, unkempt. He has every snowy crest and the mountain peaks and rocky crests for his domain; hither and thither he goes through the close thickets, now lured by soft streams, and now he presses on amongst towering crags and climbs up to the highest peak that overlooks the flocks. Often he courses through the glistening high mountains, and often on the shouldered hills he speeds along slaying wild beasts, this keen-eyed god. Only at evening, as he returns from the chase, he sounds his note, playing sweet and low on his pipes of reed: not even she could excel him in melody—that bird who in flower-laden spring pouring forth her lament utters honey-voiced song amid the leaves. At that hour the clear-voiced nymphs are with him

φοιτῶσαι πύκα ποσσὶν ἐπὶ κρήνῃ μελανύδρῳ
μέλπονται· κορυφὴν δὲ περιστένει οὔρεος Ἠχώ·
δαίμων δ' ἔνθα καὶ ἔνθα χορῶν, τοτὲ δ' ἐς μέσον ἕρπων,
πυκνὰ ποσὶν διέπει, λαῖφος δ' ἐπὶ νῶτα δαφοινὸν
λυγκὸς ἔχει, λιγυρῇσιν ἀγαλλόμενος φρένα μολπαῖς
ἐν μαλακῷ λειμῶνι, τόθι κρόκος ἠδ' ὑάκινθος
εὐώδης θαλέθων καταμίσγεται ἄκριτα ποίῃ.
  Ὑμνεῦσιν δὲ θεοὺς μάκαρας καὶ μακρὸν Ὄλυμπον·
οἷόν θ' Ἑρμείην ἐριούνιον ἔξοχον ἄλλων
ἔννεπον, ὡς ὅ γ' ἅπασι θεοῖς θοὸς ἄγγελός ἐστι,
καί ῥ' ὅ γ' ἐς Ἀρκαδίην πολυπίδακα, μητέρα μήλων,
ἐξίκετ', ἔνθα τέ οἱ τέμενος Κυλληνίου ἐστίν.
ἔνθ' ὅ γε καὶ θεὸς ὢν ψαφαρότριχα μῆλ' ἐνόμευεν
ἀνδρὶ πάρα θνητῷ· θάλε γὰρ πόθος ὑγρὸς ἐπελθὼν
νύμφῃ ἐυπλοκάμῳ Δρύοπος φιλότητι μιγῆναι·
ἐκ δ' ἐτέλεσσε γάμον θαλερόν. τέκε δ' ἐν μεγάροισιν
Ἑρμείῃ φίλον υἱόν, ἄφαρ τερατωπὸν ἰδέσθαι,
αἰγιπόδην, δικέρωτα, φιλόκροτον, ἡδυγέλωτα·
φεῦγε δ' ἀναΐξασα, λίπεν δ' ἄρα παῖδα τιθήνη·
δεῖσε γάρ, ὡς ἴδεν ὄψιν ἀμείλιχον, ἠυγένειον.
τὸν δ' αἶψ' Ἑρμείας ἐριούνιος εἰς χέρα θῆκε
δεξάμενος, χαῖρεν δὲ νόῳ περιώσια δαίμων.
ῥίμφα δ' ἐς ἀθανάτων ἕδρας κίε παῖδα καλύψας
δέρμασιν ἐν πυκινοῖσιν ὀρεσκῴοιο λαγωοῦ·
πὰρ δὲ Ζηνὶ κάθιζε καὶ ἄλλοις ἀθανάτοισι,
δεῖξε δὲ κοῦρον ἑόν· πάντες δ' ἄρα θυμὸν ἔτερφθεν

with nimble feet, singing by some spring of dark water, while Echo wails about the mountain-top, and the god on this side or on that of the choirs, or at times sidling into the midst, plies it nimbly with his feet. On his back he wears a spotted lynx-pelt, and he delights in high-pitched songs in a soft meadow where crocuses and sweet-smelling hyacinths bloom at random in the grass.

They sing of the blessed gods and high Olympus and choose to tell of such an one as luck-bringing Hermes above the rest, how he is the swift messenger of all the gods, and how he came to Arcadia, the land of many springs and mother of flocks, there where his sacred place is as god of Cyllene. For there, though a god, he used to tend curly-fleeced sheep in the service of a mortal man, because there fell on him and waxed strong melting desire to wed the rich-tressed daughter of Dryops, and there he brought about the merry marriage. And in the house she bare Hermes a dear son who from his birth was marvellous to look upon, with goat's feet and two horns—a noisy, merry-laughing child. But when the nurse saw his uncouth face and full beard, she was afraid and sprang up and fled and left the child. Then luck-bringing Hermes received him and took him in his arms: very glad in his heart was the god. And he went quickly to the abodes of the deathless gods, carrying his son wrapped in warm skins of mountain hares, and set him down beside Zeus and showed him to the rest of the gods. Then all the immortals were glad in heart

ἀθάνατοι, περίαλλα δ' ὁ Βάκχειος Διόνυσος·
Πᾶνα δέ μιν καλέεσκον, ὅτι φρένα πᾶσιν ἔτερψε.
Καὶ σὺ μὲν οὕτω χαῖρε, ἄναξ, ἵλαμαι δέ σ' ἀοιδῇ·
αὐτὰρ ἐγὼ καὶ σεῖο καὶ ἄλλης μνήσομ' ἀοιδῆς.

XX

ΕΙΣ ΗΦΑΙΣΤΟΝ

Ἥφαιστον κλυτόμητιν ἀείσεο, Μοῦσα λίγεια,
ὃς μετ' Ἀθηναίης γλαυκώπιδος ἀγλαὰ ἔργα
ἀνθρώπους ἐδίδαξεν ἐπὶ χθονός, οἳ τὸ πάρος περ
ἄντροις ναιετάασκον ἐν οὔρεσιν, ἠύτε θῆρες.
νῦν δὲ δι' Ἥφαιστον κλυτοτέχνην ἔργα δαέντες
ῥηιδίως αἰῶνα τελεσφόρον εἰς ἐνιαυτὸν
εὔκηλοι διάγουσιν ἐνὶ σφετέροισι δόμοισιν.
Ἀλλ' ἵληθ', Ἥφαιστε· δίδου δ' ἀρετήν τε καὶ ὄλβον.

XXI

ΕΙΣ ΑΠΟΛΛΩΝΑ

Φοῖβε, σὲ μὲν καὶ κύκνος ὑπὸ πτερύγων λίγ' ἀείδει,
ὄχθῃ ἐπιθρώσκων ποταμὸν πάρα δινήεντα,
Πηνειόν· σὲ δ' ἀοιδὸς ἔχων φόρμιγγα λίγειαν
ἡδυεπὴς πρῶτόν τε καὶ ὕστατον αἰὲν ἀείδει.
Καὶ σὺ μὲν οὕτω χαῖρε, ἄναξ, ἵλαμαι δέ σ' ἀοιδῇ.

and Bacchic Dionysus in especial; and they called the boy Pan[1] because he delighted all their hearts.

And so hail to you, lord! I seek your favour with a song. And now I will remember you and another song also.

XX

TO HEPHAESTUS

Sing, clear-voiced Muse, of Hephaestus famed for inventions. With bright-eyed Athene he taught men glorious crafts throughout the world,—men who before used to dwell in caves in the mountains like wild beasts. But now that they have learned crafts through Hephaestus the famed worker, easily they live a peaceful life in their own houses the whole year round.

Be gracious, Hephaestus, and grant me success and prosperity!

XXI

TO APOLLO

Phoebus, of you even the swan sings with clear voice to the beating of his wings, as he alights upon the bank by the eddying river Peneus; and of you the sweet-tongued minstrel, holding his high-pitched lyre, always sings both first and last.

And so hail to you, lord! I seek your favour with my song.

[1] The name Pan is here derived from πάντες "all." Cp. Hesiod, *Works and Days* 80–82, *Hymn to Aphrodite* (v) 198, for the significance of personal names.

XXII

ΕΙΣ ΠΟΣΕΙΔΩΝΑ

Ἀμφὶ Ποσειδάωνα, μέγαν θεόν, ἄρχομ' ἀείδειν,
γαίης κινητῆρα καὶ ἀτρυγέτοιο θαλάσσης,
πόντιον, ὅσθ' Ἑλικῶνα καὶ εὐρείας ἔχει Αἰγάς.
διχθά τοι, Ἐννοσίγαιε, θεοὶ τιμὴν ἐδάσαντο,
ἵππων τε δμητῆρ' ἔμεναι σωτῆρά τε νηῶν.
Χαῖρε, Ποσείδαον γαιήοχε, κυανοχαῖτα,
καί, μάκαρ, εὐμενὲς ἦτορ ἔχων πλώουσιν ἄρηγε.

XXIII

ΕΙΣ ΥΠΑΤΟΝ ΚΡΟΝΙΔΗΝ

Ζῆνα θεῶν τὸν ἄριστον ἀείσομαι ἠδὲ μέγιστον,
εὐρύοπα, κρείοντα, τελεσφόρον, ὅστε Θέμιστι
ἐγκλιδὸν ἑζομένῃ πυκινοὺς ὀάρους ὀαρίζει.
Ἵληθ', εὐρύοπα Κρονίδη, κύδιστε μέγιστε.

XXIV

ΕΙΣ ΕΣΤΙΑΝ

Ἑστίη, ἥτε ἄνακτος Ἀπόλλωνος ἑκάτοιο
Πυθοῖ ἐν ἠγαθέῃ ἱερὸν δόμον ἀμφιπολεύεις,
αἰεὶ σῶν πλοκάμων ἀπολείβεται ὑγρὸν ἔλαιον·
ἔρχεο τόνδ' ἀνὰ οἶκον, ἔν' ἔρχεο[1] θυμὸν ἔχουσα
σὺν Διὶ μητιόεντι· χάριν δ' ἅμ' ὄπασσον ἀοιδῇ.

[1] Tucker: ἐπέρχεο.

XXII

TO POSEIDON

I BEGIN to sing about Poseidon, the great god, mover of the earth and fruitless sea, god of the deep who is also lord of Helicon and wide Aegae. A two-fold office the gods allotted you, O Shaker of the Earth, to be a tamer of horses and a saviour of ships!

Hail, Poseidon, Holder of the Earth, dark-haired lord! O blessed one, be kindly in heart and help those who voyage in ships!

XXIII

TO THE SON OF CRONOS, MOST HIGH

I WILL sing of Zeus, chiefest among the gods and greatest, all-seeing, the lord of all, the fulfiller who whispers words of wisdom to Themis as she sits leaning towards him.

Be gracious, all-seeing Son of Cronos, most excellent and great!

XXIV

TO HESTIA

HESTIA, you who tend the holy house of the lord Apollo, the Far-shooter at goodly Pytho, with soft oil dripping ever from your locks, come now into this house, come, having one mind with Zeus the all-wise —draw near, and withal bestow grace upon my song.

XXV

ΕΙΣ ΜΟΥΣΑΣ ΚΑΙ ΑΠΟΛΛΩΝΑ

Μουσάων ἄρχωμαι Ἀπόλλωνός τε Διός τε·
ἐκ γὰρ Μουσάων καὶ ἑκηβόλου Ἀπόλλωνος
ἄνδρες ἀοιδοὶ ἔασιν ἐπὶ χθονὶ καὶ κιθαρισταί,
ἐκ δὲ Διὸς βασιλῆες· ὁ δ' ὄλβιος, ὅν τινα Μοῦσαι
φίλωνται· γλυκερή οἱ ἀπὸ στόματος ῥέει αὐδή.
Χαίρετε, τέκνα Διός, καὶ ἐμὴν τιμήσατ' ἀοιδήν·
αὐτὰρ ἐγὼν ὑμέων τε καὶ ἄλλης μνήσομ' ἀοιδῆς.

XXVI

ΕΙΣ ΔΙΟΝΥΣΟΝ

Κισσοκόμην Διόνυσον ἐρίβρομον ἄρχομ' ἀείδειν,
Ζηνὸς καὶ Σεμέλης ἐρικυδέος ἀγλαὸν υἱόν,
ὃν τρέφον ἠύκομοι Νύμφαι παρὰ πατρὸς ἄνακτος
δεξάμεναι κόλποισι καὶ ἐνδυκέως ἀτίταλλον
Νύσης ἐν γυάλοις· ὁ δ' ἀέξετο πατρὸς ἕκητι
ἄντρῳ ἐν εὐώδει μεταρίθμιος ἀθανάτοισιν.
αὐτὰρ ἐπειδὴ τόνδε θεαὶ πολύυμνον ἔθρεψαν,
δὴ τότε φοιτίζεσκε καθ' ὑλήεντας ἐναύλους,
κισσῷ καὶ δάφνῃ πεπυκασμένος· αἱ δ' ἅμ' ἕποντο
Νύμφαι, ὁ δ' ἐξηγεῖτο· βρόμος δ' ἔχεν ἄσπετον ὕλην.
Καὶ σὺ μὲν οὕτω χαῖρε, πολυστάφυλ' ὦ Διόνυσε·
δὸς δ' ἡμᾶς χαίροντας ἐς ὥρας αὖτις ἱκέσθαι,
ἐκ δ' αὖθ' ὡράων εἰς τοὺς πολλοὺς ἐνιαυτούς.

XXV

TO THE MUSES AND APOLLO

I WILL begin with the Muses and Apollo and Zeus. For it is through the Muses and Apollo that there are singers upon the earth and players upon the lyre; but kings are from Zeus. Happy is he whom the Muses love: sweet flows speech from his lips.

Hail, children of Zeus! Give honour to my song! And now I will remember you and another song also.

XXVI

TO DIONYSUS

I BEGIN to sing of ivy-crowned Dionysus, the loud-crying god, splendid son of Zeus and glorious Semele. The rich-haired Nymphs received him in their bosoms from the lord his father and fostered and nurtured him carefully in the dells of Nysa, where by the will of his father he grew up in a sweet-smelling cave, being reckoned among the immortals. But when the goddesses had brought him up, a god oft hymned, then began he to wander continually through the woody coombes, thickly wreathed with ivy and laurel. And the Nymphs followed in his train with him for their leader; and the boundless forest was filled with their outcry.

And so hail to you, Dionysus, god of abundant clusters! Grant that we may come again rejoicing to this season, and from that season onwards for many a year.

XXVII

ΕΙΣ ΑΡΤΕΜΙΝ

Ἄρτεμιν ἀείδω χρυσηλάκατον, κελαδεινήν,
παρθένον αἰδοίην, ἐλαφηβόλον, ἰοχέαιραν,
αὐτοκασιγνήτην χρυσαόρου Ἀπόλλωνος,
ἣ κατ' ὄρη σκιόεντα καὶ ἄκριας ἠνεμοέσσας
ἄγρῃ τερπομένη παγχρύσεα τόξα τιταίνει
πέμπουσα στονόεντα βέλη· τρομέει δὲ κάρηνα
ὑψηλῶν ὀρέων, ἰάχει δ' ἔπι δάσκιος ὕλη
δεινὸν ὑπὸ κλαγγῆς θηρῶν, φρίσσει δέ τε γαῖα
πόντος τ' ἰχθυόεις· ἣ δ' ἄλκιμον ἦτορ ἔχουσα
πάντῃ ἐπιστρέφεται θηρῶν ὀλέκουσα γενέθλην.
αὐτὰρ ἐπὴν τερφθῇ θηροσκόπος ἰοχέαιρα,
εὐφρήνῃ δὲ νόον, χαλάσασ' εὐκαμπέα τόξα
ἔρχεται ἐς μέγα δῶμα κασιγνήτοιο φίλοιο,
Φοίβου Ἀπόλλωνος, Δελφῶν ἐς πίονα δῆμον,
Μουσῶν καὶ Χαρίτων καλὸν χορὸν ἀρτυνέουσα.
ἔνθα κατακρεμάσασα παλίντονα τόξα καὶ ἰοὺς
ἡγεῖται χαρίεντα περὶ χροῒ κόσμον ἔχουσα,
ἐξάρχουσα χορούς· αἱ δ' ἀμβροσίην ὄπ' ἰεῖσαι
ὑμνεῦσιν Λητὼ καλλίσφυρον, ὡς τέκε παῖδας
ἀθανάτων βουλῇ τε καὶ ἔργμασιν ἔξοχ' ἀρίστους.
Χαίρετε, τέκνα Διὸς καὶ Λητοῦς ἠυκόμοιο·
αὐτὰρ ἐγὼν ὑμέων τε καὶ ἄλλης μνήσομ' ἀοιδῆς.

XXVIII

ΕΙΣ ΑΘΗΝΑΝ

Παλλάδ' Ἀθηναίην, κυδρὴν θεόν, ἄρχομ' ἀείδειν
γλαυκῶπιν, πολύμητιν, ἀμείλιχον ἦτορ ἔχουσαν,

XXVII

TO ARTEMIS

I SING of Artemis, whose shafts are of gold, who cheers on the hounds, the pure maiden, shooter of stags, who delights in archery, own sister to Apollo with the golden sword. Over the shadowy hills and windy peaks she draws her golden bow, rejoicing in the chase, and sends out grievous shafts. The tops of the high mountains tremble and the tangled wood echoes awesomely with the outcry of beasts: earth quakes and the sea also where fishes shoal. But the goddess with a bold heart turns every way destroying the race of wild beasts: and when she is satisfied and has cheered her heart, this huntress who delights in arrows slackens her supple bow and goes to the great house of her dear brother Phoebus Apollo, to the rich land of Delphi, there to order the lovely dance of the Muses and Graces. There she hangs up her curved bow and her arrows, and heads and leads the dances, gracefully arrayed, while all they utter their heavenly voice, singing how neat-ankled Leto bare children supreme among the immortals both in thought and in deed.

Hail to you, children of Zeus and rich-haired Leto! And now I will remember you and another song also.

XXVIII

TO ATHENA

I BEGIN to sing of Pallas Athene, the glorious goddess, bright-eyed, inventive, unbending of heart,

παρθένον αἰδοίην, ἐρυσίπτολιν, ἀλκήεσσαν,
Τριτογενῆ, τὴν αὐτὸς ἐγείνατο μητίετα Ζεὺς
σεμνῆς ἐκ κεφαλῆς, πολεμήια τεύχε᾽ ἔχουσαν,
χρύσεα, παμφανόωντα· σέβας δ᾽ ἔχε πάντας ὁρῶντας
ἀθανάτους· ἣ δὲ πρόσθεν Διὸς αἰγιόχοιο
ἐσσυμένως ὤρουσεν ἀπ᾽ ἀθανάτοιο καρήνου,
σείσασ᾽ ὀξὺν ἄκοντα· μέγας δ᾽ ἐλελίζετ᾽ Ὄλυμπος
δεινὸν ὑπὸ βρίμης γλαυκώπιδος· ἀμφὶ δὲ γαῖα
σμερδαλέον ἰάχησεν· ἐκινήθη δ᾽ ἄρα πόντος,
κύμασι πορφυρέοισι κυκώμενος· ἔκχυτο[1] δ᾽ ἅλμη
ἐξαπίνης· στῆσεν δ᾽ Ὑπερίονος ἀγλαὸς υἱὸς
ἵππους ὠκύποδας δηρὸν χρόνον, εἰσότε κούρη
εἵλετ᾽ ἀπ᾽ ἀθανάτων ὤμων θεοείκελα τεύχη
Παλλὰς Ἀθηναίη· γήθησε δὲ μητίετα Ζεύς.
Καὶ σὺ μὲν οὕτω χαῖρε, Διὸς τέκος αἰγιόχοιο·
αὐτὰρ ἐγὼ καὶ σεῖο καὶ ἄλλης μνήσομ᾽ ἀοιδῆς.

XXIX

ΕΙΣ ΕΣΤΙΑΝ

Ἑστίη, ἣ πάντων ἐν δώμασιν ὑψηλοῖσιν
ἀθανάτων τε θεῶν χαμαὶ ἐρχομένων τ᾽ ἀνθρώπων
ἕδρην ἀίδιον ἔλαχες, πρεσβηίδα τιμήν,
καλὸν ἔχουσα γέρας καὶ τίμιον· οὐ γὰρ ἄτερ σοῦ
εἰλαπίναι θνητοῖσιν, ἵν᾽ οὐ πρώτῃ πυμάτῃ τε
Ἑστίῃ ἀρχόμενος σπένδει μελιηδέα οἶνον·
καὶ σύ μοι, Ἀργειφόντα, Διὸς καὶ Μαιάδος υἱέ,
ἄγγελε τῶν μακάρων, χρυσόρραπι, δῶτορ ἐάων,
ἵλαος ὢν ἐπάρηγε σὺν αἰδοίῃ τε φίλῃ τε.

[1] Baumeister: ἔσχετο, MSS.

pure virgin, saviour of cities, courageous, Tritogeneia. From his awful head wise Zeus himself bare her arrayed in warlike arms of flashing gold, and awe seized all the gods as they gazed. But Athena sprang quickly from the immortal head and stood before Zeus who holds the aegis, shaking a sharp spear: great Olympus began to reel horribly at the might of the bright-eyed goddess, and earth round about cried fearfully, and the sea was moved and tossed with dark waves, while foam burst forth suddenly: the bright Son of Hyperion stopped his swift-footed horses a long while, until the maiden Pallas Athene had stripped the heavenly armour from her immortal shoulders. And wise Zeus was glad.

And so hail to you, daughter of Zeus who holds the aegis! Now I will remember you and another song as well.

XXIX

TO HESTIA

Hestia, in the high dwellings of all, both deathless gods and men who walk on earth, you have gained an everlasting abode and highest honour: glorious is your portion and your right. For without you mortals hold no banquet,—where one does not duly pour sweet wine in offering to Hestia both first and last.

And you, Slayer of Argus, Son of Zeus and Maia, messenger of the blessed gods, bearer of the golden rod, giver of good, be favourable and help us, you and Hestia, the worshipful and dear. Come and

ναίετε δώματα καλά, φίλα φρεσὶν ἀλλήλοισιν 9
εἰδότες·[1] ἀμφότεροι γὰρ ἐπιχθονίων ἀνθρώπων 11
εἰδότες ἔργματα καλὰ νόῳ θ' ἕσπεσθε καὶ ἥβῃ.
Χαῖρε, Κρόνου θύγατερ, σύ τε καὶ χρυσόρραπις Ἑρμῆς·
αὐτὰρ ἐγὼν ὑμέων τε καὶ ἄλλης μνήσομ' ἀοιδῆς.

XXX

ΕΙΣ ΓΗΝ ΜΗΤΕΡΑ ΠΑΝΤΩΝ

Γαῖαν παμμήτειραν ἀείσομαι, ἠυθέμεθλον,
πρεσβίστην, ἣ φέρβει ἐπὶ χθονὶ πάνθ' ὁπόσ' ἐστίν,
ἠμὲν ὅσα χθόνα δῖαν ἐπέρχεται ἠδ' ὅσα πόντον
ἠδ' ὅσα πωτῶνται, τάδε φέρβεται ἐκ σέθεν ὄλβου.
ἐκ σέο δ' εὔπαιδές τε καὶ εὔκαρποι τελέθουσι,
πότνια, σεῦ δ' ἔχεται δοῦναι βίον ἠδ' ἀφελέσθαι
θνητοῖς ἀνθρώποισιν· ὃ δ' ὄλβιος, ὅν κε σὺ θυμῷ
πρόφρων τιμήσῃς· τῷ τ' ἄφθονα πάντα πάρεστι.
βρίθει μέν σφιν ἄρουρα φερέσβιος ἠδὲ κατ' ἀγροὺς
κτήνεσιν εὐθηνεῖ, οἶκος δ' ἐμπίπλαται ἐσθλῶν·
αὐτοὶ δ' εὐνομίῃσι πόλιν κάτα καλλιγύναικα
κοιρανέουσ', ὄλβος δὲ πολὺς καὶ πλοῦτος ὀπηδεῖ·
παῖδες δ' εὐφροσύνῃ νεοθηλέι κυδιόωσι
παρθενικαί τε χοροῖς πολυανθέσιν εὔφρονι θυμῷ
παίζουσαι σκαίρουσι κατ' ἄνθεα μαλθακὰ ποίης,
οὕς κε σὺ τιμήσῃς, σεμνὴ θεά, ἄφθονε δαῖμον.
Χαῖρε, θεῶν μήτηρ, ἄλοχ' Οὐρανοῦ ἀστερόεντος,
πρόφρων δ' ἀντ' ᾠδῆς βίοτον θυμήρε' ὄπαζε·
αὐτὰρ ἐγὼ καὶ σεῖο καὶ ἄλλης μνήσομ' ἀοιδῆς.

[1] Translator : Ἑστίῃ, MSS.

dwell in this glorious house in friendship together; for you two, well knowing the noble actions of men, aid on their wisdom and their strength.

Hail, Daughter of Cronos, and you also, Hermes, bearer of the golden rod! Now I will remember you and another song also.

XXX

TO EARTH THE MOTHER OF ALL

I WILL sing of well-founded Earth, mother of all, eldest of all beings. She feeds all creatures that are in the world, all that go upon the goodly land, and all that are in the paths of the seas, and all that fly: all these are fed of her store. Through you, O queen, men are blessed in their children and blessed in their harvests, and to you it belongs to give means of life to mortal men and to take it away. Happy is the man whom you delight to honour! He has all things abundantly: his fruitful land is laden with corn, his pastures are covered with cattle, and his house is filled with good things. Such men rule orderly in their cities of fair women: great riches and wealth follow them: their sons exult with ever-fresh delight, and their daughters in flower-laden bands play and skip merrily over the soft flowers of the field. Thus is it with those whom you honour O holy goddess, bountiful spirit.

Hail, Mother of the gods, wife of starry Heaven; freely bestow upon me for this my song substance that cheers the heart! And now I will remember you and another song also.

XXXI

ΕΙΣ ΗΛΙΟΝ

Ἥλιον ὑμνεῖν αὖτε Διὸς τέκος ἄρχεο Μοῦσα,
Καλλιόπη, φαέθοντα, τὸν Εὐρυφάεσσα βοῶπις
γείνατο Γαίης παιδὶ καὶ Οὐρανοῦ ἀστερόεντος·
γῆμε γὰρ Εὐρυφάεσσαν ἀγακλειτὴν Ὑπερίων,
αὐτοκασιγνήτην, ἥ οἱ τέκε κάλλιμα τέκνα,
Ἠῶ τε ῥοδόπηχυν ἐυπλόκαμόν τε Σελήνην
Ἠέλιόν τ' ἀκάμαντ', ἐπιείκελον ἀθανάτοισιν,
ὃς φαίνει θνητοῖσι καὶ ἀθανάτοισι θεοῖσιν
ἵπποις ἐμβεβαώς· σμερδνὸν δ' ὅ γε δέρκεται ὄσσοις
χρυσέης ἐκ κόρυθος· λαμπραὶ δ' ἀκτῖνες ἀπ' αὐτοῦ
αἰγλῆεν στίλβουσι παρὰ κροτάφων δέ τ' ἔθειραι [1]
λαμπραὶ ἀπὸ κρατὸς χαρίεν κατέχουσι πρόσωπον
τηλαυγές· καλὸν δὲ περὶ χροῒ λάμπεται ἔσθος
λεπτουργές, πνοιῇ ἀνέμων· ὕπο δ' ἄρσενες ἵπποι.
ἔνθ' ἄρ' ὅ γε στήσας χρυσόζυγον ἅρμα καὶ ἵππους,
[αὔτοθι παύεται ἄκρου ἐπ' οὐρανοῦ, εἰσόκεν αὖτις]
θεσπέσιος πέμπῃσι δι' οὐρανοῦ Ὠκεανόνδε.
Χαῖρε, ἄναξ, πρόφρων δὲ βίον θυμήρε' ὄπαζε.
ἐκ σέο δ' ἀρξάμενος κλῄσω μερόπων γένος ἀνδρῶν
ἡμιθέων, ὧν ἔργα θεαὶ θνητοῖσιν ἔδειξαν.

XXXII

ΕΙΣ ΣΕΛΗΝΗΝ

Μήνην ἀείδειν τανυσίπτερον ἔσπετε, Μοῦσαι,
ἡδυεπεῖς κοῦραι Κρονίδεω Διός, ἵστορες ᾠδῆς·

[1] Matthiae: τε παρειαί, MSS.

XXXI

TO HELIOS

And now, O Muse Calliope, daughter of Zeus, begin to sing of glowing Helios whom mild-eyed Euryphaëssa, the far-shining one, bare to the Son of Earth and starry Heaven. For Hyperion wedded glorious Euryphaëssa, his own sister, who bare him lovely children, rosy-armed Eos and rich-tressed Selene and tireless Helios who is like the deathless gods. As he rides in his chariot, he shines upon men and deathless gods, and piercingly he gazes with his eyes from his golden helmet. Bright rays beam dazzlingly from him, and his bright locks streaming from the temples of his head gracefully enclose his far-seen face: a rich, fine-spun garment glows upon his body and flutters in the wind: and stallions carry him. Then, when he has stayed his golden-yoked chariot and horses, he rests there upon the highest point of heaven, until he marvellously drives them down again through heaven to Ocean.

Hail to you, lord! Freely bestow on me substance that cheers the heart. And now that I have begun with you, I will celebrate the race of mortal men half-divine whose deeds the Muses have showed to mankind.

XXXII

TO SELENE

And next, sweet voiced Muses, daughters of Zeus, well-skilled in song, tell of the long-winged[1] Moon.

[1] The epithet is a usual one for birds, cp. Hesiod, *Works and Days*, 210: as applied to Selene it may merely indicate her passage, like a bird, through the air, or mean "far-flying."

ἧς ἄπο αἴγλη γαῖαν ἑλίσσεται οὐρανόδεικτος
κρατὸς ἀπ' ἀθανάτοιο, πολὺς δ' ὑπὸ κόσμος ὄρωρεν
αἴγλης λαμπούσης· στίλβει δέ τ' ἀλάμπετος ἀὴρ
χρυσέου ἀπὸ στεφάνου, ἀκτῖνες δ' ἐνδιάονται,
εὖτ' ἂν ἀπ' Ὠκεανοῖο λοεσσαμένη χρόα καλόν,
εἵματα ἑσσαμένη τηλαυγέα δῖα Σελήνη,
ζευξαμένη πώλους ἐριαύχενας, αἰγλήεντας,
ἐσσυμένως προτέρωσ' ἐλάσῃ καλλίτριχας ἵππους,
ἑσπερίη, διχόμηνος· ὃ δὲ[1] πλήθει μέγας ὄγμος
λαμπρόταταί τ' αὐγαὶ τότ' ἀεξομένης τελέθουσιν
οὐρανόθεν· τέκμωρ δὲ βροτοῖς καὶ σῆμα τέτυκται.
Τῇ ῥά ποτε Κρονίδης ἐμίγη φιλότητι καὶ εὐνῇ·
ἣ δ' ὑποκυσαμένη Πανδείην γείνατο κούρην,
ἐκπρεπὲς εἶδος ἔχουσαν ἐν ἀθανάτοισι θεοῖσι.
Χαῖρε, ἄνασσα, θεὰ λευκώλενε, δῖα Σελήνη,
πρόφρον, ἐυπλόκαμος· σέο δ' ἀρχόμενος κλέα φωτῶν
ᾄσομαι ἡμιθέων, ὧν κλείουσ' ἔργματ' ἀοιδοί,
Μουσάων θεράποντες, ἀπὸ στομάτων ἐροέντων.

XXXIII

ΕΙΣ ΔΙΟΣΚΟΥΡΟΥΣ

Ἀμφὶ Διὸς κούρους, ἑλικώπιδες ἔσπετε Μοῦσαι,
Τυνδαρίδας, Λήδης καλλισφύρου ἀγλαὰ τέκνα,
Κάστορά θ' ἱππόδαμον καὶ ἀμώμητον Πολυδεύκεα,
τοὺς ὑπὸ Ταϋγέτου κορυφῇ ὄρεος μεγάλοιο
μιχθεῖσ' ἐν φιλότητι κελαινεφέι Κρονίωνι
σωτῆρας τέκε παῖδας ἐπιχθονίων ἀνθρώπων
ὠκυπόρων τε νεῶν, ὅτε τε σπέρχωσιν ἄελλαι

[1] Baumeister: ὅ τε, MSS.

From her immortal head a radiance is shown from heaven and embraces earth; and great is the beauty that ariseth from her shining light. The air, unlit before, glows with the light of her golden crown, and her rays beam clear, whensoever bright Selene having bathed her lovely body in the waters of Ocean, and donned her far-gleaming raiment, and yoked her strong-necked, shining team, drives on her long-maned horses at full speed, at eventime in the mid-month: then her great orbit is full and then her beams shine brightest as she increases. So she is a sure token and a sign to mortal men.

Once the Son of Cronos was joined with her in love; and she conceived and bare a daughter Pandia, exceeding lovely amongst the deathless gods.

Hail, white-armed goddess, bright Selene, mild, bright-tressed queen! And now I will leave you and sing the glories of men half-divine, whose deeds minstrels, the servants of the Muses, celebrate with lovely lips.

XXXIII

TO THE DIOSCURI

Bright-eyed Muses, tell of the Tyndaridae, the Sons of Zeus, glorious children of neat-ankled Leda, Castor the tamer of horses, and blameless Polydeuces. When Leda had lain with the dark-clouded Son of Cronos, she bare them beneath the peak of the great hill Taÿgetus,—children who are deliverers of men on earth and of swift-going ships when stormy gales rage over the ruthless sea. Then the shipmen

χειμέριαι κατὰ πόντον ἀμείλιχον· οἳ δ' ἀπὸ νηῶν
εὐχόμενοι καλέουσι Διὸς κούρους μεγάλοιο
ἄρνεσσιν λευκοῖσιν, ἐπ' ἀκρωτήρια βάντες
πρύμνης· τὴν δ' ἄνεμός τε μέγας καὶ κῦμα θαλάσσης
θῆκαν ὑποβρυχίην· οἳ δ' ἐξαπίνης ἐφάνησαν
ξουθῇσι πτερύγεσσι δι' αἰθέρος ἀΐξαντες,
αὐτίκα δ' ἀργαλέων ἀνέμων κατέπαυσαν ἀέλλας,
κύματα δ' ἐστόρεσαν λευκῆς ἁλὸς ἐν πελάγεσσι,
σήματα καλά, πόνου ἀπονόσφισιν·[1] οἳ δὲ ἰδόντες
γήθησαν, παύσαντο δ' ὀιζυροῖο πόνοιο.
Χαίρετε, Τυνδαρίδαι, ταχέων ἐπιβήτορες ἵππων·
αὐτὰρ ἐγὼν ὑμέων τε καὶ ἄλλης μνήσομ' ἀοιδῆς.

[1] Bury: ναύταις σήματα καλά, πόνου σφίσιν, MSS.

call upon the sons of great Zeus with vows of white lambs, going to the forepart of the prow; but the strong wind and the waves of the sea lay the ship under water, until suddenly these two are seen darting through the air on tawny wings. Forthwith they allay the blasts of the cruel winds and still the waves upon the surface of the white sea: fair signs are they and deliverance from toil. And when the shipmen see them they are glad and have rest from their pain and labour.

Hail, Tyndaridae, riders upon swift horses! Now I will remember you and another song also.

HOMER'S EPIGRAMS

ΟΜΗΡΟΥ ΕΠΙΓΡΑΜΜΑΤΑ

I

Αἰδεῖσθε ξενίων κεχρημένον ἠδὲ δόμοιο,
οἳ πόλιν αἰπεινήν, Κύμην ἐριώπιδα κούρην,
ναίετε, Σαρδήνης πόδα νείατον ὑψικόμοιο,
ἀμβρόσιον πίνοντες ὕδωρ θείου ποταμοῖο,
Ἕρμου δινήεντος, ὃν ἀθάνατος τέκετο Ζεύς.

II

Αἶψα πόδες με φέροιεν ἐς αἰδοιων πόλιν ἀνδρῶν·
τῶν γὰρ καὶ θυμὸς πρόφρων καὶ μῆτις ἀρίστη.

III

Χαλκέη παρθένος εἰμί, Μίδεω δ' ἐπὶ σήματι κεῖμαι·
ἔστ' ἂν ὕδωρ τε νάῃ[1] καὶ δένδρεα μακρὰ τεθήλῃ,
ἠέλιος τ' ἀνιὼν λάμπῃ λαμπρά τε σελήνη,
καὶ ποταμοί γε ῥέωσιν ἀνακλύζῃ δὲ θάλασσα,
αὐτοῦ τῇδε μένουσα πολυκλαύτου ἐπὶ τύμβου
ἀγγελέω παριοῦσι, Μίδης ὅτι τῇδε τέθαπται.

IV

Οἵῃ μ' αἴσῃ δῶκε πατὴρ Ζεὺς κυρμα γενέσθαι,
νήπιον αἰδοίης ἐπὶ γούνασι μητρὸς ἀτάλλων.
ἥν ποτ' ἐπύργωσαν βουλῇ Διὸς αἰγιόχοιο

[1] Plato, Diogenes, *Contest of Homer*: ῥέῃ, pseudo-Herodotus.

HOMER'S EPIGRAMS[1]

I

HAVE reverence for him who needs a home and stranger's dole, all ye who dwell in the high city of Cyme, the lovely maiden, hard by the foothills of lofty Sardene, ye who drink the heavenly water of the divine stream, eddying Hermus, whom deathless Zeus begot.

II

SPEEDILY may my feet bear me to some town of righteous men; for their hearts are generous and their wit is best.

III

I AM a maiden of bronze and am set upon the tomb of Midas. While the waters flow and tall trees flourish, and the sun rises and shines and the bright moon also; while rivers run and the sea breaks on the shore, ever remaining on this mournful tomb, I tell the passer-by that Midas here lies buried.

IV

To what a fate did Zeus the Father give me a prey even while he made me to grow, a babe at my mother's knees! By the will of Zeus who holds the

[1] The Epigrams are preserved in the pseudo-Herodotean *Life of Homer*. Nos. III, XIII, and XVII are also found in the *Contest of Homer and Hesiod*, and No. I is also extant at the end of some MSS. of the *Homeric Hymns*.

λαοὶ Φρίκωνος, μάργων ἐπιβήτορες ἵππων,
ὁπλότεροι μαλεροῖο πυρὸς κρίνοντες Ἄρηα,
Αἰολίδα Σμύρνην ἁλιγείτονα, ποντοτίνακτον,
ἥντε δι' ἀγλαὸν εἶσιν ὕδωρ ἱεροῖο Μέλητος·
ἔνθεν ἀπορνύμεναι κοῦραι Διός, ἀγλαὰ τέκνα,
ἠθελέτην κλῇσαι δῖαν χθόνα καὶ πόλιν ἀνδρῶν.
οἳ δ' ἀπανηνάσθην ἱερὴν ὄπα, φῆμιν ἀοιδῆς,
ἀφραδίῃ· τῶν μέν τε παθών τις φράσσεται αὖτις,
ὅς σφιν ὀνείδεσσιν τὸν ἐμὸν διεμήσατο πότμον.
κῆρα δ' ἐγώ, τήν μοι θεὸς ὤπασε γεινομένῳ περ,
τλήσομαι ἀκράαντα φέρων τετληότι θυμῷ·
οὐδέ τί μοι φίλα γυῖα μένειν ἱεραῖς ἐν ἀγυιαῖς
Κύμης ὁρμαίνουσι, μέγας δέ με θυμὸς ἐπείγει
δῆμον ἐς ἀλλοδαπῶν ἰέναι, ὀλίγον περ ἐόντα.

V

Θεστορίδη, θνητοῖσιν ἀνωίστων πολέων περ,
οὐδὲν ἀφραστότερον πέλεται νόου ἀνθρώποισιν.

VI

Κλῦθι, Ποσείδαον, μεγαλοσθενές, ἐννοσίγαιε,
εὐρυχόρου μεδέων ἠδὲ ξανθοῦ Ἑλικῶνος,
δὸς δ' οὖρον καλὸν καὶ ἀπήμονα νόστον ἰδέσθαι
ναύταις, οἳ νηὸς πομποὶ ἠδ' ἀρχοὶ ἔασι·
δὸς δ' ἐς ὑπωρείην ὑψικρήμνοιο Μίμαντος
αἰδοίων μ' ἐλθόντα βροτῶν ὁσίων τε κυρῆσαι,
φῶτά τε τισαίμην, ὃς ἐμὸν νόον ἠπεροπεύσας
ὠδύσατο Ζῆνα ξένιον ξενίην τε τράπεζαν.

aegis the people of Phricon, riders on wanton horses, more active than raging fire in the test of war, once built the towers of Aeolian Smyrna, wave-shaken neighbour to the sea, through which glides the pleasant stream of sacred Meles; thence[1] arose the daughters of Zeus, glorious children, and would fain have made famous that fair country and the city of its people. But in their folly those men scorned the divine voice and renown of song, and in trouble shall one of them remember this hereafter—he who with scornful words to them[2] contrived my fate. Yet I will endure the lot which heaven gave me even at my birth, bearing my disappointment with a patient heart. My dear limbs yearn not to stay in the sacred streets of Cyme, but rather my great heart urges me to go unto another country, small though I am.

V

Thestorides, full many things there are that mortals cannot sound; but there is nothing more unfathomable than the heart of man.

VI

Hear me, Poseidon, strong shaker of the earth, ruler of wide-spread, tawny Helicon! Give a fair wind and sight of safe return to the shipmen who speed and govern this ship. And grant that when I come to the nether slopes of towering Mimas I may find honourable, god-fearing men. Also may I avenge me on the wretch who deceived me and grieved Zeus the lord of guests and his own guest-table.

[1] *sc.* from Smyrna, Homer's reputed birth-place.
[2] The councillors of Cyme who refused to support Homer at the public expense.

VII

Πότνια Γῆ, πάνδωρε, δότειρα μελίφρονος ὄλβου,
ὡς ἄρα δὴ τοῖς μὲν φωτῶν εὔοχθος ἐτύχθης,
τοῖσι δὲ δύσβωλος καὶ τρηχεῖ', οἷς ἐχολώθης.

VIII

Ναῦται ποντοπόροι, στυγερῇ ἐναλίγκιοι ἄτῃ
πτωκάσιν αἰθυίῃσι, βίον δύσζηλον ἔχοντες,
αἰδεῖσθε ξενίοιο Διὸς σέβας ὑψιμέδοντος·
δεινὴ γὰρ μέτ' ὄπις ξενίου Διός, ὅς κ' ἀλίτηται.

IX [1]

Ὑμέας, ὦ ξεῖνοι, ἄνεμος λάβεν ἀντίος ἐλθών·
ἀλλ' ἐμὲ νῦν δέξασθε, καὶ ὁ πλόος ἔσσεται ὑμῖν.

X

Ἄλλη τίς σευ πεύκη ἀμείνονα καρπὸν ἵησιν
Ἴδης ἐν κορυφῇσι πολυπτύχου ἠνεμοέσσης,
ἔνθα σίδηρος Ἄρηος ἐπιχθονίοισι βροτοῖσιν
ἔσσεται, εὖτ' ἄν μιν Κεβρήνιοι ἄνδρες ἔχωσι.

XI

Γλαῦκε, βοτῶν [2] ἐπίοπτα, ἔπος τί τοι ἐν φρεσὶ θήσω·
πρῶτον μὲν κυσὶ δεῖπνον ἐπ' αὐλείῃσι θύρῃσι
δοῦναι· τὼς γὰρ ἄμεινον· ὃ γὰρ καὶ πρῶτον ἀκούει
ἀνδρὸς ἐπερχομένου καὶ ἐς ἕρκεα θηρὸς ἰόντος.

[1] Restored to metrical form by Barnes.
[2] Kuester: πέπον, βροτῶν, MSS.

VII

Queen Earth, all bounteous giver of honey-hearted wealth, how kindly, it seems, you are to some, and how intractable and rough for those with whom you are angry.

VIII

Sailors, who rove the seas and whom a hateful fate has made as the shy sea-fowl, living an unenviable life, observe the reverence due to Zeus who rules on high, the god of strangers; for terrible is the vengeance of this god afterwards for whosoever has sinned.

IX

Strangers, a contrary wind has caught you: but even now take me aboard and you shall make your voyage.

X

Another sort of pine shall bear a better fruit[1] than you upon the heights of furrowed, windy Ida. For there shall mortal men get the iron that Ares loves, so soon as the Cebrenians shall hold the land.

XI

Glaucus, watchman of flocks, a word will I put in your heart. First give the dogs their dinner at the courtyard gate, for this is well. The dog first hears a man approaching and the wild-beast coming to the fence.

[1] The "better fruit" is apparently the iron smelted out in fires of pine-wood.

XII

Κλῦθί μευ εὐχομένου, Κουροτρόφε, δὸς δὲ γυναῖκα
τήνδε νέων μὲν ἀναίνεσθαι φιλότητα καὶ εὐνήν·
ἡ δ' ἐπιτερπέσθω πολιοκροτάφοισι γέρουσιν,
ὧν ὥρη μὲν ἀπήμβλυνται, θυμὸς δὲ μενοινᾷ.

XIII

Ἀνδρὸς μὲν στέφανος παῖδες, πύργοι δὲ πόληος,
ἵπποι δ' αὖ πεδίου κόσμος, νῆες δὲ θαλάσσης,
χρήματα δ' αὔξει οἶκον, ἀτὰρ γεραροὶ βασιλῆες
ἥμενοι εἰν ἀγορῇ κόσμος λαοῖσιν[1] ὁρᾶσθαι·
αἰθομένου δὲ πυρὸς γεραρώτερος οἶκος ἰδέσθαι
ἤματι χειμερίῳ, ὁπότ' ἂν νίφῃσι Κρονίων.

XIV

Εἰ μὲν δώσετε μισθὸν ἀείσω, ὦ κεραμῆες.
δεῦρ', ἄγ', Ἀθηναίη καὶ ὑπέρσχεθε χεῖρα καμίνου.
εὖ δὲ περανθεῖεν[2] κότυλοι καὶ πάντα κάναστρα
φρυχθῆναί τε καλῶς καὶ τιμῆς ὦνον ἀρέσθαι,
πολλὰ μὲν εἰν ἀγορῇ πωλεύμενα, πολλὰ δ' ἀγυιαῖς,
πολλὰ δὲ κερδῆναι, ἡμῖν δὲ δή, ὥς σφιν ἀεῖσαι.
ἢν δ' ἐπ' ἀναιδείην τρεφθέντες ψεύδε' ἄρησθε,
συγκαλέω δὴ ἔπειτα καμίνων δηλητῆρας,
Σύντριβ' ὁμῶς Σμάραγόν τε καὶ Ἄσβετον ἠδὲ Σαβάκτην
Ὠμόδαμόν τ', ὃς τῇδε τέχνῃ κακὰ πολλὰ πορίζοι·
πέρθε πυραίθουσαν καὶ δώματα, σὺν δὲ κάμινος
πᾶσα κυκηθείη κεραμέων μέγα κωκύσαντων.
ὡς γνάθος ἱππείη βρύκει, βρύκοι δὲ κάμινος,

[1] Ruhnken: τ' ἄλλοισιν, Sources: The *Contest of Homer* adds the verse:

λαὸς δ' εἰν ἀγορῇσι καθήμενος εἰσοράασθαι.

[2] Pollux: μελανθοῖεν, μελανθεῖεν, *Life of Homer*.

XII

Goddess-nurse of the young,[1] give ear to my prayer, and grant that this woman may reject the love-embrace of youth and dote on grey-haired old men whose powers are dulled, but whose hearts still desire.

XIII

Children are a man's crown, towers of a city; horses are the glory of a plain, and so are ships of the sea; wealth will make a house great, and reverend princes seated in assembly are a goodly sight for the folk to see. But a blazing fire makes a house look more comely upon a winter's day, when the Son of Cronos sends down snow.

XIV

Potters, if you will give me a reward, I will sing for you. Come, then, Athena, with hand upraised[2] over the kiln. Let the pots and all the dishes turn out well and be well fired: let them fetch good prices and be sold in plenty in the market, and plenty in the streets. Grant that the potters may get great gain and grant me so to sing to them. But if you turn shameless and make false promises, then I call together the destroyers of kilns, Shatter and Smash and Charr and Crash and Crudebake who can work this craft much mischief. Come all of you and sack the kiln-yard and the buildings: let the whole kiln be shaken up to the potter's loud lament. As a horse's jaw grinds, so let the kiln grind to

[1] Hecate: cp. Hesiod, *Theogony*, 450.
[2] *i.e.* in protection.

πάντ' ἔντοσθ' αὐτῆς κεραμήια λεπτὰ ποιοῦσα.
δεῦρο καὶ Ἠελίου θύγατερ, πολυφάρμακε Κίρκη,
ἄγρια φάρμακα βάλλε, κάκου δ' αὐτούς τε καὶ ἔργα.
δεῦρο δὲ καὶ Χείρων ἀγέτω πολέας Κενταύρους,
οἵθ' Ἡρακλῆος χεῖρας φύγον οἵτ' ἀπόλοντο,
τύπτοιεν τάδε ἔργα κακῶς, πίπτοι δὲ κάμινος·
αὐτοὶ δ' οἰμώζοντες ὁρῴατο ἔργα πονηρά.
γηθήσω δ' ὁρόων αὐτῶν κακοδαίμονα τέχνην·
ὃς δέ χ' ὑπερκύψῃ, πυρὶ τούτου πᾶν τὸ πρόσωπον
φλεχθείη, ὡς πάντες ἐπίστωντ' αἴσιμα ῥέζειν.

XV

Δῶμα προσετραπόμεσθ' ἀνδρὸς μέγα δυναμένοιο,
ὃς μέγα μὲν δύναται, μέγα δὲ πρέπει[1] *ὄλβιος αἰεί.*
αὐταὶ ἀνακλίνεσθε θύραι· Πλοῦτος γὰρ ἔσεισι
πολλός, σὺν Πλούτῳ δὲ καὶ Εὐφροσύνη τεθαλυῖα
Εἰρήνη τ' ἀγαθή· ὅσα δ' ἄγγεα, μεστὰ μὲν εἴη,
κυρβαίη δ' αἰεὶ κατὰ καρδόπου ἕρποι μᾶζα.
νῦν μὲν κριθαίην, εὐώπιδα, σησαμόεσσαν

* * * *

Τοῦ παιδὸς δὲ γυνὴ κατὰ δίφραδα βήσεται ὔμμιν·
ἡμίονοι δ' ἄξουσι κραταίποδες ἐς τόδε δῶμα·
αὐτὴ δ' ἱστὸν ὑφαίνοι ἐπ' ἠλέκτρῳ βεβαυῖα.
Νεῦμαί τοι, νεῦμαι ἐνιαύσιος, ὥστε χελιδὼν
ἕστηκ' ἐν προθύροις ψιλὴ πόδας· ἀλλὰ φέρ' αἶψα
†πέρσαι τῷ Ἀπόλλωνος γυιάτιδος.†

[1] Ilgen: βρεμει, MSS.

powder all the pots inside. And you, too, daughter of the Sun, Circe the witch, come and cast cruel spells; hurt both these men and their handiwork. Let Chiron also come and bring many Centaurs—all that escaped the hands of Heracles and all that were destroyed: let them make sad havoc of the pots and overthrow the kiln, and let the potters see the mischief and be grieved; but I will gloat as I behold their luckless craft. And if anyone of them stoops to peer in, let all his face be burned up, that all men may learn to deal honestly.

XV[1]

Let us betake us to the house of some man of great power,—one who bears great power and is greatly prosperous always. Open of yourselves, you doors, for mighty Wealth will enter in, and with Wealth comes jolly Mirth and gentle Peace. May all the corn-bins be full and the mass of dough always overflow the kneading-trough. Now (set before us) cheerful barley-pottage, full of sesame . . .

Your son's wife, driving to this house with strong-hoofed mules, shall dismount from her carriage to greet you; may she be shod with golden shoes as she stands weaving at the loom.

I come, and I come yearly, like the swallow that perches light-footed in the fore-part of your house. But quickly bring . . .

[1] This song is called by pseudo-Herodotus Εἰρησιώνη. The word properly indicates a garland wound with wool which was worn at harvest-festivals, but came to be applied first to the harvest song and then to any begging song. The present is akin to the Swallow-Song (Χελιδόνισμα), sung at the beginning of spring, and answering to the still surviving English May-Day songs. Cp. Athenaeus, viii. 360 B.

XVI

Εἰ μέν τι δώσεις· εἰ δὲ μή, οὐχ ἑστήξομεν·
οὐ γὰρ συνοικήσοντες ἐνθάδ' ἤλθομεν.

XVII

ΟΜΗΡΟΣ

Ἄνδρες ἄγρης ἁλίης[1] θηρήτορες, ἦ ῥ' ἔχομέν τι;

ΑΛΙΕΙΣ

Ὅσσ' ἕλομεν, λιπόμεσθ'· ὅσα δ' οὐχ ἕλομεν,
φερόμεσθα.

ΟΜΗΡΟΣ

Τοίων γὰρ πατέρων ἐξ αἵματος ἐκγεγάασθε,
οὔτε βαθυκλήρων οὔτ' ἄσπετα μῆλα νεμόντων.

[1] Koechly: ἀπ' Ἀρκαδίης, MSS.

XVI

If you will give us anything (well). But if not, we will not wait, for we are not come here to dwell with you.

XVII

HOMER

Hunters of deep sea prey, have we caught anything?

FISHERMEN

All that we caught we left behind, and all that we did not catch we carry home.[1]

HOMER

Ay, for of such fathers you are sprung as neither hold rich lands nor tend countless sheep.

[1] The lice which they caught in their clothes they left behind, but carried home in their clothes those which they could not catch.

FRAGMENTS OF THE EPIC CYCLE

ΕΠΙΚΟΥ ΚΥΚΛΟΥ ΛΕΙΨΑΝΑ

ΤΙΤΑΝΟΜΑΧΙΑ

1.

Photius, Epitome of the Chrestomathy of Proclus. Ἄρχεται μὲν (ὁ ἐπικὸς κύκλος) ἐκ τῆς Οὐρανοῦ καὶ Γῆς μυθολογουμένης μίξεως, ἐξ ἧς αὐτῷ καὶ τρεῖς παῖδας ἑκατοντάχειρας καὶ τρεῖς γεννῶσι Κύκλωπας.

2.

Anecdota Oxon. (Cramer) i. 75. Αἰθέρος δ' υἱὸς Οὐρανός, ὡς ὁ τὴν Τιτανομαχίαν γράψας.

3.

Schol. on Ap. Rhod. i. 1165. Εὔμηλος . . . . τὸν Αἰγαίωνα Γῆς καὶ Πόντου φησὶ παῖδα, κατοικοῦντα δὲ ἐν τῇ θαλάσσῃ τοῖς Τιτᾶσι συμμαχεῖν.

4.

Athenaeus, vii. 277 D. ὁ τὴν Τιτανομαχίαν ποιήσας εἴτ' Εὔμηλός ἐστιν ὁ Κορίνθιος ἢ Ἀρκτῖνος . . . . ἐν τῷ δευτέρῳ οὕτως εἴρηκεν·

ἐν δ' αὐτῇ πλωτοὶ χρυσώπιδες ἰχθύες ἐλλόι
νήχοντες παίζουσι δι' ὕδατος ἀμβροσίοιο.

5.

Athenaeus, i. 22 C. Εὔμηλος . . . τὸν Δία ὀρχούμενόν που παράγει λέγων·

μεσσοῖσιν δ' ὀρχεῖτο πατὴρ ἀνδρῶν τε θεῶν τε.

THE EPIC CYCLE

THE WAR OF THE TITANS

1.

The Epic Cycle begins with the fabled union of Heaven and Earth, by which they make three hundred-handed sons and three Cyclopes to be born to him.

2.

According to the writer of the *War of the Titans* Heaven was the son of Aether

3.

Eumelus says that Aegaeon was the son of Earth and Sea and, having his dwelling in the sea, was an ally of the Titans.

4.

The poet of the *War of the Titans,* whether Eumelus of Corinth or Arctinus, writes thus in his second book: "Upon the shield were dumb fish afloat, with golden faces, swimming and sporting through the heavenly water."

5.

Eumelus somewhere introduces Zeus dancing: he says—"In the midst of them danced the Father of men and gods."

6.

Schol. on Ap. Rhod. i. 554. ὁ δὲ τὴν Γιγαντομαχίαν ποιήσας φησὶν ὅτι Κρόνος μεταμορφωθεὶς εἰς ἵππον ἐμίγη Φιλύρᾳ τῇ Ὠκεανοῦ, διόπερ καὶ ἱπποκένταυρος ἐγεννήθη ὁ Χείρων· τούτου δὲ γυνὴ Χαρικλώ.

7.

Athenaeus, xi. 470 B. Θεόλυτος . . . ἐπὶ λέβητός φησιν αὐτὸν διαπλεῦσαι, τοῦτο πρώτου εἰπόντος τοῦ τὴν Τιτανομαχίαν ποιήσαντος.

8.

Philodemus, On Piety. ὁ δὲ τὴν Τιτανομαχίαν, τὰ μὲν μῆλα φυλάττειν . . .

ΟΙΔΙΠΟΔΕΙΑ

1.

C.I.G. Ital. et Sic. 1292. ii. 11. . . . τὴν Οἰδιποδείαν τὴν ὑπὸ Κιναίθωνος τοῦ . . . ἐπῶν οὖσαν ϛχ.

2.

Paus. ix. 5. 10. παῖδας δὲ ἐξ αὐτῆς (Ἰοκάστης) οὐ δοκῶ οἱ γενέσθαι μάρτυρι Ὁμήρῳ[1] χρώμενος . . . ἐξ Εὐρυγανείας δὲ τῆς Ὑπέρφαντος ἐγεγόνεσαν· δηλοῖ δὲ καὶ ὁ τὰ ἔπη ποιήσας ἃ Οἰδιποδία ὀνομάζουσι.

3.

Schol. on Eur. Phoen. 1750. οἱ τὴν Οἰδιποδίαν γράφοντες . . . περὶ τῆς Σφιγγός

ἀλλ' ἔτι κάλλιστόν τε καὶ ἱμεροέστατον ἄλλων
παῖδα φίλον Κρείοντος ἀμύμονος Αἵμονα δῖον . . .

[1] *Odyssey*, xii. 271–4.

6.

The author of the *War of the Giants* says that Cronos took the shape of a horse and lay with Philyra, the daughter Ocean. Through this cause Cheiron was born a centaur: his wife was Chariclo.

7.

Theolytus says that he (Heracles) sailed across the sea in a cauldron[1]; but the first to give this story is the author of the *War of the Titans.*

8.

The author of the *War of the Titans* says that the apples (of the Hesperides) were guarded . . .

THE STORY OF OEDIPUS

1.

. . . the *Story of Oedipus* by Cinaethon in six thousand six hundred verses.

2.

Judging by Homer I do not believe that Oedipus had children by Iocasta: his sons were born of Euryganeia as the writer of the Epic called the *Story of Oedipus* clearly shows.

3.

The authors of the *Story of Oedipus* (say) of the Sphinx: "But furthermore (she killed) noble Haemon, the dear son of blameless Creon, the comeliest and loveliest of boys."

[1] See the cylix reproduced by Gerhard, *Abhandlungen*, taf. 5, 4. Cp. Stesichorus, Frag. 3 (Smyth).

ΘΗΒΑΙΣ

1.

Contest of Homer and Hesiod. ὁ δὲ Ὅμηρος . . . περιερχόμενος ἔλεγε τὰ ποιήματα, πρῶτον μὲν τὴν Θηβαΐδα, ἔπη ͵ζ, ἧς ἡ ἀρχὴ

Ἄργος ἄειδε θεὰ πολυδίψιον ἔνθεν ἄνακτες.

2.

Athenaeus, xi. 465 E.

αὐτὰρ ὁ διογενὴς ἥρως ξανθὸς Πολυνείκης
πρῶτα μὲν Οἰδιπόδῃ καλὴν παρέθηκε τράπεζαν
ἀργυρέην Κάδμοιο θεόφρονος· αὐτὰρ ἔπειτα
χρύσεον ἔμπλησεν καλὸν δέπας ἡδέος οἴνου.
αὐτὰρ ὅ γ' ὡς φράσθη παρακείμενα πατρὸς ἑοῖο
τιμήεντα γέρα, μέγα οἱ κακὸν ἔμπεσε θυμῷ.
αἶψα δὲ παισὶν ἑοῖσι μετ' ἀμφοτέροισιν ἐπαρὰς
ἀργαλέας ἠρᾶτο· θεῶν δ' οὐ λανθάν' ἐρινύν.
ὡς οὔ οἱ πατρώϊ' ἐν ἠθείῃ φιλότητι
δάσσαιντ', ἀμφότεροισι δ' ἀεὶ πόλεμοί τε μάχαι τε . . .

3.

Schol. Laur. on Soph. O.C. 1375.

ἰσχίον ὡς ἐνόησε χαμαὶ βάλε εἶπέ τε μῦθον·
ὤμοι ἐγώ, παῖδες μὲν ὀνειδείοντες ἔπεμψαν
*   *   *   *
εὖκτο Διὶ βασιλῆι καὶ ἄλλοις ἀθανάτοισι
χερσὶν ὑπ' ἀλλήλων καταβήμεναι Ἄϊδος εἴσω.

4.

Paus. viii. 25. 8. Ἄδραστος ἔφευγεν ἐκ Θηβῶν
εἵματα λυγρὰ φέρων σὺν Ἀρείονι κυανοχαίτῃ.

THE THEBAID

1.

Homer travelled about reciting his epics, first the *Thebaid*, in seven thousand verses, which begins: "Sing, goddess, of parched Argos, whence lords . . "

2.

"Then the heaven-born hero, golden-haired Polyneices, first set beside Oedipus a rich table of silver which once belonged to Cadmus the divinely wise: next he filled a fine golden cup with sweet wine. But when Oedipus perceived these treasures of his father, great misery fell on his heart, and he straightway called down bitter curses there in the presence of both his sons. And the avenging Fury of the gods failed not to hear him as he prayed that they might never divide their father's goods in loving brotherhood, but that war and fighting might be ever the portion of them both."

3.

"And when Oedipus noticed the haunch[1] he threw it on the ground and said: 'Oh! Oh! my sons have sent this mocking me . . .' So he prayed to Zeus the king and the other deathless gods that each might fall by his brother's hand and go down into the house of Hades."

4.

Adrastus fled from Thebes "wearing miserable garments, and took black-maned Areion[2] with him."

[1] The haunch was regarded as a dishonourable portion.

[2] The horse of Adrastus, offspring of Poseidon and Demeter, who had changed herself into a mare to escape Poseidon.

5.[1]

ἑπτὰ δ' ἔπειτα τελεσθέντων νεκύων ἔνι Θήβῃ,
οἴμωξεν Ταλαϊονίδης μετέειπέ τε μῦθον·
ὤμοι ἐγώ· ποθέω γὰρ ἐμοῦ στρατοῦ ὄμμα φαεινόν,
ἀμφότερον μάντιν τ' ἀγαθὸν καὶ δουρὶ μάχεσθαι.

6.

Apollodorus, i. 74. ἔγημεν Οἰνεὺς Περίβοιαν τὴν Ἱππονόου. ταύτην δὲ ὁ μὲν γράψας τὴν Θηβαΐδα πολεμηθείσης Ὠλένου λέγει λαβεῖν Οἰνέα γέρας.

7.

Pausanias, ix. 18. 6. πρὸς δὲ τῇ πηγῇ τάφος ἐστὶν Ἀσφοδίκου· καὶ ὁ Ἀσφόδικος οὗτος ἀπέκτεινεν ἐν τῇ μάχῃ τῇ πρὸς Ἀργείους Παρθενοπαῖον τὸν Ταλαοῦ καθὰ οἱ Θηβαῖοι λέγουσιν, ἐπεὶ τά γε ἐν Θηβαΐδι ἔπη τὰ ἐς τὴν Παρθενοπαίου τελευτὴν Περικλύμενον τὸν ἀνελόντα φησὶν εἶναι.

ΕΠΙΓΟΝΟΙ

1.

Contest of Homer and Hesiod. εἶτα Ἐπιγόνους, ἔπη ,ζ, ἧς ἡ ἀρχὴ

νῦν αὖθ' ὁπλοτέρων ἀνδρῶν ἀρχώμεθα Μοῦσαι.

2.

Photius, Lexicon. Τευμησία· περὶ τῆς Τευμησίας ἀλώπεκος οἱ τὰ Θηβαϊκὰ γεγραφηκότες ἱκανῶς

[1] Restored from Pindar *Ol.* vi. 15 who, according to Asclepiades, derives the passage from the *Thebaïs*.

5.

"But when the seven dead had received their last rites in Thebes, the Son of Taläus lamented and spoke thus among them: 'Woe is me, for I miss the bright eye of my host, a good seer and a stout spearman alike.'"

6.

Oeneus married Periboea the daughter of Hipponoüs. The author of the *Thebais* says that when Olenus had been stormed, Oeneus received her as a prize.

7.

Near the spring is the tomb of Asphodicus. This Asphodicus killed Parthenopaeus the son of Talaus in the battle against the Argives, as the Thebans say; though that part of the *Thebais* which tells of the death of Parthenopaeus says that it was Periclymenus who killed him.

THE EPIGONI

1.

NEXT (Homer composed) the *Epigoni* in seven thousand verses, beginning, "And now, Muses, let us begin to sing of younger men."

2.

Teumesia. Those who have written on Theban affairs have given a full account of the Teumesian fox.[1]

[1] So called from Teumessus, a hill in Boeotia. For the derivation of Teumessus cp. Antimachus *Thebais* fr. 3 (Kinkel).

ἱστορήκασι . . . ἐπιπεμφθῆναι μὲν γὰρ ὑπὸ θεῶν τὸ θηρίον τοῦτο τοῖς Καδμείοις· διὸ τῆς βασιλείας ἐξέκλειον τοὺς ἀπὸ Κάδμου γεγονότας. Κέφαλον δὲ φασὶ τὸν Δηϊόνος Ἀθηναῖον ὄντα καὶ κύνα κεκτημένον ὃν οὐδὲν διέφευγεν τῶν θηρίων, ὡς ἀπέκτεινεν ἄκων τὴν ἑαυτοῦ γυναῖκα Πρόκριν, καθηράντων αὐτὸν τῶν Καδμείων, διώκειν τὴν ἀλώπεκα μετὰ τοῦ κυνός· καταλαβομένους δὲ περὶ τὸν Τευμησσὸν λίθους γενέσθαι τόν τε κύνα καὶ τὴν ἀλώπεκα. εἰλήφασι δ' οὗτοι τὸν μῦθον ἐκ τοῦ ἐπικοῦ κύκλου.

3.

Schol. on Ap. Rhod. i. 308. *οἱ δὲ τὴν Θηβαΐδα γεγραφότες φασὶν ὅτι ὑπὸ τῶν Ἐπιγονῶν ἀκροθίνιον ἀνετέθη Μαντὼ ἡ Τειρεσίου θυγάτηρ εἰς Δελφοὺς πεμφθεῖσα, καὶ κατὰ χρησμὸν Ἀπόλλωνος ἐξερχομένη περιέπεσε Ῥακίῳ τῷ Λέβητος υἱῷ Μυκηναίῳ τὸ γένος. καὶ γημαμένη αὐτῷ—τοῦτο γὰρ περιεῖχε τὸ λογίον, γαμεῖσθαι ᾧ ἂν συναντήσῃ—[καὶ] ἐλθοῦσα εἰς Κολοφῶνα καὶ ἐκεῖ δυσθυμήσασα ἐδάκρυσε διὰ τὴν τῆς πατρίδος πόρθησιν.*

ΚΥΠΡΙΑ

1.

Proclus, Chrestomathy, i. *Ἐπιβάλλει τούτοις τὰ λεγόμενα Κύπρια ἐν βιβλίοις φερόμενα ἕνδεκα. . . . τὰ δὲ περιέχοντά ἐστι ταῦτα.*

Ζεὺς βουλεύεται μετὰ τῆς Θέμιδος περὶ τοῦ Τρωϊκοῦ πολέμου· παραγενομένη δὲ Ἔρις εὐωχουμένων τῶν θεῶν ἐν τοῖς Πηλέως γάμοις, νεῖκος

They relate that the creature was sent by the gods to punish the descendants of Cadmus, and that the Thebans therefore excluded those of the house of Cadmus from the kingship. But (they say) a certain Cephalus, the son of Deïon, an Athenian, who owned a hound which no beast ever escaped, had accidentally killed his wife Procris, and being purified of the homicide by the Cadmeans, hunted the fox with his hound, and when they had overtaken it both hound and fox were turned into stones near Teumessus. These writers have taken the story from the Epic Cycle.

3.

The authors of the *Thebaïs* say that Manto the daughter of Teiresias was sent to Delphi by the Epigoni as a first fruit of their spoil, and that in accordance with an oracle of Apollo she went out and met Rhacius, the son of Lebes, a Mycenaean by race. This man she married—for the oracle also contained the command that she should marry whomsoever she might meet—and coming to Colophon, was there much cast down and wept over the destruction of her country.

THE CYPRIA

1.

This[1] is continued by the epic called *Cypria* which is current in eleven books. Its contents are as follows.

Zeus plans with Themis to bring about the Trojan war. Strife arrives while the gods are feasting at the marriage of Peleus and starts a dispute between

[1] The preceding part of the Epic Cycle (?).

περὶ κάλλους ἐνίστησιν Ἀθηνᾷ, Ἥρᾳ καὶ Ἀφροδίτῃ, αἳ πρὸς Ἀλέξανδρον ἐν Ἴδῃ κατὰ Διὸς προσταγὴν ὑφ' Ἑρμοῦ πρὸς τὴν κρίσιν ἄγονται· καὶ προκρίνει τὴν Ἀφροδίτην ἐπαρθεὶς τοῖς Ἑλένης γάμοις Ἀλέξανδρος.

Ἔπειτα δέ, Ἀφροδίτης ὑποθεμένης, ναυπηγεῖται, καὶ Ἕλενος περὶ τῶν μελλόντων αὐτῷ προθεσπίζει. καὶ Ἀφροδίτη Αἰνείαν συμπλεῖν αὐτῷ κελεύει. καὶ Κασσάνδρα περὶ τῶν μελλόντων προδηλοῖ. ἐπιβὰς δὲ τῇ Λακεδαιμονίᾳ Ἀλέξανδρος ξενίζεται παρὰ τοῖς Τυνδαρίδαις, καὶ μετὰ ταῦτα ἐν τῇ Σπάρτῃ παρὰ Μενελάῳ· καὶ Ἑλένῃ παρὰ τὴν εὐωχίαν δίδωσι δῶρα ὁ Ἀλέξανδρος.

Καὶ μετὰ ταῦτα Μενέλαος εἰς Κρήτην ἐκπλεῖ, κελεύσας τὴν Ἑλένην τοῖς ξένοις τὰ ἐπιτήδεια παρέχειν ἕως ἂν ἀπαλλαγῶσιν. ἐν τούτῳ δὲ Ἀφροδίτη συνάγει τὴν Ἑλένην τῷ Ἀλεξάνδρῳ. καὶ μετὰ τὴν μίξιν τὰ πλεῖστα κτήματα ἐνθέμενοι, νυκτὸς ἀποπλέουσι. χειμῶνα δὲ αὐτοῖς ἐφίστησιν Ἥρα. καὶ προσενεχθεὶς Σιδῶνι ὁ Ἀλέξανδρος αἱρεῖ τὴν πόλιν. καὶ ἀποπλεύσας εἰς Ἴλιον γάμους τῆς Ἑλένης ἐπέτελεσεν.

Ἐν τούτῳ δὲ Κάστωρ μετὰ Πολυδεύκους τὰς Ἴδα καὶ Λυγκέως βοῦς ὑφαιρούμενοι ἐφωράθησαν, καὶ Κάστωρ μὲν ὑπὸ τοῦ Ἴδα ἀναιρεῖται, Λυγκεὺς δὲ καὶ Ἴδας ὑπὸ Πολυδεύκους· καὶ Ζεὺς αὐτοῖς ἑτερήμερον νέμει τὴν ἀθανασίαν.

Καὶ μετὰ ταῦτα Ἶρις ἀναγγέλλει τῷ Μενελάῳ τὰ γεγονότα κατὰ τὸν οἶκον. ὁ δὲ παραγενόμενος περὶ τῆς ἐπ' Ἴλιον στρατείας βουλεύεται μετὰ τοῦ ἀδελφοῦ, καὶ πρὸς Νέστορα παραγίνεται

Hera, Athena, and Aphrodite as to which of them is fairest. The three are led by Hermes at the command of Zeus to Alexandrus[1] on Mount Ida for his decision, and Alexandrus, lured by his promised marriage with Helen, decides in favour of Aphrodite.

Then Alexandrus builds his ships at Aphrodite's suggestion, and Helenus foretells the future to him, and Aphrodite orders Aeneas to sail with him, while Cassandra prophesies as to what will happen afterwards. Alexandrus next lands in Lacedaemon and is entertained by the sons of Tyndareus, and afterwards by Menelaus in Sparta, where in the course of a feast he gives gifts to Helen.

After this, Menelaus sets sail for Crete, ordering Helen to furnish the guests with all they require until they depart. Meanwhile, Aphrodite brings Helen and Alexandrus together, and they, after their union, put very great treasures on board and sail away by night. Hera stirs up a storm against them and they are carried to Sidon, where Alexandrus takes the city. From there he sailed to Troy and celebrated his marriage with Helen.

In the meantime Castor and Polydeuces, while stealing the cattle of Idas and Lynceus, were caught in the act, and Castor was killed by Idas, and Lynceus and Idas by Polydeuces. Zeus gave them immortality every other day.

Iris next informs Menelaus of what has happened at his home. Menelaus returns and plans an expedition against Ilium with his brother, and then goes on

[1] *sc.* Paris.

Μενέλαος. Νέστωρ δὲ ἐν παρεκβάσει διηγεῖται αὐτῷ ὡς Ἐπωπεὺς φθείρας τὴν Λύκου θυγατέρα ἐξεπορθήθη, καὶ τὰ περὶ Οἰδίπουν καὶ τὴν Ἡρακλέους μανίαν καὶ τὰ περὶ Θησέα καὶ Ἀριάδνην. ἔπειτα τοὺς ἡγεμόνας ἀθροίζουσιν ἐπελθόντες τὴν Ἑλλάδα. καὶ μαίνεσθαι προσποιησάμενον τὸν Ὀδυσσέα ἐπὶ τῷ μὴ θέλειν συστρατεύεσθαι ἐφώρασαν, Παλαμήδους ὑποθεμένου τὸν υἱὸν Τηλέμαχον ἐπὶ κόλασιν ἐξαρπάσαντες.

Καὶ μετὰ ταῦτα συνελθόντες εἰς Αὐλίδα θυοῦσι· καὶ τὰ περὶ τὸν δράκοντα καὶ τοὺς στρουθοὺς γενόμενα δείκνυται, καὶ Κάλχας περὶ τῶν ἀποβησομένων προλέγει αὐτοῖς. ἔπειτα ἀναχθέντες Τευθρανίᾳ προσίσχουσι καὶ ταύτην ὡς Ἴλιον ἐπόρθουν. Τήλεφος δὲ ἐκβοηθήσας Θέρσανδρόν τε τὸν Πολυνείκους κτείνει καὶ αὐτὸς ὑπὸ Ἀχιλλέως τιτρώσκεται. ἀποπλέουσι δὲ αὐτοῖς ἐκ τῆς Μυσίας χειμὼν ἐπιπίπτει καὶ διασκεδάννυνται. Ἀχιλλεὺς δὲ Σκύρῳ προσσχὼν γαμεῖ τὴν Λυκομήδους θυγατέρα Δηϊδάμειαν. ἔπειτα Τήλεφον κατὰ μαντείαν παραγενόμενον εἰς Ἄργος ἰᾶται Ἀχιλλεὺς ὡς ἡγεμόνα γενησόμενον τοῦ ἐπ' Ἴλιον πλοῦ.

Καὶ τὸ δεύτερον ἠθροισμένου τοῦ στόλου ἐν Αὐλίδι, Ἀγαμέμνων ἐπὶ θήρας βαλὼν ἔλαφον, ὑπερβάλλειν ἔφησε καὶ τὴν Ἄρτεμιν. μηνίσασα δὲ ἡ θεὸς ἐπέσχεν αὐτοὺς τοῦ πλοῦ χειμῶνας ἐπιπέμπουσα. Κάλχαντος δὲ εἰπόντος τὴν τῆς θεοῦ μῆνιν καὶ Ἰφιγένειαν κελεύσαντος θύειν τῇ Ἀρτέμιδι, ὡς ἐπὶ γάμον αὐτὴν Ἀχιλλεῖ μεταto Nestor. Nestor in a digression tells him how Epopeus was utterly destroyed after seducing the daughter of Lycus, and the story of Oedipus, the madness of Heracles, and the story of Theseus and Ariadne. Then they travel over Hellas and gather the leaders, detecting Odysseus when he pretends to be mad, not wishing to join the expedition, by seizing his son Telemachus for punishment at the suggestion of Palamedes.

All the leaders then meet together at Aulis and sacrifice. The incident of the serpent and the sparrows[1] takes place before them, and Calchas foretells what is going to befall. After this, they put out to sea, and reach Teuthrania and sack it, taking it for Ilium. Telephus comes out to the rescue and kills Thersander the son of Polyneices, and is himself wounded by Achilles. As they put out from Mysia a storm comes on them and scatters them, and Achilles first puts in at Scyros and marries Deïdameia, the daughter of Lycomedes, and then heals Telephus, who had been led by an oracle to go to Argos, so that he might be their guide on the voyage to Ilium.

When the expedition had mustered a second time at Aulis, Agamemnon, while at the chase, shot a stag and boasted that he surpassed even Artemis. At this the goddess was so angry that she sent stormy winds and prevented them from sailing. Calchas then told them of the anger of the goddess and bade them sacrifice Iphigeneia to Artemis. This they attempt to do, sending to fetch Iphigeneia as though

[1] While the Greeks were sacrificing at Aulis, a serpent appeared and devoured eight young birds from their nest and lastly the mother of the brood. This was interpreted by Calchas to mean that the war would swallow up nine full years. Cp. *Iliad* ii, 299 ff.

πεμψάμενοι, θύειν ἐπιχειροῦσιν. Ἄρτεμις δὲ αὐτὴν ἐξαρπάσασα, εἰς Ταύρους μετακομίζει καὶ ἀθάνατον ποιεῖ· ἔλαφον δὲ ἀντὶ τῆς κόρης παρίστησι τῷ βωμῷ.

Ἔπειτα καταπλέουσιν εἰς Τένεδον. καὶ εὐωχουμένων αὐτῶν Φιλοκτήτης ὑφ' ὕδρου πληγεὶς διὰ τὴν δυσοσμίαν ἐν Λήμνῳ κατελείφθη, καὶ Ἀχιλλεὺς ὕστερον κληθεὶς διαφέρεται πρὸς Ἀγαμέμνονα. ἔπειτα ἀποβαίνοντας αὐτοὺς εἰς Ἴλιον εἴργουσιν οἱ Τρῶες, καὶ θνήσκει Πρωτεσίλαος ὑφ' Ἕκτορος. ἔπειτα Ἀχιλλεὺς αὐτοὺς τρέπεται ἀνελὼν Κύκνον τὸν Ποσειδῶνος. καὶ τοὺς νεκροὺς ἀναιροῦνται, καὶ διαπρεσβεύονται πρὸς τοὺς Τρῶας, τὴν Ἑλένην καὶ τὰ χρήματα ἀπαιτοῦντες. ὡς δὲ οὐχ ὑπήκουσαν ἐκεῖνοι, ἐνταῦθα δὴ τειχομαχοῦσι. ἔπειτα τὴν χώραν ἐπεξελθόντες πορθοῦσι καὶ τὰς περιοίκους πόλεις. καὶ μετὰ ταῦτα Ἀχιλλεὺς Ἑλένην ἐπιθυμεῖ θεάσασθαι, καὶ συνήγαγον αὐτοὺς εἰς τὸ αὐτὸ Ἀφροδίτη καὶ Θέτις. εἶτα ἀπονοστεῖν ὡρμημένους τοὺς Ἀχαιοὺς Ἀχιλλεὺς κατέχει. κἄπειτα ἀπελαύνει τὰς Αἰνείου βόας, καὶ Λυρνησὸν καὶ Πήδασον πορθεῖ καὶ συχνὰς τῶν περιοικίδων πόλεων, καὶ Τρωΐλον φονεύει. Λυκάονά τε Πάτροκλος εἰς Λῆμνον ἀγαγὼν ἀπεμπολᾷ, καὶ ἐκ τῶν λαφύρων Ἀχιλλεὺς μὲν Βρισηΐδα γέρας λαμβάνει, Χρυσηΐδα δὲ Ἀγαμέμνων. ἔπειτα ἐστι Παλαμήδους θάνατος, καὶ Διὸς βουλὴ ὅπως ἐπικουφίσῃ τοὺς Τρῶας Ἀχιλλέα τῆς συμμαχίας τῆς Ἑλληνικῆς ἀποστήσας, καὶ κατάλογος τῶν τοῖς Τρωσὶ συμμαχησάντων.

for marriage with Achilles. Artemis, however, snatched her away and transported her to the Tauri, making her immortal, and putting a stag in place of the girl upon the altar.

Next they sail as far as Tenedos : and while they are feasting, Philoctetes is bitten by a snake and is left behind in Lemnos because of the stench of his sore. Here, too, Achilles quarrels with Agamemnon because he is invited late. Then the Greeks tried to land at Ilium, but the Trojans prevent them, and Protesilaus is killed by Hector. Achilles then kills Cycnus, the son of Poseidon, and drives the Trojans back. The Greeks take up their dead and send envoys to the Trojans demanding the surrender of Helen and the treasure with her. The Trojans refusing, they first assault the city, and then go out and lay waste the country and cities round about. After this, Achilles desires to see Helen, and Aphrodite and Thetis contrive a meeting between them. The Achaeans next desire to return home, but are restrained by Achilles, who afterwards drives off the cattle of Aeneas, and sacks Lyrnessus and Pedasus and many of the neighbouring cities, and kills Troïlus. Patroclus carries away Lycaon to Lemnos and sells him as a slave, and out of the spoils Achilles receives Briseïs as a prize, and Agamemnon Chryseïs. Then follows the death of Palamedes, the plan of Zeus to relieve the Trojans by detaching Achilles from the Hellenic confederacy, and a catalogue of the Trojan allies.

2.

Tzetzes, Chil. xiii. 638.

Στασῖνος ὁ τὰ Κύπρια συγγράμματα ποιήσας ἅπερ οἱ πλείους λέγουσι Ὁμήρου πεφυκέναι ἐς προῖκα δὲ σὺν χρήμασι δοθῆναι τῷ Στασίνῳ.

3.

Schol. on Homer, Il. i. 5.

ἦν ὅτε μυρία φῦλα κατὰ χθόνα πλαζομένων περ
[ἀνθρώπων ἐβάρυνε] βαθυστέρνου πλάτος αἴης,
Ζεὺς δὲ ἰδὼν ἐλέησε καὶ ἐν πυκιναῖς πραπίδεσσι
σύνθετο κουφίσαι ἀνθρώπων παμβώτορα γαῖαν,
ῥιπίσσας πολέμου μεγάλην ἔριν Ἰλιακοῖο
ὄφρα κενώσειεν θανάτου βάρος· οἱ δ' ἐνὶ Τροίῃ
ἥρωες κτείνοντο· Διὸς δ' ἐτελείετο βουλή.

4.

Volumina Herculan. II. viii. 105. ὁ δὲ τὰ Κύπρια ποιήσας Ἥρᾳ χαριζομένην φεύγειν αὐτοῦ τὸν γάμον, Δία δὲ ὀμόσαι χολωθέντα διότι θνητῷ συνοικίσει.

5.

Schol. on Il. xvii. 140. κατὰ γὰρ τὸν Πηλέως καὶ Θέτιδος γάμον οἱ θεοὶ συναχθέντες εἰς τὸ Πήλιον ἐπ' εὐωχίᾳ ἐκόμιζον Πηλεῖ δῶρα, Χείρων δὲ μελίαν εὐθαλῆ τεμὼν εἰς δόρυ παρέσχεν. φασὶ μὲν Ἀθηνᾶν ξέσαι αὐτό, Ἥφαιστον δὲ κατασκευάσαι . . . ἡ ἱστορία παρὰ τῷ τὰ Κύπρια ποιήσαντι.

6.

Athenaeus, xv. 682 D, F. ἀνθῶν δὲ στεφανωτικῶν μέμνηται ὁ μὲν τὰ Κύπρια πεποιηκὼς Ἡγησίας ἢ

2.

Stasinus composed the *Cypria* which the more part say was Homer's work and by him given to Stasinus as a dowry with money besides.

3.

"There was a time when the countless tribes of men, though wide-dispersed, oppressed the surface of the deep-bosomed earth, and Zeus saw it and had pity and in his wise heart resolved to relieve the all-nurturing earth of men by causing the great struggle of the Ilian war, that the load of death might empty the world. And so the heroes were slain in Troy, and the plan of Zeus came to pass."

4.

The author of the *Cypria* says that Thetis, to please Hera, avoided union with Zeus, at which he was enraged and swore that she should be the wife of a mortal.

5.

For at the marriage of Peleus and Thetis, the gods gathered together on Pelion to feast and brought Peleus gifts. Cheiron gave him a stout ashen shaft which he had cut for a spear, and Athena, it is said, polished it, and Hephaestus fitted it with a head. The story is given by the author of the *Cypria*.

6.

The author of the *Cypria*, whether Hegesias or Stasinus, mentions flowers used for garlands. The

Στασῖνος . . . λέγει δ' οὖν ὅστις ἐστὶν ὁ ποιήσας αὐτὰ ἐν τῷ α' οὑτωσί·

εἵματα μὲν χροὶ ἕστο τά οἱ Χάριτές τε καὶ Ὧραι
ποίησαν καὶ ἔβαψαν ἐν ἄνθεσιν εἰαρινοῖσι,
οἷα φοροῦσ' Ὧραι, ἔν τε κρόκῳ ἔν θ' ὑακίνθῳ
ἔν τε ἴῳ θαλέθοντι ῥόδου τ' ἐνὶ ἄνθεϊ καλῷ
ἡδέι νεκταρέῳ ἔν τ' ἀμβροσίαις καλύκεσσι
ἄνθεσι ναρκίσσου καὶ λειρίου· τοῖ'[1] Ἀφροδίτη
ὥραις παντοίαις τεθυωμένα εἵματα ἕστο.

*　　*　　*　　*

ἡ δὲ σὺν ἀμφιπόλοισι φιλομμειδὴς Ἀφροδίτη
πλεξάμεναι στεφάνους εὐώδεας, ἄνθεα γαίης,
ἂν κεφαλαῖσιν ἔθεντο θεαὶ λιπαροκρήδεμνοι
Νύμφαι καὶ Χάριτες, ἅμα δὲ χρυσῆ Ἀφροδίτη,
καλὸν ἀείδουσαι κατ' ὄρος πολυπιδάκου Ἴδης.

7.

Clement of Alexandria, Protrept ii. 30. 5.

Κάστωρ μὲν θνητός, θανάτου δέ οἱ αἶσα πέπρωται
αὐτὰρ ὅ γ' ἀθάνατος Πολυδεύκης, ὄζος Ἄρηος

8.

Athenaeus, viii. 334 B.

τοὺς δὲ μετὰ τριτάτην Ἑλένην τέκε, θαῦμα βροτοῖσι,
τήν ποτε καλλίκομος Νέμεσις φιλότητι μιγεῖσα
Ζηνὶ θεῶν βασιλῆϊ τέκε κρατερῆς ὑπ' ἀνάγκης·
φεῦγε γάρ, οὐδ' ἔθελεν μιχθήμεναι ἐν φιλότητι
πατρὶ Διὶ Κρονιώνι· ἐτείρετο γὰρ φρένας αἰδοῖ
καὶ νεμέσει· κατὰ γῆν δὲ καὶ ἀτρύγετον μέλαν ὕδωρ

[1] Meineke: καλλιρρόου δ' οἷ', MS.

poet, whoever he was, writes as follows in his first book: "She clothed herself with garments which the Graces and Hours had made for her and dyed in flowers of spring—such flowers as the Seasons wear—in crocus and hyacinth and flourishing violet and the rose's lovely bloom, so sweet and delicious, and heavenly buds, the flowers of the narcissus and lily. In such perfumed garments is Aphrodite clothed at all seasons. * * * Then laughter-loving Aphrodite and her handmaidens wove sweet-smelling crowns of flowers of the earth and put them upon their heads—the bright-coiffed goddesses, the Nymphs and Graces, and golden Aphrodite too, while they sang sweetly on the mount of many-fountained Ida."

7.

"Castor was mortal, and the fate of death was destined for him; but Polydeuces, scion of Ares, was immortal."

8.

"And after them she bare a third child, Helen, a marvel to men. Rich-tressed Nemesis once gave her birth when she had been joined in love with Zeus the king of the gods by harsh violence. For Nemesis tried to escape him and liked not to lie in love with her father Zeus the Son of Cronos; for shame and indignation vexed her heart: therefore she fled him over the land and fruitless dark water. But

φεῦγε, Ζεὺς δ' ἐδίωκε· λαβεῖν δ' ἐλιλαίετο θυμῷ·
ἄλλοτε μὲν κατὰ κῦμα πολυφλοίσβοιο θαλάσσης,
ἄλλοτ' ἀν' Ὠκεανοῦ ποταμὸν καὶ πείρατα Γαίης,
ἰχθύι εἰδομένη πόντον πολὺν ἐξορόθυνεν,
ἄλλοτ' ἀν' ἤπειρον πολυβώλακα· γίγνετο δ' αἰεὶ
θηρί' ὅσ' ἤπειρος αἰνὰ τρέφει, ὄφρα φύγοι νιν.

9.

Schol. on Eur. Andr. 898. ὁ δὲ τὰς Κυπριακὰς ἱστορίας συντάξας Πλεισθένην φησί, μεθ' οὗ εἰς Κύπρον ἀφῖχθαι, καὶ τὸν ἐξ αὐτῆς τεχθέντα Ἀλεξάνδρῳ Ἄγανον.

10.

Herodotus, ii. 117. ἐν μὲν γὰρ τοῖσι Κυπρίοισι εἴρηται ὡς τριταῖος ἐκ Σπάρτης Ἀλέξανδρος ἀπίκετο ἐς τὸ Ἴλιον ἄγων Ἑλένην, εὐαέι τε πνεύματι χρησάμενος καὶ θαλάσσῃ λείῃ.

11.

Schol. on Il. iii. 242. ἐπειδὴ προτέρως ὑπὸ Θησέως ἡρπάσθη . . . διὰ γὰρ τὴν τότε γενομένην ἁρπαγὴν Ἄφιδνα πόλις Ἀττικῆς πορθεῖται, καὶ τιτρώσκεται Κάστωρ ὑπὸ Ἀφίδνου τοῦ τότε βασιλέως κατὰ τὸ δεξιὸν μηρόν. οἱ δὲ Διόσκουροι Θησέως μὴ τυχόντες λαφυραγωγοῦσι τὰς Ἀθήνας. ἡ ἱστορία παρὰ . . . τοῖς κυκλικοῖς. . .

Plutarch, Thes. 32. Ἡρέας δ' ὑπὸ Θησέως αὐτοῦ περὶ Ἀφίδνας ἀποθανεῖν τὸν Ἄλυκον ἱστόρηκε, καὶ μαρτύρια ταυτὰ τὰ ἔπη παρέχεται . . .

τὸν ἐν εὐρυχόρῳ ποτ' Ἀφίδνῃ
μαρνάμενον Θησεὺς Ἑλένης ἕνεκ' ἠυκόμοιο
κτεῖνεν.[1]

[1] Cp. Allen *C.R.* xxvii. 190.

Zeus ever pursued and longed in his heart to catch her. Now she took the form of a fish and sped over the waves of the loud-roaring sea, and now over Ocean's stream and the furthest bounds of Earth, and now she sped over the furrowed land, always turning into such dread creatures as the dry land nurtures, that she might escape him."

9.

The writer[1] of the Cyprian histories says that (Helen's third child was) Pleisthenes and that she took him with her to Cyprus, and that the child she bore Alexandrus was Aganus.

10.

For it is said in the *Cypria* that Alexandrus came with Helen to Ilium from Sparta in three days, enjoying a favourable wind and calm sea.

11.

For Helen had been previously carried off by Theseus, and it was in consequence of this earlier rape that Aphidna, a town in Attica, was sacked and Castor was wounded in the right thigh by Aphidnus who was king at that time. Then the Dioscuri, failing to find Theseus, sacked Athens. The story is in the Cyclic writers.

Hereas relates that Alycus was killed by Theseus himself near Aphidna, and quotes the following verses in evidence:

"In spacious Aphidna Theseus slew him in battle long ago for rich-haired Helen's sake."

[1] *i.e.* Stasinus (or Hegesias: cp. fr. 6): the phrase "Cyprian histories" is equivalent to "The Cypria."

12.

Schol. on Pindar, Nem. x. 114.

αἶψα δὲ Λυγκεὺς
Ταΰγετον προσέβαινε ποσὶν ταχέεσσι πεποιθώς.
ἀκρότατον δ' ἀναβὰς διεδέρκετο νῆσον ἅπασαν
Ταντταλίδου Πέλοπος, τάχα δ' εἴσιδε κύδιμος ἥρως
δεινοῖς ὀφθαλμοῖσιν ἔσω δρυὸς ἄμφω κοίλης
Κάστορά θ' ἱππόδαμον καὶ ἀεθλοφόρον Πολυδεύκεα.

Philodemus, On Piety. Κάστορα δὲ ὑπὸ Ἴδα τοῦ Ἀφάρεω κατηκοντίσθαι γέγρα[φε . . .

13.

Athenaeus, 35 c.

οἶνόν τοι, Μενέλαε, θεοὶ ποίησαν ἄριστον
θνητοῖς ἀνθρώποισιν ἀποσκεδάσαι μελεδῶνας.

14.

Laurentian Scholiast on Sophocles, Elect. 157. ἢ Ὁμήρῳ ἀκολουθεῖ εἰρηκότι τὰς τρεῖς θυγατέρας τοῦ Ἀγαμέμνονος, ἢ ὡς ὁ τὰ Κύπρια, δ' φησίν, Ἰφιγένειαν καὶ Ἰφιάνασσαν.

15.[1]

Contest of Homer and Hesiod.

ὣς οἱ μὲν δαίνυντο πανήμεροι οὐδὲν ἔχοντες
οἴκοθεν, ἀλλὰ παρεῖχεν ἄναξ ἀνδρῶν Ἀγαμέμνων.

16.

Louvre Papyrus.

οὐκ ἐφάμην Ἀχιλῆϊ χολωσέμεν ἄλκιμον ἦτορ
ὧδε μαλ' ἐκπάγλως, ἐπεὶ ἦ μάλα μοι φίλος ἦεν.

[1] These two lines possibly belong to the account of the feast given by Agamemnon at Lemnos.

12.

"Straightway Lynceus, trusting in his swift feet, made for Taygetus. He climbed its highest peak and looked throughout the whole isle of Pelops, son of Tantalus; and soon the glorious hero with his dread eyes saw horse-taming Castor and athlete Polydeuces both hidden within a hollow oak."

(Stasinus?) writes that Castor was killed with a spear shot by Idas the son of Aphareus.

13.

"Menelaus, know that the gods made wine the best thing for mortal man to scatter cares."

14.

Either he follows Homer who spoke of the three daughters of Agamemnon, or—like the writer of the *Cypria*—he makes them four, (distinguishing) Iphigeneia and Iphianassa.

15.

"So they feasted all day long, taking nothing from their own houses; for Agamemnon, king of men, provided for them."

16.

"I never thought to enrage so terribly the stout heart of Achilles, for very well I loved him."

17.

Pausanias, iv. 2. 7. ὁ δὲ τὰ ἔπη ποιήσας τὰ Κύπρια Πρωτεσιλάου φησίν, ὃς ὅτε κατὰ τὴν Τρῳάδα ἔσχον Ἕλληνες ἀποβῆναι πρῶτος ἐτόλμησε, Πρωτεσιλάου τούτου τὴν γυναῖκα Πολυδώραν μὲν τὸ ὄνομα, θυγατέρα δὲ Μελεάγρου φησὶν εἶναι τοῦ Οἰνέως.

18.

Eustathius, 119. 4. ἱστοροῦσι δέ τινες ὅτι ἐκ τῶν Ὑποπλακίων Θηβῶν ἡ Χρυσηὶς ἐλήφθη, οὔτε καταφυγοῦσα ἐκεῖ, οὔτ' ἐπὶ θυσίαν Ἀρτέμιδος ἐλθοῦσα, ὡς ὁ τὰ Κύπρια γράψας ἔφη, ἀλλὰ πολιτὶς . . . Ἀνδρομάχης οὖσα.

19.

Pausanias, x. 31. 2. Παλαμήδην δὲ ἀποπνιγῆναι προελθόντα ἐπὶ ἰχθύων θήραν, Διομήδην δὲ τὸν ἀποκτείναντα εἶναι καὶ Ὀδυσσέα ἐπιλεξάμενος ἐν ἔπεσιν οἶδα τοῖς Κυπρίοις.

20.

Plato, *Euthyphron*, 12 A.

Ζῆνα δὲ τόν τ' ἔρξαντα καὶ ὃς τάδε πάντ' ἐφύτευσεν
οὐκ ἐθέλεις εἰπεῖν· ἵνα γὰρ δέος ἔνθα καὶ αἰδώς.

21.

Herodian, *On Peculiar Diction.*

τῷ δ' ὑποκυσαμένη τέκε Γοργόνας αἰνὰ πέλωρα,
αἳ Σαρπηδόνα ναῖον ἐπ' Ὠκεανῷ βαθυδίνῃ,
νῆσον πετρήεσσαν.

17.

The poet of the *Cypria* says that the wife of Protesilaus—who, when the Hellenes reached the Trojan shore, first dared to land—was called Polydora, and was the daughter of Meleager, the son of Oeneus.

18.

Some relate that Chryseïs was taken from Hypoplacian[1] Thebes, and that she had not taken refuge there nor gone there to sacrifice to Artemis, as the author of the *Cypria* states, but was simply a fellow townswoman of Andromache.

19.

I know, because I have read it in the epic *Cypria*, that Palamedes was drowned when he had gone out fishing, and that it was Diomedes and Odysseus who caused his death.

20.

"That it is Zeus who has done this, and brought all these things to pass, you do not like to say; for where fear is, there too is shame."

21.

"By him she conceived and bare the Gorgons, fearful monsters who lived in Sarpedon, a rocky island in deep-eddying Oceanus."

[1] *sc.* the Asiatic Thebes at the foot of Mt. Placius.

22.

Clement of Alexandria, Stromateis vii. 2. 19. πάλιν Στασίνου εἰπόντος

νήπιος ὃς πατέρα κτείνας παῖδας καταλείπει.

ΑΙΘΙΟΠΙΣ

1.

Proclus, Chrestomathia, ii. Ἐπιβάλλει δὲ τοῖς προειρημένοις (*sc.* Κυπρίοις) ἐν τῇ πρὸ ταύτης βίβλῳ Ἰλιὰς Ὁμήρου, μεθ᾽ ἥν ἐστιν Αἰθιόπιδος βιβλία ε᾽ Ἀρκτίνου Μιλησίου περιέχοντα τάδε. Ἀμαζὼν Πενθεσίλεια παραγίνεται Τρωσὶ συμμαχήσουσα, Ἄρεως μὲν θυγάτηρ, Θρᾷσσα δὲ τὸ γένος· καὶ κτείνει αὐτὴν ἀριστεύουσαν Ἀχιλλεύς, οἱ δὲ Τρῶες αὐτὴν θάπτουσι. καὶ Ἀχιλλεὺς Θερσίτην ἀναιρεῖ λοιδορηθεὶς πρὸς αὐτοῦ καὶ ὀνειδισθεὶς τὸν ἐπὶ τῇ Πενθεσιλείᾳ λεγόμενον ἔρωτα. καὶ ἐκ τούτου στάσις γίνεται τοῖς Ἀχαιοῖς περὶ τοῦ Θερσίτου φόνου. μετὰ δὲ ταῦτα Ἀχιλλεὺς εἰς Λέσβον πλεῖ, καὶ θύσας Ἀπόλλωνι καὶ Ἀρτέμιδι καὶ Λητοῖ καθαίρεται τοῦ φόνου ὑπ᾽ Ὀδυσσέως.

Μέμνων δὲ ὁ Ἠοῦς υἱὸς ἔχων ἡφαιστότευκτον πανοπλίαν παραγίνεται τοῖς Τρωσὶ βοηθήσων· καὶ Θέτις τῷ παιδὶ τὰ κατὰ τὸν Μέμνονα προλέγει. καὶ συμβολῆς γενομένης Ἀντίλοχος ὑπὸ Μέμνονος ἀναιρεῖται, ἔπειτα Ἀχιλλεὺς Μέμνονα κτείνει. καὶ τούτῳ μὲν Ἠὼς παρὰ Διὸς αἰτησαμένη ἀθανασίαν δίδωσι· τρεψάμενος δ᾽ Ἀχιλλεὺς τοὺς Τρῶας καὶ εἰς τὴν πόλιν συνεισπεσὼν ὑπὸ

22.

Again, Stasinus says:

"He is a simple man who kills the father and lets the children live."

THE AETHIOPIS

1.

The *Cypria*, described in the preceding book, has its sequel in the *Iliad* of Homer, which is followed in turn by the five books of the *Aethiopis*, the work of Arctinus of Miletus. Their contents are as follows. The Amazon Penthesileia, the daughter of Ares and of Thracian race, comes to aid the Trojans, and after showing great prowess, is killed by Achilles and buried by the Trojans. Achilles then slays Thersites for abusing and reviling him for his supposed love for Penthesileia. As a result a dispute arises amongst the Achaeans over the killing of Thersites, and Achilles sails to Lesbos and after sacrificing to Apollo, Artemis, and Leto, is purified by Odysseus from bloodshed.

Then Memnon, the son of Eos, wearing armour made by Hephaestus, comes to help the Trojans, and Thetis tells her son about Memnon. A battle takes place in which Antilochus is slain by Memnon and Memnon by Achilles. Eos then obtains of Zeus and bestows upon her son immortality; but Achilles routs the Trojans, and, rushing into the city with

Πάριδος ἀναιρεῖται καὶ Ἀπόλλωνος· καὶ περὶ τοῦ πτώματος γενομένης ἰσχυρᾶς μάχης Αἴας ἀνελόμενος ἐπὶ τὰς ναῦς κομίζει, Ὀδυσσέως ἀπομαχομένου τοῖς Τρωσίν. ἔπειτα Ἀντίλοχόν τε θάπτουσι καὶ τὸν νεκρὸν τοῦ Ἀχιλλέως προτίθενται· καὶ Θέτις ἀφικομένη σὺν Μούσαις καὶ ταῖς ἀδελφαῖς θρηνεῖ τὸν παῖδα· καὶ μετὰ ταῦτα ἐκ τῆς πυρᾶς ἡ Θέτις ἀναρπάσασα τὸν παῖδα εἰς τὴν Λευκὴν Νῆσον διακομίζει. οἱ δὲ Ἀχαιοὶ τὸν τάφον χώσαντες ἀγῶνα τιθέασιν, καὶ περὶ τῶν Ἀχιλλέως ὅπλων Ὀδυσσεῖ καὶ Αἴαντι στάσις ἐμπίπτει.

2.

Schol. on Il. xxiv. 804. τινὲς γράφουσι

ὣς οἵ γ' ἀμφίεπον τάφον Ἕκτορος. ἦλθε δ' Ἀμαζών,
Ἄρηος θυγάτηρ μεγαλήτορος ἀνδροφόνοιο.

3.

Schol. on Pindar, Isth. iii. 53. ὁ γὰρ τὴν Αἰθιοπίδα γράφων περὶ τὸν ὄρθρον φησὶ τὸν Αἴαντα ἑαυτὸν ἀνελεῖν.

ΙΛΙΑΣ ΜΙΚΡΑ

1.

Ἑξῆς δ' ἐστὶν Ἰλιάδος μικρᾶς βιβλία τέσσερα Λέσχεω Μιτυληναίου περιέχοντα τάδε. ἡ τῶν ὅπλων κρίσις γίνεται καὶ Ὀδυσσεὺς κατὰ βούλησιν Ἀθηνᾶς λαμβάνει. Αἴας δ' ἐμμανὴς γενόμενος τήν τε λείαν τῶν Ἀχαιῶν λυμαίνεται καὶ ἑαυτὸν ἀναιρεῖ. μετὰ ταῦτα Ὀδυσσεὺς λοχήσας them, is killed by Paris and Apollo. A great struggle for the body then follows, Aias taking up the body and carrying it to the ships, while Odysseus drives off the Trojans behind. The Achaeans then bury Antilochus and lay out the body of Achilles, while Thetis, arriving with the Muses and her sisters, bewails her son, whom she afterwards catches away from the pyre and transports to the White Island. After this, the Achaeans pile him a cairn and hold games in his honour. Lastly a dispute arises between Odysseus and Aias over the arms of Achilles.

2.

Some read: "Thus they performed the burial of Hector. Then came the Amazon, the daughter of great-souled Ares the slayer of men."

3.

The author of the *Aethiopis* says that Aias killed himself about dawn.

THE LITTLE ILIAD

1.

NEXT comes the Little Iliad in four books by Lesches of Mitylene: its contents are as follows. The adjudging of the arms of Achilles takes place, and Odysseus, by the contriving of Athena, gains them. Aias then becomes mad and destroys the herd of the Achaeans and kills himself. Next Odysseus lies in wait and catches Helenus, who

Ἕλενον λαμβάνει, καὶ χρήσαντος περὶ τῆς ἁλώσεως τούτου, Διομήδης ἐκ Λήμνου Φιλοκτήτην ἀνάγει. ἰαθεὶς δὲ οὗτος ὑπὸ Μαχάονος καὶ μονομαχήσας Ἀλεξάνδρῳ κτείνει· καὶ τὸν νεκρὸν ὑπὸ Μενελάου καταικισθέντα ἀνελόμενοι θάπτουσιν οἱ Τρῶες. μετὰ δὲ ταῦτα Δηίφοβος Ἑλένην γαμεῖ, καὶ Νεοπτόλεμον Ὀδυσσεὺς ἐκ Σκύρου ἀγαγὼν τὰ ὅπλα δίδωσι τὰ τοῦ πατρός· καὶ Ἀχιλλεὺς αὐτῷ φαντάζεται.

Εὐρύπυλος δὲ ὁ Τηλέφου ἐπίκουρος τοῖς Τρωσὶ παραγίνεται, καὶ ἀριστεύοντα αὐτὸν ἀποκτείνει Νεοπτόλεμος, καὶ οἱ Τρῶες πολιορκοῦνται. καὶ Ἐπειὸς κατ' Ἀθηνᾶς προαίρεσιν τὸν δούρειον ἵππον κατασκευάζει, Ὀδυσσεύς τε αἰκισάμενος ἑαυτὸν κατάσκοπος εἰς Ἴλιον παραγίνεται, καὶ ἀναγνωρισθεὶς ὑφ' Ἑλένης περὶ τῆς ἁλώσεως τῆς πόλεως συντίθεται, κτείνας τέ τινας τῶν Τρώων ἐπὶ τὰς ναῦς ἀφικνεῖται. καὶ μετὰ ταῦτα σὺν Διομήδει τὸ παλλάδιον ἐκκομίζει ἐκ τῆς Ἰλίου. ἔπειτα εἰς τὸν δούρειον ἵππον τοὺς ἀρίστους ἐμβιβάσαντες τάς τε σκηνὰς καταφλέξαντες, οἱ λοιποὶ τῶν Ἑλλήνων εἰς Τένεδον ἀνάγονται· οἱ δὲ Τρῶες τῶν κακῶν ὑπολαβόντες ἀπηλλάχθαι, τόν τε δούρειον ἵππον εἰς τὴν πόλιν εἰσδέχονται, διελόντες μέρος τι τοῦ τείχους, καὶ εὐωχοῦνται ὡς νενικηκότες τοὺς Ἕλληνας.

2.

Herodotus, Life of Homer.

Ἴλιον ἀείδω καὶ Δαρδανίην εὔπωλον
ἧς πέρι πολλὰ πάθον Δαναοὶ θεράποντες Ἄρηος.

prophesies as to the taking of Troy, and Diomede accordingly brings Philoctetes from Lemnos. Philoctetes is healed by Machaon, fights in single combat with Alexandrus and kills him: the dead body is outraged by Menelaus, but the Trojans recover and bury it. After this Deïphobus marries Helen, Odysseus brings Neoptolemus from Scyros and gives him his father's arms, and the ghost of Achilles appears to him.

Eurypylus the son of Telephus arrives to aid the Trojans, shows his prowess and is killed by Neoptolemus. The Trojans are now closely beseiged, and Epeius, by Athena's instruction, builds the wooden horse. Odysseus disfigures himself and goes in to Ilium as a spy, and there being recognized by Helen, plots with her for the taking of the city; after killing certain of the Trojans, he returns to the ships. Next he carries the Palladium out of Troy with the help of Diomedes. Then after putting their best men in the wooden horse and burning their huts, the main body of the Hellenes sail to Tenedos. The Trojans, supposing their troubles over, destroy a part of their city wall and take the wooden horse into their city and feast as though they had conquered the Hellenes.

2.

"I sing of Ilium and Dardania, the land of fine horses, wherein the Danaï, followers of Ares, suffered many things."

3.

Schol. on Aristoph. Knights 1056 *and Aristophanes ib.* ἡ ἱστορία τοῦτον τὸν τρόπον ἔχει. ὅτι διεφέροντο περὶ τῶν ἀριστείων ὅ τε Αἴας καὶ ὁ Ὀδυσσεύς, ὥς φησιν ὁ τὴν μικρὰν Ἰλιάδα πεποιηκώς. τὸν Νέστορα δὲ συμβουλεῦσαι τοῖς Ἕλλησι πέμψαι τινὰς ἐξ αὐτῶν ὑπὸ τὰ τείχη τῶν Τρώων ὠτακουστήσοντας περὶ τῆς ἀνδρείας τῶν προειρημένων ἡρώων. τοὺς δὲ πεμφθέντας ἀκοῦσαι παρθένων διαφερομένων πρὸς ἀλλήλας, ὧν τὴν μὲν λέγειν ὡς ὁ Αἴας πολὺ κρείττων ἐστὶ τοῦ Ὀδυσσέως, διερχομένην οὕτως·

Αἴας μὲν γὰρ ἄειρε καὶ ἔκφερε δηιοτῆτος
ἥρω Πηλείδην οὐδ' ἤθελε δῖος Ὀδυσσεύς.

τὴν δ' ἑτέραν ἀντειπεῖν Ἀθηνᾶς προνοίᾳ·

πῶς ἐπεφωνήσω; πῶς οὐ κατὰ κόσμον ἔειπες
ψεῦδος; . . . .
καί κε γυνὴ φέροι ἄχθος ἐπεί κεν ἀνὴρ ἀναθείη,
ἀλλ' οὐκ ἂν μαχέσαιτο· χέσειτο γὰρ εἰ μαχέσαιτο.

4.

Eustathius, 285. 34. ὁ τὴν μικρὰν Ἰλιάδα γράψας ἱστορεῖ μηδὲ καυθῆναι συνήθως τὸν Αἴαντα, τεθῆναι δὲ οὕτως ἐν σορῷ διὰ τὴν ὀργὴν τοῦ βασιλέως.

5.

Eustathius on Homer, Il. 326. ὁ δὲ τὴν μικρὰν Ἰλιάδα γράψας ἀναζευγνύντα αὐτὸν ἀπο Τηλέφου προσορμισθῆναι ἐκεῖ.

Πηλείδην δ' Ἀχιλῆα φέρε Σκῦρόνδε θύελλα,
ἔνθα γ' ἐς ἀργαλέον λιμέν' ἵκετο νυκτὸς ἐκείνης.

3.

The story runs as follows: Aias and Odysseus were quarrelling as to their achievements, says the poet of the *Little Iliad,* and Nestor advised the Hellenes to send some of their number to go to the foot of the walls and overhear what was said about the valour of the heroes named above. The eaves-droppers heard certain girls disputing, one of them saying that Aias was by far a better man than Odysseus and continuing as follows:

"For Aias took up and carried out of the strife the hero, Peleus' son: this great Odysseus cared not to do."

To this another replied by Athena's contrivance:

"Why, what is this you say? A thing against reason and untrue! . . . . Even a woman could carry a load once a man had put it on her shoulder; but she could not fight. For she would fail with fear if she should fight."

4.

The writer of the *Little Iliad* says that Aias was not buried in the usual way,[1] but was simply buried in a coffin, because of the king's anger.

5.

The author of the *Little Iliad* says that Achilles after putting out to sea from the country of Telephus came to land there.

"The storm carried Achilles the son of Peleus to Scyros, and he came into an uneasy harbour there in that same night."

[1] *sc.* after cremation.

6.

Schol. on Pindar, Nem. vi. 85.

ἀμφὶ δὲ πόρκης
χρύσεος ἀστράπτει καὶ ἐπ' αὐτῷ δίκροος αἰχμή.

7.

Schol. on Eur. Troades, 822.

ἄμπελον ἣν Κρονίδης ἔπορεν οὗ παιδὸς ἄποινα
χρυσείοις φύλλοισιν † ἀγανοῖσιν † κομόωσαν
βότρυσί θ' οὓς Ἥφαιστος ἐπασκήσας Διὶ πατρὶ
δῶχ', ὁ δὲ Λαομέδοντι πόρεν Γανυμήδεος ἀντί.

8.

Pausanias, iii. 26. 9. Μαχάονα δὲ ὑπὸ Εὐρυπύλου τοῦ Τηλέφου τελευτῆσαι φησὶν ὁ τὰ ἔπη ποιήσας τὴν μικρὰν Ἰλιάδα.

9.

Homer, Odyssey iv. 247 *and Schol.*

ἄλλῳ δ' αὐτὸν φωτὶ κατακρύπτων ἤισκε
δέκτῃ, ὃς οὐδὲν τοῖος ἔην ἐπὶ νηυσὶν Ἀχαιῶν.

ὁ κυκλικὸς τὸ δέκτῃ ὀνοματικῶς ἀκούει, παρ' οὗ φησι τὸν Ὀδυσσέα τὰ ῥάκη λαβόντα μετημφιάσθαι, ὃς οὐκ ἦν ἐν ταῖς νηυσὶ τοιοῦτος οἷος Ὀδυσσεὺς ἀχρεῖος.

10.

Plutarch, Moralia, p. 153 F. καὶ προὔβαλ' Ὅμηρος, ὥς φησι Λέσχης·

Μοῦσά μοι ἔννεπ' ἐκεῖνα τὰ μήτ' ἐγένοντο πάροιθεν,
μήτ' ἔσται μετόπισθεν.

6.

"About the spear-shaft was a hoop of flashing gold, and a point was fitted to it at either end."

7.

"... The vine which the son of Cronos gave him as a recompense for his son. It bloomed richly with soft leaves of gold and grape clusters; Hephaestus wrought it and gave it to his father Zeus: and he bestowed it on Laomedon as a price for Ganymedes."

8.

The writer of the epic *Little Iliad* says that Machaon was killed by Eurypylus, the son of Telephus.

9.

"He disguised himself, and made himself like another person, a beggar, the like of whom was not by the ships of the Achaeans."

The Cyclic poet uses "beggar" as a substantive, and so means to say that when Odysseus had changed his clothes and put on rags, there was no one so good for nothing at the ships as Odysseus.

10.[1]

And Homer put forward the following verses as Lesches gives them:

"Muse, tell me of those things which neither happened before nor shall be hereafter."

[1] This fragment comes from a version of the *Contest of Homer and Hesiod* widely different from that now extant. The words "as Lesches gives them (says)" seem to indicate that the verse and a half assigned to Homer came from the *Little Iliad*. It is possible they may have introduced some unusually striking incident, such as the actual Fall of Troy.

ἀπεκρίνατο δὲ Ἡσίοδος·

ἀλλ' ὅταν ἀμφὶ Διὸς τύμβῳ καναχήποδες ἵπποι
ἅρματα συντρίψωσιν ἐπειγόμενοι περὶ νίκης.

καὶ διὰ τοῦτο λέγεται μάλιστα θαυμασθεὶς τοῦ τρίποδος τυχεῖν.

11.

Schol. Lycophr. 344. ὁ Σίνων ὡς ἦν αὐτῷ συντεθειμένον, φρυκτὸν ὑποδείξας τοῖς Ἕλλησιν ὡς ὁ Λέσχης φησὶν ἡνίκα

νὺξ μὲν ἔην μέσση, λαμπρὴ δ' ἐπέτελλε σελήνη.

12.

Pausanias x. 25. 5. τέτρωται δὲ τὸν βραχίονα ὁ Μέγης, καθὰ δὴ καὶ Λέσχεως ὁ Αἰσχυλίνου Πυρραῖος ἐν Ἰλίου Πέρσιδι ἐποίησε· τρωθῆναι δὲ ὑπὸ τὴν μάχην τοῦτον ἣν ἐν τῇ νυκτὶ ἐμαχέσαντο οἱ Τρῶες ὑπὸ Ἀδμήτου φησὶ τοῦ Αὐγείου. γέγραπται δὲ καὶ Λυκομήδης . . . ἔχων τραῦμα ἐπὶ τῷ καρπῷ· Λέσχεως δ' οὕτω φησὶν αὐτὸν ὑπ' Ἀγήνορος τρωθῆναι. (*ib.* 26. 4) Ἀστύνοον δέ, οὗ δὴ ἐποιήσατο καὶ Λέσχεως μνήμην, πεπτωκότα ἐς γόνυ ὁ Νεοπτόλεμος ξίφει παίει. (*ib.* 26. 8) Λέσχεως δὲ τετρωμένον τὸν Ἑλικάονα ἐν τῇ νυκτομαχίᾳ γνωρισθῆναί τε ὑπὸ Ὀδυσσέως καὶ ἐξαχθῆναι ζῶντα ἐκ τῆς μάχης φησίν. (*ib.* 27. 1) καὶ αὐτῶν Λέσχεως Ἠιονέα ὑπὸ Νεοπτολέμου, τὸν δὲ ὑπὸ Φιλοκτήτου φησὶν ἀποθανεῖν τὸν Ἄδμητον . . . Πρίαμον δὲ οὐκ ἀποθανεῖν ἔφη Λέσχεως ἐπὶ τῇ ἐσχάρᾳ τοῦ Ἑρκείου, ἀλλὰ ἀποσπασθέντα ἀπὸ τοῦ βωμοῦ πάρεργον τῷ Νεοπτολέμῳ πρὸς ταῖς τῆς οἰκίας γενέσθαι θύραις . . . Ἀξίονα δὲ παῖδα εἶναι Πριάμου Λέσχεως καὶ ἀποθανεῖν αὐτὸν ὑπὸ

And Hesiod answered:

"But when horses with rattling hoofs wreck chariots, striving for victory about the tomb of Zeus."

And it is said that, because this reply was specially admired, Hesiod won the tripod (at the funeral games of Amphidamas).

11.

Sinon, as it had been arranged with him, secretly showed a signal-light to the Hellenes. Thus Lesches writes:—

"It was midnight, and the clear moon was rising."

12.

Meges is represented [1] wounded in the arm just as Lescheos the son of Aeschylinus of Pyrrha describes in his *Sack of Ilium* where it is said that he was wounded in the battle which the Trojans fought in the night by Admetus, son of Augeias. Lycomedes too is in the picture with a wound in the wrist, and Lescheos says he was so wounded by Agenor . . . Lescheos also mentions Astynoüs, and here he is, fallen on one knee, while Neoptolemus strikes him with his sword . . . The same writer says that Helicaon was wounded in the night-battle, but was recognised by Odysseus and by him conducted alive out of the fight . . . Of them,[2] Lescheos says that Eïon was killed by Neoptolemus, and Admetus by Philoctetes . . . He also says that Priam was not killed at the hearth of Zeus Hérceius, but was dragged away from the altar and destroyed offhand by Neoptolemus at the doors of the house . . . Lescheos says that Axion was the son of Priam and

[1] *i.e.* in the paintings by Polygnotus at Delphi.
[2] *i.e.* the dead bodies in the picture.

Εὐρυπύλου τοῦ Εὐαίμονός φησι. τοῦ Ἀγήνορος δὲ κατὰ τὸν αὐτὸν ποιητὴν Νεοπτόλεμος αὐτόχειρ ἐστί.

13.

Aristoph. Lysistr. 155 *and Schol.*

ὁ γῶν Μενέλαος τᾶς Ἑλένας τὰ μᾶλά πα
γυμνᾶς παραυιδὼν ἐξέβαλ' οἰῶ τὸ ξίφος.

. . . τὰ δ' αὐτὰ καὶ Λέσχης ὁ Πυρραῖος ἐν τῇ μικρᾷ Ἰλιάδι.

Pausanias x. 25. 8. Λέσχεως δὲ εἰς τὴν Αἴθραν ἐποίησεν ἡνίκα ἡλίσκετο Ἴλιον ὑπεξελθοῦσαν εἰς τὸ στρατόπεδον αὐτὴν ἀφικέσθαι τὸ Ἑλλήνων καὶ ὑπὸ τῶν παίδων γνωρισθῆναι τῶν Θησέως, καὶ ὡς παρ' Ἀγαμέμνονος αἰτῆσαι Δημοφῶν αὐτήν. ὁ δ' ἐκείνῳ μὲν ἐθέλειν χαρίζεσθαι, ποιήσειν δὲ οὐ πρότερον ἔφη πρὶν Ἑλένην πεῖσαι· ἀποστείλαντι δὲ αὐτῷ κήρυκα ἔδωκεν Ἑλένη τὴν χάριν.

14.

Schol. Lycophr. Alex. 1268.

αὐτὰρ Ἀχιλλῆος μεγαθύμου φαίδιμος υἱὸς
Ἑκτορέην ἄλοχον κάταγεν κοίλας ἐπὶ νῆας·
παῖδα δ' ἑλὼν ἐκ κόλπου ἐυπλοκάμοιο τιθήνης
ῥίψε ποδὸς τεταγὼν ἀπὸ πύργου· τὸν δὲ πεσόντα
ἔλλαβε πορφύρεος θάνατος καὶ μοῖρα κραταιή.
ἐκ δ' ἕλεν Ἀνδρομάχην, ἠύζωνον παράκοιτιν
Ἕκτορος, ἥντε οἱ αὐτῷ ἀριστῆες Παναχαιῶν
δῶκαν ἔχειν ἐπίηρον ἀμειβόμενοι γέρας ἀνδρί,
αὐτόν τ' Ἀγχίσαο κλυτὸν γόνον ἱπποδάμοιο
Αἰνείαν ἐν νηυσὶν ἐβήσατο ποντοπόροισιν
ἐκ πάντων Δαναῶν ἀγέμεν γέρας ἔξοχον ἄλλων.

was slain by Eurypylus, the son of Euaemon. Agenor—according to the same poet—was butchered by Neoptolemus.

13.

"Menelaus at least, when he caught a glimpse somehow of the breasts of Helen unclad, cast away his sword, methinks." Lesches the Pyrrhaean also has the same account in his *Little Iliad.*

Concerning Aethra Lesches relates that when Ilium was taken she stole out of the city and came to the Hellenic camp, where she was recognised by the sons of Theseus; and that Demophon asked her of Agamemnon. Agamemnon wished to grant him this favour, but he would not do so until Helen consented. And when he sent a herald, Helen granted his request.

14.

"Then the bright son of bold Achilles led the wife of Hector to the hollow ships; but her son he snatched from the bosom of his rich-haired nurse and seized him by the foot and cast him from a tower. So when he had fallen bloody death and hard fate seized on Astyanax. And Neoptolemus chose out Andromache, Hector's well-girded wife, and the chiefs of all the Achaeans gave her to him to hold requiting him with a welcome prize. And he put Aeneas,[1] the famous son of horse-taming Anchises, on board his sea-faring ships, a prize surpassing those of all the Danaäns."

[1] According to this version Aeneas was taken to Pharsalia. Better known are the Homeric account (according to which Aeneas founded a new dynasty at Troy), and the legends which make him seek a new home in Italy.

ΙΛΙΟΥ ΠΕΡΣΙΣ

1.

Ἕπεται δὲ τούτοις Ἰλίου Πέρσιδος βιβλία β̄ Ἀρκτίνου Μιλησίου, περιέχοντα τάδε. ὡς τὰ περὶ τὸν ἵππον οἱ Τρῶες ὑπόπτως ἔχοντες περιστάντες βουλεύονται ὅ τι χρὴ ποιεῖν· καὶ τοῖς μὲν δοκεῖ κατακρημνίσαι αὐτόν, τοῖς δὲ καταφλέγειν· οἱ δὲ ἱερὸν αὐτὸν ἔφασαν δεῖν τῇ Ἀθηνᾷ ἀνατεθῆναι· καὶ τέλος νικᾷ ἡ τούτων γνώμη. τραπέντες δὲ εἰς εὐφροσύνην εὐωχοῦνται ὡς ἀπηλλαγμένοι τοῦ πολέμου. ἐν αὐτῷ δὲ τούτῳ δύο δράκοντες ἐπιφανέντες τόν τε Λαοκόωντα καὶ τὸν ἕτερον τῶν παίδων διαφθείρουσιν· ἐπὶ δὲ τῷ τέρατι δυσφορήσαντες οἱ περὶ τὸν Αἰνείαν ὑπεξῆλθον εἰς τὴν Ἴδην· καὶ Σίνων τοὺς πυρσοὺς ἀνίσχει τοῖς Ἀχαιοῖς, πρότερον εἰσεληλυθὼς προσποίητος. οἱ δὲ ἐκ Τενέδου προσπλεύσαντες καὶ οἱ ἐκ τοῦ δουρείου ἵππου ἐπιπίπτουσι τοῖς πολεμίοις, καὶ πολλοὺς ἀνελόντες τὴν πόλιν κατὰ κράτος λαμβάνουσι. καὶ Νεοπτόλεμος μὲν ἀποκτείνει Πρίαμον ἐπὶ τὸν τοῦ Διὸς τοῦ Ἑρκείου βωμὸν καταφυγόντα. Μενέλαος δὲ ἀνευρὼν Ἑλένην ἐπὶ τὰς ναῦς κατάγει, Δηίφοβον φονεύσας. Κασσάνδραν δὲ Αἴας ὁ Ἰλέως[1] πρὸς βίαν ἀποσπῶν συνεφέλκεται τὸ τῆς Ἀθηνᾶς ξόανον· ἐφ᾽ ᾧ παροξυνθέντες οἱ Ἕλληνες καταλεῦσαι βουλεύονται τὸν Αἴαντα, ὁ δὲ ἐπὶ τὸν τῆς Ἀθηνᾶς βωμὸν καταφεύγει καὶ διασῴζεται ἐκ τοῦ ἐπικειμένου

[1] So MSS. This form is confirmed (as against Heyne's Ὀϊλέως) by Hesiod, *Catalogues*, frag. 83.

THE SACK OF ILIUM

1.

Next come two books of the *Sack of Ilium*, by Arctinus of Miletus with the following contents. The Trojans were suspicious of the wooden horse and standing round it debated what they ought to do. Some thought they ought to hurl it down from the rocks, others to burn it up, while others said they ought to dedicate it to Athena. At last this third opinion prevailed. Then they turned to mirth and feasting believing the war was at an end. But at this very time two serpents appeared and destroyed Laocöon and one of his two sons, a portent which so alarmed the followers of Aeneas that they withdrew to Ida. Sinon then raised the fire-signal to the Achaeans, having previously got into the city by pretence. The Greeks then sailed in from Tenedos, and those in the wooden horse came out and fell upon their enemies, killing many and storming the city. Neoptolemus kills Priam who had fled to the altar of Zeus Herceius[1]; Menelaus finds Helen and takes her to the ships, after killing Deïphobus; and Aias the son of Ileus, while trying to drag Cassandra away by force, tears away with her the image of Athena. At this the Greeks are so enraged that they determine to stone Aias, who only escapes from the danger threatening him by taking refuge at the

[1] Zeus is so called because it was customary for an altar dedicated to him to be placed in the forecourt (ἕρκος) of a house. Cp. Homer, *Odyssey* xxii. 334–5.

κινδύνου. ἔπειτα ἐμπρήσαντες τὴν πόλιν Πολυξείνην σφαγιάζουσιν ἐπὶ τὸν τοῦ Ἀχιλλέως τάφον. καὶ Ὀδυσσέως Ἀστυάνακτα ἀνελόντος Νεοπτόλεμος Ἀνδρομάχην γέρας λαμβάνει. καὶ τὰ λοιπὰ λάφυρα διανέμονται· Δημοφῶν δὲ καὶ Ἀκάμας Αἴθραν εὑρόντες ἄγουσι μεθ᾽ ἑαυτῶν. ἔπειτα ἀποπλέουσιν οἱ Ἕλληνες καὶ φθορὰν αὐτοῖς ἡ Ἀθηνᾶ κατὰ τὸ πέλαγος μηχανᾶται.

2.

Dionysius Halicarn. Rom. Antiq. i. 68. Ἀρκτῖνος δέ φησιν ὑπὸ Διὸς δοθῆναι Δαρδάνῳ παλλάδιον ἓν καὶ εἶναι τοῦτο ἐν Ἰλίῳ τέως ἡ πόλις ἡλίσκετο κεκρυμμένον ἐν ἀβάτῳ, εἰκόνα δ᾽ ἐκείνου κατεσκευασμένην ὡς μηδὲν τῆς ἀρχετύπου διαφέρειν ἀπάτης τῶν ἐπιβουλευόντων ἕνεκα ἐν φανερῷ τεθῆναι καὶ αὐτὴν Ἀχαιοὺς ἐπιβουλεύσαντας λαβεῖν.

3.

Schol. on Eur. Andromache 10. καὶ τὸν τὴν Πέρσιδα συντεταχότα κυκλικὸν ποιητὴν ὅτι καὶ ἀπὸ τοῦ τείχους ῥιφθείη (*sc.* Ἀστυάναξ).

4.

Schol. on Eur. Troades 31. μηδὲν γὰρ εἰληφέναι τοὺς περὶ Ἀκάμαντα καὶ Δημοφῶντα ἐκ τῶν λαφύρων ἀλλὰ μόνην τὴν Αἴθραν, δι᾽ ἣν καὶ ἀφίκοντο εἰς Ἴλιον, Μενεσθέως ἡγουμένου. Λυσίμαχος δὲ τὸν τὴν Πέρσιδα πεποιηκότα φησὶ γράφειν οὕτως·

Θησείδαις δ᾽ ἔπορεν δῶρα κρείων Ἀγαμέμνων
ἠδὲ Μενεσθῆι μεγαλήτορι ποιμένι λαῶν.

altar of Athena. The Greeks, after burning the city, sacrifice Polyxena at the tomb of Achilles: Odysseus murders Astyanax; Neoptolemus takes Andromache as his prize, and the remaining spoils are divided. Demophon and Acamas find Aethra and take her with them. Lastly the Greeks sail away and Athena plans to destroy them on the high seas.

2.

According to Arctinus, one Palladium was given to Dardanus by Zeus, and this was in Ilium until the city was taken. It was hidden in a secret place, and a copy was made resembling the original in all points and set up for all to see, in order to deceive those who might have designs against it. This copy the Achaeans took as a result of their plots.

3.

The Cyclic poet who composed the *Sack* says that Astyanax was also hurled from the city wall.

4.

For the followers of Acamas and Demophon took no share—it is said—of the spoils, but only Aethra, for whose sake, indeed, they came to Ilium with Menestheus to lead them. Lysimachus, however, says that the author of the *Sack* writes as follows:

"The lord Agamemnon gave gifts to the Sons of Theseus and to bold Menestheus, shepherd of hosts."

5.

Eustathius on Iliad xiii. 515. ἔνιοι δέ φασιν ὡς οὐδὲ ἐπὶ πάντας τοὺς ἰατροὺς ὁ ἔπαινος οὗτος ἐστι κοινός, ἀλλὰ ἐπὶ τὸν Μαχάονα, ὃν μόνον χειρουργεῖν τινες λέγουσι· τὸν γὰρ Ποδαλείριον διαιτᾶσθαι νόσους . . . τοῦτο ἔοικε καὶ Ἀρκτῖνος ἐν Ἰλίου Πορθήσει νομίζειν ἐν οἷς φησι

αὐτὸς γάρ σφιν ἔδωκε πατὴρ κλυτὸς Ἐννοσίγαιος
ἀμφοτέροις, ἕτερον δ' ἑτέρου κυδίον' ἔθηκε·
τῷ μὲν κουφοτέρας χεῖρας πόρεν ἔκ τε βέλεμνα
σαρκὸς ἑλεῖν τμῆξαί τε καὶ ἕλκεα πάντ' ἀκέσασθαι,
τῷ δ' ἄρ' ἀκριβέα πάντα ἐνὶ στήθεσσιν ἔθηκεν
ἄσκοπά τε γνῶναι καὶ ἀναλθέα ἰήσασθαι·
ὅς ῥα καὶ Αἴαντος πρῶτος μάθε χωομένοιο
ὄμματά τ' ἀστράπτοντα βαρυνόμενόν τε νόημα.

6.

Diomedes in Gramm. Lat. i. 477.

ὁ Ἴαμβος
ἐξ ὀλίγου διαβὰς προφόρῳ ποδὶ ὄφρ' οἱ γυῖα
τεινόμενα ῥώοιτο καὶ εὐσθενὲς εἶδος ἔχῃσι.

ΝΟΣΤΟΙ

1.

Proclus, Chrestomathy. Συνάπτει δὲ τούτοις τὰ τῶν Νόστων βιβλία ε' Ἀγίου Τροιζηνίου περιέχοντα τάδε. Ἀθηνᾶ Ἀγαμέμνονα καὶ Μενέλαον εἰς ἔριν καθίστησι περὶ τοῦ ἔκπλου. Ἀγαμέμνων μὲν οὖν τὸν τῆς Ἀθηνᾶς ἐξιλασόμενος χόλον ἐπιμένει, Διομήδης δὲ καὶ Νέστωρ ἀναχθέντες

5.

Some say that such praise as this[1] does not apply to physicians generally, but only to Machaon: and some say that he only practised surgery, while Podaleirius treated sicknesses. Arctinus in the *Sack of Ilium* seems to be of this opinion when he says:

"For their father the famous Earth-Shaker gave both of them gifts, making each more glorious than the other. To the one he gave hands more light to draw or cut out missiles from the flesh and to heal all kinds of wounds; but in the heart of the other he put full and perfect knowledge to tell hidden diseases and cure desperate sicknesses. It was he who first noticed Aias' flashing eyes and clouded mind when he was enraged."

6.

"Iambus stood a little while astride with foot advanced, that so his strained limbs might get power and have a show of ready strength."

THE RETURNS

1.

After the *Sack of Ilium* follow the *Returns* in five books by Agias of Troezen. Their contents are as follows. Athena causes a quarrel between Agamemnon and Menelaus about the voyage from Troy. Agamemnon then stays on to appease the anger of Athena. Diomedes and Nestor put out to sea and

[1] *sc.* knowledge of both surgery and of drugs.

εἰς τὴν οἰκείαν διασῴζονται· μεθ' οὓς ἐκπλεύσας ὁ Μενέλαος, μετὰ πέντε νεῶν εἰς Αἴγυπτον παραγίνεται, τῶν λοιπῶν διαφθαρεισῶν νεῶν ἐν τῷ πελάγει. οἱ δὲ περὶ Κάλχαντα καὶ Λεοντέα καὶ Πολυποίτην πεζῇ πορευθέντες εἰς Κολοφῶνα, Τειρεσίαν ἐνταῦθα τελευτήσαντα θάπτουσι. τῶν δὲ περὶ τὸν Ἀγαμέμνονα ἀποπλεόντων Ἀχιλλέως εἴδωλον ἐπιφανὲν πειρᾶται διακωλύειν προλέγον τὰ συμβησόμενα. εἶθ' ὁ περὶ τὰς Καφηρίδας πέτρας δηλοῦται χειμὼν καὶ ἡ Αἴαντος φθορὰ τοῦ Λοκροῦ. Νεοπτόλεμος δὲ Θέτιδος ὑποθεμένης πεζῇ ποιεῖται τὴν πορείαν, καὶ παραγενόμενος εἰς Θρᾴκην Ὀδυσσέα καταλαμβάνει ἐν τῇ Μαρωνείᾳ, καὶ τὸ λοιπὸν ἀνύει τῆς ὁδοῦ, καὶ τελευτήσαντα Φοίνικα θάπτει· αὐτὸς δὲ εἰς Μολοσσοὺς ἀφικόμενος ἀναγνωρίζεται Πηλεῖ. ἔπειτα Ἀγαμέμνονος ὑπὸ Αἰγίσθου καὶ Κλυταιμνήστρας ἀναιρεθέντος ὑπ' Ὀρέστου καὶ Πυλάδου τιμωρία, καὶ Μενελάου εἰς τὴν οἰκείαν ἀνακομιδή.

2.

Argument to Eur. Medea.

αὐτίκα δ' Αἴσονα θῆκε φίλον κόρον ἡβώοντα
γῆρας ἀποξύσασα ἰδυίῃσι πραπίδεσσι,
φάρμακα πολλ' ἕψουσ' ἐπὶ χρυσείοισι λέβησιν.

3.

Pausanias, i. 2. Ἡρακλέα Θεμίσκυραν πολιορκοῦντα τὴν ἐπὶ Θερμώδοντι ἑλεῖν μὴ δύνασθαι, Θησέως δὲ ἐρασθεῖσαν Ἀντιόπην—στρατεῦσαι γὰρ ἅμα Ἡρακλεῖ καὶ Θησέα—παραδοῦναι τὸ χωρίον. τάδε μὲν Ἡγίας πεποίηκεν.

get safely home. After them Menelaus sets out and reaches Egypt with five ships, the rest having been destroyed on the high seas. Those with Calchas, Leontes, and Polypoetes go by land to Colophon and bury Teiresias who died there. When Agamemnon and his followers were sailing away, the ghost of Achilles appeared and tried to prevent them by foretelling what should befall them. The storm at the rocks called Capherides is then described, with the end of Locrian Aias. Neoptolemus, warned by Thetis, journeys overland and, coming into Thrace, meets Odysseus at Maronea, and then finishes the rest of his journey after burying Phoenix who dies on the way. He himself is recognized by Peleus on reaching the Molossi. Then comes the murder of Agamemnon by Aegisthus and Clytaemnestra, followed by the vengeance of Orestes and Pylades. Finally, Menelaus returns home.

2.

"Forthwith Medea made Aeson a sweet young boy and stripped his old age from him by her cunning skill, when she had made a brew of many herbs in her golden cauldrons."

3.

The story goes that Heracles was besieging Themiscyra on the Thermodon and could not take it; but Antiope, being in love with Theseus who was with Heracles on this expedition, betrayed the place. Hegias gives this account in his poem.

4.

Eustathius, 1796. 45. ὁ δὲ τοὺς Νόστους ποιήσας Κολοφώνιος Τηλέμαχον μέν φησι τὴν Κίρκην ὕστερον γῆμαι, Τηλέγονον δὲ τὸν ἐκ Κίρκης ἀντιγῆμαι Πηνελόπην.

5.

Clement of Alex. Strom. vi. 2. 12. 8.

δῶρα γὰρ ἀνθρώπων νοῦν ἤπαφεν ἠδὲ καὶ ἔργα.[1]

6.

Pausanias, x. 28. 7. ἡ δὲ Ὁμήρου ποίησις . . . καὶ οἱ Νόστοι—μνήμη γὰρ δὴ ἐν ταύταις καὶ Ἅιδου καὶ τῶν ἐκεῖ δειμάτων ἐστίν—ἴσασιν οὐδένα Εὐρύνομον δαίμονα.

Athenaeus, 281 B. ὁ γοῦν τὴν τῶν Ἀτρειδῶν ποιήσας κάθοδον ἀφικόμενον αὐτὸν λέγει πρὸς τοὺς θεοὺς καὶ συνδιατρίβοντα ἐξουσίας τυχεῖν παρὰ τοῦ Διὸς αἰτήσασθαι ὅτου ἐπιθυμεῖ. τὸν δὲ πρὸς τὰς ἀπολαύσεις ἀπλήστως διακείμενον, ὑπὲρ αὐτῶν τε τούτων μνείαν ποιήσασθαι καὶ τοῦ ζῆν τὸν αὐτὸν τρόπον τοῖς θεοῖς· ἐφ' οἷς ἀγανακτήσαντα τὸν Δία, τὴν μὲν εὐχὴν ἀποτελέσαι διὰ τὴν ὑπόσχεσιν, ὅπως δὲ μηδὲν ἀπολαύῃ τῶν παρακειμένων ἀλλὰ διατελῇ ταραττόμενος, ὑπὲρ τῆς κεφαλῆς ἐξήρτησεν αὐτῷ πέτρον, δι' ὃν οὐ δύναται τῶν παρακειμένων τυχεῖν οὐδενός.

[1] Clement attributes this line to Augias: probably Agias is intended.

4.

The Colophonian author of the *Returns* says that Telemachus afterwards married Circe, while Telegonus the son of Circe correspondingly married Penelope.

5.

"For gifts beguile men's minds and their deeds as well."

6.

The poetry of Homer and the *Returns*—for here too there is an account of Hades and the terrors there—know of no spirit named Eurynomus.

The writer of the *Return of the Atreidae*[1] says that Tantalus came and lived with the gods, and was permitted to ask for whatever he desired. But the man was so immoderately given to pleasures that he asked for these and for a life like the life of the gods. At this Zeus was annoyed, but fulfilled his prayer because of his own promise; but to prevent him from enjoying any of the pleasures provided, and to keep him continually harassed, he hung a stone over his head which prevents him from ever reaching any of the pleasant things near by.

[1] Identical with the *Returns*, in which the Sons of Atreus occupy the most prominent parts.

ΤΗΛΕΓΟΝΙΑ

1.

Proclus, Chrestomathy. Μετὰ ταῦτά ἐστιν Ὁμήρου Ὀδύσσεια· ἔπειτα Τηλεγονίας βιβλία δύο Εὐγάμμωνος Κυρηναίου, περιέχοντα τάδε. οἱ μνήστορες ὑπὸ τῶν προσηκόντων θάπτονται· καὶ Ὀδυσσεὺς θύσας Νύμφαις εἰς Ἦλιν ἀποπλεῖ ἐπισκεψόμενος τὰ βουκόλια καὶ ξενίζεται παρὰ Πολυξένῳ δῶρόν τε λαμβάνει κρατῆρα, καὶ ἐπὶ τούτῳ τὰ περὶ Τροφώνιον καὶ Ἀγαμήδην καὶ Αὐγέαν. ἔπειτα εἰς Ἰθάκην καταπλεύσας τὰς ὑπὸ Τειρεσίου ῥηθείσας τελεῖ θυσίας. καὶ μετὰ ταῦτα εἰς Θεσπρωτοὺς ἀφικνεῖται καὶ γαμεῖ Καλλιδίκην βασιλίδα τῶν Θεσπρωτῶν. ἔπειτα πόλεμος συνίσταται τοῖς Θεσπρωτοῖς πρὸς Βρύγους, Ὀδυσσέως ἡγουμένου· ἐνταῦθα Ἄρης τοὺς περὶ τὸν Ὀδυσσέα τρέπεται, καὶ αὐτῷ εἰς μάχην Ἀθηνᾶ καθίσταται. τούτους μὲν Ἀπόλλων διαλύει· μετὰ δὲ τὴν Καλλιδίκης τελευτήν, τὴν μὲν βασιλείαν διαδέχεται Πολυποίτης Ὀδυσσέως υἱός, αὐτὸς δ' εἰς Ἰθάκην ἀφικνεῖται· κἀν τούτῳ Τηλέγονος ἐπὶ ζήτησιν τοῦ πατρὸς πλέων, ἀποβὰς εἰς τὴν Ἰθάκην τέμνει τὴν νῆσον· ἐκβοηθήσας δ' Ὀδυσσεὺς ὑπὸ τοῦ παιδὸς ἀναιρεῖται κατ' ἄγνοιαν. Τηλέγονος δ' ἐπιγνοὺς τὴν ἁμαρτίαν τό τε τοῦ πατρὸς σῶμα καὶ τὸν Τηλέμαχον καὶ τὴν Πηνελόπην πρὸς τὴν μητέρα μεθίστησιν· ἡ δὲ αὐτοὺς ἀθανάτους ποιεῖ, καὶ συνοικεῖ τῇ μὲν Πηνελόπῃ Τηλέγονος, Κίρκῃ δὲ Τηλέμαχος.

THE TELEGONY

1.

After the *Returns* comes the *Odyssey* of Homer, and then the *Telegony* in two books by Eugammon of Cyrene, which contain the following matters. The suitors of Penelope are buried by their kinsmen, and Odysseus, after sacrificing to the Nymphs, sails to Elis to inspect his herds. He is entertained there by Polyxenus and receives a mixing bowl as a gift; the story of Trophonius and Agamedes and Augeas then follows. He next sails back to Ithaca and performs the sacrifices ordered by Teiresias, and then goes to Thesprotis where he marries Callidice, queen of the Thesprotians. A war then breaks out between the Thesprotians, led by Odysseus, and the Brygi. Ares routs the army of Odysseus and Athena engages with Ares, until Apollo separates them. After the death of Callidice Polypoetes, the son of Odysseus, succeeds to the kingdom, while Odysseus himself returns to Ithaca. In the meantime Telegonus, while travelling in search of his father, lands on Ithaca and ravages the island: Odysseus comes out to defend his country, but is killed by his son unwittingly. Telegonus, on learning his mistake, transports his father's body with Penelope and Telemachus to his mother's island, where Circe makes them immortal, and Telegonus marries Penelope, and Telemachus Circe.

2.

Eustathius, 1796. 35. Ὁ δὲ τὴν Τηλεγονείαν γράψας Κυρηναῖος ἐκ μὲν Καλυψοῦς Τηλέγονον υἱὸν Ὀδυσσεῖ ἀναγράφει ἢ Τηλέδαμον, ἐκ δὲ Πηνελόπης Τηλέμαχον καὶ Ἀκουσίλαον.

ΑΜΦΙΑΡΑΟΥ ΕΞΕΛΑΣΙΣ

Pseudo-Herodotus, Life of Homer. κατήμενος ἐν τῷ σκυτείῳ . . . τήν τε ποίησιν αὐτοῖς ἐπεδείκνυτο Ἀμφιαράου τε τὴν ἐξελασίαν τὴν ἐς Θήβας καὶ τοὺς ὕμνους τοὺς ἐς θεοὺς πεποιημένους αὐτῷ.

ΟΙΧΑΛΙΑΣ ΑΛΩΣΙΣ

1.

Eustathius 330. 41. εἴρηται δὲ καὶ περὶ Εὐρύτου ἐκεῖ καὶ τῆς αὐτοῦ θυγατρὸς Ἰόλης δι' ἣν ἐπόρθησεν Ἡρακλῆς τὴν Οἰχαλίαν. εἰς ἣν δοκεῖ γράψαι καὶ Ὅμηρος ὡς δηλοῖ ὁ ἱστορήσας ὅτι Κρεώφυλος ὁ Σάμιος ξενίᾳ ποτε δεξάμενος τὸν Ὅμηρον ἔλαβε δῶρον ἐξ αὐτοῦ τὴν ἐπιγραφὴν τοῦ ποιήματος ὃ καλοῦσιν Οἰχαλίας Ἅλωσιν . . . τινὲς δὲ ἀνάπαλίν φασι Κρεώφυλον μὲν γράψαι, Ὁμήρῳ δὲ ἐπιγραφῆναι τὸ βιβλίον διὰ τὴν ξενίαν· διὸ καὶ Καλλίμαχος·

τοῦ Σαμίου πόνος εἰμί, δόμῳ ποτὲ θεῖον Ὅμηρον
δεξαμένου· κλείω δ' Εὔρυτον ὅσσ' ἔπαθεν .
καὶ ξανθὴν Ἰόλειαν, Ὁμήρειον δὲ καλεῦμαι
γράμμα· Κρεωφύλῳ, Ζεῦ φίλε, τοῦτο μέγα.

THE TAKING OF OECHALIA

2.

The author of the Telegony, a Cyrenaean, relates that Odysseus had by Calypso a son Telegonus or Teledamus, and by Penelope Telemachus and Acusilaus.

THE EXPEDITION OF AMPHIARAUS[1]

SITTING there in the tanner's yard, Homer recited his poetry to them, the *Expedition of Amphiaraus to Thebes* and the *Hymns to the Gods* composed by him.

THE TAKING OF OECHALIA

1.

AN account has there been given of Eurytus and his daughter Iole, for whose sake Heracles sacked Oechalia. Homer also seems to have written on this subject, as that historian shows who relates that Creophylus of Samos once had Homer for his guest and for a reward received the attribution of the poem which they call the *Taking of Oechalia.* Some however, assert the opposite; that Creophylus wrote the poem, and that Homer lent his name in return for his entertainment. And so Callimachus writes: "I am the work of that Samian who once received divine Homer in his house. I sing of Eurytus and all his woes and of golden-haired Ioleia, and am reputed one of Homer's works. Dear Heaven! how great an honour this for Creophylus!"

[1] *The Expedition of Amphiaraus, The Taking of Oechalia* and *The Phocais* were not included in the Epic Cycle.

2.

Cramer, Anec. Oxon. i. 327.
ῥωγαλέα, τὰ καὶ αὐτὸς ἐν ὀφθαλμοῖσιν ὅρηαι.
τοῦτο δὲ εὑρήσομεν καὶ ἐν τῇ Οἰχαλίας ἁλώσει.

3.

Schol. on Soph. Trach. 266. διαφωνεῖται δὲ ὁ τῶν Εὐρυτιδῶν ἀριθμός· Ἡσίοδος μὲν γὰρ δ´ φησιν ἐξ Εὐρύτου καὶ Ἀντιόχης παῖδας οὕτως, Κρεώφυλος δὲ β´.

4.

Schol. on Eur. Medea, 273. Δίδυμος δέ . . . παρατίθεται τὰ Κρεωφύλου ἔχοντα οὕτως· τὴν γὰρ Μήδειαν λέγεται διατρίβουσαν ἐν Κορίνθῳ τὸν ἄρχοντα τότε τῆς πόλεως Κρέοντα ἀποκτεῖναι φαρμάκοις. δείσασαν δὲ τοὺς φίλους καὶ τοὺς συγγενεῖς αὐτοῦ φυγεῖν εἰς Ἀθήνας, τοὺς δὲ υἱούς, ἐπεὶ νεώτεροι ὄντες οὐκ ἠδύναντο ἀκολουθεῖν, ἐπὶ τὸν βωμὸν τῆς Ἀκραίας Ἥρας καθίσαι νομίσασαν τὸν πατέρα αὐτῶν φροντιεῖν τῆς σωτηρίας αὐτῶν. τοὺς δὲ Κρέοντος οἰκείους ἀποκτείναντας αὐτοὺς διαδοῦναι λόγον ὅτι ἡ Μήδεια οὐ μόνον τὸν Κρέοντα ἀλλὰ καὶ τοὺς ἑαυτῆς παῖδας ἀπέκτεινε.

ΦΩΚΑΙΣ

Pseudo-Herodotus, Life of Homer. διατρίβων δὲ παρὰ τῷ Θεστορίδῃ ποιεῖ Ἰλιάδα τὴν ἐλάσσω . . . καὶ τὴν καλουμένην Φωκαΐδα, ἥν φασιν οἱ Φωκαιεῖς Ὅμηρον παρ᾽ αὐτοῖσι ποιῆσαι.

2.

"Ragged garments, even those which now you see." This verse (*Odyssey* xiv. 343) we shall also find in the *Taking of Oechalia.*

3.

There is a disagreement as to the number of the sons of Eurytus. For Hesiod says Eurytus and Antioche had as many as four sons; but Creophylus says two.

4.

Didymus contrasts the following account given by Creophylus, which is as follows: while Medea was living in Corinth, she poisoned Creon, who was ruler of the city at that time, and because she feared his friends and kinsfolk, fled to Athens. However, since her sons were too young to go along with her, she left them at the altar of Hera Acraea, thinking that their father would see to their safety. But the relatives of Creon killed them and spread the story that Medea had killed her own children as well as Creon.

THE PHOCAIS

While living with Thestorides, Homer composed the *Lesser Iliad* and the *Phocais*; though the Phocaeans say that he composed the latter among them.

ΜΑΡΓΙΤΗΣ

1.

Suidas. Πίγρης· Κὰρ ἀπὸ Ἁλικαρνασσοῦ, ἀδελφὸς Ἀρτεμισίας τῆς ἐν τοῖς πολέμοις διαφανοῦς, Μαυσώλου γυναικός[1] . . . ἔγραψε καὶ τὸν εἰς Ὅμηρον ἀναφερόμενον Μαργίτην καὶ Βατραχομυομαχίαν.

2.

Atilius Fortunatianus, p. 286, Keil.

ἦλθέ τις εἰς Κολοφῶνα γέρων καὶ θεῖος ἀοιδός,
Μουσάων θεράπων καὶ ἑκηβόλου Ἀπόλλωνος,
φίλης ἔχων ἐν χερσὶν εὔφθογγον λύραν.

3.

Plato, Alcib. ii. p. 147 A.

πολλ' ἠπίστατο ἔργα, κακῶς δ' ἠπίστατο πάντα.

Aristotle, Nic. Eth. vi. 7, 1141.

τὸν δ' οὔτ' ἄρ' σκαπτῆρα θεοὶ θέσαν οὔτ' ἀροτῆρα
οὔτ' ἄλλως τι σοφόν· πάσης δ' ἡμάρτανε τέχνης.

4.

Schol. on Aeschines in Ctes. § 160. Μαργίτην φησὶν ἄνθρωπον γεγονέναι ὃς ἐτῶν πολλῶν γενόμενος οὐκ ᾔδη ὅστις αὐτὸν ἔτεκεν, πότερον ὁ πατὴρ ἢ ἡ μήτηρ, τῇ δὲ γαμετῇ οὐκ ἐχρῆτο·

[1] This Artemisia, who distinguished herself at the battle of Salamis (Herodotus vii. 99) is here confused with the later Artemisia, the wife of Mausolus, who died 350 B.C.

THE MARGITES

1.

Pigres. A Carian of Halicarnassus and brother of Artemisia, wife of Mausolus, who distinguished herself in war . . . He also wrote the *Margites* attributed to Homer and the *Battle of the Frogs and Mice.*

2.

"There came to Colophon an old man and divine singer, a servant of the Muses and of far-shooting Apollo. In his dear hands he held a sweet-toned lyre."

3.

"He knew many things but knew all badly . . . The gods had taught him neither to dig nor to plough, nor any other skill; he failed in every craft."

4.

He refers to Margites, a man who, though well grown up, did not know whether it was his father or his mother who gave him birth, and would not lie with his wife, saying that he was δεδιέναι γὰρ ἔλεγε μὴ διαβάλλοι αὐτὸν πρὸς τὴν μητέρα.

5.

Zenobius, v. 68.

πόλλ' οἶδ' ἀλώπηξ ἀλλ' ἐχῖνος ἓν μέγα.[1]

ΚΕΡΚΩΠΕΣ

Suidas. Κέρκωπες· δύο ἀδελφοὶ ἦσαν ἐπὶ γῆς, πᾶσαν ἀδικίαν ἐπιδεικνύμενοι, καὶ ἐλέγοντο Κέρκωπες, ἐκ τῆς τῶν ἔργων δεινότητος οὕτως ἐπονομαζόμενοι. ὁ μὲν γὰρ αὐτῶν Πάσσαλος ἐλέγετο, ὁ δὲ Ἄκμων. ἡ δὲ μήτηρ Μεμνονὶς ταῦτα ὁρῶσα ἔλεγε μὴ περιπτυχεῖν Μελαμπύγῳ· τουτέστι τῷ Ἡρακλεῖ. οὗτοι οἱ Κέρκωπες Θείας καὶ Ὠκεάνου. οὕς φασιν ἀπολιθωθῆναι διὰ τὸ ἐγχειρεῖν ἀπατῆσαι τὸν Δία

ψεύστας, ἠπεροπῆας, ἀμήχανά τ' ἔργα δαέντας,[2]
ἐξαπατητῆρας· πολλὴν δ' ἐπὶ γαῖαν ἰόντες
ἀνθρώπους ἀπάτασκον, ἀλώμενοι ἤματα πάντα.

[1] Attributed to Homer by Zenobius, and by Bergk to the *Margites*. [2] Lobeck : ἔργ' ἀνύσαντες, Suidas.

afraid she might give a bad account of him to her mother.

5.

"The fox knows many a wile ; but the hedge-hog's one trick[1] can beat them all."

THE CERCOPES

Cercopes. These were two brothers living upon the earth who practised every kind of knavery. They were called Cercopes[2] because of their cunning doings: one of them was named Passalus and the other Acmon. Their mother, a daughter of Memnon, seeing their tricks, told them to keep clear of Black-bottom, that is, of Heracles. These Cercopes were sons of Theia and Ocean, and are said to have been turned to stone for trying to deceive Zeus.

"Liars and cheats, skilled in deeds irremediable, accomplished knaves. Far over the world they roamed deceiving men as they wandered continually."

[1] *i.e.* the fox knows many ways to baffle its foes, while the hedge-hog knows one only which is far more effectual.
[2] *i.e.* "monkey-men."

THE BATTLE OF THE FROGS AND MICE

ΒΑΤΡΑΧΟΜΥΟΜΑΧΙΑ

Ἀρχόμενος πρῶτον Μουσῶν χορὸν ἐξ Ἑλικῶνος
ἐλθεῖν εἰς ἐμὸν ἦτορ ἐπεύχομαι εἵνεκ' ἀοιδῆς
ἣν νέον ἐν δέλτοισιν ἐμοῖς ἐπὶ γούνασι θῆκα,
δῆριν ἀπειρεσίην, πολεμόκλονον ἔργον Ἄρηος,
εὐχόμενος μερόπεσσιν ἐν οὔατα πᾶσι βαλέσθαι,
πῶς μύες ἐν βατράχοισιν ἀριστεύσαντες ἔβησαν,
γηγενέων ἀνδρῶν μιμούμενοι ἔργα Γιγάντων,
ὡς ἔπος ἐν θνητοῖσιν ἔην· τοίην δ' ἔχεν ἀρχήν.
Μῦς ποτε διψαλέος, γαλέης κίνδυνον ἀλύξας,
πλησίον ἐν λίμνῃ ἁπαλὸν προσέθηκε γένειον,
ὕδατι τερπόμενος μελιηδέι· τὸν δὲ κατεῖδεν
λιμνοχαρὴς πολύφημος, ἔπος δ' ἐφθέγξατο τοῖον·
Ξεῖνε, τίς εἶ; πόθεν ἦλθες ἐπ' ἠόνα; τίς δέ σ' ὁ φύσας;
πάντα δ' ἀλήθευσον· μὴ ψευδόμενόν σε νοήσω.
εἰ γάρ σε γνοίην φίλον ἄξιον, ἐς δόμον ἄξω·
δῶρα δέ τοι δώσω ξεινήια πολλὰ καὶ ἐσθλά.
εἰμὶ δ' ἐγὼ βασιλεὺς Φυσίγναθος, ὃς κατὰ λίμνην
τιμῶμαι βατράχων ἡγούμενος ἤματα πάντα·
καί με πατὴρ Πηλεὺς ἀνεθρέψατο, Ὑδρομεδούσῃ
μιχθεὶς ἐν φιλότητι παρ' ὄχθας Ἠριδανοῖο.
καὶ σὲ δ' ὁρῶ καλόν τε καὶ ἄλκιμον ἔξοχον ἄλλων,
σκηπτοῦχον βασιλῆα καὶ ἐν πολέμοισι μαχητὴν
ἔμμεναι· ἀλλ' ἄγε θᾶσσον ἐὴν γενεὴν ἀγόρευε.

THE BATTLE OF THE FROGS AND MICE.

Here I begin: and first I pray the choir of the Muses to come down from Helicon into my heart to aid the lay which I have newly written in tablets upon my knee. Fain would I sound in all men's ears that awful strife, that clamorous deed of war, and tell how the Mice proved their valour on the Frogs and rivalled the exploits of the Giants, those earth-born men, as the tale was told among mortals. Thus did the war begin.

One day a thirsty Mouse who had escaped the ferret, dangerous foe, set his soft muzzle to the lake's brink and revelled in the sweet water. There a loud-voiced pond-larker spied him: and uttered such words as these.

"Stranger, who are you? Whence come you to this shore, and who is he who begot you? Tell me all this truly and let me not find you lying. For if I find you worthy to be my friend, I will take you to my house and give you many noble gifts such as men give to their guests. I am the king Puff-jaw, and am honoured in all the pond, being ruler of the Frogs continually. The father that brought me up was Mud-man who mated with Waterlady by the banks of Eridanus. I see, indeed, that you are well-looking and stouter than the ordinary, a sceptred king and a warrior in fight; but, come, make haste and tell me your descent."

Τὸν δ' αὖ Ψιχάρπαξ ἀπαμείβετο φώνησέν τε·
τίπτε γένος τοὐμὸν ζητεῖς; δῆλον δ' ἐν ἅπασιν
ἀνθρώποις τε θεοῖς τε καὶ οὐρανίοις πετεηνοῖς.
Ψιχάρπαξ μὲν ἐγὼ κικλήσκομαι· εἰμὶ δὲ κοῦρος
Τρωξάρταο πατρὸς μεγαλήτορος· ἡ δέ νυ μήτηρ
Λειχομύλη, θυγάτηρ Πτερνοτρώκτου βασιλῆος.
γείνατο δ' ἐν καλύβῃ με καὶ ἐξεθρέψατο βρωτοῖς,
σύκοις καὶ καρύοις καὶ ἐδέσμασι παντοδαποῖσιν.
πῶς δὲ φίλον ποιῇ με, τὸν ἐς φύσιν οὐδὲν ὁμοῖον;
σοὶ μὲν γὰρ βίος ἐστὶν ἐν ὕδασιν· αὐτὰρ ἔμοιγε,
ὅσσα παρ' ἀνθρώποις, τρώγειν ἔθος· οὐδέ με λήθει
ἄρτος δισκοπάνιστος ἀπ' εὐκύκλου κανέοιο,
οὐ πλακόεις τανύπεπλος ἔχων πολὺ σησαμότυρον,
οὐ τόμος ἐκ πτέρνης, οὐχ ἥπατα λευκοχίτωνα,
οὐ τυρὸς νεόπηκτος ἀπὸ γλυκεροῖο γάλακτος,
οὐ χρηστὸν μελίτωμα, τὸ καὶ μάκαρες ποθέουσιν,
οὐδ' ὅσα πρὸς θοίνας μερόπων τεύχουσι μάγειροι,
κοσμοῦντες χύτρας ἀρτύμασι παντοδαποῖσιν.
[οὐδέποτ' ἐκ πολέμοιο κακὴν ἀπέφευγον ἀυτήν,
ἀλλ' ἰθὺς μετὰ μῶλον ἰὼν προμάχοισιν ἐμίχθην.
οὐ δέδι' ἄνθρωπον καίπερ μέγα σῶμα φοροῦντα,
ἀλλ' ἐπὶ λέκτρον ἰὼν καταδάκνω δάκτυλον ἄκρον,
καὶ πτέρνης λαβόμην, καὶ οὐ πόνος ἄνδρα ἵκανεν,
νήδυμος οὐκ ἀπέφευγεν ὕπνος δάκνοντος ἐμεῖο.
ἀλλὰ δύω πάντων μάλα δείδια πᾶσαν ἐπ' αἶαν,
κίρκον καὶ γαλέην, οἵ μοι μέγα πένθος ἄγουσιν,
καὶ παγίδα στονόεσσαν, ὅπου δολόεις πέλε πότμος·
πλεῖστον δὴ γαλέην περιδείδια, ἥτις ἀρίστη,
ἣ καὶ τρωγλοδύοντα κατὰ τρώγλην ἐρεείνει.[1]]

[1] Lines 42–52 are intrusive; the list of vegetables which the Mouse cannot eat must follow immediately after the various dishes of which he does eat.

Then Crumb-snatcher answered him and said: "Why do you ask my race, which is well-known amongst all, both men and gods and the birds of heaven? Crumb-snatcher am I called, and I am the son of Bread-nibbler—he was my stout-hearted father—and my mother was Quern-licker, the daughter of Ham-gnawer the king: she bare me in the mouse-hole and nourished me with food, figs and nuts and dainties of all kinds. But how are you to make me your friend, who am altogether different in nature? For you get your living in the water, but I am used to eat such foods as men have: I never miss the thrice-kneaded loaf in its neat, round basket, or the thin-wrapped cake full of sesame and cheese, or the slice of ham, or liver vested in white fat, or cheese just curdled from sweet milk, or delicious honey-cake which even the blessed gods long for, or any of all those cates which cooks make for the feasts of mortal men, larding their pots and pans with spices of all kinds. In battle I have never flinched from the cruel onset, but plunged straight into the fray and fought among the foremost. I fear not man though he has a big body, but run along his bed and bite the tip of his toe and nibble at his heel; and the man feels no hurt and his sweet sleep is not broken by my biting. But there are two things I fear above all else the whole world over, the hawk and the ferret—for these bring great grief on me—and the piteous trap wherein is treacherous death. Most of all I fear the ferret of the keener sort which follows you still even when you dive down your hole.

οὐ τρώγω ῥαφάνας, οὐ κράμβας, οὐ κολοκύντας,
οὐ πράσσοις χλωροῖς ἐπιβόσκομαι, οὐδὲ σελίνοις·
ταῦτα γὰρ ὑμέτερ᾽ ἐστὶν ἐδέσματα τῶν κατὰ λίμνην.
Πρὸς τάδε *μειδιάσας* Φυσίγναθος *ἀντίον ηὔδα·*
ξεῖνε, λίην αὐχεῖς ἐπὶ γαστέρι· ἔστι καὶ ἡμῖν
πολλὰ μάλ᾽ ἐν λίμνῃ καὶ ἐπὶ χθονὶ θαύματ᾽ ἰδέσθαι.
ἀμφίβιον γὰρ ἔδωκε νομὴν βατράχοισι Κρονίων,
[*στοιχείοις διττοῖς μεμερισμένα δώματα ναίειν,*]
σκιρτῆσαι κατὰ γῆν καὶ ὑφ᾽ ὕδασι σῶμα καλύψαι.
εἰ δ᾽ ἐθέλεις καὶ ταῦτα δαήμεναι, εὐχερές ἐστιν.
βαῖνέ μοι ἐν νώτοισι, κράτει δέ με, μήποτ᾽ ὄληαι,
ὅππως γηθόσυνος τὸν ἐμὸν δόμον εἰσαφίκηαι.
Ὣς *ἄρ᾽ ἔφη καὶ νῶτ᾽ ἐδίδου· ὁ δ᾽ ἔβαινε τάχιστα*
χεῖρας ἔχων τρυφεροῖο κατ᾽ αὐχένος ἅλματι κούφῳ.
καὶ τὸ πρῶτον ἔχαιρεν, ὅτ᾽ ἔβλεπε γείτονας ὅρμους,
νήξει τερπόμενος Φυσιγνάθου· *ἀλλ᾽ ὅτε δή ῥα*
κύμασι πορφυρέοισιν ἐκλύζετο, πολλὰ δακρύων
ἄχρηστον μετάνοιαν ἐμέμφετο, τίλλε δὲ χαίτας,
καὶ πόδας ἔσφιγγεν κατὰ γαστέρα, ἐν δέ οἱ ἦτορ
πάλλετ᾽ ἀηθείῃ, καὶ ἐπὶ χθόνα βούλεθ᾽ ἱκέσθαι·
δεινὰ δ᾽ ὑπεστονάχιζε φόβου κρυόεντος ἀνάγκῃ.
[*οὐρὴν μὲν προπέτασσεν ἐφ᾽ ὕδασιν, ἠύτε κώπην*
σύρων, εὐχόμενός τε θεοῖς ἐπὶ γαῖαν ἱκέσθαι,
ὕδασι πορφυρέοισιν ἐκλύζετο, πολλὰ δ᾽ ἐβῶσεν·
καὶ τοῖον φάτο μῦθον ἀπὸ στόματός τ᾽ ἀγόρευσεν·
Οὐχ *οὕτω νώτοισιν ἐβάστασε φόρτον ἔρωτος*
ταῦρος, ὅτ᾽ Εὐρώπην *διὰ κύματος ἦγ᾽ ἐπὶ* Κρήτην,
ὡς ἔμ᾽ ἐπιπλώσας ἐπινώτιον ἦγεν ἐς οἶκον
βάτραχος ἀμπετάσας ὠχρὸν δέμας ὕδατι λευκῷ.]
Ὕδρος *δ᾽ ἐξαίφνης ἀνεφαίνετο, δεινὸν ὅραμα*
πᾶσιν ὁμῶς· ὀρθὸν δ᾽ ὑπὲρ ὕδατος εἶχε τράχηλον.

I gnaw no radishes and cabbages and pumpkins, nor feed on green leeks and parsley; for these are food for you who live in the lake."

Then Puff-jaw answered him with a smile: "Stranger you boast too much of belly-matters: we too have many marvels to be seen both in the lake and on the shore. For the Son of Cronos has given us Frogs the power to lead a double life, dwelling at will in two separate elements; and so we both leap on land and plunge beneath the water. If you would learn of all these things, 'tis easy done: just mount upon my back and hold me tight lest you be lost, and so you shall come rejoicing to my house."

So said he, and offered his back. And the Mouse mounted at once, putting his paws upon the other's sleek neck and vaulting nimbly. Now at first, while he still saw the land near by, he was pleased, and was delighted with Puff-jaw's swimming; but when dark waves began to wash over him, he wept loudly and blamed his unlucky change of mind: he tore his fur and tucked his paws in against his belly, while within him his heart quaked by reason of the strangeness: and he longed to get to land, groaning terribly through the stress of chilling fear. He put out his tail upon the water and worked it like a steering oar, and prayed to heaven that he might get to land. But when the dark waves washed over him he cried aloud and said: "Not in such wise did the bull bear on his back the beloved load, when he brought Europa across the sea to Crete, as this Frog carries me over the water to his house, raising his yellow back in the pale water."

Then suddenly a water-snake appeared, a horrid sight for both alike, and held his neck upright above

τοῦτον ἰδὼν κατέδυ Φυσίγναθος, οὔτι νοήσας,
οἷον ἑταῖρον ἔμελλεν ἀπολλύμενον καταλείπειν.
δῦ δὲ βάθος λίμνης καὶ ἀλεύατο κῆρα μέλαιναν.
κεῖνος δ' ὡς ἀφέθη, πέσεν ὕπτιος εὐθὺς ἐφ' ὕδωρ,
καὶ χεῖρας ἔσφιγγε καὶ ὀλλύμενος κατέτριζε.
πολλάκι μὲν κατέδυνεν ὑφ' ὕδατι, πολλάκι δ' αὖτε
λακτίζων ἀνέδυνε· μόρον δ' οὐκ ἦν ὑπαλύξαι.
δευόμεναι δὲ τρίχες πλεῖστον βάρος ἦσαν ἐπ' αὐτῷ·
ὕστατα δ' ὀλλύμενος τοίους ἐφθέγξατο μύθους·
  Οὐ λήσεις δολίως, Φυσίγναθε, ταῦτα ποιήσας,
ναυηγὸν ῥίψας ἀπὸ σώματος, ὡς ἀπὸ πέτρης.
οὐκ ἄν μου κατὰ γαῖαν ἀμείνων ἦσθα, κάκιστε,
παγκρατίῳ τε πάλῃ τε καὶ εἰς δρόμον· ἀλλὰ πλανήσας
εἰς ὕδωρ μ' ἔρριψας. ἔχει θεὸς ἔκδικον ὄμμα.
ἣ ποινὴν τίσεις σὺ μυῶν στρατῷ, οὐδ' ὑπαλύξεις.
  Ὣς εἰπὼν ἀπέπνευσεν ἐφ' ὕδατι· τὸν δὲ κατεῖδεν
Λειχοπίναξ ὄχθῃσιν ἐφεζόμενος μαλακῇσιν·
δεινὸν δ' ἐξολόλυξε, δραμὼν δ' ἤγγειλε μύεσσιν.
ὡς δ' ἔμαθον τὴν μοῖραν, ἔδυ χόλος αἰνὸς ἅπαντας.
καὶ τότε κηρύκεσσιν ἑοῖς ἐκέλευσαν ὑπ' ὄρθρον
κηρύσσειν ἀγορήνδ' ἐς δώματα Τρωξάρταο,
πατρὸς δυστήνου Ψιχάρπαγος, ὃς κατὰ λίμνην
ὕπτιος ἐξήπλωτο νεκρὸν δέμας, οὐδὲ παρ' ὄχθαις
ἦν ἤδη τλήμων, μέσσῳ δ' ἐπενήχετο πόντῳ.
ὡς δ' ἦλθον σπεύδοντες ἅμ' ἠοῖ, πρῶτος ἀνέστη
Τρωξάρτης ἐπὶ παιδὶ χολούμενος, εἶπέ τε μῦθον·
  Ὦ φίλοι, εἰ καὶ μοῦνος ἐγὼ κακὰ πολλὰ πεπόνθειν
ἐκ βατράχων, ἡ πεῖρα κακὴ πάντεσσι τέτυκται.

the water. And when he saw it, Puff-jaw dived at once, and never thought how helpless a friend he would leave perishing; but down to the bottom of the lake he went, and escaped black death. But the Mouse, so deserted, at once fell on his back, in the water. He wrung his paws and squeaked in agony of death: many times he sank beneath the water and many times he rose up again kicking. But he could not escape his doom, for his wet fur weighed him down heavily. Then at the last, as he was dying, he uttered these words.

"Ah, Puff-jaw, you shall not go unpunished for this treachery! You threw me, a castaway, off your body as from a rock. Vile coward! On land you would not have been the better man, boxing, or wrestling, or running; but now you have tricked me and cast me in the water. Heaven has an avenging eye, and surely the host of Mice will punish you and not let you escape."

With these words he breathed out his soul upon the water. But Lick-platter as he sat upon the soft bank saw him die and, raising a dreadful cry, ran and told the Mice. And when they heard of his fate, all the Mice were seized with fierce anger, and bade their heralds summon the people to assemble towards dawn at the house of Bread-nibbler, the father of hapless Crumb-snatcher who lay outstretched on the water face up, a lifeless corpse, and no longer near the bank, poor wretch, but floating in the midst of the deep. And when the Mice came in haste at dawn, Bread-nibbler stood up first, enraged at his son's death, and thus he spoke.

"Friends, even if I alone had suffered great wrong from the Frogs, assuredly this is a first essay at

εἰμὶ δὲ νῦν ἐλεεινός, ἐπεὶ τρεῖς παῖδας ὄλεσσα.
καὶ τὸν μὲν πρῶτόν γε κατέκτανεν ἁρπάξασα
ἔχθιστος γαλέη, τρώγλης ἔκτοσθεν ἑλοῦσα.
τὸν δ' ἄλλον πάλιν ἄνδρες ἀπηνέες ἐς μόρον εἷλξαν
καινοτέραις τέχναις ξύλινον δόλον ἐξευρόντες,
ἣν παγίδα καλέουσι, μυῶν ὀλέτειραν ἐοῦσαν.
ὃ τρίτος ἦν, ἀγαπητὸς ἐμοὶ καὶ μητέρι κεδνῇ,
τοῦτον ἀπέπνιξεν Φυσίγναθος ἐς βυθὸν ἄξας.
ἀλλ' ἄγεθ' ὁπλισόμεσθα καὶ ἐξέλθωμεν ἐπ' αὐτοὺς
σώματα κοσμήσαντες ἐν ἔντεσι δαιδαλέοισιν.
Ταῦτ' εἰπὼν ἀνέπεισε καθοπλίζεσθαι ἅπαντας.
καὶ τοὺς μέν ῥ' ἐκόρυσσεν Ἄρης πολέμοιο μεμηλώς·
κνημῖδας μὲν πρῶτον ἐφήρμοσαν εἰς δύο μοίρας
ῥήξαντες κυάμους χλωρούς, κνήμας δ' ἐκάλυπτον,
οὓς αὐτοὶ διὰ νυκτὸς ἐπιστάντες κατέτρωξαν.
θώρηκας δ' εἶχον καλαμοστεφέων ἀπὸ βυρσῶν,
οὓς γαλέην δείραντες ἐπισταμένως ἐποίησαν.
ἀσπὶς δ' ἦν λύχνου τὸ μεσόμφαλον· ἡ δέ νυ λόγχη
εὐμήκεις βελόναι, παγχάλκεον ἔργον Ἄρηος·
ἡ δὲ κόρυς τὸ λέπυρον ἐπὶ κροτάφοις ἐρεβίνθου.
Οὕτω μὲν μύες ἦσαν ἐν ὅπλοις· ὡς δ' ἐνόησαν
βάτραχοι, ἐξανέδυσαν ἀφ' ὕδατος, ἐς δ' ἕνα χῶρον
ἐλθόντες βουλὴν ξύναγον πολέμοιο κακοῖο.
σκεπτομένων δ' αὐτῶν, πόθεν ἡ στάσις, ἢ τίς ὁ θυμός,
κῆρυξ ἐγγύθεν ἦλθε φέρων ῥάβδον μετὰ χερσίν,
Τυρογλύφου υἱὸς μεγαλήτορος Ἐμβασίχυτρος,
ἀγγέλλων πολέμοιο κακὴν φάτιν, εἶπέ τε τοῖα·
Ὦ βάτραχοι, μύες ὔμμιν ἀπειλήσαντες ἔπεμψαν
εἰπεῖν ὁπλίζεσθαι ἐπὶ πτόλεμόν τε μάχην τε.
εἶδον γὰρ καθ' ὕδωρ Ψιχάρπαγα, ὅνπερ ἔπεφνεν

mischief for you all. And now I am pitiable, for I have lost three sons. First the abhorred ferret seized and killed one of them, catching him outside the hole ; then ruthless men dragged another to his doom when by unheard-of arts they had contrived a wooden snare, a destroyer of Mice, which they call a trap. There was a third whom I and his dear mother loved well, and him Puff-jaw has carried out into the deep and drowned. Come, then, and let us arm ourselves and go out against them when we have arrayed ourselves in rich-wrought arms."

With such words he persuaded them all to gird themselves. And Ares who has charge of war equipped them. First they fastened on greaves and covered their shins with green bean-pods broken into two parts which they had gnawed out, standing over them all night. Their breast plates were of skin stretched on reeds, skilfully made from a ferret they had flayed. For shields each had the centre-piece of a lamp, and their spears were long needles all of bronze, the work of Ares, and the helmets upon their temples were pea-nut shells.

So the Mice armed themselves. But when the Frogs were aware of it, they rose up out of the water and coming together to one place gathered a council of grievous war. And while they were asking whence the quarrel arose, and what the cause of this anger, a herald drew near bearing a wand in his paws, Pot-visitor the son of great-hearted Cheese-carver. He brought the grim message of war, speaking thus :

"Frogs, the Mice have sent me with their threats against you, and bid you arm yourselves for war and battle ; for they have seen Crumb-snatcher in the

ὑμέτερος βασιλεὺς Φυσίγναθος. ἀλλὰ μάχεσθε,
οἵτινες ἐν βατράχοισιν ἀριστῆες γεγάασθε.
Ὣς εἰπὼν ἀπέφηνε· λόγος δ' εἰς οὔατ' ἀμύμων
εἰσελθὼν ἐτάραξε φρένας βατράχων ἀγερώχων·
μεμφομένων δ' αὐτῶν Φυσίγναθος εἶπεν ἀναστάς·
Ὦ φίλοι, οὐκ ἔκτεινον ἐγὼ μῦν, οὐδὲ κατεῖδον
ὀλλύμενον· πάντως δ' ἐπνίγη παίζων παρὰ λίμνην,
νήξεις τὰς βατράχων μιμούμενος· οἱ δὲ κάκιστοι
νῦν ἐμὲ μέμφονται τὸν ἀναίτιον· ἀλλ' ἄγε βουλὴν
ζητήσωμεν, ὅπως δολίους μύας ἐξολέσωμεν.
τοιγὰρ ἐγὼν ἐρέω, ὥς μοι δοκεῖ εἶναι ἄριστα.
σώματα κοσμήσαντες ἐν ὅπλοις στῶμεν ἅπαντες
ἄκροις πὰρ χείλεσσιν, ὅπου κατάκρημνος ὁ χῶρος·
ἡνίκα δ' ὁρμηθέντες ἐφ' ἡμέας ἐξέλθωσι,
δραξάμενοι κορύθων, ὅστις σχεδὸν ἀντίος ἔλθῃ,
ἐς λίμνην αὐτοὺς σὺν ἐκείναις εὐθὺ βάλωμεν.
οὕτω γὰρ πνίξαντες ἐν ὕδασι τοὺς ἀκολύμβους
στήσομεν εὐθύμως τὸ μυοκτόνον ὧδε τρόπαιον.
Ὣς εἰπὼν ἀνέπεισε καθοπλίζεσθαι ἅπαντας.
φύλλοις μὲν μαλαχῶν κνήμας ἑὰς ἀμφεκάλυψαν,
θώρηκας δ' εἶχον καλῶν χλοερῶν ἀπὸ σεύτλων,
φύλλα δὲ τῶν κραμβῶν εἰς ἀσπίδας εὖ ἤσκησαν,
ἔγχος δ' ὀξύσχοινος ἑκάστῳ μακρὸς ἀρήρει,
καὶ τὰ κέρα κοχλιῶν λεπτῶν ἐκάλυπτε κάρηνα.
φραξάμενοι δ' ἔστησαν ἐπ' ὄχθῃς ὑψηλῇσιν
σείοντες λόγχας, θυμοῦ δ' ἔμπληντο ἕκαστος.
Ζεὺς δὲ θεοὺς καλέσας εἰς οὐρανὸν ἀστερόεντα,
καὶ πολέμου πληθὺν δείξας κρατερούς τε μαχητάς,
πολλοὺς καὶ μεγάλους ἠδ' ἔγχεα μακρὰ φέροντας,
οἷος Κενταύρων στρατὸς ἔρχεται ἠδὲ Γιγάντων,

water whom your king Puff-jaw slew. Fight, then, as many of you as are warriors among the Frogs."

With these words he explained the matter. So when this blameless speech came to their ears, the proud Frogs were disturbed in their hearts and began to blame Puff-jaw. But he rose up and said:

"Friends, I killed no Mouse, nor did I see one perishing. Surely he was drowned while playing by the lake and imitating the swimming of the Frogs, and now these wretches blame me who am guiltless. Come then; let us take counsel how we may utterly destroy the wily Mice. Moreover, I will tell you what I think to be the best. Let us all gird on our armour and take our stand on the very brink of the lake, where the ground breaks down sheer: then when they come out and charge upon us, let each seize by the crest the Mouse who attacks him, and cast them with their helmets into the lake; for so we shall drown these dry-bobs[1] in the water, and merrily set up here a trophy of victory over the slaughtered Mice."

By this speech he persuaded them to arm themselves They covered their shins with leaves of mallows, and had breastplates made of fine green beet-leaves, and cabbage-leaves, skilfully fashioned, for shields. Each one was equipped with a long, pointed rush for a spear, and smooth snail-shells to cover their heads. Then they stood in close-locked ranks upon the high bank, waving their spears, and were filled, each of them, with courage.

Now Zeus called the gods to starry heaven and showed them the martial throng and the stout warriors so many and so great, all bearing long spears; for they were as the host of the Centaurs

[1] *lit.* "those unable to swim."

ἡδὺ γελῶν ἐρέεινε· τίνες βατράχοισιν ἀρωγοὶ
ἢ μυσὶν ἀθανάτων; καὶ Ἀθηναίην προσέειπεν·
Ὦ θύγατερ, μυσὶν ἦ ῥα βοηθήσουσα πορεύσῃ;
καὶ γάρ σου κατὰ νηὸν ἀεὶ σκιρτῶσιν ἅπαντες
κνίσσῃ τερπόμενοι καὶ ἐδέσμασι παντοδαποῖσιν.
Ὣς ἄρ' ἔφη Κρονίδης· τὸν δὲ προσέειπεν Ἀθήνη·
ὦ πάτερ, οὐκ ἄν πώποτ' ἐγὼ μυσὶ τειρομένοισιν
ἐλθοίην ἐπαρωγός, ἐπεὶ κακὰ πολλά μ' ἔοργαν
στέμματα βλάπτοντες καὶ λύχνους εἵνεκ' ἐλαίου.
ταῦτο δέ μου λίην ἔδακε φρένας, οἷον ἔρεξαν.
πέπλον μου κατέτρωξαν, ὃν ἐξύφανα καμοῦσα
ἐκ ῥοδάνης λεπτῆς καὶ στήμονα λεπτὸν ἔνησα,
καὶ τρώγλας ἐτέλεσσαν· ὁ δ' ἠπητής μοι ἐπέστη
καὶ πράσσει με τόκον· τὸ δὲ ῥίγιον ἀθανάτοισιν.
χρησαμένη γὰρ ὕφανα καὶ οὐκ ἔχω ἀνταποδοῦναι.
ἀλλ' οὐδ' ὣς βατράχοισιν ἀρηγέμεν οὐκ ἐθελήσω.
εἰσὶ γὰρ οὐδ' αὐτοὶ φρένας ἔμπεδοι, ἀλλά με πρώην
ἐκ πολέμου ἀνιοῦσαν, ἐπεὶ λίην ἐκοπώθην,
ὕπνου δευομένην οὐκ εἴασαν θορυβοῦντες
οὐδ' ὀλίγον καταμῦσαι· ἐγὼ δ' ἄυπνος κατεκείμην,
τὴν κεφαλὴν ἀλγοῦσα, ἕως ἐβόησεν ἀλέκτωρ.
ἀλλ' ἄγε παυσώμεσθα, θεοί, τούτοισιν ἀρήγειν,
μή νύ τις ἡμείων τρωθῇ βέλει ὀξυόεντι·
εἰσὶ γὰρ ἀγχέμαχοι, καὶ εἰ θεὸς ἀντίον ἔλθοι·
πάντες δ' οὐρανόθεν τερπώμεθα δῆριν ὁρῶντες.
Ὣς ἄρ' ἔφη· τῇ δ' αὖτ' ἐπεπείθοντο θεοὶ ἄλλοι,
πάντες ὁμῶς δ' εἰσῆλθον ἀολλέες εἰς ἕνα χῶρον.
Καὶ τότε κώνωπες μεγάλας σάλπιγγας ἔχοντες
δεινὸν ἐσάλπιγξαν πολέμου κτύπον· οὐρανόθεν δὲ
Ζεὺς Κρονίδης βρόντησε, τέρας πολέμοιο κακοῖο.
Πρῶτος δ' Ὑψιβόας Λειχήνορα οὖτασε δουρὶ

and the Giants. Then he asked with a sly smile; "Who of the deathless gods will help the Frogs and who the Mice?" And he said to Athena;

"My daughter, will you go aid the Mice? For they all frolic about your temple continually, delighting in the fat of sacrifice and in all kinds of food."

So then said the son of Cronos. But Athena answered him: "I would never go to help the Mice when they are hard pressed, for they have done me much mischief, spoiling my garlands and my lamps too, to get the oil. And this thing that they have done vexes my heart exceedingly: they have eaten holes in my sacred robe, which I wove painfully spinning a fine woof on a fine warp, and made it full of holes. And now the money-lender is at me and charges me interest which is a bitter thing for immortals. For I borrowed to do my weaving, and have nothing with which to repay. Yet even so I will not help the Frogs; for they also are not considerate: once, when I was returning early from war, I was very tired, and though I wanted to sleep, they would not let me even doze a little for their outcry; and so I lay sleepless with a headache until cock-crow. No, gods, let us refrain from helping these hosts, or one of us may get wounded with a sharp spear; for they fight hand to hand, even if a god comes against them. Let us rather all amuse ourselves watching the fight from heaven."

So said Athena. And the other gods agreed with her, and all went in a body to one place.

Then gnats with great trumpets sounded the fell note of war, and Zeus the son of Cronos thundered from heaven, a sign of grievous battle.

First Loud-croaker wounded Lickman in the belly,

ἑσταότ' ἐν προμάχοις κατὰ γαστέρα ἐς μέσον ἧπαρ·
κὰδ δ' ἔπεσεν πρηνής, ἁπαλὰς δ' ἐκόνισσεν ἐθείρας.
[δούπησεν δὲ πεσών, ἀράβησε δὲ τεύχε' ἐπ' αὐτῷ.]
Τρωγλοδύτης δὲ μετ' αὐτὸν ἀκόντισε Πηλείωνα,
πῆξεν δ' ἐν στέρνῳ στιβαρὸν δόρυ· τὸν δὲ πεσόντα
εἷλε μέλας θάνατος, ψυχὴ στόματος δ' ἐξέπτη.
Σευτλαῖος δ' ἂρ ἔπεφνε βαλὼν κέαρ Ἐμβασίχυτρον.
Ἀρτοφάγος δὲ Πολύφωνον κατὰ γαστέρα τύψεν·
ἤριπε δὲ πρηνής, ψυχὴ δὲ μελέων ἐξέπτη.
Λιμνόχαρις δ' ὡς εἶδεν ἀπολλύμενον Πολύφωνον,
Τρωγλοδύτην ἁπαλοῖο δι' αὐχένος [τρῶσεν ἐπιφθὰς
πέτρῳ μυλοειδέϊ· τὸν δὲ σκότος ὄσσε κάλυψε[1]]
Ὠκιμίδην δ' ἄχος εἷλε καὶ ἤλασεν ὀξέι σχοίνῳ
οὐδ' ἐξέσπασεν ἔγχος ἐναντίον· ἤριπε δ' εὐθύς·
Λειχήνωρ δ' αὐτοῖο τιτύσκετο δουρὶ φαεινῷ
καὶ βάλεν, οὐδ' ἀφάμαρτε, καθ' ἧπατος· ὡς δ' ἐνόησε
Κοστοφάγον φεύγοντα, βαθείαις ἔμπεσεν ὄχθαις·
ἀλλ' οὐδ' ὣς ἀπέληγε μάχης, ἀλλ' ἤλασεν αὐτόν·
κάππεσε δ', οὐδ' ἀνένευσεν· ἐβάπτετο δ' αἵματι λίμνη
πορφυρέῳ, αὐτὸς δὲ παρ' ἠιόν' ἐξετανύσθη
χορδῇσιν λιπαρῇσί τε πειρόμενος λαγόνεσσιν.
Τυροφάγον δ' αὐτῇσιν ἐπ' ὄχθαις ἐξενάριξεν.

* * * *

Πτερνογλύφον δ' ἐπιδὼν Καλαμίνθιος ἐς φόβον ἦλθεν,
ἥλατο δ' ἐς λίμνην φεύγων, τὴν ἀσπίδα ῥίψας.
Φιλτραῖον δ' ἄρ' ἔπεφνεν ἀμύμων Ἐμβασίχυτρος.
[Ὑδρόχαρις δέ τ' ἔπεφνεν Πτερνοφάγον βασιλῆα,]
χερμαδίῳ πλήξας κατὰ βρέγματος· ἐγκέφαλος δὲ
ἐκ ῥινῶν ἔσταξε, παλάσσετο δ' αἵματι γαῖα.

[1] Omitted by Baumeister and by many MSS.

right through the midriff. Down fell he on his face and soiled his soft fur in the dust: he fell with a thud and his armour clashed about him. Next Troglodyte shot at the son of Mudman, and drove the strong spear deep into his breast; so he fell, and black death seized him and his spirit flitted forth from his mouth. Then Beety struck Pot-visitor to the heart and killed him, and Bread-nibbler hit Loud-crier in the belly, so that he fell on his face and his spirit flitted forth from his limbs. Now when Pond-larker saw Loud-crier perishing, he struck in quickly and wounded Troglodyte in his soft neck with a rock like a mill-stone, so that darkness veiled his eyes. Thereat Ocimides was seized with grief, and struck out with his sharp reed and did not draw his spear back to him again, but felled his enemy there and then. And Lickman shot at him with a bright spear and hit him unerringly in the midriff. And as he marked Cabbage-eater running away, he fell on the steep bank, yet even so did not cease fighting but smote that other so that he fell and did not rise again: and the lake was dyed with red blood as he lay outstretched along the shore, pierced through the guts and shining flanks. Also he slew Cheese-eater on the very brink . . . . But Reedy took to flight when he saw Ham-nibbler, and fled, plunging into the lake and throwing away his shield. Then blameless Pot-visitor killed Brewer and Water-larker killed the lord Ham-nibbler, striking him on the head with a pebble, so that his brains flowed out at his nostrils and the earth was bespattered

Λειχοπίνακα δ' ἔπεφνεν ἀμύμων Βορβοροκοίτης,
ἔγχει ἐπαΐξας· τὸν δὲ σκότος ὄσσε κάλυψεν.
Πρασσαῖος δ' ἐπιδὼν ποδὸς εἵλκυσε νεκρὸν ἐόντα,
ἐν λίμνῃ δ' ἀπέπνιξε κρατήσας χειρὶ τένοντα.
Ψιχάρπαξ δ' ἤμυν' ἑτάρων περὶ τεθνειώτων
καὶ βάλε Πρασσαῖον μήπω γαίης ἐπιβάντα·
πῖπτε δὲ οἱ πρόσθεν, ψυχὴ δ' Ἀιδόσδε βεβήκει.
Κραμβοβάτης δ' ἐσιδὼν πηλοῦ δράκα ῥίψεν ἐπ' αὐτόν,
καὶ τὸ μέτωπον ἔχρισε καὶ ἐξετύφλου παρὰ μικρόν.
ὠργίσθη δ' ἄρ' ἐκεῖνος, ἑλὼν δέ τε χειρὶ παχείῃ
κείμενον ἐν πεδίῳ λίθον ὄμβριμον, ἄχθος ἀρούρης,
τῷ βάλε Κραμβοβάτην ὑπὸ γούνατα· πᾶσα δ' ἐκλάσθη
κνήμη δεξιτερή, πέσε δ' ὕπτιος ἐν κονίῃσιν.
Κραυγασίδης δ' ἤμυνε καὶ αὖθις βαῖνεν ἐπ' αὐτόν,
τύψε δέ μιν μέσσην κατὰ γαστέρα· πᾶς δέ οἱ εἴσω
ὀξύσχοινος ἔδυνε, χαμαὶ δ' ἔκχυντο ἅπαντα
ἔγκατ' ἐφελκομένῳ ὑπὸ δούρατι χειρὶ παχείῃ·
Τρωγλοδύτης δ' ὡς εἶδεν ἐπ' ὄχθῃσιν ποταμοῖο,
σκάζων ἐκ πολέμου ἀνεχάζετο, τείρετο δ' αἰνῶς·
ἥλατο δ' ἐς τάφρους, ὅππως φύγῃ αἰπὺν ὄλεθρον.
Τρωξάρτης δ' ἔβαλεν Φυσίγναθον ἐς πόδα ἄκρον.
ἔσχατα δ' ἐκ λίμνης ἀνεδύσατο, τείρετο δ' αἰνῶς·

*   *   *   *

Πρασσαῖος δ' ὡς εἶδεν ἔθ' ἡμίπνουν προπεσόντα,
ἦλθε διὰ προμάχων καὶ ἀκόντισεν ὀξέι σχοίνῳ·
οὐδ' ἔρρηξε σάκος, σχέτο δ' αὐτοῦ δουρὸς ἀκωκή.
τοῦ δ' ἔβαλε τρυφάλειαν ἀμύμονα καὶ τετράχυτρον
δῖος Ὀριγανίων, μιμούμενος αὐτὸν Ἄρηα,
[ὃς μόνος ἐν βατράχοισιν ἀρίστευεν καθ' ὅμιλον·]

with blood. Faultless Muck-coucher sprang upon Lick-platter and killed him with his spear and brought darkness upon his eyes: and Leeky saw it, and dragged Lick-platter by the foot, though he was dead, and choked him in the lake. But Crumb-snatcher was fighting to avenge his dead comrades, and hit Leeky before he reached the land; and he fell forward at the blow and his soul went down to Hades. And seeing this, Cabbage-climber took a clod of mud and hurled it at the Mouse, plastering all his forehead and nearly blinding him. Thereat Crumb-snatcher was enraged and caught up in his strong hand a huge stone that lay upon the ground, a heavy burden for the soil: with that he hit Cabbage-climber below the knee and splintered his whole right shin, hurling him on his back in the dust. But Croakerson kept him off, and rushing at the Mouse in turn, hit him in the middle of the belly and drove the whole reed-spear into him, and as he drew the spear back to him with his strong hand, all his foe's bowels gushed out upon the ground. And when Troglodyte saw the deed, as he was limping away from the fight on the river bank, he shrank back sorely moved, and leaped into a trench to escape sheer death. Then Bread-nibbler hit Puff-jaw on the toes—he came up at the last from the lake and was greatly distressed . . . And when Leeky saw him fallen forward, but still half alive, he pressed through those who fought in front and hurled a sharp reed at him; but the point of the spear was stayed and did not break his shield. Then noble Rueful, like Ares himself, struck his flawless head-piece made of four pots—he only among the

ὥρμησεν δ' ἄρ' ἐπ' αὐτόν· ὁ δ' ὡς ἴδεν, οὐχ ὑπέμεινεν
ἥρωα κρατερόφρον', ἔδυ δ' ἐν βένθεσι λίμνης.
Ἦν δέ τις ἐν μύεσιν Μεριδάρπαξ, ἔξοχος ἄλλων,
Κναίσωνος[1] *φίλος υἱὸς ἀμύμονος Ἀρτεπιβούλου,*
οἴκαδ' ἰὼν πολέμοιο μετασχεῖν παῖδ' ἐκέλευσεν·
αὐτὸς δ' ἑστήκει γαυρούμενος ὡς κατὰ λίμνην.
οὗτος ἀναρπάξαι βατράχων γενεὴν ἐπαπείλει,[2]
καὶ ῥήξας καρύου μέσσην ῥάχιν εἰς δύο μοίρας
φράγδην ἀμφοτέροισιν ἐν ὤμοις χεῖρας ἔθηκεν·
οἱ δὲ τάχος δείσαντες ἔβαν πάντες κατὰ λίμνην·
καί νύ κεν ἐξετέλεσσεν, ἐπεὶ μέγα οἱ σθένος ἦεν,
εἰ μὴ ἄρ' ὀξὺ νόησε πατὴρ ἀνδρῶν τε θεῶν τε.
καὶ τότ' ἀπολλυμένους βατράχους ᾤκτειρε Κρονίων·
κινήσας δὲ κάρη τοίην ἐφθέγξατο φωνήν·
Ὢ πόποι, ἦ μέγα ἔργον ἐν ὀφθαλμοῖσιν ὁρῶμαι·
οὐ μικρὸν ἐκπλήσσει Μεριδάρπαξ, ὃς κατὰ λίμνην
ἅρπαξ ἐν βατράχοισιν ἀμείβεται· ἀλλὰ τάχιστα
Παλλάδα πέμψωμεν πολεμόκλονον, ἢ καὶ Ἄρηα,
οἵ μιν ἐπισχήσουσι μάχης κρατερόν περ ἐόντα.
Ὣς ἄρ' ἔφη Κρονίδης· Ἥρη δ' ἀπαμείβετο μῦθον·
οὔτ' ἄρ' Ἀθηναίης, Κρονίδη, σθένος, οὔτε Ἄρηος
ἰσχύσει βατράχοισιν ἀρηγέμεν αἰπὺν ὄλεθρον.
ἀλλ' ἄγε πάντες ἴωμεν ἀρηγόνες· ἢ τὸ σὸν ὅπλον
κινείσθω μέγα Τιτανοκτόνον ὀβριμοεργόν,
ᾧ ποτε καὶ Καπανῆα κατέκτανες ὄβριμον ἄνδρα
καὶ μέγαν Ἐγκέλαδον καὶ ἄγρια φῦλα Γιγάντων,
κινείσθω· οὕτω γὰρ ἁλώσεται, ὅστις ἄριστος.

[1] Κρείωνος, Baumeister.
[2] This may be a parody of Orion's threat in Hesiod, *Astronomy*, frag. 4.

Frogs showed prowess in the throng. But when he saw the other rush at him, he did not stay to meet the stout-hearted hero but dived down to the depths of the lake.

Now there was one among the Mice, Slice-snatcher, who excelled the rest, dear son of Gnawer the son of blameless Bread-stealer. He went to his house and bade his son take part in the war; but he himself stood exulting by the lake. This warrior threatened to destroy the race of Frogs utterly, and splitting a chestnut-husk into two parts along the joint, put the two hollow pieces as armour on his paws: then straightway the Frogs were dismayed and all rushed down to the lake, and he would have made good his boast—for he had great strength—had not the Son of Cronos, the Father of men and gods, been quick to mark the thing and pitied the Frogs as they were perishing. He shook his head, and uttered this word:

"Dear, dear, how fearful a deed do my eyes behold! Slice-snatcher makes no small panic rushing to and fro among the Frogs by the lake. Let us then make all haste and send warlike Pallas or even Ares, for they will stop his fighting, strong though he is."

So said the Son of Cronos; but Hera answered him: "Son of Cronos, neither the might of Athena nor of Ares can avail to deliver the Frogs from utter destruction. Rather, come and let us all go to help them, or else let loose your weapon, the great and formidable Titan-killer with which you killed Capaneus, that doughty man, and great Enceladus and the wild tribes of Giants; ay, let it loose, for so the most valiant will be slain."

Ὣς ἄρ' ἔφη· Κρονίδης δ' ἔβαλε ψολόεντα κεραυνόν.
πρῶτα μὲν ἐβρόντησε, μέγαν δ' ἐλέλιξεν Ὄλυμπον,
αὐτὰρ ἔπειτα κεραυνόν, δειμαλέον Διὸς ὅπλον,
ἧκ' ἐπιδινήσας· ὁ δ' ἄρ' ἔπτατο χειρὸς ἄνακτος.
πάντας μέν ῥ' ἐφόβησε βαλὼν ἐπὶ τούσδε [κεραυνόν·]
ἀλλ' οὐδ' ὣς ἀπέληγε μυῶν στρατός, ἀλλ' ἔτι μᾶλλον
ἔλπετο πορθήσειν βατράχων γένος αἰχμητάων,
εἰ μὴ ἀπ' Οὐλύμπου βατράχους ᾤκτειρε Κρονίων,
ὅς ῥα τότ' ἐν βατράχοισιν ἀρωγοὺς εὐθὺς ἔπεμψεν.
Ἦλθον δ' ἐξαίφνης νωτάκμονες, ἀγκυλοχῆλαι,
λοξοβάται, στρεβλοί, ψαλιδόστομοι, ὀστρακόδερμοι,
ὀστοφυεῖς, πλατύνωτοι, ἀποστίλβοντες ἐν ὤμοις,
βλαισοί, χειροτένοντες, ἀπὸ στέρνων ἐσορῶντες,
ὀκτάποδες, δικέραιοι, ἀτειρέες, οἱ δὲ καλεῦνται
καρκίνοι, οἵ ῥα μυῶν οὐρὰς στομάτεσσιν ἔκοπτον
ἠδὲ πόδας καὶ χεῖρας· ἀνεγνάμπτοντο δὲ λόγχαι.
τοὺς δὴ ὑπέδδεισαν πάντες μύες, οὐδ' ἔτ' ἔμειναν,
ἐς δὲ φυγὴν ἐτράποντο· ἐδύσετο δ' ἥλιος ἤδη,
καὶ πολέμου τελετὴ μονοημέρου ἐξετελέσθη.

So said Hera: and the Son of Cronos cast a lurid thunderbolt: first he thundered and made great Olympus shake, and then cast the thunderbolt, the awful weapon of Zeus, tossing it lightly forth. Thus he frightened them all, Frogs and Mice alike, hurling his bolt upon them. Yet even so the army of the Mice did not relax, but hoped still more to destroy the brood of warrior Frogs. Only, the Son of Cronos, on Olympus, pitied the Frogs and then straightway sent them helpers.

So there came suddenly warriors with mailed backs and curving claws, crooked beasts that walked sideways, nut-cracker-jawed, shell-hided: bony they were, flat-backed, with glistening shoulders and bandy legs and stretching arms and eyes that looked behind them. They had also eight legs and two feelers—persistent creatures who are called crabs. These nipped off the tails and paws and feet of the Mice with their jaws, while spears only beat on them. Of these the Mice were all afraid and no longer stood up to them, but turned and fled. Already the sun was set, and so came the end of the one-day war.

OF THE ORIGIN OF HOMER AND HESIOD, AND THEIR CONTEST

ΠΕΡΙ ΟΜΗΡΟΥ ΚΑΙ ΗΣΙΟΔΟΥ
ΚΑΙ ΤΟΥ ΓΕΝΟΥΣ ΚΑΙ ΑΓΩΝΟΣ ΑΥΤΩΝ

313[1] Ὅμηρον καὶ Ἡσίοδον τοὺς θειοτάτους ποιητὰς πάντες ἄνθρωποι πολίτας ἰδίους εὔχονται γενέσθαι. ἀλλ᾽ Ἡσίοδος μὲν τὴν ἰδίαν ὀνομάσας πατρίδα πάντας τῆς φιλονεικίας ἀπήλλαξεν εἰπὼν ὡς ὁ πατὴρ αὐτοῦ[2]

εἵσατο δ᾽ ἄγχ᾽ Ἑλικῶνος ὀιζυρῇ ἐνὶ κώμῃ
Ἄσκρῃ, χεῖμα κακῇ, θέρει ἀργαλέῃ, οὐδέ ποτ᾽ ἐσθλῇ.

Ὅμηρον δὲ πᾶσαι ὡς εἰπεῖν αἱ πόλεις καὶ οἱ ἄποικοι αὐτῶν παρ᾽ ἑαυτοῖς γεγενῆσθαι λέγουσιν. καὶ πρῶτοί γε Σμυρναῖοι Μέλητος ὄντα τοῦ παρ᾽ αὐτοῖς ποταμοῦ καὶ Κρηθηίδος νύμφης κεκλῆσθαί φασι πρότερον Μελησιγένη, ὕστερον μέντοι τυφλωθέντα Ὅμηρον μετονομασθῆναι διὰ τὴν παρ᾽ αὐτοῖς ἐπὶ τῶν τοιούτων συνήθη προσηγορίαν. Χῖοι δὲ πάλιν τεκμήρια φέρουσιν ἴδιον εἶναι πολίτην λέγοντες καὶ περισῴζεσθαί τινας ἐκ τοῦ γένους αὐτοῦ παρ᾽ αὐτοῖς Ὁμηρίδας καλουμένους. Κολοφώνιοι δὲ καὶ τόπον δεικνύουσιν, ἐν ᾧ φασιν αὐτὸν γράμματα διδάσκοντα τῆς ποιήσεως ἄρξασθαι καὶ ποιῆσαι πρῶτον τὸν Μαργίτην.

Περὶ δὲ τῶν γονέων αὐτοῦ πάλιν πολλὴ διαφωνία παρὰ πᾶσίν ἐστιν. Ἑλλάνικος μὲν γὰρ

[1] Goettling's paging. [2] *Works and Days*, 639 f.

OF THE ORIGIN OF HOMER AND HESIOD, AND OF THEIR CONTEST

Everyone boasts that the most divine of poets, Homer and Hesiod, are said to be his particular countrymen. Hesiod, indeed, has put a name to his native place and so prevented any rivalry, for he said that his father "settled near Helicon in a wretched hamlet, Ascra, which is miserable in winter sultry in summer, and good at no season." But, as for Homer, you might almost say that every city with its inhabitants claims him as her son. Foremost are the men of Smyrna who say that he was the Son of Meles, the river of their town, by a nymph Cretheïs, and that he was at first called Melesigenes. He was named Homer later, when he became blind, this being their usual epithet for such people. The Chians, on the other hand, bring forward evidence to show that he was their countrymen, saying that there actually remain some of his descendants among them who are called Homeridae. The Colophonians even show the place where they declare that he began to compose when a schoolmaster, and say that his first work was the *Margites*.

As to his parents also, there is on all hands great disagreement. Hellanicus and Cleanthes say his

314 καὶ Κλεάνθης Μαίονα λέγουσιν, Εὐγαίων δὲ Μέλητα, Καλλικλῆς δὲ Μνασαγόραν, Δημόκριτος δὲ ὁ Τροιζήνιος Δαήμονα ἔμπορον, ἔνιοι δὲ Θαμύραν,[1] Αἰγύπτιοι δὲ Μενέμαχον ἱερογραμματέα, εἰσὶ δέ, οἳ Τηλέμαχον τὸν Ὀδυσσέως· μητέρα δὲ οἱ μὲν Μῆτιν, οἱ δὲ Κρηθηίδα, οἱ δὲ Θεμίστην, οἱ δὲ Εὐγνηθώ, ἔνιοι δὲ Ἰθακησίαν τινὰ ὑπὸ Φοινίκων ἀπεμπολῃθεῖσαν, οἱ δὲ Καλλιόπην τὴν Μοῦσαν, τινὲς δὲ Πολυκάστην τὴν Νέστορος.

Ἐκαλεῖτο δὲ Μέλης, ὡς δέ τινές φασι, Μελησιγένης, ὡς δὲ ἔνιοι, Ἄλτης. ὀνομασθῆναι δὲ αὐτόν φασί τινες Ὅμηρον διὰ τὸ τὸν πατέρα αὐτοῦ ὅμηρον δοθῆναι ὑπὸ Κυπρίων Πέρσαις, οἱ δὲ διὰ τὴν πήρωσιν τῶν ὀμμάτων· παρὰ γὰρ τοῖς Αἰολεῦσιν οὕτως οἱ πηροὶ καλοῦνται. ὅπερ δὲ ἀκηκόαμεν ἐπὶ τοῦ θειοτάτου αὐτοκράτορος Ἀδριανοῦ εἰρημένον ὑπὸ τῆς Πυθίας περὶ Ὁμήρου, ἐκθησόμεθα. τοῦ γὰρ βασιλέως πυθομένου, πόθεν Ὅμηρος καὶ τίνος, ἀπεφοίβασε δι' ἑξαμέτρου τόνδε τὸν τρόπον·

Ἄγνωστόν μ' ἔρεαι γενεὴν καὶ πατρίδα γαῖαν
ἀμβροσίου σειρῆνος; ἕδος δ' Ἰθακήσιός ἐστιν,
Τηλέμαχος δὲ πατὴρ καὶ Νεστορέη Ἐπικάστη
μήτηρ, ἥ μιν ἔτικτε βροτῶν πολὺ πάνσοφον ἄνδρα.

οἷς μάλιστα δεῖ πιστεύειν διά τε τὸν πυθόμενον καὶ τὸν ἀποκρινάμενον, ἄλλως τε οὕτως τοῦ ποιητοῦ μεγαλοφυῶς τὸν προπάτορα διὰ τῶν ἐπῶν δεδοξακότος.

[1] Rzach: Ταμύραν, Flach.

father was Maeon, but Eugaeon says Meles; Callicles is for Mnesagoras, Democritus of Troezen for Daëmon, a merchant-trader. Some, again, say he was the son of Thamyras, but the Egyptians say of Menemachus, a priest-scribe, and there are even those who father him on Telemachus, the son of Odysseus. As for his mother, she is variously called Metis, Cretheïs, Themista, and Eugnetho. Others say she was an Ithacan woman sold as a slave by the Phoenicians; others, Calliope the Muse; others again Polycasta, the daughter of Nestor.

Homer himself was called Meles or, according to different accounts, Melesigenes or Altes. Some authorities say he was called Homer, because his father was given as a hostage to the Persians by the men of Cyprus; others, because of his blindness; for amongst the Aeolians the blind are so called. We will set down, however, what we have heard to have been said by the Pythia concerning Homer in the time of the most sacred Emperor Hadrian. When the monarch inquired from what city Homer came, and whose son he was, the priestess delivered a response in hexameters after this fashion:

"Do you ask me of the obscure race and country of the heavenly siren? Ithaca is his country, Telemachus his father, and Epicasta, Nestor's daughter, the mother that bare him, a man by far the wisest of mortal kind." This we must most implicitly believe, the inquirer and the answerer being who they are—especially since the poet has so greatly glorified his grandfather in his works.

Ἔνιοι μὲν οὖν αὐτὸν προγενέστερον Ἡσιόδου φασὶν εἶναι· τινὲς δὲ νεώτερον καὶ συγγενῆ. γενεαλογοῦσι δὲ οὕτως· Ἀπόλλωνός φασι καὶ Αἰθούσης τῆς Ποσειδῶνος γενέσθαι Λίνον, Λίνου δὲ Πίερον, Πιέρου δὲ καὶ νύμφης Μεθώνης Οἴαγρον, Οἰάγρου δὲ καὶ Καλλιόπης Ὀρφέα, Ὀρφέως δὲ Δρῆν, [τοῦ δὲ Εὐκλέα[1]], τοῦ δὲ Ἰαδμονίδην, τοῦ δὲ Φιλοτέρπην, τοῦ δὲ Εὔφημον, τοῦ δὲ Ἐπιφράδην, τοῦ δὲ Μελάνωπον, τούτου δὲ Δῖον καὶ Ἀπελλῆν, Δίου δὲ καὶ Πυκιμήδης τῆς Ἀπόλλωνος θυγατρὸς Ἡσίοδον καὶ Πέρσην· Ἀπελλοῦ δὲ Μαίονα, Μαίονος δὲ καὶ θυγατρὸς Μέλητος τοῦ ποταμοῦ Ὅμηρον.

Τινὲς δὲ συνακμάσαι φασὶν αὐτοὺς ὥστε καὶ ἀγωνίσασθαι ὁμόσε ἐν Χαλκίδι τῆς Εὐβοίας.[2] ποιήσαντα γὰρ τὸν Μαργίτην Ὅμηρον περιέρχεσθαι κατὰ πόλιν ῥαψῳδοῦντα, ἐλθόντα δὲ καὶ εἰς Δελφοὺς περὶ τῆς πατρίδος αὐτοῦ πυνθάνεσθαι, τίς εἴη, τὴν δὲ Πυθίαν εἰπεῖν·

ἔστιν Ἴος νῆσος μητρὸς πατρίς, ἥ σε θανόντα
δέξεται· ἀλλὰ νέων παίδων αἴνιγμα φύλαξαι.

τὸν δὲ ἀκούσαντα περιίστασθαι μὲν τὴν εἰς Ἴον ἄφιξιν, διατρίβειν δὲ περὶ τὴν ἐκεῖ χώραν. κατὰ δὲ τὸν αὐτὸν χρόνον Γανύκτωρ ἐπιτάφιον τοῦ πατρὸς Ἀμφιδάμαντος, βασιλέως Εὐβοίας, ἐπιτελῶν πάντας τοὺς ἐπισήμους ἄνδρας οὐ μόνον ῥώμῃ καὶ τάχει, ἀλλὰ καὶ σοφίᾳ ἐπὶ τὸν ἀγῶνα μεγάλαις δωρεαῖς τιμῶν συνεκάλεσεν. καὶ οὗτοι οὖν ἐκ τύχης, ὥς φασι, συμβαλόντες ἀλλήλοις

[1] Goettling's supplement.
[2] Nietzsche : ἐν Αὐλίδι τῆς Βοιωτίας, MSS.

Now some say that he was earlier than Hesiod others that he was younger and akin to him. They give his descent thus: Apollo and Æthusa, daughter of Poseidon, had a son Linus, to whom was born Pierus. From Pierus and the nymph Methone sprang Oeager; and from Oeager and Calliope Orpheus; from Orpheus, Dres; and from him, Eucles. The descent is continued through Iadmonides, Philoterpes, Euphemus, Epiphrades and Melanopus who had sons Dius and Apelles. Dius by Pycimede, the daughter of Apollo had two sons Hesiod and Perses; while Apelles begot Maeon who was the father of Homer by a daughter of the River Meles.

According to one account they flourished at the same time and even had a contest of skill at Chalcis in Euboea. For, they say, after Homer had composed the *Margites*, he went about from city to city as a minstrel, and coming to Delphi, inquired who he was and of what country? The Pythia answered:

"The Isle of Ios is your mother's country and it shall receive you dead; but beware of the riddle of the young children."[1]

Hearing this, it is said, he hesitated to go to Ios, and remained in the region where he was. Now about the same time Ganyctor was celebrating the funeral rites of his father Amphidamas, king of Euboea, and invited to the gathering not only all those who were famous for bodily strength and fleetness of foot, but also those who excelled in wit, promising them great rewards. And so, as the story goes, the two went to Chalcis and met by

[1] *sc.* the riddle of the fisher-boys which comes at the end of this work.

ἦλθον εἰς τὴν Χαλκίδα. τοῦ δὲ ἀγῶνος ἄλλοι τέ τινες τῶν ἐπισήμων Χαλκιδέων ἐκαθέζοντο κριταὶ καὶ μετ' αὐτῶν Πανείδης, ἀδελφὸς ὢν τοῦ τετελευτηκότος. ἀμφοτέρων δὲ τῶν ποιητῶν θαυμαστῶς ἀγωνισαμένων νικῆσαί φασι τὸν Ἡσίοδον τὸν τρόπον τοῦτον· προελθόντα γὰρ εἰς τὸ μέσον πυνθάνεσθαι τοῦ Ὁμήρου καθ' ἓν ἕκαστον, τὸν δὲ Ὅμηρον ἀποκρίνασθαι. φησὶν οὖν Ἡσίοδος·

Υἱὲ Μέλητος, Ὅμηρε, θεῶν ἄπο μήδεα εἰδώς,
εἴπ' ἄγε μοι πάμπρωτα, τί φέρτατόν ἐστι βροτοῖσιν;

ΟΜΗΡΟΣ

Ἀρχὴν μὲν μὴ φῦναι ἐπιχθονίοισιν ἄριστον,
φύντα δ' ὅπως ὤκιστα πύλας Ἀίδαο περῆσαι.

316 Ἡσίοδος τὸ δεύτερον·

Εἴπ' ἄγε μοι καὶ τοῦτο, θεοῖς ἐπιείκελ' Ὅμηρε,
τί θνητοῖς κάλλιστον ὀίεαι ἐν φρεσὶν εἶναι;

ὁ δέ·

Ὁππότ' ἂν εὐφροσύνη μὲν ἔχῃ κάτα δῆμον ἅπαντα,
δαιτυμόνες δ' ἀνὰ δώματ' ἀκουάζωνται ἀοιδοῦ
ἥμενοι ἑξείης, παρὰ δὲ πλήθωσι τράπεζαι
σίτου καὶ κρεέων, μέθυ δ' ἐκ κρητῆρος ἀφύσσων
οἰνοχόος φορέῃσι καὶ ἐγχείῃ δεπάεσσιν.
τοῦτό τί μοι κάλλιστον ἐνὶ φρεσὶν εἴδεται εἶναι.

Ῥηθέντων δὲ τούτων τῶν ἐπῶν, οὕτω σφοδρῶς φασι θαυμασθῆναι ὑπὸ τῶν Ἑλλήνων τοὺς στίχους ὥστε χρυσοῦς αὐτοὺς προσαγορευθῆναι, καὶ ἔτι καὶ νῦν ἐν ταῖς κοιναῖς θυσίαις πρὸ τῶν δείπνων καὶ σπονδῶν προκατεύχεσθαι πάντας. ὁ δὲ chance. The leading Chalcidians were judges together with Paneides, the brother of the dead king; and it is said that after a wonderful contest between the two poets, Hesiod won in the following manner: he came forward into the midst and put Homer one question after another, which Homer answered. Hesiod, then, began:

"Homer, son of Meles, inspired with wisdom from heaven, come, tell me first what is best for mortal man?"

HOMER

"For men on earth 'tis best never to be born at all; or being born, to pass through the gates of Hades with all speed."

Hesiod then asked again:

"Come, tell me now this also, godlike Homer: what think you in your heart is most delightsome to men?"

Homer answered:

"When mirth reigns throughout the town, and feasters about the house, sitting in order, listen to a minstrel; when the tables beside them are laden with bread and meat, and a wine-bearer draws sweet drink from the mixing-bowl and fills the cups: this I think in my heart to be most delightsome."

It is said that when Homer had recited these verses, they were so admired by the Greeks as to be called golden by them, and that even now at public sacrifices all the guests solemnly recite them before feasts and libations. Hesiod, however, was annoyed

Ἡσίοδος ἀχθεσθεὶς ἐπὶ τῇ Ὁμήρου εὐημερίᾳ ἐπὶ τὴν τῶν ἀπόρων ὥρμησεν ἐπερώτησιν καί φησι τούσδε τοὺς στίχους·

Μοῦσ᾿ ἄγε[1] μοι τά τ᾿ ἐόντα τά τ᾿ ἐσσόμενα πρό τ᾿ ἐόντα,
τῶν μὲν μηδὲν ἄειδε, σὺ δ᾿ ἄλλης μνῆσαι ἀοιδῆς.

ὁ δὲ Ὅμηρος, βουλόμενος ἀκολούθως τὸ ἄπορον λῦσαι, φησίν·

Οὐδέ ποτ᾿ ἀμφὶ Διὸς τύμβῳ καναχήποδες ἵπποι
ἅρματα συντρίψουσιν ἐρίζοντες περὶ νίκης.

Καλῶς δὲ καὶ ἐν τούτοις ἀπαντήσαντος ἐπὶ τὰς ἀμφιβόλους γνώμας ὥρμησεν ὁ Ἡσίοδος, καὶ πλείονας στίχους λέγων ἠξίου καθ᾿ ἕνα ἕκαστον συμφώνως ἀποκρίνασθαι τὸν Ὅμηρον. ἔστιν οὖν ὁ μὲν πρῶτος Ἡσιόδου, ὁ δὲ ἑξῆς Ὁμήρου, ἐνίοτε δὲ καὶ διὰ δύο στίχων τὴν ἐπερώτησιν ποιουμένου τοῦ Ἡσιόδου·

ΗΣΙΟΔΟΣ

Δεῖπνον ἔπειθ᾿ εἵλοντο βοῶν κρέα, καὐχένας ἵππων

ΟΜΗΡΟΣ

Ἔκλυον ἱδρώοντας, ἐπεὶ πολέμοιο κορέσθην.

ΗΣΙΟΔΟΣ

317 Καὶ Φρύγες, οἳ πάντων ἀνδρῶν ἐπὶ νηυσὶν ἄριστοι

ΟΜΗΡΟΣ

Ἀνδράσι ληιστῆρσιν ἐπ᾿ ἀκτῆς δόρπον ἑλέσθαι.

ΗΣΙΟΔΟΣ

Χερσὶ βαλέων ἰοὺς[2] οὔλων[3] κατὰ φῦλα γιγάντων

[1] MSS.: ἄ γέ μοι, Flach. [2] Nietzsche: ἰοῖσιν, MS. [3] Rzach: ἄλλων, MS.

by Homer's felicity and hurried on to pose him with hard questions. He therefore began with the following lines:

"Come, Muse; sing not to me of things that are, or that shall be, or that were of old; but think of another song."

Then Homer, wishing to escape from the impasse by an apt answer, replied:—

"Never shall horses with clattering hoofs break chariots, striving for victory about the tomb of Zeus."

Here again Homer had fairly met Hesiod, and so the latter turned to sentences of doubtful meaning[1]: he recited many lines and required Homer to complete the sense of each appropriately. The first of the following verses is Hesiod's and the next Homer's: but sometimes Hesiod puts his question in two lines.

HESIOD

"Then they dined on the flesh of oxen and their horses' necks—"

HOMER

"They unyoked dripping with sweat, when they had had enough of war."

HESIOD

"And the Phrygians, who of all men are handiest at ships—"

HOMER

"To filch their dinner from pirates on the beach."

HESIOD

"To shoot forth arrows against the tribes of cursed giants with his hands—"

[1] The verses of Hesiod are called doubtful in meaning because they are, if taken alone, either incomplete or absurd.

ΟΜΗΡΟΣ

Ἡρακλέης ἀπέλυσεν ἀπ᾽ ὤμων καμπύλα τόξα.

ΗΣΙΟΔΟΣ

Οὗτος ἀνὴρ ἀνδρός τ᾽ ἀγαθοῦ καὶ ἀνάλκιδός ἐστι

ΟΜΗΡΟΣ

Μητρός, ἐπεὶ πόλεμος χαλεπὸς πάσῃσι γυναιξίν.

ΗΣΙΟΔΟΣ

Αὐτάρ[1] σοί γε πατὴρ ἐμίγη καὶ πότνια μήτηρ

ΟΜΗΡΟΣ

Σῶμα τό γε[2] σπείραντε διὰ χρυσέην Ἀφροδίτην.

ΗΣΙΟΔΟΣ

Αὐτὰρ ἐπεὶ δμήθη γάμῳ Ἄρτεμις ἰοχέαιρα

ΟΜΗΡΟΣ

Καλλιστὼ κατέπεφνεν ἀπ᾽ ἀργυρέοιο βιοῖο.

ΗΣΙΟΔΟΣ

Ὣς οἳ μὲν δαίνυντο πανήμεροι, οὐδὲν ἔχοντες

ΟΜΗΡΟΣ

318 Οἴκοθεν· ἀλλὰ παρεῖχεν ἄναξ ἀνδρῶν Ἀγαμέμνων.

ΗΣΙΟΔΟΣ

Δεῖπνον δειπνήσαντες ἐνὶ σποδῷ αἰθαλοέσσῃ
σύλλεγον ὀστέα λευκὰ Διὸς κατατεθνηῶτος

ΟΜΗΡΟΣ

Παιδὸς ὑπερθύμου Σαρπηδόνος ἀντιθέοιο.

ΗΣΙΟΔΟΣ

Ἡμεῖς δ᾽ ἂμ πεδίον Σιμοέντιον ἥμενοι αὔτως
ἴομεν ἐκ νηῶν ὁδὸν ἀμφ᾽ ὤμοισιν ἔχοντες

[1] Ludwich : οὔτ᾽ ἄρ, MS. [2] τότε, Flach.

HOMER

"Heracles unslung his curved bow from his shoulders."

HESIOD

"This man is the son of a brave father and a weakling—"

HOMER

"Mother; for war is too stern for any woman."

HESIOD

"But for you, your father and lady mother lav in love—"

HOMER

"When they begot you by the aid of golden Aphrodite."

HESIOD

"But when she had been made subject in love, Artemis, who delights in arrows—"

HOMER

"Slew Callisto with a shot of her silver bow."

HESIOD

"So they feasted all day long, taking nothing—"

HOMER

"From their own houses; for Agamemnon, king of men, supplied them."

HESIOD

"When they had feasted, they gathered among the glowing ashes the bones of the dead Zeus-"

HOMER

"Born Sarpedon, that bold and godlike man."

HESIOD

"Now we have lingered thus about the plain of Simoïs, forth from the ships let us go our way, upon our shoulders—"

ΟΜΗΡΟΣ

Φάσγανα κωπήεντα καὶ αἰγανέας δολιχαύλους.

ΗΣΙΟΔΟΣ

Δὴ τότ' ἀριστῆες κοῦροι χείρεσσι θαλάσσης

ΟΜΗΡΟΣ

Ἄσμενοι ἐσσυμένως τε ἀπείρυσαν ὠκύαλον ναῦν.

ΗΣΙΟΔΟΣ

Κολχίδ' ἔπειτ' ἤγοντο καὶ Αἰήτην βασιλῆα [1]

ΟΜΗΡΟΣ

Φεῦγον, ἐπεὶ γίγνωσκον ἀνέστιον ἠδ' ἀθέμιστον.

ΗΣΙΟΔΟΣ

Αὐτὰρ ἐπεὶ σπεῖσάν τε καὶ ἔκπιον οἶδμα θαλάσσης

ΟΜΗΡΟΣ

Ποντοπορεῖν ἤμελλον ἐυσσέλμων ἐπὶ νηῶν.

ΗΣΙΟΔΟΣ

319 Τοῖσιν δ' Ἀτρεΐδης μεγάλ' εὔχετο πᾶσιν ὀλέσθαι [2]

ΟΜΗΡΟΣ

Μηδέποτ' ἐν πόντῳ, καὶ φωνήσας ἔπος ηὔδα·

ΗΣΙΟΔΟΣ

Ἐσθίετ', ὦ ξεῖνοι, καὶ πίνετε· μηδέ τις ὑμέων
οἴκαδε νοστήσειε φίλην ἐς πατρίδα γαῖαν

ΟΜΗΡΟΣ

Πημανθείς, ἀλλ' αὖτις ἀπήμονες οἴκαδ' ἵκοισθε.

Πρὸς πάντα δὲ τοῦ Ὁμήρου καλῶς ἀπαντήσαντος πάλιν φησὶν ὁ Ἡσίοδος·

[1] Flach follows Nietzsche in transposing this and the following verse and in reading ἔπειθ' ἵκοντο.

[2] Goettling's arrangement: Flach assigns the three following verses also to Hesiod.

HOMER

"Having our hilted swords and long-helved spears."

HESIOD

"Then the young heroes with their hands from the sea—"

HOMER

"Gladly and swiftly hauled out their fleet ship."

HESIOD

"Then they came to Colchis and king Æëtes—"

HOMER

"They avoided; for they knew he was inhospitable and lawless."

HESIOD

"Now when they had poured libations and deeply drunk, the surging sea—"

HOMER

"They were minded to traverse on well-built ships."

HESIOD

"The Son of Atreus prayed greatly for them that they all might perish—"

HOMER

"At no time in the sea: and he opened his mouth and said:"

HESIOD

"Eat, my guests, and drink, and may no one of you return home to his dear country—"

HOMER

"Distressed; but may you all reach home again unscathed."

When Homer had met him fairly on every point Hesiod said:

Τοῦτό τι δή μοι μοῦνον ἐειρομένῳ κατάλεξον,
πόσσοι ἅμ' Ἀτρεΐδῃσιν ἐς Ἴλιον ἦλθον Ἀχαιοί;

ὁ δὲ διὰ λογιστικοῦ προβλήματος ἀποκρίνεται οὕτως·

Πεντήκοντ' ἦσαν πυρὸς ἐσχάραι, ἐν δὲ ἑκάστῃ
πεντήκοντ' ὀβελοί, περὶ δὲ κρέα πεντήκοντα·
τρὶς δὲ τριηκόσιοι περὶ ἓν κρέας ἦσαν Ἀχαιοί.

Τοῦτο δὲ εὑρίσκεται πλῆθος ἄπιστον· τῶν γὰρ ἐσχαρῶν οὐσῶν πεντήκοντα, ὀβελίσκοι γίνονται πεντακόσιοι καὶ χιλιάδες β', κρεῶν δὲ δεκαδύο μυριάδες. . . .

Κατὰ πάντα δὴ τοῦ Ὁμήρου ὑπερτεροῦντος φθονῶν ὁ Ἡσίοδος ἄρχεται πάλιν·

Υἱὲ Μέλητος Ὅμηρ', εἴπερ τιμῶσί σε Μοῦσαι,
ὡς λόγος, ὑψίστοιο Διὸς μεγάλοιο θύγατρες,
λέξον μέτρον ἐναρμόζων, ὅ τι δὴ θνητοῖσι
κάλλιστόν τε καὶ ἔχθιστον· ποθέω γὰρ ἀκοῦσαι.

ὁ δέ φησι·

Ἡσίοδ', ἔκγονε Δίου, ἑκόντα με ταῦτα κελεύεις
εἰπεῖν· αὐτὰρ ἐγὼ μάλα τοι πρόφρων ἀγορεύσω.
κάλλιστον μὲν τῶν ἀγαθῶν ἔσται μέτρον εἶναι
αὐτὸν ἑαυτῷ· τῶν δὲ κακῶν ἔχθιστον ἁπάντων.[1]
ἄλλο δὲ πᾶν, ὅ τι σῷ θυμῷ φίλον ἐστίν, ἐρώτα.

ΗΣΙΟΔΟΣ

Πῶς ἂν ἄριστ' οἰκοῖντο πόλεις καὶ ἐν ἤθεσι ποίοις;

[1] Flach, following Nietzsche, marks a lacuna after this line.

"Only tell me this thing that I ask: How many Achaeans went to Ilium with the sons of Atreus?"

Homer answered in a mathematical problem, thus:

"There were fifty hearths, and at each hearth were fifty spits, and on each spit were fifty carcases, and there were thrice three hundred Achaeans to each joint."

. This is found to be an incredible number; for as there were fifty hearths, the number of spits is two thousand five hundred; and of carcasses, one hundred and twenty thousand . . .

Homer, then, having the advantage on every point, Hesiod was jealous and began again:

"Homer, son of Meles, if indeed the Muses, daughters of great Zeus the most high, honour you as it is said, tell me a standard that is both best and worst for mortal-men; for I long to know it." Homer replied: "Hesiod, son of Dius, I am willing to tell you what you command, and very readily will I answer you. For each man to be a standard to himself is most excellent for the good, but for the bad it is the worst of all things. And now ask me whatever else your heart desires."

HESIOD

"How would men best dwell in cities, and with what observances?"

ΟΜΗΡΟΣ

Εἰ μὴ κερδαίνειν ἀπὸ τῶν αἰσχρῶν ἐθέλοιεν,
οἱ δ' ἀγαθοὶ τιμῷντο, δίκη δ' ἀδίκοισιν ἐπείη.

ΗΣΙΟΔΟΣ

Εὔχεσθαι δὲ θεοῖσι τί πάντων ἐστὶν ἄμεινον;

ΟΜΗΡΟΣ

Εὔνουν εἶναι ἑαυτῷ ἀεὶ χρόνον ἐς τὸν ἅπαντα.

ΗΣΙΟΔΟΣ

Ἐν δ' ἐλαχίστῳ ἄριστον ἔχεις ὅ τι φύεται εἰπεῖν;

ΟΜΗΡΟΣ

Ὡς μὲν ἐμῇ γνώμῃ, φρένες ἐσθλαὶ σώμασιν ἀνδρῶν.

ΗΣΙΟΔΟΣ

Ἡ δὲ δικαιοσύνη τε καὶ ἀνδρείη δύναται τί;

ΟΜΗΡΟΣ

Κοινὰς ὠφελίας ἰδίοις μόχθοισι πορίζειν.

ΗΣΙΟΔΟΣ

Τῆς σοφίης δὲ τί τέκμαρ ἐπ' ἀνθρώποισι πέφυκεν;

ΟΜΗΡΟΣ

321 Γιγνώσκειν τὰ παρόντ' ὀρθῶς, καιρῷ δ' ἅμ' ἕπεσθαι.

ΗΣΙΟΔΟΣ

Πιστεῦσαι δὲ βροτοῖς ποῖον χρέος ἄξιόν ἐστιν;

ΟΜΗΡΟΣ

Οἷς αὐτὸς κίνδυνος ἐπὶ πραχθεῖσιν ἕπηται.

ΗΣΙΟΔΟΣ

Ἡ δ' εὐδαιμονίη τί ποτ' ἀνθρώποισι καλεῖται;

ΟΜΗΡΟΣ

Λυπηθέντ' ἐλάχιστα θανεῖν ἡσθέντα τε πλεῖστα.

HOMER

"By scorning to get unclean gain and if the good were honoured, but justice fell upon the unjust."

HESIOD

"What is the best thing of all for a man to ask of the gods in prayer?"

HOMER

"That he may be always at peace with himself continually."

HESIOD

"Can you tell me in briefest space what is best of all?"

HOMER

"A sound mind in a manly body, as I believe."

HESIOD

"Of what effect are righteousness and courage?"

HOMER

"To advance the common good by private pains."

HESIOD

"What is the mark of wisdom among men?"

HOMER

"To read aright the present, and to march with the occasion."

HESIOD

"In what kind of matter is it right to trust in men?"

HOMER

"Where danger itself follows the action close."

HESIOD

"What do men mean by happiness?"

HOMER

"Death after a life of least pain and greatest pleasure."

Ῥηθέντων δὲ καὶ τούτων, οἱ μὲν Ἕλληνες πάντες τὸν Ὅμηρον ἐκέλευον στεφανοῦν, ὁ δὲ βασιλεὺς Πανείδης ἐκέλευσεν ἕκαστον τὸ κάλλιστον ἐκ τῶν ἰδίων ποιημάτων εἰπεῖν. Ἡσίοδος οὖν ἔφη πρῶτος·

Πληιάδων Ἀτλαγενέων ἐπιτελλομενάων
ἄρχεσθ' ἀμήτου, ἀρότοιό τε δυσομενάων·
αἳ δή τοι νύκτας τε καὶ ἤματα τεσσαράκοντα
κεκρύφαται, αὖτις δὲ περιπλομένου ἐνιαυτοῦ
φαίνονται, τὰ πρῶτα χαρασσομένοιο σιδήρου.
οὗτός τοι πεδίων πέλεται νόμος, οἵ τε θαλάσσης
ἐγγύθι ναιετάουσ', οἵ τ' ἄγκεα βησσήεντα
πόντου κυμαίνοντος ἀπόπροθι, πίονα χῶρον
ναίουσιν· γυμνὸν σπείρειν, γυμνὸν δὲ βοωτεῖν
γυμνόν τ' ἀμάειν, ὅταν ὥρια πάντα πέλωνται.

Μεθ' ὃν Ὅμηρος·

Ἀμφὶ δ' ἄρ' Αἴαντας δοιοὺς ἵσταντο φάλαγγες
καρτεραί, ἃς οὔτ' ἄν κεν Ἄρης ὀνόσαιτο μετελθὼν
οὔτε κ' Ἀθηναίη λαοσσόος. οἱ γὰρ ἄριστοι
κρινθέντες Τρῶάς τε καὶ Ἕκτορα δῖον ἔμιμνον
φράξαντες δόρυ δουρί, σάκος σάκεϊ προθελύμνῳ·
322 ἀσπὶς ἄρ' ἀσπίδ' ἔρειδε, κόρυς κόρυν, ἀνέρα δ' ἀνήρ,
ψαῦον δ' ἱππόκομοι κόρυθες λαμπροῖσι φάλοισι
νευόντων· ὣς πυκνοὶ ἐφέστασαν ἀλλήλοισιν.
ἔφριξεν δὲ μάχη φθισίμβροτος ἐγχείῃσι
μακραῖς, ἃς εἶχον ταμεσίχροας. ὄσσε δ' ἄμερδεν
αὐγὴ χαλκείη κορύθων ἄπο λαμπομενάων
θωρήκων τε νεοσμήκτων σακέων τε φαεινῶν
ἐρχομένων ἄμυδις. μάλα κεν θρασυκάρδιος εἴη,
ὃς τότε γηθήσειεν ἰδὼν πόνον οὐδ' ἀκάχοιτο.

After these verses had been spoken, all the Hellenes called for Homer to be crowned. But King Paneides bade each of them recite the finest passage from his own poems. Hesiod, therefore, began[1] as follows:

"When the Pleiads, the daughters of Atlas, begin to rise begin the harvest, and begin ploughing ere they set. For forty nights and days they are hidden, but appear again as the year wears round, when first the sickle is sharpened. This is the law of the plains and for those who dwell near the sea or live in the rich-soiled valleys, far from the wave-tossed deep: strip to sow, and strip to plough, and strip to reap when all things are in season."

Then Homer[2]:

"The ranks stood firm about the two Aiantes, such that not even Ares would have scorned them had he met them, nor yet Athena who saves armies. For there the chosen best awaited the charge of the Trojans and noble Hector, making a fence of spears and serried shields. Shield closed with shield, and helm with helm, and each man with his fellow, and the peaks of their head-pieces with crests of horse-hair touched as they bent their heads: so close they stood together. The murderous battle bristled with the long, flesh-rending spears they held, and the flash of bronze from polished helms and new-burnished breast-plates and gleaming shields blinded the eyes. Very hard of heart would he have been, who could then have seen that strife with joy and felt no pang."

[1] *Works and Days*, 383–392.
[2] *Iliad* xiii. 126–133, 339–344.

Θαυμάσαντες δὲ καὶ ἐν τούτῳ τὸν Ὅμηρον οἱ Ἕλληνες ἐπῄνουν, ὡς παρὰ τὸ προσῆκον γεγονότων τῶν ἐπῶν, καὶ ἐκέλευον διδόναι τὴν νίκην. ὁ δὲ βασιλεὺς τὸν Ἡσίοδον ἐστεφάνωσεν εἰπὼν δίκαιον εἶναι τὸν ἐπὶ γεωργίαν καὶ εἰρήνην προκαλούμενον νικᾶν, οὐ τὸν πολέμους καὶ σφαγὰς διεξιόντα. τῆς μὲν οὖν νίκης οὕτω φασὶ τυχεῖν τὸν Ἡσίοδον καὶ λαβόντα τρίποδα χαλκοῦν ἀναθεῖναι ταῖς Μούσαις ἐπιγράψαντα·

Ἡσίοδος Μούσαις Ἑλικωνίσι τόνδ' ἀνέθηκεν
ὕμνῳ νικήσας ἐν Χαλκίδι θεῖον Ὅμηρον.

Τοῦ δὲ ἀγῶνος διαλυθέντος διέπλευσεν ὁ Ἡσίοδος εἰς Δελφοὺς χρησόμενος καὶ τῆς νίκης ἀπαρχὰς τῷ θεῷ ἀναθήσων. προσερχομένου δὲ αὐτοῦ τῷ ναῷ ἔνθεον γενομένην τὴν προφῆτίν φασιν εἰπεῖν·

Ὄλβιος οὗτος ἀνήρ, ὃς ἐμὸν δόμον ἀμφιπολεύει,
Ἡσίοδος Μούσῃσι τετιμένος ἀθανάτῃσιν·
τοῦ δ' ἦτοι κλέος ἔσται, ὅσον τ' ἐπικίδναται ἠώς.
ἀλλὰ Διὸς πεφύλαξο Νεμείου κάλλιμον ἄλσος·
κεῖθι δέ τοι θανάτοιο τέλος πεπρωμένον ἐστίν.

Ὁ δὲ Ἡσίοδος ἀκούσας τοῦ χρησμοῦ, τῆς Πελοποννήσου μὲν ἀνεχώρει νομίσας τὴν ἐκεῖ Νεμέαν τὸν θεὸν λέγειν, εἰς δὲ Οἰνόην τῆς Λοκρίδος ἐλθὼν καταλύει παρ' Ἀμφιφάνει καὶ Γανύκτορι, τοῖς Φηγέως παισίν, ἀγνοήσας τὸ μαντεῖον. ὁ γὰρ τόπος οὗτος ἅπας ἐκαλεῖτο Διὸς Νεμείου
323 ἱερόν. διατριβῆς δὲ αὐτῷ πλείονος γενομένης ἐν τοῖς Οἰνοεῦσιν, ὑπονοήσαντες οἱ νεανίσκοι τὴν ἀδελφὴν αὐτῶν μοιχεύειν τὸν Ἡσίοδον, ἀποκτεί-

Here, again, the Hellenes applauded Homer admiringly, so far did the verses exceed the ordinary level; and demanded that he should be adjudged the winner. But the king gave the crown to Hesiod, declaring that it was right that he who called upon men to follow peace and husbandry should have the prize rather than one who dwelt on war and slaughter. In this way, then, we are told, Hesiod gained the victory and received a brazen tripod which he dedicated to the Muses with this inscription :

"Hesiod dedicated this tripod to the Muses of Helicon after he had conquered divine Homer at Chalcis in a contest of song."

After the gathering was dispersed, Hesiod crossed to the mainland and went to Delphi to consult the oracle and to dedicate the first fruits of his victory to the god. They say that as he was approaching the temple, the prophetess became inspired and said :

"Blessed is this man who serves my house,—Hesiod, who is honoured by the deathless Muses : surely his renown shall be as wide as the light of dawn is spread. But beware of the pleasant grove of Nemean Zeus ; for there death's end is destined to befall you."

When Hesiod heard this oracle, he kept away from the Peloponnesus, supposing that the god meant the Nemea there ; and coming to Oenoë in Locris, he stayed with Amphiphanes and Ganyctor the sons of Phegeus, thus unconsciously fulfilling the oracle ; for all that region was called the sacred place of Nemean Zeus. He continued to stay a somewhat long time at Oenoë, until the young men, suspecting Hesiod of seducing their sister, killed ναντες εἰς τὸ μεταξὺ τῆς Ἀχαΐας[1] καὶ τῆς Λοκρίδος πέλαγος κατεπόντισαν. τοῦ δὲ νεκροῦ τριταίου πρὸς τὴν γῆν ὑπὸ δελφίνων προσενεχθέντος, ἑορτῆς τινος ἐπιχωρίου παρ' αὐτοῖς οὔσης Ἀριαδνείας,[2] πάντες ἐπὶ τὸν αἰγιαλὸν ἔδραμον καὶ τὸ σῶμα γνωρίσαντες, ἐκεῖνο μὲν πενθήσαντες ἔθαψαν, τοὺς δὲ φονεῖς ἀνεζήτουν. οἱ δὲ φοβηθέντες τὴν τῶν πολιτῶν ὀργὴν κατασπάσαντες ἁλιευτικὸν σκάφος διέπλευσαν εἰς Κρήτην· οὓς κατὰ μέσον τὸν πλοῦν ὁ Ζεὺς κεραυνώσας κατεπόντωσεν, ὥς φησιν Ἀλκιδάμας ἐν Μουσείῳ. Ἐρατοσθένης δέ φησιν ἐν Ἡσιόδῳ[3] Κτίμενον καὶ Ἄντιφον τοὺς Γανύκτορος ἐπὶ τῇ προειρημένῃ αἰτίᾳ ἐναλόντας[4] σφαγιασθῆναι θεοῖς τοῖς ξενίοις ὑπ' Εὐρυκλέους τοῦ μάντεως. τὴν μέντοι παρθένον, τὴν ἀδελφὴν τῶν προειρημένων, μετὰ τὴν φθορὰν ἑαυτὴν ἀναρτῆσαι· φθαρῆναι δὲ ὑπό τινος ξένου συνόδου τοῦ Ἡσιόδου Δημώδους ὄνομα· ὃν καὶ αὐτὸν ἀναιρεθῆναι ὑπὸ τῶν αὐτῶν φησιν. ὕστερον δὲ Ὀρχομένιοι κατὰ χρησμὸν μετενέγκαντες αὐτὸν παρ' αὐτοῖς ἔθαψαν καὶ ἐπέγραψαν ἐπὶ τῷ τάφῳ·

Ἄσκρη μὲν πατρὶς πολυλήιος, ἀλλὰ θανόντος
  ὀστέα πληξίππος γῆ Μινυὰς κατέχει
Ἡσιόδου, τοῦ πλεῖστον ἐν ἀνθρώποις κλέος ἐστὶν
  ἀνδρῶν κρινομένων ἐν βασάνῳ σοφίης.

Καὶ περὶ μὲν Ἡσιόδου τοσαῦτα· ὁ δὲ Ὅμηρος

[1] Westermann: Εὐβοίας, MS.
[2] So MS.: Ῥίου ἁγνείας, Flach (after Nietzsche).
[3] Goettling: ἐνηπόδῳ, MS.
[4] Friedel: ἀνελόντας, MS.; ἀνελθόντας, Flach (after Stephanus).

him and cast his body into the sea which separates Achaea and Locris. On the third day, however, his body was brought to land by dolphins while some local feast of Ariadne was being held. Thereupon, all the people hurried to the shore, and recognizing the body, lamented over it and buried it, and then began to look for the assassins. But these, fearing the anger of their countrymen, launched a fishing boat, and put out to sea for Crete: they had finished half their voyage when Zeus sank them with a thunderbolt, as Alcidamas states in his *Museum*. Eratosthenes, however, says in his *Hesiod* that Ctimenus and Antiphus, sons of Ganyctor, killed him for the reason already stated, and were sacrificed by Eurycles the seer to the gods of hospitality. He adds that the girl, sister of the above-named, hanged herself after she had been seduced, and that she was seduced by some stranger, Demodes by name, who was travelling with Hesiod, and who was also killed by the brothers. At a later time the men of Orchomenus removed his body as they were directed by an oracle, and buried him in their own country where they placed this inscription on his tomb:

"Ascra with its many cornfields was his native land; but in death the land of the horse-driving Minyans holds the bones of Hesiod, whose renown is greatest among men of all who are judged by the test of wit."

So much for Hesiod. But Homer, after losing the

ἀποτυχὼν τῆς νίκης περιερχόμενος ἔλεγε τὰ ποιήματα, πρῶτον μὲν τὴν Θηβαΐδα, ἔπη ͵ζ, ἧς ἡ ἀρχή·

324 Ἄργος ἄειδε, θεά, πολυδίψιον, ἔνθεν ἄνακτες·

εἶτα Ἐπιγόνους, ἔπη ͵ζ, ὧν ἡ ἀρχή·

νῦν αὖθ' ὁπλοτέρων ἀνδρῶν ἀρχώμεθα, Μοῦσαι.

φασὶ γάρ τινες καὶ ταῦτα Ὁμήρου εἶναι. ἀκούσαντες δὲ τῶν ἐπῶν οἱ Μίδου τοῦ βασιλέως παῖδες, Ξάνθος καὶ Γόργος, παρακαλοῦσιν αὐτὸν ἐπίγραμμα ποιῆσαι ἐπὶ τοῦ τάφου τοῦ πατρὸς αὐτῶν, ἐφ' οὗ ἦν παρθένος χαλκῆ τὸν Μίδου θάνατον οἰκτιζομένη. καὶ ποιεῖ οὕτως·

Χαλκέη παρθένος εἰμί, Μίδεω δ' ἐπὶ σήματος ἧμαι.
ἔστ' ἂν ὕδωρ τε νάῃ καὶ δένδρεα μακρὰ τεθήλῃ
καὶ ποταμοὶ πλήθωσι, περικλύζῃ δὲ θάλασσα,
ἠέλιος δ' ἀνιὼν φαίνῃ λαμπρά τε σελήνη,
αὐτοῦ τῇδε μένουσα πολυκλαύτῳ ἐπὶ τύμβῳ
σημανέω παριοῦσι, Μίδης ὅτι τῇδε τέθαπται.

Λαβὼν δὲ παρ' αὐτῶν φιάλην ἀργυρᾶν ἀνατ θησιν ἐν Δελφοῖς τῷ Ἀπόλλωνι, ἐπιγράψας·

Φοῖβε ἄναξ, δῶρόν τοι Ὅμηρος καλὸν ἔδωκα
σῇσιν ἐπιφροσύναις· σὺ δέ μοι κλέος αἰὲν ὀπάζοις.

Μετὰ δὲ ταῦτα ποιεῖ τὴν Ὀδύσσειαν, ἔπη Μ͵β', πεποιηκὼς ἤδη τὴν Ἰλιάδα ἐπῶν Μ͵εφ'. παραγενόμενον δὲ ἐκεῖθεν εἰς Ἀθήνας αὐτὸν ξενισθῆναί φασι παρὰ Μέδοντι τῷ βασιλεῖ τῶν Ἀθηναίων. ἐν δὲ τῷ βουλευτηρίῳ ψύχους ὄντος καὶ πυρὸς victory, went from place to place reciting his poems; and first of all the *Thebaïs* in seven thousand verses which begins: "Goddess, sing of parched Argos whence kings . . . ," and then the *Epigoni* in seven thousand verses beginning: "And now, Muses, let us begin to sing of men of later days"; for some say that these poems also are by Homer. Now Xanthus and Gorgus, son of Midas the king, heard his epics and invited him to compose a epitaph for the tomb of their father on which was a bronze figure of a maiden bewailing the death of Midas. He wrote the following lines:—

"I am a maiden of bronze and sit upon the tomb of Midas. While water flows, and tall trees put forth leaves, and rivers swell, and the sea breaks on the shore; while the sun rises and shines and the bright moon also, ever remaining on this mournful tomb I tell the passer-by that Midas here lies buried."

For these verses they gave him a silver bowl which he dedicated to Apollo at Delphi with this inscription: "Lord Phoebus, I, Homer, have given you a noble gift for the wisdom I have of you: do you ever grant me renown."

After this he composed the Odyssey in twelve thousand verses, having previously written the Iliad in fifteen thousand five hundred verses.[1] From Delphi, as we are told, he went to Athens and was entertained by Medon, king of the Athenians. And being one day in the council hall when it was cold

[1] The accepted text of the *Iliad* contains 15,693 verses; that of the *Odyssey*, 12,110.

καιομένου σχεδιάσαι λέγεται τούσδε τοὺς στίχους·

Ἀνδρὸς μὲν στέφανοι παῖδες, πύργοι δὲ πόληος
ἵπποι δ' αὖ πεδίου κόσμος, νῆες δὲ θαλάσσης,
λαὸς δ' εἰν ἀγορῇσι καθήμενος εἰσοράασθαι.
αἰθομένου δὲ πυρὸς γεραρώτερος οἶκος ἰδέσθαι
ἤματι χειμερίῳ, ὁπότ' ἂν νείφῃσι Κρονίων.

Ἐκεῖθεν δὲ παραγενόμενος εἰς Κόρινθον, ἐρραψῴδει τὰ ποιήματα. τιμηθεὶς δὲ μεγάλως παραγίνεται εἰς Ἄργος καὶ λέγει ἐκ τῆς Ἰλιάδος τὰ ἔπη τάδε·

Οἳ δ' Ἄργος τ' εἶχον Τίρυνθά τε τειχιόεσσαν
Ἑρμιόνην τ' Ἀσίνην τε, βαθὺν κατὰ κόλπον ἐχούσας,
Τροιζῆν' Ἠιόνας τε καὶ ἀμπελόεντ' Ἐπίδαυρον
νῆσόν τ' Αἴγιναν Μάσητά τε κοῦροι Ἀχαιῶν,
τῶν αὖθ' ἡγεμόνευε βοὴν ἀγαθὸς Διομήδης
Τυδεΐδης, οὗ πατρὸς ἔχων μένος Οἰνεΐδαο,
καὶ Σθένελος, Καπανῆος ἀγακλειτοῦ φίλος υἱός·
τοῖσι δ' ἅμ' Εὐρύπυλος τρίτατος κίεν, ἰσόθεος φώς,
Μηκιστέως υἱὸς Ταλαϊονίδαο ἄνακτος.
ἐκ πάντων δ' ἡγεῖτο βοὴν ἀγαθὸς Διομήδης.
τοῖσι δ' ἅμ' ὀγδώκοντα μέλαιναι νῆες ἕποντο·
ἐν δ' ἄνδρες πολέμοιο δαήμονες ἐστιχόωντο
Ἀργέιοι λινοθώρηκες, κέντρα πτολέμοιο.[1]

Τῶν δὲ Ἀργείων οἱ προεστηκότες, ὑπερβολῇ χαρέντες ἐπὶ τῷ ἐγκωμιάζεσθαι τὸ γένος αὐτῶν ὑπὸ τοῦ ἐνδοξοτάτου τῶν ποιητῶν, αὐτὸν μὲν

[1] This and the preceding line are not found in the received text.

and a fire was burning there, he threw off the following lines:

"Children are a man's crown, and towers of a city, horses are the ornament of a plain, and ships of the sea; and good it is to see a people seated in assembly. But with a blazing fire a house looks worthier upon a wintry day when the Son of Cronos sends down snow."

From Athens he went on to Corinth, where he sang snatches of his poems and was received with distinction. Next he went to Argos and there recited these verses from the *Iliad*[1]:

"The sons of the Achaeans who held Argos and walled Tiryns, and Hermione and Asine which lie along a deep bay, and Troezen, and Eïones, and vine-clad Epidaurus, and the island of Aegina, and Mases,—these followed strong-voiced Diomedes, son of Tydeus, who had the spirit of his father the son of Oeneus, and Sthenelus, dear son of famous Capaneus. And with these two there went a third leader, Eurypylus, a godlike man, son of the lord Mecisteus, sprung of Talaüs; but strong-voiced Diomedes was their chief leader. These men had eighty dark ships wherein were ranged men skilled in war, Argives with linen jerkins, very goads of war."

This praise of their race by the most famous of all poets so exceedingly delighted the leading Argives, that they rewarded him with costly gifts and

[1] ii. 559–568 (with two additional verses).

πολυτελέσι δωρεαῖς ἐτίμησαν, εἰκόνα δὲ χαλκῆν ἀναστήσαντες ἐψηφίσαντο θυσίαν ἐπιτελεῖν Ὁμήρῳ καθ' ἡμέραν καὶ κατὰ μῆνα καὶ κατ' ἐνιαυτόν, καὶ ἄλλην θυσίαν πενταετηρίδα εἰς Χίον ἀποστέλλειν. ἐπιγράφουσι δὲ ἐπὶ τῆς εἰκόνος αὐτοῦ·

Θεῖος Ὅμηρος ὅδ' ἐστίν, ὃς Ἑλλάδα τὴν μεγάλαυχον
πᾶσαν ἐκόσμησεν καλλιεπεῖ σοφίῃ,
ἔξοχα δ' Ἀργείους, οἳ τὴν θεοτειχέα Τροίην
ἤρειψαν, ποινὴν ἠυκόμου Ἑλένης.
οὗ χάριν ἔστησεν δῆμος μεγαλόπτολις αὐτὸν
ἐνθάδε καὶ τιμαῖς ἀμφέπει ἀθανάτων.

Ἐνδιατρίψας δὲ τῇ πόλει χρόνον τινὰ διέπλευσεν εἰς Δῆλον εἰς τὴν πανήγυριν. καὶ σταθεὶς ἐπὶ τὸν κεράτινον βωμὸν λέγει ὕμνον εἰς Ἀπόλλωνα, οὗ ἡ ἀρχή·

Μνήσομαι οὐδὲ λάθωμαι Ἀπόλλωνος ἑκάτοιο.

ῥηθέντος δὲ τοῦ ὕμνου οἱ μὲν Ἴωνες πολίτην αὐτὸν κοινὸν ἐποιήσαντο, Δήλιοι δὲ γράψαντες
326 τὰ ἔπη εἰς λεύκωμα ἀνέθηκαν ἐν τῷ τῆς Ἀρτέμιδος ἱερῷ. τῆς δὲ πανηγύρεως λυθείσης ὁ ποιητὴς εἰς Ἴον ἔπλευσε πρὸς Κρεώφυλον κἀκεῖ χρόνον διέτριβε πρεσβύτης ὢν ἤδη. ἐπὶ δὲ τῆς θαλάσσης καθήμενος παίδων τινῶν ἀφ' ἁλείας ἐρχομένων, ὥς φασι, πυθόμενος

Ἄνδρες ἄγρης ἁλίης [1] θηρήτορες, ἦ ῥ' ἔχομέν τι;

[1] Koechly: ἀπ' Ἀρκαδίης, MS. (so Flach).

set up a brazen statue to him, decreeing that sacrifice should be offered to Homer daily, monthly, and yearly; and that another sacrifice should be sent to Chios every five years. This is the inscription they cut upon his statue:

"This is divine Homer who by his sweet-voiced art honoured all proud Hellas, but especially the Argives who threw down the god-built walls of Troy to avenge rich-haired Helen. For this cause the people of a great city set his statue here and serve him with the honours of the deathless gods."

After he had stayed for some time in Argos, he crossed over to Delos, to the great assembly, and there, standing on the altar of horns, he recited the *Hymn to Apollo*[1] which begins: "I will remember and not forget Apollo the far-shooter." When the hymn was ended, the Ionians made him a citizen of each one of their states, and the Delians wrote the poem on a whitened tablet and dedicated it in the temple of Artemis. The poet sailed to Ios, after the assembly was broken up, to join Creophylus, and stayed there some time, being now an old man. And, it is said, as he was sitting by the sea he asked some boys who were returning from fishing:

"Sirs, hunters of deep-sea prey, have we caught anything?"

[1] *Homeric Hymns*, iii.

εἰπόντων δὲ ἐκείνων·

> Ὅσσ' ἕλομεν λιπόμεσθ', ὅσα δ' οὐχ ἕλομεν φερόμεσθα,

οὐ νοήσας τὸ λεχθέν, ἤρετο αὐτοὺς ὅ τι λέγοιεν. οἱ δέ φασιν ἐν ἁλείᾳ μὲν ἀγρεῦσαι μηδέν, ἐφθειρίσθαι δέ, καὶ τῶν φθειρῶν οὓς ἔλαβον καταλιπεῖν, οὓς δὲ οὐκ ἔλαβον ἐν τοῖς ἱματίοις φέρειν. ἀναμνησθεὶς δὲ τοῦ μαντείου, ὅτι τὸ τέλος αὐτοῦ ἥκοι τοῦ βίου, ποιεῖ τὸ τοῦ τάφου αὐτοῦ ἐπίγραμμα. ἀναχωρῶν δὲ ἐκεῖθεν, ὄντος πηλοῦ, ὀλισθὼν καὶ πεσὼν ἐπὶ τὴν πλευράν, τριταῖος, ὥς φασι, τελευτᾷ. καὶ ἐτάφη ἐν Ἴῳ. ἔστι δὲ τὸ ἐπίγραμμα τόδε·

> Ἐνθάδε τὴν ἱερὴν κεφαλὴν κατὰ γαῖα καλύπτει,
> ἀνδρῶν ἡρώων κοσμήτορα, θεῖον Ὅμηρον.

To this they replied:

"All that we caught, we left behind, and carry away all that we did not catch."

Homer did not understand this reply and asked what they meant. They then explained that they had caught nothing in fishing, but had been catching their lice, and those of the lice which they caught, they left behind; but carried away in their clothes those which they did not catch. Hereupon Homer remembered the oracle and, perceiving that the end of his life had come composed his own epitaph. And while he was retiring from that place, he slipped in a clayey place and fell upon his side, and died, it is said, the third day after. He was buried in Ios, and this is his epitaph:

"Here the earth covers the sacred head of divine Homer, the glorifier of hero-men."

INDEX

dau., daus. = daughter, daughters.
f. = father. s. = son. k. = king.
n. = note. w. = wife.

INDEX

INDEX

INDEX

INDEX

INDEX

INDEX

INDEX

INDEX

INDEX

PRINTED IN GREAT BRITAIN BY
RICHARD CLAY AND SONS, LIMITED
BRUNSWICK STREET, STAMFORD STREET, S.E.,
AND BUNGAY, SUFFOLK.

APPENDIX

APPENDIX

ΗΣΙΟΔΟΥ ΚΑΤΑΛΟΓΟΙ ΓΥΝΑΙΚΩΝ

19A.

Oxyrhynchus Papyri 1358 *fr.* 1[1] (3rd cent. A.D.).

. . . . ἐ]πέρησε δ' ἄρ' ἁλμυρὸν ὕδωρ
τηλόθεν εἰς Κρήτην,] Διὸς δμηθεῖσα δόλοισι.
τήν ῥα λαθὼν ἥρπαξε] πατὴρ καὶ δῶρον ἔδωκεν
ὅρμον χρύσειον ὅν Ἥ]φαιστος κλυτοτέχνης
ποίησέν ποτ' ἄγαλμα ἰδυί]ῃσιν πραπίδεσσι
καὶ κτέανον πόρε πατρὶ] φέρων· ὁ δ' ἐδέξατο δῶρο[ν.
αὐτὸς δ' ἂρ δώκεν κούρῃ] Φοίνικ[ο]ς ἀγαυοῦ.
αὐτὰρ ἐπεὶ οὕτω τ]ῆλε τανισφύρῳ Εὐρωπε[ί]ῃ
μίχθη ῥ' ἐν φιλότητι] πατὴρ ἀνδρῶν τε θεῶ[ν τε,
αὖτις ἔπειτ' ἀπέβη νυ]μφῆς παρὰ καλλικόμ[οιο.
ἡ δ' ἄρα παῖδας ἔτικτ]εν ὑπερμενέι Κρον[ίωνι,
κυδαλίμους εὐηφε]νέων ἡγητόρας ἀνδ[ρῶν,
Μίνω τε κρείοντα] δίκαιόν τε Ῥαδάμαν[θυν
καὶ Σαρπηδόνα δῖον] ἀμύμονά τε κρατερ[όν τε.
τοῖσιν ἑὰς τιμὰς δι]εδ[ά]σσατο μητίετα Ζ[εύς.
ἤτοι ὁ μὲν Λυκίης εὐρ]είης ἶφι ἄνασσε
παμπολέας τ' ἴθυνε πό]λεις εὖ ναιετάωσας

[1] For the restoration of ll. 1–16 see *Ox. Pap.* pt. xi. pp. 46–7 : the supplements of ll. 17–31 are by the Translator (cp. *Class. Quart.* x. (1916), pp. 65–67).

APPENDIX

HESIOD, CATALOGUES OF WOMEN [1]

19A.

. . . So she (Europa) crossed the briny water from afar to Crete, beguiled by the wiles of Zeus. Secretly did the Father snatch her away and gave her a gift, the golden necklace, the toy which Hephaestus the famed craftsman once made by his cunning skill and brought and gave it to his father for a possession. And Zeus received the gift, and gave it in turn to the daughter of proud Phoenix. But when the Father of men and of gods had mated so far off with trim-ankled Europa, then he departed back again from the rich-haired girl. So she bare sons to the almighty Son of Cronos, glorious leaders of wealthy men—Minos the ruler, and just Rhadamanthys and noble Sarpedon the blameless and strong. To these did wise Zeus give each a share of his honour. Verily Sarpedon reigned mightily over wide Lycia and ruled very many cities filled

[1] The following fragments from the Hesiodic *Catalogues* were published after this edition had been stereotyped, and are therefore here added as an appendix.

Ζηνὸς ἔχων σκῆπτρον· πολ]λὴ δ᾽ ἑοῖ ἕσπετο τιμή,
τὴν οἱ δῶκε πατὴρ μεγαλή]τορι ποιμένι λαῶν·
τρεῖς γὰρ ἐπὶ ζώειν γενεὰ]ς μερόπων ἀνθρώπων
μηδ᾽ ἀπογηράσκειν ἐνετεί]λατο μητίετα Ζεύς·
πέμπε δέ μιν Τροίηνδε. πολ]ὺν δ᾽ ἐκρίνατο λαόν,
λεκτοὺς ἐκ Λυκίης φῶτας, Τρ]ώεσσ᾽ ἐπίκουρους·
τοὺς ἄγε Σαρπηδὼν κρυεροῦ] πολέμοιο δαήμων.
οὐράνοθεν δὲ οἷ ἧκεν ὅ γ᾽ ἀστ]έρα, σήματα φαίνων
νόστον θ᾽ υἷι φίλῳ, Ζεὺς] ἄφθιτα μήδεα εἰδώς.
. . . .]ατοι ἀμφιβαλοῦσαις
εὖ γὰρ ἐνὶ φρεσὶ οἶδ᾽ ὅτι δὴ] Δίοθεν τέρας ἦεν.
ἦ μέγ᾽ ἀρίστευσέν τε μεθ᾽ Ἕκτ]ορος ἀνδροφόνοιο
καὶ τεῖχος ῥῆξεν· Δαναοῖσι] δὲ κήδε᾽ ἔθηκεν.
ἀλλ᾽ ὅτ᾽ ἄρ᾽ ἔμπνευσεν κρατερὸν μένο]ς Ἀργεί[ο]ισι
[Πάτροκλος . . .]κα[

40A.

(Cp. 43 and 44.)

Oxyrhynchus Papyri 1358 *fr.* 2[1] (3rd cent. A.D.).

(Slight remains of 7 lines.)

Μασσαγετῶν τ]᾽ ἐπὶ ἔργα καὶ Ἡ[μικύνων ἀγερώχων
ἠδὲ Κατουδ]αίων καὶ Πυγ[μαίων ἀμενηνῶν,
φῦλα τ᾽ ἀπε]ιρεσίων Μελανο[χρώτων Λιβύων τε
τοὺς Ἐπάφῳ] τέκε Γαῖα πελώ[ρη χρησμολόγους τε
μαντοσύν]ας τε πανομφαίο[υ Διὸς εἰδότας αἴση,
ψεύστας δ᾽, ὄ]φρα θεοῖσιν ὑφε[ιμ]ένοι ἀτασ[θῶσ]ιν

[1] The restorations are mainly those adopted or suggested in *Ox. Pap.* pt. xi. pp. 48 ff.: for those of ll. 8–14 see *Class. Quart.* x. (1916) pp. 67–69.

with people, wielding the sceptre of Zeus: and great honour followed him, which his father gave him, the great-hearted shepherd of the people. For wise Zeus ordained that he should live for three generations of mortal men and not waste away with old age. He sent him to Troy; and Sarpedon gathered a great host, men chosen out of Lycia to be allies to the Trojans. These men did Sarpedon lead, skilled in bitter war. And Zeus, whose wisdom is everlasting, sent him forth from heaven a star, showing tokens for the return of his dear son . . . for well he (Sarpedon) knew in his heart that the sign was indeed from Zeus. Very greatly did he excel in war together with man-slaying Hector and brake down the wall, bringing woes upon the Danaans. But so soon as Patroclus had inspired the Argives with hard courage . . .

40A.

(The Sons of Boreas pursued the Harpies) to the lands of the Massagetae and of the proud Half-Dog men, of the Underground-folk and of the feeble Pygmies; and to the tribes of the boundless Black-skins and the Libyans. Huge Earth bare these to Epaphus—soothsaying people, knowing seercraft by the will of Zeus the lord of oracles, but deceivers, to the end that men whose thought passes their

ἄνθρωποι,] τῶν μέν τε νόος [γλ]ωσσῆς καθ[ύπ]ερθεν·
'Αιθίοπάς] τε Λίβυς τε ἰδὲ Σκύ[θ]ας ἱππημο[λγού]ς.
ἦ ῥ' Ἔπαφος γ]ένεθ' υἱὸς ὑπερ[μ]ενέος Κρονίωνος·
τοῖο Λίβυς] μέλανές τε καὶ 'Αι[θ]ίοπες μεγάθυμοι
ἠδὲ Κατου]δαῖοι καὶ Πυγμαῖ[οι] ἀμενηνοί.
οἱ πάντες] κρείοντος 'Ερικτύπου εἰσι γενέθλη.
καὶ τούτου]ς πέρι κύκλ[ῳ] ἐθύνεον ἀΐσσοντες
]νεα μ. [. . . 'Υ]περβορέων εὐίππων,
οὓς τέκε Γῆ] φέρβουσα π[ολ]υσπερέας πολυφόρβος
τῆλε παρ' 'Ηριδανοῖ]ο βα[θυρρ]όου αἰπὰ ῥέεθρα
] πρ. [. . . . .] ἠλέκτροιο·
Νεβρῶδές τ' ὄρος] αἰπὺ κ[αὶ Αἴτν]ην παιπαλόεσσαν,
νῆσον ἐπ' 'Ο]ρτυγίην, Λαιστ[ρυγον]ίην τε γενέθλην,
ὅς τε Ποσει]δάωνος ἐρισθ[ε]νέος γένεθ' υἱός.
τὴν πάρα δ]ὶς πόλεσαν περί τ' ἀμφί τε κυκλώσαντο
ἱέμενοι] μάρψαι· ταὶ δ' ἐκφυγέειν καὶ ἀλύξαι
ἔς τε Κεφαλλ]ήνων ἀγερώχων φῦλον ὄρουσαν,
[δῆμον 'Οδυσσῆος ταλασίφρονος, ὃν μετέπειτα] [1]
εἶργε Ποσει]δάωνι Καλυψὼ πότνια νύμφη.
ἐνθ' ἵκοντ' ἐπὶ γ]αῖαν 'Αρητιάδαο ἄνακτος
]ι[. . .]α κλύον· ἀλλ' ἄρα καὶ τὰς
αἰὲν ὁμῶς ἐδίωκον ἐπι]χρονίοισι πόδεσσι.
αἱ δ' ἀρ' ὑπὲρ πόντο]ν διὰ τ' αἰθέρος ἀτρυγέτοιο

[1] The restoration of the apparent lacuna is by Mr. Lobel: see *Ox. Pap.* pt. xi. p. 51.

utterance[1] might be subject to the gods and suffer harm—Aethiopians and Libyans and mare-milking Scythians. For verily Epaphus was the child of the almighty Son of Cronos, and from him sprang the dark Libyans, and high-souled Aethiopians, and the Underground-folk and feeble Pygmies. All these are the offspring of the lord, the Loud-thunderer. Round about all these (the Sons of Boreas) sped in darting flight . . . of the well-horsed Hyperboreans—whom Earth the all-nourishing bare far off by the tumbling streams of deep-flowing Eridanus . . . of amber, feeding her wide-scattered offspring—, and about the steep Fawn mountain and rugged Etna to the isle Ortygia and the people sprung from Laestrygon who was the son of wide-reigning Poseidon. Twice ranged the Sons of Boreas along this coast and wheeled round and about yearning to catch the Harpies, while they strove to escape and avoid them. And they sped to the tribe of the haughty Cephallenians, the people of patient-souled Odysseus whom in aftertime Calypso the queenly nymph detained for Poseidon. Then they came to the land of the lord the son of Ares . . . they heard. Yet still (the Sons of Boreas) ever pursued them with instant feet. So they (the Harpies) sped over the sea and through the fruitless air . . .

[1] *i.e.* those who seek to outwit the oracle, or to ask of it more than they ought, will be deceived by it and be led to ruin: cp. *Hymn to Hermes*, 541 ff.

APPENDIX

[Uncertain Position.]

Oxyrhynchus Papyri 1359 *fr.* 1 (early 3rd cent. A.D.).

(Slight remains of 3 lines.)

εἰ δή ῥ' ἤ]μελ[λ]έν τε καὶ εἰ δίε μῦ[θον] ἀκούσ[αι
ἀθανά]των οἵ οἱ τότ' ἐναργεὲς ἀντεφάνησ[αν.
κείνη]ν δ' [ἐ]ν μεγάροισιν ἐῢ τρέφεν ἠδ' ἀτ[ίταλλε
δεξάμ]εν[ο]ς, ἶσον δὲ θυγατράσιν ᾗσιν ἐτίμ[α.
ἣ τέκε] Τήλεφον Ἀρκασίδην Μυσῶν βασιλῆ[α
μιχθε]ῖσ' ἐν φιλότητι βίῃ Ἡρακληείῃ
ὅς ῥα μεθ' ἵ]ππους στεῖχεν ἀγαυοῦ Λαομέδοντο[ς
οἳ δὴ πόσσι]ν ἄριστοι ἐν Ἀσ[ί]δι ἔτραφεν αἴῃ.
ἐκ δ' ὅ γ' Ἀμαζον]ίδων μεγαθύμων φῦλον ἔναιρ[ε
μαρνάμενος, κ]εινῆς δέ τε γῆς ἐξήλασε πάσης.
αὐτὰρ ὁ Τήλεφος] ἔτραπ' Ἀχαίων χαλκοχιτών[ων
ἀσπιστὰς καὶ ἔβησ]ε μελαινάων ἐπὶ ν[ηῶν.
αὐτὰρ ἐπεὶ πολλοὺς] πέλασεν χθονὶ βω[τιανείρῃ,
αὐτοῦ δέδμητ]ο βίη τ' ἀνδροκτασίη τ[ε

(Slight remains of 8 lines.)

[Uncertain Position.]

Oxyrhynchus Papyri 1359 *frs.* 2 *and* 3 (early 3rd cent. A.D.).

(Remains of 4 lines.)

Ἠλέκτρ[η . . .
γείναθ' [ὑποδμηθεῖσα κελαινεφέϊ Κρονίωνι
Δάρδαν[ον . . .
Ἠετίωνα[τε . . .
ὅς ποτε Δ[ήμητρος μέγ' ἐράσσατο καλλικόμοιο.

[Uncertain Position.]

. . . If indeed he (Teuthras) delayed, and if he feared to obey the word of the immortals who then appeared plainly to them. But her (Auge) he received and brought up well, and cherished in the palace, honouring her even as his own daughters. And Auge bare Telephus of the stock of Arcas, king of the Mysians, being joined in love with the mighty Heracles when he was journeying in quest of the horses of proud Laomedon—horses the fleetest of foot that the Asian land nourished,—and destroyed in battle the tribe of the dauntless Amazons and drove them forth from all that land. But Telephus routed the spearmen of the bronze-clad Achaeans and made them embark upon their black ships. Yet when he had brought down many to the ground which nourishes men, his own might and deadliness were brought low . . .

[Uncertain Position.]

. . . Electra . . . was subject to the dark-clouded Son of Cronos and bare Dardanus . . . and Eëtion . . . who once greatly loved rich-haired Demeter.

καὶ τὸν μ[ὲν φλογερῷ δάμασεν πληχθέντα
κεραυνῷ
'Ηετίωνα [χολωσάμενος νεφεληγερέτα Ζεύς,
οὕνεκα Δ[ήμητρ' ἠϋκόμῳ ἐπὶ χεῖρας ἔβαλλεν.
αὐτὰρ Δά[ρδανος ἦλθεν ἐπ' ἄκτην ἠπείροιο·
ἐκ τοῦ 'Ερ[ιχθόνιος καὶ Τρῶς μετέπειτα γένοντο
Ἶλος [τ' Ἀσσάρακός τε καὶ ἀντίθεος Γανυμήδης
νηῒ [πολυκλήϊδι λιπὼν ἱερὴν Σαμοθράκην

* * * *

. . . .] Ḳλε̣ο̣[πάτρη[1]
. . . .]δαο θυγατ[ρ
Ζηνὶ δ' ἀνήρπαξεν Γανυμήδε' 'Ερι]χθονίοιο
αἰετός, οὕνεκ' ἄρ' ἀθανάτοις περ]ὶ κάλλος ἔ[ριζε.
ἐυπλ]όκομον Δ[ιομ]ήδ[ην·
ἣ δ' 'Υάκινθον γείνατ' ἀμύ]μονά τε κρατερόν τε
]α· τὸν ῥά ποτ' αὐτὸς
Φοῖβος ἀϊδρείη̣σι κατέκτανε νηλέ]ϊ δίσκῳ.

[1] The association of ll. 1–16 with ll. 17–24 is presumed from the apparent mention of Erichthonius in l. 19. A new section must then begin at l. 21. See *Ox. Pap.* pt. xi. p. 55 (and for restoration of ll. 5–16, *ib.* p. 53). Ll. 19–20 are restored by the Translator.

And cloud-gathering Zeus was wroth and smote him, Eëtion, and laid him low with a flaming thunderbolt, because he sought to lay hands upon rich-haired Demeter. But Dardanus came to the coast of the mainland—from him Erichthonius and thereafter Tros were sprung, and Ilus, and Assaracus, and godlike Ganymedes,—when he had left holy Samothrace in his many-benched ship.

* * * *

Cleopatra . . . the daughter of . . . But an eagle caught up Ganymedes for Zeus because he vied with the immortals in beauty . . . rich-tressed Diomede; and she bare Hyacinthus, the blameless one and strong . . . whom, on a time Phoebus himself slew unwittingly with a ruthless disk . . .

4180047R00399

Printed in Germany
by Amazon Distribution
GmbH, Leipzig